To: M
From:
[signature] Ryl Goss
1/25/09

The Ecclesiastical Chronicles

Volume One: The Board

Raymond Gordon

iUniverse, Inc.
New York   Bloomington

The Ecclesiastical Chronicles
Volume One: The Board

Copyright © 2008 by Raymond Gordon

All rights reserved. No part of this book may be used or reproduced by any means, graphic, electronic, or mechanical, including photocopying, recording, taping or by any information storage retrieval system without the written permission of the publisher except in the case of brief quotations embodied in critical articles and reviews.

This is a work of fiction. All of the characters, names, incidents, organizations, and dialogue in this novel are either the products of the author's imagination or are used fictitiously.

iUniverse books may be ordered through booksellers or by contacting:

iUniverse
1663 Liberty Drive
Bloomington, IN 47403
www.iuniverse.com
1-800-Authors (1-800-288-4677)

Because of the dynamic nature of the Internet, any Web addresses or links contained in this book may have changed since publication and may no longer be valid. The views expressed in this work are solely those of the author and do not necessarily reflect the views of the publisher, and the publisher hereby disclaims any responsibility for them.

ISBN: 978-0-595-52597-3 (pbk)
ISBN: 978-0-595-51350-5 (cloth)
ISBN: 978-0-595-62651-9 (ebk)

Printed in the United States of America
iUniverse rev. 1/6/09

Chapter One
The Establishment of the Board

The radiant hues of the early morning sunlight glistened on the bonnet of Peter 'Pigeon' Goodfellow's brand new, silver Jaguar as he made his way back home after having the vehicle blessed by Reverend Perths, the vicar of St. Patrick's Anglican Church. After the brief ritual was completed the two men had sat for breakfast at MILO'S, which was about a mile away from the church on Buckingham Avenue. MILO'S was one of the most popular restaurants in Abersthwaithe and catered almost exclusively to the neighborhood's upper class and white collar professionals. The choice of the restaurant for breakfast that morning was the vicar's and even though food and the quality of service was impressive, Pigeon hated the place – and the owners who, though not classified as members in good standing, nevertheless covertly supported the unethical, subversive activities of the group who referred to themselves as the *Gold Circle*. The objective of this group was to surreptitiously rid St. Patrick's of the lower classes by every foul means possible.

Pigeon's thoughts focused on this repulsive group of upper-class Christians as he drove past the sacred edifice. He was a vestry member and an inadvertent member of the Circle until he became conscious of its existence and its objective one night during a meeting when a select group of Gold Circle members called a meeting to unveil its plans for the parish. St. Patrick's was purported to be the icon of the Anglican institution and this small group from within the so-called Gold Circle felt it inappropriate for such a large number of peasants from the two nearby squalid villages to assume membership at such a prestigious institution. As Pigeon drove past the church he observed the faithful sexton, a man from one of the impoverished villages, sitting on his bench at the entrance to the south transcept, bearing his wonted grim expression as if to repel any prospective adversaries.

St Patrick's was the seat of authority in this quasi- sanctimonious village, which was located on the eastern coast of the former British colony of Ischalton, and was the favorite house of worship for the upper class and aspirants to social elitism. Persons with social and political ambitions developed a propensity to this sacred space. Students in the more prestigious high schools around the island and those returning from universities abroad, particularly the English institutions, were groomed by their parents to take their respective places in this community. This was supposedly the correct path of life for middle class youth; become Anglican, pursue studies abroad and then return and acquire membership at St. Patrick's.

St. Patrick's had a formally registered membership of about two hundred and fifty. The other persons who were in good standing were not registered. Their names were simply recorded in a book. Nevertheless, they were considered members, and numbered about three hundred. They were categorized by the infamous group as the *Silver Circle*, the *Bronze Circle* and the *Iron Circle*. The *Silver Circle* constituted those who were potential registered members. The *Bronze Circle* was made up of those who lacked the prerequisites of potentially full membership but met the basic requirements for lower middle class status. At the bottom of the social and membership ladder was the *Iron Circle*. These were the people who merely attended the church and had the privilege of executing the menial tasks. They were allowed to participate in the services, but not become registered members, assume positions of leadership in any of the ministries or become officers of the vestry. Reverend Perths had no knowledge of this classification. He had only been assigned to St Patrick's less than two years earlier and slipped right into the order of things. Pigeon was aware of the class differences but had no knowledge of the titles which categorized one group from the other. Neither did he confront the group when sporadic displays of prejudice against the poor were revealed because he was never personally affected by them.

At the top of the social ladder were those who belonged to what was secretly referred to as the *Gold Circle*. The *Gold Circle* comprised professionals whose annual income exceeded sixty thousand dollars. Income was discreetly the sole criterion for fully registered membership at St Patrick's.

Of all the buildings in Abersthwaithe, none was more magnificent than St. Patrick's Anglican Church. The massive concrete structure stood obtrusively in all its hypocritically virtuous majesty at the corner of Buckingham Avenue and St. Patrick's Place. White was the dominant color, with light grey trimmings over the windows. The steeple seemed to reach for the sky in rapturous adoration while, simultaneously, to contemptuously abase the low, modest structures that surrounded it. The building was actually shaped like a cross, with the transepts on the north and south. St. Mary's chapel was situated in the south transept, and the door to the chapel was usually opened during the day to allow for private devotion and meditation. Rexworth Davis, the conveniently jocund sexton, guarded that entrance like a sentinel on weekdays, and warmly greeted visitors who would stop by to meditate or attend the noonday services. Some of the visitors would offer him a financial token of their appreciation for his gregariousness. By the end of the day, however, these tokens would have found their way to *Phauphen's Tavern* and exchanged for a shot or two of distilled molasses. Rexworth's wrath would surge forward like a tempestuous sea upon any member of the *Iron Circle* whom he suspected as attempting to share these gratuities by ostensibly keeping him company during his watch. Such unwanted company gravely affected his daily supplemental income.

The huge pipe organ was situated near the north transept, and there were sturdy, wooden chairs there to accommodate the overflowing crowd which usually assembled on Christmas day, Easter Sunday and Harvest thanksgiving service – or at the funeral of a member of the *Gold Circle*. The total seating capacity was approximately four hundred. Stained glass windows embellished the sacred edifice, and the main door was painted in black. St Patrick's cemetery was located in the church yard and was the oldest in the island, but there was room for a few more burials at a costly price, for to be buried there was to be a part of history. Tour buses taking visitors around the island would frequently stop by the church, and tourists would sometimes participate in the noon day services and take photographs of the tombs, some of which were dated to as far back as 1835. Over the arch between the narthex and the nave, and on a large plaque on the side of the southern door respectively, was a sign that immediately arrested one's attention. It was written in black gothic and it read:

St. Patrick's Anglican Church represents the Kingdom of God and therefore welcomes all persons, regardless of race, age, social status, nationality or sex.

One Saturday evening, Rexworth was passing the church on his way from *Phauphen's Tavern*, the local pub which was located about one mile away from the church when he noticed a few luxury automobiles parked on St Patrick's place. The church was closed but there was light in the eastern section of the building. Rex, as he was familiarly called, made a detour and approached the door on the side of the St Mary's chapel. As far as he was aware, there was nothing planned for that Saturday evening at the church. He pulled at the door, but it was locked. Believing that something odd might be taking place, or perhaps assuming that Nollie Mertins, the disgruntled organist, had left the lights on after rehearsal, as he sometimes accidentally does, Rex took his bunch of keys from his pocket and headed for the door to the undercroft. Rex always carried the bunch of keys with him, regardless of where he went. The bunch was attached to a large, silver chain that was clipped to one of his belt loops and left to dangle conspicuously down his right leg, or placed in his pocket. The bunch of keys gave him an air of authority, and certainly instilled in him a feeling of superiority to the rest of members of the *Iron Circle*, even though he was unaware of the official classification.

Having quietly entered the building and closed the door behind him, Rex made his way cautiously up the winding staircase. The higher he went the more convinced he became that something odd was taking place. He heard the sound of voices. However, the voices were not babbling; they were floating in unison at times, then at other times, they seemed to be echoing a response. The organized rhythm of the voices that responded to the versicles seemed to indicate that there was a service in progress. Rex crouched stealthily, with the calculating precision of a cat stalking its prey, to the top of the stairway and peered through the black, iron grille gate that led to the north transept. Indeed, a service was in progress.

A protracted period had elapsed before Rex began to recognize what was actually taking place. At first he thought that it was a private baptism because the two persons standing in front of the vicar were dressed in white. They were relatively new members to St. Patricks, two men of English extraction whom Rex had often seen together. After a few minutes, Rex realized that the prayers were not those he was accustomed to hearing during the sacrament of baptism. Perplexed, he contemplated the two figures in white more carefully. Then the vicar made a pronouncement that dumfounded him. He did not know what the pronouncement, 'united in a commitment of love and lifelong friendship' meant, but somehow sensed something odd about two men standing in front of a priest and staring at each other as they made the sacred and almost inaudible responses. Rex thought that the liquor which he had earlier imbibed had impaired his vision and grossly affected his hearing. However, the applause from the small gathering seemed to confirm what he thought that the pronouncement had meant, especially when the figures in white subsequently turned toward each other, embraced and kissed momentarily. Rex blinked to make sure that the liquor he had earlier consumed was not taking custody of his mental faculty. He realized that he was thinking quite logically and what he was observing was not the consequence of inebriation. Both figures in white wore satin bow-ties and cummerbunds, and white patent leather shoes. The taller of the two was clean shaven and slightly muscular, while the other sported a meticulously groomed mustache and was slightly podgy.

At that point the service seemed to have ended and the figures in white began to greet the small congregation. Then one of the ladies, whom he recognized as Maggie Billings, opened her gold, sequined handbag and took out a small, paper bag from which she distributed cylindrical bottles. The small gathering of familiar and unfamiliar faces began blowing bubbles at the figures in white. The podgy one then turned and bent slightly to the front, left pew and retrieved the small bouquet of red and white roses which was placed there sometime during the ceremony. As the podgy figure in white straightened up, the other figure in white drew closer and posed for a few photographs.

Soon the photographic session was through and the figures in white, with their guests, prepared for the traditional march. However, the figures in white did not head towards the main entrance. They turned towards the aisle that led to the black, iron grille gates, which in turn led to stairs to the undercroft. The gates were not locked because the figures in white and their guests would make their discreet exit through the undercroft. Rex's state of confusion, superimposed by semi-intoxication, did not cloud his sense of reason. He recognized that he must make a desperate and urgent dash down the stairs and through the door of the undercroft. His mild inebriation, however, affected his sense of balance, and in his endeavor to expeditiously vacate the building, his right leg tripped over his left and he went tumbling down the stairs. Fortunately, the winding staircase served to give him the advantage of rising quickly and running for cover between a family vault and a clump of bush before the onslaught of the embarrassed and worried guests. Rex concealed himself neatly between the stone and the foliage, and shaded by the cloak of late twilight, escaped any attention. The vicar, however, was the only person who ventured beyond the door. In his endeavor to quell any suspicion by any passer by, he stepped gingerly towards the gate, glancing nonchalantly at the flowering plants and vaults on either side of the pathway and approached his car which was parked in the spot marked 'clergy.' He pretended to be searching for something for a few moments, then having surveyed the surroundings to make sure that the coast was clear, he turned toward the door to the undercroft and made a subtle gesture. Suddenly, hurried footsteps could be heard rushing toward the gate. The figures in white dashed past first, followed by the rest of the guests. Soon there were the slamming of car doors and the roaring of engines. Finally, there was the sound of regimented footsteps in quick march as the vicar returned to the building and closed the door. After a few seconds, Rex darted out from his hiding place and headed for the gate. He hurried down St. Patrick's Place and turned left on Buckingham Avenue, in the direction of *Phauphen's*.

Two Sundays later, the signs over the entrance to the nave and the side of the southern door read:

> *St Patrick's Anglican Church represents the Kingdom of God and therefore welcomes all persons, regardless of race, age, social status, nationality, sex, or sexual orientation.*

That Sunday, the vicar preached a dynamic sermon on the inclusiveness of the Kingdom of God, which Rex understood as a futile attempt by the vicar to justify his part in the unholy union which he had performed that Saturday evening and to bring the congregation closer to accepting, or at least becoming tolerant of the new lifestyle of same-sex relationships which a few of those of foreign extraction had secretly brought to the island. This new lifestyle was a forbidden topic to many nationals, and others, especially those of the lower classes, were either unaware of its existence or did not understand its ramifications. Anyone whom they suspected of being even merely attracted to one of the same sex was castigated and looked upon with contempt.

* * *

Sunday services at St. Patrick's were held at 7.00 a.m. and 9.00 a.m. The first service was a said mass with hymns. The second service was the sung mass. The *Gold* and *Silver Circle* members considered themselves 'high church', which justified their aloofness form the *Bronze* and *Iron Circle* members who generally attended the earlier service. However, the demarcation was not as acute as this. There was some overlapping. Some members of the upper Circle, including Pigeon, would sometimes attend either of the two services. In addition, Pigeon would sometimes attend the office of Evensong every first Sunday at 5.00 p.m. which he thoroughly enjoyed. Visiting clergy were often invited to deliver the sermon at this office and sometimes professional singers were employed to assist the choir. Members of the *Bronze* and *Iron Circles* who enjoyed this office and who were blessed with good voices approached Mr. Mertins on several occasions and offered their talent, but were told that the choir had already had its quota. Pigeon knew this to be a blatant lie, but even though he had abhorred the prejudice against the lower classes who attended St Patrick's, he never aggressively sought to eradicate it. Nollie would take the names of these aspiring lower class members and promise them an invitation to audition at the next opening. However, choristers came and went, but invitations were never extended to the volunteers from the lower circles. Nollie Mertins' excuse was that knowledge of music was an absolute necessity. He knew, of course, that these volunteers would hardly be able to afford music lessons.

One Friday evening, a group of members from the *Iron Circle* approached Pigeon and besought him to speak with one of the members, Philbert Watts, whose musical genius was known to many thoughout the island. Pigeon subsequently approached Philbert, whose father was employed by the Lord Bishop and inveigled him into approaching Nollie Mertins and offering his talent. Philo, as he was familiarly known, was a gifted musician and a relatively close friend of Pigeon. Philbert played the piano at *Phauphen's* every Friday night and was very popular among the patrons. Sometimes he would serenade the crowd with voice and guitar. He was very popular – especially among the women, but his relationship with the Bishop restricted his response to the plethora of advances form the opposite sex. Furthermore, it was by dint of His Lordship's friendship with the proprietor of *Phauphen's*, who was a member of the *Gold Circle* at St Patrick's, that Philbert secured that gig. By special request from his lordship, Philbert would play on Monday nights when the tavern was closed to the public, but discreetly opened to a select clientele, among whom were the Mayor of Abersthwaithe, the Superintendent of Police, and His Lordship. It was therefore incumbent upon Philbert to maintain a certain level of moral rectitude – at least at *Phauphen's*.

Philbert's father was employed by the diocese as the caretaker for the grounds of Bishop's Court, as it was called. Mr. Watts was a proud man, whose employment at the Bishop's Court gave him an air of superiority. Mrs. Watts was employed as the cook, and her culinary skills were hailed throughout the diocese. She was a haughty woman, and considered herself socially superior to others of her status. Her *pseudo- English* accent, combined with her local dialect and sporadic malapropism, established her reputation as one of the most amusingly complex beings in the Anglican community. Mrs. Watts was always impeccably attired in cast-offs from Mrs. Addington, the Bishop's wife, or the First Lady, as she was sarcastically referred to by the wives of the other clergymen. It was Mrs. Addington whose keen sense of perception recognized young Philbert's prodigious talent, and whose benevolence made it possible for him to pursue private music lessons.

The lad excelled and became famous among the lower middle classes for his raunchy ballads and jazz renditions, much to the chagrin of his parents, who had hoped that he would have developed a propensity to sacred music, and one day, become the organist – at the cathedral. Such a position, they believed, would have secured their place among the upper middle class. But young Philbert was more ambitious. He imagined himself in juxtaposition with such legends as Ray Charles, Dinah Washington, Quincy Jones and Burt Bacharach, whom he greatly admired. His ambition, however, proved too lofty for such a small island and he thus resorted to mere gigs at the popular night clubs and other places that offered nocturnal entertainment. By day, Philbert was a plumber. It was purported that he worked only for the white people, most of whom were of English extraction, and a select group of the native middle class. Philbert's defense was that the *others* were overtly critical, obviously because they wanted to evade paying what he charged for his labor, and as such became too much of a vexation to the spirit. Such constant annoyance, Philbert remonstrated, was a threat to his mental health.

*   *   *

When Pigeon approached Philbert, he was reluctant to acquiesce to his request. Philbert had seen his place in the church choir as a sort of demotion, and to some small degree as a threat to his masculinity, especially since the choir consisted of a preponderance of females. However, when Pigeon's plea proved futile, a small contingent from the Iron Circle devised a second plan to succeed in their mission. They enticed Lottie Lovell, an attractive, Jamaican nursery school teacher, to seduce him. Philbert was overcome by Lottie's beauty and sensual persuasion, and after feigning resistance submitted and agreed to approach Nollie Mertins. Pigeon often chided Philbert for lending a deaf ear to his request but yielding so willingly and easily to Lottie's plea.

One Sunday, the contingent of plebs attended Evensong. Word had circulated among the lower circles that Philbert was going to approach Nollie Mertins after the service to discuss prospective membership in the choir. Consequently, a significant number from the *Bronze* and *Iron Circles* came out to support Philbert and witness what Pigeon would later describe as 'a verbal twilight tussle for the establishment of one's right to praise God without hindrance.' Philbert's success would be theirs as well, since it would lay for them the foundation for a new era in the church. The congregation who regularly attended Evensong took great umbrage at the presence of the *mob*, as the *Iron Circle* members in particular were privately called, because the office was usually followed by a sophisticated fellowship in the common room especially when visiting clergy and hired singers were employed. The *mob*, according to them, lacked the delicacy of breeding and the affluence that were the prerequisites of acceptance among the upper circles. Nevertheless, with practiced dignity they cordially greeted the *mob* with open arms and pasty grins, like hired clowns behind whose smiles lay the heavy burdens of life's diurnal tribulations. Pigeon observed the charade and perceived their falsehood with absolute disgust as he sat in a quiet corner in quiet meditation before the start of the service.

Anxiety began to creep up within the *insurrectionists* because the service had started and there was no sign of Philbert. From their expressions of disappointed resignation, Piegon could tell that they had reluctantly begun to accept what was painfully obvious; Philbert had rescinded his decision to approach Nollie Mertins. The choir had just completed the magnificat and the lector was in the process of introducing the second lesson from Ephesians 2:11-22, when the right side of the main door swung gently open as if by some supernatural command. In stepped Philbert Watts, graced with the sartorial elegance for which he had become relatively famous and with the acquired gait of a distinguished musician strutting across the stage to the thunderous applause of loyal fans. He approached the front left pew and sat. The entire congregation turned their attention towards him as he swaggered down the aisle and approached his seat. The lector, who had paused to allow him time to sit, bowed his head respectfully and continued the lesson. The *mob* beamed with pride and then they prayed quietly that the lesson would lend credence to their purpose.

The recessional hymn, *The day thou gavest Lord, is ended*, came to an end. Following the prayer of dismissal, Nollie began to play the postlude and some of the *mob* rose in preparation to leave. Philbert turned, and with the gesture of a skillful conductor, directed those members to take their seats until the postlude was ended. Pigeon smiled discreetly as he observed Philbert's calm display of breeding. The vicar was impressed, for although he had no close acquaintance with Philbert, he recognized that he must have had some formal grooming in matters pertaining to liturgy. At the conclusion of the postlude, the vicar wished all a blessed night's rest and subsequently invited them to fellowship in the common room. While the congregation headed for the black, grille gates, Philbert rose and approached Nollie, who appeared quite formidable in his black cassock and white organist's surplice. His expression was stern, and he was perspiring profusely. Pigeon assumed that he was offended by Philbert's brazen display of disrespect when he made his grand entrance during the service. Nollie rose from the organ and approached the chancel, en route to the choir room. He showed a mild gesture of respect towards Pigeon by slightly bowing his head and smiling politely. However, it was clear that he had absolutely no intention of acknowledging any of the *mob* as they lingered in gleeful anticipation of what Pigeon referred to as a holy war. Their apparent association with Philbert, however, was not the basis of Nollie Mertins' contempt. Nollie was of light complexion, being of Caucasian and Creole lineage; they were dark. His mother was an English woman from London's East End. She had come to Ischalton to work as a nanny for the children of the British ambassador and, after a brief dalliance with Jonas, the ambassador's chauffer who was from Martinique, became pregnant with Nollie. Fearing that they might be made redundant, or that she might have to return to England, posed a dismal prospect. Thus they got married. But such an ignoble background was immaterial to Nollie – Mrs. Mertins was a white woman. Most of the *mob* was black; some were East Indian and there was a Portuguese couple; but they were all natives of Ischalton. He attended and played at the sung mass and solemn evensong; they worshipped at the early mass and never attended evensong or the fellowship which followed. He lived in North Abersthwaithe; they in the east, mostly in the council flats or in Brewsters Village or Slough. But the pinnacle of his scorn was their ecclesiastical status. It was almost a solemn disgrace for any member of the two higher circles to be seen confabulating too closely or cordially with any members of such base standing, hence Nollie Mertins deemed it appropriate to display such supercilious conduct in the sacred space. It was in the chancel, in that holy place, that Philbert accosted Nollie Mertins with the modest proposal.

"Good evening, sir. That was quite a fine rendition of *Air on the G-String*," said Philbert.

"Thank you. Now if you'll kindly excuse me, but I must…"

"…before you excuse yourself," Philbert interjected gently, "may I make a suggestion?"

"*Can* you?" responded Nollie in a tone that expressed shock at Philbert's audacity.

"The altos…," Philbert continued, notwithstanding Nollie's poignant sarcasm, "…they were a bit flat…during the *Nunc Dimittis*."

"I beg your pardon?"

"And the tenors…a little sharp and much too loud, which placed the sopranos in a kind of precarious position, you know…; struggling to maintain their pitch and strike a reasonable balance. And if you don't mind me saying…the basses were a bit too beefy."

"I…I don't know you, sir." Nollie replied a dismissive tone.

"You will; in time. But right now we are addressing the choir's performance. My suggestion is that you work on refining the basses and mellowing the tenors."

"Thank you for your suggestion. I shall take it into consideration. Now I really must go."

"Before you go, I want to ask you what the requirements are for joining the choir."

"Competence in reading music."

"I would like to join this choir."

"Sure. I'll take your name and notify you when there is a vacancy...and when you acquire the necessary skills, of course," Nollie replied, smiling wryly.

"*When* are the auditions?"

"You can't read music," Nollie remonstrated. "Competence in music is a necessity."

Philbert contemplated Nollie momentarily, and then without saying another word approached the organ, took one of the books from on top of the organ and began to play *Liebster Jesu, wir sind hier* by J.S.Bach. The *mob* beamed with pride as Philbert addressed the organ with remarkable style and grace. Within minutes the vicar and most of the congregation were assembled at the foot of the chancel, with mouths agape as they beheld Philbert in all his glory. At the end of the performance there was a moment of piercingly awkward silence before the audience burst into contagious applause. Nevertheless, the *members* were too embarrassed to compliment Philbert because, only minutes before ascending from the common room, they were quietly berating him for interrupting the service by his tardiness and ironic pomposity. Apart from Mr. Haulklyn, the proprietor of P*hauphen's*, none of the other members of the *Gold* and *Silver Circles* was aware of the relationship between Philbert and the Addingtons. Furthermore, they were not going to hastily embrace him as one of their kind since they had no knowledge of his financial status. They had enjoyed his music, but his skill was not enough to qualify him for membership into the upper circles.

Philbert, however, was not only skillful; he was sagacious. In the presence of the vicar, he declared his interest in joining the choir, so that, accordingly, he could use his talent to fully glorify God. The vicar pondered, knowing that even though the registered members present had admired Philbert's talent, they nevertheless regarded him with modest contempt. He subsequently assured Philbert that his request was worth some serious consideration and that he would get back to him at some later time. But Philbert continued to coerce him into an immediate and affirmative response. Nollie, sensing the *Gold Circle's* ambivalence toward Philbert, and the vicar's quandary, immediately grasped the opportunity to asseverate that he was the minister of music, and thus was the sole authority to select persons for membership in the choir. An uncomfortable period of silence followed, during which time Philbert contemplated Nollie.

Philbert averted his attention from Nollie, in an attempt to maintain his composure, and addressed the vicar. "Excuse my asking, vicar; but isn't the hierarchal order here a little amiss?"

The *members* were shocked by Philbert's proficiency in the English language. It became clear to them at that point that there was more to status and power than wealth. For the first time their plutocracy was being threatened. Admiration for Philbert's musical genius gradually began to change to disdain.

"You aren't even a member, *you*," snarled a voice from among the privileged members.

"A member of what; the church… or the *Gold Circle?*" Philbert retorted with an air of astounding finesse.

The silence which followed was harrowing.

A voice broke in on the heavy, shrouded silence, like the church bells ringing in the dawn after a long, dark night. "Is you all goin' downstairs now, or what? I wants to turn off the lights and go 'ome."

It was Rex. Even his putrid grammar sounded like a euphonious symphony to the concourse of tense Christians, standing there on holy ground, poised for battle. The vicar grasped the opportunity to avoid any further embarrassment, "Yes…perhaps we should all just go home and calm down, then at some later time…"

"There will be no later time, Fr. Perths," snapped a rotund black woman who smelt of crude tobacco and clutched a large, gold handbag, "This confounded nonsense got to stop. Every time one of we wants to join the choir, him does say the same thing 'leh me take your name and I will get back to you,' and he don't. Him only got his big shot friends them in the choir. Well tonight, is a new beginnin'. Either Mr. Watts join the choir, or we ain't givin' a penny more to this church!"

The *mob* cheered and shouted praise to God. The *members*, however, found the woman's threat of financial pressure quite hilarious. Some of them snickered at her. Then Cynthia Faulkner, an ostentatious Portuguese woman whose husband was the chairman of Faulkner & Babbit, the largest department store on the island, stepped forward.

"Would you stoop to such severe measures, Iris Higgins, that you would encourage all of your friends to withhold their financial contributions? Do you know the repercussions of such a hard lined action? Do you really understand the problems that this church would encounter if it loses twelve dollars a year?"

The *members* chuckled at the piercing sarcasm. The *mob* gloated at the thought of their impending victory.

Philbert turned to the *mob*, "She's deriding you,"

"She doin' what?" inquired Ram, a short Indian man with a receding hairline who, with the willing assistance of his wife, a buxom black woman from one of the neighboring villages, had eleven children, and who made a modest income by selling vegetables and used clothing at the village market.

"She is making fun of your poverty and scant contributions to the church."

"Poverty?" Ram's wife surged forward with the fury of a blazing fire, "I is a healthy, regal black woman with eleven beautiful children and a nice, kind, hard working husband. You got money, and you fair skin and got good hair, but you is as barren as the sands of the Sahara!"

The crowd gasped. The *mob* cringed at the blatant disrespect and courage which Ram's wife, as she was called, displayed towards Mrs. Faulkner, a woman of such lofty, social standing. The *members* froze in shock at such scathing impertinence. The vicar hung his head in embarrassment and retreated unobtrusively down the stairs to the toilet. It was at this point that someone acquired the courage to intervene. It was Mr. Haulklyn, who had allegiances both to Philbert and the *Gold Circle*. He ordered all parties to leave while the spirit of the Lord was still in them, after such a moving service and inspiring sermon. Furthermore, he promised Philbert that he would address the issue of his membership with the vicar and Nollie Mertins when the atmosphere proves conducive to negotiation. He then turned to confirm the arrangements with the vicar. But the vicar was not there.

Mrs. Faulkner turned toward the *mob* as she prepared to leave, and addressing them all with simmering contempt, snarled, "Go boil your heads, all of you. Go and boil your heads!" She then turned abruptly, genuflected in front of the altar, and with the seasoned elegance of a ballerina, flounced towards the black, iron gates and disappeared down the stairs.

The rest followed quietly, without a mumbling word. Some of the *members* turned towards the altar, bowed reverently and left. Others genuflected and made the sign of the cross before exiting. Mr. Pilchard, a tall, dark man of a rather sclerous constitution, who was a vestry member, and a judge by profession, piously approached the altar rail and knelt in contemplation. When the last of the *mob* had descended, he whispered intercessions to God, praying assiduously that the *members* be not defeated by the devil's advocates, and that the *Gold Circle* continue to exert power and control over the affairs of the church. This petition, he concluded, was offered to the honor and glory of the Almighty God. Pigeon observed this display of impiety in amusing disgust before slipping down the stairs. Ram held his wife's hand as they descended the stairs. Philbert gently patted Mr. Haulklyn on the shoulder and headed towards the door. Rex began to turn off the lights. No one remained behind to continue the fellowship. Besides, there was nothing there of which they could have partaken. The *Gold Circle* members who remained in the common room during the skirmish, had taken great offence at Philbert's tampering with the organ and left in protest. However, before doing so, they sought to mitigate their anger by respectively transferring the pastries and crumpets from the tables to their handbags or to covered, sanitary plates.

No one saw the vicar for the rest of the evening.

*   *   *

Three days later, Eloise Pigthorne, the senior warden, called an urgent vestry meeting. She was instructed not to inform the vicar. This meeting was at the behest of Laurent Faulkner, the chairman of Faulkner & Babbit. Eloise was a large, imposing woman with the I.Q. of a mustard seed. Her late husband had amassed a large fortune through the exportation of seafood to England and the Caribbean. After his death, she sold the business to a Chinese named Young Foo, who subsequently sold it to a British Company for double the price he had paid for it. But Mrs. Pigthorne was not perturbed or embarrassed by the transaction, neither was she particularly troubled by the simile, 'as idiotic as Eloise' which was often used discreetly among Ischalton's business elite. Mrs. Pigthorne nevertheless continued to be one of the island's most respected and envied socialites by dint of her filthy affluence. She was always meticulously attired, and it was said that she rarely wore the same clothing twice. Many women, especially those of the lower classes, emulated her, and took great pride in being full figured, whether proportionately or amorphously.

Pigeon always referred to Mrs. Pigthorne as an amoeba. He was in concurrence with the vestry members that her position as warden was won on account of the vicar on whom it was rumored she had lavished her affections, with the hope of one day becoming the first Lady, a title reserved for the wives of the men of the cloth who had assumed the position of vicar or higher. Furthermore, her marriage to an Englishman would have placed her even higher on the social ladder.

According to Pigeon, everyone at some point seemed to have custody of Mrs. Pigthorne's brain. She never seemed to be able to take the initiative to do anything except to grapple with the vicar for his attention with the tenacity of a bulldog. She made no firm decisions about anything in the church, neither did she display a propensity to leadership; those around her generally dictated her actions. Consequently, she became as volatile as dough, always following the last instruction. Hence it was easy for Mr. Faulkner to manipulate her into summoning the vestry to a meeting.

Rex was not happy that night. It was his day off but he was nevertheless ordered to set up the common room for this special meeting and to remain on premises until the discussion had ended. This was most inconvenient for Rex because it conflicted with his socializing at *Phauphen's*. He had developed a relationship with one of the waitresses, Ethel Phipps, whom the patrons had affectionately nicknamed Big Ethel. Ethel's reputed husband worked at sea, on one of the ships which transported cargo around the Caribbean, and as such allowed him only sporadic visits home. Thus Ethel sought employment to keep her gainfully occupied. Rex arranged to secretly meet her in the undercroft about one hour prior to the meeting, during the course of which they would retire to the choir room for privacy. In his endeavor to create a romantic atmosphere, Rex *borrowed* two candles and a bottle of the communion wine from the sacristy. Rex also took one of the old altar cloths and spread it on the floor, so that he and Ethel could relax and listen to music on the old transistor radio someone had given him.

The vestry soon arrived and headed to the common room as they were instructed to do. Pigeon, like the rest of the vestry, was told to park his car further down the street – away from the church. Rex was told to remain at the door to let in the members, and that apart from the common room, the toilets and the corridor, no lights were to be on. But Pigeon found something unusual about the meeting; there were other members who did not belong on the vestry, about fifteen in number. They also entered the common room and sat next to each other. One other oddity struck Pigeon. It was not Eloise Pigthorne who was going to chair the meeting – it was Laurent Faulkner.

The purpose of the meeting was to create an advisory committee to the vestry. The representatives were going to be de facto officers. It was going to operate as a covert group and their main function would be to categorize the circle members, ensure that the position of chairperson on all ministries and committees, including the vestry, the choir, the Lay Eucharistic Ministry and all standing committees remain the privilege of, and under the control of, the members of the *Gold Circle*. Since the categorization of the circles was never known to the rest of the congregation, this aspect was going to be relatively easy. However, exclusion from the ministries and committees would become difficult – especially with the impending membership of Philbert Watts. Almost all agreed that Philbert would be a formidable force with which they would have to contend. Pigeon began to feel sick in the stomach at the gross impertinence of Faulkner and the rest of his group. As he contemplated the group, Mr. Haulklyn rose from his seat and requested permission to speak. Permission was granted.

"Brothers and sisters, I commend Mr. Faulkner's proposal to form an invisible committee to act as advisors to the vestry and to guarantee that the philosophies of the Gold Circle are protected and upheld. However…"

"There is no however, Haulklyn. We're dealing here with absolutes!" interjected Sam Westwater, the permanent secretary to the Minister of Education.

"*Mr.* Haulklyn. You will address me as *Mr.* Haulklyn," he replied in a reprimanding tone.

"My humble apology, *Mr.* Haulklyn,"

"Accepted. Now as I was saying, there are issues which we have not addressed. We cannot simply dismiss the members of the *Bronze* and *Iron Circles* as fools. They have found a leader who has opened their eyes to the injustices within the church – St. Patrick's in particular. And they are going to take an aggressive approach to overturning the hierarchal order here. Look what happened on Sunday evening."

"The man is an idiot!" shouted Fritz Batty, the village undertaker.

"Perhaps," said Mr. Haulklyn, "But Philbert Watts is a very clever idiot. The man was practically raised by the Addingtons. He has a very close relationship with Bishop Addington. Don't be fooled. With the Bishop on his side, he could topple us. My suggestion is that we allow him to join the choir…appease his followers, and keep the peace."

"I concur," responded Dr. Coaksley, the Dean of Abersthwaithe College for Secondary School Teachers, "To deny him membership is to open a can of nasty, slithering worms."

Paula Fields, a vestry member and one of the most successful beauticians in the island, stated her opinion, "I think that this whole thing is totally absurd…the formation of an advisory committee to the vestry. Are you insinuating that we are fools, Mr. Faulkner?"

"Paula, this particular vestry has proven itself to be most incoherent, and I am not making any ad hominem remarks here. I am speaking of the vestry as a body. All I'm trying to do is to protect what is in our best interest."

"Don't you mean, *your* best interest, Faulkner?" protested Bill Jones, the junior warden, "Does all of this have to do with the issue between Mrs. Faulkner and Ram's wife last Sunday night? Is this some kind of vendetta?"

"If you wish to remain on this vestry, and in the *Gold Circle*, my advice would be to embrace what is happening here. Let's face it, brothers and sisters; we are the power here – in Abersthwaithe and on the whole island. Membership here has its privileges. Don't let your anger cloud your judgment. This committee I have formed will be the underground, pilot group. Remember, Jesus had his underground supporters…remember when he sent his disciples to borrow the colt so that he could ride triumphantly into Jerusalem? Well, he was able to do so because…"

"Take your sermon outside to the graveyard, Faulkner, and bury it!" interjected Pigeon. Pigeon was also a barrister-at-law. "Your committee will remain underground. This vestry is a legitimate, elected board of officers and its authority will not be superseded by a bunch of power hungry, irrational communists. All of you Faulknerites can go outside with his sermon, and *him,* and bury yourselves!"

"Please, Pigeon," urged Eloise, "Give him a chance. You don't understand what's really happening here."

"Excuse me, Mrs. Pigthorne, but if there is any one at this table whose intelligence is impaired, I mean, mortally impaired, it's yours. So please, do not insult my intelligence." Pigeon charged.

"Shut up, Pigeon Goodfellow! You are not dealing with criminals in court, you know. You're talking to a bunch of intelligent people…the social elite," barked Tessie Shoehorn, an offensively obese black woman whose husband had won two and a half million dollars in the national lottery several years ago. He then expeditiously divorced her and married the twenty three year old Indian girl whom they had employed as their housekeeper two years before he won the lottery. The judge granted Mrs. Shoehorn half of the fortune.

"Shouldn't you be somewhere remote, Tessie, trying to lose weight?" snarled Pigeon.

There was a moment of terrifying silence. Then Tessie, who had become very bitter after her painful divorce, grabbed the teacup she was using and hurled it across the table towards Pigeon. He artfully intercepted it with his arm and it cannoned into a wooden figure of Jesus on the cross and smashed. The awkwardness and embarrassment bore down upon the members like a heavy, saturated cloak, and they hung their heads and nervously twiddled their thumbs in stifling anticipation of an acrimonious retaliation from Pigeon. But Pigeon's suavity would never have allowed him to respond to such ignoble conduct. Instead, he rose from his chair, and bowed politely to the gathering, "Good evening, ladies and gentlemen. Mrs. Shoehorn." Pigeon took his exit without saying another word.

Mr. Pilchard, knowing the legal ramifications of Tessie's actions, rose quickly and took control of the situation. His tall, distinguished persona and eloquent speech demanded attention from the gathering. "My friends in Christ; it is blatantly obvious that we are laying for ourselves the foundation for a disastrous mission. We are not one in heart and mind in our expedition. Our discord now is a cinch for subsequent catastrophe. Our success depends on how unified we are. We have devised a plan, scrupulously analyzed it, and are ready to put it into action. This approach, my friends, will result in success. It is expedient that this advisory group be formed and allowed to function for the good of the church and the Gold Circle. Our intention is not to usurp the authority of the vestry, but merely to guide, oversee and protect our interests. Look at the constitution of the members of this special board; most of us have at some time served on the vestry and as such are more experienced in the affairs of the church. I beg you, therefore, to trust us. We are protecting your interests as members of the Gold Circle, as well as the church's interest in your role as members of the vestry. Remember, the advantages of Gold Circle membership extend way beyond the parameters of this church. It extends across the whole island. I invite you therefore, to entrust this task of maintaining power and control to us."

"Here, here!" Mr. Faulkner voiced approvingly.

"Well said," agreed Nathaniel Francois, the actuary for the government's Department of Finance.

"However," continued Mr. Pilchard, "Before you make a decision, I want the vestry to understand that you are free to relinquish your positions on vestry or to object if you don't agree to my proposal. But remember that giving up your position on vestry or refusing to cooperate with the board will automatically mean losing your membership in the Gold Circle. Are there any objections to my proposal?"

Absolute silence followed Mr. Pilchard's intimidating didacticism.

"Would someone from the vestry therefore make a motion to accept this advisory board?" asked Mr. Faulkner.

"So moved!" responded Ruthel Pollard, the Prime Minister's maiden aunt, a tall, gaunt, ugly woman in her mid seventies who always wore a black mantilla whenever she entered any part of the church building on any occasion. The acolytes discreetly called her 'Jumbie woman.'

"I second the motion," added Mrs. Pigthorne, without understanding the long term effects of her approval.

"Those in favor?"

The motion passed unanimously, even though the show of hands revealed some slight reluctance among a few members.

"Don't worry, my dear friends. You will not regret your wise decision to elect this board. Furthermore, I will speak with Mr. Goodfellow. We are fellow Lodge brothers. He will come to his senses. Trust me," Mr. Pilchard assured the gathering.

"Now that this part is over, and the board is officially in place, we must find a private name for ourselves," Mr. Faulkner declared.

"That's already in place, Faulkner... **Friends Organized** and **Operating** to **Lead Subordinates**," asserted Sam Westwater.

"Superb. Brilliant!!" exclaimed Mr. Faulkner. The new board members burst into thunderous applause.

"Those in favor?"

"Aye!" the members roared in unison.

"Opposed?"

Silence.

"Abstained?"

Silence.

"So moved. Congratulations, brothers and sisters!" beamed Mr. Faulkner, "But before we adjourn, let us join hands in solidarity and say a closing prayer. Ms. Pollard, would you be gracious enough to do the honors?"

Ruthel clasped her hands and stepped sanctimoniously to the head of the table. She opened her arms in the symbolic gesture of universal participation in prayer which is used by clergy. "Let us pray," she slowly and solemnly spoke in an assumed voice, closed her eyes and lifted her head upwards. "Dear Lord, we thank you for sending your Holy Spirit upon us, to make us successful in our mission. We also thank you, Father, for enlightening the vestry so that they could understand what you have commanded the board of advisors to do. Father, we know that you have called us to this privileged mission and to control and protect your church. Help us, dear Lord, to know your purpose for this church, this vestry, this community, this island, and make us strong and powerful soldiers in your service. Finally, continue to bless us in all of our undertakings. Amen."

"Amen!" responded the enraptured board members.

"Let us end with the singing of the hymn, 'Onward, Christian Soldiers!'" requested Ms. Pollard.

"We need hymn books," ordered Maggie Billings, a svelte, self-righteous, fair skinned woman in her early sixties who labored under the misapprehension that her light complexion and marginal wealth gave credence to superiority. It was rumored that Mr. Pilchard was her paramour.

"Let's get some from upstairs," suggested Ms. Pollard.

"The gate's locked and the lights are off," replied Nathaniel.

"I have the keys to the choir room." said Mrs. Pigthorne.

"Let me go and get a few," offered Maggie.

"I'll come with you...help you with the books," offered Mr. Pilchard.

The pious one and the judge thus made their way to the choir room which also was in the basement but towards the other end of the building. They approached the door and Ms. Billings fumbled in the dimly lighted corridor for the right key. Having selected it, she unlocked the door. The judge glanced furtively down the corridor, and believing that they were all alone, grabbed the pious one's arm and spun her gently towards him before she could have touched the light switch and planted a long, passionate kiss on her lips. He pushed her gently away, and with his hands still on her shoulders, gazed into her olive green eyes and whispered lovingly, "There is nothing more tender and fulfilling than a stolen kiss." The judge then gently pulled her towards him again.

The pious one delicately resisted him as she batted her ridiculously long, thick, false eyelashes and tantalized him with her alluring smile, "Especially from one who belongs to another," she purred.

The judge held her firmly, "Especially when the other is not blessed with lips as meretricious as yours. Kiss me again, then, you sweet Jezebel!"

They kissed again for a few more seconds. After regaining their composure, the judge flicked the light switch. The pious one gasped. The keys fell from her hand. The judge froze in shock. There in the corner on the floor were Rex and his companion, awake but inebriated from the effects of the borrowed wine. The bottle was empty and the candle was fully burnt out. The companion addressed the judge and the pious one with glazed, unfocused eyes. Rex, more seasoned in the effects of excessive alcohol, sat up and unashamedly faced the couple, "Looking for something, sir?" he asked unapologetically. Rex was slightly perturbed by their invasion of his privacy. The pious one averted her attention from the couple.

"Are they fully clothed?" she inquired.

"Apparently," responded the judge. "Rex, this is outrageous...totally unacceptable and inappropriate! I shall have a talk with the senior warden and the vicar. Ms. Billings, you take these books to the others. I'll take care of these two."

The pious one grabbed as many books as she could and exited. "Don't say anything about this to anybody," the judge seriously warned Maggie. "Tell them to go ahead. I'll be there in a minute."

Maggie left in nervous haste.

"May I speak to you privately, Rex...in the corridor?" Mr. Pilchard solemnly requested.

Rex rose from the altar cloth and followed the judge to the corridor. The companion remained on the altar cloth, agitated and intoxicated.

"Don't worry, sir. I wouldn't say nothing," pleaded Rex as he followed the judge to the door.

The judge paused, and then he turned abruptly towards Rex. He was mortified.

"You...you saw..."

"...yes, sir," Rex interjected, "but I wouldn't tell nobody...if you don't tell the vicar."

"Very well," the judge proclaimed with a sigh of relief. "What happened here remains here. I want you to swear that your word is your honor. Raise your right hand, Rex, and swear it."

"I swear," Rex solemnly declared.

"Thank you," the judge remarked with a serious expression. "Remain here until we all leave. I will extinguish all of the lights and that will be a sign for you to exit."

When Mr. Pilchard returned to the common room, the group was singing the last verse. He stood at the entrance, and, at the conclusion, instructed everyone to leave immediately and not linger for their wonted post-meeting confabulation. He further advised that he would replace the books and secure the building, since it appeared that Rex had perhaps stepped out momentarily. The group acquiesced to his instructions and left.

*   *   *

Thus the board of advisors to the vestry was formed and officially elected. It was clearly understood that the board was going to function covertly. It was also perspicuously understood that any vestry member who did not work harmoniously with the board, comply with its wishes, or who broke the chain of confidentiality would be relieved of his or her duties on the vestry. The loss of such a position would also result in immediate expulsion from the *Gold Circle*. Since none of the vestry members who remained was willing to lose such privileges, they all swore to secrecy and total obedience to the board. However, there remained one who vehemently opposed the existence of the board – Pigeon Goodfellow. Notwithstanding, his loyalty to the judge, as a friend and to some extent, a colleague, plus his wish to remain in the *Gold Circle* for some odd reason, influenced his decision to honorably resign from the vestry without losing his membership in the circle. This was the compromise which he and Mr. Pilchard reached the day after the election. Pigeon's letter of resignation stated that he was relinquishing his duties as a vestry person due to pressing family issues.

To the vestry, the board's official title became the 'Board of Advisors to the Vestry.' To the board members, they were the 'Friends Organized and Operating to Lead Subordinates'. But to Pigeon Goodfellow, they were the Board of FOOLS.

Chapter Two

Harvest Sunday

The incident involving Philbert Watts and Nollie Mertins remained a major issue for the members of the BOARD. The ramifications of his membership in the choir were frightening. Judge Pilchard and Laurent Faulkner were especially worried by such an awful prospect because it would set a precedent for the lower circle members whom they were adamant about driving out from among them. It therefore became expedient for them to put their plan into action by intercepting Philbert's movement and as such prevent the plebs from invading the forbidden territories and reducing St. Patrick's to the status of a simple country parish. However, the struggle to subdue and eradicate the plebs would have greater far-reaching effects than anyone on the BOARD would have imagined, for while the BOARD was planning its attack, others were putting on their armor for battle in order to save their own souls and establish themselves once and for all as members of equal standing in the most powerful parish on the island. As far as each was concerned, the upcoming Harvest celebration would provide the greatest opportunity to assert himself.

Harvest Sunday ranked third in the greatest celebrations of the church year, preceded only by Easter and Christmas when it fell on a Sunday. Elaborate preparations were made for this service and the fellowship which followed. It was an especially great day for the members of the *Bronze* and *Iron Circles*. One service was held on that day and they were allowed to fully participate in the service and partake of fellowship with the members of the *Gold Circle*. The barriers which separated the body were temporarily broken down – or so it seemed. Members of the lower circles were never invited or allowed to participate in the planning process. Instructions were given to them and they followed in exhilarative obedience, rejoicing in the fact that they were counted worthy to not only celebrate the Holy Eucharist with the upper echelon but to eat of the same bread and drink of the same cup in Holy fellowship at the communion table. Later, after the service, they would sit in juxtaposition with the dignitaries at the table during the elaborate lunch in the parish hall.

Following the celebration, the *Gold* and *Silver Circles* would retire to the common room for champagne and afterwards divide the cream of the harvest crop among them before departing for their respective places of abode. A select group from among the members of the *Bronze Circle*, attired *en grande tenue*, had the privilege of serving the champagne and properly packaging the produce. In gratitude for their service, they were allowed to consume any of the champagne that was left. They could not take any of it from the room; it had to be imbibed within the confines of the common room. After the reception in the common room ended, the members of the *Bronze* and *Iron Circle* would retire to the basement where they would change from their finery to more appropriate attire for cleaning. Under Rex's supervision they would clean the church, kitchen, parish hall, common room, bathrooms and any other area that was used during the celebration. For this semi-official role, Rex would don a tie, a hat and a pseudo-British accent and issue orders in his concept of flawless grammar. When the tasks were completed, the privileged underclass would again put on their formal attire, divide what was left of the fruits of the earth and leave for their respective homes. They returned as they came – in full dress for the special celebration. Rex would subsequently secure the building and then retrieve the unopened bottles of champagne, wine or whiskey from where he was told by the vicar to conceal them prior to the celebration and take them to the vicarage, ostensibly for secure storage. Then at dusk, Rex would return to the churchyard for his bottle of champagne which he would secure in the thick foliage between the church and the Gibson family vault.

Pigeon once had enjoyed the privilege of being waited on by the lower classes during the Harvest fellowship, but this year, following his altercation with Tessie and further compounded by the formation of the BOARD, he viewed the entire celebration as an abomination and decided that he would use it as ammunition against the BOARD and the members of the so called *Gold Circle*. This year, therefore, the harvest celebration was going to mark the crucial point in the history of St. Patick's.

During the final days of the approaching Harvest celebration, the issue regarding Philbert's membership in the choir gained intensity. However, unlike former times when the voice of the 'generals' was heard and obeyed, there were now mounting tension and resistance being built in the shadows. It was the custom that on Harvest Sunday, professional singers would be employed to supplement the choir and dignitaries from all over the island would be invited to the celebration. Thus, the timing was perfect for Philbert to strike again. The members of the *Iron Circle*, under the discreet direction of Pigeon, inveigled Philbert to approach Nollie Mertins. Pigeon's plan was to use Philbert to pave the way for the lower circles to assert themselves as full members, and in doing so deflate the *Gold Circle*. Philbert was going to serve both his and their purpose well.

After a brief, passing conversation between Philbert and Pigeon on the Sunday prior to the celebration, Pigeon became fully and sadly aware that Philbert's agenda was different from his. Pigeon had never fully disclosed the true purpose of his plans to Philbert or the members whom he was using to attack the BOARD, therefore, Philbert saw the *Iron Circle* as the conduit through which he would channel the relentless pursuit of the fulfillment of his ambition as a top rated, respected musician. He thus seized the opportunity to acquaint himself with the members of the *Gold Circle* who he believed could greatly enhance his career to the status of which he had always dreamed. Philbert had grown tired of the gig at *Phauphen's*. The clientele was basically the same and the venue seemed to have lost its flair. Furthermore, the ambiance no longer seemed to impress him. He wanted to perform on stages in great concert halls around the world, receive standing ovations from the sold out audiences and all of the other accolades reserved for such entertainers as Count Basie and Burt Bacharach – musicians whom he greatly admired and respected, and to some degree, emulated. He was gradually being consumed by his delusions of grandeur. This opportunity to reach and socialize with the elite was like an answered prayer to Philbert, and he was going to pursue this possibility with the intransigence of an unethical politician.

Philbert thus sought audience with the vicar. However, the vicar was already instructed by the senior warden, at the behest of the self appointed chairperson of the insidious Vestry Advisory Board, Laurent Faulkner, to be adamant in his refusal to allow Philbert Watts membership into the choir. His presence in the choir, Mr. Faulkner warned, would shatter the very nucleus of the principles upon which the church was built, and savagely distort the image of the choir. But Philbert was unyielding in his quest for membership. He was going to persevere until the vicar submitted to his passionate appeal.

Eventually, one Sunday morning in the sacristy, the vicar succumbed to Philbert's pressure. It was the week before the harvest celebration and the choir was preparing to embark upon a series of strenuous, last minute rehearsals. Thus the vicar was caught in a dilemma. He found himself in the middle of an ethical tug-of-war. He had to decide between his loyalty to the *Gold Circle* who kept the parish, and him, in solvency and to the captions which were prominently displayed in black gothic print over the arch between the nave and the narthex and the on the wall beside the south door which remained open to visitors all day. In addition, Philbert's relationship with the Addingtons would further have complicated matters for the frightened vicar. The wrong decision could cause him his office as vicar. Consequently, the vicar arranged a secret meeting with Nollie Mertins in the vicarage that Sunday evening.

"You must regard this meeting as a conspiracy," ordered the vicar, as he poured whisky on a few cubes of ice in a glass. "Ginger…?"

"Straight, please," replied Nollie as he took his seat at the edge of the Queen Anne chair, twiddling his thumbs.

"Relax, Mr. Mertins. We're not planning a coup, you know," assured Fr. Perths. "Here you are…on the rocks." The vicar's eyes pierced Nollie's as he extended his arm with the glass.

"Thank you…"

"Philbert Watts… he …belongs in the choir. We both know it." The vicar nervously pronounced as he sipped his bourbon. "You must receive him."

Nollie addressed the vicar squarely, but remained reticent. It became obvious to Fr. Perths that Nollie was not in concurrence with his edict. Nollie took another sip and contemplated the vicar.

"You must contact him tonight and invite him to the rehearsal on Monday. Do you have any questions…concerns?"

"What can one ask when one is issued a decree as severe as what one has just received?"

Nollie's expression was stolid as he took another sip of the distilled maize. "You invite. I come. You command. I obey."

"I appreciate your candidness…and admire your sagacity," declared the vicar. "You are indeed wise to withhold your opinion. As it stands, I am caught between the devil and the deep blue sea, or as my mother used to say, God rest her soul, 'I sure got my knickers in a right twist'. You must understand my situation, Nollie. If I refuse Mr. Watts' proposal, my blood will be required by Bishop Addington. If I grant him permission to join the choir, the vestry's wrath will be upon me. So, I had to choose between my blood and their wrath."

"I suppose that these are the complexities that one encounters when one is thrown into the hurly burley of ecclesiastical management." Nollie's tone was tinged with bitter sarcasm and he wore a wry grin.

"Well, I suppose that's all I have to say – about this particular matter," the vicar responded dismissively. "Incidentally," warned Fr. Perths, "the matter pertaining to this meeting must be held in the strictest confidence. You must let the decision to embrace Mr. Watts seem unanimously…yours."

"What?"

"For my sake. You owe your loyalty to me. To betray me is to court redundancy," the vicar advised Mr. Mertins. "I'll be as frank with you as you have been with me."

Fr. Perths took another sip of bourbon.

"Is that a threat, Fr. Perths?"

"A promise," replied the vicar nonchalantly, and took one more sip. "Well," rising and wringing hands victoriously, "I guess this is all I have to say. So, are we together on this, my friend and brother in Christ?"

"Do I have a choice, good Christian fellow?" Nollie gulped the last of his whiskey, put the glass on the table and picked up his hat, turned towards the vicar and bowed reverently, "Good evening, Reverend Sir."

Fr. Perths breathed a heavy sigh of relief and closed the door behind Nollie. He had convinced himself that his actions were justifiable. His welfare, he further believed, was going to be the object of the *Gold Circle's* onslaught when they see Philbert robed and processing with the choir. Situation Ethics thus further gained legitimacy through the vicar's sense of reason. The consequences had to be evaluated. Fear of consequential reassignment by the Bishop and the quest to avoid inculpation from the vestry forced Fr. Perths to become more indurate towards Nollie. To refuse Philbert admission was to jeopardize his relationship with Bishop Addington; to allow Philbert to join the choir was to unleash the vestry's wrath. Ultimately, it was the Bishop who could inflict the deadlier blow.

Fr. Perths thus poured himself another shot of bourbon and ascended the stairs to bed, convinced that he had unilaterally brought years of an unpalatable tradition to an end. He chuckled at the thought that it was Nollie, and not he, who would have to put on the helmet and breastplate of armor to repel the deadly, piercing looks and poisonous verbal arrows that would be hurled at him on Harvest Sunday morning.

* * *

Nollie Mertins sped away from the vicarage in suppressed, semi-intoxicated anger. He did not realize how much bourbon he had actually imbibed until he hit the wind. However, he was still relatively in control of his faculties and decided that instead of heading to his home to bear left on

Buckingham Avenue towards the city. After what seemed an excruciatingly protracted journey, Nollie turned into Bishop's Court.

It was just after 8.00 p.m. when Nollie arrived at Bishop's Court. The watchman recognized him from some of the newspaper articles which chronicled reports of the many organ recitals which Nollie had arranged and at which he had performed at St Patrick's over the years.

"Is Bishop Addington here?" Nollie inquired as he stepped out of the car.

"Right upstairs, sir. Let me take you to the door," the watchman offered. "Them is good concerts you does up there in Aberths, sir…reads a lot about them. Anything new up and comin?"

"That's what I've come to tell the Bishop about. Will tell you about it when I come back down."

The watchman pressed the bell. Delicate footsteps threaded down the stairs. The door opened and a drawn figure stood silhouetted against the light in the background.

"Good evening," the figure greeted Nollie in an inquiring tone. It was Antoinette Fyrish, the housekeeper. She was in her late sixties and was slightly audibly impaired.

"Is the man with the big organ concerts up there in Aberths…he come to see me lord. Take him upstairs," instructed the watchman.

"Who is it, Nettie?" a distinguished voice came floating downstairs.

"It's the man with the big organ…from Aberths."

"Who?" the distinguished voice inquired.

"The man from Abersths, me lord…who do the big organ concerts…at St Patrick's," yelled the watchman.

Nollie entered and approached the stairway. Bishop Addington immediately recognized him.

"My lord. Good evening," Nollie greeted the Bishop with a gentle, courtly bow of the head.

"Nollie Mertins. What a delightful surprise!" exclaimed the Bishop. "Please, come right up."

Nollie ascended the stairs and approached the Bishop. They shook hands.

"Thank you for allowing me the privilege of meeting with you without prior arrangement, my lord."

"I'm happy to see you, nevertheless. Do sit down." Bishop Addington caught a whiff of alcohol on Nollie's breath. Nollie's face was flushed and he was a bit disheveled.

"A cup of tea…some…assorted biscuits, perhaps?"

"No. Thank you, my lord. Actually, this is just a quick courtesy call to let you know what I'm doing at St. Patrick's."

"Ahh…another of those great concerts, I imagine."

"Well, the harvest program, as a matter of fact. I've decided to offer Mr. Watts…Philbert…a position in the choir…and I am going to invite him to sing the lead for the anthem. I realized that the constitution of the choir was not reflective of the cross section of our membership so I am going to persuade Mr. Watts to join…and lead the anthem this Sunday…for harvest. It's my first step towards making the choir more inclusive. Plus, Mr. Watts has incredible musical talent."

"That's rather noble of you, Nollie," remarked Bishop Addington.

"Thank you, my lord," Nollie beamed like a school boy who had won his father's admiration. "I realize that you have been a major influence in Mr. Watts' life, and so if it is not presumptuous of me to ask, I would like you to come this Sunday to St. Patrick's for our special harvest celebration. Philbert would relish your being there. Your presence, I believe, would influence him to stay in the choir and in the church. I know that a man of your position must have many duties on a Sunday but if at all possible, my lord, I beseech you to come…for Mr. Watts' sake."

"Well, how does one refuse such an invitation when it is presented like this? It is fortunate that this Sunday, I was going to be conducting private devotions in the chapel here at half past seven. I'll be finished in time for the service at St Patrick's."

"May I ask one more favor of you, my lord?"

"Certainly," assured the Bishop.

"Could you keep this a secret…I mean…my coming here…and make your visitation …well…appear as a surprise visit?"

"I think that I can. But I will just come and sit in the congregation. I will not officially participate, if that will be alright. Mrs. Addington and I shall be there," advised his lordship.

"Wonderful!" replied Nollie gleefully. "Could you give me the exact address for Mr. Watts. I don't quite remember the house."

"Three twenty one Charlotte Road…small white house on the left, facing New Market Street…"

"Thank you, my lord. Now I must bid thee farewell. Au revoir." Nollie rose and tipped his hat respectfully.

Nollie took brisk steps to maintain his balance as he descended the stairs and approached his car. He beamed with satisfaction at the success of the first part of his clandestine plot to deflate Fr. Perths in front of the Advisory Board and the Vestry. As he closed his car door and started the engine, the watchman came running towards him.

"So how's things up there, at St Patrick's?"

"Good," replied Nollie.

"Tell me, is that cockroach, Rex Davis, still buggin' round me cousin's wife?"

"What?" expressed Nollie.

"Rex and me cousin…Ethel Phipps…you know…Big Ethel…"

"Don't know who you talking about."

"Well, me cousin does work at sea, and she does work at *Phauphen's*, where Philbert Watts does sing and play the piano."

"Dunno. Don't go into *Phauphen's*. I live in North Abersthwaithe."

"Well, I hear say that the two of them is a item. Rex like to play like he holy, and look what he doin'. When me cousin come back from sea, I goin' to tell him to go up there and galvanize Rex behind," the watchman swore.

"Well, got to go. Nice talking to you." Nollie feigned a smile as he reversed from the driveway and sped off along King's Drive.

Within ten minutes Nollie arrived at the small, white house. It was shortly after eight forty five when he knocked at the faded, brown door. The curtains parted and a grim face peered through the glass. Nollie took a deep breath. The door opened and a man in a plaid pajama pants and a tattered, dingy white vest opened. It was Philbert's father.

"Can I help you?" the feeble voice inquired.

"Good evening, sir. I am Nollie Mertins, the organist and choir master at St Patrick's in Abersthwaithe. I've come to ask a favor of Philbert, your son."

"Just a minute." Mr. Watts turned and headed towards the kitchen where a dim light was burning. The tantalizing aroma of stewed fish effused from the kitchen. A figure appeared at the kitchen and contemplated Nollie from a distance. The figure was clad in an ankle length duster, with feathers around the neckline and down the front. Slightly withered hands held the middle opening together. Nollie thought for a moment that the figure in the robe must be awfully warm or very cold.

"Is who?" the robed figure inquired in a suspicious tone.

"The organist from St. Patrick's," the old man replied. "He want to see Phil."

"Let the man inside, Lennie," ordered the robed figure.

"Come in, Mr. Mertins. Have a seat."

Nollie entered, acknowledged the robed figure and sat in the chair closest to the door.

"So you is a organist?" the robed one addressed Nollie, in a thick, localized English accent.

"Yes, mam." Nollie suppressed the laughter.

"We did want our son to consume a position like that …at the cathedral," confessed the overdressed individual, "but he choosed to work at some old heathen night club in Abersths. Of course, his father and me was ablutely disappointed," the robed one cried in despair.

The robed one's malapropism, superimposed by her hired British accent made it very difficult for Nollie to easily understand what she was saying. Furthermore, it seemed that she had already placed her dentures in storage for the night. The slightly muffled sound thus aggravated matters.

"I suppose you are Mrs. Watts; Philbert's mother?"

"Yes. I'm sorry that I didn't induce me'self earlier. I am Philbert's mum."

Philbert appeared in the corridor and approached Nollie. He was puzzled. It was Nollie with whom he had had the confrontation a few night earlier, who had blatantly displayed his disdain towards him in front of the congregation. Nollie rose as Philbert drew close.

"Your eminence!" Nollie extended his arm and greeted Philbert. They shook hands. "I know that my visit no doubt surprises you," admitted Nollie.

Philbert's art of subtle diplomacy concealed his surprise at Nollie's unexpected visit and his suspicion about Nollie's strangely hyperbolical greeting.

"I would rather say that it amazes me," Philbert remarked. "Nevertheless, what can I do for you, sir?" Philbert inquired in the tone of a wary businessman.

"Don't make this visit sound so formal," Nollie besought him.

The hint of alcohol accosted Philbert's nostrils. He stepped back and contemplated Nollie with a little more suspicion. It became obvious to Philbert that Nollie was under the influence of alcohol and thus was merely bordering on rationality. Philbert therefore decided that judiciousness must guide his response to the semi-inebriated Nollie Mertins.

"Have a seat, Mr. Mertins. I must say that I am very flattered by your visit. I feel so unworthy to be visited by one as distinguished as yourself."

"Thank you, my dear friend." Nollie sank into the chair, in a desperate attempt to cling to sobriety. Philbert concealed his amusement.

Philbert dismissed his parents and sat opposite Nollie. "I understand that you seek a favor of me?"

"Yes. If indeed you would be gracious enough to oblige."

"I'm sure. What is it?" Philbert realized that he must act quickly before Nollie became fully overcome by the alcohol.

"Harvest…the anthem…I want you to join the choir and take the lead for the harvest anthem this Sunday."

Philbert was flabbergasted. Nevertheless, he sensed that there was something sinister about Nollie's request. "Are you sure, Mr. Mertins, that you would like me to sing the solo for the anthem?"

"I am. You see, Mr. Watts, I thought of what took place last Sunday and as I was leaving, I turned to close the door behind me and I read, perhaps for the first time, the caption on the plaque by the South door…that speaks of the inclusiveness of the Anglican church, and I thought, for the first time, that I have an obligation to welcome all persons into the household of God, so why not invite Philbert to join the choir."

"I see," Philbert interjected. "How very noble of you, Mr. Mertins. When do I come for the rehearsal?"

"Well, you wouldn't," Nollie replied. "I will bring the music to you. We will rehearse privately. No one will know that you will be taking the lead until they see you in the procession and hear you sing. I want it to be a surprise. It's time for me to stand up for what I believe to be morally correct…true, just!"

"Then why take such a clandestine approach?"

"The impact of the surprise, Mr. Watts. The impact!"

"Then I shall be happy to abide with your wish, Mr. Mertins," Philbert assured him.

"Well, that's all. Goodnight." Nollie rose awkwardly from his chair, put on his hat and left without saying another word. Philbert stood watching his strange and unexpected guest until his car disappeared around the corner.

* * *

Sunday morning came like the final advent. The bells chimed at 5.00 a.m. and the villagers welcomed the happy morning with the joy of souls who have come out of some great tribulation. They rose with the bells as the light of dawn broke over the eastern horizon and put the darkness of the long night of anticipation to flight. It was a glorious morning. The monochromatic hues of grey and blue were superimposed by the subtle tones of orange and red and the brilliance of the light of the rising sun. There was the illusion of green slightly above the horizon, where the orange and the blue gently kissed. As the morning sky above flaunted its kaleidoscope of color, the people below prepared to deck themselves with garments that paralleled the festivity of the celebration. The *Iron Circle* members were especially notorious for clothing themselves in symbolic attire. They were the ones who planted farms and worked in the cane and rice fields; they were the housekeepers to the wealthy professionals and English emigrants; they were *Phauphen's* main clientele. They were the fishmongers and market vendors; they were the laborers. They worked hard and they lived hard; they produced many children – that was their sole legacy. Ruthel often spoke disparagingly of the legacy of the men of the *Iron Circle* as two large breasts and a dozen children.

There were, however, certain characteristics of the members of the *Iron Circle* which, as Pigeon often discussed with the vicar, warranted great admiration – and respect. Poverty might have dictated their standard of living and determined their social status, but they possessed an ironic sense of peace and contentment. They lived as a community, not as isolated individuals living in juxtaposition to each other. They were neither shaken by the harsh vicissitudes of life nor intimidated by life's dismal prospects. They did not yearn for material affluence – their wealth was their love and support for each other. When there was a marriage or baptism, the word spread around and they came in droves, with their cattle and sheep and chickens – and liquor. They feasted, they drank, they made merry; they fought, they sang, they slept; then they returned to their respective homes. No formal invitations were ever issued – they responded to the word. Similarly, in the event of a death, they came bearing edible gifts – and liquor. They offered sympathy, they hugged, they wept in unison; they sang, they slammed dominoes on the table, they imbibed to a stupor, they kept vigil, they fought, they slept and then they rose and buried their dead – their faith in God and their love for each other being their only strength and consolation. Friendship with the deceased or the family was irrelevant – they responded to the word.

Religion dictated the order of life for the *Iron Circle*. A weathered bible could be found in almost every home – and its contents were demonstrated relatively well among the people. No provision was ever made for them to pursue bible study at St. Patrick's. Such studies were the privilege of the two higher circles. It was not that the vicar was not interested in expounding the scriptures to them – it was because he was forbidden to allow them to share the same class and nature of studies with their superiors. Furthermore, it was believed that the Theology would be too complex for their simple minds. Thus they knew no Theology but they knew the raw, pure gospel. They did not theologize or philosophize but they lived the gospel in their unique way. The word was their hope, their faith and their life. They cared for nothing else. Consequently, their concept of harvest differed vastly from that of the upper class conservatives. These characteristics Pigeon saw as the foundation which he could use to develop his plan of attack on the BOARD.

The members of the *Iron Circle* understood the festival as a celebration of God's act of providence and of God's care for them on a communal and individual level. All that they had, they vehemently believed and argued, came from God. It was all they had to live on, and all for which they lived. Thus Harvest Sunday was *their* day, *their* festival.

Harvest Sunday was also Rex's day to assert himself as a figure of some basic level of authority. He sought to impress the *Gold Circle* members by his display of arrant disrespect for the members of the *Bronze* and *Iron Circles*. He spoke to them disdainfully and harshly, especially when anyone of consequence was within hearing distance. He directed them to the rear of the nave, and if any should escape his attention when they entered and subsequently assume a position towards the front of the nave or in either of the transepts, he would request their immediate removal so as to make room for the government officials and other people of importance who were expected to attend. The children of the soil would graciously acquiesce to his commands and proceed to the rear.

This year, however, circumstances would set a new tone for the Harvest celebrations and for St. Patrick's on the whole. Maudie Springer, a tall, buxom woman in her late fifties entered the church through the south door and sat in the front pew in the south transept. Maudie was a proud woman. She referred to herself as a regal black woman who might have been a queen if she were born in Africa. Maudie wallowed in her delusions of grandeur and considered herself aloof from the uncultured villagers who would be classified as the *Iron Circle*. It was therefore not surprising that she would deign to sit in the transept rather than at the rear of the nave.

Having taken her seat, Maudie opened her large, white handbag and took out her bible and hymn book. She was organized and wanted everything to be in easy reach when needed. Maudie wore a green, ankle length skirt which was held at the waist by a wide gold belt. The tightly drawn belt which was strapped around the waist in quiet repose, like the calm before the storm, was followed by an impetuous protuberance of green that curved like a semi-circle at Maudie's rear mid-section before tapering off at the ankle. The white cotton blouse seemed a bit too close for someone who was blessed with such a healthy endowment of mammary glands, but the audacious, double stranded, green necklace and matching earrings created a subtle diversion from the hefty bosom to the small, dark, round face under a huge, gold hat. White, wedge heeled shoes and white, lace gloves completed the ensemble. When Maudie returns home, the entire outfit would be aired and then replaced in a trunk until the following harvest.

As Maudie made herself comfortable and bowed her head in prayer and contemplation, Rex observed her from the north transept. The pews were quickly being filled and he was bringing chairs from the undercroft and placing them along the side aisle. Realizing that he was the center of attention as he organized the seats and pranced about in his crisp, starched, black cassock which a member of the *Gold Circle* had brought for him from England several years ago, he made his way over to Maudie, never averting his attention from her as he approached the pew. His expression was as adamant as flint as he considered her gross impertinence. On reaching the pew, he tapped loudly on the polished wood to attract Maudie's attention. Maudie raised her head in anger at the crude interruption of her private meditation. Rex said not a word but raised his arm and pointed toward the rear of the nave. Maudie studied him momentarily and then calmly resumed her meditation. The congregation watched in silence. Those who knew Maudie

Springer held their breath. Rex slammed his hand against the pew a second time. Maudie continued her meditation without raising her head again.

"Get to the back!" snapped Rex as he thumped on the pew a third time.

"I'm trying to say me prayers, ok," Maudie responded with quiet severity.

"Your place is at the back!" Rex retorted brusquely.

"Look, don't let me sin me soul this early harvest Sunday morning, Rexworth Davis. Bug off!" Maudie warned the persistent sexton. "I'm tryin' to say me prayers."

"Then get to the back of the church where you belongs and say them there. God goin' to hear you better at the back where you belongs…with the others!" Rex ordered.

"You wants me to go to the back?" Maudie inquired.

"Yessss!" Rex replied, leaning forward towards Maudie's face.

"Fine!"

Maudie rose with haste, collected her books, replaced them in her handbag and hung the bag strap over her arm. Then without uttering another word, rocked the pew until the clamps that fixed it to the floor became loose, and with great skill and gargantuan strength, maneuvered the bench into the side aisle and dragged it to the back. Silence engulfed the church as the congregation beheld Maudie's tempestuous outburst. Some of the distinguished visitors rose to their feet, with mouths agape at Maudie's display of superhuman strength and rabid defiance toward the robed sexton. Mr. Pilchard, who had arrived and was seated close to his wife in one of the pews along the center isle, rose from his seat and approached the visibly agitated and embarrassed Rex.

"Don't stoop to her level. Let the hog wallow in the mud where she belongs," he advised. "We shall replace the pew after the service ends."

The crowd could see that Rex felt overwhelmed by the surge of defeat, and it pleased them. But they could also see the beam of pride etched across his face as the judge came over and consoled him. They were unaware that Rex and the judge had become dear friends; that they were sealed in a contractual friendship that began in the undercroft a few weeks earlier, the sexton and the judge, blasphemous partners bearing secrets which if revealed could cause one his job and the other his honor and his marriage. The crowd could never have known that these two men were sworn to secrecy like the men of the cloth or that there was a specific reason why they suddenly began to display moral support for each other privately and publicly. Furthermore, how could they have known that the two men were being faithful to their truce or that the foundation of their friendship was built on fear, the fear of a revelation that could destroy them both? If they could, they would know that it was this very fear that drove the judge to publicly display his sympathy towards Rex during his time of anguish.

To the *Gold Circle*, Rex was the ammunition to be used to attack or subdue the *Iron Circle*. It was Rex who inadvertently stood at the line of fire between the *Gold* Circle and the *Bronze* and *Iron Circles*. Rex served their purpose well and they compensated him handsomely at Christmas and on his birthday. Technically, Rex belonged to the *Iron Circle* but the *Board* which represented the cream of the *Gold Circle* membership thought it sagacious to use one from the lower circles to attack the lower circles. It was Rex who defended the *Gold Circle* when they came under a hail of criticism from the lower circles. It was he who kept the lower circles in place when they sought to lift themselves from the dust upon which the *Gold Circle* treaded. He was the betrayer of his people, the one utterly despised by both circles but embraced by the one to whom he paid obeisance. Rex became a wandering stranger in his own territory.

Mr. Pilchard was one of Ischalton's most respected citizens. He was tall, dignified and always impeccably attired. He was regarded by Ischalton's elite as the quintessential gentleman, refined in speech and polished in his mannerism. His wife was the epitome of delicate breeding, a gentle woman with a kind heart, whose only fault was her unconscious membership in the *Gold Circle*. She argued that Maudie's actions were perhaps obstreperous, but nevertheless justified by provocation. To those who knew Mr. Pilchard, the socialite, he was the famous judge. However, to Pigeon Goodfellow, who was one of his closest acquaintances for many years, he was privately but jocularly referred to as the notorious judge. It was Pigeon who later would coin the term, famnotorious, to describe the judge, an adjective which would later be adopted by the Abersthwaithe elite to describe the famous who had fallen from grace.

Thus Mr. Pilchard came to Rex's rescue. The members of the *Bronze* and *Iron Circles* observed the entire incident with a mixture of amusement, anger and jealousy. They were amused because they were not particularly fond of Maudie Springer or Rex but angered because Rex was attempting to humiliate one of their own in front of the elite members of the congregation. However, they were jealous because of Rex's apparently close acquaintance with the judge. Some of them, by their display of humility and accepted inferiority expressed in words and actions towards the members of the upper circles, publicly revealed a longing for such a relationship with one of the island's most respected socialites. Nevertheless, they were baffled by the sudden closeness between the two, as revealed by questions and knitted brows, and therefore determined to uncover the story behind the bonding of what Maudie Springer described as 'the unequally yoked.'

As Rex and the judge retreated from the area of controversy, the bell rang thrice to signal the start of the service. By this time the church was packed and the ushers were trying to find seats for the late arrivals. Only one pew was available for seating – that in which Maudie Springer sat. No one else joined her. It was her pew that day. It was she who had solicited it for her comfort; it was she who fought for the right of occupancy. She had denied no one a seat. The people made a deliberate choice not to sit in a pew that seemed to have been placed there by accident or just left there as a favor to the lower class visitors who crammed the church that Harvest Sunday. The late comers all chose alternative seats. Even Stella Dawkins, nicknamed 'the Pirate', who peddled bootlegged DVDs and CDs among the *Iron Circle* during the sermons on Sundays opted for another seat which would have proved more lucrative because of the possibility of a more protracted sermon.

The vicar invited the congregation to bow their heads for the opening prayer, after which the organ blasted a fanfare that introduced the opening bars of the hymn, 'We plough the fields and scatter the good seed on the ground.' The hymn was a favorite for Harvest Sunday and the congregation bellowed its praise to God for his gracious acts of providence. The procession entered the church and marched with solemnity and dignity down the aisle towards the altar. The verger lead the procession, stepping as though he had been mechanically wound up, with his head held high and his attention fixed on the huge cross hanging majestically from the wall at the rear of the altar. The choir followed immediately behind the thurifer, the crucifer and the torch bearers. Pomp and circumstance was the order of the service. The choir wore red robes and surplices trimmed with lace. The clergy, who were visiting St Patrick's for the celebration perhaps with the dim hope of being sent to serve there sometime in the very near future, were impressive in their regal attire. The vicar was the last in the procession and he shrouded himself in a green and gold cope embellished with gold tassels. A pair of the smallest acolytes walked on the right and left of him, holding the cope open. He nodded reverently to the congregation who sat along the centre aisle. For some strange reason, he held his right arm slightly forward as if he were carrying a crosier. Some of the women of the *Iron Circle* who were crammed at the rear of the nave bent their knees slightly and bowed their heads as he passed by. The vicar beamed.

Toward the conclusion of the epistle, there was a slight commotion at the rear of the church. As some of the congregation looked back, gasps were heard almost in unison. Bishop and Mrs. Addington had arrived and were waiting to be ushered to their seats by the excited usher. The watchman and Antoinette Fyrish accompanied them and were standing slightly behind Mrs. Addington. Rex met them at the door and directed the ushers to find seats for the watchman and Antoinette among the *Iron Circle*. Bishop Addington, however, forbade the usher from carrying out the instruction. He instructed Rex to find a pew where all four could have sat together.

The lesson had ended, but Nollie Mertins paused from introducing the sequence hymn until the Addingtons had been seated. There was no pew that could have accommodated four additional persons – except the one in which Maudie Springer sat. Maudie rose and beckoned the party to join her. There was room, she whispered. Before anyone could stop the Addingtons, the Bishop proceeded towards Maudie. The rest followed him, trying desperately to minimize the attention. As they tiptoed towards Maudie, some of the members of the *Bronze* and *Iron* Circles delicately applauded. Rex, as well as some members of the upper circles, especially Mr. Pilchard and Mr. Faulkner, was livid with rage. The Addingtons seemed quite content to sit among the peasants.

"A pretty picture indeed," whispered Ruthel Pollard to her nephew, who also was a member of St. Patrick's. "Like the pearls before the swine." She glanced at the Addingtons disapprovingly.

The opening bars of the sequence hymn, 'Now Thank we all Our God', echoed across the building and the congregation stood. The members at the rear of the nave sang lustily. The men, in particular, composed impromptu harmonies that defied the melody – harsh, cacophonous tones that were the evident after effects of the harvest vigil and celebration which took place in the village among the members of the lower circles. At the vigil, food was prepared in large pots all night and there was eating, excessive drinking of locally made wines from rice and corn and illegally distilled spirits from the sugar cane. Thus they sang with spirit, literally. Nevertheless, the Addingtons relished such spirited singing which was quite a startling contrast to the excruciatingly stiff conservatism of the Cathedral and many of the other Anglican churches around the island.

Canon Hutchfield preached a convincing sermon on Providence. However, the Theology, set in the most ornate language, made no impact on most of the congregation which was seated at the rear of the nave. It never did. They never could understand the Theology, for they were not academic geniuses. The Gospel was their strength, but alas, it was rarely preached from the pulpit at St. Patrick's. It did not matter on this day, however, to the members of the *Iron Circle*. They were graced by the distinguished presence of Bishop and Mrs. Addington in their midst.

During the announcements, Fr. Perths specially acknowledged the presence of the Addingtons. There was enthusiastic applause. Bishop Addington gently refused the vicar's invitation to 'come up higher.' He stated that he and Mrs. Addington were enjoying the rare privilege of sitting among the flock, sharing uplifting fellowship. He thanked the vicar for his kindness, however.

After the other visitors were welcomed, the special blessings were performed and announcements were made, the vicar pronounced the offertory sentence and the choir rose to perform the anthem. The harvest anthem had always been one of the highlights of the celebration. Everyone braced himself for what in the past had invariably been an emotional performance. Specially hired professional singers usually sang the lead while other specially invited persons assumed supplementary roles. This year, Nollie told the choir that he was unsure of who would be the soloist and therefore he was going to assume the role throughout the rehearsals until he found a suitable vocalist. He avoided any questions or conversations regarding the soloist.

The anthem began with the introduction from the organ. Nollie's ostentatious display of his musical adroitness led him to digress from the introduction which he had rehearsed with the choir to a complicated improvisation of the score. Nevertheless, the choir stood erect, waiting patiently for their note to begin. They knew Nollie well and had come to expect this unnecessary flaunting of musical genius over the years. Nollie closed his eyes in emotional ecstasy as he made love to the organ, seducing the key board and the musical score with a surge of sporadically impetuous mordents and acciaccaturas. The congregation watched this stupendous display of musical skill with great appreciation. The *Gold Circle* regarded Nollie Mertins as one of the island's seven wonders – as one of the assets that place St. Patrick's as the pinnacle of conservative Anglicanism and as the point of gravity for ecclesiasticism.

Then the members of the lower circles who instantly recognized Philbert gasped and opened their eyes wide in amazement, as if the heavens suddenly opened up before them, as Philbert Watts appeared from the direction of the altar with the grace and grandiosity of an angel coming to proclaim the dawning of the Kingdom. His appearance demanded steadfast attention as he strutted down the chancel, robed in a crisp, new red cassock and brilliant white surplice which was devoid of lace trimming. He held the book open in his right hand and, having reached the place where he was instructed to stand, waited for his cue. The choir had their eyes fixed on Philbert. They seemed unsure of his purpose but nevertheless maintained their composure. The members of the *Gold Circle*, especially the BOARD and Vestry members, beamed with pride as the figure in red and white stepped down the chancel. The whole presentation, they thought, was dramatic and awesome. Then one by one, they began to recognize the figure and their jaws dropped in shock. Mr. Faulkner turned and addressed the judge with his eyes before turning again towards the vicar. Unspoken demonstrations of acrid disapproval among some members of the *Gold Circle* cast an aura of cold hostility across the front and middle sections of the nave. However, emotions of delight were ignited at the rear of the nave as Philbert stood in the center of the chancel, as motionless and regal as a sculpture of a king. Then Nollie gave the cue.

The four part harmony of the opening verses engulfed the church like a cloud of sweet smelling incense. The euphonious sound of the well trained choir seemed to have obliterated every trace of anger or displeasure at Philbert's appearance. Ironically, none of the Board or Vestry members had yet associated Nollie Mertins with Philbert's assault on St. Patrick's. After the choir had sung another verse, Nollie played a few more bars that served as a bridge. Eight staccato base notes followed, then like a rush of mighty wind, a powerful, refined baritone voice issued forth from the robed figure in the center of the chancel. The entire church fell silent as all eyes beheld Philbert. His amazing voice transcended every range from second bass to top tenor as he glorified the Lord and paid homage to the composer of the Harvest anthem. Ambivalent thoughts seemed to play a frenzied game of see-saw in the minds of the Board members as their expressions switched from joy, at what appeared to be the excellence of the presentation before the distinguished visitors, to anger at their resentment towards Philbert.

Laurent Faulkner must have realized that Philbert's presence and flawless rendition would present even more grave possibilities for St. Patrick's. He quickly whispered to the judge that the BOARD must act quickly to diffuse any thoughts of embracing any member of the *Bronze* or *Iron Circles* at this level, for any such participation in major occasions or decisions by any member of these circles was formally forbidden. They knew, however, that unearthing Philbert would pose extreme difficulty, especially after the standing ovation he received at the end of the anthem, a sign of highest appreciation that was led by Bishop Addington himself and followed immediately by the members of the three lower circles, then by the distinguished guests and the reluctant members of the *Gold Circle*. Such homage had never before been paid to the choir or any soloist during a service at St. Patrick's.

The service ended with the usual pomp and circumstance. However, at the end of the postlude, the visitors and the elated members of the lower circles flocked the Addingtons as they stood at the entrance to the main door – and Philbert Watts, who was still in his robe and whom Bishop Addington had made it his duty to congratulate after embracing the vicar. Fr. Perths was a little more than an incidental figure that morning as the excited congregation sought to individually welcome the Bishop and Mrs. Addington. Meanwhile, some of the leading members of the Board accosted Nollie Mertins at the organ before he had the chance to seek refuge at the Bishop's side.

"What the hell was the meaning of that…that sacrilege that took place during the offertory anthem?" the judge snarled.

"I have no comments to make," Nollie protested as he closed the organ and sorted his music.

"The height of impertinence!" barked Gladys Barnwell, a frustrated, middle aged mulatto woman whose husband paid her little attention.

"Am I not free to choose the person I think best for the solo parts? Haven't I always been correct in my choice of soloists over the years? What is the big issue now?"

"Riff-raff, Mr. Mertins… riff-raff!" screamed Gladys.

"Look, kindly excuse me," requested Nollie. "I need to speak with his Lordship,"

As he attempted to move, Mr. Faulkner intercepted him. "You're going nowhere until you give us an acceptable explanation of what took place here!"

One of the members of the *Iron Circle* noticed that the members of the *Gold Circle* were surrounding Nollie in what appeared to be a hostile exchange. He quietly nudged his wife, who brought the confrontation to the attention of a few of the others, including Ram and his wife. They hurried towards the chancel. They knew that the man who gave Philbert an opportunity to represent them was in trouble and dashed over to defend their new friend and supporter. As they drew closer, they observed Mr. Faulkner speaking and waving his index finger threateningly in Nollie's face. His body language suggested hostility.

"Is what happening here, Brother Mertins?" inquired Ram's wife.

Mrs. Pigthorne, who feared the repercussions of the Board, was standing next to the judge in an attempt to gain his favor. She fixed Ram's wife a chilling stare.

"Shouldn't you be over in the Parish Hall preparing to serve the guests, you?" The scorn was piercing. "Get over there and change your clothes and see to the guests, please," Mrs. Pigthorne commanded.

"I know that you ain't talking to me. You *couldn't* be talking to me." Ram's wife's voice was seething with venom.

"You have to be a stupid woman to assume that she is not speaking to you. Do you see any of your specie standing up here?" Maggie Billings interjected sarcastically.

"You go and bury yo' head, yo'ugly, dried up, freckled face' red nigger!" Ram's wife sizzled with bitter retort.

"Woman! You are standing in sacred space!" charged Mr. Pilchard.

"Mrs. Ramgalam! That's me name! Not woman. Mrs. Ramgalam!" Ram's wife yelled. "And look who talkin' 'bout sacred space, look who…!"

"Just go over to the hall and do as you were told," ordered Gladys.

"You say one more thing to me this morning, and I goin' tear that ugly, lace frock off of you…right in this *sacred space*, expose you fully, so that the Lord can see just what you and all of y'all up there is like….a bunch of flaming hypocrites!"

"That would be a sight to behold, Gladys…," said Nollie, imbued with sudden courage at the realization of support from the spokesperson of the forbidden group, "…the sight of a naked woman of such formidable proportions. Now kindly excuse me. I need to have a tete -a- tete with his Lordship."

Nollie retreated to the choir room as Ram's wife continued to batter Gladys Barnwell and Eloise Pigthorne with a hail of angry words. The rest of the small, embittered, opposing group regarded Nollie with contempt as he made his silent and hurried retreat.

"I goin' over to the hall," Ram's wife concluded, "and tell the others to make sure that the Bishop and his wife and the other priests get something to eat. Is every man for himself after that! Come, Ram!" The small group stormed out of the church and headed for the parish hall.

"We must take immediate control of things around here, Eloise. As our warden, you have failed us…miserably. Look what happened today, right in our very face…a gross insult to our intelligence and disregard for our status. We have to pull out all of the stops. It's do or die, and we're going to stay alive. I promise you. I swear in the name of the Almighty God – the *Gold Circle* will prevail!" declared the judge.

The protestors headed towards the hall for the reception. By then there were only a few of the ushers and some of the members of the congregation who were in the church replacing the pew which Maudie Springer had moved to the back and removing some of the sugar cane stalks that had decorated the church for the harvest.

Rex was returning from the parish hall where he had been taking the produce from the altar. Mr. Pilchard intercepted him as he approached the high altar.

"Am I to believe that you have been talking, Rex?" he asked.

"About what, sir?" the perplexed Rex inquired.

"About our little secret."

"You mean…?"

"Right," responded the judge.

"Why 'you askin'me that, sir?"

"Because Ram's wife, that impertinent jennyass, made a suggestive remark…"

Rex paused. "No, sir. Nothing. Nothing like that. I ain't say nothing to nobody."

"You swear?"

Rex paused again. "Yes, sir, on me grandmother's grave. I ain't tell nobody nothing."

"Thank you. Thank you. Very much," sighed the judge in relief. He patted Rex on the shoulder and exited.

Pigeon, who was quietly observing the whole angry exchange and the judge's conversation with Rex from behind one of the huge pillars near the iron gate, slipped stealthily downstairs and left the building through door to the undercroft. He knew that he had amassed sufficient ammunition for the day to now begin to aggressively plan his strategy to destroy the BOARD.

* * *

Chapter Three

The Annual General Meeting

November was a hectic month at St. Patrick's. It came on the heels of the Harvest celebration in October and immediately preceded the busy Advent and Christmas periods.

The most significant activity for November was the Annual General Meeting. At this meeting, reports from all of the ministries, guilds and committees were submitted, read, discussed and when appropriate, voted upon and ratified. It was a politically charged meeting and only one service was held that day so as to encourage every member to attend. Naturally, the *Bronze* and *Iron Circles* merely voted. Almost invariably, they voted for anyone whom they felt had shown even the slightest inclination to friendship with them. Thus, those seeking office knew how to amass their votes. The members of the lower circles knew instinctively whom the possible candidates would be. These potential candidates would suddenly begin to cordially greet them upon seeing them in church and inquire of the welfare of their respective household members. In addition, they would appear at the early service to worship and have fellowship with them. Sometimes they even deplored the attitude of the other members of the *Gold* and *Silver Circle*. Pigeon Goodfellow often referred to these politicians as 'brazen hypocrites who smile at God but frown upon his image.'

The months preceding the Annual General Meeting were usually filled with surreptitious plots and downright appalling schemes to overthrow the wardens and other legal officials of the corporation. Aspiring members stopped at nothing to usurp the position and power of those in authority. The BOARD members, however, were never entangled in such an imbroglio; they were after all an illegal, discreet body whose main function was to control the vestry. More power, they believed, could be exercised from the outside. All that mattered to them was that the persons elected to the vestry be 'willing to work *cooperatively* with them for the good of the parish.' Furthermore, there were no canons or by-laws by which they were bound. Consequently, the assumption of a position on the vestry would be considered a descent from grace.

The members of the *Bronze* and *Iron Circles* also were never a part of the political confusion. However, it was their lowly status that kept them outside the parameters of such privilege. Superficial acknowledgement of their presence at church and insincere cordiality by their affable fiends during the fellowship were the dictates of their respective votes.

This year, the Annual General Meeting was going to be more dramatic because the position of senior warden was open for nomination. There were also four vestry positions open, one of which was the vacancy resulting from Pigeon's resignation. The BOARD, however, wanted to fill all four positions with persons who would be loyal to them. They were not impressed with Mrs. Pigthorne's performance as senior warden, but she was as manipulative as clay in a sculptor's hand and therefore would be perfect for their dishonorable purposes.

One of the primary objectives of the BOARD was to relieve Nollie Mertins of his duties as the organist and choir director. They were convinced that Nollie was part of a sinister plot to overthrow them or to assume full control of the recruitment process for the choir. This possibility drove the greatest fear into the BOARD because they saw Nollie's actions as a means through which he would break down the walls that separated the circles.

Nollie's sudden change of attitude toward the *Bronze* and *Iron Circles* was perplexing to the Faulkner. It was Nollie who earlier was most adamant against inclusion, now he suddenly seemed to have developed a strange propinquity to the lower circles. The prospects were frightening to Faulkner and he immediately began to work towards a plan to get rid of Nollie.

The BOARD thus embarked upon its mission of destruction. The plan of action would be to fill the vacancies on the vestry with pliant members and then subsequently inveigle the vestry to make Nollie's position redundant. There was also a subtle plan to placate the members of the lower circles by creating and forming subservient ministries and giving them positions of authority. Those in authority would be the most malleable and would serve as conduits through which the BOARD would exercise control over the brood. They firmly believed that the *Bronze* and *Iron Circles* would be grateful for this social advancement for they had perceived on several occasions how far these people of the soil would go to be a part of their company. The BOARD believed that these simple people were going to be so intensely focused on their own affairs that they were going to be totally unaware of the more fortified walls that the *Gold Circle* would be erecting to ostracize them permanently. It was toward the achievement of this purpose that a select body of the vestry members was summoned by the BOARD to an exigent meeting. The evening of the vicar's off day was the time chosen for this meeting. Mr. Faulkner notified Rex of the meeting and instructed him to be present, and to notify him should the vicar appear on the premises for any reason.

* * *

Monday night was Rex's night off from the pub. It was therefore convenient for him to be present at the church to carry out Mr. Faulkner's instructions. However, this was the particular evening that Pigeon sought to meet with him. Rex knew that a private meeting with Pigeon would be a flattering experience for him, but that under the influence of a few drinks, he would reveal more than was necessary. It was therefore incumbent upon him to calculate how he would avail himself to both parties without either one knowing of the request of the other. Pigeon's offer was enticing and Rex would never allow such an opportunity to pass him. On the other hand, his covenant with the judge would never allow any courtship with disloyalty. Rex therefore sought to notify Pigeon that he had had a previous engagement with a family member that night but was willing to meet him later, at ten o'clock, if the time was convenient. Pigeon agreed, and informed Rex that the discussion would take place over a few drinks. This immensely pleased Rex, and he swore to Pigeon that nothing on the face of this earth or below the sea, or in the sky above, neither principalities nor powers could prevent him from fulfilling his promise. Rex could see that his promise had pleased and relaxed Pigeon, for his face radiated with a sense of accomplishment.

Tension resonated heavily in the common room that evening, for the invited vestry members knew that they would be the first to experience the unyielding power of the BOARD as it conducted its first meeting. They knew that they would be at the frontline in the battle between loyalty and deviousness, between duty and conscience, between courage and cowardice – between good and evil.

* * *

The meeting started on time, and Mr. Faulkner chaired the session. "Ladies and gentlemen," he addressed the gathering, "I call this meeting to order. I will begin by asking Mrs. Barnwell to provide the opening prayer."

"A prayer…for this…this clandestine gathering, Mr. Faulkner? Our intentions border on malevolence," protested Art Kimble, a God-fearing man who firmly believed in retribution. "Asserting our place at St. Patrick's is one thing, but beseeching divine assistance in something that deep inside we know to be destructive and basically evil is another thing. I wish that you hadn't invited me to this meeting, Brother Pilchard."

The members were astounded by Art's courageous remonstration and beheld him with shocked expressions. Persis Bentham, a woman in her late fifties who sewed her own clothes and had developed the art of shifting her dentures from side to side during times of intense concentration or agitation, gasped at Art's protest.

"The height of impertinence!" Persis remarked, and slightly shifted her dentures to the left. "I am appalled," she cried, "at such a course outburst of…such unwarranted juvenile behavior." Then she shifted her dentures to the right.

"One might have thought that you would be more appalled at your husband's frequent outbursts when he comes home drunk and begins to thump you around the house like an old dust cloth," Art retorted.

"That's none of your damn business, Art Kimble. That has nothing to do with this meeting!" Persis snapped.

"It does, as a matter of fact." Art assured her. "The frequent thumps to the head have left you devoid of any common sense. Incidentally, Persis, you were supposed to shift your dentures to the left after your last absurd remark," Art added as he contemptuously contemplated Persis.

"That will be quite enough of that, thank you, Mr. Kimble," ordered the judge. "We're in this together!"

"If the demands of the Board are too stringent for you, Kimble, you are free to resign like Pigeon Goodfellow; or you could cower in the background while the others fight your cause." Mr. Faulkner added.

"One of those, eh?" cried the judge, "the bible in one hand and the dagger in the other."

"What we are doing, ladies and gentlemen, is not right. If we are going to strive for power and control, then let us do so, on our own accord. But I protest the invocation of the Holy Spirit to guide us in this covert scheme. I fear the repercussions of such a vain and vulgar use of the name of the Lord!"

"Then would you rather not pray, Kimble?" Mr. Faulkner inquired of the ambivalent sexagenarian.

"I would like that very much." Art responded with a sigh of relief.

"Good. Now that the chicken has been spared the pot, let's get on with it!" cried Leola Featherstone, who with her husband, was the owner of a chain of fast food restaurants across the island.

"Aww, get stuffed, Featherstone!" barked Art, totally disgusted with the whole sordid affair.

"*Shall* we pray, pleeeease?!" Gladys Barnwell besought the gathering.

"Desperate, aren't we, eh, Gladys...*desperate*," Art sneered.

"Enough!" shouted the judge. "Go ahead, Gladys," he ordered.

"Thank you, Mr. Pilchard," said Gladys, and scrutinized Art once more from head to toe before whispering a slew of nasty names and vulgar suggestions. "Let us pray," she subsequently invited the gathering as she piously extended her arms.

"Dear Heavenly Father, we the Board of this church are in a dilemma. Our call to oversee and protect the interest of this institution is being challenged by those who seek to usurp our authority and overturn the orderliness you have called us to maintain. We beseech you, dear Father, to confound those whose purpose is to cause dissention and promote disorder in your church. Give us that power to always subdue them and create an establishment where we all come to know and understand our respective roles and purposes, where authority is respected, where all men and women are welcome, and where all people enjoy a wonderful fellowship. This we ask in the name of our Lord and Savior, Jesus Christ. Amen."

"Amen...Amen!" The gathering responded enthusiastically.

"Wonderful...wonderful, Gladys. That was an excellent prayer," cried the Judge.

All but one member concurred.

"Yes indeed. Wonderful...just wonderful." Art responded with acerbic sarcasm. "We have just besought the Lord to enable us to do what we have convinced ourselves is the right thing to do. We approach the Lord justified in our wrongness, so we automatically shut our ears to the rightness."

"As soon as the sermon is over we shall continue with the meeting," the judge declared.

"It is over. As far as I am concerned, it is over. You may proceed, your honor," Art responded.

"Thank you, Mr. Kimble." Mr. Faulkner replied with a slight bow of the head and a polite smile. "Now, my fellow members in Christ, it is as plain as day that our authority is being challenged. I know that you are uncomfortable with the manner of our approach to maintaining order and control, Kimble, but we are charged with the responsibility of keeping this parish afloat, aloof from the others and in accordance with the reputation for which it has come to be known throughout the Caribbean. Furthermore, the Annual General

Meeting is less than a month away, so urgency and judiciousness will be the dictates of our discussion and planning. The floor is now open, ladies and gentlemen, for any ideas."

"Sack the organist," commanded Fritz Batty. "He is the cause of all of this confusion. He is the one who put that Watts man to stand in the chancel and sing on Harvest Sunday. Do you all have any idea how embarrassing that was...in front of all the dignitaries...a mere commoner leading our choir?"

"And that is exactly what gave the rest of the brood the impetus to approach us with such scathing impertinence," Gladys Barnwell chimed in. "Imagine that a woman like Ram's wife should have the audacity to even *approach* a member of the Gold Circle, let alone *speak*..."

"She didn't just speak, Gladys. She battered you with explosive abuse," added Sam Westwater. "This is exactly why this meeting is so urgent. Those people aren't fools as we believe them to be. They might be low on the social scale, but they aren't fools. One has nothing to do with the other. My suggestion is to allow Mr. Watts to join the choir, and so keep the rest of those mudheads quiet."

"That's out of the question. Definitely out of the question!" cried the Judge.

"To reiterate Fritz's suggestion, fire the organist. He is a great organist, we all can attest to that. But he is also a threat to our existence as an exclusive group," advised Dr. Coaksley. "We already have established our reputation as *the* church of Ischalton, so we *can* get rid of him. We can always bring in an organist from England. That will place us even higher on the scale."

"A valid point, Doc," stated Mr. Featherstone.

"Aye Aye," echoed Sam.

"Motion?" inquired Mr. Faulkner.

"So moved," said Fritz.

"Second," added Ruthel Pollard.

"Those in favor?"

All but Art agreed with the motion.

"You have a problem, Mr. Kimble?" inquired the judge.

"No, your honor. Just abstained, that's all"

"Motion carried," cried Mrs. Shoehorn.

"I am amazed at how shallow you all are," Art pointed out. "Do you actually believe that Nollie acted alone? Go on. Give him the sack. See what you will accomplish by that."

Silence followed.

"What exactly are you saying, Kimble?" asked the judge.

"Hasn't it occurred to you that Fr. Perths has said nothing about all that took place on Harvest Sunday?"

"Are you implying that Fr. Perths was aware of Nollie's plan?" Nathaniel Francois inquired.

"I'm neither stating nor implying anything. All I am doing is cautioning you before you make any rash and foolish decisions, that's all."

"Then someone will approach Fr. Perths and ask him plainly about his feeling about, or his part in, this whole thing. Judging from his answer, we will come to know the truth, and act accordingly," suggested Mr. Faulkner.

"And having found the truth, whatever it is, what do you do?" Art added phlegmatically.

"He must be reprimanded...severely," decreed the judge.

"Who will bell the cat, your honor?" Art asked, with his eyes fixed furtively on the judge.

"The senior warden, of course, under our instructions," the judge wryly declared.

"Me?" No sir. Not so. Not me!" Mrs. Pigthorne vehemently protested.

"Whom do you suggest, then, madam senior warden?" questioned Mr. Faulkner.

"You. You do it. After all, it was your decree," responded Art, with a sinister grin.

"Are you implying that I am scared to do it, Mr, Kimble?" asked the now agitated Faulkner.

"You said it, your eminence. You said it."

"Then I will. First thing tomorrow, I will."

"Make sure you record this in the minutes, Maggie. Laurent Falkner has promised to approach the vicar and inquire about his knowledge or his part in the incident on Harvest Sunday," Art ordered.

"And what do we do about the vacancies. Any recommendations to fill the vacant positions on the vestry?" inquired Sam Westwater.

"Al Foster and Darlene Burrows for the two, three year positions," Mr. Faulkner suggested.

"Darlene Burrows?" exclaimed Ruthel, "Why, the woman is as daft as a stone!"

"What's your point?" asked the judge.

"Point taken," said Ruthel.

"And what about the vacancies left by Pigeon Goodfellow and Edward Goodridge?"

"What about Nekada Dufries and Sam Galloway?" suggested the judge.

"Good choices. Both are very cooperative," agreed Mr. Faulkner.

"Don't you mean very pliable...intensely stupid?" added Art.

"Prone to serve us well...?" continued the judge.

"Point taken," Art responded in a tone of resignation.

"Motion to accept the slate?" asked Mr. Faulkner.

"So moved," motioned Nathaniel.

"Second," added Mrs. Shoehorn.

"Those in favor?"

All but one abstained.

"Another don't know, eh, Kimble?"

"No. Just another vestige of wisdom," Art responded.

"One last thing," cried Mr. Faulkner.

"What?" inquired Sam.

"Committees. Committees for the riff-raff....to keep them preoccupied,"

"Yes. Indeed," agreed the judge. "Any ideas?"

"Yes," cried Dr. Coaksley excitedly. "Three, as a matter of fact. One , the Beautification Committee; two, the Special Activities Committee and three, the Public Relations Committee."

"And your wisdom in creating such committees, bearing in mind that we already have the Property Committee and the Human Relations Committee?" cautioned the judge.

"Well, the beautification Committee is just a big name for ...well, sophisticated scavengers, you know, to do the actual cleaning of the buildings and grounds under the direct supervision of Rex and the indirect supervision of the senior warden. Think of it. We could use them to keep the property in pristine shape and get rid of the hired landscapers. Think of the money we will save."

"Brilliant, brilliant indeed!" exclaimed the Judge. The others concurred.

"And the special Activities Committee?" the judge further inquired.

"Who is going to prepare the place when we have special activities, you know, like the annual tea party, the parish fair and such like? We need persons to prepare the place and clean up afterward. It would save us from soliciting volunteers from among ourselves. Let the laborers soil their hands."

"Agreed," Mr. Faulkner stated.

"As for the Public Relations Committee...," Dr. Coaxley continued.

"...Public Relations Committee? Are you suggesting that those *mules* represent our public interests? " Ruthel Pollard interjected.

"No, my dear Ruthel. *We* have the Human Relations Committee who will address our, well, *human* issues. *They* will have the Public Relations Committee to address *their* issues. *We* aren't the *public*. *They* are. By establishing such a committee, we will use them to control *them*."

"You are indeed the eight wonder of the world, Dr. Coaksley," the judge declared.

"All well and good," agreed Sam Westwater. "But who will chair these committees and who will make up these committees?"

"Someone whom they listen to…look up to…respect," suggested Fritz Batty.

"Ram's wife," Art recommended, "to chair the Public Relations Committee." Silence followed.

"Brilliant!" exclaimed the judge. "But who will approach her about this?"

"Leave it to me, your honor. Leave it completely to me," assured Art.

Mr. Faulkner and Mr. Pilchard exchanged glances.

"Can we trust you on this, Kimble?" the judge inquired.

"My word is my honor, Pilchard."

"So let it be done," commanded the judge.

"I think that that tall, dark man with the donkey carts…I don't know his name, but they all refer to him as Uncle Ed, you know him…he would be good for the position of Chairperson of the Beautification Committee. He is the mogul of the village. He is highly respected among the plebs," Fritz stated. "I can speak to him."

"Excellent. Thank you, Fritz," said Mr. Faulkner. "Now that leaves us with the Special Activities Committee."

"Nellie Sweetwine. She is the one who organized the Bronze Circle to do the work for the Harvest celebration this year. She can work in conjunction with you, Bill, in you capacity as the jr. warden. Apart from the incident in the church, I think that things went very well," remarked Mr. Hauklyn.

"Good suggestion, Hauklyn," the judge concurred.

"So there; we are just about ready for action. Are there any questions from the vestry?" Mr. Faulkner inquired. "Apart from Hauklyn, you all have been rather quiet."

"What else does one do when one is subjected to this kind of humiliation? A self appointed Board has assumed control over the vestry; the Board calls a meeting and we respond by attending. Does it matter if we remain reticent or speak? Ultimately, it is the Board that will make the final decision about the matters arising," Bill Jones remonstrated.

"I don't think I like the tone of your remark, Jones," the judge stated.

"Well, I'm sorry if my tone or remark has offended you, sir, but I am simply making a statement on behalf of the vestry members present. I assure you, your honor, that there is no insult intended," Bill replied.

"Then am I, as chairperson of the BOARD, to postulate that the BOARD and the Vestry are working amicably and cooperatively towards a common goal?" Mr. Faulkner asked the slightly agitated Bill Jones.

"You have my word, sir," Bill replied as he gently tapped his left leg to suppress his discreet anger and noticable nervousness.

"Then I assume that you will approach Nellie Sweetwine and solicit her assistance?" Mr. Faulkner continued as he fixed his eyes firmly on Bill.

"...And that the purpose and details of this meeting will be held in the strictest confidence?" the judge added as he too fixed his eyes squarely in Bill's eyes, never averting them until after Bill nervously responded.

"As I said earlier, sir, you have the fullest cooperation of the vestry." Bill's breathing became heavier and he pounded his foot a little heavier on the floor.

All eyes were laid on Bill as his agitation became more obvious.

"Let me stress here and now," warned the despotic judge, "that this board is very serious about its mission to maintain order and control in this parish, for the obvious good of the people who financially support it. We have a duty to see that the tradition is held and that this parish remains socially and financially aloof from the other parishes in Ischalton. Our reputation as a formidable force in the Anglican community is known and respected well beyond the confines of Ischalton and it is going to stay that way. Any member of this vestry who therefore seeks to burst the chain of confidentiality, or who is perceived to be a threat to the mission and purpose of the BOARD, will be removed from office, one way or the other, and subsequently blackballed from the Gold Circle. Any questions?"

"More of a comment," Art Kimble responded. "The BOARD has stressed cooperation in its mission to maintain the health of this parish, the social and financial health, that is. However, I find it most ironic, or shall I say, depressing, that the spiritual health has not once been mentioned, which to me and this vestry, I'm sure, is *the* mission of the church. Notwithstanding, I..."

"...Enough of your sermonizing, Kimble," growled Sam Westwater. "If our mission is a problem to you, then you are free to resign from the vestry."

"I never said that I had a problem, Westwater. It would behoove you to shut up and let me finish my comments," Art replied.

"Let him speak, Westwater. Let the BOARD hear his litany of concerns. Let the boy plead his case," the judge ordered.

Art turned and momentarily addressed the judge with his eyes. Bill Jones gently placed his hand on Art's shoulder, implying that he discontinue his comments.

"I dismiss my case, your honor," Art stated. "The *boy* has chosen to refrain from any further comment."

A brief period of nerve wrenching silence followed.

"There being no further questions, or comments, I beg to have this meeting adjourned." Mr. Faulkner interjected.

"So moved," a voice bearing a heavy tone of disgust scudded across the table.

"Second," another followed instantaneously.

A resounding chorus in unison voiced their favor. All subsequently rose and began leaving. The atmosphere was shrouded with a cloak of uneasiness. No prayers were offered at the conclusion of the meeting. The judge and

Mr. Faulkner studied Art Kimble and Bill Jones as the two vestrymen left the room together. No wishes for a good night's rest were exchanged among the four men.

The last of the group to leave the building was the judge. He beckoned to Rex and ordered him to set the alarm and lock the door. Rex rose and complied with the instructions. However, he did not make an immediate exit but waited for the judge to leave the building. Rex watched him from the window as he approached his car and sat for a few minutes. As Rex was about to leave, he peered through the window again but the judge was still there in his car. His eyes were closed and he appeared to be sleeping or trying to regain his composure after what Rex assumed to be a mentally harrowing meeting. Rex therefore shut the window and hurried to the gate. He hurried towards Buckingham Avenue and St. Patrick's Place and stood there stealthily, as though expecting someone. After a short while, he heard the roar of the judge's vehicle and began to walk briskly to the next corner. He put his head down as he hurried towards the next intersection. Suddenly, a black car pulled up and stopped briefly. Rex recognized it and quickly got in and the car sped off. When Rex looked back, Judge Pilchard's Rover had not yet reached the corner of Buckingham Avenue.

*   *   *

Pigeon Goodfellow turned into his driveway and parked beside his silver Jaguar. He used the black Toyota on casual occasions and for minor errands around North Abersthwaithe and the jaguar for official business, church events and formal occasions. The only minor occasion for which he used the Jaguar was for golfing. Image was important for the members of the King Edward Golf Club, and Pigeon strove to make a good impression. However, he hated such superciliousness and would have withdrawn from the club had it not been fertile ground for high profile clientele. Many of the men and women whom Pigeon represented in court and in other legal matters made their initial contact with him on the golf course. Copious private and personal deals were made during a putter and subsequently ratified over drinks in the club house. Pigeon thus could not afford to divorce himself from such ignoble company. Furthermore, to sever his membership would be to fall from grace and to give the impression that he could no longer afford to maintain membership at this ultra-inclusive club – a fate which had befallen a few members over the course of the years. Pigeon was well acquainted with the proverb which was used in the legal world to describe those who were sinking: "A dying lawyer is his own undertaker." There was no way that Pigeon was going to be added to this list of causalities.

Similar problems on the vestry plagued Pigeon's conscience. However, such arrogance and lust for power and control affected him differently. The establishment of the BOARD was an affront to his intelligence and his position as one of the most prominent lawyers in Ischalton. It was not the BOARD's disrespect towards the vestry as a whole or their utter disdain for the lower social circles that was the germ of his displeasure; it was their attack on his ego. Pigeon took their approach subjectively and would rather die than tolerate it. Furthermore, membership on the vestry, he had remarked during his meeting with Mr. Pilchard, offered him no personal, financial or social advantages, and thus he could walk away 'with his tail raised in victory.' However, Pigeon was consumed by fervid anger and resonant anguish. He was never before a victim of such gross humiliation. In his capacity as a district magistrate, Pigeon was used to receiving the plaudits of his colleagues and the respect and admiration from the elite. Now, however, he was deflated by those to whom he had discreetly considered himself superior, and consequently made a vow to utterly destroy them.

Pigeon thus planned his attack. Over the last few days, he had collected much information to begin his assault. Now he felt that the time was right. Sagacity dictated that he begin by crippling the power behind the force, the indomitable Laurent Faulkner and the despotic Adolph Pilchard, and subsequently overthrowing the BOARD. For his assault on the judge, Pigeon would entangle the naive Rexworth Davis in a deadly web of deception. The course of Laurent Faulkner's fate would be chartered later and through a more subtle and deadly source – the president of the King Edward Golf Club.

Apart from the house and ground staff, Rex was the first in his social class that Pigeon had allowed to enter his home as a guest. Rex was enthralled by the exquisite décor which comprised some of the most elegant furniture he had ever seen and made copious remarks to Pigeon about the quality and style of the furniture and decoration. He led Rex into his study which was off to the left of the sitting room. He switched on the lights but did not part the drapes which hug majestically from the cathedral like sash windows. The room was quite bijoux but practical, definitely a man's room, as Pigeon would often remark to visitors to his home, by the style of furniture and the polished, mahogany paneled walls.

"Welcome to my home, Rex," Pigeon exclaimed as he opened his arms and pasted a wry grin. He noticed that Rex was a bit tense. "Please, make yourself comfortable…anywhere," he pleaded.

"Nice house, Mr. Goodfellow," Rex remarked.

"Thank you. Please, Rex, call me Pigeon. When you are here, we're friends, man, good friends. You need only address me as Mr. Goodfellow in public, like, you know, at church. In my home, we're friends," Pigeon assured the mildly overwhelmed but elated sexton. "So, what can I get you …to drink?"

Rex was still so mesmerized by the magnitude of such flaunting opulence that he did not hear Pigeon's question. His attention was focused on one of the oil paintings which was hanging over the polished, mahogany desk.

"What about a glass of cognac…top brand…no, let me give you a glass of wine, the finest wine you'll ever taste. Mrs. Goodfellow and I bought this while we were in the south of France last year."

Pigeon knew that Rex was far from being a connoisseur, but nevertheless addressed him as one equal in social standing. This was Pigeon's way of making Rex more emollient for the assault. "Look," he continued as he held up the bottle, "do you see the dark, brownish color and the streaks that appear on the glass? This testifies to the viscosity of the wine."

Rex nodded in agreement as he gazed with a blank expression and an idiotic grin at the bottle, "Aye aye, sir.…good vosticy…the wine…nice vosticy."

"Hungry, Rex?"

"A lil' bit, sir…sir Pigeon."

"Here," Pigeon poured the wine and served it to Rex. "Let me check to see if there is anything around. The maid has gone for the night and my wife is asleep. Hope I find you something to go with that wine… Wait a minute before you drink the wine. One should have something in one's stomach before one imbibes."

Pigeon returned after a brief period carrying a half of a loaf of plaited bread and a few crude slices of cheese on a plate. "Sorry, my friend. This is all that I could find that doesn't warrant any cooking. I'm afraid that I have not been blessed with culinary skills. I'm not a cook."

After placing the bread in front of Rex, Pigeon poured himself a little wine.

"Well, cheers, my friend!" Pigeon raised his glass in a toast to the unholy friendship. "Eat, my friend…eat," he invited Rex. "Let us break bread and drink wine in the covenant of friendship!"

Thus Rex sealed himself in another blasphemous fellowship of camaraderie; first with the judge, and now with the insidious Pigeon Goodfellow. Nevertheless, Rex was filled with the gentle rhapsody of self-glorification, counting himself lucky to be called and chosen by the cream of the upper-echelon and united with them in an impious matrimony. At last he had arrived. By dint of ignoble birth, he was deemed a member of the *Bronze Circle*, but by obsequious association an illegitimate fellow of the *Gold Circle*, a privilege that would ultimately strip him of his dignity as a human being and cause his allegiance to oscillate like a pendulum from one mendacious disciple to the other.

There was no knife to slice the bread, so they broke it and ate each piece with a bit of cheese. Rex took sporadic sips of wine in between as Pigeon presented the details of his request to have Rex manage the staff in his home while he and Mrs. Goodfellow were away for a few days. All of this power seemed to please Rex immensely, for he smiled brightly and raised his glass, and agreed without any hesitation to undertake the task.

"Now let me give you a sample of what the very rich use to toast when they seal multi-million dollar deals. Here. Have a sip of this." The crafty lawyer handed Rex another glass containing a moderate amount of inexpensive whiskey. He continued this trend by offering the dim-witted sexton a variety of alcoholic drinks until Rex began to show signs of mild inebriation. Pigeon Goodfellow was a charming man and hence he was able, with moderate effort, to seduce the unsuspecting Rex almost to the point of hypnosis. The die was now cast. Pigeon prepared to move in for the final assault. He had sought the weak, blemished lamb and had trailed behind him like the King of the Beasts stalking its prey, until the opportune time.

"Now that we have sealed our friendship in the breaking of bread and the drinking of the wine, there is one thing left for us to do," the subtle lawyer proposed. "We must endorse our friendship by sharing a secret about someone dear to us…like a good friend. But it must be a mutual friend…the same friend. In this way, our bond in brotherhood will never be broken, for the secret will be sealed in blood. I will share my secret first and then you will divulge…tell me yours. Are you willing to seal our friendship, brother, friend, honorary member of the Gold Circle?"

"My word…hic…is…my…hic…honor," Rex spurted out as he rose awkwardly from his chair, with his arm extended to take another toast.

"Good. Excellent," Pigeon responded gleefully. "So…let me see…whom do we both know…ahh, Mr. Pilchard, the good judge; my dear, dear friend. Let's share something about him that no one else knows…alright."

"Anything you asks, sir…sir Pigeon. I am your…your…hic… 'umblest servant…hic… I am 'appy to be the friend of …hic…the best…hic…damn lawyer…on the ..hic…whole friggin' island!"

"Well, the good judge is going to be retiring within the next two years. Now, he doesn't want anyone to know…anyone," Pigeon warned. "Only you and I share this secret. Now let us take a toast to seal my friendship"

Rex took a gulp of the vodka and slammed his glass on the marble coffee table. Pigeon realized that he must act expediently, for Rex was quickly being overcome by the effects of the vile, unorthodox mixture of cheap alcohol which he had received over the years as tokens of appreciation from clients for whom he had waived or reduced his legal fees.

"What's your secret about the judge? Tell me quickly so that we can seal our friendship," Pigeon entreated the semi-irrational sexton.

"I see 'im...hic...he...and...and...hic...Billings...Maggie Billings...in the choir room... that night at the meeting in the common room...they was kissin'...right in front of me...and ...hic...he tell me not to say nothing...to nobody...so...I never...say...hic...nothing..."

"If we are going to be friends, Rex, you have to tell me a true secret. You can't make up anything..."

"I swear, on me grandmother grave, sir Pigeon."

"Then repeat everything you just said to me..."

"I did see...Mr. Plichard...and ...hic...hic ...Billings...They was kissin' in the choir room...and she take ...the books...hic...and...hic...run. And he tell me not to say nothing...hic...to nobody."

Pigeon became almost numb with shock. After a momentary period of absolute silence, he made a few slow, aimless steps across the room and then turned and scrutinized Rex suspiciously. "You're sure about this, my friend...absolutely sure?"

"Yes, sir Pigeon. The place was dark and I ...hic...was sleepin' in a chair...in the dark...and he and Miss Billings, sir...they open the door... hic...and they start...they kiss up one another...and when they turn on the light...they see me there...and she scream...and...hic...she run...with the books that he gave her... and he tell me not to...hic...say nothing to nobody...hic...," Rex swore.

"I believe you. I believe you. Thank you." Pigeon pondered briefly again. Then a sinister grin came across his face. "Let's seal this secret that endorses our friendship." Rex and Pigeon thus raised their glasses once more to ratify their iniquitous covenant of brotherhood. "Come. Let me take you home before it gets too late. Your dear wife is probably getting quite worried. Tell her that you were in good company."

*   *   *

The black car pulled up in front of Rex's house just after 11.20 p.m. Pigeon expressed effusive gratitude to Rex for his valuable friendship and he and Rex swore over their respective grandparents' graves that their meeting would remain a secret to their own graves.

Pigeon drove off from Rex's house and swung left at the next corner, which lead to Beach Road. Beach Road was a relatively desolate road at night, especially in Brewster's Village where many of the members of the *Bronze Circle* lived. On the right of the Road was the beach. It was in this area that one went to purchase fresh fish and shrimp early in the morning when the villagers brought in their catch. There, one could get a better bargain for the seafood before the fishermen and women reached the market which was further in the village. On the left were small farms which provided income for the villagers. Small, crudely built homes made of zinc sheets and unpainted wood told the grim tale of this squalid community. Pigeon rolled down his windows to inhale the fresh, riparian air as he ruminated on the details of his meeting with Rex. Feelings of ambivalence consumed him as guilt and justification yanked at his mind in a passionate game of mental and spiritual tug-of-war as he contemplated the information he had received from the malleable Rex. He knew that he had gathered the information about the judge by surreptitious means and that such a method was grossly unethical. Furthermore, he had caused Rex to commit a grave sin by breaking the covenant he had made with the judge, and worse, he knew that to denigrate the judge – his friend, colleague, and most of all, a fellow Christian brother and member of the same parish – would be an act of unmitigated shame which could eventually bring about his own bitter demise. Suppose, he pondered, Rex should similarly break the covenant they had made; or that the judge should find out that he was the nucleus of the germ, a rumor that would ultimately spread across the church like a deadly pestilence, stealthily and indiscriminately gnawing away at the very heart and soul of the congregation until every vein of moral rectitude and spiritual uprightness is wasted away in an agonizing death.

Other thoughts also prevailed, however, thoughts which would preponderate and stamp their seal of approval on Pigeon's conscience. Faulkner and Pilchard had shattered his ego. He earlier had privately contemplated assuming the office of senior warden at this coming election, but even if he wins, the BOARD would dictate his actions. Also, it was now the time for someone to step in to usher in a new era at St. Patrick's – an era whereby all members would be equal and the barriers which had separated them would be broken down. This upcoming election would offer the best opportunity for Pigeon to assume the office of senior warden, a powerful position indeed – at St Patrick's Church.

The assumption of such a position in this prestigious parish was one of howling esteem, at least to Pigeon. Ecclesiastically, it came second only to the Bishopric, and politically, to the office of Prime Minister. Such a position would be good for him, he thought. It would take him high up on the social ladder. He had established immense fame and prestige in the legal arena and he was aware of the ramifications of that position. Now he must likewise conquer the ecclesiastical sphere – by whatever means necessary. He must meet his opponents on their terms, and defeat them. Thus he was not going to pursue this victory through spiritual or mental martyrdom, for his mission was ultimately not for the purpose of the masses, but for his own aggrandizement.

Having justified his intended actions, Pigeon pulled off the road and parked for a brief period. He turned off the engine so as to allow himself to be embraced by the gentle quietness of the still night. After a short while he rolled up his trousers, took off his moccasins and stepped out on the cool, damp sand. He walked toward the ebbing tide and stood in the shallow water while gazing up at the magnificence of the constellation. He then smiled, closed his eyes and clasped his hands.

"Dear God," he whispered, "how awesome is your name; you are worthy of the highest honor and glory; how magnificent are the works of your hand; your glory is beyond our comprehension. Give me, your humble servant, the strength and wisdom to crush your enemies who seek to destroy your church. Enable me, your unworthy and humble servant, to assume the office of Senior Warden so that I can scatter the proud who oppress the lowly and thus bring order to the church of St Patrick. Grant me the power to destroy those who are the stumbling block to your purpose and let the congregation see and come to know I am the one chosen to establish and execute your purpose at St Patrick. Grant me, your humble servant, this power in your holy name. Amen."

As Pigeon turned and processed toward his car, he was overcome by a surge of spiritual rejuvenation. He raised his head toward the moonlight sky again and paced slowly to his car in his imaginary chausable of protection and cope of peace. The hushed, unremitting sound of the ebbing tide seemed like a heavenly chant sanctioning his rebaptism and commissioning to carry out the work he felt justified in doing.

Pigeon started the engine again and headed off down Beach Road. Suddenly, a sinister thought overcame him. This time, however, there was no reason to wrestle with conscience for he was now commissioned, so he earnestly believed, to do whatever he deemed fit to do in his plan to vanquish the enemy and achieve the position of senior warden. Thus Pigeon Goodfellow, the newly commissioned Archenemy of the BOARD and Foul Fiend of the people, turned left on to Westminster Lane and slowly drove past Maggie Billings' home. The house was in darkness except for the polished bronze lanterns on either side of the high, iron gates and the solitary light in what appeared to be the sitting room. As he approached the corner, which was about three hundred feet from the house, a black Mercedes Benz caught his eye. It was parked discreetly under the shade of one of the almond trees that lined Westminster Lane and in front of a black Navigator, which made it mildly obtrusive for anyone driving down the one way street. Nevertheless, Pigeon was able to easily spot it because he was on an expedition to seek verification of Rex's secret; and he did. The black Mercedes Benz was indeed the one belonging to the honorable judge. This discovery was enough proof of the authenticity of Rex's secret and it propounded a stunning revelation for Pigeon; it became perspicuously evident to him that God had validated his mission. Henceforth, Pigeon would embark on the relentless pursuit of the destruction of the BOARD and the assertion of his position as senior warden with a clear conscience.

* * *

The week leading to the Annual General Meeting was marked by subtle politicizing, unusually blatant interaction between the members of the *Gold Circle* and those of the lower circles and frenzied, last minute efforts to gain support for the slate which was presented to the congregation two weeks prior to the meeting, as set forth by the canons. The vestry had presented the names of the persons whom the BOARD had recommended and the new, subordinate committees which the vestry was instructed to form were in place. Also, all of the prospective chairpersons for these sub-committees had delightfully agreed to function in their respective capacities. Even Ram's wife, who was most hostile towards the BOARD and vestry, had submitted joyfully to their request and was now respectfully addressed as Mrs. Ramgolam. Everything seemed to fall in the BOARD's favor. They too, felt justified in their actions. They too had prayed assiduously to God for spiritual guidance as they planned and embarked on their clandestine mission to usurp the authority of the vicar and the vestry, control all matters pertaining to ministry at St. Patrick's and to destroy anyone or anything that did not conform to their devilish agenda.

The battle lines were thus drawn between Pigeon and the BOARD, with each side convinced that God was on its side.

* * *

On Wednesday morning, a Vauxhall van drove up to Maggie Billings' home. As the driver stepped out, the care-taker approached the gate.

"Delivery for a Maggie Billings…" the driver said.

"Right place, sir," the care-taker replied as he unlocked the gates.

The driver opened the back door of the van and removed a large bouquet of roses. "You gotta sign for these, sir," the driver informed the puzzled care-taker.

After the care-taker signed, the van drove off and he took the flowers to the back door and gave it to Annabelle, Maggie's malicious housekeeper. The arrival of a bouquet of flowers at the Billings' home must have been a rare occurrence, for Annabelle's interest was instantly aroused. She immediately determined to know whom the bouquet came from, especially since Maggie was never married and there was never any sign of a prospective suitor. She once had heard a rumor in the village about Maggie's dalliance with the judge but no one ever dared to even attempt to substantiate it. Furthermore, this rumor was spread several years ago and only among a few people. According to Annabelle, if it were true, it would have been revealed by now. Nevertheless, she saw it fit to open the envelope which was attached to the bouquet and read the note:

> Dearest Maggie:
> If beauty were a song, you'd be a symphony.
> If diamonds were to assume a human form, it would be you.
> If love could fly, we'd be above the stars on gossamer wings.
> But alas! Nothing is there to compare with your beauty.
>
> Adolph
> xxx

Annabelle hardly understood the ornate poetry but she immediately recognized the name. Even if there were another Adolph around, Annabelle knew only one. She hurriedly replaced the card and took the bouquet to Maggie, who was on the telephone. On the table in front of her was a list of names and telephone numbers of members of St Patrick's. Maggie had been on the phone for most of the morning amassing support for the BOARD's agenda. Annabelle entered the room with the bouquet.

"These is for you, mam. Sombody jes delivered them for you."

"Flowers...for me?"

"Roy jes bring them to me. He say a man jes now delivered it for you."

"Hold them off, Annabelle! Is there a card? Who could possibly be sending me ...roses? It must be from someone who obviously doesn't know me well, who doesn't know that I am allergic to flowers."

"Here, mam...this must be the card."

Maggie took the envelope and removed the card and opened it. She read the contents. However, no expression of joy came across her face, but bewilderment and a hint of intense fear.

"Thank you...Annabelle... Put the flowers in a vase, outside on the verandah, and later, you may take them home. I...I can't keep flowers in the house."

Annabelle was perplexed by her mistress' response to the beautiful bouquet. She knew that she was allergic to flowers, but her reaction to the gift and the card aroused much concern.

"Who the flowers is from, mam?" the inquisitive Annabelle asked in feigned ignorance.

Maggie raised her head towards Annabelle, contemplating her crass impertinence in asking such a question.

"An acquaintance…" she answered. "She was …visiting the island …on holiday from England…and sent these to me. She said that she was sorry that she was not able to drop by. How very nice of her. A pity she wasted her money on these flowers. I'll write her. Go. Go on, Annabelle . Take them outside before my eyes begin to itch."

Maggie sighed with relief at the thought that she was able to avoid rousing Annabelle's suspicion. Immediately upon Annabelle's exit, Maggie snatched the receiver off the telephone and nervously began to dial Mr. Pilchard's personal number.

"Pilchard," the distinguished voice answered.

"Adolph, why on earth would you send me flowers…and sign the card… flowers… You know that I am allergic…"

"…Maggie, calm down. What flowers are you talking about?" the judge interjected.

"The roses. You just sent me roses."

"Poppycock! I sent you nothing. Why on earth would I want to do that?" the judge questioned.

"The card… you sent me a card attached…expressing you love,…a card with your name…"

"What card?"

"Didn't you send me flowers…a bouquet of roses, with a card attached?"

"Why would I do that? When would I have had the time to do that, anyway? That is precisely why I asked you to make those calls for me. I'm extremely busy. Maggie, calm down. Perhaps you read the card incorrectly. Have you been drinking, Maggie?"

"Don't be foolish, Adolph. I'm neither illiterate nor drunk. I know what I've read. The card has your name…as having come from you."

"Maggie…" the judge's voice became very somber, "maybe…it could be that…somebody knows …about us."

A dreadful silence followed.

"I'll come over this evening. For all we know, it probably is some kind of innocent mix-up…perhaps something purely coincidental… or some sick joke. I'll have it sorted out by the end of the day. Don't worry," the judge solemnly assured Maggie.

"O.k. I should so hope." Maggie's voice was somber as she hung up the phone and sat in the chair, terrified almost to a stupor at the thought that her relationship with the judge could become the most shocking public scandal to launch an assault on Ischalton.

During the same day, members were receiving letters signed by Mrs. Pigthorne soliciting support for the slate, and especially for the names presented by the nominating committee who were all members of the BOARD. There was also an impressive outline of a five year plan which included the formation of three sub-committees whose purpose was to create a more inclusive form of participation in the church's ministry. This letter made a favorable impression on the members of the *Bronze* and *Iron Circles*. They were flabbergasted at the fact that they were counted worthy to receive letters from the senior warden and displayed their excitement by bringing to her gifts of the produce of the earth. Even those who were illiterate deemed it an honor to receive word from the senior warden, after the literate shared the contents of the letter with them. They thus vowed their support for their new hero and heroines – Uncle Ed, Mrs. Ramgolam and Nellie Sweetwine.

The three chair-persons of the newly formed sub-committees became instant celebrities in Brewster's Village. Men began tipping their hats to Uncle Ed, and the villagers almost immediately began to address him as 'Sir Edward.' Ram's wife bought a blond, synthetic wig for the Sunday of the installation, a preposterous bundle of false hair that sat on her head like a cheap, straw hat – a ridiculous, amorphous mass of curly, flaxen straw that was tossed upon her cranium like an abandoned bird's nest. Mrs. Ramgolam wore this wig like the weathered crown of dethroned and forgotten royalty – a head piece which bestowed upon her the rather uncanny obeisance as 'Brewster's Village First Lady.' This headdress would become a permanent part of Mrs. Ramgolam's persona. Mrs. Sweetwine, however, remained the same. Her gentle character and quiet disposition, superimposed by an attractive simplicity and a persuasive charm, had already etched an indelible mark on the minds of the villagers whose cooperation she had solicited for the last harvest celebration. These three became an unholy trinity who would be revered by the simple, unsuspecting masses comprising the *Bronze* and *Iron Circles*. Eloise thus telephoned the BOARD members one evening after receiving some fruits of the earth to tell them that the BOARD was on its way to achieving a resonating victory.

* * *

Maggie Billings took a scented bath that night and donned a red, silk negligee which she had bought in Paris a few years ago. It was trimmed with black and red feathers and drawn at the waist by a simple, satin band which formed a delicate bow at the left side of her tiny waist. She had spent a miserable day. Thoughts of her illicit affair with the respectable and powerful judge being the topic of conversation among the upper class were tearing her apart. Furthermore, and perhaps even worse, was the awkwardness and penetrating embarrassment she would feel in the presence of her dear friend, Mrs. Pilchard, whose serene dignity and natural grace would earn her heartfelt pity from the public. She, on the contrary, would become the object of sizzling contempt. Maggie and Mrs. Pilchard had often sat for afternoon tea and a tete-a tete on Maggie's verandah which overlooked the garden, and planned many church sponsored charitable events which would be attended by the elite, the bourgeois, and those social aspirants who paid the exorbitant ticket prices simply to mingle with the high and not-so-high society. However, the crux of Maggie's concern was neither the public contempt nor the shame in the presence of the noble Mrs. Pilchard, but the possibility of losing her paramour. The judge was the only man she had ever loved – and would ever have loved. He was perhaps the most admired and feared man in Ischalton – a tall, dark man with a grim countenance and hefty bank account – an influential, intimidating leader who brought grown men to tears and the powers that be to their knees. Women of all classes adored him; some made subtle advances and disguised propositions towards him, hoping to catch him in a moment of manly weakness but perhaps knowing deep inside that such a decent and ardent Christian man, as he was often described by the great, public figures, a man who devoted himself to establishing justice and serving the church so faithfully, would never succumb to their salaciousness. This was the only man to whom Maggie would have surrendered her love. No one else was worth her time. No one else could raise her to the social level which, from as early as her pubescent years, she had desired. However, Maggie now came to the harsh and bitter realization that without the judge, she was just another insignificant member of the society who yearned for status without the prerequisites. For Maggie, the prospects of death were more bearable than the loss of social status. Consequently, it became expedient that she resort to the most deadly and powerful of means to maintain her relationship with the judge – the flesh.

*   *   *

The familiar touch of Maggie's door bell announced the arrival of the judge. He had a key to the house but never entered without first announcing his arrival by pressing the bell in his unique way. However, this time he chose to wait for Maggie to open the door. Maggie remembered that he once had told her that the only time he would ever end their affair was if it had come to light. Now she knew, deep inside, that that awful time had come, and that this very night, he would either have to fulfill that promise or break it. He was pensive as Maggie slowly opened the door. His jaw dropped as he beheld her, silhouetted against the lights in the sitting room. The aroma of pineapple and baked chicken accosted his nostrils and taste buds, causing him to smile and take a deep breath in anticipation of a sumptuous meal. The pensive expression disappeared and he became enraptured as his eyes became fixed on Maggie's seductive attire and alluring pose. The judge's heart pounded as he embraced her, and she knew instantly that his decision regarding the relationship would warrant immense courage and strength.

"I'm sorry to be so late...," the judge apologized. "I see that you're ready for bed but I was..."

"Shh... No need to explain," Maggie whispered as she wrapped her slender, delicately oiled arms around the judge and planted a passionate kiss on his lips. "I know what you're going to say, and I know that it is going to be hard for you to say it, just as it is going to be hard for me to hear it. So hush, hush, my darling. Come, let us eat together, one last time, before we bid each other farewell. Let us take our last sip of this elegant wine before we part and then let us take our last journey to the stars on gossamer wings. If we must part, then let it be a sweet farewell. Let us leave the tears for our moments of painful solitude."

Maggie had made it easier for the judge to end their twelve year affair by her dramatic monologue on the acceptance of her grim fate. Ironically, however, it was this dramatic monologue that seemed to make matters more difficult for the judge. As Maggie turned to approach the table, the judge firmly placed his hands on her shoulders and gently spun her around.

"Do you honestly expect me to have the strength to resist you now, Maggie? Even under the most threatening of circumstances, no man in his right mind could ever make such a foolish decision as to walk away from someone who radiates with such beauty...such femininity...who shatters the iron walls of one's resistance with just a blink of the eyes. Maggie, the mere sight of you sends my heart beating like a thousand jungle drums...takes me to the zenith of enthrallment. I'm brought to my knees in weakness before you."

He gripped Maggie more firmly and pressed his lips against hers, a long, fervid kiss that drained him of the little energy he had left after a long, harrowing day in the court. Suddenly, he drew a deep breath, turned away and took a few short steps towards the red Queen Ann chair and rested his hand on the chair back. His back was turned and his head was raised towards the ceiling.

"Maggie... I...I..."

"You're calling it quits." Maggie's voice was tense with emotion.

"Temporarily," the visibly agitated judge replied as he turned towards his mistress.

"Really? For just how long?" Maggie inquired, her eyes fixed on the nervous judge.

"I...I cannot say...right now. All I know is that we must, for the moment, call it a day."

"So, what was all this talk about a minute ago...my radiant beauty... your jungle drums?"

"And what was all that talk about 'sweet farewell' when I came through the door? You gave me the impression that you had anticipated my decision and that you were prepared to accept it."

"I was expecting you to hold me in your arms and tell me that nothing, no matter what, would ever take you away from me!" Maggie's voice was tinged with anger and hurt.

"So, you were just playing a game with me...playing dead to see what funeral you'd have. Well, now you see. Pitiful, lachrymose obsequies. No flowers, no eulogy; just torrents of hypocritical tears from the many who have not shown up to pay their last respects."

"You have never loved me, Adolph, or you would have been man enough to confront whoever sent me those flowers. I believe that you know who has sent those flowers. For all I know, maybe it's you who sent them...a coward's way out!"

"Maggie! Cut this out at once!" the judge's voice was stern and compelling as he approached her and held her firmly. "It's the sensible thing to do. Either we part for a period or we ignore the possibilities and suffer the consequences. Sweetheart, if we agree to a temporary separation, then if either of us is approached and asked about our relationship, we will be able to deny it and be truthful in our denial. After the rumors subside, then we can rekindle the spark," the judge implored.

"Meanwhile, I suppose, you go back to your lovely wife and I to empty arms. And I am supposed to wait like the dutiful mistress until her paramour gallantly returns on his horse from some distant land and sweeps her up in a moment of unbridled passion, and then ride off again into the horizon while she weeps and beats her breast in agony until he returns when he sees fit. Well, I'm afraid that this is not going to happen, Adolph. You will stand up to pressure like the man you are known to be and you will do whatever is necessary to protect this sacred love we share. I will not be your closet concubine...your *kept* woman, to be picked up and put down when convenient. I am prepared to face the music, and dance; and so should you."

"And risk my honor!?" The judge raised his voice and pounded his fist on the coffee table. "Be reasonable, Maggie. You are beginning to sound like a bordering lunatic. I have much more to lose. I cannot sacrifice my honor for a roll in the hay."

"Oh…is this what it is…a roll in the hay?" Maggie's tone reeked with venom and emotional pain.

"That's not what I mean…"

"What then do you mean, Adolph. What exactly do you mean?" Maggie's eyes sought his.

"What I mean is that I cannot substitute my honor for a fleeting dalliance. Maggie, this relationship we have is special…beautiful….and intensely passionate. I love you. You know that. But now, right at this juncture of our relationship, we are standing at dangerous crossroads. Somebody is watching us closely. The wrong decision can cost both of us our dignity…respect…honor. To stay is to come to complete ruin. To go is to preserve our love and rekindle it later. Use your common sense, Maggie. Think. Think!"

"I have been thinking, Adolph. And I've heard you very well; very clearly. Let me say something to you now, after which we may sit down to dinner as if this conversation never took place. You are free to leave. I will not hold you against your will. However, when you do, be assured that by the time you arrive home, I shall have called your dear wife and related every sordid detail of our relationship. And then I will apologize to her for your unfaithfulness and my naivety, my gross stupidity for ever believing you when you said that you would one day leave her for me. And then I will have a word with Father Perths, after which I will submit my resignation from the vestry on account of moral turpitude. After that, I will have a clear conscience, for I have no spouse to apologize to or no marriage vows by which I will be judged. You have much more to lose, Adolph. So, you are the one who needs to think, not I. Now, if you want to go, you may go. Go on. Get out! Don't tire me any longer. Your presence casts a heavy shadow over me."

The judge made a few feeble, uncertain steps towards the door and stopped.

"Oh, incidentally, you need not leave the key. I'll have the locks changed, first thing tomorrow." Maggie hissed.

The judge stood by the door. He trembled with fear and anger at Maggie's threat. When he regained his composure, he approached the dining table, like a terrified lamb that had narrowly escaped the vicious fangs of a savage wolf, and sat with his eyes unfocused and his head hanging listlessly to the side.

"Shall we dine? You must be very hungry now." Maggie stared at the judge as she simpered her question and comment. The sarcasm bore heavily down over the dining room like dark, tempestuous clouds as Maggie turned away and headed for the kitchen.

A few minutes of morbid silence followed. Then a timid, subdued voice came floating across the room as Maggie returned to the kitchen for the last dish.

"Let me see the note that came with the flowers, Maggie. With any luck, I might be able to decipher the handwriting, and make a wild guess as to who would probably carry out such a prank…to intimidate you, that's all. It is nothing more than a flagitious attempt to make you admit something without interrogation, so as to get to me…to deflate me. My guess without even looking at the handwriting is that it must be Art Kimble or Bill Jones who is the…the miscreant."

Maggie stopped and turned abruptly, "Why on earth would you assume that? I like Bill *and* Art. I don't see why they would do something like that."

"There is something about those two blokes that doesn't warrant trust. I perceived a subtle, venomous opposition at the meeting the other night. The two of them left the meeting together. I could have sensed the poignant resentment towards Faulkner and me. Something told me that they were going to do something to subvert my authority, but I never could imagine anything like this…sons of bitches!"

"Adolph…?"

"Sorry. But I am convinced that one of the two of them is behind this. But act normal. They will be watching you to see what your reaction would be. If you display any nervousness in their presence, they will interpret it as a sign of the truth. And remember, any questions or accusations…just deny it. Denial is a powerful defense."

"But my concern is where or from whom could they have got any hint of this? My intuition tells me that Rex might have something to do with this. But how, or why, would he want to mention anything to the two of them, of all people."

"Rule out Rex. Trust me on this. Rule out Rex. My covenant with Rex on this is sealed tight. He is true blue."

"I guess you're right."

"Look, let's forget this whole thing about those flowers. As far as you are concerned, it never happened. Tell yourself that it didn't happen and it will be like it actually never happened. Just leave it alone. If I hear anything about this, I am going to deal with the person or persons very seriously. And I think that they are aware of that. That's why they attacked me indirectly…through you." The judge rose and took Maggie's chin and raised it gently until their eyes met, "Maggie, listen to me. I'll take care of this. You have nothing to worry about. Remember, I am practically invincible…a man feared and in some cases, revered by the members of this society. My stern, powerful reputation and moral rectitude precede me. Those chickens can never harm you, or me. Trust me."

The judge's fanfaronade greatly impressed Maggie and boosted her courage. As long as she was the judge's mistress, she believed, she was safe.

Once more, they kissed passionately, as if to endorse the judge's promise of protection. Maggie turned and approached the kitchen again, this time beaming with joy and pride that she, a woman of such moderate consequence, could vanquish such a powerful man, mould him like clay in the hands of a potter; that she, a woman of such comparative unimportance, could bring this invincible tyrant, this man who is feared and revered by the society, to his knees in perfect submission. When the table was fully set, they sat down to dinner.

*   *   *

That night, while the judge was comforting the pious one with promises of protection and seducing her with his self portrait of power and quasi-reverence, a discreet meeting was in progress at *Phauphen's Tavern*. The select group consisted of a small cross-section of the congregation – from the *Gold Circle* to the *Iron Circle*. Pigeon Goodfellow had called the meeting and, in conjunction with Mr. Hauklyn, devised a plan to overthrow the illegitimate regime. Mr. Hauklyn had agreed to host the meeting in the closed pub on condition that he be absent from the proceedings and that he be considered ignorant of the purpose of the gathering, should any of those attending prove untrustworthy and report the events of the evening to the judge or Mr. Faulkner. These two dictators and Mr. Hauklyn had a cordial relationship, so it was necessary for Mr. Hauklyn to appear naïve and aloof from Pigeon and his subversive group. About twenty eight members made up the covert gathering, and after Pigeon had spent a fair amount on drinks and cutters, he called the meeting to order. Mr. Haulklyn subsequently retired to the office at the back, as pleased as punch with the financial intake for the night.

Pigeon stepped in front of the group and motioned with his raised arms to turn their attention towards him. "Friends, I call this important meeting to order. I am indebted to you for your attendance here this evening. It is indeed a pledge of your support."

A mild applause followed. The attendees were meticulously selected. Pigeon knew who were the disgruntled members of the vestry, those who were ignorant of the existence of the BOARD and would frown contemptuously upon its members were they made aware of their identity, those who despised the judge and Laurent Faulkner but were afraid to publicly express their feelings and those members of the *Bronze* and *Iron Circles* who would easily support him and discreetly influence the simple minded villagers. Pigeon had made a careful study of the persons present and was convinced that each would faithfully serve his purpose. At a corner table across the room sat Bill Jones and Art Kimble.

"Brothers and sisters, we who are ardent supporters of the Church of St Patrick are faced with a serious crisis. I understand, from reliable sources which I rather not mention, that there is a group in the church that wants to control everything and everybody – even the priest, the vestry, and his Lordship, Bishop Addington. They have formed a discreet group and their purpose is to divide the parish into social classes, whereby the financial and professional elite will form the ruling class and all others become their subjects. I further understand that they have presented a slate for the coming vestry election which consists of persons of relatively dull intellect who could easily be controlled. Comrades, I have called this meeting tonight to make you aware of their unscrupulous, lawless agenda."

"Who are the members of this board?" The question came from Silas Davies, the proprietor of a small fabric store just outside Brewster's Village.

"Let's not take a subjective approach to our mission, Davies. My aim is not to roll heads but to challenge a system."

"Who's behind all of this, Pigeon? I mean, who started up this whole divide and rule thing?" Silas continued.

"Faulkner and Pilchard!" cried Art Kimble from the corner table.

The gathering turned towards him, but the subdued lights in that corner produced merely a shaded outline of his face.

"Yeah...," echoed a husky voice from the same subdued corner table, "Moloch and Mephistopheles."

"Gentlemen, please. Let's deal with this issue as objectively as possible. Don't let us indulge in *ad hominem* remarks..."

"...But they ask me wife to be in charge of the Public Relations Committee," Ram interjected, "so I doesn't believe that them wants to control things. That ain't true."

"Did you see what took place after the service on Harvest Sunday?" asked Pigeon. "This is precisely why I had to call this meeting. Did you see how they swarmed Nollie Mertins like killer bees because he allowed Philbert Watts to sing the solo for the anthem? Look below the surface, my friends. Philbert Watts is a symbol of St. Patrick's underclass. When he succeeded that Sunday, you succeeded. And that was a searing threat to their power and control, a blistering insult to their illusive superiority."

"Right...yes...we were witnesses to that....," admitted Teacher Lovell, the proprietor and self-appointed headmistress of her small, bottom house, elementary school in Brewster's Village. "I saw the whole thing with me own two eyes. It was scandalous and embarrassing."

"Yes, me dear," added Phyllis Cummings, who had a crudely built concession stand in front of Brewster's Village Methodist School where she sold home made confectionery, pickled mango slices, tamarind balls and custard-blocks. Teacher Lovell had requested that she come to the meeting. "I did want to get up there pun that altar and plant me fist right in that Maggie Billings' face. But it was too soon after church."

"Well, I'm glad that you didn't," Pigeon responded. "Now, my friends, you're beginning to understand what I'm trying to say to you, hence the urgency of this meeting. I tip my hat to you. Ladies and gentlemen, if we allow these folks on the BOARD to succeed in their agenda, then we are to be pitied, for we are nothing more than fools. We cannot, and must not, allow this to happen. It behooves us to rise up and save our church and our selves."

"So, tell us, Pigeon, what is your plan to fight the enemy within?" The calm voice belonging to Bart Nuckles, who had earned the reputation as Brewster's Village most skillful coffin maker and Fritz Batty's deadly rival, came sailing across the room.

"Remove Eloise Pigthorne from office and elect a new Senior Warden, someone who can stand up to Faulkner and Pilchard," Pigeon replied. "They carry out their dirty agenda through Eloise. Friends, my reason for inviting you here this evening is to let you know of my intention to run for that position of senior warden, and I am beseeching your support."

An awful, terrifying silence engulfed the room. Moments later, a slow, uncertain applause came from the direction of the subdued, corner table. This was followed by a surge of striking palms demonstrating approval and support. This sign of approval motivated Pigeon to publicly disgrace the members of the BOARD by denigrating their character, mocking their simmering stupidity and exposing their skullduggery.

"No ad hominem remarks, Goodfellow!" jeered Art Kimble. Suppressed laughter from the subdued corner table followed.

Pigeon artfully presented his case and convinced the gathering to support his agenda. However, his nomination was to be made from the floor. This approach, he believed, would catch the BOARD off guard and thwart their plans. He further besought the gathering to discreetly canvass support from individuals who were known to be opposed to the vestry and the BOARD. Since, however, the BOARD was more or less a covert group, the disdain for and opposition towards the vestry would have preponderated. Furthermore, Pigeon had received a verbal report of the sub-committees that were being formed from the gentlemen at the subdued corner table. This strategy by the BOARD was perhaps going to pose the biggest threat to Pigeon's success in his bid for the position of Senior Warden. Thus Pigeon sought to resort to the 'divide and rule' policy – a strategy he would subsequently describe to the men at the subdued corner table as 'a piece of management legerdemain.' Pigeon judiciously appointed Ram as the campaign manager for Brewster's Village. This appointment was met with robust approval. Pigeon vehemently believed that support from the *Bronze* and *Iron Circles* would be a cinch for his success in the election at the upcoming Annual General Meeting. Ram, however, was given the privilege of unilaterally announcing his position, describing his role and presenting the strategy to his dear wife, who subsequently would be implored to swear to secrecy. The gathering was asked to pray earnestly for Ram as he embarked on this dangerous expedition. After everyone had vowed his support for Pigeon and had sworn to confidentially, the meeting closed with a prayer led by Rocky De' Souza, the landlord of a few dilapidated tenement houses in the village.

As the gathering left the tavern, cloaked in the darkness of the still night, the gentlemen who sat at the subdued corner table exchanged wishes for a good night's rest with Pigeon and Mr. Hauklyn and approached their cars which were parked in the rear of the parking lot.

"How do you like that, Kimble?" Bill Jones asked.

"You mean…"

"Right. The announcement to run for Senior Warden."

"Not surprised."

"But, how come he never mentioned his intention when he spoke to us on the phone?"

"Don't know. Maybe it was a last minute decision." Art responded.

"Don't you think that as junior warden, he should at least have said something to me first… I mean, don't I deserve that respect?"

"Aww…don't take this personally, Bill. I'm sure that it was not meant to be an ad hominem attack…"

The two men laughed as they ignited their respective engines. Art Kimble tuned his radio to the jazz station and sped off into the still night. Bill Jones pondered a while before slowly exiting the parking lot.

*   *   *

The trip home for Ram was plagued with agonizing considerations. He saw his support for Pigeon as the conduit for social advancement. If Pigeon were to achieve victory in his bid for the prestigious office of Senior Warden, he thought, then maybe he would be appointed to some official position in the church. This would mean assuming some degree of power and interacting with the upper class. This thought brought a smile to Ram's lips, for although he was pleased with his wife's appointment as Public Relations Chairperson, and puffed up with pride, he nevertheless bore a discreet streak of jealousy. Her advancement in the ecclesiastical and social sphere implied his inferiority and threatened his position as the head of household. The accolades that were lavished upon her by the villagers simultaneously served as subtle reminders of his insignificance as the male. Immediately, these dismal, belittling thoughts propelled him to approach his role as campaign manager with the intransigence of a raging bull. The true test of his tenacity, however, was going to be the imparting of the information regarding his position and role to Mrs. Ramgolam. Ram thus sought to boost his courage by making a social call at 'Blackie's', one of the most notorious rum shops and bars in Brewster's Village. He ordered a bottle of illegally distilled spirits and joined four other men with whom he was acquainted and who were already mildly drunk.

As the five men sat confabulating and imbibing, Granny Durkins, a short, relatively thick woman in her early seventies, who was fairly active for her age, appeared and began to collect the empty bottles that were strewn about or piled in a wooden carton box. She had made a modest income from this meager trade. By day she functioned as a char woman at the Government Department of Health office across the street from Blackie's. Granny Durkins was a shrewd businesswoman and took this nocturnal trade very seriously. She worked long and hard to support her two daughters, three sons and eight grandchildren. Blackie's was her territory. She had made friends there and had established a healthy working relationship with Mr. Blackman, the proprietor. Mr. Blackman had allowed her certain privileges, one of which was the right to collect all empty bottles and offer them for resale to any one who would purchase them. Granny Durkins had amassed quite an impressive clientele, and she served them with dignity and efficiency. She and Mr. Ramgolam indulged in a light banter upon her arrival and he offered her a drink, which she gratefully accepted before resuming her task.

Shortly before midnight, Pinky Beckles, nicknamed 'Coconut Woman' or 'Monkey Queen', by virtue of her concubinary relationship with a coconut vendor familiarly known as 'Monkey King', approached the five men, carrying a canvas bag. She, like Granny Durkins, was an unregistered member of St Patrick's and consequently was classified as a member of the '*Iron Circle.*' By dint of her membership at St Patrick's, she was causally acquainted with the men at the table and Granny Durkins. Pinky and the men acknowledged each other but no one offered her a drink. She headed over to the box containing the empty bottles and began to place some of the bottles in the canvas bag.

"You can't tek none of them bottles, Pinky," Arthur Jackson, one of the men at the table cautioned her. "Them bottles belongs to Granny Durkins."

"These bottles doesn't belong to nobody," Pinky loutishly replied. "They is in the garbage. I ain't see Durkins' name pun none of these bottles."

At that moment, Granny Durkins came out of the bar with a few bottles which she was going to store in the box until it was time for her to leave and observed Pinky executing the brazen loot. Granny rested her bottles on another table and called Pinky over to her. As they spoke, Ram could not help but observe the striking contrasts between the two 'fat cats' of Brewster's Village bottle industry. Granny Durkins was a short, thick, dark skinned woman with short, cropped grey hair which she kept covered under a head tie and a tattered Yankee baseball hat. She bore a peaceful, pleasant countenance in spite of the problems associated with her useless children and her three estranged, reputed husbands. Coconut Woman, by contrast, was a relatively tall, light skinned woman in her late forties or early fifties, who appeared to have been the beneficiary of life's harshest circumstances. She was inclined to pugnacity even at the mildest level of provocation and her expression carried the permanent mark of disgruntlement and tepid anger. Pinky's attire had the power to evoke a chuckle from even the most somber of persons. Her trademark outfit was a colored tee shirt over a pair of short shorts, which pronounced rough justice upon her flaccid, blotchy, melon thick thighs and lean legs that sported varicose veins. Thick white socks and an exhausted pair of sneakers usually complimented the ensemble. The two women seemed to be settling their dispute quite amicably. This quelled Ram's fear for the older woman who appeared to be standing in the shadow of the towering, formidable foe. Ram thus resumed his conversation with the men at his table.

 Granny Durkins eventually turned away from Coconut Woman and headed towards the table on which she had earlier placed the bottles. Coconut Woman likewise turned around, went back to the box and continued to place the bottles in her canvas bag. Granny Durkins again approached Coconut Woman. This time, however, Ram heard her pleading with Coconut Woman to desist from interfering with her bottles. Coconut Woman completely ignored her and continued to plunder Granny Durkins' merchandise. Suddenly, without any warning, and with rapid force and precise calculation, Granny Durkins swung a left hook which connected to Coconut Woman's right side jaw. The sudden, powerful, unexpected blow caused Coconut Woman to topple over the right side of the box to the ground. Granny Durkins wasted no time. She quickly removed her dentures from her mouth and placed them on Ram's table before arming herself with one of the empty bottles. Ram and the other patrons rose impulsively from their respective tables in order to avoid any injury and to get a clear view of the fight. Ram, however, was afraid for Granny Durkins' sake. He knew that Coconut Woman was skilled in the art of physical combat because he had witnessed Monkey King and her on several occasions slugging it out, right on the street by the coconut stand, in front of their customers. Ram therefore sought to intervene so as to save Granny Durkins from Coconut Woman's wrath. However, before he could step forward, Granny Durkins charged forward and began to batter Coconut Woman with the empty rum bottle as she tried in vain to regain her footing. Then, by a stroke of miscalculation, the bottle missed Coconut Woman's forehead and smashed against one of the tables. Coconut Woman seized the opportunity to retreat far enough to assume her footing. She rose with incredible speed and charged forward towards Granny Durkins, barring her teeth and bellowing like an enraged bull. Granny Durkins braced herself for the vicious onslaught by raising her arms and clenching her fists like a defensive heavyweight boxer, but Coconut Woman launched forward with such indomitable force that Granny Durkins lost her footing and they fell to the ground. Ram knew then that Granny Durkins would certainly suffer the bitter consequences of Coconut Woman's torrid fury. Once again, he made a desperate attempt to intervene; again, Granny Durkins effortlessly proved her competence. She wrestled with the skill and ardor of a prized fighter struggling with his last ounce of energy in the final round to defend his honor. Granny's agility proved advantageous. She managed to negotiate a turn which enabled her to pin Coconut Woman to the ground, between the fence and the gutter. From that position, she was able to keep Coconut Woman relatively subdued with her weight and with the right hand, while she slugged mercilessly to the face with the left hand. The cacophony of voices which urged the fighters and offered combative tips, superimposed by the sound of falling tables, chairs and bottles brought Mr. Blackman to the scene. Upon noting the reason for the noise, and worse, realizing that Coconut Woman was involved in the fight, he hurled a string of profanities at her before dashing back into the bar and immediately returning with a short, stout piece of wood which he kept hidden by the register – a weapon which over the years had subdued many an unruly or dishonest customer. The realization of Mr. Blackman's intense anger and the desire to save Granny Durkins from any unlucky blow from the notorious piece of wood impelled Ram and one of the other men to separate the two women. Coconut Woman sprang to her feet, and with lightning speed grabbed her canvas bag and fled across the street, oblivious of the passing vehicles. When she crossed the street and realized that no one was in pursuit, she began to scream curses at Granny Durkins, Mr. Blackman and the customers as they began to rearrange the furniture and assist Granny Durkins in composing herself after the challenging but victorious ordeal.

 Soon order was restored, and Ram and his friends, along with the other customers, once again sat down to indulge in conversation and finish their respective rounds. Mr. Blackman returned to the cashier's register and Granny Durkins resumed her task of collecting the empty bottles and placing them in the box. All seemed quiet until one of the customers rose impetuously from his table, knocked over his chair in the frantic process and dashed for cover in the shop.

"Look out, fellas'. Run!" he yelled.

As Ram turned to see what the commotion was all about, a Pepsi bottle, which was followed by a hail of miscellaneous bottles hurtling through the air like missiles, struck him in the face; Coconut Woman was firing glass rockets from across the street towards the shop in rapid succession. The terrified customers scrambled for cover as the bottles crashed against the walls and the fallen furniture. Men panicked and women screamed in fear as the surge of bottles cannoned against the concrete building. Suddenly, as if catapulted from a falconet, Mr. Blackman shot past the frightened customers with the stout piece of wood raised in anticipation of deadly assault and charged across the street towards Coconut Woman, while blasting her with an avalanche of poisonous expletives. By this time, Coconut Woman had exhausted all of her ammunition and, knowing from practical experience the crippling effects of the infamous piece of wood, took off with supersonic speed down the dry, dusty road, banked the corner and disappeared in a cloud of dust. When Mr. Blackman returned, he closed the bar for the night.

Two of the men who were imbibing with Ram took him home. He was mildly intoxicated but badly bruised from Coconut Woman's violent attack. One of the men put him to sit on the step and knocked on the door. As the light in the sitting room came on, they fled for their own mercy's sake. Neither of them was courageous enough to face the sometimes bellicose Mrs. Ramgolam and explain the unfortunate chain of events that took place at Blackie's Bar.

The door swung open and Mrs. Ramgolam, looking fair in attire and foul in expression, was confronted by the sedentary form of her husband on the top of the step, limp with semi-inebriety and bruised and swollen from Coconut Woman's brutal assault. A desperate cry for the mercy of God emanated from her lips when she noticed the swelling and dried blood just above Ram's right eye brow.

"Murdah…murdaaaah…help!!" she yelled as she threw herself upon him and wrapped him in her arms.

"Hush ya *##@*, Gloysis, before you wakes up the neighbors and the children them," Ram ordered in a harsh but subdued tone. "Take me inside quick; leh me lie down pun the chair," he instructed, "and close the door fast before anybody see."

Once they were safely inside and Ram was placed on the chair, he begged his wife to sit with him and place his head on her lap while he recalled the grossly exaggerated details of the fight and his misfortune. When he thought that he had aroused enough of his wife's concern, sympathy and anger against the men at the table and Coconut Woman, he cunningly interjected the details of the meeting at *Pauphen's* and in particular, his appointment and role as Pigeon's Campaign Manager in preparation for the Annual General Meeting. The sympathy which impaired Mrs. Ramgolam's judgment thus served to spare Ram the agony of her wrath at the sight of his intoxication. Furthermore, she was so flabbergasted with the appointment that her anger towards the men, and especially Coconut Woman, was temporarily appeased. Even the alcohol that reeked from Ram's breath did not bother her – not that night. The appointment warranted celebration and took precedence over every other thing that night, even Ram's injuries. Immediately, Ram and his wife discussed the urgent need to employ someone to manage the stall. The market was now no place for the Public Relations Chairperson of St. Patrick's Church and a Campaign Manager to be seen haggling with penurious customers over used items. They both agreed to offer the position to one of Ram's older cousins, Lenny Ragnauth, nicknamed 'Pissy Ragnauth', due to the hint of urine that invariably effused from him. Nevertheless, he was deemed trustworthy enough to be offered the job which they both knew that he would gladly accept when Ram approaches him early the following morning.

Ram and his wife thus went to sleep that night, having given thanks to God for leading them into green pasture – a metaphor which symbolized their new social status and the opportunity to mingle with St Patrick's upper echelon. That night also, before Ram fell asleep, he thanked God for the injury he received as a result of the fight and he promised his wife that he was going to purchase a new outfit the following morning for the execution of his noble task.

*   *   *

The day before the Annual General Meeting was always a busy day for Fr. Perths. It was a day spent overseeing the preparation and completion of all the committee reports, meeting with the wardens, ensuring that the parish hall was prepared for the meeting and spiritually preparing himself for the Advent Sunday Mass. The most important of the activities of the day, however, was his meeting with the wardens during which they discussed a strategy for conducting the upcoming meeting. The wisdom of this approach was that they would be prepared to present themselves as a united, fortified team at the Annual Meeting. However, the wardens rarely made any major contributions to the discussions; it was the vicar who generally dictated what was going to be presented and how the presentations were going to be made. This Saturday meeting was also the time to reinforce the importance of soliciting votes for the candidates whom he previously would have recommended to the nominating committee. These recommendations, according to Fr. Perths, would ensure a healthy constitution of vestry persons who would serve the church, and him, faithfully; who would support him in everything he says and agree to everything he does. Such cooperative teamwork, he affirmed, was vitally important for effective leadership and control, especially in the church where the judicious application of guilt and abuse of religion almost invariably serve as powerful weapons to subjugate the masses who come believing that they are unworthy creatures and that their salvation will be justified by blind obedience to the priest, moral probity, or misdirected faith. He defended these principles by appealing to eudemonism.

Fr. Perths was basically a good man – a kind, gracious and discreetly generous person who was exemplary in his prayer life and erudite in the scriptures. He loved his congregation, irrespective of social status, and was extremely popular among the children. In addition, he was considered a religious and political icon among the poor and oppressed whom he represented and defended most gallantly at town meetings and at private meetings with the most influential and powerful of politicians. However, by dint of his creaturely imperfections, he was well aware of certain deficiencies of his character, inadequacies which often caused him and the congregation arrant shame. He was frequently the object of thundering disgrace at social gatherings as a result of his uncontrollable imbibing and gluttony, and the target of public mockery at political affairs when the excessive alcohol took custody of his brain. The Pentecostal churches, especially those in the poor villages surrounding Abersthwaithe, were notoriously critical of this man of the cloth – and consequently the Anglican Church. Ironically, many of the poor and oppressed whom he valiantly defended at the town meetings were members of these very churches. These were the very people who hailed him with one breath and nailed him with the other. However, Fr. Perths was not perturbed by their hypocrisy; he dismissed it as one of the many frailties of human nature.

After the official business of the meeting had ended, Fr. Perths and the wardens became involved in trivial conversation over tea and crumpets which Olga Nurse, the self-appointed chairperson and sole member of the of the Vicar's Guild, had prepared. Suddenly, Laurent Faulkner appeared at the door and requested to seek audience with Fr. Perths. The wardens instantly became uneasy, especially Bill Jones, who almost immediately began to tap the desk with his fingers and knock his knees together in agitation. They knew the reason for Mr. Faulkner's visit and therefore sought to hastily excuse themselves, ostensibly to attend to matters arising out of the meeting, and in particular, the last minute campaigning effort.

"Busy day, I imagine," Faulkner calmly stated as he began the interrogation with a litany of small talk. "Looks like rain later."

"Yes. The forecast has predicted a late day shower," the unsuspecting vicar responded. "You know how unpredictable the weather is at this time of the year. Sun one minute, then baps! Down come the torrents."

"Good for the plants, good for the garden, bad for business. The store does poorly on rainy days. Very poorly," Faulkner whined.

"So, what brings you here today?" inquired the vicar who by now was beginning to become suspicious of the aimlessness of Faulkner's conversation and the surprising visit on a Saturday morning.

"Nollie Mertins." Faulkner's response was slightly muffled as he poured himself some tea and popped a biscuit into his mouth.

"What of Nollie Mertins?" Fr. Perths inquired nonchalantly.

"Were you aware of his plan for Harvest Sunday?" Faulkner took a sip of the hot, lemon grass tea.

"What precisely are you referring to?" Fr. Perths asked as he began to clear the papers and folders from the table in a sudden inundation of apprehensiveness.

"Philbert Watts." Faulkner turned and looked at the vicar squarely in the face.

"Can't say that I understand the connection between the two," the vicar confessed as he averted his attention.

"You were aware that he was going to offer the solo to Philbert Watts."

"Is that a question or statement?"

"A suspicion, to be exact," Faulkner coldly replied as his eyes sought the vicar's.

"An awful presumption on your part, Mr. Faulkner," the vicar likewise responded as he assumed full height and fixed Mr. Faulkner a frigid stare.

"So, how does one account for Mr. Watts' blatant disrespect?"

"Blatant disrespect for what, Mr. Faulkner, or may I say, for whom?"

"The purity of the liturgy...the congregation...the...the..."

"...the masked, hooded crusaders who refer to themselves as the BOARD?" the vicar interjected with a sudden gush of courage and disgust.

The vicar's rhetorical question caught Mr. Faulkner by surprise for he appeared to lose his voice for a few seconds. The members of the BOARD knew that the vicar was vaguely aware of the class distinction within the parish, but it just became obvious to Fr. Perths that Mr. Faulkner only now seemed to realize that he was also fully aware of the existence of the covert group of dictators whose tentacles reached far beyond the precincts of St Patrick's. However, Faulkner quickly regained his composure after this staggering, psychological upper-cut which almost left him speechless.

"The BOARD, my friend, is merely…well… more like a force of suggestion; neither here nor there. An agent of order, one might say, rather than a body or a person."

"Indeed…like the force of evil…as opposed to an incarnation of the same."

"Not quite," Faulkner replied with a wry smile. "Am I therefore to assume that you had no cognizance of Nollie's plans?"

"Why this cross-examination, Mr. Faulkner? Even if I were to say that I knew of Nollie's plans, or anyone else's for that matter, what purpose would such an acknowledgement serve?"

"It would serve to reveal what the vestry and the prominent members of the church believe – that there is a sinister force at work to undermine the power and control of the very people who seek to keep this church financially savvy and socially aloof, and pay you." Faulkner indicated.

"Interesting indeed," Fr Perths responded. "And whom do you think they might be referring to. Do any names come to mind?"

"No. Not really."

"Yet you approach *me* on a Saturday morning to interrogate me about this surreptitious force at work among us to destroy the so-called powers that be. Admit it Faulkner; I am the object of your suspicion, aren't I?"

"I thought that you might have overheard something, know of something or at least have some mild suspicion, that's all."

"Well, I'm sorry, but I have no information to offer to you," confessed Fr. Perths.

"Then I suppose that I can safely say that you know absolutely nothing of any plot by Mr. Mertins to subvert the authority of the vestry…?"

"…or the BOARD? The answer is no. I'm sorry. I have absolutely no knowledge of any subversive plot by Mr. Mertins. Please convey my apology to the BOARD."

Fr. Perths collected his folders and approached Mr. Faulkner, "I'm sorry, Mr. Faulkner," he added dismissively as he patted him on the shoulder, "but if there are no other…ah…*important* issues to discuss, I beg to be excused. I have an awful lot to do before tomorrow."

"Thank you for your time, Fr. Perths. Good morning." Mr. Faulkner bowed slightly as he tipped his hat. He then turned towards the door and exited without adding another word.

The stridency of Mr. Faulkner's footsteps as he marched down the hallway testified to the intensity of his anger at being dismissed so unceremoniously by the vicar. Intuitively, Fr. Perths knew that the time had eventually come for him to don the helmet and breastplate of protection in preparation for battle against the forces of one time friends whose superciliousness he had for years condoned for the sake of his own financial comfort and social acceptance. He had lived in quiet dread of this day, for he knew that these social elites, this brood of sanctimonious bigots, as he often referred to them whenever he was angry with them or had imbibed too much, by dint of their insatiable desire for power and control, could never ultimately be faithful to him or each other and that any friendship that was formed would be only superficial and temporary. Nevertheless, he had nurtured this very brood by the verisimilitudes of friendship and by his reticence about their gross disrespect for authority and lethal disdain towards the poorer members of the community and parish. Now, he thought, he must pay the heavy price for his sin, and theirs, which he had encouraged. Now he must summon his true friends, those whom he once regarded with sizzling contempt, to wage war against the true enemy; now he must gather his new allies to do battle against the old foe and the faithful to struggle against the unfaithful. Fr. Perths now must, without shame or compunction, approach the *Bronze* and *Iron Circles* and beseech their protection against the flaming verbal swords and the bitter wrath of the *Gold Circle*. The vicar must now befriend those whom he once despised for the sake of his welfare. These will be the new friends for whom love is not an art, but a way of life; these are the ones who are not consumed with the passionate desire to be in control but blessed with the sincere yearning to serve. The vicar must now embrace the scornful, seek their mercy and ignominiously join hands with them in a brotherhood and sisterhood of love. He must act expeditiously so as to gather his army in time for the Annual General Meeting when, he believed, the enemy will strike with rabid vengeance and unrelenting terror. The terrified vicar thus sought to contact Philbert Watts to gather the forces together. He thus immediately abandoned his plans for the rest of the day and sped off to Charlotte Road to meet Philbert.

*   *   *

Rexworth Davis also was preparing for the Annual Meeting. It was another of his days to assert himself as the vicar's '*aide de camp*' by issuing orders and directions to the members on the vicar's behalf. He was especially notorious for his bluntness and coarseness towards the members of the two lower circles on these election Sundays when both congregations would assemble for one service, followed by the Annual General Meeting. This year's meeting was especially significant to him because of the covenants of friendship he had sealed with the judge and Pigeon Goodfellow.

Bill Jones had authorized Rex to supervise the setting up of the hall for the meeting and to issue directions to the Fellowship Committee who were preparing this special breakfast. The committee was made up of *Bronze* and

Iron Circle members only. This Saturday, Bill Jones introduced the newly appointed Chairperson of the Special Activities Committee, Nellie Sweetwine, to the Fellowship Committee. Her first task as the chairperson was to direct the culinary logistics and seating for the Annual General Meeting. The members of the committee took great umbrage at this appointment and complained bitterly to Rex, and although they all had possessed a moderate degree of respect and liking for Nellie, they nevertheless considered her appointment a gross insult to their ability as a team and more so as individuals. No one said a word during the introduction, but the stifling reticence and disapproving looks towards Rex, Bill Jones and Nellie Sweetwine created an aura of hostile disagreement. Bill Jones excused himself immediately after the introduction and made a hasty exit towards the side gate. Rex walked alongside him, carrying a box of paraphernalia which Bill was going to sort out in preparation for the upcoming meeting. As Bill approached his car, which was parked in front of the gate, Thelma Mullins, the now defunct chairperson of the Fellowship Committee, appeared behind him.

"Excuse me, Mr. Jones," the icy, wounded voice accosted his ear as he turned the key to the door, "but is just like that you all does do things 'round here?"

"What precisely are you talking about, Mrs. Mullins?" Bill inquired in a tone of feigned ignorance as he continued to open the door.

Bill's pretense immediately antagonized Mrs. Mullins. She straightened herself, and with hands akimbo, pressed her upper body against the side of Bill's right arm, while her head swayed from side to side. "Nellie Sweetwine, that's what!"

"Mrs. Sweetwine's appointment," Bill remarked as he stepped slightly backward, "has absolutely nothing to do with you or any member of the Fellowship Committee. She was chosen by the vestry to assume the position with immediate effect, and all I have done is to carry out the vestry's instruction to introduce her to the committee. If you are offended by the vestry's decision, then I suggest that you write a letter to them, or speak to the priest."

"Well I ain't writing a fartz or speaking to nobody," Mrs. Mullins barked. "Y'all tek it 'pun yourselves to appoint a new chairperson, now go tek it pun yourself to prepare the breakfast for tomorrow!"

"May I remind you, Mrs. Mullins, that your place on this committee is solely at the vestry's discretion…"

"…and I can leave at me' own flippin' discretion," Mrs. Mullins furiously interjected.

"But until then," Bill warned the irate ex-chairperson, "you *will* prepare everything as planned, and you will, as the assistant to Mrs. Sweetwine, give your fullest support."

"Or else?"

"No one is indispensable, Thelma." Bill maintained his calmness and dignity as he turned and entered his car. "Have a lovely day, Mrs. Mullins," he added dismissively from the open window as he ignited the engine and sped off.

Mrs. Mullins, breathing heavily in hissing rage, picked up a large stone from the side of the street and hurled it at the speeding car as it swung the corner. The flying object was accompanied by a peel of thundering profanities and threats as she made a futile attempt to reach the retreating vehicle. However, Mrs. Mullins did not possess the skill of an archer, and the stone which was intended for Bill connected to another target. Mrs. Mullins heard the impact but did not recognize the vehicle, but upon realizing that she had missed her intended target turned and made a hasty retreat into the churchyard. On entering, she encountered Rex, who had witnessed the whole thing, and spent a few minutes with him, airing her grievances and sharing the details of her encounter with Bill Jones. Her plan, which she shared with Rex, was to return to the kitchen, call a meeting and persuade the members of the committee to protest Mrs. Sweetwine's appointment by boycotting the whole event. Soon after, however, as the members gathered around her in servile obedience, the kitchen door opened and Rex entered, accompanied by the Mayor's chauffer and two policemen.

"Look she over there," Rex said calmly as he pointed towards Mrs. Mullins.

"Yes, she look like the person I saw running after the brick hit the car...," the chauffer testified as he moved towards Thelma in close scrutiny. "It's her...she is the person I see running in the church yard. I recognize the dress and the hat."

The committee members stood with mouths agape as the police approached Mrs. Mullins.

"You threw this brick at the Mayor, mam?" the policeman asked as he displayed the object in his palm.

"Me...pelt the mayor? No sah. Never done, never done. I would never do such a thing. No sah. Not me. I was in here with these women all the time," Mrs. Mullins swore.

Mrs. Mullins' testimony was relatively believable until she added the last sentence. Then Rex, in his endeavor to ingratiate himself with the mayor and his staff, spoke boldly as he pointed towards Thelma.

"You jes' tell me that you pelt a stone at the warden and that it hit somebody' car. You jes now tell me that." Rex stated accusingly.

"Me? Me, Rex? I never tell you such a thing...no sah," Mrs. Mullins insisted.

"Maybe I can help to clear this up, officer," Nellie Sweetwine intervened with an air of authority.

"And who are you?" the officer respectfully inquired.

"I'm Mrs. Nellie Sweetwine, the chairperson of the Fellowship Committee. This woman was with us in here preparing for a celebration tomorrow. She only stepped out for a moment to discuss something with the warden. If she threw a stone at the mayor's car, I'm sure that it was only an accident. I'm sure that it was not *intended* for the mayor."

A period of a tense silence followed as all eyes turned and focused on Thelma Mullins in anticipation of any further defense. Mrs. Mullins stood there, scrutinizing Nellie and Rex and deliberately averting her attention from the police. Rex realized that she was caught in a quandary. The woman she had only minutes ago held in such contempt was now the one whose hand was stretched to pull her from the quicksand of shame and disgrace. Rex could see from her expression that she was thankful for Nellie's assistance, but at the same time intensely angered that it was Nellie's help that she had to receive. Hence there was no gratefulness on Mrs. Mullins' part.

"I doesn't need you to represent me, Nellie Sweetwine!" Thelma snapped. "I didn't pelt no stone at anybody car, so mind your damn business."

Thelma Mullins' ungratefulness and lies became too much for the patient policeman to bear. He shook his head in disgust, unlocked the handcuff from his side and approached her, "I think you'd better come with me, mam."

"Why? For what…eh, for what? What I do?" Thelma vehemently protested.

"You pelt the mayor with a big brick, that's what you done," Rex responded nonchalantly.

"Is the priest here, sir?" the officer inquired.

"No, officer. He jes now left to go out." Rex answered.

"Mam…?" the gentle officer invited Mrs. Mullins to turn and place her arms behind her back.

Mrs. Mullins nevertheless folded her arms in defiance and averted her attention from the officer. Her expression bore the stamp of truculence as she batted her eyelids and began to hum "Amazing Grace" while she gently shook her hips and tapped her right foot.

"You're going to come willingly, mam, or do I have to take you by force?" the officer threatened.

Mrs. Mullins remained non-compliant and completely ignored the officer. The members of the committee by now had begun to beseech her to obey the policeman, who by this time was on the verge of breaking the bonds of his patience. Still, Mrs. Mullins remained unyielding. Suddenly, the officer grabbed her arms, and in spite of some moderate resistance from the stubborn ex-chairperson, he managed to clasp the handcuffs around her wrists.

"Let's go, gentlemen," the officer calmly instructed the constable and the chauffer as he led Mrs. Mullins towards the door. "When you get in touch with the priest, let him know that we have escorted this woman from the church and that she is being held at her majesty's pleasure."

The committee stood in shock as the police departed with the ex-chairperson of the Fellowship Committee in handcuffs. Rex accompanied the party to the gate as Mrs. Mullins, with the humility of a sacrificial lamb, entered the police car and sat without uttering a single word. She held her head high as the cars pulled away, not once looking at the small crowd which had gathered at the front of the churchyard or the committee members who stood transfixed in a sea of shock and embarrassment. Rex saluted as the car drove off.

"Ok, let's get back to work, comrades," Rex commanded the committee as he closed the gates. The female spectators on the street who had witnessed Mrs. Mullins' departure seemed impressed with Rex's apparent position of authority. One of the women who had gathered outside blew Rex a kiss as their eyes met. Rex smiled as he clapped his hands twice and ushered the committee members inside, much to the chagrin of the newly appointed chairperson.

*   *   *

A significant amount of time had elapsed before Fr. Perths reached Pilbert Watts' home on Charlotte Road. The traffic had become heavy as he approached the city. However, the slowness of the traffic allowed him extra time to plan his strategy. He had developed great respect for Philbert – a regard which, however, had stemmed from fear rather than admiration for his talent and intelligence. Urgency required immediate friendship with this man who was so close to his Lordship and Mrs. Addington.

Fr. Perths approached the door, took a deep breath, whispered a prayer and knocked. Mrs. Watts opened the door and contemplated him in shock before regaining her composure. This was the second visit to the Watts home by one upon whom they had lavished honor and great respect. Fr. Perths could see that it was flattering to Mrs. Watts that he, the vicar of St Patrick's, should deign to visit her humble home. He contained his amusement as she glanced furtively to the left and right to see whether the neighbors were witnessing the arrival of this distinguished visitor to her home. No one whom she would have liked to impress seemed to taking any particular notice, except a few half naked children playing marbles in the adjacent yard. He felt awkward as they paused to observe with discreet amusement his rotund figure in his black cassock, which was drawn above the waist by a worn, black leather belt and further complimented by a pair of dusty, tattered brown sandals and white socks. His slightly bald head was protected from the harsh, morning sun by a paisley flop hat. He removed his hat and bowed respectfully to the lady of the house.

"Good morning, mam," the vicar greeted the proud figure at the door.

"Good morning, Parson," Mrs. Watts replied. Her acknowledgement was accompanied by a slight curtsey and a broad smile.

"From the old school, no doubt," the impressed vicar responded to the gracious welcome.

"Yes, Parson, the one on Prince William Street – St James-the-Less Primary. But I did only go to third standard."

"Really?" Fr Perths managed to respond as he struggled to suppress his amusement. "Ah, I'm here to see your son…would like to know if he would be gracious enough to have audience with me this morning."

"I'm afraid that he only jes' now had breakfast, Parson," Mrs. Watts apologized. "He would hardly be hungry so soon after. You might jes' have to have your yaudence by yourself. Please to come in and have a seat. I could whisk up a nice porridge for your yaudence while you talk to Philbert."

"Thank you, Mrs. Watts. But I am not really hungry either. I'll come by at some other time and partake of fellowship with you over a nice meal. How's that?"

"That would be rather lovely," the gracious hostess added in her quasi-British accent after momentarily studying the vicar. "I'll get Philbert."

Mrs. Watts disappeared around the narrow corridor. Fr. Perths took a few deep breaths in order to control his nervousness. He was amazed at his own anxiety. Under normal circumstances, it would be Philbert who might have been nervous about meeting him. However, it was he who sat twiddling his fingers in anticipation of what would be an ignominious experience.

The sound of strident footsteps heralded the approach of the arrogant musician, who upon receiving word that the vicar had come to see him, seemed to assume an air of pomposity. Fr. Perths believed that Phil had realized that he had come to his home only to seek a favor of him, for he had never been there before, even when Phil was sick. The vicar also believed that Phil's respect for him as a man of some distinction was beginning to wane by Phil's apparent lack of excitement upon entering the room. For a fleeting moment, therefore, Fr. Perths felt that his visit would be in vain, for although he knew that propriety would dictate some degree of sympathy, on Phil's part, towards him, he knew that Phil would not be the kind of person who would be prepared to sell his soul for a pound of flesh. Consequently, he would deal with Phil as he would an opponent in a game of chess. As Philbert thus approached, the vicar stood up respectfully and extended his arm.

"Your eminence!" Fr. Perths addressed the prudent musician with a broad smile.

"Reverend Sir," Philbert returned the flattering acknowledgement as he extended his right arm.

The two men shook hands and embraced like old friends.

"Please, Fr., have a seat. What warrants such a surprising visit by one as distinguished as yourself?"

Fr Perths realized that Phil was playing a game of cat and mouse with him, and decided to play along.

"Please. Dispense with such rigid formalities, Philbert. I'm here as an old friend and a humble servant to seek a favor of you," the vicar briskly, but nervously replied.

"I'm at your service, Fr. What can I do for you?"

Philbert's warmth and simulated obsequiousness deluded the vicar, who thus wasted no time with flippant overtures, but went straight to the purpose of his visit.

"I need your help. I have reason to believe that the vestry and some of the prominent members of the church are going to attempt to subvert my authority as vicar at the meeting tomorrow. I understand that your participation in the Harvest anthem has sparked some bitter protest among them. They hold me responsible..."

"Are you?" Philbert interjected with a leery expression.

The reverend gentleman paused, for revealing the truth would further open the floodgate for other issues that were far more troubling that the present one. On the contrary, lying would take him to an emotional pinnacle of ease but would subsequently send him hurtling to the ground in thundering disgrace. He raised his eyes towards Philbert and their eyes met. Philbert looked intently at him in anticipation of an answer. The silence was harrowing as the vicar once more lowered his eyes in tense hesitation. His invidiousness pierced the atmosphere like the arrow that flies by night, but from Philbert's expression, the vicar could see that his heart was hardened against him. He trembled as he contemplated Phil, who sat staring at him and paitently awaiting his response.

"It would not be unreasonable for one to postulate that Mr. Mertins did not act unilaterally..."

"Were you responsible?" Philbert reiterated.

"Let me just say that I did not intervene. It is precisely because of my lack of intervention that I am being sought after by this very irate group which has accused me of *mingling* the *gold dust* with the *mud*."

"I see. And no doubt I constitute a part of the mud," Philbert added with a simpering smile.

"It's merely a matter of opinion, my brother... their warped opinion," the vicar sneered.

"Why exactly are you telling me all of this now, as opposed to earlier?" inquired Philbert.

"I'm telling you all of this now because...well...because...I...I...have come to the point where I find such behavior to be most...ah...unchristian and poignantly irritating." Fr Perths confessed.

"So, what is it that you want me to do, Fr...Join the choir – to prove a point?"

"You should. You've got the voice and the talent. However, I want to ask you to do a little more than that. I want you to run for the office of warden." The vicar's expression was stern and his tone was businesslike as he fixed his eyes on Philbert.

"Me? This...this embodiment of mud, to laud it over that of the gold dust, Father? Wouldn't that be blasphemous?"

"Nevertheless, I am beseeching you to run for office. I think that you stand a great chance of winning. Of course, you will have to be nominated from the floor. However, if you will accept the invitation, I myself will arrange to have someone influential nominate you and someone to second it. So what do you say?" The vicar's plea was almost convincing.

"Isn't this rather sudden, Fr., all due respects? Is there something sinister behind this sudden decision to have me run for warden of St Patrick's...I mean, St Patrick's Anglican Church, when only a few weeks ago, I wasn't even eligible to sing in the choir?"

"The Holy Spirit moves in mysterious ways, my friend. Who am I, or anyone else for that matter, to thwart the will of God. I was inspired to come to you, Philbert."

"And you are convinced that it is the Holy Spirit that has guided you here to me?"

"Let me say that I *believe* that it is the working of the Holy Spirit," the crafty vicar replied.

"Isn't it a bit late to run a successful campaign, Fr.? I mean, this is the last hour."

"Are you doubting the power for the Holy Spirit, my friend?"

Philbert paused in profound contemplation as the cunning vicar fixed him a penetrating stare. He then rose from his seat and stepped toward the window. The vicar's eyes anxiously and nervously followed him.

"I'll give it a try, Fr.," Philbert assured the tense vicar as he turned towards him. "At least it's worth a try. If I win, then I'll be convinced that it was indeed the working of the Holy Spirit. If I don't, then I suppose that all of this would have been nothing but your vain attempt to subdue the vestry by appealing to the *mud* people. Fair enough?"

"I'll be bold enough to trust that it is God will," the relieved but frightened vicar proclaimed.

"Then so be it." Philbert extended his arm. "I'll leave immediately for Brewster's Village as soon as I finish my task here."

The vicar rose and they shook hands to endorse the pact. They embraced briefly in irreverent brotherhood before the man of the cloth bade farewell to the covertly ambitious musician.

The vicar departed in uneasy quietude, unashamed of his opprobrius conduct to achieve his own ends, but nevertheless mortally afraid of the repercussions of having misused and abused the name of the Holy Spirit to entangle Philbert in his web of treachery.

* * *

Brewster's Village was a hive of political confusion the day before the Annual General Meeting. This heap of confusion resulted in the fragmentation of a community which once had a common heart and mind. Ram's campaign was underway, but directed to a select group. Mrs. Ramgolam busied herself by going from door to door encouraging the members of St. Patrick's to attend church and to vote at the meeting. This year, the BOARD was counting especially on the votes from the *Bronze* and *Iron Circles* in order to succeed in establishing their agenda. As far as the BOARD was concerned, their victory was going to be a cinch, for their strategy had won them the support from the lower circles. In particular, the formation of the sub-committees and the subsequent appointment of the respective chairpersons made them very popular. With their well executed plan in place, the BOARD now felt poised for a landslide victory.

The big part of Mrs. Ramgolam's mission was to amass support for Eloise Pigthorne in her bid for re-election to the position of senior warden, as well as support for the persons on the slate. Mrs. Ramgolam worked passionately to prove her worth and consolidate her position as Public Relations Chairperson. Her campaign attire was impressive, except for the synthetic mass of light gold which cascaded from her head to a little below her shoulder – a voluminous assemblage of greasy, blond fiber and colorful tricho-embellishments that made her look like the caricature of a fourth place winner in a carnival costume competition. Nevertheless, her effort was worthwhile until Philbert made his usual grand appearance in the village and announced his intention to run for the prestigious office of senior warden.

The news spread like pollen on a windy day, and those who received word rejoiced that this man of the soil would pave the way for their advancement in the affairs of St Patrick's. They were ignorant of the classification of the members, but they nevertheless were fully aware of the absence of any representation from their community in the offices of the church. Now one of their own was paving the way for their social advancement, and they were thrilled. Philbert therefore effortlessly dismantled what Mrs. Ramgolam so tediously built up during her campaign.

The news of Philbert's intention shocked and intensely angered Mrs. Ramgolam. She received the news when she entered Blackie's Pub during the final hour of her campaign. She was going to encounter many of the *Iron Circle* members there that evening and she had planned to speak to them before the alcohol affected them and impaired their judgment for the meeting the following morning. However, as she approached the first table, Harry Goolcharran, who with his wife Clowdette operated a four room *guest house*, 'Garden of Eden', across the street from Blackie's, met her with the news.

"Hail!" he announced to the men at his table, "the blond queen of Brewster's Village…Philbert Watts' archrival!"

The men at the table rose and greeted her with mocked obeisance as Harry proceeded to humiliate her in front of the patrons.

"How's the campaign going, Blondie?" Harry grinned.

"Good, man. Good," Mrs. Ramgolam replied with a broad smile in spite of the taunting from the spirited Harry. "This is me last stop. After this, I done. I goin' to tek a beer and then go home and prepare for tomorrow. I wants to talk to y'all 'bout the election tomorrow. I wants y'all to go out and vote for…"

"…Aww, piss off, Blondie," snarled the half drunk Egbert Hutchins. "We votin' for Philbert Watts. That's our man!"

"Who?"

"Watts, the musician. He runnin' for warden tomorrow. He got we vote. All of we voting' for 'im." Egbert replied.

"Yeah… he already @#*%#@ been here to ask we to *#@#&* vote for him. He jest now buy us these *%#@#* drinks. So we has to #@#*&%#@ support him," added 'Bobo' Jensen, a fisherman.

Mrs. Ramgolam stood there, shocked, speechless and humiliated like a batsman in a cricket match who was beguiled and stumped by the onslaught of a curved ball. As she stood there, motionless and enraged, two of Blackie's patrons, a man in his late sixties and a skinny, disheveled, drunk woman who appeared to be in her late thirties, approached Harry. The man gave him eight dollars and he in turn gave the man a key. The couple immediately staggered across the street towards 'Garden of Eden.'

"Buy us two drinks, me dear, and we'll swing our vote," drawled a short, stout man at Harry's table.

"Come sit on me lap, sweetheart," another voice echoed across the table, "leh me run me fingers through you' 'air, and I goin' to do whatever you wants me to do tomorrow."

Mrs. Ramgolam could no longer stand the cruel taunting, and in the short time that she stood there, she had exhausted all of the dignity she had adopted for the prestigious position. She turned to observe the other patrons in the pub. No one else seemed to be paying her any attention. Unable to contain her anger at the avalanche of derision that plummeted down on her, she turned towards the men at Harry's table and splattered the group with a wash of filthy language that made Bobo Jensen's words seem like a canticle of praise. As she poured the verbal acid on the men, they mercilessly derided her by making animal noises and jeering her. The noise attracted the attention of Mr. Blackman, who approached the table and besought both parties to refrain from such obstreperous behavior. The men stopped immediately, but Mrs. Ramgolam turned on Mr. Blackman and began to blast him with a fire of hellish expletives. Mr. Blackman wasted no time trying to appease or reason with the angry woman. He abruptly turned and dashed into the shop and, with the ferociousness of a hungry pit bull, returned and charged forward towards Mrs. Ramgolam, with the infamous piece of wood raised for crippling assault. Mrs. Ramgolam realized that she had antagonized the shopkeeper to the point of irrationality and thought it best to flee from the premises rather than attempt to apologize. She therefore swung around and bolted from the pub with remarkable speed. However, Mr. Blackman proved more agile, and before Mrs. Ramgolam could reach a safe withdrawal, he stretched out his arm and grabbed the mass of blond fiber from her head. Mrs. Ramgolam nevertheless continued her desperate retreat down the street, leaving the irate proprietor with the heap of blond confusion in his hand. When she realized that Mr. Blackman was no longer in pursuit and that her wig had been confiscated, she resumed the verbal abuse from a safe distance, demanding that he return the bundle of hair immediately. Mr. Blackman yielded to her fervid request, but not before turning the outside pipe on it and thoroughly soaking it. He then threw the clump of wet, blond fiber across the street, accompanied by a few moderate profanities, and returned to his business. The laughter from the patrons who witnessed the incident penetrated the encroaching darkness of the evening as Mrs. Ramgolam grabbed the saturated, entangled clump and made a hasty retreat around the corner.

That night, the rain poured incessantly, as if the sins of the church were being purged by the water from above as it prepared for a new, transformed ministry whereby all of its members would dwell in harmony and peace;

whereby the *Gold Circle* and the *Iron Circle* would sit together at table in holy fellowship; whereby the social walls which divided the congregation would be broken down and there will be one flock, united in a common bond; whereby the dignity and talents of all members would be respected. This was what Pigeon was promising the people in his campaign.

While the rain was pouring, the people were praying. Pigeon was praying for his success at the polls; the BOARD members had decided at the last meeting that they would all fall on their knees at precisely nine o'clock on this election eve to pray that God's plan for them to rule and defend the church would come to fruition; Philbert and his mother also were on their knees praying that the Lord would bless them as they deserved by granting the parishioners the wisdom to recognize that it was He who was calling and sending Philbert to assume the position of senior warden; Ram's wife was offering petitions on behalf of herself and her husband, that they would be counted worthy enough to be numbered among St. Patrick's elite; Mrs. Ramgolam was also praying diligently for Mr. Blackman's demise – that the Lord would strike him with some deadly disease and bring an abrupt end to his business; Thelma Mullins was praying passionately from the detention cell that Bill Jones would be struck by some severe illness that would ultimately deprive him of his manhood, and that the fellowship breakfast would be a bellowing disaster; Bill Jones was praying for a legitimate excuse to miss the service and elections the following day.

Reverend Perths did not pray that night; he was sure that the Lord was on his side and that victory was already won. He thus went to bed that rainy night, basking in the sure confidence of a howling success at the elections in the morning.

Chapter Four

Election Sunday

The rainbow which bedecked the sky on the morning of election Sunday was interpreted by some as a sign of the validation of God's approval for the petitions which were offered the previous night. Never was there such a bustle of excitement at St Patrick's like this Advent Sunday morning. Long before the members began to fill the pews, they were abound with joy and enthusiasm. Rex had placed the extra chairs along the side aisles on Saturday so that he could be free to parade in his starched, black cassock like a pompous clergyman and lord it over the members of the *Bronze* and *Iron Circles*. Furthermore, it was the first day in which he would publicly issue orders to the newly formed 'Special Activities Committee.' Rex opened the church one hour earlier than usual in order to accommodate those members of the upper circles who would be there earlier than usual so as to find good seats. Mrs. Sweetwine and her crew arrived earlier than usual in order to execute their tasks with efficiency and orderliness. Mrs. Sweetwine had made it her duty to arrive earlier so as to ensure that none of the members would enter the parish hall prior to the end of the service in order to secure seats for them and their friends. In order to put an end to years of such an ignoble practice, the newly appointed chairperson instructed Rex to lock the main door leading to the parish hall. Persons attempting to enter the hall before the service was over would have to use the door that led from the kitchen to the hall. In this case, the members of the committee would be able to politely intercept them and redirect them to the church. This was Nellie Sweetwine's instruction.

As the time drew closer to the start of the service, the members continued to fill the pews. Some of them had not attended church for the entire year, but had come to support their candidates who were running for office. Pigeon had already arrived and had taken a seat in the right, rear section of the nave. By this time also, Nollie was sitting at the organ, spiritually caressing the congregation with the gentle notes of the solemn prelude which he had prepared especially for this Advent Sunday. It was an appropriate piece because it helped to establish the tone for this penitential season, and as Nollie had hoped, to keep the congregation subdued before the spirited meeting which was to follow.   However, his obversance of so many lapsed members entering the church and directing themselves to specific seats, and near to particular people, foreshadowed a fierce political affair in the parish hall. Tension and confidence danced a quivering and irreverent waltz among the members of the *Gold Circle* as certain lapsed members entered and made their way over to Pigeon, who had taken his seat among the members of the *Bronze* and *Iron Circles*. Hostile glances were being made across the nave as some presumptuous members of the lower circles assumed seating positions among the two higher circles. However, wisdom on the part of the members of the *Gold* and *Silver Circles* dictated that they remain silent, and pretend to love their neighbors as themselves by smiling and making room for them in the tightly packed pews. Common sense and experience directed Rex to ignore these impertinent people of the soil who dared to sit among the elite, and to focus on other concerns which had nothing to do with the allocation of seats. However, in spite of the tension and the sudden appearance of lapsed members, the *Gold Circle* remained assured of victory in their well designed plot to maintain control at St. Patrick's. However, by the beginning of the service, tension once again became the leading partner in this agitated waltz as the absence of two prominent members of the *Gold Circle*, Bill Jones and Maggie Billings, became poignantly noticeable among a few of the members of the BOARD, some of whom had approached Nollie and inquired of their whereabouts.

*   *   *

The Great Litany was sung with much liturgical grace and dignity. The acolytes and choir members looked regal in their black cassocks and crisp, white surplices as they solemnly processed behind the stiff, grim verger. Fr. Perths brought up the rear in his richly embellished violet cope, which was held open by two tiny acolytes. He sang the litany in perfect pitch.

When the Litany ended, Fr. Perths turned towards the congregation to offer the salutation. He opened his arms to utter the opening words, but paused as he stared down the center aisle. The perplexed congregation addressed him momentarily until murmuring and sighs of amazement emanating from the rear of the nave and echoing across to the front accosted their ears. Everyone turned inquisitively towards the rear of the center aisle. Mr. and Mrs. Ramgolam had arrived, attracting to themselves the kind of attention that was lavished upon such distinguished visitors to the church like the Prime Minister or Bishop and Mrs. Addington. The Ramgolams held hands as they strutted down the aisle. Mrs. Ramgolam bowed her head and smiled politely to the gaping members as she stepped clumsily in large, white platform shoes towards the front of the nave. She was clad in a mortally inappropriate dress that was deceptively dignified in the front but boasted too low a neckline at the back; consequently, the majority of her back was exposed right down to the waistline. Ripples of dark brown on either side of where the principles of anatomy had placed the waistline assaulted the eye as the mountainous posterior convulsed under a thin layer of floral, imitation silk. In order to emphasize the low-cut back, Mrs. Ramgolam swept up the blond mass in a large bun which seemed too cumbersome for her to balance. Perched on top of the bun was a distressing floral arrangement, comprising roses and a few wild flowers and leaves. A short piece of dyed, mosquito netting fell from under the arrangement and rested just above Mrs. Ramgolam's prominent cheek bones, which were daubed with a heavy layer of what appeared to be a red powder. The floral headdress on the clump of blond synthetic directed the morbid mind to a weathered wreath resting on a mound of dirt in the burial ground. Ram's wife completed the ensemble with a profuse array of genuine gold on her ears and around her neck and arms. A small, white, child's handbag dangled foolishly from her left shoulder.

Mr. Ramgolam complemented his wife's outfit by sporting a mustard green suit and pumpkin yellow shirt. A broad tie with the preponderance of purple hung neatly from his neck. Brown hushpuppies and white socks stepped gingerly down the aisle as he headed towards the front pew. Fr. Perths remained speechless at what he perceived to be a deliberate and vain attempt by the Ramgolams to attract as much attention from the members of the upper circles and to be accepted by them. He watched helplessly as members made disparaging remarks or displayed expressions of approval.

"An interesting work of homemade artlessness," Ruthel Pollard remarked of Mrs. Ramgolam's hat as she stood reasonably close to the lectern.

"It is as plain as the nose on my face that the BOARD has created a pompous and impertinent twit by offering that woman that position," Eloise Pigthorne added as she tossed a disapproving look at Mrs. Ramgolam's frock.

"Where does that piece of dirt think he's going?" Mr. Faulkner inquired with regard to Mr. Ramgolam. "Give these plebs an inch and they'll take a bloody mile," he whispered to the vicar from the Lay Eucharistic Minister's chair.

"Why has everyone stopped focusing on the service and turned their attention on two people who clearly seem to be happy to be here?" Mrs. Pilchard quietly asked her husband who had maintained his dignity throughout the whole dramatic entrance. "These people are so easily distracted," she noted.

The judge seemed hardly to have heard a word she had said, for he made no response. His thoughts seemed far, far beyond the precincts of the church.

The Ramgolams were offered seats in the front pew on the left. It was a tight squeeze, but the members who were occupying the seat reacted to the urgency of the moment, so that the mass could go on uninterrupted.

Fr. Perths gave an outstanding sermon on the wisdom of preparation. He emphasized social change as the priority in the hierarchy of needs at St. Patrick's and in the wider community. The sermon seemed a bit protracted for election Sunday when there usually would be a short sermon because of the subsequent lengthy address which was delivered in the hall at the Annual General Meeting. During the sermon, Fr. Perths sternly admonished an unidentified group of persons in the congregation for their persistency in 'waging a covert and deadly war against theocracy.' Only a few of the congregation who understood his ornate language nodded in the affirmative. The reverend gentleman spoke of that great day at St. Patrick's when old and young, rich and poor, peasants and bourgeois and clergy and laity will dwell together in perfect harmony, with none having more than the other and all being equal in a common bond of humanity. The man of the cloth concluded the sermon by challenging all present to search their consciences and root out the evil that lies within so as to be duly prepared to meet the Lord when he comes on that last, great advent day.

Fr. Perths could tell by the fidgeting and the furtive glances towards him that certain members of the congregation were offended by the sermon. However, after the service, he was made to understand that Laurent Faulkner had reported the details of their meeting to the disgruntled members and further advised them to dismiss the urgency of his sermon as nothing more than 'bordering socialism' and 'the vain pursuit of self-justification.'

Stella Dawkins nevertheless spent a lucrative fifty minutes during the sermon peddling a variety of bootlegged CDs and DVDs among the members of the two lower circles who occupied most of the seats in the rear of the nave. She did especially well with the sale of the adult movies, and took several orders which she would deliver the following Sunday.

During the announcements, the last of the three notifications regarding the Annual General Meeting was made. The church was deathly quiet during the reading of the slate. No one made a sound or moved as the names of the slate were called. The silence was terrifying, like the eerie calm before the deadly storm.

The vicar concluded the announcements by offering an apology on behalf of the junior warden. "Mr. Bill Jones, our beloved junior warden," he stated, "begs to be excused from today's meeting due to a mild injury he incurred as a result of a fall down the stairs in his home. He has been treated and he will be fine. However, his doctor has ordered complete bed rest for a couple of days. He asks that we remember him in our prayers today and he hopes that we have a very productive meeting. He has also asked me to convey the best of British luck to those running for the various offices." There was no word on Maggie Billings.

The service ended with the singing of the recessional hymn, 'Onward, Christian soldiers.' The members who sat at the rear of the nave sang with the passion and determination of terrified soldiers preparing to face the enemy on the battlefield. After the postlude had ended, and Fr. Perths had given the dismissal, several small groups of persons from the Bronze and *Iron Circles* surged forward respectively towards certain individuals. The members of the BOARD observed these small, pre-election gatherings with expressions of discreet amusement. They were not the least perturbed, for Faulkner had bluntly stated earlier that their victory was already ordained by God. One of the larger groups, however, attracted Fr. Perth's attention more magnetically than the others and appeared to slightly challenge the confidence of some of the BOARD members who had huddled together with worried faces, whispering and casting looks of disapproval towards the group. It was the group that had gathered just outside the front door; Pigeon Goodfellow was standing in the middle, and the group was looking intently at him and paying rapt attention as he appeared to quietly issue final instructions.

*   *   *

Breakfast was organized and well received. Those persons who had left the church immediately upon receiving Holy Communion in order to secure comfortable seats for themselves and members of their cliques were politely requested to return to the sacred space until the appropriate time. However, the disgruntled individuals chose to remain outside under a large tamarind tree and later complained to Fr Perths and speak disparagingly of Mrs. Sweetwine rather than to face the intense humiliation of returning to the church. They inquired about Thelma Mullins, but at that time, no one seemed to worry too much about her absence.

After everyone had been served, Fr. Perths called the meeting to order. Immediately after the opening prayer, he expressed effusive gratitude to Mrs. Sweetwine and the committee for the lavish, delectable breakfast which was served. Applause came on the heels of his expression of gratitude. It was then that serious questions regarding Thelma Mullins' absence began to surface. Everyone professed ignorance of her whereabouts. Even the fellowship committee feigned ignorance, as they were advised by Nellie Sweetwine to refrain from sharing the details of the arrest. Rex, however, by dint of his being outside Mrs. Sweetwine's jurisdiction, revealed the sordid details of the incident to the judge and Pigeon, who in turn were made to swear to secrecy. Neither of these two men was aware of the other's knowledge of the incident.

The adoption of the agenda was carried unanimously and the business of the meeting proceeded quite smoothly. Fr. Perths gave an impressive speech, which included expressions of gratitude to the various guilds, committees, ministries and some individuals. He also spoke of a new era at St. Patrick's. Towards the end of his speech, he welcomed the appointed chairpersons of the newly formed committees. He then invited them to stand so as to be publicly and officially acknowledged. As they stood to accept their acknowledgment, Mrs. Ramgolam stepped forward and sought permission from Fr. Perths to give a brief response to the warm welcome. No one objected. The judge was pleased that the BOARD's plans seemed to be working to their advantage for he whispered to Fr. Perths that whatever Mrs. Ramgolam was going to say was going to please the members of the two lower circles and consequently consolidate the BOARD's victory. Laurent Faulkner and the judge exchanged nods and gave each other a wink to express their joy at what seemed to be the beginning of the path to an overwhelming success on all sides. Fr. Perths offered Mrs. Ramgolam the microphone. The members burst into applause when she accepted the microphone. She plunged her hand into her cleavage and removed a folded sheet of paper, opened it and rested it on the podium. Ruthel Pollard and a some of the other female members of the *Gold* and *Silver Circles* gasped in disbelief and averted their attention from Ram's wife as she stood there, boldly fumbling in her hallow for the script. A few of the men who were sitting at the rear tables heckled her mercilessly as she began her speech. However, Mr. Pilchard rose hastily and sharply rebuked them.

"Ladies and gentlemens...," Mrs. Ramgolam began, notwithstanding the abuse from the rear, "I greets you in the name of our Lord on this most ass-spacious occasion. In my kaypacity as the Public Relations afficah', I is going to represent all of y'all consorns to the vestry. I will do me very bess' to make all'yah proud. I wants to t'ank the vestry them for afferin' me this noble position and I beg y'all to vote for the peoples on the list and to support the vestry them. T'ank you."

The audience applauded excitedly. Some of the members of the *Iron Circle* gave her a standing ovation.

"Devoid of any eloquence, but honest and succinct," remarked Laurent Faulkner.

"To those who understand her dialect," Gladys Barnwell added with modest amusement.

At the conclusion of the vicar's report, the audience was invited to make comments or ask questions. Claude Roachford raised his hand.

"The floor recognizes Mr. Roachford," Fr. Perths announced.

The audience turned to observe Mr. Roachford, who rarely spoke to anyone, but who nevertheless always bore a peaceful countenance and acted politely and respectfully towards everyone. He was sitting relatively close to Pigeon but was not engaged in any conversation with him during the meeting. The BOARD and the vestry appeared anxious to hear this gentleman's questions or comments.

"Reverend sir," he began, "during your sermon, you alluded to a covert group which you have accused of waging war against the ecclesiastical authority. Do you mind elucidating your statement? How can we eradicate such a group without knowledge of who these…ahh…*vile wretches* are?"

The silence which followed was as terrifying as the fear of death. The members of the lower circles were merely inquisitive; the *Gold Circle* and the vestry were as tense as autumn leaves just before their descent from the tree on a blustery day. The man of the cloth became as motionless as a statue as he desperately prayed for the wisdom to answer the usually reticent gentleman without offending anyone.

"To…ah…attempt to…ah…identify those…ahh…*vile creatures* would be to pronounce judgment on people who may very well be innocent of any theocratic warfare," the vicar replied. "Furthermore, I was referring to this group more as, well, an abstract agent, rather than *persons* per se. I don't actually accuse any particular person," the nervous, cowardly priest confessed.

"I will ignore your semantic fiasco, Reverend sir. However, would you by any chance be referring to this cloak–and-dagger group which refers to itself as the BOARD; 'Friends Organized and Operating to Lead Subordinates?" Mr. Roachford looked intently at the petrified vicar who, after regaining his composure, stuttered profusely in a vain attempt to conceal his knowledge of this covert group who claimed responsibility for his financial comfort.

"Is…is…that…an..o..opi…opinion,   or…or…are…you…you… attempt…ting… to lead the…wit….wit….ness…?" Fr. Perths managed to utter in a strangely timid voice.

"Is that a rhetorical question, irreverent sir?" yelled Horace Littlejohn, the assistant superintendent of police, who, after service on Sundays, always left the church without ever partaking of fellowship in the parish hall. His question evoked an uproarious laughter among the visiting, lapsed members and bitter, verbal reaction from some of the more prominent members of the BOARD.

"Don't cast aspersions, *Little*john," Fritz Batty snarled. "Act like the man you're not and spell it out!"

"Aww, go lay in your coffin, Batty, and bury yourself!" Mr. Littlejohn snapped in savage retort. "I speak as an authority. I have solid evidence of this group which is operating to control things here. I should have all of you arrested for attempted usurpation!"

"You're not talking to a bunch of criminals here, you know, Littlejohn," Mr. Pilchard added defensively. "We are a bunch of intelligent men and women."

"Is this a confession, honorable judge, or are you admitting the existence of such a group?" Mr. Littlejohn inquired.

"No. It is the public declaration of your madness," Laurent Faulkner interjected.

"Are you going to stop this, Fr Perths?" asked Nora Nesbeth, the recently appointed matron of the public hospital, "or shall I get up and leave? We've just come out form church and here we are, devouring each other like cannibalistic, wild dogs!"

"Please, ladies and gentlemen," Fr. Perths raised his hands, "let us conduct ourselves with a little more Christian decorum."

Silence followed immediately and order was temporarily restored. No further questions or comments were directed to the vicar.

The clerk of the vestry was then invited to present the slate. The invitation was attended by the shuffling of feet and murmuring from across the floor. As the slate was being read, there was a slight commotion from the rear of the hall. Thelma Mullins had arrived, escorted by Mr. Mullins, a burly, jet black man with a receding hairline and a cropped mustache. His enormous size and fierce countenance made him quite minatory as he scanned the hall as if searching for some particular individual. Mrs. Mullins stood slightly behind him. However, her odd appearance created a bigger stir than that of her imposing husband who hovered menacingly over the audience who sat by the door. Mrs. Mullins was always relatively well attired. Her outfits were generally cheap but well coordinated and her hair was invariably well groomed. She flaunted colorful costume jewelry and wore patent leather shoes which always seemed too tight for her thick, little feet. Furthermore, she was never without a handbag, although her choice of bag seemed to be based on practicality rather than on color coordination. However, on this day, Mrs. Mullins was attired in the same outfit she was wearing when she was taken away by the officer. Her clothes seemed very disheveled and crumpled as if she were lying on the floor for a protracted period. The well groomed afro hairdo she so proudly and neatly sported was badly disfigured. The right side was flat and the top was twisted. It appeared as though she was lying on her right side for a long time, enough to affect the symmetry of the usually impeccably formed and balanced afro. An expression of extreme tiredness and fatigue veiled her face, and the heavy bags under her eyes told the grim tale of mental and physical anguish.

As all eyes studied Mrs. Mullins in bewilderment, Phil Bathersfield, a cobbler who conducted a modest trade in Brewster's Village market, rose and approached the couple.

"Rudolph! Whu you doin' here? Ain't see you in a long time, man? You lookin' fuh somebody?"

"Jones…the warden' fuh the chu'ch," the gruff intruder barked. "Where he deh? I wants to talk to 'im."

"You mean Bill Jones, the senior warden?"

"Yes; that %**&#@. I wants to talk to 'im."

"He's not here. He didn't come today. He sick at home, they say. Why?"

"He ain't come, eh? He know why…@##@%^ coward."

"Shh…come, leh we go outside, man. You can't cu'ss like this in the church. God goin' vex with you. Come, leh we talk outside." Phil implored.

As the men retreated outside, Mrs. Mullins cast a dirty look on the audience before turning and flouncing through the door. Fearful respect for the imposing Rudolph Mullins demanded total silence from the audience. Some, however, exchanged puzzled expressions regarding Mrs. Mullins. The women on the Fellowship Committee, who knew what had transpired the day before, glanced at each other and then turned and entered the kitchen without uttering a solitary word.

Fr. Perths rose from his seat and approached the door, hoping that his presence would dismiss any thoughts of fighting.

"Whu happen with you and Jones?" Phil inquired as they exited the building.

"He mek me wife get lock up, that's what…" Rudolph Mullins growled, "and give somebody else the position as chairperson of the group that does tek charge o' things pun a Sunday."

"You was in the lock up, Thelma?" the astonished Phil asked.

"Whole @%&**% night, that's what!" Rudolph affirmed. "If I catch 'im I goin' break his **&%^** hands, two o' them both, that's what!"

"Look, Rudolph," Phil patted the irate man on the shoulder in an attempt to appease him, "I goin' to talk to Jones when I sees him. Don't get you'self in trouble with the police over this. It ain't worth the trouble. Besides, look the pries' standin' up deh too. Show some respect, man. And Thelma, if they tek away you' position, let them keep it. Just come back to church and continue to praise God."

"She ain't comin' back here no more, that's what!" snapped Rudolph, "I goin' send she to another church. All o' them people in this church is ^&&***% hypocrites, that's what, @@$#%^&* hypocrites!"

"You tekin she to *your* church, eh?" Phil sarcastically inquired.

"He don't go to church," Thelma confessed. "He say that the church full o' hypocrites...."

"Yeah...power hungry *@@#*, that's what," Rudolph interjected. "I says me own friggin' prayers at home. Come, Thelma...leh we go 'ome. You tell Jones that I goin' twist his *%%$@ face when I catches him."

As the couple mounted the bicycle on which they had come, Bobo Jensen, as well as two other men who had come to church on this Sunday specifically to vote for Philbert Watts, appeared from the parish hall to check on Phil.

"You alright, Phil?" Bobo inquired as he addressed Rudolph suspiciously, "they's goin' to do the votin' soon."

Several months ago, Bobo and Rudolph were involved in a fierce altercation over a woman at Blackie's, and although they had subsequently met at the bar and at several social occasions in the village without any antagonism, Bobo's concern for Phil's welfare somehow seemed to unearth some buried hostility in Rudolph.

"Whu' you come out here for like some bad man?" Rudolph dismounted his bicycle as he addressed Bobo in a threatening tone.

"Whu' happen? You got a problem with somebody here?" Bobo responded with equal rancor.

"Yea, all of you %%$@# hypocrites, that's what. I goin' to **%$@ all of you..." Rudolph's expression and tone were savage as he tossed the cycle to the ground while Thelma was still sitting on the bicycle bar. Both landed in a small puddle which was formed by the heavy downpour the previous night.

Bobo perhaps perceived Rudolph's pugnacity as a direct threat and challenge not only to the church members, but to him personally. Consequently, he advanced, throwing off his red, plaid blazer and undoing his green and orange paisley tie. The two men drew close to each other, sizing up each other with their arms poised for battle.

"Gentlemen, please!" Fr. Perths pleaded from the doorway.

"Y'all cut that &&%@ out, man," Egbert Hutchins implored from the steps of the parish hall. "Y'all deh pun holy ground. Y'all go out pun the road and fight!"

Bobo responded to Egbert's plea and turned to make his way towards the road. Rudolph thus seized the opportunity to launch his assault from behind and pounce on Bobo's back, while locking off his neck with his powerful left arm and punching him mercilessly with his right hand. This cowardly attack intensely provoked the two men who had come out with Bobo, and they instantly forgot that they were still standing on holy ground. They charged forward in unison with so much force that they knocked the two struggling men to the ground, where upon they quickly subdued Rudolph and began to administer a fleet of blows across his face and body. Rudolph retaliated with the ferocity of a hungry lion but was no match for the three angry men. Thelma sought to come to her husband's aid by grabbing a piece of wood from the side of the fence and issuing blows across the bodies of her husband's assailants. One of the men reluctantly grabbed her by the arm, seized the piece of wood, spun her round while bending her arm backward and upward, pushed her forward against one of the trees and walloped her buttocks with the piece of wood.

"Murdah…Murdaaaaah!" Thelma yelled at the top of her voice.

The noise of the commotion brought the congregation to the door. They were mortified at the sight of a fight in the churchyard on this election Sunday. The altercation cast a sheet of electrifying embarrassment on the members and the vicar. Someone immediately summoned the police.

"Gentlemen, stop it at once!" demanded Fr. Perths, who was the only one brave enough to approach the scuffle. The sight of the man of the cloth in his black cassock and priest's collar brought some arrest to the battle. However, before the fight actually ended, the three men grabbed Rudolph, Thelma and their bicycle and threw them out on the street. As the couple rose in a futile attempt to further retaliate, the sound of sirens began to pierce the air. Desiring no further confrontation with the police, Rudolph and Thelma Mullins hastily mounted their bicycle and sped off, while hurling curses at the congregation, promising to later continue the fight in the village and threatening to set fire to the church. However, by the time the police arrived, the couple had disappeared around the corner. Fr. Perths, in his urgency to complete the meeting, and in his quest for peace and quiet on this Advent Sunday, advised the congregation to return to the parish hall while he assured the police that the miscreants had gone and that order had been restored. The members of the *Gold Circle*, however, returned to the hall, intensely angered and disgraced by the incident which was caused by the plebs who were allowed to participate in worship and fellowship at St. Patrick's. They therefore vowed to revisit and arduously pursue the plan to have a small church built in the village; this was going to be the first item on their agenda after the installation of the new vestry.

After the commotion caused by the altercation had simmered down, the congregation resumed its business. Meanwhile, news of Thelma Mullins' overnight detention at the Queen's pleasure had reached the ears of the members, and the *Bronze* and *Iron Circle* members immediately requested that Mrs. Ramgolam investigate the manner in which Thelma's deposition was executed and report to them at a special meeting which was going to be called the following Saturday at Volda Bradshaw's house in the village.

* * *

Volunteers began to distribute the ballot sheets as the clerk of the vestry proceeded to announce the names on the slate to fill the positions as vestrypersons. The motion was made by Mr. Pilchard to cast one ballot for the four uncontested vestry positions. The motion carried; thus Darlene Burrows, Al Foster, Nekada Dufries and Sam Galloway acceded to the office of vestrypersons for their respective terms. In like manner, the names of delegates to Synod were approved and ratified. All, so far, of the BOARD's plans were coming to fruition. Stolen expressions of victory and satisfaction were exchanged among the members of the BOARD and the vestry when the nominations were approved without any hitches.

The crucial moment came when the clerk presented Eloise Pigthorne as the candidate to assume the prestigious office of Senior Warden. Within a few minutes, Faulkner stated boastfully, the first part of the BOARD's agenda would have been completed and they would be on their way to a resounding victory. He thus displayed no anxiety, especially in the wake of the earlier uncontested positions which were approved by the casting of one ballot. The final position and name on the slate was then announced – that of Senior Warden.

A momentary period of silence followed.

Laurent Faulkner rose and raised his hand in the assurance of a smooth closure to part one of the BOARD's vile agenda. "I beg to have one ballot cast for…"

"Not so fast, Faulkner," the voice was that of Bart Knuckles, Fritz Batty's arch rival in the coffin industry. "I beg to nominate Peter Goodfellow for the position of Senior Warden."

"I second the motion," echoed Silas Davies.

An awful silence engulfed the parish hall. The expression on the judge's face changed instantly from one of victorious confidence to absolute horror, like condemnation on judgment day. The nomination hit the members of the BOARD like an iron ball to the chest. For the first time since the formation of this insidious group, their discreet and unlawful authority was being threatened. Faulkner further realized the precariousness of the BOARD's position when Pigeon's name was announced. He realized that they could no longer function as a covert entity. The die was cast. Their Judas had betrayed them. He had used their very weapon to attack and subdue them.

The war of the underworld thus began. What appeared to the lower circles to be merely another nomination was in fact more than a superficial competition for office. In Faulkner's analysis, if Pigeon were to assume this powerful and prestigious position, the BOARD would immediately be stripped of its power and the walls dividing the social classes would be broken down, thus creating what he later described as a *communist ecclesiasticism*, whereby the *Gold*, *Silver*, *Bronze* and *Iron Circles* will lie down together. Such a fate would result in the fall of the minuscule empire of St Patrick's and bring to naught the so-called powers. It therefore became a matter of rabid urgency for Faulkner to seek to deflate this impertinent and ambitious Bolshevist before his revengeful agenda could take its place.

After the first few moments of intense shock had passed, a hushed discussion opened among a few of the members of the *Gold Circle* who were sitting in close proximity.

The clerk then announced, "If there are no more nominations, I beg that someone…"

"Just a minute," Laurent Faulkner requested.

After a few more tense seconds had elapsed, Mr. Faulkner raised his hand and stood. "I beg to nominate Mr. Adolph Pilchard for the office of senior warden."

"Second!" shouted Fritz Batty.

This nomination appeared to have dealt Pigeon a severe blow, for he gasped and straightened up in his chair and opened his eyes wide as he made eye contact with some of his supporters. He had mentioned earlier that morning to some of the people that his only rival was going to be the dull and malleable Eloise Pigthorne, for whom he and his supporters had little regard and against whom victory was therefore a cinch. He also had expressed a profound faith which, as he also told the gathering, was built on the confidence won that night on the beach, when he was convinced that his victory was purposed and confirmed by God. However, Faulkner also held the similar belief that God had blessed their plans and had already granted them victory by dint of their fervent intercessions in their respective homes at nine o'clock on the previous night.

"How they sseek to divide the Trinity in a combat against itself," Faulkner remarked to the vicar, "by holding legitimacy to God's generalship on the battlefield of their selfish ambitions!"

Faulkner tapped his feet anxiously as tension, determination and desperation locked arms in an unholy trinity as the supporters of Adolph

Pilchard and Pigeon Goodfellow took up their positions on the battlefield. He was going to employ every measure in order to ensure success. Faulkner therefore dictated that Eloise Pigthorne withdraw from the race, so as to permit the judge to muster enough votes to gain victory in the race for the position of ultimate power. However, Faulkner's confidence was once again shattered when, with the calm assurance of an athlete about to cross the finish line way ahead of the group of exhausted runners in vain pursuit, Joseph Chung Wee, who specialized in the sale of firewood, coals and kerosene oil at his shop in Brewster's Village, stood and raised his hand.

"I beg to nom'nate Phibe't Watts."

"Oi second dhat!" The voice came form Hetty De' Santos, a stout, ebony colored Barbadian woman who was married to Arnold De'Santos, a Portuguese man who bought stolen goods and sold them for a huge profit from his grocery. It was Adolph Pilchard who had sentenced him to five years detention at her majesty's pleasure. Mrs. De' Santos thus bore a scorching hatred towards the judge. Nevertheless, he was one of her many clients who bought her famous souse and sweet-bread which she made and sold from her home on Saturdays to support herself and nine children which she bore for Mr. De'Santos.

Suddenly, the atmosphere at the rear of the hall became alive with a strange excitement at Philbert's nomination. However, the supporters of the other two candidates became mildly agitated. Adolph Pilchard and Laurent Faulkner became strangely silent. They turned towards Fr. Perths and addressed him coldly with their eyes, as if holding him responsible for Philbert's audacity.

There were now three candidates running for the position of senior warden – one motivated by revenge and ambition; another out of necessity and the desire to control, and the other in response to the request of the vicar. No further names were presented and the motion was made that nominations be closed. The motion passed and the polls were opened.

*   *   *

Laurent Faulkner hung his head and placed his hand on his forehead as he pondered on the fate of the BOARD and the tone that he and others had set in the parish over the years. He seemed overwhelmed by the unexpected attendance at this year's Annual General Meeting. In previous years, the *Gold Circle* maintained control and everyone accepted it, some because they did not deem it their business to get involved in the leadership of the church, others because they were content to allow others to undertake the difficult task of sharing the ecclesiastical duties and managing the financial affairs while they simply remained in the background and complained about everything, while the rest were lead to believe that their place in society had judged and sentenced them to unworthiness of any participation and subservience to those of higher, social status. Now all of this was on the verge of changing. The eyes of the plebs were opened by Philbert's participation in the Harvest anthem and more so by the tendentious appointments of Mrs. Ramgolam, Nellie Sweetwine and Uncle Ed. The BOARD's sinister plan to create new ministries and appoint the three persons from the village as chairpersons, ostensibly to encourage inclusion and more active participation in the church's ministry, would become the accuser, judge and sentence that would be passed on them. Their own wickedness and ironic stupidity would thus form the very earth which would be heaped upon them in their amplified, premature burial. Faulkner raised his head and sighed heavily as he pondered on this grim possibility.

Various reports were read and discussions followed during the hour in which the polls, by law, had to remain open. Not many members had participated in the discussions, however, since the interest was on the elections and not particularly in the current ecclesiastical affairs. In any case, much of the discussion was beyond the comprehension of the members of the lower circles who, on this particular morning, represented the majority. The lapsed members who had turned out in large numbers were eligible to vote by virtue of their attendance at mass on Christmas, Easter and Harvest Sunday. Their monetary contribution, though scant, was augmented by their generous contributions at Harvest. Furthermore, their protracted absences served to please the upper circles, who were happiest the less they were around. In addition, their names were merely recorded in the parish register so that St. Patrick's could maintain its parish status. According to the numbers on the register, St. Patrick's boasted the largest congregation on the island. However, according to the *Gold Circle*, the two lower circles were considered *recorded* members, as opposed to *registered* members. Whereas in other congregations the two forms of membership would be the same, at St. Patrick's, there was a subtle difference.

*   *   *

Fr. Perths, unlike Faulkner, was exceptionally elated to see so many members in attendance on this day. Philbert's success at the polls would represent a victory for him for several reasons: it would bring about the dissipation of the BOARD; provide him with a more trustworthy senior warden and servile vestry; surround him with more loyal and respectful members; enable him to exercise more control in his position as vicar; make him the recipient of abundant gifts from the peasants who would revere him as their religious, English icon; finally, and most importantly, it would place him in good stead with Bishop Addington. It therefore behooved the vicar to pray assiduously for Philbert's success. Philbert would be the key to opening up a new era at St. Patrick's. He was, after all, an individual whose character and social status exceeded the definition of any of the four circles. He stood aloof from the other candidates – dignified and sophisticated – a man who demanded great respect and bore enviable popularity and fame. He was the man of the moment.

The vicar knew, however, that Philbert was not the man who was really feared among the BOARD. It was Pigeon whom they feared more. He was the one who could meet them at their level, and win; he was the one who could expose their cunning and heap burning coals of shame and disgrace upon them; he was the one who could cause some of them to change their allegiance – a terrifying likelihood indeed. But a more dismal prospect than all of the above was the fear that under his leadership, the despised could become the revered – the powerless become the powerful and the formidable become the vulnerable.

The reverend gentleman also realized that Adolph Pilchard's bid for office came as an unexpected but necessary move from the floor. To have left Eloise to compete against the other two illustrious candidates would have been to court lachrymose failure for the BOARD. The stamp of dazzling stupidity and malleability which marked her character was the signature for certain failure at the polls. Furthermore, there was a preponderance of lower circle members who had absolutely no regard for her position as senior warden, and who consequently would never have voted for her, for she neither represented their interests nor associated with them – as Philbert did.

*   *   *

The tellers returned to the hall, bearing the ballot report. As the clerk assumed her position at the podium and placed the microphone to her mouth, the buzz of nervous excitement came to a terrifying halt. All eyes pierced her with poignant anticipation. Some of the members supporting the three candidates closed their eyes and raised their heads upward, as if offering the last, desperate prayer for the victory of their respective candidate.

"Ladies and gentlemen," the clerk slowly and deliberately began, "I hereby present the tellers' report of the ballots which were cast for the election of senior warden of St. Patrick's Anglican Church, located in the village of Abersth…"

"...Aww, shut up, Pauline! We knows where the church is. Just give we the damn results, man!" yelled Joshua Chandrapaul, who ran a small fabric store in front of his home in Brewster's Village. The other men who were seated beside him in the rear burst into raucous laughter. The congregation turned and contemplated them momentarily in disgust. However, the disapproving expressions on the faces which addressed them only served to provoke the impatient storekeeper into hurling more insults at the timorous clerk, who immediately began to stutter as she continued with the preamble.

"Ladies a...a...and gen...gentlem... mm... men..."

"Aww, get on with it, man. And the winner is..." Joshua again interjected.

"Mr. Chandrapaul. Please!" pleaded the vicar.

"She wastin' we time, parson, with a lot o' stupidness. Just tell we who win so that we can go 'ome. Me wife waitin' fuh me, man," the disgruntled store keeper protested.

"Yea. He got to go mek breakfast!" a voice boomed from the rear.

The congregation burst into laughter. Mr. Chandrapaul spoke no more.

"The ma...majority needed to win the election," Pauline continued, "is two thirds. There were four hundred and fourteen votes cast. Of these, Mr. Adolph Pilchard received one hundred and ninety seven votes, Mr. Philbert Watts, one hundred and fifty four and Mr. Peter Goodfellow, eighty three votes. We therefore have to cast another ballot."

The results were met with laborious sighs and groans. However, it remained clear to Reverend Perths that no one was prepared to leave without ensuring that the candidate for whom he or she voted had gained victory. Fresh ballot sheets were thus distributed for the second time and the members cast their votes. During the second count, however, the congregation broke into small, spontaneous groups, talking and laughing or partaking of the food which was laid out in abundance. Some of the members of the *Bronze* and *Iron Circles* who were seated in the rear burst into song, at first belting out favorite hymns, and later, popular folk songs, much to the chagrin of the two upper circles who were involved in serious discussions regarding the election, and who furthermore had absolutely no tolerance for folklore, which they associated with the poor and lowly. During the fellowship, however, the vicar also noticed that the three candidates barely spoke to each other. The judge, in particular, was the most reserved and offered not a solitary word to Philbert Watts, whose popularity at the polls had dealt the *Gold Circle* a savage blow. The judge's brief conversation with Pigeon bore the mark of a delicate hostility. Reverend Perths, struggling with fear and the awkwardness resulting from a guilty conscience, retreated to the vicarage for a moderate period, supposedly to take his medication. However, upon his return, the familiar hint of alcohol effused from his breath, the odor which through the years had become his characteristic mark in times of stress.

Within twenty five minutes, the tellers returned with the results. There was applause, after which the congregation took their seats and nervously fixed their attention on the vestry clerk. The results, however, took a surprising twist.

"Ladies and gentlemen," Pauline announced more confidently, "the results of the second ballot are as follows..."

The silence filled the hall with a holy terror, and the expressions on the faces of the congregation became like those of the statues on the tombs of the wretched in a cemetery – transfixed on the sky in dreaded anticipation of the roll-call to announce their fate.

"...Mr. Adolph Pilchard, one hundred and twenty seven votes. Mr. Peter Goodfellow, one hundred and..." Pauline seemed to be experiencing momentary difficulty in deciphering the handwriting.

"Pauline!" screamed Lottie Greenidge, a thick, fair skinned woman from Brewster's Village who took in washing from the lower middle class who lived on the border of Abersthwaithe. "If you can't read the flippin' thing, give somebody else it. You only mekin' people nervous!"

"Why doesn't you sit down, Lottie, and leh the woman 'lone. Ya'll is the ones who got the poor woman nervous. Ya'll ain't got no damn manners!" Mrs. Ramgolam angrily responded in her endeavor to once again impress the Vestry members and the *Gold Circle*, close to whom she had chosen to sit.

Some of the men in the rear began to heckle Mrs. Ramgolam and ruthlessly berate her for betraying her social class. None of the upper circles whom she was so desperately trying to impress came to her rescue. Ruthel Pollard, for instance, never would have sacrificed her claimed superiority in order to defend Mrs. Ramgolam by groveling in the social mud pit with such base creatures. Mrs. Ramgolam therefore deemed it necessary to retaliate, in a further futile attempt to impress her superiors, by hurling crude insults across the hall. Mr. Ramgolam thought it wise not to interrupt his wife.

"All ya' at the back there behavin' like a bunch o' blasted anti-men!" she shouted angrily. "Ya'll doesn't have no flippin' respect for the parson or no body. Ya'll jest sittin' down behind there laughin' at everybody. I ain't come out here this mornin' for nobody to mek me a flippin'monkey!"

"Dat is jes' what you look like from the back 'ere with that t'ing pun top you head, sweetheart!" Lottie Greenidge yelled from the back.

"Yeah...," echoed Ivan "Ashy" Bell, nicknamed because of his dark, dry, ashy skin, "Go climb a tree and swing like a monkey...from that pile o' rope pun ya head!"

The members who were seated at the back burst into throes of uncontrollable laughter. The more refined members were appalled at such course behavior and cast disapproving looks at the disruptive group in the rear, and the vicar in the front.

"Fr. Perths," protested Dr. Griffin, the Dean of the Ischalton Agricultural School, "What kind of meeting is this? You have to control these people. This is outrageous and grossly unacceptable behavior for a church!"

"People!" Fr. Perths raised his hands in order to restore order, "Please… let's show some respect for each other!"

The laughter subsided and order was gradually restored.

'Please, Pauline. You may continue," Fr Perths advised the visibly shaken clerk.

"Mr. Pe… Peter Go…Goodfellow, one hundred and sixty nine votes and Mr. Philbert Watts, one hundred and eighteen. Nobody has a two thirds majority vote. We therefore have to vote again."

Fritz Batty thus rose from his seat and raised his hand amidst the sighs of growing disgust and expressions of tiredness.

"Reverend Perths, I beg permission to make a brief suggestion."

"Permission granted, Mr. Batty."

The congregation paused in rapt attention as Mr. Batty approached the podium and placed the microphone to his lips. "Reverend Perths, Vestry, ladies and gentlemen…," his respectful acknowledgement seemed to subdue the vociferous group at the back and arrest their attention, "…I would suggest that we have these three gentlemen come to the podium and give us a synopsis of their background, the main reason why they wish to run for the office of senior warden and a brief description of how they see themselves functioning in this privileged position. This would result in a more informed vote by the people and make the voting process swift and final. We can't spend all day here."

Everyone applauded in approval of what he or she agreed to be a sensible suggestion. Fr. Perths, however, did not applaud for he realized that Mr. Batty had made the suggestion solely as a ploy to increase the judge's chance of winning the position. The now worried vicar was convinced that neither Pigeon Goodfellow nor Philbert Watts had the ability to match the oratorical skills of the celebrated judge, which therefore cemented Mr. Batty's ploy to set the foundation for a guaranteed victory for the BOARD. Fr. Perths also believed that those ignorant of the existence of the *Circles* and the BOARD, as well as the naïve among the members, regarded Fritz's suggestion as an unbiased opportunity for all three of the candidates to win the position, and furthermore as a means to hasten the end of the excruciatingly stressful and painfully tedious voting process. The prospects of victory for his candidate thus began to grow dim.

Pigeon Goodfellow was chosen by Mr. Batty to be the first to speak. Again Fr. Perths construed the invitation for Pigeon to speak first as another ploy by the cunning Fritz Batty to allow the judge more time to prepare his speech and also to hear Mr. Goodfellow's plans so that he could build on it. Furthermore, he noted Fritz's display of total disregard for Philbert by placing him last at the podium. This last thought was justified by the remark which Fritz was heard to make to the members after the meeting; "a mere courtesy extended to a pitiable fool." Pigeon thus took his place at the podium.

"Reverend Sir, Wardens and members of the vestry, ladies and gentlemen; it gives me great pleasure to stand here before you on this glorious morning and give you a brief autobiography, share with you why I would be the best candidate for the position of senior warden and explain how I would execute my task as the same."

Bobo Jensen tapped Holly Atkins, who was seated in front of him, on the shoulder. "Whu he just say 'bout some car?"

"Ain't sure…" Holly whispered.

"It sound like he say he was givin' 'way some car…he auto…," explained Bobo.

"Oh…his autobiography," Holly responded.

"Whu kind o' car that is?" Bobo inquired in a subdued tone.

"It ain't a car, Bobo. He talkin' 'bout his autobiography… 'bout himself."

"Then why the @#&&% he don't say that, instead o' confusin' people and raisin' up they hopes like that," Bobo remonstrated.

"As you all know," Mr. Goodfellow continued, "I am one of the island's most successful barristers at law. I was born in the village of Farmington on the West Coast, and I am the third of four children. I was brought up in the church and my parents raised us to be humble and respectful citizens. I attended St. Sidwell's Primary school in Farmington and pursued my secondary education at King George College. Some of you might remember that I was among the top three students to pass the secondary school entrance public examinations, and after successfully completing my advanced level examinations, I went on to England where I completed my law degree. My friends, my ignoble background as a child in Farmington gives me the advantage of being able to identify with the needs of the lower social classes, and my profession as a lawyer exposes me to the grave injustices perpetuated on the poor and lowly. Brothers and sisters, I am a Christian. I have always been involved in the work of the church. My standing here today is in response to what I believe to be God's direct call to serve him in the capacity as your senior warden. Consequently, I am by far the best candidate for this position. I can represent all of you at every level, and as your senior warden I will endeavor to serve you with integrity and love, and open to every member of this congregation the opportunity to participate in the full ministry of St. Patrick's. Thank you."

A moderately loud applause followed.

"Quite condescending," Ruthel Pollard whispered to Gladys Barnwell.

The members of the BOARD maintained their dignity and delicately applauded the man whom they considered to be the greatest threat to their purpose. From the expressions on the faces of the members of the two lower circles, Fr. Perths could see that they could not have comprehended most of Pigeon's speech, but the mention of his birth in Farmington seemed to have created some familial bind that mildly served to his advantage.

"Are there any questions for Mr. Goodfellow before I invite the next candidate to the podium?" the vicar asked.

"As a matter of fact, there is." The voice came from Laurent Faulkner, who subsequently rose from his seat as he posed his question. "How would you, Mr. Goodfellow, a man who recently resigned from the vestry because of, quote, 'pressing family issues,' find the time to function effectively in a position as time consuming as that of senior warden of St. Patrick's?" Mr. Faulkner clasped his hands and rubbed them together as if satisfactorily completing the task of cementing the crafty Pigeon in an inescapable slab of his own treacherousness.

The vicar realized instantly that the question was asked to deliberately embarrass Pigeon in front of the members to whom he was pretending to be of service. He further perceived the profound resentment in Mr. Faulkner's tone and sardonic smile, and convinced himself that Mr. Faulkner's question was the result of some contemptuous discussion among the BOARD about Pigeon's resignation and character. Nevertheless, Pigeon responded to the question with the wisdom and subtlety of a serpent.

"At the time of my resignation, my dear friend, you will recall my allusion to my wife's situation at her job and the necessity for me to avail myself for the supervision of our two children who have since left for boarding school in England. I now have the time to give myself unstintingly to the work of the church. Furthermore, I am willing to make any sacrifices that will be required of me to attend to matters pertaining to the church. You see, my brothers and sisters in Christ, I am a faithful husband to my wife and a dedicated father to my children. This alone testifies to my faithfulness to this church and my commitment to serve you as your warden." Pigeon paced his words regimentally and solemnly, like the slow march of a funeral possession, as he fixed his eyes on the judge to whom the last two sentences of his response were directed. No one dared to ask him any more questions.

His response was followed by an enraptured applause from his growing group of supporters. Diplomacy dictated that Mr. Pilchard, along with other members of the BOARD, give at least a half-hearted applause. The judge appeared very uneasy as Pigeon completed his remarks, like one whose mind was reeling in turmoil, and as Pigeon returned to his seat, the judge hung his head and cast Pigeon a deadly glance.

"Thank you, Mr. Goodfellow," Fr. Perths said as he graciously accepted the microphone from the eloquent lawyer. "I now invite the honorable judge, Mr. Adolph Pilchard, to approach the podium." The man of the cloth bowed respectfully to the approaching judge as he handed him the microphone. A tepid round of applause from the BOARD accompanied the honorable gentleman as he assumed his position at the podium.

"Thank you." The judge paused as he made eye contact with the audience and gave a polite and dignified smile.

"Reverend Perths, Madam Senior Warden, members of the vestry, my dear brothers and sisters…"

"…And Members of the BOARD!" a powerful, male voice interjected from the vicinity of the mid section of the hall where many of Pigeon's supporters were congregated. "Don't forget to mention the BOARD, Honorable Sir!"

A hushed laughter echoed across the hall. Notwithstanding the remark, the judge continued, visibly unshaken, but intensely angry. He realized by this time that Pigeon had turned against him and the BOARD, and was going to utterly humiliate, embarrass and destroy them if he were to succeed in his bid for the position. The judge thus decided to employ extreme, defensive measures, like an unrelenting army general.

"I must begin my speech by congratulating my Christian brother for being a faithful husband to his wife and a dedicated father to his children. These, my friends, are admirable and virtuous qualities which are quickly disappearing from our society. However, what does one say when such impeccable values are juxtaposed with an insatiable desire for money, to the extent that a man would willingly sacrifice his moral rectitude for a dollar. However, I digress." The judge's eyes met Goodfellow's momentarily.

Mr. Pilchard's remark shot across the hall like a deadly arrow, and it appeared to have dealt the arrogant lawyer a psychological wound more deadly than that inflicted by Apollyon's fork, for he raised his head abruptly and glared at the judge. The two contemplated each other momentarily before the judge smirked and continued his address. Nevertheless, Pigeon remained as motionless and stoic as a statue at the gate of a shrine.

"I, unlike my jurisprudent brother across there, was born and raised in a privileged home but was exposed at an early age to oppression, social affliction and gross injustices, by dint of my late father's profession as one of our nation's most respected politicians and my recently deceased mother's unmatched voluntary work among the poor and disabled. In addition to all of that, I was raised a staunch Anglican and attended church every Sunday – to this day. I have never wavered in my faith or strayed from the church. I am a man of moral integrity and gentleness of spirit, despite my somber expression or foreboding appearance. I am, after all, a judge, and my days are spent facing, addressing and judging the many ills within our society…"

"What about your nights?" another voice echoed from the mid section.

The question evoked a hail of sporadic laughter from certain sections of the hall. Nevertheless, the judge appeared unscathed by the piercing question and maintained his dignity as he proceeded with his speech.

"My friends, I know right from wrong, good from evil, justice from injustice, courage from weakness, light from darkness. The person you need to represent you as your Senior Warden should possess these qualities, be a man of the moment and simultaneously a man of the future, for this is what our hope as a church is based on. My brothers and sisters, I desire to be your senior warden because I firmly believe that it is my duty to be so, so that I can properly represent you and assist the good Reverend in making St. Patrick's the place where all of you can find the needed help in realizing your God given potentials. Friends, I served on this vestry for two terms in the past, and I remained faithful to the call even when I was faced with the strenuous demands of the home. This is a sign that I will never forsake you when the going gets tough, but will endure to the end, serving you humbly and faithfully. Thank you."

The applause from the BOARD and from some members of the vestry was deliberately spirited. Mrs. Ramgolam gave the judge a standing ovation. A few others from across the hall followed her in their expression of appreciation. The members of the BOARD, however, remained seated as they applauded, since they never would have deemed it appropriate to imitate one of such a sordid social status.

Hostile glances were again exchanged between the Judge and Pigeon as the former made his way to his seat amidst the roar of applause. Reverend Perths then invited the last speaker to the podium. He wisely downplayed Philbert's introduction, as if this candidate's presentation were merely incidental. However, Philbert's name was hardly announced when the members in the rear rose to their feet and filled the hall with tumultuous applause and shouts of encouragement. The BOARD, in particular, took intense umbrage at the vulgar display of support for, as Faulkner remarked to the vicar during Pilbert's speech, "this *rodent* who, if successful, would gnaw away at the established order, social demarcation and political structure of St. Patrick's, which the *Gold Circle* had long imposed and tenaciously guarded for years, until nothing is left but the skeletal remains of what once was the ecclesiastical glory of Ischalton, remains which would be overtaken by the ghouls and scavengers of the Anglican community." The prospect, he added, though dismal and frightening, was nevertheless impossible, since the BOARD was practically invincible. Philbert thus took his place at the podium, and had to raise both hands for almost thirty seconds before the applause could subside.

"Reverend Sir, distinguished members of the vestry, ladies and gentlemen; it is with great pride that I stand before you today in my endeavor to win your vote for a position on which I believe I have been judiciously selected to serve. My friends, I will not boast of my background, for much of it is neither relevant nor appropriate for this presentation. I will state, however, that I am a simple man, endowed with gifts which I believe will be of great asset to this church and to the community. I further believe that a church is a presage of the heavenly Kingdom, and therefore should embrace all persons, regardless of social status, race or creed…"

The audience in the rear and part of the mid-section burst into avid applause.

"…However, my brothers and sisters, there must be order, respect for tradition and a sense of creatureliness that must remind us that we are God's children, dwelling in the same household and depending on the Heavenly Father for our strength and sustenance. In my capacity as your senior warden, it will be incumbent upon me to exercise my duties in cooperation with the priest, vestry and congregation. I will be your humble servant and I will endeavor to make the necessary sacrifices to serve you with joy and humility. Thank you."

Once again, the applause was so loud that it reverberated throughout the hall like roar of the surfing sea at high tide. More persons than before stood up and cheered the popular candidate as he bowed his head over and over again in gracious appreciation. Again, the BOARD gave mild applause. Mr. Hauklyn, however, joined the enthusiastic supporters and gave Philbert a standing ovation. Eyebrows were raised among the BOARD as they beheld what Ruthel referred to as 'the traitor among them' displaying such appreciation for 'so dishonorable a candidate.' It became evident, she remarked, 'that the serpent had slithered into the *Circle* and was inflicting them, one by one, with venom more deadly than the disease that lays waste at noonday.'

No one asked any questions when invited to do so. The lower circles barely understood what Pilbert had said, but knew instinctively that he was on their side. The upper circles, and especially the BOARD and vestry, never would have offered Philbert the satisfaction of knowing that he had held their attention, or have given him the respect he deserved by engaging in any conversation with one of what Faulkner deemed as being of 'such low esteem.'

After the applause died down, the clerk again opened the polls. The uneasiness encircled the hall and cast a pall of fear, like storm clouds before a tempest, over the congregation. However, some of the members of the upper circles and the majority of the lower circles, were not perturbed by the prospects. Some of Philbert's most ardent supporters joined hands and prayed quietly. The BOARD retired to an adjoining room to craft an emergency plan in the event that the judge emerged unsuccessful in his bid for office. Pigeon and his supporters discussed plans for the future of the Church on his assumption of office. The group of disruptive men at the rear of the hall shared a small bottle of rum amongst themselves by raising the bottle to their lips and imbibing mouthfuls of the distilled molasses in anticipation of Philbert's resounding success. Stella Pirate Dawkins made a last, desperate effort to dispose of the remaining bootlegged, amateur adult videos and cassettes comprising sacred music for two dollars lower than the original asking price. Her business ploy proved highly successful for the sacred cassettes, but her customers bought none of the videos for fear that God would have punished them by causing Philbert to lose in the election. However, a few of them promised her that pending Philbert's victory, they would meet her outside in the burial ground, by the fence behind the Gonsalves and Monsanto family vaults, on condition that the videos be further reduced by two dollars. Stella was reluctant but finally acquiesced to their demands. The BOARD returned to the hall with the look of earnest resignation on their faces.

Suddenly, the hall was overcome by a tense silence. The tellers entered the room in steps moderate and solemn, bearing the envelope with the results like prison officers escorting a prisoner to the execution cell. Their expressions bore the grim news that one of the candidates had finally won the election and that the results might be met with some degree of hostility.

"Ladies and gentlemen," the tense clerk announced, "you have elected a new senior warden who will serve you and represent you for the next three years. According to our by-laws here at St. Patrick's, should the office of Senior Warden become vacant at any time within the three year term, the person amassing the second highest number of votes at the election will automatically assume office, unless he or she shall decline, whereby the priest, in conjunction with the remaining warden and vestry, shall appoint a member to take office."

The members sat still and held their breath. Pigeon, however, seemed quite relaxed in anticipation of a howling victory, and bore an inward, confidential smile that drove a morbid fear into the heart of the uneasy judge, as well as the other members of the BOARD who beheld him with hateful expressions.

"Ladies and gentlemen, the results are as follows." The clerk spoke deliberately and slowly as she opened the envelope. Not a sound other than the rustling of the envelope being opened was heard. Mouths hung agape and eyes opened wide in tense anticipation as the clerk nervously proceeded to read the results.

"Mr. Philbert Watts – sixty eight."

Absolute silence followed.

"Mr. Adolph Pilchard…," the clerk paused and raised her head as she addressed the crowd with limpid, frightened eyes, "sixty seven…"

The BOARD gasped. They were mortified by the devastating report. The supporters of Pigeon Goodfellow rose to their feet in thunderous applause, but Fr. Perths raised his hand in silent appeal for silence and order.

"Mr. Peter Goodfellow – two hundred and seventy nine. Congratulations!"

Once again, Pigeon Goodfellow's supporters burst into tumultuous applause. Pigeon rose and raised his hand as he turned full circle to express his gratitude to the cheering crowd. Fr. Perths, wishing to end the meeting immediately for fear of turbulent repercussions, raised his hand and invited silence to take its place in the hall. When the noise and applause subsided, he expressed effusive gratitude to the members for their attendance and participation and to the Fellowship for the sumptuous meal. He subsequently requested a motion to adjourn the meeting, and after the motion was unanimously passed, offered the closing prayer.

The defeated reverend gentleman watched helplessly and fearfully as the congregation dispersed amidst the hotchpotch of emotions. The deflated BOARD members collected their paraphernalia and proceeded *en masse* to their respective cars, quietly and pensively, like mourners retreating from a burial plot after the final obsequies. During the final voting process, Faulkner had instructed them to retreat to one of the rooms to devise a plan of action should Mr. Pilchard be defeated by the ambitious and vindictive Pigeon Goodfellow. However, the surprising and ironic twist in the results revealed to him something new and shocking, something which he had never considered; the frightful verity that those who earlier would swear their allegiances to BOARD would in fact acutely betray them, and even worse, give their loyalty to one who was either their deadliest enemy or to one whose audacity to run for office was a virulent insult to their intelligence and superiority. The psychological wound was mortal, but Faulkner was too embarrassed to lick his wounds publicly, and hastily departed from the building.

*   *   *

Adolph Pilchard was the most affected by Pigeon's victory. His wounds and fear had penetrated more deeply than that of any of the other members of the BOARD. The defeat brought him face to face with his mediocrity. When most of the others had left, he requested that Rex open the church for him, where he withdrew to the back of the nave for a few minutes of solitude and contemplation. He had been stripped of his crown and scepter and had received in its place the tattered hood and walking stick of an aged and afflicted mendicant, the symbol of his lost and forgotten humility. He became the BOARD's foremost target for his traitors – who were among his closest acquaintances. The cross of guilt and shame upon which he would be nailed for his adulterous affair with Maggie Billings was in fact to be the object of his transformation; the judgment which he for years had passed on others became his own accuser and condemned him to the hell of a troubled conscience. He was further gravely distressed by his ignominious loss to Philbert Watts at the polls by one vote – one solitary vote which stripped him of his honor and respect and caused him to fall, like Lucifer, from grandiosity to the pit of disgrace. He held Maggie Billings and Bill Jones responsible for his demise. The urgency and importance of the single vote became real to him, and he therefore poured burning coals of corrosive contempt upon the heads of his mistress and the junior warden. Furthermore, at the ad hoc meeting which Laurent Faulkner had called during the balloting, he was advised by Sam Westwater to graciously step out of the race so that the BOARD and vestry members could place their votes on Philbert Watts. The rationale behind that thought, Sam explained, was that it would be a sure way to prevent Pigeon Goodfellow from achieving victory. He further explained that the BOARD would more likely be able to control Mr. Watts than the unpredictable Pigeon Goodfellow. Most of the BOARD had concurred, but the arrogant judge considered the suggestion preposterous and dismissed it. It was this arrogance which would subsequently lay the red carpet on which his shame would tread.

Minutes later, the judge closed the black, heavy doors behind him and drove away from the church a bitter and broken man, panting for revenge on his betrayers and thirsting for the blood of the conqueror.

*   *   *

Pigeon tuned in to the BBC for the program of Solemn Evensong which was aired on Sundays at three o'clock in the afternoon. He sang along to the *Magnificat* as he cruised along Beach Road and stopped at the spot where he believed he was commissioned to serve in the prestigious capacity of Senior Warden of St. Patrick's. Once more he rolled up his trousers, removed his shoes and stepped into the water, oblivious to the few persons strolling along or relaxing on the beach or tossing pebbles into the ebbing tide. This time, his prayer was one of thanksgiving and not a petition, and he swore to do an excellent job. He then returned to his car and drove off towards his home, rejoicing that with God's help, he had overcome the enemy.

* * *

Philbert Watts' pragmatism spared him the agony of the defeat. He was proud of the way he had presented himself and delivered his speech, but his crowning glory was his obvious popularity over that of the judge. He had come in a distant second to Pigeon, but he nevertheless bore the same degree of joy at having defeated the famous judge. Two votes seemed like two thousand at that moment, and as he turned the corner at Buckingham Avenue, he beamed at the fleeting thought of assuming the office of Senior Warden as a result of an ill wind that would blow the coldness of some debilitating or mortal affliction upon Pigeon Goodfellow.

* * *

Stella Dawkins waited behind the vaults by the fence, in spite of Philbert's loss, with the hope that at least one of Philbert's gravely disappointed supporters would appear so as to purchase one of the adult videos to revive his broken spirit. Alas! No one ventured close.

* * *

Grand celebrations were in held in Brewster's Village, for although Philbert failed to win the position, the people were nevertheless equally ecstatic at Pigeon's success, for either of the two men would be the pioneer of a new era for them. Ram was especially thrilled, for he firmly believed that Pigeon's success was as a result of his effective campaigning. He thus was sure that Mr. Goodfellow was going to offer him some official position in the church. In order to ensure this social advancement, Ram threw an impromptu party in honor of Pigeon's victory – and in anticipation of his own success. The villagers assembled in Ram's yard, bearing food, drinks and a juke box. Noel Cumberbatch and his wife Flossie, who reared cattle and chickens, and who were considered two of the most respected people in Village, slaughtered a cow for the occasion. Mr. Xingwee, a close friend of

Mr. Goodfellow and the proprietor of 'Shanghai Temple', a moderately posh Chinese restaurant on Buckingham Avenue, provided the plastic cutlery and the sanitary cups and plates.

Mrs. Ramgolam's joy at her husband's success, however, was superimposed with a mild layer of jealousy. She was joyful because, as she revealed to Ram on their way home from church that day, his advancement would automatically mean hers, in whatever form it would come. But she also hinted that Mr. Pilchard's defeat would probably result in her loss of status. In retrospect, Ram perceived this hint of jealousy which he believed would reveal itself sporadically when she would yell at him for no justifiable reason or refuse to attend to his needs like the dutiful wife she had always claimed to be.

The ironic and surprising twist in the polls resulted in the certainty of change for all parties. Some looked forward to a brighter future while others gazed through the fog to a melancholy prospect. The vicar, however, was the only one standing on the line of demarcation dividing despair from invidiousness. He worried himself to a stupor about the prospect of losing certain privileges under, and as a result of, Mr. Goodfellow's wardenship; but he also mused on the awkwardness of now having to develop an amicable and trusting relationship between himself and the man whom the BOARD both feared and hated the most.

*   *   *

This Election Sunday would mark the beginning of a new era in the history of St. Patrick's Church. Vices and virtues which for years had lain dormant will now rise to engage in mortal combat; the oppressed will become the oppressor; friends will become enemies and enemies will become friends; St. Patrick's will become simultaneously the temple of peace and the scene of the Armageddon.

That evening, Reverend Perths sat in prayer and contemplation in his car which he had parked on Beach Road; he had decided to go there to relax so as to avoid the awkwardness of having to attend the party in the village. The tide was high and the waves slammed violently against the rocks as the water hissed and foamed in its ordained fury. The vicar closed his eyes and thanked God that the very water, which now was hurling its rage against the passive rocks, will soon ebb in a gentle and humiliating retreat, while the rocks, bruised and battered by the onslaught of the tempestuous waves, will remain dignified, unyielding, invincible.

Chapter Five
The Aftermath

Bill Jones' telephone rang incessantly as members of the vestry and the BOARD, as well as a few others from the *Gold Circle*, called to inquire about his welfare. He had earlier received the news of Pigeon Goodfellow's unprecedented victory at the polls that morning from the vicar who had stopped by after the meeting to pay a pastoral visit and to reiterate his loyalty and gratitude to the vestry and to the unofficially appointed and covert BOARD for their love and support. He further asked the cowardly junior warden to convey his blessings upon the discreet existence and leadership of the BOARD, stating that their knowledge and expertise were valuable assets to what he described as a sometimes fickle minded and incoherent vestry. Bill had prepared a written excuse explaining the nature of his supposed accident and the details of his injuries for the sake of consistency in his report to the many anticipated callers and well wishers. No one challenged the authenticity of his story, but expressed wishes for an expeditious recovery so as to be able to attend the first vestry meeting which would be held under the wardenship of Pigeon Goodfellow on the Thursday evening following the commissioning of the new vestry.

On the evening of the election, Pigeon embarked upon his expedition to destroy the BOARD, and in particular the judge and Laurent Fulkner, his aide-de-camp, whose idea it was to form the tyrannous, illegal organization. Pigeon knew that the best approach to accomplishing his mission would be to adopt the divide- and- rule strategy. His first task would therefore be to conquer the loyalty and support of the vestry, at any cost, and if possible, ingratiate himself with some of the members of the *Gold Circle* who bore some quiet animosity towards the judge and Laurent Faulkner – an aversion which blatantly manifested itself in the lack of support for the judge at the polls. Also, he would endear himself to Philbert Watts' and solicit his assistance in planning and directing many cultural programs involving the villagers, whose numbers alone would sustain him and to some extent, protect him from the possible wrath of the BOARD. All of these plans Pigeon considered urgent. However, of all these urgencies, the most immediate, challenging and compelling would be the taming of Maggie Billings. Pigeon considered this task a life-or-death gamble, and he was prepared to die in his vain endeavor to claim absolute power and control at St. Patrick's than to be controlled by the BOARD.

Election Sunday thus became the day when not only a new era began at St Patrick's, but it also marked the inauguration of the short period in St. Patrick's history which Sam Westwater would later refer to as "the age of Pigeonism."

*   *   *

Nature seemed to share Adolph Pilchard's gloom and humiliation and to endorse his desire for revenge by brewing storm clouds to cover the moonlight and galaxy of diamonds which earlier in the evening had illuminated the sky. The distraught judge feigned a quiet resignation that night as he and his wife shared a delectable dinner at home. He had convinced Mrs. Pilchard that he was not the least perturbed by the election results and confessed that his decision to run for the position was the result of a thoughtless, last-minute effort by the BOARD to keep Pigeon Goodfellow in his place. Reluctantly, he added, he had acquiesced to their request. His loss, therefore, was a blessing in disguise as he had no desire to bear such a heavy burden for three or six years. Consequently, he avoided the unnecessary consolation which he knew that his wife was prone to make on occasions like these, when he appeared to suffer any kind of major loss or humiliating defeat.

Immediately after dinner, the judge left for his office ostensibly to look over some files in preparation for a long, harrowing day on Monday. His custom was never to bring any work home. That aspect of his life, he would stress, was to be left in the court and in his office; his home was his place of refuge. He therefore was able to rid Mrs. Pilchard of any concern that he was leaving in the midst of drizzling rain to attend to his business. She thus performed her nocturnal rituals before retiring to bed, and before he left, he kissed her. She held him close, and as she gazed into his eyes she expressed abundant joy and pride that she had 'married a noble man whose passion for justice was so intense that he would disregard the weather and sacrifice a soft, warm bed and the comfort of a loving wife to drive to the city on such a wet, melancholy Sunday night.'

The jazz music that the judge played as the black Mercedes Benz cruised majestically along the tree lined Manchester Avenue where he lived did not serve to mitigate his anger. Too many of the people he had trusted had disappointed him earlier that day. Apart from Maggie and Bill, he could not identify his other betrayers. Their identity had to be left to his imagination and he had no proof that he was right, which gravely aggravated matters. He cursed whomever he had suspected in the vilest language as he hummed along sporadically to the tunes. The judge was quickly becoming irrational with rage as certain members of the BOARD whom he had suspected came to mind. Nevertheless, his pride would compel him to bear a pleasant countenance and appear nonchalant while in the presence of the vestry and BOARD. He then pondered on the future of the BOARD under the new leadership of Pigeon Goodfellow. He envisaged the diminution of power as the BOARD succumbed to Pigeon's dictatorship. This thought of powerlessness to one for whom he had lately developed so intense a hatred directed him to a small liquor shop on one of the arterial streets in the city, where he purchased and quaffed two glasses of well aged rum on the rocks. On returning to his car, he switched to the religious station and headed straight towards Westminster Lane.

Cautiously, the judge inspected the surroundings on Westminster Lane as he parked a few doors from Maggie's house. He remained in his car for about fifteen minutes so as to allow the alcohol to take mild effect so that he could muster up the courage to tell Maggie exactly how he felt. As he sat in his car, engulfed by the darkness of the wet night, he contemplated the streetlights as they cast beams of light that penetrated the darkness and the slightly dense fog. He thought of the scriptural passages which speak of the light which ultimately overcomes the darkness, and a hopeful smile briefly came over his face.   He eventually put on his hat and emerged from the vehicle. As he walked towards the house, trying to dodge the persistent drizzles and the small puddles, the trees seemed to loom grotesquely over him, as if deriding his failure or bearing some grim prophecy. The lights that shone behind the sheer curtains in Maggie's sitting room caught the judge's attention as he approached Maggie's gate. That room was used only when Maggie entertained guests, especially those who were not frequent visitors to her home. He hesitated as he reached the gates. However, before he could finally decide to retreat, a male figure in a black trench coat emerged from the shadows, near the front door and opened a large, black umbrella. The figure offered a dignified wave to the person inside the building and shut the door. As the silhouette hurriedly approached the judge, he could feel the pangs of jealousy rising like the crescendo of jungle drums in a frenzied, war dance. He stood erect to his full height, in an intimidating posture, and braced himself to intercept what appeared to him to be an unknown rival. The two figures came face to face with each other at the gate. The silhouette in black that was retreating from Maggie's home moved the umbrella aside as he drew closer. The judge's jaw dropped and he gasped in horror. The nocturnal visitor was none other than Pigeon Goodfellow. Neither of the two men acknowledged the other for a moment. Pigeon, however, seemed undaunted by the judge's exuding rage.

"What the hell are you doing here, Goodfellow?" snapped the judge, who by this time had lost some composure as a result of the alcohol and the sight of the man whose victory at the polls had humiliated him.

"As your new senior warden, I think that I have an inalienable right to visit my people and acquaint them with my plans for the next three years, don't you think?"

"Poppycock! You are not yet officially the warden!" the judge exclaimed in seething retort.

"Some things can't wait, can they? So, my friend, what business brings *you* here, on wet, dreary night like this?" Pigeon maintained a calm, amicable tone.

"Like you, I'm here merely to seek after the welfare of a valued parishioner whose absence from the Advent Sunday mass is a cause for concern," the judge replied as he struggled to maintain his composure and conceal his blazing fury.

"You might have phoned, like the others, instead of risking a cold and fever from this rain. However, I must admire your loyalty," Pigeon replied sarcastically. "However, have a good night."

The judge and Pigeon shook hands, after which Pigeon made a hasty departure down the street. The judge contemplated him contemptuously as he hurried to his car, and remained at the gate until the car turned the corner. Breathing heavily in compressed anger, he approached Maggie's door and turned the key. The safety latch was employed so he had to press the bell. Delicate footsteps descended the stairs and switched on the light in the foyer.

"Adolph...," the judge announced from the other side.

Maggie unlocked the safety locks and opened the door. "A bit late, isn't it?" she said in a soft, gentle voice that was tinged with hurt.

The judge contemplated her momentarily. The hate in his eyes was like daggers cast into her chest. "I'm sorry to have awakened you, but I could not have come any earlier. I have a wife… remember?"

"O yes; that woman. How often I forget," Maggie replied sarcastically as she turned and ascended the stairs. "I'm sorry to hear about your loss," she added in an incidental tone.

No response came from the judge. He closed the door and followed her up the stairs.

"Shall I reheat dinner?"

"Forget dinner. Where the blazes were you this morning?" the judge snapped.

"Thank you for asking. I see that you have been really concerned. The whole day has passed, and now you come, at half past nine in the night, to wake me from my sleep to inquire of my welfare; how thoughtful!" Maggie replied.

"Well, I'm sorry to have fallen short of your lofty expectations, my dear, but these are the kinds of complications that face persons in a relationship such as ours. All that is needed, Maggie, is some tolerance…understanding… patience. Why the hell are you so ratty tonight?"

"You might have at least called…like all the others who called since church was finished….even before the meeting got started," Maggie griped. "Adolph, I'm not going to be your prized object on the shelf, for you to pick up when you're in the mood and then put back down on the shelf to harbor dust."

The judge approached Maggie and put his arms around her. "I haven't come to argue with you, sweetheart. I've come to find comfort in your arms after a long, stressful day and …"

"Please…," Maggie interrupted the judge as she gently freed herself from his grip. "This is exactly what I mean. You need comfort so you come over here. I'm sure if you had won the position you would not have reached this house; you would have stayed home, as you have been doing for the last couple o' nights, and expressed your joy in *her* arms."

"My wife will always come first, Maggie. We've already discussed this, at length," the irate Judge stated.

"Then go back there. Let her comfort you, if she can!" Maggie snapped.

"Maggie! Stop this at once. Stop it!" The judge held her by the shoulders gave her a mild shake. "You know that I love you more than anything else in the world. I *happen* to be married, that's all, but I love you. So just stop this nonsense. What's come over you?"

The visibly distraught woman pulled away again, but this time, turned her back on her paramour as she placed both hands on the Queen Anne chair. "I'm sorry, but I guess that I'm just very angry that you lost the election and I don't know what to say or do. I feel bad…guilty for not having gone to support you. But the incident with the bouquet of flowers is still fresh in my mind and it troubles me greatly. Therefore, I thought it best to just stay away for a while," Maggie turned and faced the judge, "and I want you to do the same, so as to quell any further suspicion. But the ambivalence is killing me. I want you to go and yet I can't picture my life without you…not for one fleeting moment."

Unable to control his emotions, the amorous judge grabbed Maggie and planted a passionate kiss on her lips. "I don't intend to go anywhere, darling. Neither my wife nor any troublemaker will make me leave you, not even for a split second!"

For the third time, Maggie managed to free herself from the judge's arms. "But you must, Adolph. You must go. It is imperative that you do. I would rather lose you for a few days or weeks than to lose you forever. At least I can find some joy in knowing that you'll return to me if we part for a few weeks. But if I lose you altogether, I might as well be dead. I'll be much better off dead than alive without your love."

"Maggie, I care for nothing else than your love, but if my presence brings you such great distress, then I'll leave… for two weeks; not a day longer. I'll take Mrs. Pilchard to Europe for a two week vacation, somewhere far. You'll have the time to flush this fear from your system, and whoever the culprit is will be thrown right off track; trust me," the judge swore.

Maggie smiled for the first time that evening. "That will please me greatly. We both need time to think and time to quell any further suspicions."

"Then so be bit…reluctantly, however…reluctantly. Mrs. Pilchard will be thrilled when I mention going on a two week vacation."

"Let's drink to this, darling." Maggie suggested.

The two toasted with a glass of fine, red wine. "Here's to us," the judge raised his glass. They sipped as they sat close to each other. Maggie was tense. The nervous judge could see that Maggie was tense.

"Let's make this temporary parting a sweet farewell," the judge whispered as he drew Maggie closer. This time however, Maggie did not resist, and the next twenty minutes took them to the stars on a magic carpet of love. However, they soon returned to the harsh realities of their earthly circumstance. The judge rose, donned his rain coat and once more kissed his lover passionately before heading down the stairs. They held hands at the bottom of the stairs as they gazed into each other's eyes once more. Maggie held her glass of wine in one hand and the judge's hand in the other. He looked intently into her eyes. She returned the stare. However, there was something distant in her eyes; they were focused on the judge but her stare penetrated his eyes, his face, his heart, and appeared to rest on someone or some place else.

"Maggie," the judge whispered.

"Sweetheart," Maggie responded as she looked at him with large, limpid eyes – eyes which for the first time appeared distant, insincere, frightened.

"What was Pigeon Goodfellow doing here?"

Maggie gasped and the glass fell from her hand and splintered on the floor. The red wine meandered along the highly polished wooden floor like blood trickling from a wounded heart. Maggie was shocked into speechlessness. The large, green eyes began to well up with tears which trickled down her soft cheeks.

"When exactly were you going to tell me that that shit head was here?"

Maggie made no response. The judge's anger, intensified by the rum and wine concoction, and the memory of the day's events, erupted like a volcano. "You bloody traitor! You're playing the harlot with my emotions? You wallow with the hogs, you'll smell like them; lie with dogs and you'll scratch fleas like them!" The judge grabbed the frightened woman's shoulders and shook her moderately. "What the bloody hell was that devil doing here!?"

"He came to solicit my help with the program he will present to the congregation, that's all… that's all…he didn't come to…"

"Bloody liar!" the infuriated judge yelled. "I would have left here and you would have said nothing, nothing!"

"Adolph, please…,"pleaded the terrified woman.

The judge became irrational with anger. He pulled Maggie towards him by the shoulder of her silk duster and slapped her across the left cheek before pushing her away with such force that she tumbled to the royal blue Persian rug that accentuated the floor. "Traitor!" he bellowed.

Maggie reeled to the floor, screaming in terror. "Adolph…stop…stop. You're hurting me…stop, please!"

The judge remained by the door, glaring at the delicate woman writhing in pain on the floor. His eyes were bloodshot from the alcohol and ablaze with rabid hate. "I don't believe a damn word you just said; not a bloody word!"

"Get out!" Maggie hissed as she lay crouched on the floor. "Get out… before I call your wife!"

Once more the judge raised his hand to assault the defenseless woman, but before he could get close enough, she rose up and slid slightly backwards. "Touch me once more, and I'll reveal everything to your wife and to the BOARD; everything! Go on!" she screamed, "I dare you, you irascible old fool; go on!"

The enraged judge froze and then abruptly turned and stormed out of the building, slamming the door behind him and leaving his mistress in terror and anguish on the floor.

Almost immediately, he could hear the clicking sound of the security latch and the double locks being turned. The judge stood there, motionless and emotionally torn. He wanted to go back inside and fall at Maggie's feet in remorse, but his arrogance forbade such a display of weakness and humility in front of a woman –especially by a man of his social standing. He thus stormed towards the gate, having stopped twice in a fierce mental struggle between common sense and egoism. The distressed judge stomped out to the street, grumbling and swearing under his breath as he headed towards his car. As he approached the vehicle, another car which was parked close to Maggie's house suddenly pulled out, temporarily blinding him with its harsh, white flood lights. The vehicle stopped momentarily as it passed him, and the driver thrust his head out of the window.

"Working overtime, lover boy…?"

The individual burst into a spate of sardonic laughter as the black car sped off and disappeared like a phantom into the night, leaving the petrified judge standing with mouth agape in the middle of the dark, lonely street. Within a few seconds he regained his composure and stumbled to his car, semi-intoxicated, alarmed and confused. He could not recognize the individual because he was disguised in a pair of dark sunglasses and a black knitted cap that caressed his cranium and covered most of his forehead. Overcome with fear, the judge ignited the engine and sped off.

That night, he dreamt that he was on trial in court. When he awoke, he could not remember the nature of the crime for which he was being tried, but his memory remained etched with the indelible image of Pigeon Goodfellow presiding at the trial, pointing accusingly at him and bearing the sinister grin of a skull on the brink of winning one more lost soul for the devil. As he turned to face the jury in one last, futile plea for mercy, he froze in horror as he recognized the grim faces of thirteen BOARD members contemplating him – condemning him, with the odious glare of eyes without pupils – to the unbearable depths of hell. He awoke in a cold sweat, shivering in fear. Mrs. Pilchard lay next to him in a sound and restful sleep, like an angel in pink satin and with a peaceful countenance, oblivious to his mental anguish. The judge rose from his bed, groped his way through the semi-darkness to one of the sofas in the sitting room and burst into tears.

The next few days brought further agonizing signs of harsh realities to Judge Pilchard. He had made a quiet but keen observation of Rex's sudden change in loyalty. Pigeon's victory seemed to have necessitated a sudden change of allegiance for Rex. Judge Pilchard realized that Rex was avoiding him like the plague and offering him only the basic acknowledgements when it could not be avoided. Consequently, he began to draft hazy sketches in his mind of what he perceived to be Rex's involvement with Pigeon, the bouquet of flowers which was delivered to Maggie and the mysterious individual in the sunglasses and knitted cap. If Rex had broken his covenant with him by allying himself with Pigeon, then Rex stood to suffer the fullest brunt of his wrath. However, on account of the unreliability of mere suspicion, there was not enough evidence to sentence Rex. Nevertheless, the judge kept close scrutiny of Rex's behavior, and in a matter of three weeks became almost totally estranged from him – the one whom he had dared to trust to bear a secret that could bring him to the furnace of flagrant disgrace.

*   *   *

On the first Friday night after the election, the meeting involving the ousting of Thelma Mullins from the position of Chairperson of the Fellowship Committee was held at Volda Bradshaw's place in Brewster's Village. The attendance was not as large as was expected perhaps because the meeting was held in the wake of the Annual General Meeting. Furthermore, most of the political fervor within the lower circles had subsided because of Pigeon's howling victory. He was their man of the moment, the pioneer of their struggle for equality, and because of him – and Philbert – they were on their way up the social ladder. They had suffered no significant consequences in the wake of Thelma's demise. In addition, the Mullins' skirmish with the three men in the church yard had caused a bitter division among those who had befriended the couple and those loyal to Bobo Jensen. Nevertheless, an impressive cross section of the Brewster's Village community attended the meeting.

The meeting was held in Volda's back yard. The Bradshaws had a large, tarred, canvas tent permanently erected in their back yard, which they rented for special occasions, like parties and weddings, and used as a night club when there was no rental. Colored lights were strung diagonally across the ceiling and the sides were enclosed with a thick superimposition of coconut branches. Potted palm trees, locally made wooden chairs and tables covered with checkered, plastic tablecloths completed the décor. The dirt floor was always clean swept and there was a medium sized, wooden platform, which was used primarily for dancing, in the center of the tent. A bar was situated on the side closest to the house. Two latrines were located further behind the tent, and served both sexes respectively. Toilet tissue was never kept in the toilets because it was often stolen by unscrupulous guests attending large functions. Anyone who had an urgent need for the commodity while on the premises was therefore required to purchase the same from Mrs. Bradshaw at five cents for eight sheets. This preposterous sale of toilet paper generated a modest income, and it was purported that whenever the Bradshaws offered a complimentary sweetmeat at parties or weddings, they would discreetly add prunes; this generous gift was offered only to those whose guest lists exceeded one hundred. Brad's Palace, as it was called, was Brewster's Village most sophisticated social hall, and only the villagers who owned their own small businesses or made a reasonable income through other sources could afford to host functions there or socialize there on nights when the club was open. It was the Taj Mahal for Brewster's Village upper class, like the Ramgolams, and the mecca for those at the very bottom of the social ladder, like Bobo Jensen and the Mullins.

Scores of villagers assembled at Brad's Palace for the meeting. Many of them, however, merely attended for the opportunities it afforded – one of the main ones being the privilege of using a commode with an overhead tank. This was a modern convenience in Brewster's Village, and it was generally found only in the homes of the village's indigent plutocrats like the Bradshaws and Uncle 'Sir' Ed. Sometime later in life, those less fortunate villagers would be able to boast about having been to Brad's Palace to attend a function, sip a quiet drink and retreat for a bladder release or business of the bowels.

Mrs. Ramgolam presided over the meeting. She had a wooden plaque made of varnished wood, bearing her name and office in bold letters, prepared for the occasion. It read: **GLOYSIS RAMGOLAM: PUBIC RELATIONS CHAIRPERSON**. The plaque was placed on the front of the desk at which she sat. Sir Ed sat on her left and Dottie 'Teacher' Lovell, whom she had appointed as her personal secretary sat adjacent to him. Teacher Lovell enthusiastically accepted the position immediately upon being approached. She boasted to Uncle Ed of the business advantages that the position would have offered her as the owner of an elementary school, but on a grander scale, of her chances of being placed on the list of Brewster's Village prospective social elites and consequently, among St. Patrick's crème de la crème. Joshua Chandrapaul sat on her right. Nellie Sweetwine was not officially told of the meeting. The suggestion was made to invite the newly elected Senior Warden to the meeting, but Mrs. Ramgolam rejected it because she deemed it a subtle ploy to have her office upstaged by one whose election had placed him high on the list of the most powerful laymen in Ischalton's ecclesiastical arena. Harold Carrington, the owner of the only photo studio in Brewster's Village, was invited to take photographs of Mrs. Ramgolam's first official public duty. Protocol dictated that no fee be charged for the First Lady's inaugural meeting. Complimentary juice was served and the crowd guzzled it. The members who were accustomed to socializing at Brad's Palace merely sipped the concoction as they confabulated.

Many came to the meeting bearing grudges against Mrs. Sweetwine for copious reasons. Uncle Ed sat observing the crowd as they gathered. He knew from the sardonic remarks, which he had been overhearing during the course of the week following the elections, that some of the people present had interpreted Nellie's appointment as a form of social advancement, and that it offended them and made them green with envy. He knew, therefore, that they had come only to publicly vilify her, and that others attended specifically because they were drawn to political sensationalism; Mrs. Mullins' deflation had had absolutely no effect on them. Uncle Ed also realized that a few of them saw the opportunity to visit Brad's Place as the crowning glory of their life, while the rest attended the meeting to objectively discuss the Mullins incident. He therefore anticipated a moderate display of animosity and conflict.

The meeting started on time, and Mr. Chandrapaul invited Sir Ed to offer the opening prayer. Sir Ed prayed for order and fairness in the discussions and thanked God for allowing Mrs. Ramgolam to become the chairperson of the Public Relations Committee. He concluded his prayer by beseeching God to grant the people of Brewster's Village the power to 'prevail at St. Patrick's Church.' After the audience endorsed the petitions with a resounding 'amen,' they burst into vivacious applause. The crowd was in the process of settling when a dark blue Vauxhall appeared at the entrance. A tall, slim man stepped out of the vehicle. He was impressively attired in a pair of starched, black trousers, a white shirt and black tie. A black chauffeur's cap rested jauntily on his head. He stepped gingerly towards the right rear door and opened it. A more casually dressed figure emerged from the vehicle and approached the tent. All eyes turned towards the well coordinated individual as he strode pompously towards the front table. When he drew close to the table, Mrs. Ramgolam recognized him and smiled submissively. Others also had recognized him but refrained from any response to his presence until the First Lady gave them the cue. On sensing amicability, they responded with greetings and modest applause. The figure by now had reached the table and had begun shaking hands with the four self-deemed elites. A chair was brought for him and he respectfully accepted the graciousness. He subsequently sat, and the rest of the audience recognized him as Sam Westwater. Everyone had assumed that the First Lady had issued an invitation to him. However, after he left, it was discovered that Mrs. Ramgolam was ignorant of his coming and that no one there had invited him to the meeting. One day later, Uncle Ed was told by reliable sources that Sam was instructed by Laurent Faulkner to attend the meeting so as to ensure that those 'fickle minded simpletons' were not aligning themselves with Pigeon Goodfellow.

"Ladies and gentlemen," the delighted Joshua Candrapaul announced, "we are happy to have Mr. Westwater down here with we. Welcome, sir." The audience paid him homage with enthusiastic plaudits and loud greetings in their most eloquent dialect. Mr. Chandrapaul then invited him to address the crowd, but he declined and insisted that Mrs. Ramgolam proceed with the agenda.

Mr. Chandrapaul again rose from his seat. "Ladies and gentlemen, the peoples of Brewster's Village is proud to recognize our..." he turned to see the writing on the plaque, "...our Pubic Relations Chairperson and we congratulates her to this elevation post."

The audience burst into passionate applause and rose to their feet. Sam Westwater remained seated, but mildly applauded. After the surge of appreciation had abated, the First Lady rose to speak. Her outfit caused a great stir, especially among the women. As she began to speak, she stepped from behind the table and proceeded to the front of the centre aisle. Mrs. Ramgolam had studied and committed to memory the idiosyncrasies of the speakers at the Annual General Meeting as they addressed the congregation, and determined to emulate them should she be placed in such a prominent position. The request to investigate the Mullins incident and give a report therefore pleased her tremendously, for she knew that she soon would have to address groups of people in the same way as the vestry clerk and the others had done at the annual meeting. Mrs. Ramgolam passionately prepared for this day and spent all week coordinating her outfit. Less emphasis, however, was placed on researching the incident. Nevertheless, she believed that she had compiled enough information to warrant a meeting.

"T'ank you....t'ank you, ladies and gentlemens... I appreciates your kind applauds..." Uncle Ed hung his head and twitched his fingers as he listened to Mrs. Ramgolam's putrid grammar. Amusement and embarrassment wrestled passionately in his head as he cast furtive glances at the plaque and at the overdressed chairperson of the Public Relations Committee. As he mused on the misspelled word on the plaque, his mind began to wander as he studied Mrs. Ramgolam's form and the many children which she and her husband had produced. The irony of her position as Pubic Relations Officer as spelt on the plaque, struck him so powerfully that he found it extremely difficult trying to maintain his composure.

"As your Public Relations Ahffisah," she continued, "I have been entrested with the task of givin' all yah the infahmation 'bout Thelma Mullins....how they tek she out from the Fellowship Committee as Chairperson and hand it to Dorothy Sweetwine."

The audience paid rapt attention as Brewster's Village First Lady poured out the details of the whole sordid affair.

"The vestry put Dorothy in charge of the Fellowship Committee. They didn't tek Thelma out; they jes' put Dorothy in charge and they tell Thelma to support she. She get vex 'cause they give Dorothy the position, and she tek and shy a brick at the senior warden car. But the brick miss and it hit the mayor car. So the police come and lock she up. But it was a accident. She didn't mean to hit the mayor car. She jes' miss Mr. Jones' car, that's all."

All of the people sat quietly, listening keenly and shaking their heads in agreement. Mrs. Ramgolam spoke confidently, and sought to impress Sam Westwater by showering the vestry with unnecessary accolades. Stanley 'Turkey' Hodges stood and raised his hand.

"Excuse me, Miss Ramgolam," Stanley inquired. "Who decide to tek out Thelma and put Dorothy in? I doesn't see no sense in that?"

"That's right!" yelled a course female voice from the rear. "Dem playin' politics, that's what…friggin' politics!"

"The vestry ain't got no damn business tekin' out Thelma jes' like that… dry so," protested Iris Higgins, an itinerant fishmonger who peddled seafood door to door in Brewster's Village and in the neighboring village of Slough. She and Dorothy Sweetwine were once involved in a terrible fight early one Saturday morning, which stemmed from a simple argument between their two sons – who subsequently became good friends. The two women never spoke to each other after the brawl. "I ain't know who tell that Sweetwine that she can run any food committee. She can't cook a fartz for me, that's all I know. All ya tek out Thelma and put in somebody like Dorothy Sweetwine. That is confounded nonsense…ain't mek no sense!" she remonstrated.

Perceiving from the comments that a bitter debate – which could lead to an outright brawl in a place like Brewster's Village – was brewing, Sam Westwater interjected. "Ladies and gentlemen, the method by which the change was made might have appeared harsh, or personal, but let me assure you that it was done with every good intention. Mrs. Mullins was doing and excellent job, but she was holding that position for over two years, and we can't expect one person to be burdened with such a heavy responsibility for such a long time. We were concerned about Mrs. Mullins. We wanted to free her a bit so as to be able to spend more time with her family. If you were holding such a position for such a long time, wouldn't you want to get a break from it and let someone else carry the burden. That's exactly what we did for Mrs. Mullins. However, we were not able to explain things to her before the change. Furthermore, we asked her to assist Mrs. Sweetwine. That's what managers of a company do when someone assumes a new role. The person stepping down assists the new person. So you see, Mrs. Mullins is still actually the second in command, like the assistant manager. Furthermore, the vestry found a way to give all members the opportunity to take on leadership roles. As such we appointed Mrs. Ramgolam as the chairperson of the newly formed Public Relations Committee, so that your voice can be represented; Mr. Ed Burrows, whom you refer to as Uncle Ed, as chairperson of the Beautification Committee and Nellie Sweetwine as the chairperson of the Fellowship committee. Now, I don't know what the new vestry will do – under the leadership of Peter Goodfellow. We have to wait and see."

The gullible audience believed every word. They shook their heads in the affirmative as Sam delivered his tendentious speech.

"Does anyone have any questions or would like to say anything?" Sam asked.

There was some murmuring among the audience before Valerie Thomas, a well known seamstress from the village of Slough, raised her hand and stood.

"Mam, you have a question?" Sam inquired.

"I wants to say something...." Valerie replied.

"Go ahead."

"This confounded nonsense got to stop. That woman mek it look like the vestry just tek and kick she out like that, and put Dorothy in she place. Everybody was mad 'bout the whole thing. Now you come and explain everything to we, and we understands. This is jes' what does cause all kinds of story in the church…this kind of maliciousness. I wants to t'ank you fuh comin' to explain things to we. We feels better now," she confessed.

Applause followed.

The members of the audience who had taken umbrage at Thelma's apparent demise voiced their satisfaction and their concurrence with Valerie's comments. It was this display of tractability which gave Sam Westwater the courage and opportunity to present the vestry's plan for the people of Brewster's Village for the coming year. He thus invited Mrs. Ramgolam to take her seat.

"Ladies and gentlemen," Sam rose and stepped out to the centre of the audience, "I think that now would be the time to share some wonderful plans which the vestry, under the leadership of Mrs. Pigthorne, has made for the people of Brewster's Village and the surrounding villages."

The audience sat still, intensely focused on Sam as he paced up and down the aisle. Their faces bore the expressions of children in nervous and gleeful anticipation of Santa Clause on an impecunious Christmas Eve night.

Suddenly, a beer bottle came hurtling across the room and smashed against the front edge of the table, narrowly missing Sam Westwater. He froze in terror, but the audience, who were accustomed to such impetuous outbursts and expressions of rage, ducked and turned almost in unison to see the source of the object. Two of the men ran to the gate as a figure on a bicycle sped like a bullet up the street and banked the corner. The men made a futile dash behind the bicycle, pelting stones, empty cans and bottles that littered the street at the figure on the cycle, while hurling the most nauseating obscenities. However, the figure disappeared into the darkness of the evening. After the commotion subsided, the audience directed Sam to continue. The two men who had chased the figure on the cycle remained as guards at the entrance.

Sam, slightly timid at first, resumed his speech. "At its last meeting," he continued, "the vestry discussed an idea which was brought up during an earlier conversation involving the good Mr.Pilchard, Mr. Faulkner and myself. We were very concerned about you people having to walk or hire a taxi all the way to St. Patrick's every Sunday. So we discussed the idea of building a small church right here in Brewster's Village, where most of you live, so that you can worship right near your homes and you can be appointed to all of the leadership positions in the church."

The audience gasped and their jaws dropped. Their faces became aglow with ineffable joy. A tidal wave of explosive applause swept across the room as some of them stood and pounded their feet in excitement. Sam breathed a sigh of relief as the naïve crowd endorsed the iniquitous plan to have themselves effaced from the hallowed walls of St. Patrick's. However, Uncle Ed was not in approval of the plan, but kept his feelings and comments to himself, until the opportune time.

During the meeting, some members of the audience were observed making sporadic visits to the toilet, with sheets of tissue in their hands and a key which they had received from Mrs. Bradshaw, who for some odd reason, sat at the cash register throughout the meeting. The frequency to the toilet increased during the course of the evening, but no one was particularly alarmed.

Eventually, the meeting came to an end. Sam gave no specific time for the start or completion of the proposed plan, and no one asked. Having received the response which he and the BOARD had hoped for, and for fear of another bottle attack, Sam made a hasty departure during the singing of the closing hymn, *'Onward, Christian soldiers.'*

At the conclusion of the hymn, the members surrounded Mrs. Ramgolam and lavished her with flattery and pledges of loyalty and support. Some of the members, however, did not linger, but made urgent departures, leaving a malodorous trail of flatulence in their wake.

No one knew whether the bottle which was hurled into the room was intended for Sam Westwater or Mrs. Ramgolam, but some postulated that it might have originated from Rudolph Mullins. Consequently, the remaining members unanimously agreed that the two men who chased the mysterious figure on the cycle would function as personal bodyguards to Sir Ed and Mrs. Ramgolam respectively. Another man volunteered to function in the same capacity for Mrs. Sweetwine. However, Uncle Ed did not deem it necessary for him to have a bodyguard and refused the offer, but Mrs. Ramgolam was intensely thrilled by the suggestion and offered effusive gratitude to the members for their loyalty. She requested that the protection begin immediately and that subsequently, her bodyguard be attired completely in black and carry a stick that was fashioned after a constable's truncheon. The members concurred.

Uncle Ed expressed wishes to everyone for a good night's rest and departed on his personal horse drawn cart which he used specifically for social engagements. He offered a few of the older women a ride to their respective homes before heading to his own home on Canal Road. Profound thoughts of Sam's remarks occupied his mind as he made his solitary way to his abode. He decided that he would call a discreet meeting with Pigeon Goodfellow, with whom he and established a casual relationship which began during Pigeon's campaign.

After everyone had left, the Bradshaws closed the gates and secured the premises. As Mrs. Bradshaw counted the coins which she had collected that evening, she complimented her husband on the brilliant suggestion to offer the audience free refreshments consisting of a mixture of lemonade and a preponderance of prune juice.

*   *   *

Advent Sunday not only marked the beginning of the Christian calendar and the start of the penitential season in preparation for Christmas; it inaugurated a period of a deadly ecclesiastical civil war that shook the very foundation of St. Patrick's. During the election process, the BOARD had met briefly in one of the rooms to devise a plan of action to maintain their control if Pigeon Goodfellow were to win the election. However, the plan lacked any definition, because deep inside they believed that a victory for him was highly unlikely. When, therefore, the results proved them wrong, they became too stupefied to speak and too humiliated to linger; thus they quickly departed, wounded and stripped of their pride – their hearts pounding with the desire for the blood of those who by their vote had betrayed them and their eyes glowing with the incandescence of hell's fire. They had met on the Tuesday evening following the election. It was there that they had received word of the meeting which was going to be held at Brad's Place; it was then that they decided to immediately put the first part of their plan to destroy Pigeon into action. They thus appointed Sam Westwater as the general of their army of darkness to invade the privacy of the peasants' meeting in Brewster's Village, under the guise of comradeship. Sam subsequently reported to the BOARD that his mission was a glowing success.

On the Saturday morning following the meeting at Brad's Palace, Pigeon received a call from a public telephone in Brewster's Village.

"Goodfellow's...."

"Good morning, sir." The voice on the other side seemed distant and slightly muffled. There was a hint of familiarity in the voice, but Pigeon could not identify the person.

"Ed Bancroft here...Uncle Ed... from Brews..."

"...Yes....yes indeed. My good friend, Ed Bancroft...from Brewster' Village...Uncle Ed," Pigeon interjected. "How do you do, my old friend?"

"Good, but not so good," the voice replied.

Pigeon realized that this manner of contradiction was characteristic of persons whose limited command of the English language often prohibited them from accurately describing their feelings. He therefore postulated that Uncle Ed was troubled by something.

"How can I help you, old friend?" Pigeon inquired.

Pigeon sensed a tone of relaxation and comfort in Uncle Ed's voice after the warm reception. However, Pigeon decided to temper his cordiality so as not to sound too condescending.

Uncle Ed continued. "I'd like to speak to you 'bout something serious... 'bout some church that the vestry want to build in the village. You know 'bout dat?"

"Where did you get that from?" Pigeon's tone became very businesslike. "I mean, has someone been asking you to be involved in that scheme?"

"Nah. At the meetin' las' night, you know, over at Brad's, ah..."

"What meeting?"

"The meetin' 'bout Thelma...Thelma Mullins...you know, 'bout why they throw her out o' the Fellowship Committee."

Pigeon's tone became very somber. "Who called that meeting for something as trivial as that?"

"Dunno, but a big crowd was there, and Sammy Westwater come and he say that they's buildin' a church here in Brewster's Village so that we doesn't have to come all the way to St. Patrick's. Who say that we doesn't want to come to St. Patrick's? Something don't sound right 'bout dat, you know... something."

"Who called this meeting?" Pigeon's voice was bubbling with urgency. "Somebody had to call such a meeting. I wouldn't put it past Pilchard or Faulkner to plan something like that and stay in the background. So, when is this church supposed to be built?"

"Dunno. All I know is dat I ain't in agreement with it. I is a member of St. Patrick's, I been a member of St. Patrick's all o' me life, and I ain't leavin' there to come to no lil' wodden chu'ch in the village, to sit on no blasted wooden bench with no backrest. And who's goin' to be in charge if they builds it? We ain't got nobody in the village with enough common sense to run no chu'ch," Uncle Ed expostulated. "And I believe," he continued with conviction, "dat if they goes ahead and build dat chu'ch, they's goin' to make Mrs. Ramgolam the senior warden…dat damn fool …turn up at the meetin' yesterday with dat blasted husk o' dry fiber pun top she head. Then what you think they do…they puts Bertie Hackett to be she bodyguard 'cause somebody come in at the meetin' and pelt she down with a beer bottle."

Pigeon burst into an uncontrollable fit of laughter.

"Dis is serious, Mr. Goodfellow. Everybody at the meetin' was happy 'bout the plan, but I doesn't agree with buildin' no chu'ch in this village."

Pigeon breathed a heavy sigh. "Look, Ed, I'll find out what this is all about. I am appreciative of your trust in me and in my ability as your newly appointed senior warden to take care of something as serious as this. Thank you."

After the conversation ended, Pigeon sank into his large, red, leather sofa in his study and mused over the conversation. He was cautious about saying too much to Uncle Ed, who in spite of his status in the village and acquaintance with him, was of plebian extraction – one who, however, had justifiably earned his respect and pity. Furthermore, Pigeon had dissimulated ignorance of the erection of the church in the village. He remembered vividly that the concept had been brought up during his time on the vestry, but he had never voiced any protest. Now the idea had been shared with the villagers, and according to Uncle Ed's report, they joyfully embraced it. It thus became frightfully obvious to him that the BOARD had already won the loyalty of the villagers on whom he was depending to serve him faithfully in his quest to overthrow them. It was on his red, leather sofa that Pigeon thus devised a plan that could warrant the salute of the legions of angels in the deepest recesses of hell.

*   *   *

The haunting shadow of dusk cloaked Pigeon with its hooded black cape as he moved stealthily through the semi-darkness towards Eloise Pigthorne's large, cast iron gates. The old watchman greeted him respectfully after he introduced himself as the new senior warden of St. Patrick's, and then retreated behind some evergreens to the side of the large, brick house, where he announced Pigeon's arrival. After what seemed an unnecessarily protracted period of waiting, the grim sentinel returned and unlocked the gate.

"Come with me, sir," he beckoned to Pigeon with a slight motion of the hand. He led him to the front door where a rotund black woman with a cheerful countenance greeted him and led him up the stairs and into the drawing room.

"Please to sit down, sir. Madam is goin' to be with you shortly. She jes puttin' on she brassiere. She like to look proper whenever guesses comes to the house," she unashamedly confessed.

"I agree…wholeheartedly," Pigeon replied after overcoming the shock of the housekeeper's bluntness. "She should. She must."

Pigeon knew that the housekeeper's basic intelligence would never have detected his sarcasm, so he chuckled to himself as she exited the exquisitely decorated room. As he sat in the ultra soft, cushioned chair, he admired the impressive porcelain figurines which his instinct told him were collected from the various countries which the Pigthornes might have visited before Eloise became widowed. The oil paintings which in quiet stateliness graced the light brown, paneled walls, and the rich tapestry which draped the oversized sash windows seemed to create the atmosphere of an insouciant opulence. However, the object which arrested Pigeon's attention was the huge portrait of Eloise which hung on the wall, above the baby grand piano. It was a vignette of Eloise before her hair began to show hints of grey. Pigeon could see traces of what once was a relatively beautiful woman – a gentle and virtuous woman with eyes that exuded kindness and a quaint naivety. Now, as he contemplated her form, he wondered what could have gone wrong in that relatively short period of time. The attractive innocence that gazed gently from the portrait had in reality now become a vacuous and distant stare; the elusive beauty which the artist had managed to capture had faded and was replaced by an almost indefinable mass of fat upon which were stuck a pair of lips, a nose and two eyes that gazed in bovine amazement behind thick, gold framed spectacles. Mrs. Pigthorne had always been proportionately plump, but now she had grown large and top-heavy, with breasts that were sentenced to confinement in firm, structured supports. As Pigeon cogitated on Mrs. Pigthorne's full, unconfined mammary glands, a mischievous smile came across his face and he hung his head in quiet, private amusement. He struggled to maintain his dignity as the sound of confident but delicate footsteps made their way to the room. Upon raising his head, he beheld the elegantly attired figure of Mrs. Pigthorne stepping gracefully into the room. He was amazed at how such a stupid woman could carry herself with such enviable grace and elegance – at how much she was both admired and envied by a large cross section of women from every corner of the island – at how impressionable a woman of her age and status could be.

Pigeon had focused on Mrs. Pigthorne's malleability as he drove to her home. Her pliability was the Achilles' heel through which he was going to shoot his arrow of treachery and destruction. He was going to convince her that the BOARD had acted on a premeditated plan to nominate her for a second term of office so that they could continue to exert their power through her and to subtly inveigle her into declining her bid for office should any one be nominated for the position from the floor. His aim was to poison her mind against the BOARD and to win her favor towards him; this he had planned to achieve by employing any necessary devious craft.

"Good evening, Mr. Goodfellow," Mrs. Pigthorne beamed as she entered the room. She seemed thrilled but slightly perplexed that the man whom both the vestry and BOARD had feared so morbidly had come to make a social call at her home.

"Madam Senior Warden!" Pigeon returned the warm greeting by rising and bowing slightly.

"It's a pleasure to be graced by your distinguished presence in my humble abode," she added as she extended her arm with the inherent dignity of a princess.

"I think that it is I who am humbled by your distinguished presence and this royal ambience...very tastefully decorated, I must say," Pigeon looked around approvingly.

"Thank you. My late husband had employed decorators from England to..."

"...decorators...from England?" Pigeon interjected with dramatized astonishment.

"Well," Mrs. Pigthorne confessed, "they were already here on the island doing some decorating for the Governor General's wife, so Mr. Pigthorne seized the opportunity."

"Impressive." Pigeon remarked.

"Do sit down Mr. Goodfellow. And may I congratulate you on your victory at the elections. I wasn't aware that you were considering this office." Mrs. Pigthorne sat erect towards the end of the chair, with her left leg crossed behind her right leg and her hands resting on her right thigh. Pigeon briefly contemplated her breasts and wondered what they must look like without such rigid confinement. The light from the brass floor lamp which was reflecting on the light blue silk bodice seemed to augment her already obtrusive organs. For the first time, Pigeon felt intimidated by a woman – and especially one of such dull intellect and imposing proportions. So lost was he in erotic contemplation that he never heard her invitation for a cup of tea or a drink.

"...Mr. Goodfellow...?"

"Uhh....uh...ahh...sorry, did you say something?" the embarrassed, elected senior warden inquired as he regained consciousness.

"I was offering you a cup of tea...or a drink," the gracious hostess calmly repeated with a polite smile.

"Uhh…no…no. Thank you," he replied. "I am actually here only for a very short visit to formally meet with you so that the transition to my elected office would be a smooth and amicable one. Contrary to suspicion, I am prepared to work with the vestry in a harmonious relationship and, if you would graciously oblige, to seek your advice from time to time."

Mrs. Pigthorne stared at Pigeon in utter amazement. She seemed flabbergasted by his magnanimous overtures.

"Thank you for your kind remarks and your willingness to work harmoniously with us on the vestry. Of course, you are most welcome to call upon me for any kind of help or any advice regarding ecclesiastical matters. I'm most willing to oblige." Mrs. Pigthorne clasped her hands in delight, leaned her head modestly to the right and flashed a coy smile.

Pigeon reciprocated the smile. However, his was sinister, for behind his apparent delight were disparaging thoughts about Mrs. Pigthorne and his iniquitous plans to destroy the BOARD.

"Perhaps you could assist me by calling a special vestry meeting tomorrow morning after church…" Pigeon's eyes sought hers as she made a vain attempt to avert her attention from his arresting and intimidating gaze.

"A vestry meeting…tomorrow?" The fear in her voice was pronounced.

"Yes, immediately after the service; to give me the opportunity to officially meet the members and lay out my plans for the next term. Wouldn't that be the ethically correct thing to do? Actually, it would say volumes about you… your graciousness, your professionalism…not to mention your strength, you know, to stand on your own; to make decisions on your own. I think that the BOARD has usurped your authority, and you should at least make one final effort to assert yourself as the senior warden in these last few weeks of your term. It would tell them something…trust me. One of the main reasons for my resignation from the vestry was that I could no longer bear the disrespect that was shown to you in your capacity as warden. Mrs. Pigthorne, you are a woman of character, a role model to the hundreds of women who wished that they were in your place…a brilliant woman. Call a meeting. You are within your rights to do so. And you owe no one any explanation…none!"

Mrs. Pigthorne listened to Pigeon's plea with passionate enthusiasm. Her chest seemed to have puffed up almost to double its size with pride, and her eyes glowed in appreciation at his flattering plausibility. "But isn't it a little rushed to call a meeting for tomorrow morning?"

"Perhaps; but the nearness of your departure from office should instill some sense of immediacy to their response, don't you think?"

"I guess you're right. After all I *am* the warden."

"By the way," Pigeon implored, "Don't divulge the true purpose of the meeting. Just tell them that you'd like to, well, wrap things up before you leave."

"This means that I have to start calling now. It's already late. I just hope that…"

"Oh…another thing," Pigeon interjected, "order the members not to inform anyone on the BOARD of this meeting. And bind them to confidentiality."

"I will," Mrs. Pigthorne swore.

"And one last request; don't let any one know that I was here…giving you this advice or seeking this favor of you."

"Of course not." Mrs. Pigthorne promised.

"Well," Pigeon rose and gave a slight and polite bow, "I must be going. I appreciate your trust in me and your promise of support."

"And I your candor," the compliant warden responded with a delicate smile as she rose from her seat and bowed her head respectfully and graciously to the side.

"Thank you. I'll be seeing you in the morning." Pigeon nodded respectfully and stepped gingerly from the room.

A cool, gentle breeze brushed across Pigeon's face as he cruised along Kingston Boulevard. He bore a sardonic smile as he hummed along to the hymns that were playing on one of the local radio stations. His mission was successful. He had molded Eloise Pigthorne like clay in the potter's hand, and through her, he was going to win the vestry's affection and support the following morning after church; it was imperative that he do, and he was going to ensure that his plans were not foiled. He was going to do anything that was necessary to win their favor. As far as he knew, he had won the support of the congregation – the votes testified to his popularity. He knew that there was power in numbers, but he also knew the destructive power of a disgruntled minority. The votes attested to the congregation's trust and confidence in him, but there were enemies in the shadows. It therefore became obvious to him that in order to establish the full control for which he was yearning, he would have to ultimately win the favor of his enemies – or destroy them completely. He thus increased the volume of the radio as the St. Peter's Cathedral Choir sang the 69th psalm.

*   *   *

Eloise Pigthorne had completed the last telephone call and had retired to her bed. There was little disagreement to her request for a meeting the next day. No one aired any suspicions. Bill Jones had agreed that she should call such a meeting and promised that he would be there to personally express gratitude to her for the excellent job she had done during her term in office. Ironically, he also thought it appropriate to request Pigeon Goodfellow's presence – as a goodwill gesture. Bill had tried to convince her that it would be within her best interest to develop an amicable relationship with the new senior warden, who traditionally, would be numbered among Ischalton's most prominent citizens. Eloise told him that she would think seriously about his proposal and would make a decision after she had completed her nocturnal devotions.

Midnight drew near as Eloise tossed restlessly in her king sized bed. Visions of betrayed BOARD members in black robes with hoods descending the stairs to some dark, dismal dungeon plagued her mind and caused her to perspire profusely in her state of somnolence. Then one of the figures turned to gaze upon her one last time before it disappeared into the fissure. She slowly and fearfully approached the apparition, but she could not recognize its features, for the hood had cast a shadow over its face. Then the figure raised its hands and gently pulled back the hood from its face. She froze in terror. It was an emaciated caricature of Adolph Pilchard. His eyes were red and tears rolled down the skeletal contours of his face. The figure studied her momentarily. It neither judged her nor condemned her; her guilt was precipitated by her own sorrowful conscience. After a few agonizing moments, the figure replaced the hood on its badly mangled head and turned towards the stairs. Eloise made a futile attempt to chase after it and implore its forgiveness, but try as she would, she could not move. The figure slowly descended the stairs and disappeared into the abyss. Eloise was awakened by her own screams.

Guilt and remorse racked Eloise's mind as she wrestled with ambivalence. She had seized the opportunity to act assertively in her last few weeks of office, and Pigeon's inveiglement served as the catalyst for her courage. Discreetly, she had resented the BOARD's usurpation of her office, but she nevertheless subjected herself to their control so as to maintain a relationship of good standing. Now she had overcome the enemy within. Unilaterally, she had summoned the members of the vestry to an urgent meeting – a meeting that did not conform to the canons which required forty eight hours notification of any such gathering of the legal officers of the church. Eloise was proud of herself, and she condemned herself for not having sooner established rapport with Pigeon. In the short period that Pigeon spent at her home, he had endowed her with the strength to finally break the psychological chains which had bound her to the post of servile obedience to which the BOARD had sentenced her.

The thrill of assertiveness gave Eloise a new hold on life, but it also drove a rabid fear into her. In the dead of night, on the eve of the Sunday morning Eucharist and fellowship to which she always looked forward, Eloise was being haunted by ghastly visions of betrayal. As if facing the BOARD after

Pigeon's visit would not be extremely difficult for her, relating to Adolph Pilchard would be almost impossible. It was Mr. Pilchard with whom she once had had a torrid affair while Mr. Pigthorne was still alive – an affaire de Coeur which came to an abrupt end when Mr. Pigthorne, in his endeavor to pleasantly surprise his wife on one of her many overseas trips to the strangely frequent Mothers' Union conventions, found the judge, clothed only in a pair of silk, Scottish plaid boxers and a pair of bedroom slippers, hiding in the bath tub, behind the shower curtain. Eloise vehemently denied any involvement in a romantic relationship with the judge. Her claim was that he was visiting his relatives on the island and had only come over to the hotel to relieve himself and to shower because his relatives' bathroom and latrine were at the back of the dark, muddy yard. During the confrontation, the judge called Mr. Pigthorne a stupid, insipid buffoon for believing that his wife would do such a shameful thing, upon which Mr. Pigthorne, infuriated by such witless effrontery, swung a powerful right hook to the judge's jaw, which tossed him to the floor and which caused the top row of his dentures to eject from his mouth and fall to the ground. Mr. Pigthorne confiscated the grinning 'gnashers' and left the room without saying another word to his wife. Two days later, Mr. Pigthorne posted the dentures by registered mail to Mrs. Pilchard, accompanied by an anonymous note which informed her of where the plate was found, but without any revelation of the identity of the woman with whom her husband was caught.

One night, a few weeks after Eloise had returned home from the convention, Mr. Pigthorne took her to dinner at *The Lighthouse*, the island's most exclusive restaurant. While they were having dessert, he calmly informed her of his plan to remove her from the will and to contact his lawyer the following week to begin divorce proceedings. Three days later, Mr. Pigthorne died of a massive heart attack. Mrs. Pigthorne, by virtue of her social standing, was able to avert a post mortem. All suspicion was thus buried with Mr. Pigthorne that rainy Thursday afternoon in September.

* * *

After another hour of agonizing restlessness, Eloise rose from her bed and picked up the phone. Nervously, she dialed and waited.

"Pilchard's," the voice was feeble, but it was unequivocally that of the judge, awakened from a deep sleep.

"Adolph?"

"This is he." The voice had resumed its depth and power.

"It's…"

"Maggie… is this you?" The judge glanced at his wife as she lay in peaceful slumber and tiptoed from the room. "Maggie, what the hell do you mean by calling me at this hour when…"

"It's not Maggie!" The response was blunt and the tone, piercing. "It's Eloise!"

"Oh…Eloise….what…what's wrong. Are you alright?" the judge inquired in a loud whisper as he crept further along the corridor towards the drawing room.

"Yes. But I am troubled by something that happened earlier tonight." Eloise's tone was penitential.

"What?" The judge's voice bore only a hint of concern.

"It's about Pigeon Goodfellow. He was here earlier."

"What!?" the judge bellowed with rage. "What the blazes was he doing there…what the bloody hell did he want?"

"He wanted me to call a vestry meeting in the morning…after church… to make a smooth transition." Eloise's voice was barely more than a whisper, for she was overcome with fear.

"And what did you say?" Mr. Pilchard's voice became calm and somber, as if waiting to pronounce judgment.

"I…I…I told him that I was not keen on doing it, but…he…forced me to agree and call all of the members…"

"You called the vestry members, and never informed me? You summon the vestry to a meeting and do not notify me?" The judge's tone was reprimanding and condemning. "You get behind the BOARD's back and join with Pigeon Goodfellow to attack us….you @##%** traitor!" Mr. Pilchard's voice was deafening as Eloise held the receiver nervously to her ear.

"Look, Adolph, I am having a difficult time dealing with my actions. In retrospect, I should have sought your permission, but he stood right over me, psychologically breaking me down until my resistance succumbed to his power. Adolph, you must understand my plight. I am a mere woman. He is a man, a very powerful man in the community. What else could I have done?" Eloise pleaded.

"You know what you could have done. But you wanted to do what he said. You could have told him to get the **##@ out of your house before you call the police! But you wanted to do it. You know that you wanted to…!" The judge's voice roared like a lion in a rival battle.

"The fact that I am telling you now about this testifies to my loyalty to the BOARD. I am not a traitor." Eloise's voice bore a trace of defensiveness and hurt. "Look, I want you to accidentally show up at the meeting, ostensibly to look for something, and then act surprised when you see the meeting in progress. This is the reason for my call. I am a sincere supporter of the BOARD. I will never betray the BOARD."

The judge breathed a heavy sigh of resignation. "You know, I am going to watch carefully what happens in the morning. If no one tells me about this meeting, then I'll know for a fact that the vestry is among those who betrayed me at the elections. As for my dropping by accidentally at the meeting, you can forget it. That will never happen. I will never lower my dignity by subjecting myself to such gross humiliation. Goodnight."

Before Eloise could utter another word, the judge had slammed the receiver. A sudden pall of intense fear overcame her as she gently replaced the receiver on the telephone. Immediately, she proceeded to the liquor cabinet and poured herself a potent shot of bourbon which she guzzled in one gulp before retiring to bed. She awoke the following morning to the faint and distant peal of the bells of St. Patrick's.

*   *   *

There was nothing unusual about the service that morning. However, there was a strangely tense aura which prevailed among the vestry and some of the members of the BOARD throughout the period of worship. The vestry members in particular appeared subdued, and very few of them exchanged the peace with the judge or Laurent Faulkner after the confession and absolution. Father Perths preached an eloquent sermon on preparation and watchfulness, and challenged the congregation to profound introspection as they awaited the coming of the Christ child at Christmas. Mr. Pilchard had spent most of the service quietly observing the members of the vestry, and made mental note of those whom he had suspected of being Pigeon Goodfellow's supporters and his betrayers. Ironically, it was the ones of whom he was most suspicious who had made it their duty to approach him during the service to exchange the peace, through languid handshakes and cold, repulsive kisses. He and Pigeon exchanged the peace and made brief inquires about each other's welfare. He and Eloise merely acknowledged each other by polite bows of their heads.

The mass ended with the hymn, "*When we all get to heaven*", which the congregation sang lustily. Following the dismissal, Mr. Pilchard shared a light banter with some of the members of the BOARD and the vestry, briefly acknowledged the vicar who was greeting the parishioners in the narthex, and then proceeded to his car. Mrs. Pilchard had voiced mild concern about her husband's strangely hurried departure from the church to the vicar, who explained that it might have been nothing more than a residue of the embarrassment of having lost the elections so badly.

As the congregation filed into the parish hall for fellowship, the vestry slipped quietly into the common room. After the last member entered the room and took his seat, Bill Jones closed the door and Eloise called the meeting to order.

"Ladies and gentlemen, I want to thank you for your willingness to come to this meeting at such short notice. As I promised you last night, it's going to be a short meeting…"

Jason Coleman, who had made his living by his private accounting business, raised his hand.

"Mr. Coleman?" Eloise acknowledged him.

"Tell me," Jason said as he pretended to look around for someone, "Shouldn't the BOARD be here…I mean, *you* are chairing this meeting?" His sarcasm provoked a round of laughter which eased the tension and fear in the room.

"How much did you have to pay for *this*, Eloise?" Fenton Skeete yelled from the back of the room where he was sitting and smoking a cigarette. "…must have cost you quite a bit, eh, such a privilege?"

The members roared with laughter.

"On a more serious note, is it legal to call a meeting without the BOARD's knowledge and permission? In other words, would the judge find us guilty of committing a heinous crime?" Paula Fields stood as she asked the question.

Contagious laughter engulfed the room once more.

Eloise artfully restored order and seriousness to the meeting by interjecting her remark before anyone else could speak. "If we don't hurry and get out of here, the BOARD might find out; so let me get straight to the point. The purpose of this meeting is to officially make a smooth transition of wardens. I have invited Mr. Goodfellow to say a few words to you as I officially step down from office. My term does not officially end until the last day of December, but I shall be away during the first part of January, so I have chosen to do this now. I know that such a transition was never done before, but I have chosen to do it this way; it is the ethically correct thing to do."

"Here here!" Fenton Skeete shouted.

Some of the vestry expressed their concurrence by applauding mildly. However, Eloise could sense some discomfort among some of them as she opened the door to invite Pigeon into the room. Upon entering, Pigeon made a furtive glance across the room and Eloise wondered if he was trying to detect any signs of quiet protest or resentment from the members towards him. Instantly, she could see from his expression and protracted stare that he had placed his mark on two persons in the room. One of them was Aaron Ishmael; the other was Tessie Shoehorn.

The hilarity which only a few moments ago had engulfed the room had dissipated and was replaced by an aura of apprehensiveness. Eloise knew that Pigeon was surrounded by some of his most discreetly loyal supporters, and this knowledge helped her to relax. However, she also was well aware of the possibility and the danger of the enemy within. Pigeon nevertheless appeared calm and unthreatened, and he addressed them all as his comrades and verbally lavished them with spurious affection.

"My friends in the Lord's service," Pigeon began, "I thank you for your presence here today. Before I go any further, I beg for one minute to express personal gratitude to Mrs. Pigthorne for the wonderful job she has so far done in her capacity as senior warden. It is a performance that would be almost impossible to beat. I am but a mere shadow in the light of her immense achievements. However, by dint of my profession and my unique idiosyncrasies, I envisage a different manner of leadership. I believe that I have been called and chosen, not only by you, my friends, but by the Holy Spirit, to assume this position so that I can bring some semblance of order and coherence to this privileged group of persons here as we undertake the business of this great church. I believe that the person who assumes this position to which I have been elected must embrace democracy, and shun every form of leadership which borders on despotism. As a vestry, we are the leaders of this church, the legal officers who have a divine right to rule and govern the affairs of God's church. We have been duly elected for this office and we must not, under any circumstance, allow insidious intrusions into our midst to usurp our authority."

"Here, here!" Fenton shouted again from the rear.

"However," Pigeon continued, "statistics have shown that democracy does not always serve as the most effective form of government. As leaders elected to serve in God's church – and especially a church in which demons lurk in the shadows, we must practice some degree of autocracy. Our word must sometimes be the order of the day. It's the only way we will be able to exercise power and abate those who lurk in the shadows to usurp our authority. My dear friends, my beloved brothers and sisters, we must also practice and uphold timocracy, for ultimately it is our honor which is at stake here; our honor as individuals and as a vestry must be protected. We must be strong, courageous, determined. My friends, there is no room on this vestry for pusillanimity. We must be sensitive to the concerns of all of our members, and seek to serve with integrity. We are called to be sensitive, yet indurate; public, yet intensely private; willing to listen, but ready to ignore; quick to praise, yet prepared to condemn. My beloved, need I continue this prolixity? The message is clear; we are called to be all things to all men."

It was from this moment that Pigeon began to lose his credibility, for the earlier expressions of delight on some of the faces of his audience began to change. During his speech on election Sunday, he had impressed the audience and won their vote by virtue of his apparent honesty and respect for the dignity of every member of the congregation. He seemed to have transcended the ugliness of the prejudices which haunted the parish and to have embraced democracy. Now, as he stood before the vestry, some of whom had elected him, his countenance began to assume a different form and his words seemed to unearth some form of uneasiness in them. Beneath his gentle, trustworthy façade lay a nefariousness which some of the members seemed to have perceived and which seemed to have given them second thoughts of having voted for him. A few of them began to exchange worried glances.

As the group sat quietly, contemplating Pigeon's address, Pigeon paused to analyze the expressions of the faces which beheld him and realized that there was a silent and deadly resentment which burned in some of the eyes that stared at him. While he stood there before those faces which were etched with mixed emotions, the door behind him opened. Pigeon turned abruptly and froze in shock as his eyes came into full contact with those of Laurent Faulkner, who stared at him with such blazing venom that his blood instantly began to boil with the fire of white hot hatred.

"What the bloody hell are you doing here, Faulkner? This is closed vestry meeting!" Pigeon's voice trembled with sizzling rage.

"You are not yet the warden, Goodfellow. What you are doing is unlawful!" Faulkner shouted as he pointed accusingly at Pigeon.

"This is a special meeting which has been called by the present senior warden for a particular purpose which has already been declared to the members; and this makes it lawful. It is your intrusion that is unlawful – and completely out of order!"

"Here, here!" Fenton once more yelled from the rear.

"I see that you're here, Bill, supporting this," Faulkner bellowed accusingly. "Where does your allegiance lie, Bill; with the senior warden or *him*?

"I'm here simply at the behest of the senior warden. Have I committed a crime?" Bill replied sarcastically.

"This is a legal gathering, Faulkner," Jason Coleman added defensively. "I received a call last night from the senior warden, inviting me to attend this special meeting of the vestry. There is absolutely nothing here that is being illegally done."

Some of the members nodded in the affirmative in their support of Jason's comments.

"Now I will assume that this compurgation will put your accusations to rest, Faulkner," Pigeon calmly stated in a tone of resignation.

"Madam Senior Warden," Mr. Faulkner warned, "I forbid you to continue this meeting at once! If not, I will have no choice but to report you and this entire vestry to higher authority."

"Don't you mean the BOARD, Faulkner? I don't consider them as higher authority. In fact, I don't even consider them an entity," Pigeon retorted.

"I suppose you consider the Bishop as higher authority, Goodfellow," Mr. Faulkner replied, "because that's exactly whom I'm going to report you all to. Does that answer your question, Mr. depraved Goodfellow?"

"Madam Chairperson," Pigeon requested, "I beg that you please expel this avatar of unethical garbage from our midst. His smell is most offensive!"

Laurent Faulkner and Pigeon Goodfellow glared at each other in deadly contemplation for a few seconds, after which Mr. Faulkner turned abruptly and exited without uttering another word. A terrifying silence engulfed the room.

Pigeon turned and addressed each member suspiciously with his eyes. His stare was particularly sustained when he addressed Aaron Ishmael and Tessie Shoehorn. "I would rather believe that Mr. Faulkner is blessed with clairvoyance than to believe that there is a traitor among us." Once more, he focused his attention on Aaron and Tessie. Aron averted his attention to the large crucifix which stood on one of the corner tables.

"If you ask me," Fenton Skeete growled from the rear, "the traitor sits right in front of you….as large as life."

Tessie Shoehorn, who was extremely sensitive about her size, straightened up and swung slightly to her left and glared at Fenton. "You go to hell, Fenton Skeete. For all we know it could be you who went and said something!"

"How do you know that he was accusing you, Tessie? He didn't mention your name," Jason interjected.

"He didn't have to," added Louis De'Santos, the owner of *Louis D's*, an exotic seafood restaurant in the city. "He said that the traitor was as *large* as life."

The murmur of suppressed laughter came floating from the rear. The hushed response infuriated Tessie, and she rose and stomped across the room to Louis' chair. She placed one hand on her hip and pointed the other in Louis' face as she leaned aggressively forward, "Yes…large…large and beautiful as life, Louis De Santos," she yelled. She then opened her arms wide as she turned gracefully in a complete circle. "See, large and beau-ti-ful as life, ya confounded jackass!" Tessie then turned and swaggered back to her seat.

"Yeah, Tessie," shouted Fenton in a tone of mockery, "abundant life; the fullness of life…tetchy, old cow!"

A gush of raucous laughter erupted from the rear. Tessie turned again and contemptuously scrutinized Fenton.

"Mrs. Shoehorn…gentlemen!" Pigeon shouted in a commanding tone, "This is not going to work. We cannot begin a new term of office with this kind of antagonism toward each other. Let us stop this at once. If there is indeed a traitor among us, the Lord who called me to this office will reveal that person's identity to me. There is no need for us to act like this. If we are divided, then it would be easy for the BOARD to infiltrate our midst and reek havoc."

"I concur...," stated Orland Dalghetty, the diocesan treasurer and chairman of *Liverpool Associates*, a British financial company located in the down town area.

"Brothers and sisters, I wish to comment on one more issue which I intend to address at the first vestry meeting in January – the surreptitious plan to build a church in Brewster's Village. I want you to know that I am aware of this plan and I vehemently oppose it. This plan does not serve to bring this congregation together; rather, it serves to further separate us by keeping the people of a certain class in their place. My friends, this will be the first item on my agenda when I officially assume office. I therefore warn you to prepare for a resounding veto against the plan."

Absolute silence followed Pigeon's remark. Once again, however, Tessie Shoehorn and Aaron Ishmael exchanged glances. Pigeon quietly observed them.

"Once again," Pigeon reiterated, "I thank Mrs. Pigthorne for this opportunity to meet you and to facilitate a smooth transition to what I hope will be an effective and coherent vestry."

A moderate round of applause followed Pigeon's remarks, and Mrs. Pigthorne again voiced her appreciation to the vestry for their response to her request to attend the meeting. Everyone then exited the room. As the members filed past the desk, Pigeon analyzed their expressions, and in the deadly silence of his prejudgment, determined those whom he will condemn to psychological torment.

* * *

That night, Mr. Pilchard parked his car on Midland Avenue, put on his black flop hat and strolled three blocks over to Maggie Billings' home. The rays of light from the street lamps which shone on the thick foliage and patulous branches of the flamboyant trees which lined the avenue cast copious shadows which served to protect his identity. Maggie's home appeared particularly far that night, and as the judge drew closer, his heart seemed to pound more heavily with the gush of anxiety. He therefore paused in a dark spot, by a clump of bush, to compose himself. Behind the bush was an alleyway which formed a kind of demarcation between *The Victoria Mansion*, an upscale apartment building where many English denizens and wealthy locals resided, and the section of Queenstown which comprised the large, middleclass family homes. Maggie's home was located in the middle of Westminster Lane, which was around the corner from the alleyway. As the judge stood in the shade of one of the flamboyant trees, deeply inhaling the fresh cool air, he heard the rustling of paper emanating from the dark alleyway, behind the thick clump of bush. Stealthily, he edged forward to investigate the source of the sound. As he peered behind the clump of bush, he gasped in a sudden gush of fear at the stooping, semi-nude figure of a vagrant nicknamed 'Bunzo'. Bunzo was a short, fat, pot bellied man in his late thirties who roamed the city streets and who spent every penny he received at the *El Dorado Bakery*, where he bought coconut buns. The proprietor, Walter Conrad, used to give him, as well as the other homeless persons who congregated in front of the bakery to spend the nights on cardboard boxes, generous amounts of the sweet bread and other cakes every evening before the bakery closed. Bunzo would later exchange his pastries and bread for coconut buns. Bunzo was relieving himself in the privacy of the dark alleyway, and feeling threatened by the invasion of his privacy, rose impulsively and dashed forward towards the judge. Mr. Pilchard darted down the dark street, with the half naked vagrant in hot pursuit, assailing him with stones, dust and a string of virulent expletives. The judge swung the corner on to Westminster Lane with Bunzo close behind, still yelling profanities and pelting the terrified judge with whatever he could find on the side of the road. The brouhaha attracted the attention of the dogs which began barking furiously behind large iron gates and the residents who turned on their lights and parted their drapes so as to peer outside. Having reached Maggie's house, the judge quickly opened the gate and dashed inside the yard. He braced the gate in order to prevent the angry derelict from entering the yard. As Bunzo reached the gate and was about to force his way inside to get to Mr. Pilchard, he suddenly stopped and his eyes opened wide in recognition of the judge.

"Judge Pilchard…your honor…oh **#@#*; is you, judge Pilchard! I didn' know was you was standin' there when I was koongseein…"

Mr. Pilchard nevertheless held the gates firmly. "Yes…it is I, judge…judge…Pilchard. I…I…didn't know that…that… some….somebody was there…I…I…heard a sound, so I just stopped to …to see…see if somebody was…was…in trouble…. I didn't mean to spy…on…on you…"

"Dis is where you livin, judge?" Bunzo asked with a broad smile.

"No. No. I'm just visiting someone… Go on. You may go now…go on…"

"Gimme a small piece, eh judge…loose me wild with a dollar, eh, your honor…" Bunzo wasted no time in capitalizing on the chance encounter.

"Here…take it and go…go on…and put on your clothes…please!" the judge implored as he fumbled through his wallet and pulled out a fifty dollar bill. He had no time to figure out the denomination in the semi-darkness.

As Bunzo expressed exuberant gratitude for the generous act of charity, neighbors stared through their respective windows in utter shock at the tall, distinguished silhouette of the judge standing behind Maggie's gates, pleading with the rotund, half naked figure clad only in a tattered jersey and a pair of worn, weathered shoes, with his trousers and underpants rolled up in one hand and a piece of crushed newspaper in the other. The light in Maggie's foyer came on and Maggie, robed in an elegant silk duster and high heeled slippers, appeared at the front door with Cleopatra, her well groomed poodle.

"Oh…you visitin' you' girl, eh…?" Bunzo remarked as he moved his head from side to side to get a better view of Maggie as the light from the foyer reflected partly on her svelte body draped in the flowing silk duster. "That's a sexy ole' bird you got there, judge…a real ole' tart she be, judge. Goodnight, mam!" he yelled as he waved at Maggie. Maggie averted her attention from the semi-nude night visitor.

"Go on now…just go…before the police come and lock you up…," the judge craftily advised Bunzo.

The judge's mention of the police served its purpose well. Bunzo dashed up the street without another uttering word. As the judge made one last furtive glance at the surrounding houses, he observed parted curtains being closed and lights being extinguished. He immediately hurried towards the front door and disappeared inside.

"I notice that your unexpected visit has caused quite a stir in the neighborhood," Maggie nonchalantly remarked.

Mr. Pilchard was still too shaken, humiliated and embarrassed to respond. His face was contorted with rage and he was breathing heavily from exhaustion as he mounted the stairs. Maggie and Cleopatra followed in silence as the judge threw himself on the leather sofa.

"A glass of water…or a smidgen of brandy, perhaps, to calm your nerves?" Maggie asked as she put Cleopatra to sit on the Queen Anne chair.

The judge gave no answer, but raised his head and studied Maggie in cold contemplation.

"One would assume that you at least would have the decency to offer an apology for making such a coarse and public announcement of your arrival at an otherwise quiet neighborhood.

"I'm beginning to think that my only apology is to myself for being foolish enough to come here," the judge snapped.

"It's not too soon to come to your senses, you know," Maggie responded in angry earnest.

The judge glared at Maggie in sinister silence. "Are you still a member of St. Patrick's, Maggie?" he finally asked.

"Is there somewhere else that you are suggesting that I go?"

"That's not the question." The judge barked.

"Where else would I go, Adolph?"

"Then you *will* be at church. Every Sunday!" the judge commanded.

"What's bringing this on, Adolph? Why the sudden decree that I attend church every Sunday?" Maggie inquired.

"Because I suddenly feel surrounded by traitors...covert enemies... double-crossing bastards. You now are one of the very few that I trust, Maggie, and I need you there...to keep your eyes open...to protect me," he pleaded.

"Oh...just as I thought; motivated by self interest as usual," Maggie cried.

"Maggie, its either you are for me or against me. It's as simple as that!" the judge rejoined.

"Right now, Adolph, it is much easier for me to be against you. However, I will stand by you, for this is what a woman does when she is in love. She remains faithful to her man, even when the faithfulness is not reciprocated and even when she knows that in the end, she will never ever have full claim to him."

The two contemplated each other momentarily. The judge's eyes suddenly became aflame with passion.

"Come here," he ordered.

Maggie slowly approached the visibly moved judge, who stretched his arm and gently pulled her on the sofa. They kissed passionately.

"Maggie," the judge whispered as he slowly released her and leaned backwards on the chair, with his head gazing up to the ceiling. "Goodfellow, the son–of-a-bitch, it was he who sent you those flowers; I have no proof, but I'm sure that it was he who sent them. He knows of us."

Maggie sat up and stared blankly at the judge.

"What I don't know is how he knew...how he could have found out," the judge pondered.

"He met you here the last time, didn't he?"

"The flowers were sent before that. Remember?" he reminded the now agitated Maggie.

"Rex. Rexworth Davis, who else...," Maggie suggested. "...the night in the choir room."

The judge turned and looked at Maggie, but his stare was distant. "You believe that Rex would betray me?" he quietly asked as he tapped his right foot and averted his attention to his black Barker wingtips.

"No proof, "Maggie whispered, "Just a mere hypothesis."

"You don't think that it is possible that someone might have known or said something before that time?" the judge asked.

"Highly improbable...not impossible; just very highly improbable," Maggie reasoned.

"Maggie, I am prepared to deny any accusations...to lie blatantly...to do anything to protect my honor."

"*Your* honor?"

"Well, ours. But you know what I mean. I am a public figure, Maggie," the judge stated.

"And a married man, Adolph. Don't forget that. As a matter of fact, that is precisely what you mean by a public figure. You can't allow your beloved wife to hear about us, can you?" Maggie replied. "Incidentally, what about the holiday you said that you were going to take with Mrs. Pilchard?" Maggie inquired. "That should quell much of the suspicion, if at all there is any."

"I changed my mind. Quite frankly, I didn't think that that was going to solve anything. Sooner or later, I'll have to come back, wouldn't I?" the judge noted.

"What if it isn't Pigeon who is responsible for any of..."

"...Maggie," the judge interjected, "you're being naïve. All evidence points to Pigeon. He cast aspersions at the annual meeting. He looked me in the face and hurled burning coals of sarcasm on my head. I know what he was referring to."

"Why are you running when no one is chasing you?" Maggie put her hand in the judge's right hand and leaned her head on his shoulder. "I think you are over reacting; you're imagining more than it is."

Mr. Pilchard rose from the chair and approached the bar. He poured himself a shot of brandy. "Something for you?"

"No."

"Maggie," the judge said as he walked slowly towards the window and parted the drapes slightly, "I feel threatened." He turned and faced Maggie, who was sitting elegantly at the edge of the sofa. The subdued lights from the lamp behind the sofa created strands of gold tinsel at the back of her head where the blond colored hair caught the light. She looked alluring in her black, silk negligee which was partly exposed under the flowing black and red duster. Her light, peanut brown complexion glowed as the light reflected on her delicately oiled and perfumed skin, and her large, olive colored eyes projected a magnetism that seemed to draw the judge to the precipice of self control and emotional sanity. Once before, when their relationship was threatened by the thunderbolts of gossip and peals of scandal, the judge, in his endeavor to protect his honor, had come to Maggie's home to sever the relationship. However, the course of the evening somehow had already been charted by their concupiscence and twisted convictions, and after several minutes of what the judge would later describe as a torrid copulation, sealed their relationship by making vows that would bind them to their unholy union until they are parted by death. Now the dark night which had sanctified their irreligious union and protected the privacy of their adulterous affair was being put to flight by the monochromatic hues of the dawning sky and the rays of alizarin crimson which radiated from the rising sun. The judge and his mistress thus were faced with the threat of exposure for the second time. In this instance, however, it was not a solitary beam of light which was vainly penetrating the thick darkness of their blasphemous union; it was the very light of the sun which would scatter the darkness of the long night. Their rapture which endured for the night was going to become the lachrymation which cometh in the morning.

"The last time our relationship was threatened," the judge continued, "we weathered the storm. But this time the tempest is too powerful for us. Either we swim or we sink, and I do not intend to go down, Maggie. I have no intention of losing your love because of Goodfellow…the flaming bastard!" The judge took a sip of the brandy and turned away from Maggie. "I'd have him killed first," he mumbled.

"Adolph…?" Maggie cried in dismay.

"Come on; you know what I mean." He explained.

A ghastly silence followed. He once again turned towards Maggie.

"Do you love me, Maggie?" The judge's expression was stern and his eyes were livid with rabid hate.

"Of course I do, Adolph," Maggie replied as she recoiled on the sofa in fear.

"Are you sure?" the judge pressed.

"Of course I'm sure. Why?"

The judge drew a deep breath. "What sacrifices are you prepared to make for someone you love…and someone who loves you more?"

"Whatever is necessary, Adolph. I've gambled my dignity to save our love; I've endured emotional and physical abuse from you to hold on to your love; I have been kept awake many a night by the relentless struggle between guilt and justification on the battleground of my conscience; I have paced this floor like a zombie many a night because you chose to cling to your dear wife while my passions blazed in its own funeral pyre. Yet you question the authenticity of my love?"

"Then we must get rid of Goodfellow." The judge's eyes pierced her like toxic needles and his voice trembled with abhorrence as he pronounced the death sentence.

"Ok. But how?" Maggie asked in a soft, calm voice.

The judge contemplated Maggie. He was amazed at her naivety, but nevertheless pleased, for he perceived that this very innocence could precipitate his exoneration.

"By whatever means necessary, Maggie," he answered. "All I need to know is that you are prepared to stand behind me, whatever the cost."

"I am." Maggie's tone was cogent as she gazed lovingly at the man who juggled her emotions in their private romantic circus. She could see from the coldness in his eyes that he was harboring some flagitious thought, but convinced herself that the man she loved so deeply was above reproof.

"How can I be so sure?" The judge fixed her a rigid stare as he took another sip of the bourbon.

Maggie rose elegantly from the sofa and undid the satin bow which held the duster at the waist, and without averting her attention from him, seductively slipped the duster off her shoulders and let it fall to the floor. The judge's eyes opened wide in amazement and his jaw dropped as he raised his head from the glass. Once again, the woman whom he was forbidden to love – the one for whom he risked his honor – his kept woman – the one whose face appeared when he was being tender to his wife – had spun her web around him, and with her eight psychological fingers, caressed every vein in his weak heart until he finally succumbed to her poisonous, romantic overtures.

That night they made another covenant. They would vehemently deny any accusations made against them, and should the truth of their relationship be exposed, the judge would immediately resign from office and subsequently leave his wife, for there would be no more need for pretense. They kissed once more, as if to seal their profane covenant, before the judge made his way to the door.

*   *   *

The drapes in the neighboring houses which were parted during the judge's dramatic arrival to Maggie's home were closed and the houses were in darkness as he made his way hurriedly along the street. The umbriferous branches of the flamboyant trees which arched Westminster Lane protected him from the penetrating rays of the street lights as he darted along the sidewalk like a phantom of the night. Suddenly, like an apparition released from the deepest recesses of hell, a slim figure of a man dressed in a pair of black trousers and a black blazer over a black jersey, appeared behind him. The figure wore a black fedora and a pair of black hushpuppies. The startled judge turned sharply to his right and looked over his shoulder to identify the figure.

"Good evening, sir. I didn't mean to startle you," the stranger said in a refined, baritone voice.

"Good evening," the judge responded as he sought to recognize the stranger's face.

"Your face looks rather familiar," the stranger noted as he edged past the judge.

"Does it?" the judge responded. His fear of the figure in black subsided when he heard the refinement in the stranger's voice.

"Ah...I know," the stranger answered. "You bear a slight resemblance to that famous judge...what's his name....ah..."

"...if you mean Adolph Pilchard..." the judge interjected.

"Yes...yes; that's right...Judge Pilchard, ain't it?" the stranger guessed.

"I am he," the judge replied.

"Well, bless my heart! How do you do, your honor?" The stranger extended his arm and they shook hands.

"Pretty good for an old man, as we say after we reach sixty," the judge jovially replied. "And you are...?"

"It's a bit dangerous for you to be in this area at this time of night, don't you think? There are a lot of vagrants who roam this area at night, seeking a quiet place to rest until morning," the stranger warned, without responding to the judge's question.

"Yes. I know. I saw one of them earlier this evening...by the alleyway." the judge agreed. "Nasty fellah..."

"Yes. I know," the stranger admitted.

"You...you saw him too?" the judge asked surprisingly.

"Yes," the stranger responded brusquely. "He was chasing some bloke up the street."

Mr. Pilchard immediately began to be wary of the stranger, who after shaking his hand, never looked him in the face, but kept his head forward and his attention focused, as if being guided by some unseen entity.

"You see, your honor, I keep vigil in this neighborhood, and particularly on this street. I have interests in this street and I protect my interests." The stranger kept his face forward as he spoke. His voice was crisp and deep, and his expression was somber.

The men reached the intersection of Thames Drive and Midland Avenue. The judge turned to the stranger and extended his arm for a parting handshake. "Well, I guess that fate will bring us together again some time. This is where I turn. I'm parked half way up Midland Avenue. It's been a pleasure, Mr..."

Again the stranger ignored the judge's attempt to get his name. This time also, he made no response to the judge's attempt to exchange parting handshakes, but kept his face forward.

"I too am parked on Midland Avenue," the stranger said dryly. "I'm right behind you."

A cloak of uneasiness overcame the judge as he turned his face abruptly towards the stranger. His mind raced back to the stranger in the black car who had accosted him as he was leaving Maggie's house after his last visit. Mr. Pilchard therefore sought to subtly divorce himself from the uncanny stranger's company by crossing the street. Without uttering a solitary word, the stranger crossed the street as well and kept his pace beside the judge. Nothing else was said by either of the men, and the stranger never turned his attention towards the judge.

When the judge reached his vehicle, the stranger stopped and turned towards him as he entered his car. The judge did not lower the window to express wishes for a good night, but locked the doors as he fumbled nervously to ignite the engine. The stranger merely stood there, watching him like a sentinel. For the first time, the judge was able to fully observe the stranger's facial features. He was dark man with sharp features. His high cheek bones gave his dark, sunken eyes a ghostly appearance and his thick eyebrows were joined at the center of his forehead. The fedora cast a shadow over the upper part of his face and he bore a sepulchral expression. His impeccably groomed mustache bore traces of grey and his chin was clean shaven. The judge realized that the stranger must be a man of some significant social standing, but mentally impaired and potentially dangerous. After artfully maneuvering the sleek, black Mercedes from between the cars which sandwiched him, the judge sped off along MidlandAvenue. As he glanced through his rear view mirror, he realized that the stranger never moved from the spot on which he was standing when he entered his car, but stood there, as motionless as a statue, watching the car until it disappeared around the corner. The terrified judge drove along Sutton Avenue until he came to Shell Road where he made a right turn. On reaching Normandy Highway, he made another right turn and continued along that road until he came to Midland Avenue, where he made another right turn. He drove slowly along Midland Avenue in an attempt to gain sight of the stranger, but there was no trace of him. The cars which were parked behind him were all still there, and as he drove past Thames Drive, he looked down the road to catch a final glimpse of the stranger, but the street was desolate. It was as if the stranger had disappeared into the darkness of the night.

As Mr. Pilchard drove home, his thoughts of the stranger were so terrifying that he quickly forgot his earlier confrontation with Bunzo and the ecstasy he shared with Maggie. Something had gone terribly wrong. His nocturnal visits to Maggie's home were becoming more unnerving rather than exciting; someone was apparently building a case against him to bring about his downfall; those whom he had trusted had betrayed him; the BOARD which he was instrumental in founding was beginning to lose its power; those with whom he sat at table in fellowship were privately deriding him. Somewhere in the equation, he strongly believed, Pigeon Goodfellow was executing a festering conspiracy against him. Nevertheless, he would continue to conduct a publicly civil relationship with the man he feared most so as to divert all suspicion when St. Patrick's bells begin to toll.

When the judge entered his living room, he found three messages obtrusively placed on the coffee table closest to the entrance. One was from Tessie Shoehorn and one was from Laurent Faulkner. The other was from Bill Jones.

* * *

Torrents of rain fell that Tuesday morning as a Brewster's Village bus rolled into the city terminal. The passengers quickly disembarked and rushed towards into the terminal building. The last two persons to alight were buttoned up in matching plastic rain coats. He wore a rain hat and she covered her head with a rain-mate. They shared a large, black umbrella as they rushed across the street to the taxi stand. Within minutes they were riding in the back seat of a beige Morris Oxford along Water Street towards *Walters and Goodfellow*, a posh legal office located on West Regent Street in the heart of Georgetown, Ischalton's busy capital. The couple entered the building and headed for the receptionist's desk where they requested an audience with Mr. Goodfellow.

"Do you have an appointment?" the receptionist politely asked.

"We doesn't," the woman replied. "But jes' tell him that the Public Relations afficah from St. Patrick's church is 'ere to talk to 'im."

"Sure. Just a minute," the woman said. She rose from her seat and knocked on the door marked *Peter Goodfellow, Esq.* "He'll be with you in a minute. Please take off your coats and have a seat; make yourselves comfortable," she said upon her return.

The man assisted the woman in removing her coat. The receptionist gasped at the sight of the woman's attire after the coat was completely removed. She wore a black and white polka dot dress which was gathered at the waist with a broad, white band tied in a huge bow on the side. The skirt fell just above the knees and about three inches above the black knee high stockings. A pair of off-white, wedge heeled shoes with broad straps and huge buckles fitted snugly around her thick feet. Large, gold earrings, several gold chains and a large, white handbag completed the ensemble. The blond fiber on her head was gathered together at the back by a white ribbon bow and formed a plaited pony tail which fell just past the shoulder. The inclement weather had proved prohibitive to a more elaborate hairstyle, she would subsequently explain to Mr. Goodfellow when, in private amusement, he offered flattering remarks to her about her tasteful attire. As soon as the coat was removed, she approached the receptionist's desk with some degree of urgency.

"All ya got a toilet in 'ere? I does got to pee a lot when the rain fallin' like dis," she confessed.

"Down the hall; first door on your right," the receptionist replied, in suppressed amusement.

"She does got to wee wee a lot, you know. After she had the tenth baby she start' havin' problems with she bladdah'," the man explained.

The receptionist seemed not to hear the man's remark and resumed her task. The man was more modestly attired, but that his tie was discordant. Nevertheless, the briefcase he carried lent an air of humble professionalism. Within seconds of the woman's return from the bathroom, Mr. Goodfellow emerged from his office.

"Mr. and Mrs. Ramgolam, my dear friends...my dear, dear friends!" the warden elect exclaimed as he approached the couple with his arms opened wide.

The couple respectfully rose from their seat. He stood straight and dignified. She crossed her legs, held her skirt and awkwardly curtseyed, almost falling over in the process. The receptionist's eyes momentarily met Pigeon's and she turned away from the couple in order to prevent herself from bursting into throes of laughter.

"Do come inside," Mr. Goodfellow invited them after the greeting and hand shaking ritual. "What brings you here, in such awful weather?" Pigeon inquired. "Ahh... I know...the preparation of your will...ready to divide the millions from your business, eh?"

Mrs. Ramgolam sat facing Pigeon with her arms clasped and her arms resting on her thighs. Her handbag hung from the side of her right arm and her back was slightly arched as she leaned forward on the chair, with her knees spread apart and her feet turned inward. She did most of the talking since she earlier had forbidden her husband from saying much on account of his improper English.

"We wants to congratulate you on your successfulness at the election," she explained.

"Thank you!" Pigeon exclaimed. "I'm flattered that you should come all this way in this inclement weather to congratulate me."

"We was talkin' jes the oddah day, and we say 'dat we bes' come an' tell you how happy we was that you was goin' to be the senior warden. We hear that you has a lot of nice plans and we wants to help."

"Well, actually I do. And I'm pleased that you are supportive of my plans," Pigeon stated with a polite smile.

"Gloysis," Mr. Ramgolam urged his wife, "'urry up an' talk, nah. Mr. Goodfellow gat a lot o' work to do, ya know."

Mrs. Ramgolam stole a reprimanding glance across the mahogany coffee table to her husband.

"Is there something that I can do for you, Mrs. Ramgolam?" Pigeon inquired.

"I did jes want to ask you if I is still goin' to be the chairperson of the Public Relations Committee. Me hear say that you was goin' to liquefy the committee."

Pigeon suppressed his laughter. "Well, I should." He suddenly assumed a serious expression. "Mrs. Ramgolam, the reason why that committee was formed, as well as the others that Uncle Ed and Nellie Sweetwine have been put in charge of, is because certain elements, whom I will not name, want *you people*, if you know what I mean, to be focused on other duties so as to keep you separate from them. That is precisely why they want to build a church in Brewster's Village; to keep the villagers from coming to St. Patrick's. Do you understand?"

Ram was appalled. "They doesn't want we with them pun Sundays?" he asked.

Pigeon said not a word but solemnly shook his head in the negative.

"And what 'bout you, Mr. Goodfellow?" Mrs. Ramgolam inquired.

The question seemed to catch him by surprise. "Mrs. Ramgolam!" He responded in a tone of mild hurt.

"And what 'bout 'im?" she added, pointing to her husband. "You still wants me 'usband to be you' campi'n manager for Brewsters Village?"

"Well, the campaign is over, isn't it? I've won the election, haven't I?" he responded with a wry smile.

Ram interjected, "Whu' she mean is, you doesn't want we at the church either?"

"That's an absurd thought, Mr. Ramgolam." Pigeon stated defensively. "You're always welcome at St. Patrick's. We're one big family, aren't we?"

"Then how come you doesn't come to church for the 7.00 o'clock service with we, you know, the peoples from the village?" Ram further inquired.

Pigeon soon began to show visible signs of discomfort at the Ramgolams' interrogation.

"I like the high mass at 9.00 o'clock, you know, the incense, the organ and choir…all the pomp and circumstance, you know," he artfully replied.

"We likes the high mass too, but they doesn't like we to come to that. They does turn up they face at we. That's why we doesn't go the 9.00 o'clock service." Ram complained.

"Mr. Goodfellow," Mrs. Ramgolam suddenly thought, "you should let them mek we come to the nine a'clack service pun a Sunday."

"Yeah," Ram enthusiastically agreed. "That would be good. Then everybody could be like one, you know…one big family, like you jus' say."

"Yes….that….would…be….nice indeed. But that will take time, a long time to get done." Pigeon nervously explained. 'Look, I'm very sorry, but I have a client coming to see me shortly, I'm afraid that I …"

The Ramgolams rose from their seats.

"But you didn't say, Mr. Goodfellow. I is still the chairperson? And is me 'usband still you' campai'n manager?" Mrs. Goodfellow reiterated.

Pigeon paused and nervously scratched his head. "Look, let me be frank with you Mr. Ramgolam. You served me well as my campaign manager in the village, but the election is over. I've won, and I'll always be most grateful to you. With regard to the Public Relations position, you may continue as the chairperson, Mrs. Ramgolam. It was, on the second thought, a very clever idea by the vestry."

"T'ank you…t'ank you very, very much!" Mrs. Ramgolam beamed with excitement. "Come, dumplin', leh we go." She grabbed her husband's arm and headed out of the office.

The Ramgolams took their leave in the pouring rain. Throughout the journey home, Mr. Ramgolam was sullen and quiet. As the bus rolled past West Buckingham Avenue, on its way to Brewster's Village, the bells of St. Patrick's rang the angelus. A tear fell from Mr. Ramgolam's eye.

"He use me," he mumbled. "All he do was use me…"

Mrs. Ramgolam realized that her husband was profoundly hurt by the man to whom he had offered his loyalty and trust. Ram had firmly believed that his role as Pigeon's campaign manager for Brewster's Village was his passport to social advancement. Pigeon's rejection had plunged a sharp, emotional dagger right through his heart and completely deflated him. His only hope for any semblance of self worth was to bask in the light of his wife's prominence as the Public Relations Chairperson of Brewster's Village. However, his anger at Pigeon and his discreet frustration of having to now stand in his wife's shadow in the socio-political arena forbade him to celebrate her success at the meeting or share her joy. Try as Mrs. Ramgolam might to lift her husband's spirit, he continued to sink further into a state of depression.

"You ain't doin' nothin' for that dog Goodfellow, you know Gloysis," he decreed. "He goin' to **#@* use you too. Ya'hear?"

"I's the Public Relations Afficah, Jo Jo. 'Ow the @#**# I goin' to not do nothin' for the man? He goin' to be the seniah warden. Me can't do 'im like that."

"Well you got to figure that fo' ya'self, Gloysis; but yo' ain't doin' a #@@#** for 'im, ya' hear me?" Ram insisted.

Mrs. Ramgolam folded her arms and averted her attention from her husband, who continued to stare at her in a threatening manner. She pouted her lips and batted her eyelids defiantly as she clutched her handbag as if it were a comforting source. Nothing more was said by either of them for the rest of the trip. When the bus reached the Public Road and Roraima Street junction, the Ramgolams disembarked and headed up Roraima Street towards their home. Mrs. Ramgolam covered herself with the umbrella and walked away from her husband who came traipsing a modest distance behind her, sulking and weather beaten from the pouring rain.

*   *   *

Tuesday remained a wet and melancholy day, and as evening fell, a thick mist enveloped the village of Abersthwaithe. The rays of light which penetrated the mist from the lamp posts created an enchanting and mysterious aura. Churchill Street seemed desolate, and the residents in the posh homes along the street seemed to have taken early retirement for the night. However, one of the houses seemed a striking contrast to the other dark and closed up palatial homes on the street. It was the home of Laurent Faulkner, the chairman of the BOARD. A special vestry meeting was being held to discuss and vote on the building of the church in Brewster's Village before the new warden assumed position. The aim was to have the plan approved and ratified so that Pigeon would not be able to thwart their plans and so that construction could begin immediately upon receipt of town and diocesan approval. *Faulkner & Babbit*, as well as some of the more affluent members of the BOARD, was going to fund the capital. Mr. Pilchard's role, as one of the island's most powerful and respected citizens, was to inveigle Fr. Perths into arranging an urgent meeting with the two of them and the Lord Bishop.

The cars began arriving shortly after eight o'clock, and by eight twenty all of the members, as well as Fr. Rerths, were present. After a long and passionate opening prayer by Ruthel Pollard, the discussion began with a detailed report from Bill Jones of Pigeon's remarks and plans which he presented at the vestry meeting, with the emphasis being on his plan to veto any vote to erect a church in Brewster's Village. Bill therefore stressed the necessity of the vote which must be made prior to the new vestry's first meeting which was only a little over four weeks away.

Eloise Pigthorne thus presented the plan. "Reverend Perths, the vestry is especially pleased to be graced by your presence this evening at this special vestry meeting. We are also happy to have among us this evening, some of our distinguished parishioners who are here to make a generous donation to the plan we are here to discuss, pending your approval of the plan, of course. As you all know, we do not hold the monthly vestry meetings in December because, according to our by-laws, the Annual General Meeting takes precedence over the vestry meeting. I say all of this to remind you that this is the last vestry meeting that I will be functioning as your senior warden. Effective January, Mr. Peter Goodfellow will take his place as your senior warden. Reverend Perths, we have called this meeting to discuss and approve the erection of a church in Brewster's Village. Pending approval from all parties, we hope to begin building in February and we plan to dedicate the church on the eleventh of June, on the feast of St. Barnabas."

It had become obvious to Fr. Perths that Eloise was primed prior to delivering her speech. Her occasional glances across the room to Laurent Faulkner had convinced the vicar that she was merely repeating what was dictated to her some time earlier. However, the rapacious priest found it sagacious to ingratiate himself with the BOARD members in order to continue enjoying the financial benefits of self-abasement. Thus he had already given his nod of approval to the plan when the villainous judge met with him earlier to convince him to arrange a meeting between the two of them and Bishop Addington. Fr. Perths knew that what he was agreeing to was wrong, but he nevertheless was willing to dispense with moral rectitude for social acceptance; sacrifice his dignity for financial comfort; forsake his vows of ordination for the pledge of foul allegiances; surrender his Christian principles for the ruthless laws of survival. He justified his actions by appealing to the doctrine of grace and by periodically offering small sums of money to the destitute whom he would encounter on his rare visits to the villages around Aberstwaithe.

Several vestry members were vehemently opposed to the plan. However, none was more in disagreement than Lois De Santos for he had fully understood the need to have the *Bronze* and *Iron Circles* maintain their unregistered membership at St. Patrick's. He recalled that they had agreed to the social demarcations and the formation of the committees which would have forced the lower circles to concentrate on their own issues. They also had seen the wisdom in the appointments of Uncle Ed, Nellie Sweetwine and Mrs. Ramgolam as their lackeys through whom they would control the *Bronze* and *Iron Circles*. However, he now argued that the erection of another church in Brewster's Village would result in their having to do the so-called menial tasks which otherwise might have been assigned to the lower circles. He furthermore argued that their social prejudices could become a flagrant object of arrant shame, especially in the eyes of the Roman Catholics and the Pentecostals who were more welcoming of the lower classes. In spite of his opposition, however, he neither abstained from voting nor excused himself from the gathering for fear of losing his status, especially since it was all which he, like some of the others, had in his quest for aggrandizement. Thus he sat quietly in an unspoken dissent, absorbed in the vileness of his self interest as the BOARD crafted its abhorrent plan to contradict its faith by ostracizing the poor from its midst.

"You have my blessings on this project," Fr Perths proclaimed. "I think that it is a testimony to our lives as Christians. It is tangible proof of our mission mindedness and our desire to give some sense of identity to the otherwise insignificant members of our community. May God bless our project!"

A round of applause followed the vicar's pronouncement, even from those who were in opposition.

"Then I ask someone to make a motion to embark on the project pending approval from Bishop Addington and the town board," Eloise begged.

"So moved," cried Aaron Ishmael.

"Second." added Paula Leitchfield, whose husband was the general manager of the Rice Marketing Board.

The motion passed unanimously. Once again, there was brisk applause.

"Tell me," Fenton Skeete inquired, "Isn't five months a rather short time to allot for the building of a church, I mean, with all of the possible delays one faces when one embarks on such a project?"

"It's not St. Patrick's we're building, you know," Laurent Faulkner replied.

The members burst into laughter.

"In spite of the hilarity," Fenton continued, "this is a serious project we are embarking on, with significant ramifications."

"And I concur," Laurent Faulkner responded. "But the fact is that a simple, wood frame structure with a zinc roof does not require architectural genius or constructional artistry."

"Is that the extent of the building?" Jason Coleman asked.

"There'll be a room for the priest, a sacristy for the altar paraphernalia, and two toilets – outside – of course," Mr. Faulkner replied dryly.

"What about furniture? Where are we purchasing that from?" Fenton pressed for more answers.

"Purchase?" Mr. Faulkner seemed shocked at the question. "We're having them locally built. Benches made of greenheart and stained with dark varnish. The local men will be employed to do the building of the church and the furniture."

"*We* are building a church for the local village people and *we* are determining the details. Don't these people have a say in what their church should look like?" Fenton once again questioned the arrogant Faulkner.

"What say? We are providing the funds. We are directing the project. What would they discuss with us…the color of the tiles on the bathroom walls…central cooling as opposed to overhead fans…stained glass windows instead of louvers or sash…or wood, for that matter?" Faulkner replied.

Mild laughter sailed across the room.

"I mean, what could they…" Faulkner continued.

"…I get your point, Faulkner!" Fenton angrily interjected.

"Very well. Then keep your opinions to yourself. If you don't like what we're doing to help these people, then you are free to resign like Goodfellow." Faulkner snapped.

A hushed and awkward silence followed.

"May I say something?" Mr. Pilchard asked.

"The floor is yours," replied Eloise.

"I get the impression that there is some underlying resentment to the vestry's plans to build this church. As a matter of fact, I have been sensing some antagonism against the BOARD, against me, against certain individuals on the vestry. May I remind you, friends, that the BOARD is merely a group of dedicated members working with the vestry in a spirit of fellowship. Contrary to belief, we are not a board of dictators. We are attempting to do something that would be of tremendous benefit to the people of the surrounding villages. Let's face it, comrades, we are high church. Furthermore, the sermons preached here are above their ability to comprehend. What they need is a church of their own, with their own officers working under the direction of St. Patrick's, and on special occasions, they come across here for a joint celebration, you know, like…"

"…like harvest, eh, when they bring all of their best produce for you vultures to feast on and then serve you like stooges and clean up after you all like dogs eating up the crumbs that fall from your table. Is that what you mean, your honor? Have you forgotten that those *peasants*, as you all like to call them, are equally high church, like you all?" Jason Coleman remarked sardonically.

"I perceive that you are one of the traitors that Mr. Pilchard was just referring to, Coleman? You know what to do if you don't agree to what we are doing," Laurent Faulkner interposed.

Jason rose from his seat, "No, Mr. Faulkner, I am not a traitor, any more than you and the whole lot of you sitting here are. What you all are doing is immoral. And you call yourselves Christians. And I am surprised at you, Fr. Perths, for allowing this devilishness to continue. I have held my tongue for a long time, and I have put up with a lot of foolishness from this vestry and this BOARD, but tonight I will speak my mind. I want no part of this vile plot against the poor. Yes, I failed in my duty as a Christian by allowing this wickedness to continue to this point, but tonight it ends. It ends for me. I want no part of this; I want no part of this vestry and this incorrigible lot which calls itself the BOARD. Furthermore, I want no part of this church!" The irate Jason marched forward to the coat rack to retrieve his rain coat and umbrella. Silence engulfed the room.

"No amount of rain will stop this parade, Jason Coleman, so you can go to hell!" Tessie Shoehorn shouted from the corner chair.

"And I'd like to take you with me, fatty, but there ain't enough space in the pit!" Jason retorted with a foul expression stamped on his face. "So bug off, you splenetic old cow!"

He stomped out of the house and slammed the door. A few of the members turned and contemplated Tessie, as if in expectation of a response. Tessie batted her eyelids and raised her head towards the ceiling. Sniggering from a few of the vestry members echoed across the large room.

"Does anyone else wish to go with him?" Faulkner asked in a gentle but stern tone.

No one responded.

"Friends, we'll have to move very quickly on this. But don't be afraid. There is nothing that anyone can do to stop this. The vestry has already approved the project," Mr. Faulkner stated.

"Yeah, but the Bishop hasn't. Neither has the town board," Fritz Batty warned.

"Hence the immediacy of our action," Mr. Pilchard added. "Reverend Perths and I have a meeting with Bishop Addington on Friday morning. I suggest that we do not wait for his approval before we approach the architect. Let's call Mr. Horwood in the morning. A drawing for such a simple building should not take long. I suggest that you speak to him, Fr. Perths, and stress the urgency of a plan before Friday so that immediately upon receiving the Bishop's approval we can proceed directly to the town hall. I will call Jeff Hutchins in the morning and tell him to expect us on Friday, Fr. Perths.

"Superb!" Mr. Faulkner exclaimed.

"Let's take a toast to our defeat of the enemy!" Ruthel Pollard announced.

The members toasted, and after another hour of fellowship departed in high spirits, confident that their plan to permanently ostracize the poor from their midst will be achieved in only a few months. Fr. Perths also left in good spirit, knowing that he had redeemed himself and that the BOARD was once again on his side. His sense of security was thus restored, and he made a private vow to never again gamble with his financial stability.

* * *

Late that night, Pigeon was awakened from his sleep by the ringing of the telephone. He fumbled in the dark to take up the receiver before it disturbed his wife. "Goodnight," he answered in a loud whisper.

"Goodnight. Jason Coleman here," the voice answered.

"Jason!"

"Sorry to disturb you at this hour, Mr. Goodfellow," he apologized, "but there is something that I must share with you tonight. Time is critical."

"What's wrong, Jason?"

"I just left Faulkner's house. There was a meeting there tonight…the vestry and the BOARD, about building the church in Brewster's village."

"What happened?"

"I walked out. I've left the vestry. I've left St. Patrick's. Can't deal with it any more," Jason confessed.

"What? Who called that meeting?" Pigeon asked.

"That imbecile, Pigthorne. Bloody idiot!"

Pigeon rose from his bed and stumbled through the dark room to the corridor and put on the light. He sat in one of the chairs. "I bet she called that meeting at the direction of Faulkner or Pilchard. The bastards! When did she call you?"

"On Sunday night."

"Just as I thought…Aaron Ishmael or Tessie Shoehorn…just as I thought. They probably called Pilchard or Faulkner no sooner the meeting was finished on Sunday and repeated everything. I'll take care of them." Pigeon swore.

"No. It wasn't either of the two of them. It was your good friend, Bill Jones…relayed every bit of information…everything you said…the whole works." Jason reported.

"What?" Pigeon exclaimed in utter shock.

"That's right. The son-of-a-bitch…repeated everything!" Jason reiterated. "Listen to me, Goodfellow; I know that this must hurt you. But here is what I've been thinking. Go see the Bishop tomorrow morning, first thing tomorrow, and lay down your case before him before they do. Pilchard and Fr. Perths have made an appointment to see him. I don't know when, but I know that it's some time soon."

"Thanks, Jason. I'll call him tomorrow morning and …"

"No!" Jason interrupted him. "Don't call. Just go. Turn up at his door. He'll see you. He's a very gracious man. He'll see you."

"Thanks, Jason. Thanks for being a loyal friend. Thank you."

"And one more thing, Goodfellow; this call is highly confidential." Jason stated.

"Don't worry, friend. As far as I know, you never called. I shall keep this in utter confidence," Pigeon promised.

"Goodnight."

"Yes...goodnight." Pigeon hung up the telephone and slipped back into bed, deeply hurt by Bill's betrayal, but enthralled by Jason's loyalty. Before falling asleep, he made a solemn vow to take reprisals against Bill Jones and deal the judge one final blow.

*   *   *

The following morning remained overcast and grey as Pigeon got dressed and headed to the city to see the Bishop. The Christmas music which was being aired on the radio station did very little to lift his spirit. The pain of betrayal and the desire for revenge racked his mind and spirit as he maneuvered through the heavy morning traffic. On his arrival to Bishop's Court, he was intercepted by the diligent watchman, who stood in front of the oncoming car and raised his hand like a traffic policeman. Pigeon stopped and rolled down his window as the man approached his car.

"Can I 'elp you, sir?" the watchman inquired.

"Morning. Here to see Bishop Addington. Urgent," Pigeon replied.

"Jes park yonder by the palin' over there," the watchman directed Pigeon. "I goin' to let the Bishop know that you's come to see 'im. What's ya' name, sir?"

"Peter Goodfellow."

"Jest a minute, sir."

The watchman retired to the rear of the building and soon returned. "'E's goin' to see you in 'is office. Please to come 'round 'ere with me."

Pigeon locked his car and followed the watchman to the bishop's office on the ground floor. Bishop Addington was there to greet him.

"My friend, the good fellow! How do you do?" Bishop Addington extended his arm as he graciously welcomed Pigeon.

"Good morning, my Lord!" Pigeon responded to the warm greeting as they shook hands.

"Let me first apologize for calling on you without an appointment and for coming so early..."

"Ahh, don't mention it. I'm happy that I'm here to receive you. I was in the process of making a call to the Archbishop to discuss a few issues, you know, the usual diocesan problems that keep us bishops gainfully occupied… Please, have a seat. Shall I get you a cup of tea…a sandwich?"

"No. Thank you. Mrs. Goodfellow insists on serving me a heavy breakfast before releasing me to deal with, quote, 'the pressures of the public.'"

The two men enjoyed a few more minutes of light banter before the matter at hand was introduced.

"Bishop," Pigeon's expression became very serious. "As you might have heard by now, I was elected as senior warden of St. Patrick's…"

"Ah…yes, yes. Congratulations!" the Bishop replied. "It's going to be quite a challenge, you know."

"It already is, my Lord. I'm already engaged in a fierce battle with the vestry and a covert group which calls itself the BOARD."

"Board? Board of what?"

"Board of Fools, my Lord. Pardon the expression." Pigeon remarked. "Bishop, they have embarked on a devilish mission to oust the people from Brewster's Village and Slough from St. Patrick's by building a church – some two by four wooden structure – in Brewster's Village, ostensibly to save them the long, arduous trip to Aberstwaithe on Sunday mornings, and to give them the opportunity to quote, 'worship in a way that is relevant to them.'"

"But they can't attempt such a thing without my permission, so there is no need to worry about that," Bishop Addington calmly assured Pigeon.

"Precisely, my Lord. This is exactly why I have come to ask you – to deny them permission to do so. Those people love to worship at St. Patrick's. They want to play an active part in the ministry at St. Patrick's but they are denied the opportunity to do so, and now that I'm the senior warden, they are afraid that I will allow them to assume positions of leadership in the church, positions which they believe should be offered only to a certain group who refer to themselves as the *Gold Circle*."

"What in heaven's name is happening there? Fr. Perths has never made mention of any such group to me. I know of their politics, but this…," Bishop Addington admitted.

"It's always been a discreet entity, Bishop, more like, say, a force of suggestion. But it became more pronounced, more viciously incarnate, after Philbert Watts sang the solo at the Harvest Sunday celebrations…" Pigeon continued to reveal the sordid details of the harvest episode to the bishop, who stared at him with his brows knitted and his mouth agape in disbelief.

"Oh, so now it all falls into place," the bishop added calculatingly. "Tell me, what was Nollie Mertins' role in all of this?"

"He once had despised those people from the village. To be honest, Bishop, I really cannot figure him out. One day he treats Mr. Watts with piercing disdain, and the next day he is embracing him like a brother and putting him to take the lead on Harvest Sunday. And need I mention, now that you have brought it to my attention, that I have not seen any further association between the two. It was almost as if Mr. Mertins was up to some surreptitious plan."

"Now I see," the bishop reiterated. "Now the puzzle is beginning to fit together."

"What puzzle, my Lord?"

"Oh…nothing. Just contemplating. So tell me, what was *your* role in all of this? I mean, how long did you know of all of this before you decided to come to me. And why have you only now decided to report all of this to me?" Bishop Addington inquired.

The question caught Pigeon by surprise but he artfully dogged the impact. "I…I didn't …think…that it…it was my duty to report this to you. I felt that this information should be brought to your attention through the vicar or the present senior warden."

"Are you telling me that your vicar and your senior warden were aware of all of these things?"

"I don't know to what extent Fr. Perths was or is aware of any of this. He has a tendency to be rather naïve at times, but I know that Mrs. Pigthorne was well aware of all of this nefariousness." Pigeon testified.

"And…she…"

"Bishop," Pigeon interjected, "Mrs. Pigthorne's role as senior warden is, perhaps, like that of a supernumerary. It is the BOARD that speaks…that dictates. She merely acts out their commands."

"I see," the Bishop responded.

"My Lord, I was made to understand that Mr. Pilchard and Fr. Perths have made an appointment to speak with you. The erection of the church is the topic that they are coming to discuss. They are seeking your permission to embark on their hellish mission. I beg you, Bishop, do not grant them permission to ostracize the poor, for ultimately, that is exactly what they are seeking your permission to do," Pigeon besought the bishop.

"I will listen to them, and I will make a decision, but only after much consideration, so I hope that their intention is not to begin building with any degree of urgency." Bishop Addington stated.

"I believe that it is, my Lord. I understand that they are ready to act on it. They already have secured the funds from *Faulkner & Babbit*, as well as from some of the Board members, and they are sometime later to approach the town board." Pigeon declared.

"It doesn't matter whom they receive permission from. Nothing can be done without my stamp of approval. However, I do owe them the respect of listening to their plans and rationale."

"Well," Pigeon rose, "I thank you for your graciousness, my Lord, in giving me a few minutes of your precious time. I myself have a rather busy day today but this matter was of great urgency. Please convey my respects to Mrs. Addington."

"I shall," Bishop Addington replied as he rose and escorted Pigeon to the door. "I shall be fair in my judgment of the whole matter. And I suppose that your visit is to be treated as a matter of utmost confidence..."

"Thank you, Bishop. Good morning."

The two men once more shook hands and Pigeon returned to his car, confident that he had unilaterally deflated the BOARD. He ignited his engine and turned on the radio once more to the Christmas music. This time, however, he sang along to the tunes. As his car approached the gates, the inquisitive watchman again intercepted him. He rolled down the glass.

"You's from Abersths, eh?"

"Yes. North Abersthwaithe," Pigeon answered.

"...could tell by yo' fancy car. Rich people up there, eh?"

"So it is said," Pigeon replied.

"Got a dollar or so?" the watchman begged, "something for the Chris'mas?"

Pigeon offered him a ten dollar bill. The watchman opened his eyes wide with joyous surprise.

"T'ank you, sir. T'anks much. You goes to St. Patrick's too, wit' them rich folks, eh?"

"Yes. I worship at St. Patrick's...with all kinds of people" Pigeon replied with a smile.

"Rex, you know, the sexton...he beefin' round' me cousin's bird, you know. Me cousin comin' back from sea for Christmas. He goin' flap 'im up, dhat Rex."

"I'm sure that they'll talk things over like good Christians. Anyway, I have to go. Good morning."

Pigeon roared off towards the corner, satisfied that his mission was successful. As he glanced through his rear view mirror, the watchman was still standing there, staring at the ten dollar bill.

*   *   *

Rain poured throughout the morning, and by afternoon sections of Brewster's village were swamped with almost two inches of water. In many of the streets puddles appeared almost everywhere, and travel, whether by foot or donkey cart, became extremely difficult. In addition to the gloom brought on by the inclemency of the weather, the village was in a state of sorrow.

Marjorie Pickins, affectionately called 'Neighbor' Pickins or 'Ma' Pickins', who lived with her extended family in one of the tenement yards had died and was being buried on this day. Ma Pickins was the village's centurion, and when she reached one hundred years old, the neighbors celebrated the event with one of the biggest parties ever hosted in Brewster's village. It was a quintessential village celebration, where people came from all over the village bearing enough food and drinks to serve the guests. Invitations were extended orally to everyone whom anyone met. The celebration was held in the pasture, and a team of villagers, which included children, had gathered that morning to clean the pasture and set up all of the paraphernalia necessary to host the village's biggest party. The celebration began at four o'clock in the afternoon and ended the next day, shortly before six o'clock in the evening. Within one hour, as the dusk began to set in, the pasture was completely cleaned and the animals were able to graze the next morning. It was a grand celebration which was kept only for residents of Brewster's Village who had reached one hundred years old. The last such celebration was six years earlier when Edris Jackson, known as 'Aunty Baby' reached that milestone. Today, however, the village had gathered again to mourn a revered member of its community. Nevertheless, they celebrated, again. They knew how to mourn – in a way that was unique. Joyous mourning was one of the village's idiosyncrasies. They were solemn; they were frivolous. They were sacrosanct; they were jovial. They cried; they laughed. They hugged; they fought. They burst into euphonious song; they engaged in cacophonous squabble. They slept; they kept courtly vigil. Above all, they gave themselves totally to the mourning family – their time, their food, their few pennies, their prayers. No one ever mourned in solitude.

The cemetery was flooded, but the villagers had donned their Wellingtons and made their way to the graveside in order to carry out the most significant part of the ceremony – the singing of the hymns as the dirt is being thrown on the coffin. It was customary that one of the older women, armed with an old, tattered hymnal, would call the words and the rest of the mourners would echo the words in song. Women would wail and throw themselves to the ground while able bodied men lifted them bodily away from the gravesite. Many women began their concubinary relationships in this manner. The men would escort them home after the mournful drama, and before the night was over, physical expressions of affection would be issued and relationships would be born. This time, however, the flooded ground prohibited the excessive demonstrations of sorrow, so the mourners were only able to sing the hymns.

Some of the men had congregated about thirty feet away from the grave in order to carry out their ritual of imbibing locally brewed rum. Ram was among the coterie of men who, much to the chagrin of his wife, was consuming the distilled beverage. Normally, Ram would be standing close to his wife on occasions like this. However, the two had been estranged since their visit to Pigeon's office earlier in the week and Ram was enjoying the freedom. His wife stood in the middle of the crowd, casting disapproving glances at her husband. One of the men then offered Ram a large bottle of rum, and as Ram was about to place the bottle to his lips, his wife pushed her way through the crowd.

"Jo Jo!" she yelled. "You tek one more sip o' dat' t'ing an' it goin' to be me and you this afternoon, right in this burial groung'!" She approached Ram and stretched her arm to take the bottle.

"Look Gloysis move ya black, ugly @##@* from 'ere, yeh!" Ram yelled as he brushed her arm away.

One of the men grabbed the bottle from Ram in a desperate endeavor to save the contents. "All ya don't fight with dis bottle in ya hand before y'all spill all this good stuff pun the ground."

Ram was infuriated because he was denied a sip of the alcohol. "Why the **#@#* you doesn't go back over deh and sing ya *@#@*#?" he shouted.

"Why the hell you doesn't go ya coolie *@@#**# back over deh and show some respect for the dead, you damn fool!" she yelled in bitter retort.

"No!" Ram yelled defiantly. "You go ya #$#@* back over deh!"

All during the argument, no one except a few mourners at the edge of the crowd was paying any particular attention to the couple. The crowd around the graveside continued to sing while the small group of men, bonded in an intoxicating fellowship of brotherhood, shared their precious commodity. Suddenly Ram's wife, unable to bear the humiliation any longer, swung her large, white handbag at Ram's face. He artfully intercepted it, grabbed it and flung it into the air towards the crowd. The bag landed in the half-filled grave. The pastor, who was also the founder of *The Tabernacle Pentecostal Church*, froze in horror, and upon regaining his composure made a hasty exit. Mourners began to follow the pastor with great urgency as Ram, armed with a large twig which he had broken off from a nearby tree, tried desperately to retrieve the object. The grave diggers stood by watching the confusion but unwilling to help because of the superstition surrounding such an incident. Ram's wife also had hastily exited the cemetery and had darted off down the wet, slippery road. Within two minutes, all the mourners, except Ram and the gravediggers, had fled from the cemetery. The gravediggers, however, were not afraid, for both of them wore silver bracelets and chains. Nevertheless, they found it sagacious to stand by and allow Ram to take his wife's handbag from the grave.

After about seven terrifying minutes, Ram was able to retrieve the bag. He immediately dashed home, placed the bag on the road in front of the house, gathered some old newspapers, wrapped them around the bag and lit the object afire. He subsequently collected the ashes and threw them into the trench. Only after Ram had burnt the bag and disposed of the ashes was he was allowed to enter the house. All connections between the dead and Mrs. Ramgolam's bag were thus severed, hence the fear of Ma Pickins' ghost returning for Ram's wife completely diminished. Nevertheless, Mrs. Ramgolam went to bed wearing a blue strip of cloth tied around her arm as an extra precautionary measure. That night she served her husband his dinner but no conversation was exchanged. They ambled around the house, bearing blithe regard for each other because of Pigeon Goodfellow.

*   *   *

Rain, accompanied by monstrous peals of thunder and fork lightning, heralded the dawn of Friday morning. Fr. Perths spent a longer period of time that morning praying assiduously for success in his mission. It was the day that the judge and he were scheduled to meet Bishop Addington regarding the erection of the church in Brewster's Village. At precisely eight thirty, the judge's black Mercedes pulled up in front of the vicarage, which was about a half of a mile from the church. Fr. Perths donned his black trench coat and, hidden under his large black umbrella, hurried through the pouring rain to the car.

"An awful mess, this weather," the judge greeted him.

"Hope it's a sign of something good to come out of this meeting," the vicar responded.

"Should be a success," the judge assured him. "Incidentally, I spoke with Jeff Hutchins last night. Getting the permit will be a cinch. As soon as Mr. Horwood issues the drawing, I'll take it over to Jeff."

"We'll have to choose our words judiciously when we present out proposal to Bishop Addington," Fr. Perths advised.

"I suggest that you let me do the talking. You merely support. We'll let the positives preponderate. However, the art of successful persuasion is the striking of a delicate balance between the positive and the negative. *We* must present the negatives so that it will be perceived that we have indeed considered both sides," the judge explained.

"Brilliant!"

The Mercedes turned into Bishop's Court a few minutes before nine thirty. The watchman appeared from the guard hut which was at the side of the house and approached the car. His identity was hidden under the umbrella until he reached the car. The judge briefly rolled down the window.

"Good morning, Gilbert," Fr. Perths greeted the watchman.

"Oh…good mornin' Parson!" Gilbert reciprocated the warm greeting. "Good mornin' your honor."

"Still as diligent as ever, eh Gilbert?" Fr. Perths continued.

"I was expectin' y'all but I been waitin' in the hut 'cause of the rain," he explained. "I has a spare brolly under me arm in case you needs one," he offered.

"No. Thank you. We've got our umbrellas." Fr. Perths replied.

" 'ere, Bishop's goin' to see y'all upstairs. Follow me," Gilbert indicated as he led the two men toward the huge, oak front door. Before entering, he pressed the bell. Antoinette the housekeeper awaited them at the top of the stairs.

"Tell Bishop that the parson and the judge them is here," he ordered the fragile, aging figure at the top of the staircase. Greetings were exchanged and Antoinette curtseyed before retiring to the back to notify the bishop. The watchman escorted the men upstairs and offered them seats.

Anntoinette soon returned and approached Fr. Perths. "Bishop Addington will be with you shortly. He ask me to tell you that he's having fun with Mrs Addington."

"At this time of the morning?" Fr. Perths whispered to the judge.

"Such an activity does not conform to the dictates of time, or place for that matter." The judge quietly explained.

"Would you all likes a cup of tea?" the gracious housekeeper inquired.

"No. Thank you," Fr. Perths replied.

"Neither," echoed the judge.

"Bishop will be with you as soon as he's done with his wife. Please to excuse me." Again Antoinette curtseyed and made her exit.

"The impertinence of that woman to broadcast the bishop's privacy like that!" the judge exclaimed.

"How on earth did she know that the bishop was being tender to his wife?" Fr. Perths whispered again.

"She works here. She's probably familiar with his morning rituals."

Seconds later, the approaching sound of brisk footsteps was heard and Bishop Addington appeared. The two men rose respectfully.

"He's still rather energetic after such a rigorous ritual," Fr. Perths commented with his hand over his mouth.

"Gentlemen!" The Bishop greeted them with arms extended. "Such a delight!"

"My Lord," the judge replied with a slight bow of the head.

"Right Reverend Sir!" Fr. Perths responded.

After the brief acknowledgements were made the bishop invited the two visitors to sit. "I'm sorry to have you waiting, but I was on the phone with Mrs. Addington. She is away in Bermuda, spending some time with her sister."

"Oh, on the phone…" echoed Fr. Perths with a sigh of relief.

"Yes.…I asked Antoinette to let you know…"

"…She did. She did," interjected the judge. "So, how do you do, my Lord?"

"Brilliant," replied the bishop. "And I suppose that you gentlemen are doing fine…busy with all that work at St. Patrick's."

"Quite," responded Fr. Perths.

"As a matter of fact, it is with reference to all that hard work that we now seek audience with you," Mr. Pilchard declared.

"Wonderful. How can I be of assistance to you?" Bishop Addington inquired with simulated ignorance.

The judge presented a compendious explanation of the BOARD's plan to erect the church building in Brewster's Village. The bishop listened attentively as Mr. Pilchard presented the details of the project proposal. Fr. Perths remained obediently silent throughout the judge's presentation.

"The plan sounds wonderful," Bishop Addington admitted as he crossed his legs and began to twiddle his fingers. "What, if I may ask, was the motivation behind the vestry's plan to construct such a building? Did the people in the village indicate that the distance was prohibitive?"

"No, bishop," the judge replied. "But we realize the struggle that they go through in order to get to St. Patrick's, especially during the rainy seasons like now."

"Have you noticed a decline in attendance among the villagers, Father? I mean, your being here this morning seems indicative of your support of such a plan. Am I correct?" The Bishop's eyes pierced the obediently reticent priest.

"Well, yes. To a great extent, my Lord," he replied.

"To a great extent in what; your support or in decline in attendance?" the bishop inquired in his quest for further clarification.

"Well, both…both…," Fr. Perths answered.

"He believes that he will greatly miss the presence of the people from the village, my Lord, but he, like many of us, recognizes the urgent need for such a structure," the judge craftily intercepted.

"I see," the bishop responded. "Entangled in the web of sentimentality, Father?"

"I guess," the now visibly shaken priest confessed.

"Father, did you meet with the members from the village to get their feelings on this matter, or is it that the vestry has made a unilateral decision?" Bishop Addington pressed.

"One of the vestry members was assigned to do just that, bishop," Mr. Pilchard again cut in with an answer.

"To do what, inform the villagers or seek their input?" The bishop once more sought clarification.

"Both, my Lord." replied the judge.

"And they fully concurred?"

"From all accounts, they did, my Lord." Mr. Pilchard replied.

"There were no objections...."

"From all accounts, none, my Lord," the judge testified.

"Are you convinced that whoever this person was, who went to address the villagers about this, gave an accurate report of his meeting, Father. Do you feel that he has chosen to omit any objections?" Bishop Addington once more cross-examined the vicar.

"I believe that he has given me an authentic report, my Lord," the vicar sheepishly replied.

"Alright, gentlemen; I am willing to approve the plan but I will do so only after I have met the members – from Slough and Brewster's Village, of course – and discussed the project with them. You see, gentlemen, one has to be very careful when one is making decisions that affect different classes of people. One's decision, regardless of how fair it ultimately may be, can easily be misconstrued as favorable toward one group and biased toward another and consequently place one in a rather awkward position. So Father Perths, I want you to arrange a meeting with the villagers – at St. Patrick's of course. Tell them that I wish to address this issue with them and that I want their honest opinion. Encourage full attendance. I can come any time after Christmas but preferably before the end of January. As soon as you have notified them and you agree on a date, please contact me. But it must be before February."

"Certainly, my lord; I shall so do," Fr. Perths dutifully responded.

"Well, your honor," the bishop rose and extended his arm toward the judge, "it has been a pleasure. I do look forward to coming across to St. Patrick's in January."

"And Reverend Father," the bishop again extended his arm, "as soon as the date is set, please call the office and let Clementine know. I will fit it into my schedule."

"Certainly, my Lord," the deflated vicar swore.

The bishop remained at the top of the stairs after he closed the meeting with a brief prayer. The two men – the perfidious judge and the immodest priest, despondent and psychologically battered, stepped out into the drizzling rain. So mentally downtrodden were they that they did not even remember to open their umbrellas. Gilbert saw them hurrying toward the car and ran out to meet them with his umbrella.

" 'ere, sirs. Let me shelter y'all from the rain before y'all gets a cold," he offered.

"Thank you, Gilbert. But it's only a drizzle. We're fine," the judge responded.

The excessively gracious watchman remained beside the car until the two men got in and buckled themselves. Gilbert made one last attempt to seize the day by carping about the inclement weather. "Y'all be careful how y'all is drivin' back to Abersth in this nasty weather. Man, enough is enough, you know…almost four days in a row, this stupid rain. I can't go nowhere 'cause of this rain, and 'cause I ain't got no money. Imagine, Christmas jes' 'round the corner and I ain't got no money. What could be worse, eh Parson, wet and broke, heh heh!"

Reverend Perths fumbled in his pocket. "Alright Gilbert, let me give you something for Christmas."

"I'll give him, Father," Mr. Pilchard offered.

The judge lowered the window further and gave the dauntless mendicant a twenty dollar bill. "Have a happy Christmas, Gilbert!"

"T'ank you, your honor. This is me lucky week," the beaming watchman declared. "This is the second visitor from St. Patrick's to come 'round 'ere in one week."

"Oh yes?" the judge nonchalantly remarked as he ignited the engine. "Who else was here?"

"That man…with the silver jag…ah…."

"Silver jaguar…you…don't…mean…Peter Goodfellow, do you?" the judge inquired with a serious expression.

"Ah…yes, dhat's 'im, dhat's the bloke. Said 'is name was Peter Goodfellow. He was 'ere on Wednesday mornin'. Nice man. Good man," the watchman added.

"Yes. Good man. Good man." Fr. Perths reiterated. "You take care now."

The Mercedes pulled gracefully out of the driveway and swung left on King's Drive. The two men were quiet, tense, reserved. The rain began to pour and lash against the vehicle. After a prolonged period, the judge broke the silence.

"Awful…the rain, that is." The judge kept his attention on the road as he spoke with the solemnity of a death sentence.

"I wonder what he said to the bishop," Fr. Perths expressed in a distant tone.

"Worse than that; there is a traitor among the vestry. Someone has breached the vow of confidentiality," the pensive judge replied.

"Fenton Skeete, you think. He took stark objection to the project," Fr. Perths suggested.

"Highly unlikely; would be too obvious. He's too clever for that," the judge reasoned.

"Guess you're right," the vicar agreed. "Or Jason…perhaps…?"

"Only one thing left to do," the judge declared.

"What?"

"Prep the peasants. Get them on our side. Stall the process," the judge advised. "If we can delay the meeting until after January, then it is highly unlikely that the bishop will again find the time to get over to St. Patrick's to deal with such an insignificant matter."

"But he stated clearly that he wants to meet the people," the vicar protested.

"Perhaps because he might have been told that the people were not in agreement with the plan. Don't forget that Pigeon Goodfellow was there before us. You don't know what was said to the bishop. We have to cover all sides," the judge argued persuasively.

"Judge, we can't base our actions on groundless suspicion, or mere assumption. We are supposing that Mr. Goodfellow's visit was in regard to the project. He couldn't have had enough information to warrant a visit to the bishop. Furthermore, the fact that he was able to meet with the bishop before we did proves that the appointment was made even before the meeting at Faulkner's."

"Good point," the judge agreed.

"In addition, we can't blatantly disregard the bishop's orders. We're duty bound to call the meeting," Fr. Perths insisted.

"And a meeting there will be," the judge promised, "but at a later stage. Trust me Father, Bishop Addington will not roll our heads if a meeting in January is not possible. My belief is that he will appoint one of us, a neutral person or team, to conduct a meeting with the people and then report to him. Remember, he does not personally disapprove of the plan. All he wants to know is that the people are in agreement with it. It's as simple as that."

"I wish," Fr. Perths mumbled.

"Father," Mr. Pilchard proposed, "let me take care of this. Tell the bishop that you have placed the project in my hands. In my capacity as a judge, he will consider the political ramifications before attempting any drastic reprisals. He can discipline you, but he can't touch me. Let me captain this ship."

"I will, reluctantly, but I will, in faith," the timid but relieved vicar agreed.

"Good. Then I will go over to see the architect as soon as I drop you back to the vicarage. I'll start the ball rolling until we receive Bishop Addington's approval. This project will come to fruition, Father. I, Adolph Pilchard, am in the captain's seat. I, the famous judge, have spoken," Mr. Pilchard proclaimed.

Fr. Perths turned and studied the arrogant judge as he casually manipulated the steering wheel of the sleek, luxurious Mercedes. If this calm control were redolent of power, the frightened vicar thought, the transference of the Bishop's order would then be justified by ebullient success.

Chapter Six

Happy Holidays

Christmas week began with the Festival of Advent Lessons and Carols which was held on the Sunday evening. The festival was always followed by a Pre-Christmas party which was hosted by the vestry for the children of the community. However, none of the children from Brewster's Village or Slough was ever invited or encouraged to attend the party, even though some of them would attend the service with their parents. The custom was to have each of the children from Abersthwaithe bring a gift which would subsequently be delivered by appointed members of the vestry to the children in the surrounding villages. This year however, under the direction of Laurent Faulkner, invitations were issued to the children of the village. In addition, a slight change to the custom was made; none of the children was required to bring any gifts. *Faulkner & Babbit* provided the Santa Clause and the gifts – stuffed toys and Christmas crackers for the girls and cap-guns and cowboy hats for the boys. More than three hundred children and their parents attended the festival and party, but the children from the privileged homes in Abersthwaithe did not socialize with the children from Slough or Brewster's Village; nor did their parents encourage any fellowship among them. Such snobbery, however, neither daunted the young plebs' spirit nor hastened their departure. They sang, they danced, they played games, they ate and drank as if there were no tomorrow. Most of the privileged children made hasty exits immediately upon receiving their respective gifts from Santa Clause. Others stayed but remained in their own cliques.

The vestry and BOARD members made a salient effort to socialize with the peasants by serving them snacks and forming basic conversations. However, the wiser guests from the poor villages perceived their insincerity but nevertheless maintained their simple and unpretentious dignity. Teacher Lovell complained about the vestry's condescending manner and swore that she would never attend another Christmas party at St. Patrick's.

After all of the guests had departed, the BOARD met briefly with the vestry in the common room, as planned, so as to evaluate their progress. They closed and locked the door because the members of the Special Activities Committee, under Rex's supervision, were still in the building cleaning the parish hall.

"Well, I think we have been able to win their loyalty," Laurent Faulkner asserted after Ruthel provided the opening prayer.

"To some extent, I'd say," Sam Westwater partially agreed.

"What do you mean, Sam? Didn't you see how that horde guzzled the food and drinks? They probably have never eaten or drunk like that in their lives, you know what I mean; plus Santa…the gifts. Come on, Sam. We've practically got them eating out of our hands!" Bill Jones argued.

"Agreed. But there's more to those people than meets the eye," Mr. Pilchard warned. "And now that we know that Goodfellow's been seeing the bishop, we can't assume anything. Furthermore, we have all established that there is a traitor among us. Heaven knows what those people are thinking. It therefore stands to reason that they may be playing the very game that we are playing."

"I concur," Aaron Ishmael voiced from the far corner. "And if I may be so presumptuous, I would dare to say that my suspicions of the traitor rest with Maggie Billings. Notice she hasn't been around too much lately."

"And how do you suppose she was able to do that, Ishmael, when you perspicuously stated that she has been absent?" the judge inquired in a tone that was laced with disdain.

"Please, don't take it personally, Pilchard. This is not a personal attack on anyone. I'm merely stating my feelings. It stands to reason that she, or Jason Coleman, or even Pigeon Goodfellow, may be equally guilty. Isn't one entitled to think, and express one's opinion?" Aaron asked defensively.

"Yes. But when one's reasoning borders on irrationality, or absurdity for that matter, one should keep one's thoughts to oneself," the judge snapped.

"You kiss my…"

"Gentlemen!" Laurent Faulkner interjected, "let us focus on our mission. We can't afford to enervate ourselves by attacking each other like this. And

Ishmael, we wouldn't tolerate this kind of impertinence. You're speaking to the most prominent judge in the land, a man who is respected and held in honor by the citizens of this country!"

"And I am Aaron Ishmael, equally respected by those who know me, and I will not tolerate his impertinence either. We both are men alike, cut from the same cloth!"

"Like bloody hell we are, Ishmael!" the judge shouted.

Aaron momentarily contemplated the judge with a deathlike silence and then rose and took up his bag and umbrella. "You're right, Pilchard. To think that you and I are cut from the same cloth is absolutely preposterous. Good evening and merry Christmas to you all."

"This meeting is not over, Mr. Ishmael. Please take your seat!" Mr. Faulkner ordered.

"It is for me, Faulkner. It has been for a long time but I am only now officially taking my leave," Aaron replied.

"If you walk out of that door, Ishmael, you can forget about ever returning," Faulkner threatened.

"I do not plan on returning, Faulkner. And even if I did, you don't have the authority to prevent me. So go to hell. *You* can kiss my ass, you shameless arriviste!" Aaron took one final, murderous glance at the judge and departed.

"How much more of this are we going to have to endure, Madame Pigthorne?" Art Kimble asked. "Can't we as a vestry see what is happening right in our faces? First there was Goodfellow, then Coleman, now Ishmael."

"Perhaps you will be kind enough to explain to us what is happening, Kimble?" Faulkner retorted sarcastically.

"This," Art indicated with the showing of the hand, "this usurpation of the vestry's authority; this blatant disrespect for the officers of this church. Even if your intentions as a BOARD are ultimately honorable, they come across as grossly offensive."

"Pardon our intrusion, Kimble, but this BOARD has not usurped the vestry's authority. All we are trying to do is to assist you all by offering advice and support. I hardly find that offensive," Faulkner explained.

"Speak for yourself, Art Kimble," Eloise Pigthorne added defensively. "This vestry has no objections to any assistance from the BOARD."

"You're even too daft to realize that you have absolutely no power in your capacity as senior warden, eh, Eloise?" Art rejoined.

"That's not the point, Kimble!" Eloise snapped.

"You can go too, Kimble, like the rest of them," Tessie Shoehorn interposed. "Then we would have gotten rid of all the stupid, troublemaking buffoons."

"No one's speaking to you, Tessie. And who the hell are you calling a stupid buffoon, you fat, tetchy, insipid walrus!" Art replied.

"I like this meeting, comrades. I really like it. It's one of the most productive meetings I've ever attended. We've achieved absolutely nothing. Not a damn thing," Sam complained. "Meanwhile, the so-called traitors are probably planning a powerful counter attack."

"You can call me all the names you want, Kimble. I still rest my case, flippin' idiot." Tessie grumbled.

"And I rest mine too, Tessie. It's too fat and heavy to be carried around," Art retorted.

"Can we please return to the matter at hand, ladies and gentlemen? I've had a long, tiring, stressful day," Ruthel pleaded.

"And it shows," Art responded.

The sanctimonious old woman gasped and fixed Art a piercing stare, but said nothing.

Mr. Pilchard rose and stepped to the front of the room. "Ladies and gentlemen, do we wish to continue our project in Brewster's village, for if we don't, then I beg to adjourn this meeting right now and forget everything. The BOARD will step away and the vestry will be left on its own, to the mercy of the riff-raffs."

Silence followed.

"I take it then that your reticence is indicative of your willingness and readiness to get to work and to stop this foolishness right now…right now!" the irate judge demanded.

Silence again prevailed.

"Mr. Faulkner, you may continue," the judge ordered and returned to his seat.

"As we were saying, my friends, I believe that we have made a positive impact on the peasants. We should now proceed to stage two," Mr. Faulkner suggested. "Does anyone have another opinion?"

The silence continued.

"Then our next step, my friends, is to arrange a meeting with Mrs. Ramgolam. She will be the one through whom we will execute our plan. Meanwhile, Mr. Pilchard has already approached the architect and the town hall official. Both parties are with us on this."

"What about the bishop? He is the crucial factor in all of this," Fritz Batty inquired.

"The plan is to get the people on our side; get them to buy the idea and convince the bishop that they are as excited as we about the new church in Brewster's Village. It's their response that the bishop wants, not ours. Our success with this project is contingent upon our success with the people, and I think that the party this evening has put us in good stead."

"Here, here!" Fritz remarked.

"Then onward, Christian soldiers! I'll invite Mrs. Ramgolam to a special planning meeting at my home on Tuesday evening. Mrs. Pigthorne, Mr. Pilchard and I will sit with her and set the wheels in motion," Faulkner announced.

"Excellent!" Sam exclaimed.

"May I make a suggestion?" Glayds Barnwell begged.

"Permission granted," Faulkner replied.

"Our Old Year's Night Party," Gladys suggested, "could we invite a select group from Slough and Brewster's village. It's rather late now but they'll be thrilled to come. If nothing gets them on our side, this certainly will."

A few seconds of silence followed before the judge stated his opinion.

"Gladys, that is a brilliant idea; an absolutely fantastic idea. I agree."

"So moved," cried Sam.

"Second," added Ruthel.

"Those in favor?" Faulkner inquired.

The vote was unanimous. The preparation of the guest list and the distribution of invitations were assigned to Eloise who graciously accepted the responsibility. The meeting thus drew to a close. As the members prepared to leave, Fritz stepped out to the subdued corridor and made his was toward the toilet. A shadow flashed across the wall ahead of him, followed by the sound of hurried, delicate footsteps and the gentle closing of a door. A momentary fear seized the undertaker and by the time he regained his composure and sounded an alarm, the phantom had completely disappeared. Some of the men subsequently searched the building but all the members of the Special Activities Committee had gone and the lights in the kitchen and parish hall were extinguished. Before they finally departed, the judge implored all of them to be on guard for any signs of traitorous behavior among the remaining vestry members or by those who had relinquished their positions.

* * *

Within five minutes of the vestry and BOARD's departure, the rain began to drizzle again. Minutes later, torrents from the saturated clouds began pouring down on the black Mercedes as it circled Westminster Lane for a safe and discreet parking spot. Mr. Pilchard regarded the downpour a blessing since it gave him the opportunity to completely conceal himself in his black trench coat, hat and large, black umbrella. More advantageously, it allowed him to carry Maggie's gift unobtrusively through the dark street.

The profuse, colorful fairy lights which embellished some of the houses made little impact on the darkness of the wet, December night as the judge crept stealthily beneath the black pall of night toward his mistress' house.

Christmas music echoed from the house as the judge approached the door. He breathed a sigh of relief as he turned the key and closed the door behind him. Normally, he would press the bell so as not to alarm Maggie by his sudden appearance, but his time he crept up the stairs, bearing the gift in his outstretched arm. It was customary for the judge to have Maggie's gift delivered on Christmas Eve day. Under the guise of platonic friendship, he would have a huge basket comprising fruit and sweetmeats sent to her house, as well as to other households consisting of family members and close friends. However, because of the tension in the church and the phantoms which have been appearing in the night as he approached or exited Maggie's house, he thought it wise to refrain from ordering Maggie's fruit basket this year. When he bought Maggie's gift, he gave the saleswoman the impression that it was for a relative who had always been especially good to him. In order to further quell any suspicion, he signed the card in her presence and put a fictitious name on the envelope. Thus his secret mission was successful. He managed to purchase the gift and enter Maggie's home unobtrusively. However, halfway up the slightly curved staircase, he heard the sound of Maggie's voice engaged in conversation with another person. The other voice was sonorous and hauntingly familiar. The judge paused. He was too embarrassed and afraid to proceed or retreat. He contemplated making a sound so as to announce his presence, but before he could act on the thought, he recognized the voice. He froze in horror. The rich baritone of the mysterious stranger who had appeared out of the darkness and had accompanied him to his car during his last visit, accosted his ear like the roll call on doomsday.

"Perhaps, Margaret, transferring your membership to St Paul's might be the best thing for you to do, don't you think?" The tone was persuasive.

"Your suggestion is wise, but merely temporary – not to mention impractical. I am looking for permanent comfort, security, love that I can call my own. Transferring is not going to provide that, Wilberforce." Maggie's voice bore a hint of urgency.

"Then what do you think would be the best thing for you to do at this point?" the voice inquired.

"Remain at St. Patrick's, but be as infrequent in my attendance as I am now until such time."

"And what if such a time does not materialize?" the voice pressed.

A surge of ambivalence swept over the judge. He wanted to know the subject of the discussion, but he also thought it wise to vacate the premises without their knowledge of his presence. However, jealousy directed him to proceed further up the stairway, but as he made the first step forward, the visitor rose from wherever he was sitting and headed toward the stairs.

"Margaret, I know that you will do ultimately what is best for you. You have always been the wiser of the two of us, so I know that you will achieve what you set out for. I have no doubts about that. I hope that you will like your gift. Merry Christmas!"

The brief silence that followed suggested some physical embrace. Mr. Pilchard quickly concealed the gift under his now unbuttoned coat, and with brisk steps, mounted the rest of the stairway. His appearance startled the couple as they stood in casual embrace.

"Adolph! When did you arrive?" Maggie asked as she gently pushed the visitor aside.

"Just got here. Didn't you hear the door? Well, I guess you *couldn't...*" the judge sarcastically remarked as he placed his hat and umbrella on the coat rack.

The two men momentarily studied each other in absolute silence. Maggie trembled in fear and began to nervously rub her hands together as she awkwardly beheld the two men contemplating each other in a deathly coldness.

"Good evening, sir," the stranger greeted the judge with a slight bow of the head. "It's a pleasure to see you again."

"Likewise," the judge replied with a stolid expression.

"Do you two men know each other?" Maggie asked with a forced, nervous smile.

"Casually," the judge answered as he averted his attention from the stranger and approached the coat rack again to remove his coat without revealing the gift.

"Yes. Casually," the stranger echoed in his polished, baritone voice as he stared at the judge. "By happenstance we met one night as he was scurrying through the darkness to his car. We shared a light banter before heading to our respective homes."

The judge made no comment but turned slightly to acknowledge the stranger. As the stranger spoke, he looked directly at the judge and their eyes met briefly. Mr. Pilchard was able for the second time to look the stranger squarely in the face. This time, the colored lights from Maggie's Christmas tree and the lamps threw light on him and the judge was able to make a more detailed mental sketch of his facial features. The stranger was a relatively handsome man, dignified, exquisitely groomed and impeccably attired. The judge felt the pangs of jealousy gnawing at his emotions, but sagacity dictated that he conduct himself with augustness.

"I trust that you are in the process of leaving," the judge quipped with an air of grandiloquence. "And as you trudge through the mire toward your modest abode, I pray the Lord be with you."

"I live in *The Victorian Mansion*," the stranger retorted. His expression became rigid and his sunken eyes fixed the judge a gorgonian stare.

"Impressive. I never knew that there were janitor's quarters there," the judge nonchalantly remarked as he poured himself a shot of bourbon.

"Yes, there are," the stranger replied, "but my three bedroom flat is located on the third floor, overlooking the garden and fountain."

The judge said nothing more to the stranger, and as he turned toward Maggie, he noticed that the stranger was still staring him in the face.

"Pray have a good night, sir, and a blessed and peaceful Christmas," the stranger proclaimed. "And oh, incidentally, as you creep through the darkness back to your wife, I pray the Lord have mercy on you. Goodnight, Margaret."

The stranger gave Maggie one more kiss on the cheek and left without uttering another word to the judge, who remained at the bar with the glass in his hand.

"That was quite an interesting re-acquaintance, I must say," Maggie remarked after the stranger left.

Mr. Pilchard slammed his glass on the bar counter and stormed across the room to Maggie. "What the hell was that man doing here? And who the hell is he?"

Maggie turned away and began to clear one of the coffee tables of the china which she had used to entertain the stranger. The judge grabbed her forcibly and swung her round to face him.

"Woman, I am speaking to you. Who the hell is that man…that blasted jackass who has the impertinence to speak sarcastically to me?"

"I am equally perplexed to know how *you* became acquainted with him. You obviously know each other well enough to stand in my drawing room and spit venom at each other."

The infuriated judge grabbed Maggie by the arm as she attempted to turn once more to clear the china from the table. "I want an answer, Maggie; now!"

Maggie assumed her full height and glared at him. "Take you hand off of me, Adolph Pilchard," she hissed.

"Is this what you've been up to all this time, eh, playing the bloody harlot, with that …that ostentatious nigger!" the judge snarled as he grabbed Maggie closer.

"Kindly remove your person from me, Adolph. I resent your insinuations and your arrogance. How dare you come into my house and cast insulting and sarcastic remarks to my guest! I believe that I deserve more respect than that, don't you think, Adolph?"

"I get it. Of course I get it," the judge complained as he removed his hand and turned away. "You want out…all of the suspicions scare you, eh, so you seek comfort in your neighbor's arms. And why not; after all, he's only a stone's throw away, literally. He doesn't place you second to his wife, I suppose. When you need company, all he's got to do is climb the fence and he's up here, up under your skirt!"

"Adolph!" Maggie shouted. "Stop it, at once! He's merely a friend, a very good friend in whom I confide. We've known each other for years."

"Doesn't he have anything to do at home on a night like this, you know, like trim a Christmas tree or something? The man looks as mad as a hatter!" the judge remarked with scorn.

"He's lonely, that's all. He stops by every now and then. He merely came to spend a few minutes with me and have a cup of tea for the Christmas season."

"Interesting. Any other man would have a shot o' scotch or bourbon or something. He comes over for a cup of tea. I know, Maggie, you didn't expect me here tonight. So my sudden appearance surprises and angers you. Cup of tea my foot; he came for his Christmas gift, early enough to beat the crowd. Goodnight, Ms. Billings. I'm sorry to have come unannounced. I forgot that I needed to call to reserve a number." The judge stormed across the room to the coat rack and donned his coat and hat. "Oh, by the way, happy Christmas." He removed the gift from the coat pocket and handed it to Maggie, who stood observing his odd behavior.

"No. Thank you, Adolph. I accept cash only for my favors." Maggie gathered the china and exited toward the kitchen without another word.

The judge followed her to the kitchen and stood at the entrance. "I'm sorry, Maggie, but the mere thought of another man even talking to you drives me to the brink of irrationality. I love you beyond human understanding."

"And I love you too, Adolph. But such behavior can expose us," Maggie explained as she wiped her hands in the Egyptian cotton kitchen towel.

"Sometimes I don't care, my love. Sometimes I want the whole world to know, but I don't think that humans have developed enough or have reached the level of sophistication enough to fully understand that a man can love another woman as much as, or more than, he loves his wife; and so I am bound to stay married. But my love for you is as boundless as the ocean, Maggie," the judge confessed.

Maggie turned from the sink and beheld the man for whose love she would die. She gave him a coy smile and stepped across the marble tiled floor towards him. "Christmas is not a time to foster anger and harbor hatred. Kiss me, you jealous devil!"

After a passionate expression of affection, the judge again offered Maggie the gift. He insisted that she open it immediately. Her large, heavily made-up eyes became as bright as the star on her Christmas tree. The diamond sparkled like a thousand colorful lights.

"Oh, Adolph!" her eyes became teary as she took the necklace from the box. The diamond pendant hung from a chain of white gold. Once more, they kissed. "Shall I present my gift to you now, sweetheart?"

"When have I ever refused anything from you?" the judge replied.

"Then wait here until I summon you. I can't bring it to you; you have to come and get it for yourself," Maggie said with a tantalizing expression.

"But Maggie, how will I slip something large into the house without Mrs. Pilchard noticing…"

"…shhh!" she interrupted him as she sauntered towards her bedroom.

About ten minutes had elapsed before Maggie opened the bedroom door and invited the judge to get his gift. However, she did not appear at the door, but the gentle fragrance of roses and wild thyme effused from the candle lighted room. The judge took a deep breath and entered the room. He gasped as he beheld his mistress reclining seductively on her new, queen sized, canopy bed. Her flowing silk negligee of leopard skin pattern was slightly parted to reveal the seductive undergarment of similar design. She had caressed her skin with scented creams and set her hair to fall carelessly about her shoulders. Beside her was a pair of silk boxers of similar leopard skin design. The light from the scented candles cast suggestive shadows across the room as the judge stood at the door with mouth agape and eyes opened in taurine amazement. When he finally regained composure, he closed the door.

The chime of the grandfather clock as it heralded the midnight hour echoed throughout the house. The poignancy of the chimes awakened the judge from his deathlike slumber. He jumped off the bed in a state of delirious agitation and threw on his clothes. They both agreed that the pair of boxers would remain at Maggie's house to be used only on special occasions. Within minutes, the judge was descending the stairs in desperation. He had promised Mrs. Pilchard that he was going to return early enough to trim the Christmas tree as was customary every year on the evening of the service of Advent Lessons and Carols. It was now eight minutes after midnight and he was scampering through his mistress' garden towards the gate as the annoyance of the drizzling rain seemed to chide him for his unfaithfulness. He darted along the dark street, consumed with thoughts of a reasonable excuse to make to his wife, until he reached his car. As he fumbled through his pockets for his keys, he felt the overwhelming presence of something dark and sinister behind him. He spun around in terror as a deep, cultured voice greeted him from the car that was parked obliquely opposite his Mercedes.

"Good morning, judge Pilchard," the unexpected, but terrifyingly familiar voice pierced his heart and soul as he stood there, too shaken to move. The car door swung slowly open and a tall, dark, familiar figure wearing a black coat and fedora stepped out.

"Isn't it strange – these ironic encounters between you and me? We seem to be meeting at all and sundry places, at these odd hours of the night when I should be relaxing with a book and a cigar, and perhaps a glass of wine in my leather recliner; and you, you should be at home relaxing with your wife on the sofa in front of the television. Nevertheless, here I am on the street on a wet, cool night like this, and here you are, creeping from your mistress' house at ten minutes after midnight. Mere randomness or part of some divine purpose, you think?"

As the figure drew closer, the judge recognized the dark, handsomely sculptured face and the penetrating, sunken eyes. "What in the blazes do you want? Why the hell do you keep haunting me like a demon in the night? What do you want?" the judge clamored.

The figure beheld him momentarily. "What's mine. You have yours. Leave mine alone!" the stranger commanded in a deep, threatening tone.

"What the hell are you referring to?" the judge inquired as tension mounted within him.

"The woman I love. The one whose pasture you've obviously just been grazing in. You smell of it, you lecher!" the stranger stepped closer to the judge, almost brushing against him.

The judge backed away and opened the door. "Go to hell. Go to bloody hell!"

"You come back here one more time, and you'll be going with me, judge!" the stranger warned.

"Is that a threat?"

"No. It's a promise!" the stranger declared. "It's because of you that Margaret wouldn't surrender her love to me. You come here with your charm and your prestige, to seduce my woman, then go home and cuddle your wife. You have what is yours and still covet what's mine!?"

"I guess that some of us are just blessed. That's the way of life," the judge responded as he entered his car dismissively and turned the key.

The stranger rushed to the front of the vehicle to intercept it. "You son of a bitch! You bloody hypocrite! You want her, eh, you'll have to kill me. Go ahead. Run me over, because I'm not going to give up until she's mine, you hear; mine, all bloody mine!"

The judge revolved the engine in a futile attempt to intimidate his seemingly irrational rival. "Get your mad ass from in front of my car before I run over your ugly face!" the judge yelled from the half opened window.

The stranger bent over by the side of the road and picked up a huge stone, almost the size of a cement block and raised his hand to hurl the deadly object towards the windscreen, in the direction of the judge's face. "Flaming adulterer, I'll tell your wife!"

The judge quickly put the car into gear and pressed the accelerator. The vehicle thrust forward with a deadly force and knocked the stranger about ten yards away. As he struggled to rise from the wet road, the judge, in sizzling rage, drove the vehicle towards him and ran over him. The car continued down the street and banked the corner.

It was about two hours later when the stranger's body was discovered by the side of a dark blue Fiat which was parked about fifty yards from Maggie's house. Maggie never heard of her friend's death until Christmas Eve morning, when the report of a hit-and –run accident appeared on the front page of The Argosy, Ischalton's most widely circulated newspaper.

Mrs. Pilchard was fast asleep when the judge returned home. He was trembling in fear as he entered the house, and breathed a sigh of relief when he realized that Mrs. Pilchard was soundly sleeping. He quietly slipped into his pajamas, and after guzzling a potent shot of whiskey, crept into bed, terrified by the ordeal he had just gone through, but nevertheless comforted by the fact that the man who had threatened to bring about his downfall was no more; that the man who was making him afraid to venture into Westminster Lane was out of the way; that the man who was his rival could no longer conquer woman whom he loved so much. He had eventually solved the puzzle that had been baffling him for a long time – the bouquet of flowers and the stranger in the car that night after he left Maggie's house. He had wrongfully accused Pigeon Goodfellow. Now the true culprit was dead, and all of the judge's secrets will be buried with him. The judge thus fell asleep with the thought that he would rise a few hours later, happy that Maggie Billings was an intimate part of his life, and that they would continue to be together for a long time.

* * *

Christmas Eve day was as wet as the previous days. Sporadic downpours of rain descended upon the island as the stores in Georgetown overflowed with last minute shoppers. The radio stations were airing the old Christmas favorites as the bustling crowd braved the showers for gifts. In Brewster's Village, puddles were growing into swamps as the deluge continued to create havoc on the dirt roads. The aroma of black cake and pepperpot filled the air as the villagers prepared their outfits for the Christmas Eve vigil and mass at St. Patrick's. Christmas Eve was another of those rare occasions when the four social circles worshipped together. However, the lavish Christmas dinner in the parish hall, which followed the service, was attended only by the two upper circles. The lower circles had the privilege of serving, as they did on Harvest Sunday. Consequently, the villagers who were on the select list of servers were not only preparing their attire for the mass, but also their serving outfits which were going to be put in a bag and taken out at the end of the service when they would assume their honorable roles. This year, however, a select number of villagers from both Brewster's Village and Slough were invited to attend the function. It was the first for them and so it brought them much attention in the villages. The guest of honor for this year was the outgoing senior warden – Mrs. Eloise Pigthorne. The function was also the place where the incoming warden and newly elected vestry members were given the traditionally special welcome. In addition to the honorees, the elected chairpersons of the newly formed Public Relations Committee, Beautification Committee and the Special Activities Committee were invited. However, Uncle Ed, the chairperson of the Beautifications committee, declined the invitation, ostensibly to attend a family celebration.

Mr. Ramgolam left his stall in the market earlier than the other vendors because he was a guest at the Christmas dinner, by dint of his wife's position as Public Relations Chairperson. He left his cousin, Pissy Ragnauth to manage the stall which was busier than usual because of the holiday season. After Ram severed his relationship with Pigeon, he returned to his stall on a daily basis, but he told Pissy to remain in the position as storekeeper, just in case Pigeon had sought his favor again. Over the last few weeks, Ram and his wife had been mildly estranged as a result of their political differences. However, Ram took advantage of the opportunity to attend such a prestigious function and dine with the social elite. He got a haircut and had his hair dyed jet black. Mrs. Ramgolam remained at home to prepare herself for the grand occasion. Ram's sudden enthusiasm to attend the dinner had convinced his wife that his opposition to her cooperation with Pigeon and the BOARD was motivated by jealousy, thus she told her husband that she would dismiss any thoughts of abandoning her office as Public Relations Officer. Furthermore, she decided that she would support the BOARD and vestry in their plan to erect the church in Brewster's Village because, she explained to Ram, they were most likely going to appoint her as the senior warden – a position which she assumed would place her in the same position in Brewster's Village as her counterpart in Abersthwaithe.

The villagers might have relished the idea of attending the dinner as guests – or even servers, but they had their own celebrations. They would congregate at various places and partake of highly potent local wines made of corn and rice, and locally distilled rum. Food was prepared in abundance and there would be singing of favorite Christmas hymns and songs, and dancing. Sporadic outbursts of swearing and fighting under the influence of the alcoholic beverages would emerge but would quickly be brought under control by the residents who strove to maintain the peace of Christmas. However, none of the local celebration would begin until the people had returned from church. In addition, food was prepared and given to members of the community who lacked the means to celebrate Christmas. Also, homemade gifts were exchanged or given to the most senior members and poorer children of the community. Some of the men in the village would parade as Santa Clause in locally made outfits which were funded by some of the business owners in the village. In Brewster's Village and Slough, every effort was made to celebrate Christmas as a community. However, the privacy of those who chose not to participate – like Maudie Springer and Rexworth Davis – was respected.

Nine o'clock drew close as the rain continued to drizzle across the island. The bells of St. Patrick's Church were programmed to chime Christmas carols every hour, and at eight o'clock, it chimed a verse of *Silent Night*. Earlier in the day, Pigeon had arranged to give Jason a ride to church for the Christmas Eve service. At precisely eight thirty, the silver jaguar pulled up in front of Jason's home. Pigeon had encouraged his wife to drive the other car to the church ostensibly because he was going to make a brief stop in Brewster's Village after the dinner, so as to attend one of the celebrations at *Brad's Palace*. Once Jason entered the car, they began to discuss the issues at the church with no hindrances.

"...Any further progress with the Bishop?" Pigeon inquired as he pressed the play button of the vehicle's impressive stereo system.

"No. But I understand that he is requesting a meeting with the villagers," Jason replied.

"How'd you know?"

"From Fenton Skeete," Jason answered. "...Spoke to him today...ran into him and his wife...shopping at Bookers."

"Well, this is what I want you to do for me, Jason. I want you to befriend Fenton..."

"...We *are* friends," Jason interrupted.

"Really? Well, I want you to get the man in bed with you, Jason – not literally, of course," Pigeon commanded the young, impetuous Jason. "Through Fenton, we could bring the BOARD to its knees. If you do this for me, Jason, I will raise you up, ecclesiastically and socially. Remember, I'm not only one of the island's most successful barristers, but I am now the senior warden at St. Patrick's – I've scored two concurrent sixes. I need a faithful team, and I am depending on my most trusted friends, like you.

You are relatively young and you will be an asset on that vestry, especially in bridging the generation gap. We have a lot of young professionals returning from the mother country, young people who are seeking to assert themselves. My plan is to get them on board, you know – fresh, active creative minds."

"I see," Jason responded.

"Can we toast on this at the dinner tonight?" the crafty Pigeon Goodfellow proposed.

"It's a promise," Jason swore.

"Tonight, I want you to stay close to Fenton. Set things up tonight. But be very subtle. The BOARD will be watching you like hawks. Then, before we go home I want you to come to Brewster's Village with me. However, don't tell Fenton about it. It will make things too obvious and rouse suspicion."

"Got it!" Jason replied as he took one last puff of the cigarette.

The two men continued in conversation about a variety of subjects, including Jason's accounting business which was beginning to wane as a result of a new British accounting firm, *Adams & Perverly*, which had opened offices across the island and was recruiting the students who were returning from universities abroad, and in particular, the British institutions. The returning students who were Anglican were going to be among the next generation of *Gold Circle* members who would assume their position at St. Patrick's and in society.

The church was nearly filled by the time Pigeon and Jason arrived. Rex was directing two men from the Beautification Committee who were placing additional chairs along the side aisles. As usual, he was directing the members of the lower circles to the back of the nave. Most of the villagers had worn their Wellingtons because of the swampy roads in the village, but once the women reached the church, they removed theirs and donned patent leather shoes which matched their festive attire. Maudie Springer had arrived earlier and chose to sit on one of the additional chairs along the side aisle. Rex maintained his distance from her.

As Pigeon entered the church, the Ramgolams arrived in a specially hired car. The vehicle was old and the wheels and bumpers were covered with the red mud that constituted the arterial roads in the village. There was still a mild drizzle, but a man came out of the front passenger's side of the old Morris Oxford, bearing a large umbrella, and opened the vehicle's back door. Mrs. Ramgolam stepped out while her husband exited from the other door. The man escorted Mrs. Ramgolam to the front door and closed the umbrella while he waited for Mr. Ramgolam to enter the building. The ushers gasped as they beheld the Ramgolams in their formal attire. The man who stood regimentally by Mrs. Ramgolam's side was the man whom the villagers had appointed to be her bodyguard after she was nearly assaulted by a bottle throwing scoundrel at the meeting at *Brad's Palace*. The escort took the bulletins from the usher and proceeded ahead of them down the center aisle towards the front pews. Half way down the aisle, Rex intercepted them. He gave no verbal directions but directed them back to the rear with an outstretched arm and extended index finger, accompanied by a stern expression. The bodyguard stopped and glared at him, and the two men stood facing each other in stark defiance as the Ramgolams stood in rehearsed dignity behind the bodyguard. Pigeon beheld the couple with quiet amusement as they held hands in the center of the aisle. Mr. Ramgolam wore a black suit and a pair of brown leather shoes. A green and red diagonally stripped tie and white shirt, with a black fedora, completed the outfit. Mrs. Ramgolam created quite a stir among the congregation with her ruffled, black skirt which fell just above her knees, to reveal the top of her knee-high white, fish net stockings which, she later boasted, someone had brought for her from a recent trip to the United States. Her red and green long sleeved blouse featured large symmetrical motifs of diamante. A broad, gold leatherette belt was drawn tightly around her waist and clasped by a huge, resplendent buckle. She was shod in a pair of black, patent leather boots which rose just below her calves, while a tiny, sequined gold bag was strung stupidly across her right shoulder and rested on her left hip. A profuse assortment of jewelry completed the ensemble. However, it was the blond, synthetic mass that drew the most attention – and suppressed laughter from the congregation. Rejuvenated curls cascaded at the back while the top was gathered into a huge bun. Red and greed satin ribbons held the bun in place. The front was combed forward and trimmed just above the eyebrows. Mrs. Ramgolam donned a large, white circular pair of spectacles for added effect. She stood erect, with her head raised almost to the ceiling as if oblivious to the gaping crowd.

Pigeon contemplated the couple as he whispered to Jason. "Imagine that those two had the audacity to visit me at my office, seeking to work with me in my capacity as warden – those two. I pray that they would choose not to sit beside me – or even close enough to exchange greetings publicly. Do you know how embarrassing that would be!"

"You got to sit at the back. There ain't no more seats up in the front," Rex commanded the bodyguard. Pigeon breathed a sigh of relief.

In order to flaunt his new position as supervisor to the Beautification Committee, Rex added a rector's cape, which fell elegantly around his shoulders. He stood in the center of the aisle with his chest puffed up with pride.

"Damn fool," Pigeon again whispered to Jason. "Look at him. He thinks that the smiles on the faces of the upper circles are indications of admiration. They're only laughing at him…and his cape, knowing them."

"I see some empty seats in the front," the bodyguard protested, "why we can't sit deh?"

"Cause them seats is for important peoples," Rex snapped.

"Well these people is important people, so move from in front o'me!" the bodyguard warned the arrogant sexton, "'fore I drag you outside an' bust you' old wrinkle up face."

One of the men sitting nearby rose and whispered something to Rex, who subsequently moved aside for the trio to proceed to the front and take their seats. Shortly before the service began, Maggie Billings arrived and was escorted to the pew in which the Ramgolams sat. She cast a disapproving look towards them but smiled politely when the bodyguard perceived her snobbery. Even when she averted her attention, the guard still stared menacingly at her. She seemed agitated throughout the service. Mr. Pilchard and his wife sat in the opposite pew, and bowed their heads respectfully as Maggie acknowledged them. Pigeon made sporadic glances towards the judge as he sat between his wife and mistress, and pointed out his uneasiness to Jason. However, he did not share the reason for the judge's agitation. When the service began, Pigeon drew Jason's attention to the fact that Rex no longer wore the rector's cape. The two men suppressed their laughter.

The service was magnificent, and the choir sang a wonderful and spirited anthem. Philbert's rich, mellifluous tenor voice could be heard soaring across the church as he sang the more difficult tenor harmonies. Some of the members described Philbert's presence in the choir as the only negative aspect of the entire celebration. Nevertheless, they congratulated Fr. Perths for the way in which the celebration was conducted. That night, the vicar preached an ironically dynamic sermon on the inclusiveness of God's salvation through the incarnation, stressing that all persons sitting in the congregation were brothers and sisters in God's household. During the sermon, Stella Dawkins sold over twenty bootlegged videos and Christmas cassettes. She had a strict policy of never pushing adulterated videos during the Christmas, Holy Week and Easter services. That night, she placed a generous offering in the collection plate.

At the end of the mass, the select members of the congregation proceeded to the parish hall for the customary festive dinner. The others headed back to their respective villages through the heavy drizzle. At the end of the service, Pigeon had suggested to Reverend Perths and some of the members that the congregation remain in the church and sing Christmas carols until the rain stopped. However, neither the vicar nor the privileged members who remained were particularly concerned about their Christian brothers and sisters having to brave the drizzle and potential downpour as they hurried back to the squalor of the village. They replied that it was best for the people to return to carry out their traditional celebration.

As the remaining congregation entered the parish hall, they were greeted by waiters and waitresses bearing trays covered with drinks and an array of delectable hors-d'oeuvres. Pigeon drew close to Jason as the guests filed into the hall.

"There's Fenton. Go over and talk to him. Don't let him get away. Catch him and fish out every bit of information before he becomes intoxicated. I am going to ignore you for the rest of the night so as not to evoke any suspicion. And listen, Jason, I don't know where I stand with him, so if he should vilify me, play along with it; just do whatever it takes to get information," Pigeon whispered.

"Right," Jason agreed and headed across the hall to Fenton Skeete as he was taking a seat at one of the corner tables.

"My brother!" Jason greeted the unsuspecting Fenton. "All the best for the season."

They shook hands as Fenton reciprocated the greeting. "Haven't seen you since the meeting at Faulkner. How's it going? We miss you."

"Brilliant!" Jason responded. "Anyone sitting here?"

"No. Mrs. Skeete had to hurry back home to complete the baking. She had left the oven on low while we were in church. I'm just here to show my support, you know how it goes... Please, sit."

"Thank you." Jason wasted no time in seizing the opportunity to subtly charm and interrogate the trusting Fenton. "May I get you a drink? I'm going to get one for myself."

"Thank you. A scotch on the rocks, please."

Jason headed over to the bar where Pigeon was standing and observing him, and confabulating with Bill Jones and two other men who were neither on the vestry nor on the BOARD.

"Jason Coleman. So, how is it going with you, my brother?" Pigeon inquired in feigned surprise.

"Very good, chief!" he responded. "Gentlemen," he added in acknowledgement of Bill Jones and the other two men. The men merely nodded in response.

"I'm glad that you're taking the reins, Goodfellow," Bill stated. "We need some honest, level headed people on this vestry; good, strong men, like you, to bring some semblance of integrity around here. Eloise was of no substance. Faulkner and Pilchard called the shots. She followed; the bloody amoeba."

"Well, I intend to make a change around here, Bill, even if it means getting Fr. Perths to ask some of the present vestry members to resign. I am convinced that I have been elected senior warden by divine purpose and I already have the people's vote. I'll do what it takes to turn this church back into a church; put an end to this social club and all of the socialites. The Pigeon era is going to be remembered for generations to come," Pigeon swore.

"Aye aye, captain!" Bill agreed as he patted Pigeon on the shoulder. He then stepped aside for a tete-a tete with Eloise Pigthorne, who was about to formally begin the program.

The celebration proceeded smoothly with the formal welcoming ritual and a lavish feast. Jason and Fenton kept each other company for the entire night, even though other members periodically interjected with brief conversations. The two wardens and the vicar sat at the head table, while the newly elected senior warden and vestry members sat together at another table close to the head table. The guests from the neighboring villages sat together at the last table in the hall. No speeches from the newly elected officers were allowed at this function, thus the formalities concluded in a relatively short time and the members began to leave. Mr. Pilchard and Mr. Faulkner approached the last table where the villagers sat and personally wished them all the best for the season. They shook hands with the men and kissed the women, and reminded them of the Old Year's Night Ball.

Ram, in his state of semi-intoxication, interpreted the gestures as a sign of acceptance into the elite circle, and as he and his wife left the building, he apologized to his wife for his failure to see the benefits of maintaining her position as Public Relations Chairperson. He also thanked her for making it possible for them to be received into high society. Once again, therefore, Ram decided to give full management of the stall to his cousin, Pissy Ragnauth, since this apparent rise to a new social status would have deemed his management of a market stall most inappropriate. Mrs. Ramgolam laughed as she walked beside the body guard, who held her husband firmly as they strode towards the waiting hired car.

Faulkner and Pilchard subsequently proceeded to the head table as the last of the members were wishing each other a merry Christmas and taking their leave.

"I think we made a very good impression on the plebs, don't you think?" the judge remarked.

"You can say that again," Bill agreed. "We've got them like putty in our hands."

"This man is a genius, vicar!" Faulkner stated as he patted the judge on the shoulder. "In a few short months, St. Patrick's will be, well, pure *Silver* and *Gold*."

"Don't start the party yet, gentlemen. Saint Pigeon has a plan," Bill cautioned the group.

"What do you mean?" Fr. Perths inquired as he attempted to rise from his chair. The scent of alcohol from his breath was strong and offensive.

"First, the man believes that he was elected by divine purpose. Second, he is going to *tell* you, Fr. Perths, to ask certain members of the vestry to resign, and third – listen to this – he is going to turn St. Patrick's from a social club, back into a church," Bill reported.

"That arrogant fool. Divine purpose? Ha!" the vicar sneered.

"The bloody pettifogger!" Mr. Pilchard scoffed.

"My advice is to make sure that the BOARD is unified so as to stand up to him. I get the impression that Pigeon has an underground team working for him already. Just be careful with what you say and whom you say it to," Eloise warned.

"True. He's a dangerous man…very cunning. If there's any one here who knows the man, it is I," the judge admitted.

"Nevertheless, we shall proceed with our plans, gallantly…powerfully! We shall not be overcome by any kind of adversity, or adversary, for that matter!" Fr. Perths swore as he made a second futile attempt to stand.

Laurent Faulkner, who was strangely silent during Bill's revelation of Pigeon's plans, suddenly raised his hand. "Bill, Pigeon seems to trust you. The fact that he revealed his plans to you indicates some level of trust. My advice therefore, is that you stay close to him. Offer him your support and win his trust – all of it. Promise him sincerity of friendship, not imply it; swear your loyalty to him, and keep us informed – of everything. Whatever you share with us, we will keep in utmost confidence. Remember, *you* are our warden, not he."

"Think you can handle that, Bill? Think we can trust you to do this, warden of the BOARD?" the judge riterated.

"I will. I swear on my honor. My loyalty is to you, to the BOARD and to Fr. Perths," Bill replied.

"Let's take a quick drink to that, brothers and sister in Christ!" Fr. Perths responded. However, as he attempted once more to rise from the chair, he toppled backward and almost fell. His face was red with physical fatigue from the affect of the alcohol and his eyes were glazed and unfocused. In Bill's endeavor to break the vicar's fall, he accidentally knocked over the empty champagne bottle and a few of the glasses which were on the table. The noise attracted Rex and some of the villagers who were still in the process of clearing and cleaning the room. It was only then that the small group remembered that they were not alone as they connived with Bill to betray Pigeon. Immediately, they changed the conversation and, on the judge's advice, began to "praise the scavengers for the excellent job done." They subsequently departed, with Mr. Faulkner taking the intoxicated priest back to the vicarage.

* * *

Brewster's Village was alive with the festive activity as the silver jaguar maneuvered through the swamps and poodles of the arterial dirt roads towards *Brad's Palace*. The village's upper crust, like the Ramgolams and Uncle Ed, gathered there every Christmas Eve. The celebration was a little more elaborate at the Bradshaw's place, and those who could afford the small fee went there. Some of them, however, would stop by the other home thrown parties on their way to *Brad's Palace* to socialize and to deliver food, cakes or items for the hampers which would be distributed to the poorer residents later on Christmas morning.

Pigeon arrived to the applause of the crowd who had gathered at the Bradshaws. He had reluctantly allowed Jason to ride home with Fenton. He was hoping to gather some information immediately, but Jason convinced him that he would be able to amass much more if Fenton took him home, and promised to contact him later on Christmas day. Furthermore, he would be able to consolidate their friendship the longer they spent in each other's company. On realizing the warmth with which he was received, Pigeon's spirit soared and he forgot his mission with Jason. As soon as he had settled, he set to work on his expedition to destroy the BOARD's plan to erect the church in Brewster's Village. His approach was subtle, and after a series of brief conversations with random individuals, he was able to identify those whom he could trust to assist him in his surreptitious plan to overthrow the BOARD and thwart their plan. He thus gathered a small group of those he deemed the most intelligent, influential or socially ambitious guests around one of the tables in the rear. The group comprised Uncle Ed, Ram, Petulia Nobles, Dotty Cambridge, Joshua Chandrapaul and Harry Ying We, who recently opened a grocery in the village. Pigeon relayed the BOARD's subtle plan to oust them from St. Patrick's by building them their own church. He was hyperbolical in his details, and his captive audience swore their allegiance to him after he was finished.

"I am truly your friend, even more than I am your warden," he stressed. "I would rather step down from my position than to allow those devils to castigate you like this. They refer to you as mules and plebs, low class citizens who have no business worshipping with them at St. Patrick's. However, in our counter attack, we must be careful, as wise as serpents. I want us to keep all of this information between us. Nobody, you hear me, no body is to know of what I just told you, except that the church is being built to keep them out of St Patrick's. But don't tell them who gave you this information! When we defeat them, I as your warden will see to it that all of you at this table sit next to me in my position of prominence."

The group swore their loyalty and support, except Uncle Ed, who, though in agreement with Pigeon, chose to remain dormant and refrain from becoming too involved in the ugly politics. However, he swore never to divulge any of the information which Pigeon had shared with the group.

"There is one more thing, comrades," Pigeon continued. "I understand that Bishop Addington has requested a meeting with the people of Brewster's Village and Slough, to get your feelings about this new church. My belief is that someone from the BOARD or vestry will try to call a meeting with the people so as to influence you all before the bishop comes to St. Patrick's. Don't agree to any meeting with them – the BOARD or vestry, I mean. Rather, send a representative to the bishop, requesting that he come here instead, to *Brad's Palace*, to meet the people and to enjoy the hospitality of the people who live here. Prepare a lavish feast, in true country style, and influence the villagers to vote against the plan to build a church here. Tell them that St. Patrick's is their church and that they have every right to worship there."

The group agreed to Pigeon's plans and vowed their support. They subsequently chose Ram and Petulia Nobles to pay the bishop a visit on the morning after Boxing Day. Pigeon encouraged them to waste no time, and to go without an appointment, as he did. He offered to take them himself. He reminded them of the bishop's graciousness and his policy to never turn anyone away.

The group concurred. When Pigeon fully realized that he had won the group's support and loyalty, he mingled with the crowd for a short time and then departed. Again, the guests applauded when he wished them a merry Christmas and drove off in his impressive Jaguar. The Bradshaws expressed joy and pride that the elected senior warden had condescended to share fellowship with them on Christmas morning.

Pigeon skillfully negotiated the swamps and potholes as he proceeded slowly through the wet, narrow streets of Brewster's Village. The rain had stopped but the sky was still heavily overcast and threatening. There was no urgency in reaching home, since he knew that Mrs. Goodfellow would already be asleep and that there was no need to rise early on Christmas day. Consequently, he decided to make a right turn towards William Street, which would have ultimately taken him past *Phauphen's Tavern*. He doubted whether there would by any activity at this hour of the morning on Christmas day, but nevertheless decided to drive past the night club. As he drew close, he noticed that there were more cars than usual parked in front of the building. He drove slowly past in an attempt to recognize any of the vehicles. On failing to do so, he parked safe distance away from the tavern and walked towards the building. He donned his rain coat, hat and a pair of sunglasses and made his way to the foyer. From there he sought to identify the patrons in the subdued room. Some of the faces he recognized but none of them was significant enough to warrant any suspicion or motivate his interest to go further. The maitre d' merely acknowledged his presence with a polite bow of the head and mannerly smile. As he turned to exit, two figures standing by the bar attracted his attention. One was Fenton Skeete. The other was Jason Coleman. Pigeon concealed himself in a dark corner of the room and observed the two men for a while before leaving. As he exited the building, he noted that the time was eight minutes after three.

* * *

Christmas day was relatively quiet. The villagers never did much on the day itself, but resumed the celebration on a grander scale on Boxing Day, when friends would go from house to house, feasting, imbibing excessively, and bursting into Christmas carols and old favorite hymns. Abersthwaithe remained calm during both days. The residents there were too conservative to indulge in socializing on a grand scale like the villagers. However, relatives from various parts of the island would visit on Boxing Day, but the celebrations remained extremely private.

The rain poured heavily during Christmas day and Pigeon spent most of the day in his study. He was tense all day, for he had not received the expected call from Jason. The days ahead were crucial, for he was officially going to be installed as the senior warden on the first Sunday in January, so it was imperative that he know what the vestry and the BOARD were planning before he assumed his role. At six fifteen in the evening, he telephoned Jason, but no one answered the phone. He called several times during the rest of the evening, and finally left a message. However, he got no response.

* * *

Maggie spent most of the day trying to understand how her neighbor met his horrible and sudden fate. Annabelle tried desperately to comfort her mistress by reminding her that Wilberforce was mildly eccentric and might have got into an altercation with one of the vagrants who roamed the desolate neighborhood at night seeking a quiet place to rest until daylight. However, Maggie dismissed the idea as impractical, especially since the reported stated suspicion of a hit-and –run accident. The distressed woman spent the entire day trying to get herself mentally and spiritually prepared for the funeral, which was set for the day after Boxing Day.

Deaths by such a suspicious manner always made the headlines, since they were such rare occurrences in Ischalton, and Wilberforce's demise drew much public attention. Since the victim was known to be a frequent visitor to Maggie's home, the police paid her a visit to seek any information that might to help them solve the mystery. Maggie admitted that the deceased was there earlier in the evening, but did not mention anything or anyone to her that would have roused any suspicion. She did not mention the judge's presence and the antagonism she had sensed between the two men. Furthermore, her suspicions did not for a single instant rest on the judge, especially since he had left much later in the drizzling rain. On Boxing Day, an article in one of the less read newspapers, *The Ischalton News*, stated that the murdered man was last seen on his way to the home of a neighbor. It further implied that they were having an affair. Maggie vehemently denied the allegation when interviewed by a reporter from *The Argosy*. Roy, her caretaker, as well as Annabelle, supported his mistress. Maggie was thus never detained for any questioning, but rumors of her affair with the judge began to surface and gather impetus among St. Patrick's elite. Consequently, she temporarily withdrew from St. Patrick's and began to worship at St. Paul's cathedral in Georgetown.

*   *   *

Boxing Day was the day when the Pilchards hosted a sumptuous holiday lunch for the family members and very close friends. One of Mrs. Pilchard's sisters, Dorset Hudson, had known of the purported affair between her brother-in-law and Maggie Billings for a long time, but had never mentioned anything to her sister. Dorset and the deceased were neighbors in a middle class area in Versailles, which was on the north coast of the island, until he moved into *The Victoria Mansion*. They had remained friends and made infrequent telephone calls to each other over the years. Dorset had heard from the deceased, about two years earlier, that the judge was a frequent nocturnal visitor to Maggie's home, but she never revealed the relationship between herself and the Pilchards, thus Wilberforce inadvertently shared much of the details of the relationship between himself and Maggie, and the little he knew of Maggie and Judge Pilchard. Dorset never believed that her brother-in-law would have gambled his respectability for an adulterous affair, and thus dismissed Wilberforce's comments as mere groundless suspicion. However, during Wilberforce's last conversation with Dorset, he had jocularly shared with her the judge's altercation with the semi-nude vagrant and his subsequent meeting with the judge that night as they walked to their cars. He had told Dorset that his intention was to intimidate the judge, and that he had sat in his car and waited for him until he left Maggie's home. After Wilberforce's death, that last conversation suddenly began to reverberate in Dorset's head. She became more suspicious when the judge kept changing the conversation whenever the subject of the murder arose.

"Why are you so persistent in raising such a morbid conversation on a day like this?" the judge asked his wife when she expressed her sorrow at such a violent death "especially during the Christmas season."

"Adolph, don't be so heartless," she responded. "The poor man probably has a family that's torn with grief. I would expect you to be more sensitive to such suffering."

"No. He lived alone," Dorset revealed.

"You know him?" one of the family friends asked.

"Yes. When he moved back from England to here, he lived down the street from me before he bought the flat in *The Victoria Mansion*. As a matter of fact, he had spoken to me a few nights before he died." She added.

"I heard that he and Maggie Billings were romantically involved. Was that true?" Mrs. Pilchard inquired.

The judge did not seek to interrupt the conversation this time, and Dorset perceived that he was interested in hearing what she knew.

"I don't know. I knew that he was in love with her, but according to him, she was involved with someone, some married man, I hear, and was not keenly interested in him. The poor fellow..." She cast a furtive glance at the judge to observe his reaction to her response.

"What on earth do women expect to get out of being romantically involved with married men? The men don't leave their wives – generally," Mrs. Pilchard remarked.

"I think that married men who do that should be shot," a female relative added in disgust. "Here is a man, obviously of some breeding, who is in love with a single woman, but can't get anywhere with her because another man, who already has a wife, has seen fit to covet what might have been the other's. Oh the shame! The shame!"

"Come on, folks, let's get this lunch on the road. I'm famished!" the judge interrupted, again.

This time, however, Dorset chose to change the conversation. For the first time, she had come to believe that Wilberforce's story was true. She did not think that the judge had anything to do with his murder, but she had begun to believe that he was indeed involved in an adulterous affair with Maggie Billings. She thus made a vow, that very minute, never to indulge in any conversation involving her brother-in-law, whom she had loved so much and for whom she had such abundant respect. However, from that moment, she noticed that the judge made every effort to avoid her, and never looked her squarely in the face – ever again.

* * *

Towards the end of Boxing Day, when the evening drew close, the saturated clouds began to disperse. The stars that bedecked the sky appeared more resplendent than ever after the protracted period of heavy rainfall. The jeweled sky seemed to herald the dawning of a peaceful era as the island celebrated the incarnation of the Christ child. However, Pigeon was restless and agitated, for he still had not heard from Jason, despite additional calls during the day. At sunset, he told his wife that he was going to pay a visit to the vicar to discuss matters pertaining to his newly elected office, and left. He got into the black Toyota and sped off towards the vicarage, where he spent less than fifteen minutes in casual conversation with the vicar, who was experiencing the delayed effects of an alcoholic dissipation. Upon leaving the vicarage, he headed towards North Abersthwaithe where Jason lived. The stars appeared more numerous as Pigeon drove along the lonely stretch of road towards Amsterdam Drive. He turned the radio station to the program of Evensong so as to calm his spirit, but the canticles and hymns seemed to chide him for the way in which he was manipulating the trusting, naïve villagers, and using them to achieve his own ends. He therefore switched to the jazz station, so as to keep his mind focused on the music and not on Jason's seemingly irrational, irritating behavior.

Pigeon parked his car and proceeded to Jason's gate. The 'Beware of the Dog' sign that was displayed on the gate prohibited him from going any further. Instead, he banged on the metal template with his silver ring. The sound attracted the dog's attention and it began to bark ferociously from its kennel. Pigeon stood with both hands in his trouser pockets as he waited for a response. For a few seconds he gazed up the narrow street at the parked cars, and assumed that many of the residents were entertaining visitors. As he turned to knock on the metal sign a second time, he caught a glimpse of what he presumed to be a figure pulling back from the window to seek refuge behind the curtain. Pigeon pretended not to notice it and knocked again. The dog began to bark wildly for a second time. Still, no one appeared. Pigeon noticed, however, that many lights were on in the sitting room, and that in spite of the noise from the ravenous canine, no one was answering. As he turned to leave, he noticed a familiar figure stepping very cockily toward him. As the figure drew nearer, he realized that it was Bart Knuckles, one of the newly elected vestry members. Pigeon was only mildly acquainted with Bart, but knew that he was an extremely conceited individual who held a senior position at the Ischalton National Bank.

"Mr. Goodfellow!" Bart greeted Pigeon. "My goodness, it's a pleasure to be in your company this evening. I should have known that you'd be at the get-together."

"How are you, Bart?" Pigeon maintained his calm composure as he tried desperately to conceal his hurt. The men shook hands.

"You're leaving?" Bart inquired as he glanced at his watch. "The party's only just started."

"I…I've only just got here, and I …ah…I just realized that I had to make an important stop by Fr. Perths, so I am going to go there now…first, before I join the party. I don't want to go there too late," Pigeon embarrassingly replied.

"Well, don't stay too long now. We'll be looking for you," Bart added as he approached the gate.

"I'll try," Pigeon promised and headed back to his car. When he drove past the house, he realized that in that short period, Bart had already entered the house.

Jason's strange behavior was most perplexing to Pigeon. Try as he might, Pigeon could not comprehend Jason's sudden avoidance. Only two nights earlier, Jason had ridden with him to the church and had sworn his allegiance to him. Now he seemed to be avoiding him like the plague. To some degree, Pigeon held Fenton responsible for Jason's apparent disloyalty. Furthermore, Pigeon could not understand why he was not invited, or even told, of the so-called get-together. If Fenton was invited, then Pigeon's suspicions of betrayal would be justified. He thus decided to proceed to *Pauphen's Tavern* for a quiet drink.

The tavern was surprisingly crowded. Pigeon selected a seat that was located in a secluded corner. He recognized some of the clientele but they were merely acquaintances. He ordered a shot of whiskey and ginger, and as he sipped his drink in solitude, his mind conjured up images of Jason sharing the details of their conversation with his guests. Suddenly a surge of rabid hate overcame him, and he swore to avenge Jason's unfaithfulness. In a chair which was next to where he sat, there were two folded newspapers which he realized were already read and left to litter the pub; one was *The Argosy*, the other was *The Ischalton News* which contained the report of Maggie Billings' purported affair with the murdered man, Wilberforce Gaskins. He tucked the second newspaper by his side after glancing across the front page. He was going to read the article when he returned home. He replaced the other newspaper.

A round of contagious applause soon interrupted his vengeful thoughts of Jason, and as he turned his attention towards the small stage, he noticed that Philbert Watts was taking his place at the piano. The resounding plaudits lasted for about twenty five seconds and Philbert bowed elegantly and blew the ladies a kiss before sitting. Pigeon was highly impressed with Philbert's professionalism and stage grace, and all through his performance, Pigeon kept calculating the ways in which he could use him to help confound the

BOARD, control the vestry and destroy the judge. However, if Jason were proved to be disloyal, he would deal with him – privately.

As Philbert was performing his last song, Rexworth Davis walked into the tavern. Pigeon had never before seen Rex in such casually elegant attire, and found it even more interesting when one of the waitresses, a full busted woman with a noticeable absence of posterior, approached him and stood next to him for the duration of the song. When the song ended, the small crowd burst into applause again, and Philbert rose from the piano, bowed gracefully and exited the stage as the appreciative patrons shouted for an encore. The woman who stood near to Rex disappeared at the back. Philbert returned to the stage, acknowledged the appreciation with a stately bow and assumed a sedentary position at the piano again. As he enchanted the audience with his silky tenor and ostentatious pianism, two men came into the tavern and slipped quietly to one of the back tables. They ordered two beers. Pigeon recognized one of the men as Bishop Addington's watchman.

When Philbert finally left the stage, amidst the roar of appreciation, the busty waitress appeared again. However, she had changed her work attire and had donned a tight black dress. She once again approached Rex, who was still standing in a dark corner by the stage, and after what seemed like a brief conversation, the couple left the tavern. Immediately, the two men rose and exited the building. Pigeon followed quietly, with the newspaper hidden at his side.

Upon reaching the outside, he noticed that the two men had intercepted the couple and were accosting them. Pigeon hurried towards his car and entered it. As he turned to observe the small group, he realized that the man who and accompanied the bishop's watchman was having a wrangle with Rex. Suddenly, the man fired a powerful right hook which knocked Rex against the car that was parked nearby. Rex retaliated by charging forward defensively and throwing sequence of calculated punches. A series of mutual blows followed, and Rex's agility surprised Pigeon. As the men fell to the wet ground in their brutal assault of each other, the busty one darted up the street, screaming for murder and begging for help. Pigeon could no longer see what was happening since the two men were on the ground and the watchman was obstructing his view. However, as the patrons became aware of the scuffle, they came rushing out of the tavern towards the two men, who were still locked in a furious battle. Suddenly, the watchman broke the beer bottle he was still carrying and charged towards the men. Pigeon spared no more time at the scene, he quickly started his car and sped off in the opposite direction. As he swung the corner, he prayed that someone would intercept the watchman and protect Rex from the awful possibilities of the broken bottle and the two men who undoubtedly were going to combine their efforts to thrash him. He assiduously prayed also for Rex's safety, for it was Rex upon whom he would depend most to assist him in destroying the judge.

As ten o'clock drew close Pigeon slipped into his pajamas, made himself a cup of tea and served himself a thick slice of fruit cake. He subsequently retired to his study, where he reclined on the divan with a glass of wine, the newspaper which he took from the tavern, his prayer book and the bible. The article regarding Maggie's supposed affair with the murdered man proved to be of great interest to him. He already knew that the judge was having an affair with Maggie and that he was a frequent visitor to Maggie's home. If he could prove that the judge was aware of the victim's interest in Maggie, then he knew that he might be able to build a case against him. He further thought that even if the judge had nothing to do with the murder, his adulterous affair at least would be exposed. However, he thought it better to connect the two so as to produce a more crippling effect. With regard to Jason, if he was discovered to be unfaithful, he would apply a more deadly form of revenge; he would create a vicious rumor that Jason and Fenton Skeete were instigating a covert plan with the BOARD to excite an insurrection against the Bishop if he refused them permission to erect the church in Brewster's village. Such a lie, he figured, would immediately impair the friendship between the two men and consequently weaken the power of their assumed attack on him. Having made these decisions, he thus opened his prayer book and besought the Lord to give him victory against his adversaries.

* * *

Saturated clouds once again covered the sky on Friday morning as the silver jaguar approached Bishop's Court. Ram and Petulia disembarked a short way off from the entrance. The plan was that Pigeon would take them, and that they would subsequently ride the bus back to the village. Later that evening, Pigeon would meet them at Petulia's home to discuss the details of the visit.

Pigeon then drove off towards Westminster Lane. It was the day of Wilberforce's funeral, and having read of Maggie's purported relationship with the man, he decided to pay Maggie a visit, ostensibly to express his condolences. As he parked the car, a short chubby man stood by the alleyway observing him. When he reached Maggie's gate and looked back, the man was still standing there, quietly observing him.

Annabelle met him at the door and afterwards escorted him to the drawing room where she invited him to take a seat while she prepared him a pot of tea. Several minutes later, Maggie entered the room and Pigeon rose and bowed respectfully.

"My lady! It's so wonderful to see such a refreshingly beautiful face so early in the morning!"

"Thank you. Such flattery gets one anywhere," Maggie graciously replied as she approached him. He hugged her gently and kissed her on the cheek. After they sat, Annabelle entered with a tray from which she served tea and cream filled biscuits.

"I know that my visit this morning no doubt has surprised you, but having read about the death of your close friend, I decided to drop by on my way to work. I understand that the funeral is this afternoon?"

"Yes. At the cathedral…the Roman Catholic Cathedral. He was Roman Catholic," Maggie replied. "However," she added emphatically, "we were not romantically involved."

"Contrary to the newspapers," Pigeon stated.

"Precisely," Maggie replied.

"But don't you think that there might have been, well, at least a little interest there… on his part, I mean. I mean, look at you, Maggie. I'm sure that he might have been at least a little interested," Pigeon remarked.

Maggie gave a coy smile and admitted to his love for her, but explained that his was an unrequited love. Pigeon then posed a question that startled his gracious hostess.

"Did Pilchard know that the deceased was enamored of you?"

"What?"

"Did judge…"

"I heard you," Maggie interjected. "Why such a question?"

Pigeon knew that he had struck a sensitive chord. "Well, there have been rumors…about the two of you, plus I have, well, some evidence of the same."

Maggie became visibly agitated after Pigeon's revelation. He leaned back more comfortably on the chair and crossed his legs with the confidence of one who had scored a major victory. "Let's not beat about the bush, Maggie; you and the good judge are romantically involved."

Maggie uttered not a single word, but stared at Pigeon in shock and terror. Her eyes welled up with tears as he continued to psychologically batter her with the crippling verities of her affair with the honorable judge.

"Look, Maggie, I am not here to condemn you, or judge you, or even threaten you. I'm here as a friend, to protect you from certain grim possibilities – matters which may arise as a result of your romantic involvement with the judge – complications which may stem from the murder of this man who rivaled the judge for your affection. You understand where I am coming from, Maggie?"

Maggie continued to stare at Pigeon, speechless and transfixed to her seat like a condemned man in the electric chair at the moment of his execution.

"You do understand the ramifications of all that I have just pointed out to you, do you?" Pigeon addressed the petrified woman. As he stared into her eyes, she suddenly lowered her eyelids and began to twiddle her fingers nervously. A tear rolled down her cheek. She patted the corner of her eye with the back of her hand.

"Was judge Pilchard here the night that Mr. Gaskin was killed?" the agonizing interrogation continued.

Maggie kept her head down and raised her eyes to meet Pigeon's. She made no response.

"I assume that by your reticence, your answer is in the affirmative," Pigeon stated.

"For a short while," Maggie admitted in a timid voice. "He was here, but only for a very short time. And the two never met. Mr. Pilchard never knew of Mr. Gaskin."

"But Mr. Gaskin knew of him."

"Yes. Of course. Mr. Pilchard is a very well known man in the community," Maggie replied.

"I'm talking of his involvement with you," Pigeon explained.

"I never actually told him. He only might have suspected. If he had believed that there was such a relationship, it would have been based on mere implication."

"I understand that Mr. Gaskin came by the night he was killed."

"Yes. But he left a long time before Mr. Pilchard came by. Please, Mr. Goodfellow, I don't wish to talk about this. Furthermore, I don't know where you are trying to lead this conversation, but Mr. Pilchard…"

"…Was indeed here the night that Mr. Gaskin was killed, but you did not mention this to the reporter – or to the police, for that matter." Pigeon interrupted the dismissive woman.

"What is your point, Mr. Goodfellow?" Maggie snapped.

"The point is that you might, just might, be protecting the famous judge from…"

"…From what, Mr.Goodfellow; from the crime of murder?" Maggie interjected angrily.

"Well…"

"I am trying to preserve my privacy, and protect the judge's marriage, that's what. Are you implying that Mr. Pilchard might be somehow responsible for Mr. Gaskin's death, and that I am trying to cover up something?"

"Is that a confession, or mere analysis, Ms Billings?" Pigeon asked with a wry smile.

Maggie rose impetuously and strode across the room to the door of the drawing room and swung it open. "Get out, Mr. Goodfellow! I demand that you leave this house immediately!"

Pigeon rose slowly, and bearing a derisive smile approached the antagonized woman and offered her a business card, "Just in case you need a good lawyer. My service for you is gratis."

"Go to hell, Pigeon Goodfellow!" Maggie hissed and flung the card across the room.

"If I were you, Maggie, I wouldn't treat this matter with such dismission. You could end up in big trouble. And I'll tell you, if that were to happen, the judge will be saved by his reputation alone, but nobody really knows you. Furthermore, the very judge that you seek to protect so vigilantly will deny any romantic involvement with you, to save his reputation and his marriage, and you'll be left hanging like a vintage garment in a museum closet."

Maggie averted her attention as she held the door for Pigeon to pass. "Annabelle," she beckoned, "kindly escort Mr. Goodfellow to the door, and ask Roy to lock the gates behind him."

"Yes, mam," Annabelle replied obediently. "Sir...," she said as she stretched out her arm towards the stairs to indicate that he should leave.

Pigeon turned once more to Maggie and contemplated her. "Good morning, Miss Billings."

Maggie again averted her attention as he descended the stairs.

"Don't worry, mam," he advised the housekeeper. "I know my way out."

Pigeon closed the gate himself and headed towards his car which was parked further down the street. As he approached the vehicle, the short, chubby man appeared from the alleyway again and approached him. Pigeon assumed that he was one of the vagrants who frequented the areas around town at night.

"Good morning, sir. Nice car you got."

"Thank you," Pigeon replied as he turned the key to the door. As the stranger came closer, Pigeon held his breath and got into the vehicle.

"Got a dollar...so I could get some coconut buns for breakfast?" the stranger asked.

As Pigeon opened his wallet, the stranger held the door open. "Been to see the ole'girl, eh, dhat ole' tart in the big 'house yonder, eh?"

"I don't know anybody like that, sir," Pigeon responded calmly so as not to antagonize the man.

"Yea...the big 'ouse yonder. Lots o' people goes there, mostly mens... especially at nights. She real popular," the vagrant inadvertently testified.

"How do you know that?" Pigeon inquired as he removed a five dollar bill from his wallet. He held it in his hand for the man to see it clearly.

"Cause I comes 'ere at night to sleep, over there in the alleyway," the vagrant replied.

"Then you know of the murder…the man who…"

"Oh yeah," the vagrant replied enthusiastically. "I was lyin' down over there in the alleyway, and I hear shoutin', but I get frighten, cause I thought that it was peoples come to chase me from there and throw away me things, so I stay quiet. The rain was fallin' and I cloak up under me plastic so I wouldn't get wet. Then I hear a car start up, and then I hear baaps, like the car hit something, and the car speed away. Then I get up and I come right deh, by the fence, and I peep, but the car did done turn the corner. Then later, I see police cars and I tek up me things and run; I run back so…down the other side of the alleyway and I climb over the fence and run down the next street. And then I hear say that somebody did get knock down with a car, and dead."

Pigeon began to interrogate the man. "Did you see anybody go to that woman's house that night?"

"No, cause the rain was fallin' real bad, so I stay under me plastic," the vagrant apologized as he gazed at the five dollar bill.

"Do you know any of the men who go to that house?" Pigeon continued to question the man.

"No. But once, I did see that… tall man…ah…"

"Judge Pilchard…?"

"…Yea…Yea, Judge Pilchard! You knows 'im?"

"Yes. Good friends. We're good friends," Pigeon remarked. "Who else do you see?"

"And I knows that man who does live in them nice houses over there. Wilb'force he say 'is name was. He does carry food and things for she. I does see 'im passin' when I comes in the alleyway to sleep. He does give me money when I aks 'im. But I ain't see 'im since Christmas Eve. I think he must be gone away somewhere," the man continued, "or he would a' give me money for Christmas…five dollars, like he does always do."

Pigeon was amazed at the wealth of information he was gathering from the strange and unsuspecting witness. However, he could not tell the stranger that Wilberforce was the victim of the very accident to which he was partly a witness.

"I wonder if Wilberforce ever met the judge at the house down the road, you know. Maybe they were all just good friends. Who knows?" Pigeon craftily remarked.

"They was. I did see them walkin' down the street together, once. They was talkin'…they was goin' that way, together," the vagrant explained.

Before Pigeon could ask another question, the man snatched the five dollar bill and darted through the alleyway. Pigeon was too shocked to move, and by the time he regained his composure, the vagrant had disappeared. Pigeon thus started the engine and drove off, enraged at being violated but pleased that he had gathered so much information. However, as the anger dissipated, he began to challenge the authenticity of the vagrant's report, and to suppose that the information might have been fabricated in anticipation of the five dollar bill. In further analyzing the vagrant's conduct, Pigeon believed that he might have been mixing lies with some truth, and perhaps laboring under the assumption that he was not really going to be given the money, resorted to thievery. Pigeon therefore thought it wise to ponder on the information a little longer and not place his hopes in such questionable information.

*   *   *

The crimson and golden hues of twilight were like the heavenly chant of angels at vespers – in contrast to the dismal grey of the monks' dirge at matins, which earlier in the day had covered the sky and drizzled like persistent tears as Maggie walked away from the gravesite of the man whose advances she had spurned. Throes of remorse gnawed away at her bleeding heart with each footstep she took as she contemplated the many times her heart had pleaded with her to surrender her love to a man whose affections were devoted to her – and her alone. She knew that she had suffered sporadic attacks of immense desire for him, and therefore had thought it sagacious to counteract her feelings by treating him disdainfully whenever he expressed his love for her. She could have been happy with the man whose love was directed only to her, she thought, the man with whom she could have walked hand in hand in the brightness of the noonday, or upon whose shoulders she could have rested her head in public. Instead, she succumbed to her devilish pride which guilefully persuaded her to seduce the judge into the abandonment of his wife. Maggie's quest for victory in the forbidden rivalry for the judge gave her a greater sense of happiness and self-worth than Wilberforce's overtures. She nurtured this sense of self-worth by deeming herself more beautiful, gracious and desirable than the judge's wife; and the affections of a man who was revered by society placed her on a pedestal from which no one could remove her. Therefore, she was content to share the love of a man whom she realized she would never ultimately have, but nevertheless dared to believe that she could completely and solely possess.

Tears rolled down Maggie's cheeks as she stepped gracefully towards her car, clutching her handbag close to her for comfort. The black veil which fell over her face served to conceal the grief from the large crowd which had assembled to pay their respects to the man of distinction who had met such an ignoble and controversial manner of death. Roy, who functioned as her caretaker and occasional chauffer, opened the rear door for her as she approached the vehicle. Whispered talked emanated from the curious onlookers who had assembled at the entrance to the cemetery hours before the lengthy cortege arrived. The men tipped their hats as Maggie passed and some of the women bowed their heads and gave quiet, respectable smiles. Maggie realized that by the respectful acknowledgements from the onlookers, they had assumed that by dint of her distinguished attire and regal appearance, she was a woman of means and character, for such displays of respect from the underclass were generally reserved for the socialites and persons of high political standing. Maggie savored the moment and held her head high as she stepped past her obvious inferiors.

Once in the car, Maggie's thoughts again focused on the details of Pigeon Goodfellow's visit earlier that day. Terror and grief seemed to take their seats on either side of her as she rode in the lonely rear seat of her shell white Desoto. Maggie, like many, had great respect for Pigeon's intelligence, and knew that there could be some vague element of truth in his concept of the incident. If he turned out to be correct, then her romantic involvement with the judge would become a headliner in all of the nation's newspapers and tabloids. Such a shocking revelation, she further reasoned, could result in a permanent estrangement between herself and the married judge, or perhaps, she thought, a similar separation between the judge and his wife. She vividly remembered his words that night when he met Wilberforce at her house. Such words, Maggie figured, would only be used by a man who had at some point contemplated leaving his wife for another woman. However, the bright ray of unholy hope suddenly gave way to a pall of gloom as Maggie's thoughts suddenly swung back to her late suitor. She now realized, for the first time, how foolish she was for having refused his affection in favor of the married judge's; she now realized that she could end up a lonely, bitter woman, who gambled with love, and lost – miserably; she now realized that she had spurned that which was certain for that which was a dismal and unlikely prospect. Visions of Wilberforce in his coffin consumed her thoughts as she mused on her egregious stupidity and his scintillating and sincere expressions of affection. It was as he lay in peaceful repose that she, for the first time, had deeply contemplated his facial features for a considerable period of time, and noted that indeed, he was a very handsome man. She remembered wishing all through the service that he would awake from his deathlike slumber and reach for her, and together they would walk hand in hand towards the horizon of eternal happiness. Then suddenly, reality struck her a powerful blow, and for the first time since his death, she burst into a shower of bitter, uncontrollable tears.

*   *   *

The colored fairy lights which were strung around the inner walls of *Brad's Palace* created a festive ambience as the surge of subdued conversation from the patrons swirled around the room. The Christmas tunes that were being played were hushed and the sound of tinkling glasses echoed across the room like the chime of Christmas bells. In a corner on the far side of the building, Pigeon, Ram and Petulia Nobles were seated at a table discussing the details of the meeting with the bishop, which was held earlier that day. Pigeon was imbibing heavily. Bishop Addington had agreed to visit Brewster's village and meet the members at *Brad's Palace* on the evening of the first Monday in January. The Bishop had told Ram and Petulia that he would forego his wonted Monday night fellowship meeting in order to meet his people to discuss this most urgent matter. Petulia was given the task of preparing the letter announcing the meeting and Ram was issued the responsibility of ensuring its distribution to every member who resided in Brewster's village and Slough. The Bradshaws agreed to host the meeting, and as a sign of their support for Pigeon, promised to offer a complimentary drink to each of the attendees.

As the trio continued to plan their strategy in the dim corner of the night club, Howard 'Howie' Bobsemple, who was employed as a watchman at *Fruity Fletcher's*, a large, wholesale grocery store that specialized in the sale of fruits from all over the Caribbean and North America, approached the table. His approach seemed calculated to Pigeon, who had acknowledged his presence earlier in the evening when he had just entered the nightclub to deliver two cartons of assorted fruits. Howie drew a chair and sat facing the chair back as he sought the group's immediate attention.

"Mr. Goodfellow, sir," Howie whispered with the urgency of a secret agent, "they's plannin' to do you in…"

"What are you talking about, Howie?" Pigeon nonchalantly inquired.

"Them…the judge, Fr. Perths, Mr. Faulkner, Mr. Jones…they's planin' to do you in!"

"What do you mean, Howie?" Pigeon again sought clarification.

"Chris'mas Eve night, after everybody lef' and we was cleanin' the hall, them was tellin' Mr. Jones to tell them everything dhat you say. And them say that you ain't their warden. Don't trust none o' them, Mr. Goodfellow sir…none of them; not even the parson," Howie warned the newly elected senior warden.

Before anyone could say or ask anything else, Howie rose hastily from his chair and exited.

"That son-of-a-bitch...Bill Jones. Could you imagine? He must have told them everything I said to him at the dinner...every bloody thing!" Pigeon remarked.

"What you gwine to do, sir?" Ram asked the visibly agitated and antagonized Pigeon.

There was tone of sincerity and concern in Ram's voice as he gazed at the troubled man.

"Jes ignore them, Mr. Goodfellow. Dem is a bunch of hypocrites. And I'm surprised at Fr. Perths. He should be ashamed of 'e'self; the damn fool!" Petulia declared.

Pigeon forthwith brought the meeting to an end and departed with haste. In blinding rage and semi-intoxication, he sped towards Bill's home on Cedar Avenue, in North Aberthswaithe. It was imperative that he accost him before the New Year's Eve ball and the commissioning of the vestry on the Sunday immediately following New Year's Day.

Pigeon's unimpressive black vehicle arrived on Cedar Avenue within eleven minutes of having departed Brewster's Village. The hurt and irate warden elect parked the vehicle and stormed towards Bill's gate and knocked. Bill's car was parked on the driveway. Two fierce Dobermans dashed forward from the side of the house and began barking ferociously. Almost immediately, the glass door that led from the sitting room to the verandah slid open and one of Bill's daughters stepped out.

"Mr. Goodfellow!" she greeted the angry man. "How nice to see you!"

"Hello, Carletine," Pigeon responded with the refinement of a fine, old, English gentleman. "...such a delight to see you!"

"You just missed daddy. I think that he went to Mr. Haulklyn's place... there is supposed to be some meeting there, I think. Mr. Coleman just picked him up," the young woman disclosed.

"Thank you. I'll see if I catch him there."

"Incidentally, congratulations...on your election," Carletine added. "I told daddy that you'll make a perfect warden."

"Thank you. That's very good of you to say that. All that I can say is that I'll try my best to live up to your expectations. Goodnight!"

As Pigeon made his way to *Pauphen's*, he realized that the enemy was joining forces to attack him. However, an even more grim reality struck him; those whom he had considered his trustworthy friends – those who, at various times, had professed brotherly affection and had claimed that they had supported him in the elections– had betrayed him. He suddenly felt alone, like a forlorn army oficer on the battlefield, critically bruised and mentally anguished. There was none that he could trust any longer. His enemies and friends were all alike, and wore masks that disguised their true nature. Pigeon thus realized that he was caught in the game of civil war in the jungle. He therefore would be watchful of the enemy and suspicious of friends; he would spare none the bullet in the wake of threat.

Upon turning on to Langley Place, he switched off the flood lights and slowly drove past the tavern. He studied the vehicles that were parked along the street, but recognized only three of them. The tavern did not appear crowded from the outside, so he parked his car and approached the building. From the dimly lit foyer, he observed the few patrons and noted that across the room in the far left corner, a group of five persons seemed immersed in conversation. As his eyes became accustomed to the subdued lights, he recognized the faces and the pensive expressions that they bore as they sipped what seemed to be some kind of liquor. Each of them was taking turns in speaking while the others were paying rapt attention. The aura around the table did not give credence to a holy fellowship, and the members seemed to be casting furtive glances around them like insurrectionists plotting a major revolution. He therefore decided that the only way to know whether they were discussing the issues of the church – or him – was by suddenly approaching them in the middle of a sentence. He thus observed them calculatingly, like a lion stalking its prey, and as they leaned attentively towards Bill Jones, he strode swiftly and stealthily towards the unsuspecting group.

"Season's greetings, gentlemen!" Pigeon greeted the group with a sinister expression.

The group gasped at the sudden and unexpected appearance of what Pigeon instantly realized was obviously the subject of their conversation. His forbidding stare penetrated the semi-darkness like the beam of a watchman's torch on a gang of thieves. The conversation came to an immediate and abrupt end as the group fumbled to respond to his sarcastic greeting.

"I'm sorry to have startled you by my sudden appearance, but I trust that I am not interrupting a private gathering," Pigeon apologized.

"No...no...not...not in the least...I...mean..." Mr. Pilchard managed to reply.

"...Then I'm sure that you wouldn't mind if I join you gentlemen for a drink for the season. I mean, we can take one toast to end the year and another to welcome the New Year with all of its possibilities, its mysteries and its uncertainties. Mam...!" Pigeon drew a chair as he summoned the attending waiter. "A bottle of your best champagne, please. This one's on me, gentlemen."

The awkwardness that emanated from the group was piercing. Notwithstanding, Pigeon sat and instigated a conversation on the vestry's proposal to erect a church in Brewster's village. "So, I heard that there is a lot of work in store for me for the new year!" he began with a sarcastic mile. "…Talking about that new church in Brewster's village."

"Aye aye, Captain!" Fenton Skeete responded with a broad smile.

"It's all charted out for you, my good man," the judge added.

"That's what I like; a challenge. But do you think that the Bishop will approve the plan?"

"Don't see why not," Sam Westwater replied. "The plan makes much sense, at least to me."

The waiter approached the table with a bottle of *Jean Brutant* and six champagne glasses. Pigeon popped the bottle and poured. "Gentlemen!" he exclaimed, "all the best for the new year. May all of our plans come to fruition!"

The toast was made and the group thanked Pigeon for his generosity. However, Pigeon could feel the discomfort of the members pressing against him like an evil and oppressive spirit. Nevertheless, he decided that he would remain and wear them out. He further noted that Jason and Bill were reticent throughout the duration of time that he sat at table with them. Their awkwardness was the sign that Pigeon interpreted as proof of the treachery which they were plotting against him. Thus he continued to humiliate them by probing questions about the church in Brewster's village.

"Tell me, has any one sat down to discuss the building of this new church with the members in Brewster's village, or in Slough; or is this another clandestine plot to keep the plebs in their place?" Pigeon stared each of them directly in their face, but none responded directly to the question.

"If I were living in Brewster's village, or Slough, for that matter, I would have rejoiced in the decision to have a church built in my own neighborhood," Sam stated.

"Whose decision; theirs…yours, or the BOARD's?" Pigeon continued his interrogation.

"Whose idea it is or was, is totally irrelevant, Pigeon. I would concentrate on the advantages of worshipping in my own neighborhood," Bill spoke for the first time.

"Then how come you, or anyone else for that matter, never pushed for a similar building to be erected in North Abersthwaithe, which is even further from St. Patrick's than Brewster's village or Slough?" Pigeon inquired.

"We have cars, Pigeon, come on. They don't. Getting to church on a Sunday must be a terrible hassle for most, if not all, of them," Sam added defensively.

"Did they complain, Sam? I don't ever remember any of them complaining about the distance. They just always seem to come with great joy, unless, of course, I am unaware of any disgruntlements on their behalf," Pigeon remarked.

"Perhaps," the judge added dismissively. "Gentlemen," he continued as he rose from his chair, "I beg to be excused. Mrs. Pilchard is expecting me home at a reasonable time…"

"…Tonight," Pigeon interjected sarcastically as he stared the judge squarely in the face. "She wants to make sure that tonight is her night." Pigeon bore the sardonic expression of a grinning skull.

"Yes. Something like that, I suppose. She knows what happens when I'm out with the boys," the judge wittily replied. "Goodnight gentlemen. I guess I'll be seeing you all at the New Year's Eve Ball."

Before making his exit, the judge placed a twenty dollar bill on the table and cast one last deadly glance towards Pigeon. "My contribution for the drinks, guys. Goodnight again, gentlemen."

Pigeon continued to stare at the judge until he disappeared behind the wall of the foyer. "Well, shall I order another round, gentlemen?"

"As a matter of fact, I was just about leaving when you arrived, but I remained so as to spend at least five minutes in your distinguished presence. But now duty calls. I, also, beg to be excused." Fenton rose, placed a ten dollar note on top of the twenty dollar bill and made a hasty exit.

Jason rose and donned his cap. He slipped his hand into his pocket and took out his wallet.

"Sit down, Jason," Pigeon ordered the fleeing turncoat. "I need to discuss something with you."

Sam and Bill rose almost simultaneously in preparation to leave.

"Shall I contribute towards the champagne, Pigeon?" Sam asked as he put on his black fedora.

"It's all on me, Sam. Thanks!" Pigeon graciously replied.

"Then I'll leave you two gentlemen to confabulate. Goodnight." Sam leaned forward and extended his arm. He and Pigeon shook hands. Sam turned towards the entrance.

"Here's my contribution for the tip for the waiter, fellas," Bill added as he placed a five dollar bill on the pile and leaned over to shake Pigeon's hand. "Please give my respects to the lady of the house…"

"You sit too, Bill. We need to talk," Pigeon commanded the retreating informant.

The two men tried to appear calm as they took their seats and stared at Pigeon. Their posture appeard tense and their expressions bore the mark of anticipation of some embarrassing confrontation.

Pigeon poured a shot of the remaining whiskey and leaned back on his chair. "Tell me, is this how we are going to deal with each other as wardens, vestry members, parishioners…friends…?"

"What are you talking about, Goodfellow?" Bill responded in feigned ignorance.

"Don't insult my intelligence, Mr. Jones," Pigeon snapped. "I know what was going on here, and what has been going on."

"What are you insinuating here, Goodfellow?" Bill's tone was tinged with anger.

"I'm not insinuating anything, Bill. I'm making a statement," Pigeon replied.

"Then say it, for heaven's sake. I'm not going to sit here all night while you fumble with the English language to make a point," Bill voiced with increasing anger.

"Then I'll say it, Jones, loudly and clearly. The two of you are sons o' bitches; a nasty set o' mother #@**#@ traitors!" Pigeon bellowed as he pointed his index finger in Bill's face.

The noise attracted the attention of some of the patrons who were scattered across the room.

"Look, I'm not going to sit here and endure this kind of coarse accusation and disrespect from you, Pigeon," Bill protested as he rose from his chair.

Pigeon rose impetuously from his chair and intercepted Bill as he attempted to leave. "You're not going anywhere, Jones, until you've heard what I have to say to you. And I want this other traitor sitting here to hear what I have to say too!"

"Would you kindly excuse me, Mr. Goodfellow," Bill requested in a stern and threatening tone. "I would like to leave."

Pigeon stepped aside to allow Bill to pass. However, as Bill turned to leave, Pigeon followed him, hurling accusations and insults at him. "Joining with those dogs to bite me wouldn't get you anywhere, Billy boy. Telling them what I said ain't going to put you nowhere, you damn lackey! I am the senior warden, not you; so none of you can't do me a shit, you hear me, not a shit! And you can tell them what I said too, you yellow bellied sissy. I'm going to flap all of you up, you wait!" Pigeon yelled as he waved both arms in the air.

The patrons all stared in shock at the magistrate's obstreperous behavior. While Pigeon was following Bill to the door, Jason slipped across to the other side of the room and made a discreet escape. When Pigeon returned to the table and realized that Jason was gone, he became intensely angry and began shouting again. This time, however, there was no one at the table, and the security guard was summoned to escort him from the building. Mr. Hauklyn witnessed the entire incident from the wings. It was he who had summoned the security personnel.

*   *   *

By eleven o'clock that night, the news of Pigeon's disorderly conduct was already in circulation among the members of the *Gold Circle* who were in opposition to his wardenship. Shortly before eleven fifteen, Maggie's telephone rang and she was informed of the incident. However, unlike the other members of the circle, she did not see it as the golden opportunity to 'dethrone the emperor'. Instead, the report struck terror in her, for she knew that what had taken place at *Pauphen's* was not simply a drunken outburst; it was the battle cry of an enraged and irrational warrior whose vicious attack on the enemy was indirectly going to bring about her shameful demise. The wound inflicted upon her heart as a result of Wilberforce's death was fresh and excruciatingly painful. She was paying the price for her stupidity and, if Pigeon's suspicions were true, for the guilt of having inadvertently caused Wilberforce's death. Maggie thus swore to herself that night that she would never suffer like this again. Earlier that day, she had stood in the cemetery, as helpless and ineffective as an idol in a temple, while the man whom she knew had adored her was lowered into oblivion. Now, the man whom she loved was standing in the shadow of a premature burial, and worse, he was going to take her with him, for she knew that it was through her that Pigeon would launch his merciless attack upon the judge. It became obvious to Maggie that she would now have to choose between the foe and the lover. The conundrum facing her threw her into a state of immense fear and anxiety. To be faithful to the judge would be to bring about her own destruction, for she would have to publicly deny their affair and consequently lose him to his wife forever. To be faithful to Pigeon would be to bring about the judge's professional and marital demise, for she would have to admit to the adulterous relationship. However, her unfaithfulness to the judge and her loyalty to the enemy may be her only chance of winning the judge forever, even in the wake of his professional downfall. She thus decided that she would invite Pigeon over to dinner on New Year's Night, while the judge and the BOARD were recuperating from the New Year's Eve festivities.

Maggie thus slipped under the cover of her queen sized, canopy bed, knowing that if she wins the gamble, she will no longer have to count sheep during the lonely nights when insomnolence strums his cacophonous lullaby.

*   *   *

St. Patrick's bells heralded the rising of the sun on the last morning of the year, and the residents of Abersthwaithe and the surrounding villages rose to greet the day and prepare for the traditional celebrations. Private parties after the services at St. Patrick's and the Roman Catholic Church were the custom of the affluent residents of Abersthwaithe.

In the villages, the households prepared peas and rice, cassava bread and stewed beef, pork and chicken. The amount prepared was determined by affordability. However, even the poorest households made every effort to prepare this traditional meal, because it was a sign of a prosperous year. Consequently, those who raised cattle, pigs or chickens would share some of the raw meat with those who suffered extreme poverty, with the hope that the coming year would bring them good fortune. Those who did not cultivate livestock or own farms would purchase extra meat and vegetables and distribute them to the poor. The villagers believed that it was their duty to assist the poor, for a poor man's fortune would be their fortune – the poor man's woes would be theirs, for it would be a sign of God's blessing or wrath upon them.

Brewster's village was alive with activity even before the bells of St. Patrick's heralded the dawn of the last day of the year. The villagers were already slaughtering the animals and chickens for the preparation of the traditional meal. Furthermore, since it was believed that God's blessings were commensurate to the degree of generosity to the poor, those who reared livestock were eager to be the first to distribute their gifts to the poor. Old Year's Day was also the day when Uncle Ed offered the free service of his donkey and horse drawn carts to those who were distributing meat to the poor; it was his sacrifice for abundant blessings in the following year.

After the service at St. Patrick's and the other churches around Abersthwaithe and the surrounding villages, the residents of Brewster's village and Slough would go from house to house and partake of food and potent, local wines. There would be dancing and singing, a couple of fights between inebriated guests, and a few of the intoxicated males might end up in various trenches around the village. The overall tone, however, would be one of joy and celebration.

Nightspots like *Brad's Palace* and *The Sugar Cane* would host paid parties for the select clientele who could afford the cover charge. The village elite like the Ramgolams and Uncle Ed, as well as those who considered themselves socially superior to the common villagers, like Maudie Springer and Constance Weatherspoon, would attend these parties. There were also the self righteous villagers who would remain on their knees in their respective churches until the clock struck midnight, after which they would rise and subsequently find their way to the many celebrations around the village. However some chose to begin the new year in solitude and closed their doors and turned off the lights so as not to attract any unwanted visitors.

This year, the Ramgolams were among those who were going to be guests at the Faulkners' Old Year's Night Ball. Consequently, they merely distributed a few parcels of meat, which they had bought, to some of the poor families and offered their apologies for not being able to attend any of the local celebrations that night. At about nine o'clock, Mrs. Ramgolam went over to Molly Mc Kenzie, who ran an unlicensed, bottom house beauty salon, to have her blond wig washed and set for the function that night. Mr. Ramgolam therefore chose that time to go over to Petulia's home to collect the flyers announcing the Bishop's visit to Brewster's village. He had not shared any of the details of his meeting with Pigeon with his wife, who he knew would have been bitterly opposed to the plan. Furthermore, it was he who earlier had forbidden his wife to have any association with Pigeon. Now, however, he was assisting the very Pigeon in plotting against the persons who had elevated his wife to her present status. Ram knew that even though Mr. Goodfellow had allowed his wife to maintain her position after he had won the election, it was not to him that she gave honor, but to the BOARD, and especially to Laurent Faulkner and Adolph Pilchard.

In order to distribute the fliers as expeditiously and discreetly as possible, Ram gathered twelve children and offered each of them twenty five cents to distribute the fliers throughout the village, while he rode the bus to Slough and, in like manner, gathered five teenage boys and paid them a dollar each to make the distributions among the people. Ram therefore returned to Brewster's village quite quickly, but instead of returning home, diverted to *Blackie's* where some of his close associates had already gathered to begin the New Year celebrations. It was there that he made his announcements of the Bishop's visit to the patrons as they came and went. By noon, the news of Bishop Addington's visit on the following Monday had circulated the village, and great excitement was aroused.

Mrs. Ramgolam was still at Molly's salon when she received the flyer, and she was overcome with immense joy. She later boasted to Ram that the meeting would present another opportunity for her, as the Public Relations Chairperson, to be in the limelight, and to stand side by side with Bishop Addington in front of what she began to describe as the *villagers*. However, Ram mentioned nothing to his wife about his role in the upcoming meeting. Even when Mrs. Ramgolam voiced her surprise at not being informed by anyone on the vestry about the Bishop's visit did Ram mention anything about his role or the nature of the Bishop's visit. Ram told her to stop worrying, for he was sure that later that night, at the service or at the ball, she was going to be duly notified.

* * *

The service was well attended, and again, Philbert Watts assumed the lead part in the anthem. However, the members of the *Gold Circle* were not as perturbed as they were on Harvest Sunday, for they knew that by Easter Sunday, according to Ruthel Pollard, 'the mules shall have acquired their own green pasture and still waters in which to graze and be silent.' Mrs. Ramgolam, however, was more surprised when none of the vestry or the *Gold Circle* members – or even Reverend Perths - mentioned anything about the Bishop's visit which was scheduled for the following Monday. She kept inquiring from her husband as to the time of the announcement.

Pigeon Goodfellow's aloofness from the vestry that night was poignantly noticeable. He merely shared the peace and wished those with whom he came into contact abundant blessings for the new year. At the end of the service, he mingled briefly with some of the members of the lower circles and a few of his close acquaintances before departing with his wife for a family gathering in Georgetown. No conversation was shared between him and Jason or Bill Jones. The former maintained his distance from the latter two, and they in turn seemed to avoid any interaction with him. Maggie Billings was surprisingly sociable that night, and she and the judge shared a brief conversation. However, she did not attend the ball hosted by the Faulkners, but retired to her home to quietly welcome the new year.

At the stroke of midnight, the bells began to chime to the tune of *Auld lang syne*, and the members of the congregation who were still milling around burst into song and hugged and kissed each other. For the duration of the tune, the social barriers were temporarily broken down, and the members of the various circles embraced each other and celebrated the arrival of the new year in harmony and peace. However, no sooner had the chimes ceased that the members departed for their respective celebrations, with none desiring to have further fellowship with the other. The members of the *Bronze* and *Iron Circles* who were still present when the upper circles and the select few from the two impoverished villages departed for the Faulkners stood with awe as Mr. and Mrs. Ramgolam, escorted by Bertie, Mrs. Ramgolam's bodyguard, held hands and stepped ceremoniously towards the specially hired car. Mrs. Ramgolam, in particular, had very little to do that night with any of the members from Brewster's village or Slough, but waved to them with the failed finesse of unrefined royalty as she proceeded to the waiting vehicle. The bodice of her red, satin, home made gown was covered with an ostentatious display of resplendent, gold colored motifs and she wore a gold tiara which seemed to sit enthroned on the mass of rejuvenated curls which fell just above her bust line. Ram was appropriately attired in his black suit and red bow tie.

It was later learned that the black bowler hat and white gloves which he wore against his will was at the behest of his wife. He later confessed to Pigeon that he had acquiesced to his wife's command to wear the hat and gloves so as to appease her in anticipation of her bellowing rage when she discovers that he was part of the planning for the Bishop's visit.

Sometime during the celebration at the Faulkners, the judge and Mr. Faulkner, as well as Bill Jones, expressed gratitude to Mrs. Ramgolam for the impressive job she was doing in her role as Public Relations Chairperson, and urged her to encourage the people to support the plans for the new church. Mr. Faulkner reiterated the compliments and requests during his speech at the dinner. This time, however, the other specially invited guests pledged their support and vowed to stand firm on their word when the Bishop comes two days later to meet the members at *Brad's Palace*.

The guests gasped and their jaws dropped upon hearing the pledge of support from the peasants.

"I beg your pardon?" Laurent Faulkner responded in utter shock.

"We's goin' to support the plans for the new church when Bishop Addington come to see we on Monday night," Moses Abrams repeated.

"The bishop is coming to Brewster's village on Monday, and no one mentioned anything?" the judge remarked.

"Where did you get that information from, Moses?" Mr. Faulkner asked.

"Some boys was givin' out the notice…pun a piece of paper that say that the Bishop comin' to meet we at Brad's Palace pun Monday night at ha' pas' six," Moses replied.

Silence engulfed the room as the guests contemplated each other in disbelief.

"Who the hell arranged this meeting? Who invited the Bishop to go to Brewster's village?" Mr. Faulkner yelled as he pounded his fist on the table.

"It could only be Goodfellow. He was over at the Bishop the other day. The bishop's watchman told me. He saw him there," the judge replied.

"That man has gone too far," Bill declared. "Someone has to put a stop to his madness. Last night he verbally attacked me and Jason…and…"

Mr. Pilchard raised his head abruptly and fixed Bill a forbidding stare. Bill paused.

"Yes," Jason added. "He has to be the one who arranged the meeting, I'm sure. He would do something like that."

"That's the man you all voted for to run the church," the usually reticent Mrs. Pilchard piped.

Bill rose from his seat and stood in the center of the group. "I have a suggestion, brothers and sisters, a plan that would put this man in his place once and for all."

"What is that, Bill? The man is your new warden. You all voted him in," Mr. Faulkner responded. "What could you possibly do now?"

"Look, the man disgraced the church in public last night," Bill protested. "I have witnesses. He cursed like a sailor and made threats. The people were appalled. I say we circulate a petition to have him removed from office. I myself will draw up the petition and oversee its circulation. Mrs. Ramgolam, I'm sure, will organize its circulation in Brewster's village and Slough. Could we count on your support, Mrs. Ramgolam?"

"You has all of my support, Mr. Jones," Mrs. Ramgolam swore.

Mr. Ramgolam sat quietly and nervously tapped his feet.

"Just a minute," Dr. Griffin interjected. "We can't sign a petition to have him removed from office."

"And why not?" Fritz Batty inquired.

"Because we never officially installed him," Dr. Griffin stated. "Think, folks. The man has not yet been commissioned. He has not yet assumed office. He is only the warden elect."

"He's right," the judge declared.

"O.k., we take the position from him, and what do our by-laws say…it says that the person receiving the next highest votes will assume office until such time that the next Annual General Meeting is held. That leaves us with Philbert Watts," Mr. Faulkner announced. "Is that what we want?"

The guests refrained from voicing their true feelings because of the presence of the specially invited members from the two villages. Nevertheless, they agreed that Bill's suggestion should be put into action. A motion was made and a vote was thus cast. The motion received a majority vote. However, there was a small number who abstained. It was further agreed that Mr. Pilchard and Mr. Faulkner would approach Philbert and Reverend Perths with regard to the plan. They were also going to offer Philbert the honor of BOARD membership. However, this privileged position would last only for the duration of his office as warden. No one anticipated any problems or opposition to the decision. In addition, it was decided that Fenton Skeete and Nathaniel Francois would attend the meeting at *Brad's Palace* and report the details to the BOARD.

Mr. Faulkner then raised his glass. "Ladies and gentlemen, let's take a special toast to seal our agreement and celebrate our success in all of our plans for this new year!"

The guests toasted and cheered, and the live band burst into a calypso which brought the guests to their feet in an uninhibited display of frenzied gyrations.

* * *

Around four thirty on New Year's morning, Pigeon was awakened by the sound of his telephone which seemed magnified in the quiet of the wee hours of the new day. He fumbled in the dark to pick up the receiver before his wife could be disturbed.

"Good morning and happy new year." Pigeon's voice was breaking from tiredness and the sudden awaking.

"They're going to circulate a petition to oust you from office…just giving you a heads up. They planned it at the party over at Faulkner's."

The husky voice spoke quickly and urgently, and the informer hung up before Pigeon could say another word. He could not identify the voice, and assumed that the individual had wished to conceal his identity and thus disguised his voice. However, he also thought that it might have been a hoax in order to make him do something that would indeed bring about his own downfall.

Pigeon did not immediately return to bed but ambled to the cabinet and poured himself a potent shot of brandy to calm his nerves. He had been looking forward to his meeting with Maggie later that evening, but he suddenly began to reconsider his affirmative response to her invitation. Irrational thoughts began to consume his mind, and he pictured Maggie serving him a drink which was laced with some powerful narcotic or worse, a poisonous substance, after which the judge would appear from some hidden corner of the house and interrogate him before hacking him to pieces and disposing of his body in some remote area. Furthermore, he knew that the honorable judge's reputation would save him from any accusation – even in spite of the faintest intimation of suspicion. Notwithstanding, Pigeon decided that with the necessary precautions, he would visit Maggie that night, in case she wanted to reveal something about the judge's role in Wilberforce's murder, or to make a confession regarding her role in the same.

After realizing that a fair portion of time had elapsed, and that the brandy was beginning to affect his sense of reason, Pigeon retired once more to bed. He knew that the time had come for him to clear the threshing floor of the chaff which could ultimately suffocate him.

*   *   *

Friday morning brought dark, grey clouds and inclemency. Abersthwaithe and the surrounding villages were relatively quiet after the night of frolic and revelry. Apart from a few small groceries, all of the other shops and stores were closed for the day, as was the custom. At about ten o'clock, Mrs. Ramgolam donned her yellow plastic raincoat, a pair of Wellingtons and her slightly tattered umbrella, and departed for *Brad's Palace* to investigate the issue regarding Bishop Addington's visit on the coming Monday. Ram was still sleeping and recovering from the after-effects of excessive alcohol and excessive revelry from the previous night when his wife left the home. She gave specific instructions to the eldest of the four remaining children at home to prepare his breakfast when he awoke and to refrain from divulging her whereabouts to him if he awoke before she returned.

Brad's Palace was still closed when Mrs. Ramgolam arrived, and she proceeded to the front door of the house and knocked. Mrs. Bradshaw opened.

"Eh eh, Gloysis…whu you doin' pun the road in all this rain, this early new year's mornin'?" Mrs. Bradshaw greeted her visitor.

"Ah come to discuss dhis t'ing 'bout the bishop visit pun Monday night," Mrs. Ramgolam replied.

Soon the two women were engaged in pertinent conversation over two enamel cups of hot cocoa and two saucers of salt biscuits served with fried smoked herring and boiled green plantains.

"How come you askin' me 'bout all this?" Mrs. Bradshaw inquired after swallowing a mouthful of the hot beverage. "You mean to say that you' husband ain't tell you 'bout it?"

"Ram ain't know nothin' bout it. Dhat's why I come to aks you. I is the Public Relations afficah and y'all got a meetin' with the bishop and nobody ain't tell me nothing? I is the one who is supposed to let the people know and all dhat. When they talk 'bout it las' night at the ball over deh at the Faulkners them, I was apllaud. So whu time is this meetin?" Mrs. Ramgolam further asked.

"Half pas' seven. Look Gloysis, go aks you' husband 'bout the meetin. I ain't supposed to say nothing 'bout it to nobody. Mr. Goodfellow tell me not to say nothin' to nobody," Mrs. Bradshaw responded.

"Oh… is a secret. Ya'll doin' all o' dis behind me back. I see. Well leh me tell you something, Volda, you is a snake in the grass. You join with them people to prevent the vestry them from buildin' the chu'ch here. Well leh me tell you something; don't mind whu y'all does, we goin' still build that church, so you an' all of them, whoever they is, could carry all ya' @#*#. You is a traitor…a nasty backstabbin' bitch. But we goin' see who got the power here, Volda; I goin' to show you who is the boss here," Mrs. Ramgolam swore as she rose from her chair and headed towards the door.

Mrs. Bradshaw was appalled by Mrs. Ramgolam's attitude and the coarse, undeserving insults that were hurled towards her; but worse, she was intensely angered by the Public Relations Officer's blatant disrespect for her home and arrant disregard for her hospitality. She stood at her door in shock and mounting indignation as Mrs. Ramgolam descended the stairs, still casting disparaging remarks about her and her husband for their audacity. However, it was Mrs. Ramgolam's mention of Mr. Bradshaw that finally thrust Mrs. Bradshaw into an uncontrollable inferno of fury.

"Gloysis Ramgolam, you know you blasted eyes pass me and me husband," yelled the irate Mrs. Bradshaw. "You bring yo' pickey hair *#@*% right upstairs in me house this early new year's morning, sit down and lick down me' breakfast and then cuss me and me husband out over something that we ain't know nothing' 'bout. You bes' move you' @#@**# from in front of me house before I come down deh and galvanize you' backside!"

"Come nah; come and try it if you bad, Volda. Come an' galvanize me backside if you think you bad, you dry head, insipid, bufumbra rat. I'd hand you a new years lickin' you'd never forget!" Mrs. Ramgolam retorted.

Mrs. Ramgolam's threat and abuse unleashed a wave of white hot anger in Mrs. Bradshaw, who normally was a relatively quiet and unassuming woman. In her fury, she charged down the stairs without even realizing that she was still clothed only in a duster and a pair of old, house slippers. The shouting from the verbal exchange had attracted the attention of some of the neighbors who were nonchalantly carrying out their morning chores, and who consequently rushed to the scene. Mr. Bradshaw appeared at the door, and upon noticing that it was his wife that was involved in the New Year's Day brawl, dashed back inside to put on a shirt and quickly slip his feet into a pair of Wellingtons. By the time he returned to the door, a crowd was already formed and the two women were engaged in a fierce battle – the night club proprietress and the Public Relations 'Afficah', slugging it out like two ruffians in a drinking bar. Most of the crowd was offering advice to Mrs. Bradshaw whose reciprocity they hoped would be shown to them at some later date when the Bradshaws would host their lavish, monthly, Sunday buffet brunch and dancing, which the village elite would attend for a modest fee, and to which the Bradshaws would invite a few of the other villagers who could not afford the fee, for good luck. Mrs. Bradshaw always held fast to the passage in the New Testament in which Jesus teaches that when one hosts a party or a banquet, one must invite those who could not reciprocate in like manner.

"Cuff she pun she mouth good, Volda. She talk too much!" shouted Ruby Cozier, Mrs. Bradshaw's closest neighbor.

Mr. Bradshaw forced his way through the thickening crowd in order to reach the two women who had since tumbled to the ground and were wrestling on the wet grass and sloppy mud. Half of Mrs. Bradshaw's duster was already ripped off, and Mr. Bradshaw removed his shirt in order to cover his wife's exposed torso. Mrs. Ramgolam's plastic coat was ripped in several parts and her clothing was covered with mud. Mr. Bradshaw was soon able to subdue his wife, and with the unwilling assistance of two other male bystanders, to separate the two women.

"What the hell the two y'all goin' on with, man. What kind o' disgraceful, common place behavior y'all getting' on with?" he reprimanded the two women.

"Is she!" screamed Mrs. Bradshaw. "Is she start it!"

"Is she come outside and knock me firs' because I ask she a simple question," Mrs. Ramgolam responded defensively. "I ain't do she nothing!"

"You see how these people in Abersthwaithe got you all. Y'all getting' jes' like them. They lyin' down in they fancy bed in they fancy house, and the two y'all fightin' out here like two mad people, 'cause o' them!" the infuriated Mr. Bradshaw shouted. "They got y'all livin' jes' like how they does live, like dogs bitin' one another…jes' like them. Volda, get you backside back upstairs and have some respect for y'self!"

Ruby Cozier took Mrs. Bradshaw by the hand and led her back to the house. The crowd began to disperse after Mr. Bradshaw started to admonish the two women. They did not want to arouse Mr. Bradshaw's anger against them and thus lose their chance of being invited for a free brunch.

"Leh we move from 'ere, Brian," one of the bystanders advised his friend, "'fore Mr. Bradshaw see we and don't invite we to he Sunday party like he does do sometimes to dhem other people."

The two men made a hasty retreat to their respective homes.

"And you, Mrs. Ramgolam, you go 'long you way. You come all the way here to fight with me wife. Whu kind o' behavior is that for a flippin' Public Relations Offisah? You ain't got no pride in yo'self?!" Go 'long, go over to Abersthwaithe now, leh dhem people see whu you look like now with mud all over you skin and you' clothes all tear up, tear up. See if they goin' even let you inside they gate. Go 'long, yo' fool!"

Upon being rebuked so harshly and dismissed so shamefully from the scene, Mrs. Ramgolam turned and flounced away from the crowd, while nevertheless hurling a string of profanities at the jeering crowd. Some of the men began to boo her as she retreated from the scene, and in retaliation she raised the back of her dress and bent over to expose a pair of muddy, home made, off-white, cotton underwear.

"Go bleach them drawers, Gloysis!" Mabel Richardson yelled.

"Yeah," echoed Egbert Hutchins, who lived across the street from the Bradshaws. "And wash you' batty with Dettol 'fore you get ringworm from the mud!"

The remaining crowd burst into throes of boisterous laughter before Mr. Bradshaw turned his attention on them and chided them for their simplicity of mind and failure to interrupt the shameful scuffle between the two women.

Within one hour, the news of the fight had spread all through the village and into Slough. However, Ram was still asleep when his wife returned home, and by the time he awoke, she had already showered again and tidied herself.

She mentioned nothing to him about her encounter with Mrs. Bradshaw, but while he was having his breakfast, she accosted him about his role in the upcoming meeting on Monday.

"Who tell you that I know 'bout it?" Ram defensively asked his wife.

"That Volda Bradshaw," she replied. "She say to aks you. She mus' know. And she say that she ain't supposed to say nothin' 'bout it to nobody."

"That Volda Bradshaw talk too much. Nobody ain't give she no message," Ram snapped. "And how come she tell you that? She jes' up so and tell you that?" he further inquired.

"I been over there this morning. Me and she had it out," Mrs. Ramgolam explained.

"What you go over there and pick 'pun the woman for? Who aks you to go over there and aks the woman anything, Gloysis? She ain't got nothin' to do wid it. We only keepin' the meetin' deh. Why you doesn't stay you *%#@@ in you' house and mind you' business!"

"I is the Public Relations Afficah, and I is supposed to know everything that goin' on 'bout the church!" she yelled.

"Well, keep outta dis. It ain't got nothin' to do wid you," Ram warned.

"You see you, Ram, you is a jealous, two faced, coolie dog. You' vex 'cause I is the Public Relations Afficah and you ain't nobody. Is only because o' me dhat you went to the ball at the Faulkners dem las' night. Is only 'cause o' me that you up deh wid the big shots dem. But you ain't no damn body!" the irate, humiliated woman berated her husband. "You is a traitor!"

"Look Gloysis, move you black behin' from in front o' me, yeah. Gwan!" the infuriated Ram barked as he waved his hand dismissively.

"Dhat's all you good for, to cuss people, nothin' else, yo' coolie dog!" Mrs. Ramgolam retaliated.

"I ain't cuss you, Gloysis..." Ram argued.

"So whu you always tellin' me 'bout black dhis and black dhat, yo' coolie..."

"...Gloysis!" Ram interjected angrily. "Since when black is a cuss? You is a black woman. Whu color you expec' you behin' to be? How is dhat a cuss? If you think dhat black is a cuss, then is not me cussin' you, is you' cussin' yo'self. You doesn't hear me complainin' when you call me a coolie, 'cause I is a coolie. They ain't nothin' wrong 'bout bein' a coolie. I ain't shame 'bout bein' a coolie, so you shouldn't be shame 'bout bein' black. I doesn't know why black people does get vex when you call dhem black. Is a mystery I would never unda'stan'."

"Don't change the subject. You is a traitor. Leh me tell you something, I goin' to go to the meetin' pun Monday, and I goin' to sit right next to the bishop at the front table. I is the Public Relations Afficah and I goin' to..."

"Look Gloysis, gimme a chance 'bout dhis 'Public Relations Afficah' stupidness. Dhem people only usin' you, and you knows it. You ain't goin nowhere!" Ram decreed.

"An' all dhis time you sit down deh at the ball, an' hear Mr. Faulkner dhem talkin' bout dhis meetin' and yo' sit down dhere like you ain't know nothing. You is a bad man… a wicked man!" Mrs. Ramgolam declared. "You plottin' 'gainst you own wife, you own friggin wife!"

"You ain't goin' to the meetin', Gloysis. I don't care what you say." Ram then rose from the table and headed towards the front steps where he sat and lit a cigarette.

"Where you goin? I ain't done wid you yet!" Mrs. Ramgolam screamed.

"I done wid you, though, Gloysis. I done a long time," Ram replied dismissively as he drew his first puff.

Mrs. Ramgolam, already infuriated from the incident over at the Bradshaws, hurled the enamel cup of left-over coffee at her husband. The cup grazed against the left side of Ram's head and tumbled down the stairs. Ram became intensely angry and picked up the cup and threw it towards his wife. The object struck her in the forehead and fell to the floor. Mrs. Ramgolam immediately seized the piece of wood which was used to hold one of the wooden windows open, and chased her husband, cursing him and his generation as the children stood by, screaming in fear. Ram dashed up the street, with his wife in hot pursuit and a few neighbors trailing her, begging her to compose herself and conduct herself like that of a true Public Relations Officer. The pursuit ended when Ram swung the corner and increased the distance between them. When Mrs. Ramgolam realized that she could not reach her husband, she threw the stick aimlessly towards him, and it missed and struck an old, abandoned car which for years had been parked by the bridge which pedestrians used to cross over the canal to Slough. Mrs. Ramgolam aborted the chase when Mr. Ramgolam ran across the bridge, and upon turning back, straightened up and strutted back to the house with the gait of a princess, as though nothing had happened. The children met her half way along the road, and holding hands, escorted her home as if the family was returning from a walk to the park.

*   *   *

Evening came on eagles wings, and Pigeon got dressed and left his home at about seven fifteen. He had decided that he would make a surprise visit to Jason's home. As he drove, he contemplated on his friendship with the man whom he had respected and loved like a younger brother. Jason's unfaithfulness had severely affected him, and even though he pretended that he was not the least perturbed by such strange behavior, his mind was restless. He had trusted Jason, and had great plans for him when he officially assumed the office of senior warden. Jason was going to be his right hand man, and he was going to prime him for the role of junior warden when Bill's time was up at the end of that year. Of all the disappointments he had had, and all the pains he had suffered at the hands of those to whom he had opened himself, Jason's actions hurt him the most. He needed to know where he stood with Jason before he proceeded to Maggie's place. He knew that he could only defeat his enemies if he had an undercover ally, someone whom he trusted and cared deeply about, and he believed that Jason was such a person. For some strange reason, however, he could not bring himself to despise Jason, and decided to give him another chance at loyalty.

As Pigeon drew closer to Jason's home, he thought deeply about him. He remembered the first time he met the relatively young accountant. He had attended the Easter Sunday service that day, and during the fellowship in the Parish Hall, he mentioned that he had just returned from England where he had spent many years working as an account after his graduation. He took a great liking to him, as a younger brother, and the two men developed a close, brotherly relationship. However, as the years progressed, and Jason met other friends in his profession and developed other interests, he and Jason grew gradually apart. However, they still held a very high degree of mutual respect. Pigeon remembered Jason as a rather gullible individual, and he often warned the young man of the dangers of readily believing things that were said to him without first analyzing the facts. He also remembered chiding Jason many times for his naivete, and cautioning him of the awkwardness in which he could find himself. He and Jason had shared many intimate stories about themselves – in their personal lives and in their professions – stories which he had never shared with anyone else, even with Mrs. Goodfellow. These memories made it very difficult for him to shun his once closest friend. He was nine years older than Jason, but Jason's sincerity and loyalty placed him on the top of his list of closest friends.

At one time, Jason had confessed that he had developed strangely deep affections for Maggie Billings, with whom he was assigned by the vicar to do some volunteer bookkeeping for the church; Jason had wanted a different level of intimacy to develop between them. However, Pigeon was able to redirect Jason's affections to a young woman who had worked as an intern in his office. He never asked Jason anything about that relationship and determined never again to discuss it with the young man, especially since he subsequently had heard rumors about him and Maggie going on private midweek retreats together at one of the Roman Catholic monasteries in a place called Leitchfield on the east coast. Jason likewise never again brought up the issue of his deep affection for Maggie, but it was shortly after his confession that the two men began to drift apart.

Now, as he drew closer to Jason's home, he began to wonder if Jason was deliberately avoiding him because of some discreet relationship with Maggie, something of which Pigeon had perspicuously expressed his disapproval. However, he had no proof of any present relationship between Jason and Maggie. Neither did he worry about any questionable company that Jason kept – except that of Fenton Skeete – whom he had considered to be a subtle opportunist. Furthermore, he thought that unless Jason had ceased to be the sincere and loyal person he knew him to be, he was not going to shun him because of relationships to which he was vehemently opposed. He respected Jason for his noble character, and that would be the only dictate for their renewed friendship.

Pigeon parked the black Ford about twenty five yards from Jason's gate, and remained in the vehicle for approximately five minutes, praying for patience with Jason and for Jason's willingness to speak with him and to cooperate with him in his war against the BOARD and vestry. At exactly seven thirty five, he stepped out of the vehicle and proceeded to the gate. He knew that if he had knocked, the dogs would have begun to bark and this would have given Jason the opportunity to evade him. Thus he stepped cautiously towards the front door, praying passionately that the dogs were in their kennels. He had decided that if the dogs were not contained, and had attacked, he would jump on top of Jason's car for refuge. He thus proceeded and pressed the bell. The sound of firm footsteps approached the door and opened. Jason was petrified. His jaw dropped as he beheld Pigeon, standing there with a disarming smile. Pigeon noted that whatever bitterness Jason might have developed towards him seemed to have been temporarily shelved for the duration of the visit.

"My friend!" Jason managed to compose himself and display delight at seeing Pigeon.

Pigeon could see that Jason's excitement was not genuine, and that his unexpected visit had caused him some discomfort and mild anger.

"Jason," Pigeon responded in his usual calm voice. "How do you do, my brother?"

Pigeon knew his friend well, and could see that he was quite perplexed by his strange calmness. He could also see by Jason's expression that he was wrestling with a troubled conscience, but even more perturbed by his sudden appearance.

"Wha…what …brings you here this evening?" Jason stuttered nervously as he maintained his place at the entrance of the door.

"You," Pigeon replied with a wan expression, "your questionable attitude…towards me, for instance. What is the matter with you, Jason? You seem distant…strange…almost like a completely different individual. I'm here because you and I need to talk. Christmas Eve night we sat in my car and we spoke about a couple of things, and you promised to cooperate with me, work harmoniously with me. Then, a couple of nights ago, you wake me from my sleep and you fill me in with the details of a meeting which you walked out from because you were not in concurrence with what they were doing. Now you are avoiding me like poison. What's up, Jason? You owe me some kind of explanation, don't you think. After all, we're friends; at least I'd like to think that we are."

Throughout Pigeon's lament, Jason stared at him without any hint of remorse. He merely stood there without making any comment or even an excuse for his strange behavior. He did not invite Pigeon inside.

"Are you going to invite me inside, Jason, or you're going to speak to me at the door as if I'm a gypsy selling trinkets, or a Jehovah's Witness pushing erroneous doctrine?" Pigeon was beginning to lose patience with his one time best friend.

"Yes…yes, I suppose you can come in," Jason replied after a momentary period of obvious reluctance. "Bu…but I can't really entertain you right now. I…I'm trying to finish some work here."

"Looks like things are picking up again," Pigeon remarked as he was directed to the chair nearest to the door.

Jason remained tense as Pigeon sat observing him keenly. Jason offered his estranged friend no drink, and remained standing with his arms folded.

"Sit down, Jason. I know that you have work to do, but at least give me the respect I deserve. I'm not going to carry on a conversation with you standing over me like a security officer."

"Look, Pigeon, like I said, I've got a lot of work to do. You'll just have to excuse me." Jason's tone was harsh and unfriendly.

Pigeon nevertheless ignored him and made himself more comfortable. "Could I get a drink, or something? I mean, it's New Year's Day."

Jason began to show signs of severe agitation.

"Jason, is something wrong? You are obviously very uneasy…tense," Pigeon stated as he stared at Jason with a blank, but nevertheless notoriously intimidating expression. If my presence is making you this uncomfortable, then I suppose that it is no use trying to resuscitate a moribund friendship."

The rejected Pigeon thus rose to leave. He ambled reluctantly towards the door and then stopped and turned to face the man whom he once had held in such high esteem. "You know, Jason, I had perceived that our friendship was dying a slow, painful death, but I was hoping, deep inside, for a miracle cure. But I can see that it is pointless. So I am going to beg you for at least a glass of water before I leave. A dying man usually thirsts for one thing or the other. May I please have a glass of water before I leave?"

Jason briefly studied his one time friend before he ascended the stairs to the main floor. Pigeon used the opportunity to rush over to Jason's desk to note the nature of the work he was attempting to complete with such urgency. He noted that Jason had several opened files on the table. However, it was the closed file which struck him a powerful blow; it was thick and bound in what appeared to be a brown, leather cover on which was etched, *Faulkner & Babbit.* Immediately, Pigeon felt the surge of fury rising in his head as he began to make sense of Jason's sudden change of attitude towards him. As he turned to hurry back to the door, he heard subdued voices in conversation upstairs. One was Jason's. He was unsure of the other, but realized that it was that of another male. Pigeon decided that he would dispense with propriety and mount the stairs – one last time – in a desperate attempt to understand the source or reason for his former best friend's sudden change of attitude towards him. Without sparing one more second, he dashed up the stairs, with the stealth and speed of a cat that has sensed the presence of a mouse, to the second floor. On reaching the top, he froze and his mouth fell agape as he beheld two figures seated at the dining table, engaged in some sort of meeting. Files and sheets of paper were on the table, and they each held a pen. The figures turned in shock to behold the unwelcomed, intruding visitor. Their eyes met, and they contemplated him momentarily before any greetings between the parties were exchanged.

Pigeon stepped briskly across the room to the table with his arm extended to shake hands. "My my...! What a pleasant surprise to see you here!"

One of the figures suddenly rose to intercept him before he could reach the table. They shook hands, but the figure prevented him from going further by gently patting him on the shoulder and turning him towards the door. As Pigeon turned, he noticed that the other member made some subtle effort to conceal the contents of the papers on the table by leaning forward over them and covering them under his arms.

"No insult intended, Goodfellow, but this is a private meeting...a confidential matter," the figure explained.

"I see, Pigeon stated. "Is that the petition that's being circulated to oust me from office?"

The question caught the group by surprise.

"What are you talking about, Pigeon?" Jason asked with a somber expression.

"Aww, never mind; just one of those incidental remarks made in jest," Pigeon replied. "I'm sorry to have intruded on your private meeting, gentlemen. Goodnight."

"You asked for water," Jason said as Pigeon headed towards the stairs.

"Don't bother yourself, Jason. I'll soon be home. I'll serve myself a drink when I get there," Pigeon replied as he briefly studied the figure who intercepted him from approaching the table. He tipped his hat gallantly, "Gentlemen…"

As Pigeon descended the stairs, the men glanced briefly at each other. The figure stepped forward to follow him to the door.

"I know my way out," Pigeon curtly remarked as he turned and stared piercingly and coldly at the man.

The man stopped abruptly. Pigeon descended the stairs and closed the door quietly behind him and left. As far as he was concerned, his relationship with Jason was now completely severed. He now was no longer bound to any loyalty to him or sympathy towards him. Whatever was the offence he had committed to turn his friend so abruptly and bitterly against him, he would never know. Nor did he care to know. Jason was now, more than anyone else, on his list to be utterly destroyed. However, his hatred towards Jason was so suddenly intense that he set to work immediately to destroy him.

Pigeon strode briskly towards his car and sat patiently, like a serpent concealed in the bush, waiting for the unsuspecting prey. He was overcome with despondence as he sat in his vehicle, reminiscing about his friendship with Jason. It became obvious that Jason was never a faithful friend. They had spent much time together, but Jason's recent actions made it very clear that he had been working with the enemy all through the time he had sworn loyalty to him.

As Pigeon sat contemplating Jason's sudden change of attitude, he noticed one of the figures leaving his former friend's property. The individual was one of the more recent members of the church, and obviously one who had already been drawn into the *Silver* or *Gold Circle*. He studied him furtively as he strode towards his vehicle which was parked further away in the opposite direction. Five minutes later, the other individual, the one who had intercepted him, appeared. However, he was carrying a large envelope. He walked past the car, oblivious of Pigeon observing him. No sooner had he passed that Pigeon, now filled with rabid hate, stepped out of his car.

"Excuse me there, sir," Pigeon called out.

The man turned as Pigeon was about ten feet away from him. He displayed evident uneasiness on realizing that it was Pigeon who was so approaching him in the dark of the evening. He placed his hand with the envelope behind him and forced a nervous smile.

"Oh, it's good to see you again, Mr. Goodfellow, sir," he said as his frightened eyes stared at Pigeon.

"Good to see you again too. I actually don't know your name. I know your face, of course, from seeing you at the church, but I'm afraid that I don't know your name," Pigeon confessed.

"Austin…Austin Johanson," the tall, well built young man replied. His voice was shaking with nervousness.

Suddenly, Pigeon's countenance changed and he stretched forward his arm. "I believe you have something there for me, Johanson?"

"Something like what?" Johanson inquired, as he backed away fearfully from Pigeon.

"Something like that envelope behind your back. Give it to me," Pigeon demanded.

"I…I can't. I am taking it to Mr. Faulkner. He's expecting me in a few minutes. It…it's nothing about you," Johanson swore.

"Nevertheless, let me see it." Pigeon's tone was cold and threatening.

"I can't, Mr. Goodfellow. The whole group's confided in me. I have to do as I promised. If you wish to see the contents of the envelope, I would suggest that you speak with Mr…."

"…Give me the damn envelope, Johanson," Pigeon interjected as he pulled out a revolver from the inner pocket of his blazer and pointed it towards the trembling man.

Johanson immediately surrendered the envelope and turned to rush to his car.

"Where do you think you're going, Johanson. You wait here until I check the contents of this envelope. *I* will decide when you go," Pigeon ordered.

Johanson stood trembling as Pigeon ripped open the envelope. There were several sheets of paper with scores of signatures. The accompanying letter was a petition to abrogate Pigeon's election to office. Pigeon took the envelope and dismissed Johanson.

"You can go. I'll take this to whomever you were going to take it to. I know who it is that you were supposed to take it to; don't worry, I know who it is," Pigeon advised Johanson.

"But Mr. Goodfellow, I can't not take this envelope over. Mr. Faulkner is waiting for me. We just spoke with him."

"Good. Then think of the surprise he'll get when *I* take it to him," Pigeon said with a wry smile.

"Look, sir, please, you can't…" Johanson pleaded.

"…Can't what?" Pigeon interjected. "A few minutes ago at Jason's house you were trying to intimidate me. Now you're begging for mercy? Well here it is; get your effeminate ass in the car and get out of my sight. And one more thing," Pigeon stepped close to Johanson and pointed the gun to his chest, "you will tell Faulkner that a vagrant who hangs around the area at night snatched this envelope from you and ran away through the alley. Trust me, they will believe you. Mr. Pilchard knows the man who sleeps in the alleyway. And remember, if you mention anything about this, I'll take care of you. Believe me. Furthermore, no one will believe you, and nothing can happen to me. Look around…see…there are no witnesses. So It's my word against yours. Remember, I'm a lawyer. I know the game. Now go…get… the #**%# outta my sight!"

Johanson jumped into his vehicle without another word and disappeared round the corner. Pigeon placed the envelope under the driver's seat and headed back to Jason's house and knocked on the door. Jason opened, and the sight of Pigeon a second time shocked him. However, Pigeon remained calm, and stood erect with his hands hanging listlessly at his side.

"Good night again, Jason," Pigeon greeted his visibly puzzled, former friend.

Jason smiled nervously as he beheld Pigeon standing motionlessly at the door. "Hi, Pigeon. I …I am glad to see you again, but as I told you earlier, I'm rather busy. I can't talk to you right now. I'm trying to…"

"…Shut up, Jason and go and sit down. I need to talk to you, whether you have the time or not!" Pigeon's countenance was sombre and his eyes penetrated Jason like a poisonous dagger.

Jason turned mechanically like a robot and proceeded to the desk, and turned to face Pigeon. He sat at the edge of the desk as if awaiting a fatal chastisement.

"What the hell was that meeting upstairs all about?" Pigeon glared at the visibly frightened Jason.

"Just…just a little gathering to discuss something that I was commissioned to do," Jason managed to squeak.

"Commissioned by whom to do what, Jason?"

"Look, I'm not supposed to be divulging any of what was discussed here tonight. You can't come into my house to interrogate me like this," Jason protested. "I've sworn to condfidentiality."

"That's good. Very noble, I say. But let's get serious, Jason. Both you and I know that your skill in the art of confidentiality is like a monk doing stand-up comedy in an X-rated night club. It was you who woke me from my sleep a couple o' weeks ago to tell me what the BOARD was planning, remember. I'm sure that all of that was said to you in confidence. They would be shocked, mortified, if they knew that you have shared that information with me. What's happened to you, Jason? What's happened to you, to us, between then and now?" Pigeon implored.

"Look, Pigeon, things don't always go as planned. Things happen. People change," Jason claimed.

"Don't I know it!" 'Pigeon remarked. "But don't you think that as your friend, or should I say, as your former friend, I am entitled to some sort of explanation regarding your behavior towards me, Jason?"

"Look, I'm sorry if my behavior's offended you, Pigeon," Jason apologized. "But I have to see to my own welfare. Nobody is going to do that for me."

"What do you mean?"

"Business was waning. Nobody offered me any help; not even you. All you kept saying was that I should hold on and be strong…patient. Then I spoke to Fenton that night you asked me to. He spoke to Mr. Faulkner, and here I am. Things have picked up and I am doing great. No thanks to you. You are a powerful man in this society, Goodfellow. You could have helped me if you wanted to. Yes, I agree; you were a close friend to me, but I don't need friends now. None of my so called friends helped me. It was Fenton Skeete, the man you sent me to deceive, who made connections to the man who had become my enemy, the man whom you taught me to hate, *Good*fellow. That's right. It was Mr. Faulkner who came to my rescue. Now, he's asked me to do something, I have no choice but to conform. I no longer make friends, Pigeon; I take hostages. You give me what I want, and I'll give you what you ask. That's my new philosophy of life. It's as simple as that," Jason explained.

"It's like that now, eh, Jason?" Pigeon responded.

"I'm sorry…"

"That's alright, Jason. Just remember, however, that hostage negotiations don't always work in either party's favor. The outcome can sometimes be deadly. Remember that."

Pigeon stared coldly at his former friend for a moment before turning abruptly and proceeding to the door. He suddenly turned and fixed Jason a murderous stare. "You are a son-of-a-bitch, you know; a nasty, rotten bowelled, son-of-a-bitch, Jason."

Jason hung his head but raised his eyes to return Pigeon's stare. After a moment of cold, rigid, reciprocal stares, Pigeon stormed through the door.

*   *   *

Jason approached the window and watched his former friend exit the gate. He remained at the window until Pigeon's car sped past the house. Immediately, he proceeded to the gate and locked it, after which he let the two fierce watch dogs out of their kennels. On returning inside the house, he went straight to the telephone and dialled.

"Hello...Mr. Faulkner..."

"This is he," the voice replied.

"Jason here. Goodfellow was just here. But he didn't see anything. Johanson had already taken the sheets with everything and he's already on his way over to you."

"What was Goodfellow doing there?" Faulkner inquired.

"I don't know why he came. He just appeared at the door, asking me what happened between him and me. I told him that I'm busy now and that I don't have the time to spend with him as before, that's all. So he got angry, cursed me and left."

"Good man, Jason. Very good. Don't let him intimidate you. Stand up to him, and he'll back off; face him like a man!" Faulkner charged.

"Tha...thank you, sir."

"Jason, you sound scared. Are you alright?"

"Slightly. He...he *is* a powerful man, sir," Jason confessed.

"Look, I'll have an eye out for you. He can't touch you, alright. He wouldn't dream of it. Leave him to me," Mr. Faulkner consoled the terrified Jason. "The petition which Johanson is bringing over is only step one of his demise. And yes, he might be a powerful man, but only in the court when he is dealing with criminals like himself. But this time he's dealing with me, Laurent Faulkner, and Mr. Pilchard, two men of consequence; one being among the wealthiest on the island, and the other one of the most powerful and influencial. Don't worry, Jason. You're covered – one hundred percent! Oh, I hear the door bell. It might be Johanson with the signed petitions. Take courage, my friend. The fall of the Goodfellow Empire has begun!"

"Thank you. Thank you. Very much," the relieved Jason replied.

*   *   *

Pigeon turned into Westminster Lane and parked opposite *The Victoria Mansion*. He had thought it best to park in a discreet spot just in case Mr. Pilchard decided to pay an unexpected visit. He had considered this meeting to be of a highly confidential nature, and he was going to do whatever was necessary to protect Maggie from suspicion or blame. As far as he was concerned, Maggie was the one who held the key to the vault containing Adolph Pilchard's secrets and vices, secrets if discovered, would bring the imperious judge to his knees in howling disgrace. Pigeon thus approached the house and knocked on the door. Delicately heeled footsteps descended the stairs and opened the polished, mahogany door.

"Peter Goodfellow!" Maggie greeted the emotionally wounded warden-elect with a warm, dignified smile.

"Maggie...," Pigeon responded.

"Do come in," Maggie besought him.

"Thank you. Please excuse my lateness. I was taking care of a personal matter which ran overtime," Pigeon apologized.

"I'm happy that you could be here. That's what matters. Please, let's proceed upstairs."

As Maggie ascended the stairs, her hips swayed gently and seductively under an ankle length, diaphanous, floral patterned dress which was supported by two narrow straps over the shoulder. Her hair was gathered at the back and held in place by a richly embellished ornament which glittered in the light from the chandelier which hung majestically over the staircase. Her svelte figure was almost the epitome of physical perfection for a woman of her years, and her skin appeared very smoothe and soft. For a moment, Pigeon felt a gentle brush of envy towards the judge as he admired the woman who only a few days earlier had requested that he leave her premises. Upon reaching the top of the stairs, Maggie turned towards him and offered him a seat in one of the chairs closest to the bar. For the first time, Pigeon realized how beautiful Maggie really was. He knew that the true features of her face must have been concealed under layers of make-up, but she nevertheless appeared stunningly beautiful that evening – and strangely provocative.

"Please accept this bottle of *Claude Guiteau*, compliments of Peter Goodfellow," Pigeon said as he offered Maggie the black and gold paper bag containing the very expensive liqueur.

"Thank you," Maggie beamed as she accepted the gift.

Pigeon felt his chest pounding as Maggie smiled and batted her eyelids upon receiving the gift. He could not help but admire her pearly white teeth and seductively made-up eyes. He thus sighed and turned his focus on Jason so as to regain his composure.

"May I get you a drink before I serve dinner?" Maggie approached the bar and placed some ice in a glass.

"Thank you. A shot of your best whiskey, please; whatever you've got."

Maggie fixed her guest a drink and proceeded to the kitchen. Pigeon was impressed with Maggie's charm and delicacy. He thus began to muse on Mr. Pilchard's relationship with her, and for a second, wished that the judge would show up at the house and engage in a duel with him for Maggie's affections, and that he would effortlessly defeat him and conquer her. He was so comsumed with thoughts of battle with the judge that he did not hear Maggie inviting him to the table. He thus apologized profusely for his mental distraction, and explained that he was contemplating the many challenges he was likely to face in his new role as senior warden of such an influencial and prestigious parish church.

The sumptuous dinner began with a brief prayer, in which Maggie thanked God for the opportunity to have fellowship with Pigeon and besought his blessings on their renewed friendship. The couple discussed a variety of topics, but Pigeon knew that they were merely gallivanting in desultory trivialities until one of them builds enough courage to introduce the main topic. They had consumed almost half of the bottle of liqueur and were just completing dessert when Maggie introduced the subject of Wilberforce's death.

"You know, Pigeon, I am very grateful to you for coming over this evening for dinner. I have been in a very melancholy mood since Mr. Gaskin's death," she lamented.

"That's understandable," Pigeon responded as he fixed his eyes intently on Maggie.

"He was in love with me; very much so," she admitted. "But I was foolish. I never yielded to his pleas for my affections. Instead I surrendered to someone who, deep inside, I knew would never ultimately be mine. Now, Wilberforce is gone, and the man to whom I gave myself has more or less deserted me. Now that the fire is being ignited, in the wake of Wilberforce's death, I'm alone, dejected, left to sink into oblivion like a dated garment while he...he is locked in the arms of his wife; the best of both worlds for him, I guess."

"How does that make you feel?"

"Bitter. Angry. Very angry, and hurt. I loved him. I gave entirely of myself to him," she confessed. "He claimed that he loved me more than he loved her, but could do nothing because of his position in society, you know, the scandal and all that...and the complexities of loving two women when you are married to one of them..."

"But you should have known that this would have been the outcome of such a relationship," Pigeon stated.

"My brain kept telling me just that, but my heart wouldn't listen," Maggie rejoined. "However, now I'm ready to let my brain take custody of my heart, and I want you to help me."

Pigeon was shocked by Maggie's request but responded very cautiously. He was not sure whether Maggie's plea was genuine or an attempt, in conjunction with Mr. Pilchard, to ensnare him in some deadly trap. He fixed his attention on Maggie for a moment before responding.

"What are you seeking my assistance to do, Maggie?"

"I want you to make it public that Adolph Pilchard and I are romantically involved, and have been so for years. I can't do it, because it could backfire in my face. He would accuse me of trying to destroy his marriage for my benefit, and not only deny the truth but spurn me in its wake. Furthermore,

I cannot do this with just anyone. I need a trusted friend, like you. I cannot trust any of those people on the BOARD. I am beseeching you, as a friend, to assist me," Maggie pleaded.

"You are asking me to destroy a man's marriage, Maggie? Yes, Pilchard and I are more or less antagonistic towards each other, especially since the elections; but I cannot, in all good conscience, attack the institution of marriage. Furthermore, I have tremendous respect for Mrs. Pilchard. She is a decent woman…a woman of exemplary character."

"Then at least," Maggie begged, "help me to bring him to the point where *he* decides to leave her. In that case, the decision would be entirely his, not yours or mine."

"You have a point," Pigeon agreed.

"Then help me. Please," Maggie cried.

"What specifically do you want me to do?" Pigeon inquired.

"Just let the public know of our relationship," Maggie suggested. "I will give you some information. You can then take whatever you deem worthwhile, compile a report and submit it to the *Argosy*."

"In that case you can do it yourself, can't you?" Pigeon replied.

"Yes. But that's not all. I want you to sign the report as Wilberforce Gaskins…"

"What!?" Pigeon gasped as he leaned back in his chair and beheld Maggie in shock, "You are asking me to tell a blatant lie on a dead man?"

"Wilberforce is dead, Pigeon. Furthermore, he was the only person who knew of my affair with Adolph. In addition, Wilberforce wanted to expose him a long time ago, but I dissuaded him from doing so. Trust me, Pigeon, Wilberforce will rest peacefully if you were to do this," Maggie swore.

The sound of a barking dog resounded from one of the closed rooms.

"You keep that mutt in the house with you?" Pigeon inquired incidentally.

"Only at nights, or if it rains incessantly during the day," she replied.

"Going back to our conversation; are you telling me that it is highly possible that Pilchard could be somehow involved with Mr. Gaskin's death?"

"I would never believe that, let alone imply it," Maggie declared. "What I am asking you to do has nothing to do with Mr. Gaskin's death. Please, just leave that alone. Any accusations could lead all of this into another direction."

"I'm sorry," Pigeon apologized.

"So, are you going to do this for me, Pigeon? It's your only chance of being rid of him once and for all. If you let this opportunity slip by, there would be nothing else by which you could bring a man of such social standing to his knees. In other words, your help will be beneficial both to you and to me. If I could have done this by myself, I would have done so. But my conscience would rip me apart if I were to do this and then he has to leave his wife, and asks me to marry him. How will I ever look him in the face?"

"Come back to earth, Maggie," Pigeon ordered the emotional wanderer.

As Pigeon pondered on the request, he began to feel the effect of the unorthodox mixture of the whiskey and the liqueur. He gazed at Maggie and realized that her magnetic, tantalizing stare was an attempt to weaken him and entangle him in her web of perfidy. At that moment, he did not care. He felt valiantly ready for anything.

Maggie leaned towards the now vulnerable accomplice to her treachery and began to caress his hand with her fingers. Pigeon's eyes met hers as she continued to run her beautifully polished nails up his arm. Pigeon closed his eyes and swallowed. Maggie rose and approached him, and began to run her fingers gently through this tightly matted hair.

"If you agree to help me, Pigeon, we could seal our agreement. I could show you what keeps Adolph's heart chained to my bed posts. We could make this our private covenant. Furthermore, you will forever have the advantage over him, for you would have plucked and tasted of the grapes from his vineyard."

Maggie then unclasped the ornament that held her hair in place. The light brown tress fell wildly over her face and shoulders as she shook her head seductively. Pigeon rose and turned to face the alluring temptress. They gazed into each other's eyes for a moment before Maggie drew him close and delicately kissed his lips. She pulled back gently as she gazed passionately into his eyes. "Your lips are warm, and send a shiver right down my spine," she purred.

"Just shut up," Pigeon whispered, "and kiss me again, before I plead insanity."

The two kissed passionately before Pigeon picked up Maggie and lifted her across the room. He laid her gently on the couch while he remained standing and began to unbutton his shirt. Suddenly, as if awakened from a trance, he stopped unbuttoning his shirt and gazed at Maggie in shock.

"What's the matter? Scared? Can't handle this?" Maggie teased the retreating Pigeon.

"Maggie, I…I will help you, but…but I…I can't do this. I…I'm a married man…you know…I …I have…have a wife…." Pigeon was most apologetic as he continued to button his shirt.

Maggie made no verbal response, but rose elegantly, slid the straps from her shoulders and slipped her dress to the floor. As she stepped out of it, she gazed seductively into Pigeon's eyes. Pigeon made several attempts to avert his attention, but Maggie's provocative undergarments drew him towards her once more like a magnet.

Pigeon awoke shortly before mid-night. He was horrified at the realization of himself lying naked and prostrate on the large sofa. Immediately he sprung to his feet in a desperate attempt to clothe himself. As he leaned over to retrieve his trousers from beneath the coffee table, he froze in terror and embarrassment at the sight of Maggie, fully clothed and relaxing on one of the brick-red, leather recliners in front of the television. She was watching the eleven o'clock news.

"Coffee?" she asked with her eyes still fixed on the television.

"No!" Pigeon snapped.

"Do you want anything?" she inquired nonchalantly.

"Yes," Pigeon barked. "I want to know what the blazes just happened here!"

"As a matter of fact, I asked myself the same thing before I got dressed," Maggie replied sarcastically.

"You bloody seduced me!" Pigeon shouted accusingly.

"Did I?" Maggie responded drily and gently. "Were you actually there?" As she spoke, she never averted her attention from the television.

"Nothing happens when a man is seduced by a succubus – against his will!" Pigeon retorted. "I'm bloody going home, and I never want to see your face again…ever! And as far as doing what you brought me here to ask me to do, you can forget it!"

Pigeon stormed down the stairs and slammed the door behind him. As he strode furiously towards the gate, Maggie stepped out to the verandah.

"Mr. Goodfellow, if I were you, I'd think again about breaking our covenant. I have photographs of you lying naked on my sofa, with your deficiencies exposed," Maggie warned the fleeing warden elect.

Pigeon stopped abruptly and turned towards the verandah. "Bitch!" he snarled.

"Have a blessed night's rest. I'll call you," Maggie responded with a simpering smile and retreated into the house. She slid back the glass door, closed the drapes and extinguished the lights.

In a fit of rage, Pigeon charged forward towards the front door and began banging on the polished mahogany and making threats. The light in the foyer came on and the sound of descending footsteps was soon heard. The door opened, and as Pigeon opened his mouth to issue the last round of threats, he noticed the fierce looking mastiff at Maggie's side. Pigeon turned immediately and bolted towards the gate. The dog instinctively darted behind him, with Maggie pleading in vain for it to abandon its pursuit. Pigeon's agility propelled him to the top of the gate in one athletic leap. However, the canine was twice as nimble, and it jumped behind the fleeing lawyer as he scaled the gate and its sharp teeth ripped the back of his trousers. Pigeon landed on the other side of the gate and, without stopping to assess the degree of damage to his grey tweed, sped off down the street to his car, with the animal barking savagely at the gate. By the time the car rolled past the gate, Maggie and the animal had disappeared inside the house.

The journey home for Pigeon was racked with mental inquietude. His conscience was tearing him apart; he had succumbed to Maggie's flagrant forwardness, and in doing so entangled himself in her web of treachery from which there was no escape. Furthermore, he was confronted by the stark recognition of his own weaknesses and the appalling limitations of his purported strength and sagacity. The realization of his finiteness threw him into a paroxysm of rage and he began to swear at the members of the BOARD and vestry, and utter strings of blasphemy against God for abandoning him and making him fall victim to the snares of the enemy. In addition, the humiliation of being chased by Maggie's canine and having his trousers ripped by the savage animal planted the virulent seeds of revenge against the brazen woman and intensified his desire to avenge those upon whom he had stamped the fourth seal.

On reaching home, Pigeon took a quick shower to physically purge himself and slipped into a pair of blue, cotton pajamas. He disposed of the ripped trousers, and then proceeded to pour himself a shot of twenty year old rum which he used only on special occasions. He threw himself on the leather recliner and sunk into deep contemplation. There was much to consider – who should be the first to be the object of his wrath; the manner by which his anger and revenge should be inflicted, and the time-line for the completion of his judgement. There were so many to hate – so many to avenge – that the burden on his chest forbade any possibility of a peaceful slumber.

Pigeon nevertheless went to bed that night convinced that all that was happening to him was part of God's plan for him, in that it was precisely in the wake of all of this persecution and evil apportioned to him that he, like Moses, was being purged and molded for God's service by the fire of purification.

*   *   *

Saturday morning caught the members of the BOARD in a quandary. They had received the distressing call from Laurent Faulkner about the assault on Johanson and the theft of the brown envelope. The installation of the new vestry was going to take place on the following day and time was heavily against them in their quest to oust Pigeon before he could be commissioned. After a series of telephone calls among themselves, they decided that Mr. Pilchard and Mrs. Pigthorne would make an urgent call on the vicar that afternoon to request that he postpone the commissioning of the new vestry until the last Sunday in January, ostensibly to bring closure to all unfinished business so that the incoming officers could begin *tabula rasa.*

No one doubted Johanson's story because Mr. Pilchard was able to verify the existence of the vagrant who sought nocturnal refuge in the alleyway near to Maggie's home. The judge recalled a distorted account of his own experience of being confronted by the hostile vagabond "while he was conducting his 'stewardship visitation' at Ms. Billings home one evening last year." It was his testimony that lent credulity to Johanson's story.

At about three o'clock, Mr. Pilchard and Mrs. Pigthorne met in front of the church and drove over to the vicarage. The BOARD had agreed that it would be unwise to mention anything about the stolen petition and that the focus of the meeting be directed to the erection of the church in Brewster's village. Fr. Perths was in the process of preparing his sermon when the unexpected visitors arrived. Nevertheless, he warmly welcomed them. Pearl the housekeeper, served tea and petit fours as they waited for the vicar to join them.

After apologizing for the unexpected visit, the judge went straight to the purpose of their mission. "We are here, Father, because we are confronted by a seriously irritating obstacle."

Fr Perths knitted his brow in perplexity, but said nothing.

"Peter Goodfellow. We have to delay the commissioning until the end of the month," the judge decreed, "until the present vestry seals or completes it plans for the building of the church in Brewster's village. Bishop Addington is going to meet the members at Bradshaw's place over there in Brewster's village, as you probably recall. If Goodfellow is commissioned tomorrow, his influence on the vestry and the people may affect the Bishop's decision."

"Wouldn't that be unconstitutional…the postponement of the commissioning, I mean?" Fr. Perths inquired.

"Absolutely not!" the judge replied. "We are not postponing the Annual General Meeting. We *can* postpone the commissioning without the vote and approval of the people."

"How so?"

"The by-laws state that the new vestry will assume office in January. It doesn't specifically say what date in January," the judge explained. "We have traditionally done it on the first Sunday, but it's not a stipulation. Furthermore, the assumption is that the new vestry only becomes effective from the date of the commissioning, but again, nothing in the by-laws mentions anything about the exact date of the commissioning, so the decision is not beyond the dictates of the constitution."

At first Fr. Perths appeared reluctant, but subsequently accepted Mr. Pilchard's hypothesis. "You have a point," he agreed. "But how do I notify the officers by tomorrow? And what will people say"

"Madam senior warden will notify them; and as for the people, I don't think that it would be gravely problematic. And forget the reaction from those ignorant brutes from the village. They wouldn't understand anything even if you were to explain your decision to them," the judge explained.

Mrs. Pigthorne gasped, for she did not expect to be burdened by any such task. "Wouldn't they think it out of order that I, as outgoing warden, should …"

"…you *will* do it, Eloise. That's the duty of a senior warden," the judge commanded the timid woman. "Furthermore, Fr. Perths is preparing his sermon. He has no time today to deal with such trivialities. For once, Eloise, stand up and be counted!"

After several minutes of insignificant conversation, the judge and Mrs. Pigthorne departed, proud that their mission was so easily fulfilled.

"One thing that we can give our vicar much credit for," the judge remarked as they approached their vehicle, "is his naivete and overt stupidity…ha ha ha. Wouldn't trade him for any other…"

Eloise smiled, but in her telephone conversation later that evening with Darleyne Burrows, one of the newly elected vestry members in whom she confided, she cursed the judge and berated him for his arrogance and gross disrespect towards the vicar, and more so for his asperity towards her. She knew that the BOARD had considered her a fool, she complained, but she thanked God that she had the intelligence to discreetly vote for Pigeon in this last election. She explained that it was her way of proving to herself that she could indeed be instrumental in ordering the course of affairs at St. Patrick's, and bold enough in avenging Adolph Pilchard's total disregard for her position and the BOARD's usurpation of her office.

Chapter Seven

Ecclesiastical Tremors

When the congregation arrived on the first Sunday morning in January in expectation of the traditional installation festivities, it was obvious that the news of the postponement had not fully circulated. Members filled the church for the only service of the day, in anticipation of the special fellowship brunch in honor of the newly installed vestry. A wide variety of dishes was brought to the parish hall by the villagers and presented to Nellie Sweetwine and her team for the celebration. Fifteen minutes before the start of the service, the church was almost filled, and Rex was supervising the members of the Beautification Committee to place additional chairs along the side aisles. Rex was strangely subdued throughout the morning, and his oddly mild disposition caused some of the members of the *Gold Circle* to worry about his mental and physical health. However, to the few who knew of the incident between Big Ethel's reputed husband and him outside *Pauphen's*, attributed his calm demeanor to the effects of his purported humiliating defeat.

At precisely nine thirty o'clock, the mass began, and as Fr. Perths mounted the chancel steps, Pigeon and Mrs. Goodfellow entered the church from the right transcept. One of the ushers, Mildred Lovell, who was stationed at that door, greeted the couple and turned to lead them towards the front pew where the newly appointed warden and vestry persons would be seated until the commissioning, after which they would ascend to the chancel and sit in special chairs alongside the choir stalls. However, it was at that moment that Mildred was informed that there were no specially assigned seats in the front of the nave or chairs in the chancel. She thus paused, and Rex, standing across the other side by the organ, looking grim and circumspect in his starched cassock, motioned her to proceed to the rear. Mrs. Goodfellow, already embarrassed by their lateness, turned immediately to follow Mildred down the side isle. However, Pigeon reached out and gently grabbed her arm and motioned her to remain next to him.

"We especially have to sit in front today for the installation of the new vestry," he whispered to his wife. "Have you forgotten?"

"But it's filled," she replied in her delicate voice. "Can't you see there are no seats for us? We have to find alternative seats," she advised her husband, who now was beginning to reveal the first pangs of intense anger.

As the couple stood there, the congregation contemplated them. The village women scrutinized Mrs. Goodfellow, who was always impeccably attired, and the BOARD members, who were congregated in their usual section, studied Pigeon as he stood in the passage peering across the crowded pews, looking for appropriate seats. Mildred approached the couple and leaned towards Mrs. Goodfellow and whispered something in her ear. Once again, Mrs. Goodfellow attempted to follow the usher, but this time Pigeon held her arm tightly and glared at Mildred. When Pigeon looked around the church, everyone was staring at them.

The processional hymn had already ended and Fr. Perths had paused to allow them to find seats. However, Pigeon's pertinacity gave a clear indication of his refusal to be humiliated in front of, or by, the phalanx who refer to themselves as the BOARD, whose aim he knew was to deflate him by blatantly disrespecting him and inveigling his most trusted friends to betray him. Pigeon realized that his belligerence was attracting much attention and therefore seized the opportunity to state his claim. As he defiantly stood there, firmly but gently gripping his wife's hand, Rex marched across the front with the confidence and gallantry of an army General and approached him. Pigeon knew that Rex enjoyed moments like this when all eyes were on him, and therefore allowed him to flaunt his limited authority. Furthermore, he and Rex had a made secret pact which he could not have allowed an insignificant incident like this to sever.

"You got to sit at the back, sir. They ain't got no more seats up front for you." Rex's expression was as adamant as flint and he was unflinching as he looked at Pigeon squarely in the face.

"I'm the senior warden now," Pigeon calmly explained. "I'm being commissioned today. There must be a place for…"

"...There ain't no commissinin today, Mr. Goodfellow sir," Rex interjected. "Dhat been put off 'till later. You has to go to the back. All the seats up front is full. Follow me."

Upon being informed of the postponement of the commissioning, Pigeon froze in shock and his jaw dropped. The firm grip with with he held his wife unconciously slackened and his eyes opened wide as he stared at Rex in disbelief.

"Come. Let's follow him. Don't make a fuss. Please," Mrs. Goodfellow begged.

The couple followed Rex, who now was beaming with pride at the attention he was receiving. He strode erect down the aisle, with his shoulders pulled back and his chest pushed out. However, as he strutted down the aisle in his crisp, ironed cassock, two men who would have been classified as members of either the *Silver* or *Gold Circle* rose and offered their seats to the Goodfellows. When Rex reached the rear of the nave, and turned to direct the Goodfellows to a pew which was occupied by some of the members from Brewster's Village, he gasped at the sight of the two men standing behind him.

"Thank you," the taller of the two said as he slid past the sexton. The members who were sitting in the rear and observing the whole ignominious episode burst into currents of hushed laughter as Rex stood there trying to figure out where the Goodfellows had gone. Rex turned to glare at them and his eyes met Maudie Springer's. The two contemplated each other for a few tense seconds before Maudie scrutinized him and averted her attention as she mumbled an imprecation.

There were no further disruptions and the service proceeded gloriously until the time of the *pax*. The members shared the kiss of peace with each other, but remained within the realms of their respective circles. It was not usual for them to cross social barriers. However, Pigeon reversed the order of tradition by offering the kiss of peace to the members of the two lower circles, even more than he did to the members of his own social class. The members were thrilled to be embraced by their new warden, and made audible vows of assiduous support as they hugged or shook hands.

The taller of the two men who offered the Goodfellows their seats remarked on Pigeon's benignancy and thus arranged with him to have a brief conversation after the service so that they could become more profoundly acquainted.

Pigeon remained at the rear of the nave during the exchange of peace, but furtively observed the vicar as he made his way down the center aisle, hugging and kissing the members of the upper circles. As soon as the vicar reached the center of the aisle and was in the process of turning to make his way back to the altar, Pigeon hurried down the side aisle to the front.

"See," Pigeon pointed out to his wife, "the lily-livered reverend sees me and turns back before I could reach him. He's avoiding me. Well, I'll follow him!"

As Reverend Perths approached the chancel steps, Pigeon intercepted him.

"Peace, Fr. Perths!" Pigeon greeted the retreating vicar with a long, close embrace.

"Peace, my brother in the Lord!" Fr. Perths replied with a forced smile as he glanced awkwardly across the front pews to Mr. Pilchard and Laurent Faulkner. The two men observed the charade with stern expressions.

"I understand that the commissioning of the new vestry has been postponed?" Pigeon inquired as he gripped the vicar's elbow with one hand and impeded his movement by firmly placing his other hand on his shoulder.

"Ah…yes…yes…" Fr. Perths timidly replied and averted his attention to the altar as though he was in a hurry to continue the service. He made a mild attempt to extricate himself from Pigeon's grip but was more vigorously contained by the resolute warden-elect.

"Why? Who decided this?" Pigeon continued to interrogate the vicar who by now had burst into beads of nervous sweat.

"Well…it was decided by some of the officers who…who felt that …that it was rather a bit too soon in the month…to…to…"

"Which officers? I am the senior officer here, as of January. I am the senior warden, Fr. Perths. If such a decision was made, then I should have been a part of it. Did no one see fit to ask my opinion? This is covert behavior, and will be reported to the bishop!" Pigeon fixed the vicar a cold, intimidating stare as he chided him for his unethical behavior.

"Look Mr. Goodfellow; let us discuss this after church. I must proceed with the service…please," Fr. Perths pleaded as he gently released himself from Pigeon's firm grip.

Pigeon contemplated the dishonorable vicar as he proceeded to the altar. Suddenly, Pigeon mounted the chancel steps and approached the lectern.

"Good morning…," he greeted the congregation with a broad smile.

Fr. Perths stopped abruptly and turned towards the lectern. The BOARD members gasped as they beheld Pigeon standing before the congregation.

"Will the newly elected vestry please come forward for the induction ceremony. Thank you." Pigeon remained standing at the lectern until the puzzled members rose and slowly began to approach the chancel steps.

The members of the BOARD were infuriated. They glanced at each other in anger, shock and disbelief. Nevertheless, the vestry members approached the chancel and stood there, with confused expressions. Bill Jones ambled up the asile and stood at the back of the group. He kept glancing at the BOARD members as if awaiting some explanation.

"I know that you were told that the induction was postponed, but Fr. Perths and I were able to sort things out. Fr. Perths…" Pigeon summoned the man of the cloth to the front.

The shocked vicar responded to Pigeon's command with the servile obedience of a zombie.

"Why the hell is he proceeding with this?" Judge Pilchard inquired.

"Fear. What else?" Faulkner responded. "Goodfellow has his supporters at the back. It's obvious that Perths does not want to offend *them*… Look, don't you see…they've come out in their finery in anticipation of the commissioning and the celebration after. Perths can't disappoint them. They'll trample him with their hooves. Or perhaps he's afraid of the bishop. Either way, the fool's afraid, that's all."

Fr. Perths thus acquiesced to Pigeon's command. The cunning Goodfellow graciously invited Bill Jones to stand beside him, and as Bill reluctantly took up his position, Pigeon turned and stared defiantly at the members of the BOARD. As his eyes met Mrs. Pigthorne's, she winked and gave a gentle, discreet nod of approval and bowed her head.

At the conclusion of the induction, the newly commissioned vestry turned towards the congregation, as was customary, in anticipation of the vicar's welcoming remarks, which included the plea for support from the congregation. However, Fr. Perths stretched out his arms and pronounced the offertory sentence. The vestry, who by now appeared even more confused, began returning to their respective seats, but Pigeon raised his hand and requested that they remain momentarily. Fr. Perths, who had already reached the altar, turned and glared at the impertinent senior warden, but wisely chose not to interrupt him.

"Brothers and sisters," the new warden began, "I thank Fr. Perths for the gracious favor of commissioning the vestry this morning. I believe that this induction ceremony marks the beginning of a new era in the history of St. Patrick's. Under my leadership as your warden, the walls that divide us as a family will be dismantled. We shall dwell together in harmony and respect. The *wolves* and the lambs will co-habit; Abersthwaithe and Brewster's Village shall lie down together, and Slough shall cover them with her pinions. My primary objective, brothers and sisters, is to root out the evil from among us, in all of its ugly forms, and create in its place a family abiding in atmosphere of peace, love and harmony. This vestry will lead this parish, and nothing will break the chain that will bind us together; no one will usurp our authority, and nobody…nobody will divide this congregation by erecting any church in Brewster's Village…!"

The members at the rear of the nave burst into passionate applause, and voiced sporadic exclamations of 'Amen!'

"…This church belongs to all of us," Pigeon continued. "It is my home and it is your home, and here we all shall stay. My friends, welcome to a new epoch!"

A large number of the congregation burst into spirited applause. Some of the members of the lower circles gave Pigeon a standing ovation. He glanced at some of the members of the BOARD with quiet amusement. He knew that he had put them in a dilemma. Their failure to applaud would have exposed them as the nefarious entity about whom he had spoken; on the other hand, their applause would have suggested not only the acceptance of a humiliating defeat, but bitter remorse and mortifying surrender.

The BOARD eventually began to slowly and mildly applaud while their facial expressions remained serious and distant. Pigeon contained his amusement.

Ironically, the service ended with the hymn, "How sure a foundation," after which the members of the two lower circles surrounded Pigeon to offer their congratulations and pledge their support. As he stood amidst the crowd, acknowledging their expressions of immense joy, Rex approached him and informed him that the vicar had requested his immediate presence in his office. Rex's familiar warmth had dissipated, and as he relayed the vicar's message, his face was contorted with rage against the audacious senior warden who, according to Faulkner, had "dared to disrespect the vicar and the BOARD, and blatantly display his ill-gotten camaraderie with the savages whom he once had despised and subjected to base humiliation."

The enthusiastic group which surrounded Pigeon made it difficult for him to immediately respond to Fr. Perth's request, and Rex voiced his disapproval of what he misconstrued to be a deliberate delay in responding to the vicar's summons.

"The boss want to see you…now!" Rex barked. "Stop cacklin' wid' dhese peoples and go an' talk wid' 'im!"

Before Pigeon could respond to Rex's vulgar self-assertion, Dotty Cambridge and Joshua Chandrapaul launched a massive verbal attack on him.

"Rexworth Davis, you bess' move yo' nasty, dutty self from here, yeah. You doesn't see the man is talkin' to we, yo' fool!" Dotty snapped.

"He ain't goin' nowhere 'till he done talkin' to we. So go and tell Fr. Perths dhat, yo' scavenger!" Joshua added.

"You mekin' dhese peoples get you in trouble," Rex warned. "I goin' and tell the parson dhat dhese peoples turnin' you 'gainst 'im, and dhat you…"

"Look, move you frowsy self from here, Rexworth, 'fore I tek dhis bible and bash in you' face wid' it!" Petulia Nobles furiously interjected.

The group of supporters began to scoff derisively at him.

"You want another cut-ass like you had pun boxin'night in front of *Phauphen's*?" Joshua asked before he proceeded to further taunt the now humiliated sexton.

Joshua's comment shocked the arrogant sexton almost to the point of numbness. Rex froze and fixed Joshua a cold stare, then stormed off through the crowd towards the stairs. The raucous laughter from the group attracted the attention of the members of the BOARD, who tossed disapproving glances at them and cast caustic remarks about their character and Pigeon's coarse opportunism. None of the members surrounding Pigeon responded to them.

Eventually, Pigeon was able to disengage himself from the excited crowd which surrounded him and make his way to the vicar's office. As he proceeded down the aisle, other supporters from the two upper circles offered their congratulations and demonstrated their approval by briefly shaking hands or patting him on the shoulder as he passed them. On reaching the stairs that lead to the undercroft, the taller of the two men who had offered their seats to his wife and him intercepted him and introduced himself, after which he made an appointment to meet Pigeon in his office on Tuesday morning.

Pigeon descended the winding stairs and continued to Fr. Perth's office. The door was closed, but he could hear subdued voices coming from the room. Before knocking, he considered returning to the nave or proceeding to the parish hall until the persons in the vicar's office have left, so he could have private audience with the clergyman who had summoned him so urgently. However, he chose to knock on the door rather than leave and be mocked by his own conscience with regard to his cowardice.

"Mr. Goodfellow!" Fr. Perths greeted the warden as he opened the door. "It has taken you a while to get here. I was beginning to think that your defiance has assumed a new dimension," he added with a wry smile. "Please, do come in."

Pigeon sensed Fr. Perth's scathing remark, but nevertheless chose to ignore it. Upon entering the office, he realized that Laurent Faulkner, Bill Jones, Tessie Shoehorn and Fritz Batty were sitting in the room in chairs which were arranged in a semi-circle in front of Fr. Perth's desk. Beside Bill Jones was a vacant chair which Pigeon assumed was placed there for him to sit during whatever interrogation or reprimand that was in store.

"You wish to speak with me, Fr. Perths?" Pigeon inquired brusquely.

"As a matter of fact I do. Have a seat." Fr. Perth's tone was reprimanding and lacking in its usual warmth. This served to evoke Pigeon's anger to the point of refusing to speak with the vicar in the presence of the others.

"If you wish to speak with me, what are these...*people*...doing here?" Pigeon inquired.

"These *people*," replied Fr. Perths, "are here at my request, just as you are. So please, Mr. Goodfellow, let's leave our puerility outside. I've called this meeting to discuss what happened in church this morning and the ramifications of your actions."

"Excuse my asking, Father; but is this meeting your idea…or these *people's*?" Pigeon asked.

"That's beside the point, Goodfellow," snarled Fritz Batty. "What you did this morning is inexcusable and completely out of order! The induction was postponed until the end of the month and you had no darn business defying the vicar's order."

"Go suck an egg, Batty!" Pigeon snapped. "Who the hell do you think you're talking to? Do I look like one of those bloody corpses that you cajole into becoming limp, so that you can dress them and make them up to look like formidable clowns?"

"My business has nothing to do with your lack of respect for authority. What you did was out of order and you will be reported!" Fritz retorted.

"Good! Then do what you have to do, Batty! And while you're at it, give an account of your dishonest dealings with the vulnerable people who come to you at their time of grief; the people you fleece so mercilessly while they are mourning their dead," Pigeon rejoined. "Tell me, Batty," he continued, "those gold teeth in your mouth; did you purchase them or did you rip them out of the mouth of a corpse?"

"Mr. Goodfellow. Please!" Laurent Faulkner pleaded. "We are addressing an ethical issue here. You stood in front of the entire congregation and defied the priest…disrespected him!"

"Like you do, Faulkner – you and the BOARD – that illegal group that has usurped the vestry's and the vicar's authority. Let me say something to you, Faulkner, you don't have a shit over me, O.K., not a damn thing over me. You act as though you are some kind of sovereignty around here. Do you think that the success of your business gives you the right to control things around here and disrespect the officers of this church, you bloody highway robber! Or are you assuming that your whiteness gives you carte blanche to dictate things here. This is the Caribbean, Faulkner – native Indian territory – Carib region, developed by the sweat and blood of African slaves which you people forced into serving you. Ever tried figuring out how many black people have shares in *Faulkner & Babbit*, by dint of their ancestors' blood, Faulkner, eh, have you, have you!?"

"Mr. Goodfellow, I demand that you stop this at once!" Fr. Perths interjected. "What does race have to do with this? As you have just mentioned, this is the Caribbean. Race is never an issue here. We are a people – a conglomerate – not a bunch of races scrambling for oxygen in a cell with a solitary window. So please, Mr. Goodfellow, let us deal with this issue objectively."

"Of course you will see things as you do, Fr., because you and Faulkner are of the same foreign extract, and on this island your kind has inherited the privileges that were bestowed upon your forefathers – our slavemasters. This is the kind of thing I have to deal with on a daily basis in the court – the distortion of justice and the intimidation of people of color. One would never imagine that the same battles have to be fought in the church. This is exactly what the two of you are trying to do here now, with the help of these two golliwogs and this confused red nigger, Fritz Batty. But none of you is going to intimidate me; none of you!"

"Who the hell you' calling a golliwog?" Tessie screamed.

"Excuse me, Fr, but do you have a mirror to lend Tessie? I think that the image on the other side of the mirror will help her to figure out whom I'm talking to. The puffy, black face coated with white powder; the two thick lips smeared with some kind of pink substance; the cheeks daubed with red chalk; the expressionless eyes surrounded by some ridiculous blue paint and something that looks like charcoal marks…craftsmanship at its most grotesque! Go Tessie, look in the mirror and tell me what you see," Pigeon calmly replied.

Tessie made no response, but heaved her chest and glared at Pigeon with the hatred of a fallen angel.

"If we may return to the purpose of our meeting, Mr. Goodfellow," Fr. Perths nevertheless continued, "my reason for summoning you to my office is to inform you that the commission ceremony was unconstitutional and therefore null and void."

"What?" Pigeon exclaimed. "Could you repeat that, Fr. Perths?"

"I think you heard him the first time, Goodfellow," Mr. Faulkner drawled.

"Unconstitutional? You stood up in front of the congregation and inducted the vestry and now you call me quietly in here to tell me nonsense about unconstitutional. Indeed, I deem you insane, Fr., bloody insane!" Pigeon declared as he pointed accusingly at the vacillating priest.

"He might be insane, Pigeon Goodfellow," Tessie stated, "but he's right and he has my support."

"And that's mighty *large* support, Tessie, coming from you. But I have larger support, fat girl. I have the support of the people; so there!" Pigeon snapped. "Furthermore, if we ae talking about unconstitutional, what's more unconstitutional than this so-called BOARD?"

"There is no documentation or written evidence of any such group, Goodfellow, so your accusation is baseless and will not hold up in court; you know that," Mr. Faulkner replied defensively.

Pigeon ignored Laurent Faulkner's comment. "Tell me, Fr. Perths, who put you up to this? This sort of attitude is not compatible with your character. Whose idea was this to deem the induction unconstitutional? I notice that Pilchard is not here in the room. Was it his idea? Did he sow the seeds of this wickedness and then retreat like a thief in the night, or better yet, a coward in the dark? Well, it's one magistrate against the other. I'll have a talk with Bishop Addington. As far as I am concerned, I am the senior warden, duly elected, and duly installed, and I will assume the duties of the senior with immediate effect. Bill, are you with me on this as my junior warden?"

Bill gave a dry, sinister laugh. "You're not *my* senior warden, Goodfellow…"

"Don't beat about the bush, Jones," Pigeon snarled. "Either you're for me or you're against me. Now which is it?"

"I'm afraid that I have to be on the side of what I believe to be the right thing," Bill replied.

"Then I take it that you are against me," Pigeon stated as he rested his eyes heavily and coldly on Bill.

"Well, since you have judged yourself to be in the wrong, then I have no choice to but support Fr. Perth's decision," Bill stated.

Pigeon glared at Bill for a few seconds, "I see…I see."

He then paced slowly towards the door and turned. "If this is how you feel, Bill, and if this is what you are proclaiming, Fr., then it's too bad. I and the majority of the congregation who witnessed the induction consider it valid, and so it is. If you wish to settle this in an ecclesiastical or legal court, be my guest. And Bill, if you and I are going to work together, I advise that you rid yourself of any close association with this meddlesome brood…as soon as possible. Good morning."

Pigeon closed the door softly behind him and proceeded along the corridor. Suddenly, the creaking sound of Fr. Perth's office door was heard behind him, and Bill's voice reverberated along the narrow passage.

"Thanks for the advice, Goodfellow sir, but you can offer it to your new junior warden. I've just relinquished my position, with immediate effect!"

The verbal bullet struck Pigeon straight through this back, and he froze momentarily. However, when he turned, Bill had already retreated to the room and shut the door. Pigeon thus drew a deep breath and continued up the stairs and across the now quiet, empty nave towards the parish hall. On crossing the front of the altar, he genuflected and whispered a prayer, beseeching God to protect him from his enemies and to give him victory over them.

* * *

Early in the evening, the judge left his home to visit a close friend who had solicited his wise counsel on an urgent business matter. However, about twenty five minutes later, he turned into Westminster Lane and parked about fifty yards from Maggie's house. It was the first time that he would pass the spot where he had taken Wilberforce's life. He began to hum one of his favorite hymns 'Amazing Grace', so as to convince himself of his exoneration and God's forgiveness. He also prayed that the incident would sink into oblivion and that Wilberforce's avenging ghost would not torment him by gnawing at his conscience. However, as he passed the spot where Wilberforce died, a pang of guilt and immense fear suddenly struck him in the chest and he broke into a profuse sweat. He increased his pace and hurried to Maggie's gate. So harrowed was he that he did not realize that Maggie had opened the kennel to allow Basil, the mastiff, to enjoy his regular evening exercise around the yard before retiring to the house for the night. Mr. Pilchard closed the gate behind him and dashed towards the front door. As he fumbled for his key, the dog appeared at the side of the house, and upon spotting the judge, stopped and uttered a ferocious growl. Mr. Pilchard froze with his hand still stuck in his pocket. He once told Maggie that he had heard somewhere that when confronted by a fierce canine, one should remain as motionless as a statue and fix the animal a forbidding stare. However, this animal seemed to have felt threatened by the tall, dark figure with the grim aspect and barred its fangs. The judge thought it sagacious to do likewise so as to intimidate the fierce animal, but upon barring his dentures, the dog charged forward viciously. Mr. Pilchard sprang on top of Maggie's car bonnet and kicked wildly and desperately as the enraged animal sought to maul him by snarling and jumping at his brown, leather Barkers. He yelled desperately for help, but it was the screams of the two children who were playing next door in the verandah which eventually attracted Maggie's attention and the attention of several neighbors.

"Basil!" Maggie shouted as she rushed outside, wrapped only in a large, white, bath towel and shod in a pair of mauve bedroom slippers. A shower cap adorned her head. "Basil! Get back to your kennel at once!"

The canine made one more attempt to assault the judge before scurrying away to the back, barking furiously.

"Come quickly, Adolph," Maggie directed the embarrassed and intensely angry judge. "Jump down and run into the house."

Mr. Pilchard alighted from the car bonnet and dashed into the house and closed the door, while Maggie restrained the savage animal. After Maggie had confined the dog to the kennel, she hurried back to the house. The judge was already upstairs at the bar, pouring himself a shot of brandy.

"Get rid of that dog, Maggie," he brusquely ordered her.

"Please, don't get carried away," Maggie replied. "He isn't always like that. I think that he must have…"

"…I said to get rid of him!" the judge crudely interjected as he glared at her.

"You're serious, are you?" Maggie paused as she contemplated him.

"Damn right I am!" he snapped. "I'll kill the bastard if I put my hands on him!"

"You seem quite nonchalant about taking lives these days, aren't you?" Maggie remarked.

Mr. Pilchard stopped abruptly. Suddenly, he turned and observed Maggie in utter shock for a few moments. "What in hell is that supposed to mean?"

"Nothing, Adolph. Just an incidental comment," she calmly responded as she proceeded to her bedroom.

"That was not an incidental remark, Maggie. What did you mean?" he pressed as he put down the glass of brandy and slowly approached her, with his eyes fixed firmly on her.

"Nothing," she swore. "I was just simply reacting to what you just said… about killing my dog."

"Liar!" the judge barked as he grabbed her by the shoulders. "You're implying that I had something to do with …with…Mr. Gaskin's death, aren't you?"

"Let go of me, Adolph…" Maggie hissed.

"How dare you, Maggie. How dare you!" The judge's voice quivered with rage. "How dare you even think such a thing!"

"Don't be stupid, Adolph. I have never thought or implied such a thing!" Maggie explained. "It was your insensitivity towards me that incited my remark; nothing else. You threatened to kill my dog, Adolph. You threatened to take a life!"

The judge remained silent, but his expression was like that of a condemned man without a blindfold, standing before a firing squad. It was the first time that he felt that the dawn was breaking on his dark secret, for he was not convinced that Maggie's remark was incidental. He had analysed her statement, and thus vehemently believed that she was referring to more than just the demise of her canine. Sagacity therefore dictated that he immediately concoct a story in his defence – a story which he knew instinctively that he might soon have to relate in court in order to exonerate himself. However, he knew that he would have to bring Maggie to a point of total surrender and submission in order to make her believe his concoction and stand beside him through his impending ordeal.

"Maggie, sweetheart…," he thus implored, "forgive me my irrational outburst. It's just that I've been going through a lot these days…mentally…"

"That's alright, dear," Maggie replied.

"No. It's not. I should have spoken to you before, but I …I was not sure…and I'm still not sure, how you would …deal with…handle…this." The cunning judge hung his head in feigned despair like a puppy beseeching his master's pardon and sat at the edge of the sofa, with his elbows on his knees and his hands on his forehead.

"What is it, sweetheart?" Maggie inquired as she sat next to him with her head on his shoulder.

The judge turned towards Maggie and held her in his arms. He massaged her gently on her shoulder as he began to craftily weave his mendacious account of Wilberforce's death. "Maggie, there is something that happened that night between Wilberforce and me the last night he was here…something that …I think…was …was building up for along time. It…it… sort of reached its bitter climax on that last night."

Maggie's eyes opened wide and her body became rigid as if expecting either of them to explode into bloody fragments of flesh and sinew across the room.

"You must believe what I say to you now, Maggie. I did not mention anything that was happening before because…it would have aggravated an already tense situation. But Wilberforce had threatened my life several times…"

"What do you mean?" Maggie interjected.

Mr. Pilchard immediately became defensive. "You were in love with the man, Maggie. I know…he told me…"

Maggie became petrified. Her mouth fell agape. The judge thus launched his crippling assault on the now vulnerable, embarrassed and confused woman.

"He warned me to keep away from you and threatened to kill me if I didn't. He would lay wait for me almost every night and threaten me, harass me. Then on that last night, as I was hurrying to my car, he appeared from nowhere, bearing a large stone. I dashed to my car and shut the door and started the engine, but he held on to the car, pounding at the glass in a vicious attempt to assault me. I…I was mortally afraid…and …and I…I pressed the accelerator in a desperate effort to escape. I sped off, but…but he held on to the handle and …I…I swerved to avoid hitting the other cars that were parked on the other side of the street, and he…he must have fallen. When I looked back…I…I saw him…getting up and still trying to chase after me with the stone raised in the air. But then, another car turned the corner behind him…as he chased after me…with the stone. I then turned the corner. The next day, I read of the death. Maggie, I swear that it is the truth but I couldn't tell you. I was angry, and I still am angry…intensely angry that you were having an affair with him behind my back. How could you lie to me like that? I was on the verge of leaving my wife for you… for you, Maggie, and look what you were doing. If I report what happened to the police, what do you think they will believe – that Mr. Gaskin and I were involved in some rival conflict – and your name will be dragged into the mud. I have kept silent to protect you, Maggie, to guard your honor, to maintain our relationship. That's how much I love you, Maggie. This is how much I care for you…with all my heart," the aging romancer confessed.

Maggie's taciturnity and horrifying expression clearly displayed that she was convinced by the judge's story and that she was mortally afraid of the possible disgrace which public knowledge of the judge's story could bring her. Thus she threw her arms around her lover's neck and burst into tears. "I'm sorry, Adolph…but…it was hard sometimes being here, dying for your love and knowing that you cannot be here. Wilberforce was only mere company in my solitude, but it's you that I love…it's you that I have always loved… only you, Adolph…it's your love that I live for – no one else's…" she cried.

The judge held her close and comforted her with promises of his everlasting love for her, and a litany of the many times he had wished to be with her but was unable to do so by dint of his unsatisfying marriage to a woman whose caress lacked the electrification of hers, and whose lips were bereft of the passion which was quintessesentially Maggie's. The moments of consolation were followed by several minutes of intense copulation, after which Maggie served a delectable dinner comprising roasted capon and Spanish rice, with an entremets consisting of shreaded saltfish, pumpkin and raisins. Thirty minutes later, the couple swore eternal faithfulness to each other and the judge left, happy that his mistress had believed his story and that once again, he had emerged the champanion in the illicit affair.

*   *   *

Several hours later, Maggie lay tossing in her bed as her heart and mind wrestled fervently over her relationship with the judge. The brain was warning her of the folly of her affair with a married man whose social position will never allow him to leave his wife for her, and therefore her affair should be dictated by reason and common sense. The heart, however, insisted that true love is unconditional, and therefore warrants some degree of trust. It further stressed that it is love, more than any other factor, which matters in any relationship and that it is love which ultimately binds all things together. In the end, it was the heart that preponderated, and Maggie made a decision to pay Pigeon Goodfellow a visit at his office early the next morning. Shortly after midnight, she pulled the covers over her and fell into a deep, refreshing sleep.

* * *

Monday morning arrived in the company of saturated clouds and heavy mist which veiled the southern section of the island. At eight thirty, Maggie arrived at Pigeon's office. He had not yet arrived and the receptionist invited her to take a seat in one of the conference rooms. Maggie proceeded to the assigned room and removed her rain coat before continuing to the ladies room to refresh her make-up and comb her hair which she had tucked under her rain-mate. As she walked along the narrow corridor on her way back to the conference room, Pigeon arrived and hurriedly proceeded to the gentlemen's quarters after a long, harrowing drive on the busy, slippery roads. The urgency with which he bolted to the toilet prevented him from fully recognizing Maggie, and thus he merely acknowledged the passing figure. After he had relieved himself, and had returned to a rational state, he returned to his desk without further acknowledging the figure in the subdued conference room. After a light banter with the receptionist, he approached his office door.

"Oh, Mr. Goodfellow, there is someone waiting to see you. She's in the conference room," the receptionist advised him.

"Indeed...I did see someone...a woman, as I was rushing to the toilet," Pigeon acknowledged. "Who is it?" he whispered.

"A Margaret Billings...says that she didn't have an appointment," the receptionist explained.

Pigeon stopped abruptly. His expression became alarming. "Who?"

"...said her name was Margaret Billings," she reiterated. "Should I have told her that you were not going to be able to ..."

Pigeon interrupted her by raising his hand in a halting gesture like that of a traffic policeman. "No. It's alright. You didn't know..."

"I'm sorry if I ..."

"It's alright. Don't worry," Pigeon assured the worried receptionist. "I wasn't expecting her, that's all. Please, send her in."

The troubled receptionist relayed the message and escorted Maggie to the office.

"Mr. Goodfellow?" Maggie greeted the wary lawyer as she entered the room.

"Ms. Billings? What a surprise to see you...an unexpected delight on a melancholy Monday morning, shall I say?" Pigeon remarked with a respectable, but nervous grin.

"Thank you," Maggie graciously replied.

"Please. Do sit."

"I'm sorry for intruding on you like this, without an appointment, I mean," Maggie apologized. "I know that you are a very busy person, so I wouldn't take too much of your time; that's if you would be gracious enough to allow me the privilege of a few minutes to seek a favor of you."

"Be my guest, Maggie. How may I help you?" Pigeon inquired tersely as he sat facing her. His expression remained somber. He knew that he had to play the game well, and win, for up to this point, she had had the advantage by dint of the nude photograph.

"I know that the last time we met…things got…a bit out of hand…," she began to speak slowly and deliberately.

"A bit…?"

"Well, perhaps …I should have said, *rather* out of hand," she continued with a tense and awkward smile, "and we left on not the best note…"

"Are you seeking my forgiveness, Ms. Billings?" Pigeon asked with a sinister grin and penetrating eyes.

"Is this an unreasonable favor to ask?"

"Without surrendering the photograph of me lying naked on your floor – I'm afraid that it is," Pigeon replied.

"Well, better than that," Maggie continued as she unzipped her handbag and placed her hand inside. "I've brought the camera," she said as she handed Pigeon the camera.

"How do I know that this was indeed the camera and the film you used?"

"You may remove the roll yourself and develop the film yourself, then destroy the photograph," Maggie answered.

Pigeon took the camera and studied Maggie for a few seconds, after which he agreed to her suggestion. "I know that this is a great risk to take this film to the studio, but I would rather know for certain that this is indeed the roll you used. I have a friend at *Superflash Studios*. I'll ask him to develop the roll for me. I'll tell him that it was my wife who took the photograph during one of her frivolous moods if he mentions anything to me."

"Now," Maggie continued, "is my forgiveness in order?"

"Tentatively. Let's get the photograph first," Pigeon bargained, "then the pardon will take immediate effect."

"Thank you," Maggie beamed.

"Well, is that all?" Pigeon inquired as he rose from his seat.

"Actually, there is one more thing, one more favor…one greater than the first," Maggie responded.

"O yes? And that is…?" Pigeon inquired as he resumed his seat.

"Adolph. I know that I had asked you to help me to bring him to a shameful and scandalous demise, but I have been thinking deeply about it, and I have cancelled our contract…our verbal contract. I want you to forget it…abandon the plan."

"I never made any contract with you, Maggie," Pigeon stated with a serious expression.

"Well, perhaps contract is a strong word," Maggie sought to explain with a gentle smile.

"The *wrong* word, definitely!" Pigeon added brusquely.

"But you will forget it nevertheless," Maggie insisted.

"Why the sudden change of heart, Maggie?" Pigeon asked.

"I am too much in love with the man to destroy him like that," Maggie confessed. "Furthermore," she continued, "I will never be truly happy winning him under such conditions. Part of his heart is bound to be left with *her*, and I will *not* wrestle with memories of a lost love."

"I see. You want me to just forget everything that happened the other night because you woke up this morning in love with Pilchard? I don't buy your story, Maggie. Furthermore, I don't trust you," Pigeon stated. "I believe that you *have* indeed thought about your plan and realized that *you* stand to lose more than he. So now you come to beg me to forget everything. Or is it because you now have realized that I have the upper hand here?"

Maggie remained reticent as she stared at Pigeon. Her large olive eyes were filled with fear and desperation, like that of a cornered, frightened animal.

"And what about my trousers, Ms. Billings, the expensive pair of trousers made of pure, Scottish wool which your dog destroyed? Have you been thinking deeply about that, or is that bastard, Pilchard, your only source of concern?" Pigeon's tone was bitter and his expression severe.

"Please, Pigeon, we're talking here of a man's honor, a man's life, a marriage; and you are fussing about a piece of wool. I will pay for your trousers, whatever it cost. But right now, this is not the issue. I am beseeching your mercy on behalf of someone who means everything to me," Maggie desperately pleaded.

"Mercy? Mercy?" Pigeon roared as he pounded his fist on the chair handle. "You know for yourself how much Pilchard has been seeking to destroy me. And he hasn't finished yet. The man is seeking daily to destroy me, Maggie. Everybody knows that!" Pigeon rose from his seat and began to pace the floor, breathing heavily in order to maintain his composure. "And now you come here, nonchalantly requesting my mercy on that arrogant, jurisprudent dog!"

Maggie remained silent, and as she stared in shock at Pigeon, her eyes began to well up with tears. It was her lachrymose expression that ultimately served to appease Pigeon, and he immediately stopped raving.

"Look, I'm sorry, "Pigeon apologized. "I should not be taking out my hatred for Pilchard on you. I'm sorry. But you must understand that Pilchard does not have my well being at heart. Maybe he conceals it from you, but I know what he is doing and saying behind my back. However, for your sake, and to some extent mine, I will forget all that happened. But this had better be the roll of film, the only roll that you used when you took my photograph. If I find out that you have lied, it would be a clear sign that you and Pilchard are in concert and I will inflict my wrath upon both of you. Don't forget, I now am armed with secrets about the two of you that can make both of you the headlines for weeks! Are we clear on this?"

"Yes. And I sincerely thank you," Maggie replied as she rose from the chair. She approached Pigeon and kissed him on the cheek. "Thank you. Thank you. Very much."

*   *   *

The distraught but somewhat relieved woman buttoned her coat and donned her rain-mate. After reiterating her gratitude, she left the office, and on her way out, she expressed abundant gratitude to the receptionist for her graciousness. On returning to her car, she pondered on Pigeon's threats. She had entered his office with good intentions, but upon further contemplating and analyzing the details of the conversation, and especially Pigeon's last remark, she realized that she had made herself vulnerable to a man whose machiavellianism knew no boundaries. An instantaneous fear overcame her and she immediately instructed Roy to head for *Superflash Studios.*

On arrival at the studio, Maggie whispered a prayer that she would find Jefford Outridge, the manager, in his office. He would be her only hope of protection from the fury of the tempestuous and sometimes irrational Pigeon Goodfellow. Upon entering the building, her heart lept for joy and she offered a quiet prayer in thanksgiving for what she interpreted to be a sign of God's favor; Jefford was standing by one of the machines giving instructions to one of the employees. He turned calmly to see who had entered the studio, and upon recognizing Maggie, immediately put down the teacup from which he was sipping coffee and approached her.

"Margaret Billings! What a marvelous surprise!" he exclaimed.

"Indeed!" she replied as she placed her umbrella against the counter.

They embraced, and he invited her into his office.

"May I get you a cup of tea…coffee…something to take the dampness out of your system?" he asked with a beaming smile.

"Nothing. Thank you. I'm rather in a hurry, but I've stopped by to seek a great favor of you. I can't explain everything now because I am on my way to a meeting," she explained.

"Anything for you, Maggie. My goodness; it's been a while. You look as lovely as ever. And need I tell you how much I have been longing to see you again," Jefford remarked.

"I'm flattered," Maggie replied. "But we can talk about that later." Maggie was nervous, and thought it wise not to waste time absorbing anymore of the excessive flattery.

"How can I help you?" Jefford asked in a businesslike tone.

"I know that you and Pigeon Goodfellow are acquainted with each other…" she began.

"Ahh…, Peter Goodfellow…the man…yes…my sporadic golfing partner!" Jefford responded as he gleefully threw his arms in the air.

"Jefford," the impatient and slightly agitated Maggie interrupted, "this is a serious request. Please."

Jefford approached her and assumed a serious expression. "What's wrong, Maggie?"

"Well, it's a long story which I promise I will explain to you later. But now, I want you to just listen to me, please," she pleaded.

"I'm sorry. Please…continue," Jefford apologized.

"Mr. Goodfellow may be bringing a roll of film to be developed today or sometime soon. I want you to oversee the development of the film and discreetly have another set made for me," she requested.

"I …can't do that. It's against the law. I could get into serious trouble. Furthermore, he is a lawyer. The man knows the law like the back of his hand." Jefford explained.

"I am aware of that – hence the discretion. He would only know if *you* tell him. I need your help, desperately, Jefford. You must help me," Maggie pressed.

Jefford turned away from Maggie and sighed deeply. He turned towards her again and sat on the edge of his desk, contemplating her deeply as she tensely awaited his response.

"Why are you asking me to do this? And what's in this for me? You're not only asking me to risk my job, but my honor. Come on Maggie, I'm a man of integrity," Jefford remonstrated.

Maggie studied the reluctant Jefford momentarily. "Do you mean that all that we've shared in the past is of no consequence, Jefford?" Maggie asked as she drew closer to Jefford, who had begun to breathe heavily and swallow hard. "If you do this for me, Jeff, I would ignite the flame that once blazed in our hearts. This is how badly I want a copy of the films. And I promise, he would never know. You will never have to lose sleep over this, trust me," Maggie swore as she caressed his lips with the tip of her delicately scented index finger. "Or have you forgotten how happy I've made you in the past."

Jefford remained silent as he closed his eyes and took a deep breath. "Just a minute," he whispered hoarsely and proceeded to the door. "Miss Neptune, don't let anyone disturb me for a few minutes. I'm having an important meeting with...this ...saleswoman."

"Yes sir, "the timid Miss Neptune replied.

Maggie observed Jefford as he closed back the door and quietly locked it. She had had a torrid affair with him during the first three months of the previous year. As he turned, his mouth fell open as he beheld her standing by the coat rack with her olive green, cotton blouse partly unbuttoned and her rain coat tossed across the desk.

"You... really...mean business..." Jefford panted as he gazed upon Maggie in her svelte perfection. "Fortunately, it's raining heavily so the studio is practically empty...a perfect day for personal business."

"I *am* a business woman, Jefford, and I play fair," she purred.

Jefford approached the sizzling temptress and seized her in his short, chubby arms. He was much shorter than she, and had gained quite a few pounds since their romantic encounter ended as suddenly as it had begun. They kissed passionately as they backed against the wall. The coat rack fell to the floor in the wake but they paid no attention to it. In less than two minutes, Jefferson raised up on his toes, trembled violently, gasped and sank to the floor. His belly heaved and shook like jello as he lay panting on the floor, with his trousers half way down his short, fat thighs. Maggie buttoned her blouse and zipped up her skirt before she raised the exhausted Jefford from the floor and helped him to reorganize himself. After she helped him to his chair, he swore to keep his promise, and she made a vow to make him happier upon receipt of the photographs. They kissed once more and Maggie hurried to the door. She swung open the door in a desperate endeavor to exit the building before the rain stopped and customers began to flood the studio. As she stepped out, she froze in shock as she beheld Pigeon Goodfellow completing a transaction with one of the employees. She quickly gained composure, and with lightning speed, dashed back into the office and closed the door. Jefford was still sitting in his chair with this head leaned on the desk in a state of exhaustion.

"He's out there. My mind told me that he was going to come some time today. Quick, you have to go out there and see to the film. I don't know what he's told the girl. Go on...catch him before he leaves!" Maggie cried.

Jefford rose wearily and ambled to the door, still panting.

"Wait!" Maggie ordered, and offered him a glass of water which she drew from the wash basin in Jefford's private toilet. "Drink this, quickly. You can't go out there panting like that!"

Jefford drank the water, and having composed himself, opened the door. However, Pigeon had already left and the young woman with whom he had been speaking saw Jefford and immediately approached him.

"Mr. Outridge, a gentleman named Mr. Goodfellow just bring a roll of flim, and he aks me to give you the flim and the note. Everything deh in dhis bag."

"Thank you, Miss Culley," he replied and once again retired to his office. However, before entering the office, he discreetly removed the envelope and inserted it into his pocket.

"What does he want? Is it the film that he's brought?" Maggie inquired.

"Yes. Here it is," he revealed. "Don't worry. I'll keep my promise."

"But where is he? Is he still out there? Has he driven off?" Maggie further inquired nervously.

"Calm down," the mildly irritable Jefford advised. "I'm sure that he's left. It's raining out there. Why would he linger around?"

"Please. Would you kindly go and see. Make sure. Please!" Maggie nevertheless insisted.

Jefford once more exited the office and proceeded to the entrance to the studio. There was no sight of the silver jaguar and he returned to the office with the happy news. Instantaneously, but vigilantly, she raced to her car. Roy opened the door for her and upon igniting the engine, sped off along Lombard Street.

*   *   *

Jefford subsequently returned to the office and opened the envelope. The note read:

> *Good Morning, Jeff:*
> *This roll of film contains evidence needed for a minor court case. It is highly confidential, so would you please personally oversee its development. When you have finished developing the pictures, please give me a call. I will collect them as soon as possible. I appreciate your assistance, brother! We'll talk. Thank you.*
> *Pigeon*

Jefford suddenly began to feel faint. His bodily passions for Maggie persuaded him to honor his word to her. However, his sense of ethics dictated that he be faithful to the man who called him 'brother.' Ambiguity thus wrestled passionately in his mind, but eventually, his promise to Maggie prevailed. Jefford then breathed a heavy sigh of relief and immediately set to work.

* * *

The day labored on with sporadic, heavy downpours which threatened to cancel the big meeting in the village. Much preparation had been made, and the villagers were zealous to meet the bishop and present their case. Consequently, the inclemency of the weather was of minor threat. *Brad's Palace* remained closed for the day in order to prepare for the major event. Word had circulated that certain prominent members of St. Patrick's had inveigled a few of the villagers to advocate the building of the church. However, Pigeon's supporters were prepared to convince Bishop Addington that their place was at St. Patrick's, and therefore will neither support the plan to build nor transfer their membership to any church in the village. It became clear that the villagers were prepared to brave even the most severe weather in order to win their respective case.

By six fifteen, there was no more room to accommodate the mammoth crowd which had turned out to meet the bishop. There was a clear demarcation between the rival groups and the atmosphere was tense. However, there were some who were there only for the sake of experiencing an evening at *Brad's Palace*. Complimentary drinks flowed abundantly, and the coins for the use of the toilet multiplied in like manner, with lines sometimes being formed in front of the latrine and men discreetly relieving themselves behind large trees at the back of the yard.

Shortly before six twenty, a silver jaguar turned the corner and pulled up in front of *Brad's*. As the vehicle approached the club, the children who were lingering outside ran alongside it. Everyone's attention was drawn to the luxurious vehicle and the crowd surrounded the car to welcome their hero. The door opened and Pigeon disembarked. Those who had pledged their allegiance to him burst into zealous applause and extended their arms for a welcoming handshake. The vehicle pulled away and Pigeon stepped with dignity through the crowd, shaking hands and inquiring about their welfare. He also offered sporadic words of encouragement as he proceeded to the front of the room where he was escorted by Ram and Harry Ying We to one of the special seats which were set aside for him and the other distinguished guests. He sat next to Petulia Nobles and Agustus Sealy, one of the quiet members who lived in North Abersthwaithe. The three soon became engaged in a quiet conversation.

Suddenly, a strange silence engulfed the room as Mrs. Ramgolam, accompanied by her bodyguard, as well as Fenton Skeete and Nathaniel Francois, appeared at the entrance. Mrs. Ramgolam looked ridiculously impressive, like an indeterminate caricature of a chorister in her white cotton blouse with a Fontainebleau collar and long, puffed sleeves with a frill at the end. Her wig was combed in a bun and she carried a mildly tattered briefcase. The make-up was reminiscent of a clown who had lost his identity – whose colors had faded like the sunset which yields to the insipid hues of the dusk. No one made any disparaging remarks about the Public Relations Officer for fear of her bodyguard and respect for Fenton and Nathaniel. Mrs. Ramgolam, as well as Fenton and Nathaniel, was directed to the front of the room and offered seats just behind Pigeon. Insincere greetings were exchanged before the trio took their seats.

A surge of excitement emanated from the rear, followed by contagious applause as a black Morris Oxford approached the entrance to the pub and stopped. The chauffeur in his crisp, starched, black trousers and white terylene shirt emerged from the vehicle and opened the rear door. Bishop Addington disembarked and immediately began to greet the exhilarated crowd. He looked dignified and imposing in his black suit and violet clerical shirt. The bishop was known to be a gracious man, one well respected and loved by all walks of people. He smiled warmly at the children in their tattered finery which they had donned to meet the man of such distinction. Pigeon immediately rose and pushed through the crowd to welcome the man of honor and to escort him to his seat which was placed behind the table in the front of the room. On reaching him, they embraced and Pigeon invited him to the front. The crowd burst into rapturous applause as the bishop made his way to the front. The tension which earlier had hung over the room like a dark cloud had temporarily dissipated, and for that moment the crowd was of one heart and mind.

Pigeon stood in front of the table and raised his arms. The applause gradually diminished and the crowd became silent.

"Ladies and gentlemen, it gives us great pleasure to welcome his Lordship, Bishop Michael Addington, to Brewster's village. As you all know, His Lordship has graced us with his distinguished presence specifically to address the issue of the church being erected here in Brewster's village – a plan to which we are vehemently opposed…"

" 'ow de hell he expec' we to understan' whu' he sayin' if he goin' to talk fancy like dhat?" Monty Archins, known as 'Turtle', drawled.

"Dhat's whu does 'appen when you doesn't read, Turtle," Phil Dawkins, Stella Dawkins' husband replied.

Turtle raised his hand and spoke without permission. "Is we or isn't we goin' to build de chu'ch?"

"Kindly hold your question, sir. We'll get to your question in a minute," Pigeon replied.

"Well you has to talk so we can understand. Nobody ain't know what you sayin' wid dem fancy words dem!" Turtle complained.

"*I* does, Turtle," Ram's wife responded with an air of contempt for the ill clad sexagenarian. "So hush up yo' mouth!"

"Aww, go boil yo' head, Gloysis," Turtle growled. "You ain't understan' nothing. You' English is as bad as me own."

A few of the audience merely chuckled because of their respect for the bishop. Pigeon nevertheless continued.

"The purpose of this meeting, my friends, is to let Bishop Addington know how much you, the people of Brewster's village and Slough, feel about building another church here. During the discussion, Mr. Sealy shall be your moderator. Bishop Addington will reserve his remarks after you all have shared your views. We shall now begin the meeting with a prayer, after which the floor will be opened for discussion."

Bishop Addington invited the audience to stand for the prayer. After a brief but powerful invocation and a few gracious remarks from the bishop, Pigeon declared the floor open.

Immediately, Mrs. Ramgolam rose from her seat and stood at the head of the center aisle, at an angle where she could see both the bishop and the audience. It was obvious that she had received some coaching prior to the meeting. "Bishop Addington, Modirater, ladies and gentlemens; in my kaypacity as your Public Relations Offisar, I speaks on behalf of the members of St. Patrick's Anglican Church in Abersthwaithe. We feels dhat the church in Brewster's village will enable the peoples dhem from the two villages to go to church without havin' to walk so far and all dhat, especially pun rainy days. If we builds a church here, the peoples dhem will be very 'appy. Furthermore, me' lord, I has a partition in me briefcase that the peoples dhem sign to say dhat they wants dhem own church in the village." Mrs. Ramgolam took up her briefcase.

"Be careful, bishop. She got roaches in she briefcase too!" yelled a voice from the rear.

A wave of suppressed laughter swept across the room but stopped abruptly as Pigeon rose and cast the crowd a disapproving look.

Mrs. Ramgolam then opened her briefcase and presented a thick pile of papers to the bishop. "Dhem is the partitions dhem, me lord," she said confidently.

"Those are the petitions which we asked the members to sign, my lord, so as to show you how many people want this church built. The signed petitions represent more than half of the congregation, my lord," Nathaniel Francois explained and then turned towards Pigeon with a mocking grin.

Bishop Addington slowly and gently flipped the pages as he skimmed through the scores of names which appeared on the petition sheets. Pigeon's jaw dropped as he turned towards the crowd. Many of them hung their heads as Pigeon's eyes rested upon them. The shock of betrayal left him stupefied. It became obvious to him that the very people whose dignity he was seeking to defend had turned against him. As he stood there, too dumfounded to speak, Petulia rose impetuously from her seat and turned towards the crowd.

"This woman tellin' lies pun you all!" she screamed. "I *know* that y'all didn't sign no petition." She then turned towards the bishop. "Bishop, could I see that list? I wants to see if them people…"

"You can't see nothin', Petulia. Them papers is confidensheyal," Mrs. Ramgolam interjected as she stretched her arm wide open so as to prevent Petulia from reaching the table.

"Gloysis Ramgolam, you bes' move you han' from in front o' me before I stuff you in dhat ugly, stupid briefcase! Nobody ain't even invite you here!" Petulia warned as she glared at Mrs. Ramgolam.

"Ladies, please let us exercise some dignity in front of the bishop," Pigeon eventually spoke as he regained his composure.

"She *does* have a right to see the petitions, Mrs. Ramgolam," Bishop Addington calmly informed the Public Relations Officer. "It *is* public information."

"Thank you, Bishop," Petulia said as she reached for the papers. After a few seconds of desultory reading, she recoiled in shock. "Bishop, they got dead people pun this sheet!"

"Dah' aint true. All o' dem people is **alive**." Mrs. Ramgolam responded defensively.

"Ms. Pickins, me' dear; you got **Marjorie Pickins** name pun the sheet here with she name signed. Ms. Pickins **in** the burial groung, love." Petulia calmly stated as she showed Mrs. Ramgolam the sheet.

"Well, somebody must be mek a **mistake**, me lord," Mrs. Ramgolam explained. "Dhese names is real people, **me** lord."

"How many more mistakes are on that sheet, Madam Public Relations Officer?" Pigeon added. "Furthermore, when could you have possibly had these names signed?"

Fenton Skeet raised his arm. He was given permission to speak.

"My Lord, a few of the concerned members of St.Patrick's vestry conducted this petition with the assistance of some of the members who live in Brewster's village and Slough. We did it during the course of New Year's Day. The signatures are authentic, my lord, and the people are enthusiastic about the prospects of a new church which will serve their purpose and which will be most convenient for them. You see, Bishop, the people who live in these villages boast a rich culture, quite different from those in the other areas, and we feel that a church of their own will prove more meaningful to them. We conducted a detailed investigation, my lord, and this proposal was made after indepth consultation with these villagers." Fenton explained.

"I would like to ask a question, Mr. Moderator," Pigeon requested.

"Permission granted, Mr. Goodfellow," Mr. Sealy replied.

Pigeon rose and turned towards the audience. "I would like to ask an important question. Did all of you who are purported to have signed this petition…you know, those who Mr. Skeete said signed this paper…did you understand what was being said to you? Were you forced or bribed to sign this petition?"

"I object to Mr. Goodfellow's cross examination of these …ah…*people*, Mr. Moderator. This is not a court," Nathaniel protested. "He's insulting their intelligence, Bishop!"

"I think what you mean is that *you* are guilty of doing just that; you, the vestry and the BOARD," Pigeon remonstrated. "You are the ones who refer to these people as *brutes*; you all are the ones who don't want them in the same church with you. Now you come here to stand in front of the bishop as if you have these poor people at heart. You should be ashamed of yourself, Skeete!"

"Mr. Goodfellow has a personal agenda, Bishop. He doesn't really care about any of these people. Trust me," Fenton interjected.

Pigeon then took the petition from the table and ran his fingers down the first page. He suddenly stopped, raised his head and glanced across the room. "Jeremy…Jeremy Rudder… come to the front…come here."

Jeremy slowly and embarrassingly approached the front. All attention was on him as he approached the table. Pigeon lay the petition on the table directly in front of the bishop. He offered Jeremy his pen.

"Here, Jeremy," he said quietly. "Sign your name here…just here, next to your signature.

Jeremy hung his head and rubbed his hands together nervously as he made several glances at the bishop and Pigeon.

"Go on, son," Bishop Addington gently persuaded the young man. "Sign your name for us."

The young man momentarily contemplated the bishop. His eyes became teary. "Me…me …can't write, me lord. Me ain't know how to read…or write," he confessed.

Pigeon and the bishop studied each other briefly.

"I rest my case, my lord," Pigeon affirmed. "They made you tell a lie, Jeremy. They made you tell a lie to the bishop. You may return to your seat, Jeremy. Thank you."

Immediately, the distraught and embarrassed young man turned and bolted from the room, for among the villagers, it was considered a mortal sin to lie to a priest – let alone a bishop. Furthermore, such an offence was purported to be followed by bad luck.

None of the people from the villages knew what had happened at the table, but supposed that it was something particular that Jeremy might have done, which the bishop, by virtue of divine intuition, had come to know, for the villagers had believed that men of the cloth were blessed with supernatural powers to detect sin and wrongdoing. The crowd thus became deathly quiet, and one by one some of the village's most notorious men rose quietly and slipped through the crowd and departed in beads of sweat.

Bishop Addington whispered something to Agustus, who subsequently rose and approached the front of the room.

"Ladies and gentlemen, please raise your hands if you want to have your own church built in Brewster's village," Agustus asked as he glanced around the room.

Sporadically, a few hands were raised. Fenton then rose and addressed the crowd with his eyes. Slowly, other hands went up. Soon, more than a half of the crowd had their hands raised and their heads hung.

Pigeon studied them. He gazed upon them in utter disbelief. Suddenly, he turned towards the bishop. "I'm sorry to have wasted your time, Bishop," he apologized in a hushed tone. "I'm very sorry to have got you involved in this...imbroglio." Pigeon then turned towards the people, "I'm sorry to have attempted to prevent something which most of you clearly want to have done. You may have your church. I hope that you never regret your decision. Thank you for coming out this evening." Pigeon then embarrassingly returned to his seat, hurt, angry, humiliated and shocked almost to a trance.

The silence which followed was cutting, and Agustus immediately sought to ease the awkwardness by inviting the bishop to give his remarks. As soon as the bishop rose, the crowd burst into applause. However, some members of the audience withheld their plaudits and sat stoically as they observed the excitement of the howling defeat. Augustus raised his arms and the applause immediately subsided. The bishop approached the front of the room.

"My friends," he began as he clasped his hands and smiled peacefully at the exhilarative crowd, "this evening you have proved to yourselves that you are capable of making major decisions and standing up for it. Your presence here tells me volumes about your character as Christians who are prepared to fight for what you believe is right. I therefore grant you permission to erect your church – the church in the village – the church that will give you all the opportunity to direct your own affairs in ways that are meaningful to all of you..."

Again, the crowd burst into passionate applause as they rose from their seats. The standing ovation lasted for almost a minute, after which Augustus once again raised his arms and the people sat.

"Let me stress, however," Bishop Addington continued, "that with this permission come responsibilities and the need for accountability. After the novelty of having your own worship space shall have worn off, the real work will begin. A priest has to be employed and wardens and a vestry – or bishop's committee – must be elected. In addition, standing committees and other ministries must be formed and must act in accordance with the stipulations of the diocese. I will therefore appoint Fr. Perths, in conjunction with your Archdeacon, of course, who knows you all by name and who perhaps knows best the degree and diversity of talents and skills with which you have been blessed, to spearhead this project and address all of the ecclesiastically pertinent issues at the local level. In addition, I appoint Mr. Peter Goodfellow, your newly appointed senior warden, and Mr. Adolph Pilchard, to oversee and direct the structural issues and supervise the day to day activities during the erection of the building. *I* will preside over the entire project, and I will give all the support and encouragement needed right up to the time of the dedication of the new church. My dear friends in Christ, I congratulate you on the initiative you have taken to spread the gospel through making the church accessible to all people. May God bless you in this ambitious endeavor to take his gospel to highways and byways, to the mountains and the valleys and to the ends of the island. Thank you."

The crowd once more rose to their feet and burst into ebullient applause. This time, however, the applause was accompanied by shouts of appreciation and love for Bishop Addington. Even those who were opposed to the project stood respectfully and applauded. Immediately after the standing ovation, Bishop Addington did the benediction. Once again, he personally greeted Pigeon, Fenton, Nathaniel, Mrs. Ramgolam and a few of the crowd who were close to him as he made his way towards the exit. The applause started again as Bishop Addington entered his car. After a final dignified wave, he rode off in his impressive, but modest, black vehicle. The children ran alongside the car until it turned the corner and sped off.

"Well," Agustus remarked, "if we can't beat them, I guess it is better to join them than to continue fighting. It might be a good opportunity for you to…"

"I'd rather die than join that bastard Pilchard in this project, Guss. I'd rather drop dead!" Pigeon snapped.

"Bishop Addington is a very clever man, Pigeon – a godly man. Don't spurn him or dismiss his wisdom as folly," Augustus warned the intensely irate opposition leader.

"He saw for himself how fraudulent that petition was! He knows how deceitfully these fellahs are operating, yet he allows them to proceed with their plan!" Pigeon protested. "What the hell was that all about, eh, putting me to work with Pilchard to supervise the very thing to which that I'm vehemently opposed? Is this some sort of mockery…his way of humiliating me in front of all these…these…damn illiterate numskulls? Look at them, just look at them, jumping up and down like a troupe of monkeys on a bloody high! Don't worry, Guss, this shit is going to come back to haunt Bishop Addington. See, it all goes back to the same thing – they all got this thing for Pilchard…all of them…and nobody's got the balls to stand up to him. But don't worry, Guss, I've got it all figured out, watch me…just watch me!"

Agustus stood by quietly as Pigeon ranted and raved over the bishop's decision. He merely patted Pigeon on the shoulder before taking up his folder and making a quiet exit through the excited crowd as they surrounded Fenton, Nathaniel and Mrs. Ramgolam, shaking hands and hugging passionately. Ram, Harry, Petulia and Joshua remained in a corner of the room, nursing their wounds from the crushing defeat. Pigeon crossed the room towards them and thanked them for their loyal support, and swore to them that the blow was not final. He then expressed gratitude to the Bradshaws for their hospitality. After a brief conversation with Mr. Bradshaw, he proceeded to the front of the building, and upon noticing the silver jaguar across the street, headed out towards the imposing vehicle and rode off unceremoniously.

Word of the bishop's approval spread rapidly across the Brewster's village and Slough, and the villagers celebrated in quintessential Brewster's village fashion. News of sporadic scuffles between rival parties was reported and there were threats to hinder the progress of the building by vandalism and fire. In addition, there was word that someone threw a chamber-pot of urine in Mrs. Ramgolam's face and darted off down the dark, dirt road, with the bodyguard in hot pursuit. However, the culprit outran the bodyguard, jumped across the muddy trench and disappeared through the cane field.

*　　　*　　　*

On receiving word of the bishop's decree, Mr. Pilchard telephoned the members of the BOARD and instructed them to immediately stop whatever they were in the process of doing, and to fall on their knees and thank God for the resounding victory. "This defeat of the enemy is the stamp of God's approval of the existence of the BOARD," he testified to Lauent Faulkner. "Furthermore this joint supervision is the ultimate opportunity to finally humiliate and disgrace Pigeon publicly, and I will do so until the weight of embarrassment and humiliation became too heavy for him to bear and consequently cause him to resign from his position as senior warden."

*　　　*　　　*

Pigeon meanwhile returned home that night with the dagger of disappointment stuck through his heart.

"My heart bleeds from the wound of betrayal," he cried as he twisted and turned next to Mrs. Goodfellow throughout the long, dark night. He shared with her his story about that night on the beach when he received his commissioning for the task which he believed he was divinely called and sent to perform. Pigeon thus made an oath that he would wrestle to the end with the enemy rather than submit to the bishop's edict. He swore to his wife that he would fight fire with fire, and that he was not going to extinguish his flame until he had consumed the last of the enemy in one final showdown. This last enemy, he pronounced, was now Bishop Michael Addington.

* * *

Tuesday morning approached with the dolefulness of a brumous day in a desolate burial ground. The sky was heavily overcast and the drizzle was persistent and annoying as the people set about to address their cares and execute the occupations of their daily life. People huddled about in raincoats or covered themselves in plastic tablecloths as they made their way to their respective occupations or to take care of their personal business. Pigeon solemnly ambled around the house as he mused on the humiliating defeat of the previous night. Mrs. Goodfellow tried to convince him over breakfast that the villagers should be able to pursue what they believed was best for them in the same way as he was tenaciously holding on to what he believed was the right thing for him to do. However, his pride would never have allowed him to surrender to a man whose status he had fervidly envied and whom he hated with a deadly passion. Had it not been for Mr. Pilchard, he might have accepted the bishop's decision with less acrimony, but he believed that he was in total control of the reins that could lead the judge to absolute destruction, and he intended to masterfully and ruthlessly steer him into an uncompromising path to annihilation.

Heavy downpours fell intermittently as Pigeon headed for his office. However, *en route* to the office, he swung on to Lombard Street for a brief stop at *Superflash Studios*. The young woman with whom he had left the film and the letter immediately recognized him and proceeded to notify Mr. Outridge.

"Sorry, sir," she whispered as she pushed the door slightly, "Mr. Goodfellow…"

"What about him, Miss Cully?" Jefford petulantly inquired as he paused from his telephone conversation.

"He deh outside, sir. He say dhat he come fuh de flims dhem," she informed her boss.

Jefford sighed impatiently. "Miss Cully, you *must* do something about your English. I have important people coming here to conduct business, and I wouldn't have them assume that I can't afford to hire proper people. It is most irresponsibile of anyone to speak as badly as you do. Just go…tell him that I'll be out in a minute," Jefford instructed the nervous and humiliated young woman. "But then again, don't…don't bother. I'm coming right now," Jefford added and hung up the phone.

The two men embraced and Jefford invited Pigeon into his office. Pigeon apologized for the demand he had made on his friend but did not explain any of the details of his request. It was Jefford who shared all of the sordid details between Maggie and himself. He offered Pigeon a cup of coffee, and the two friends indulged in a casual tete-a-tete, during which they reminisced about their boyhood, grammar-school days together after Pigeon noticed a photograph of his friend in his grammar-school uniform hanging on the wall.

Jefford suddenly deviated from their path down memory lane. "You know, Pigeon, these memories of our wonderful days of brotherhood have done something to my conscience. I feel badly doing this, but there is something I must know. Tell me, what does this …film…have to do with Maggie Billings?

Pigeon straightened up and he stared at Jefford as if the latter were an apparition from the depths of hell who had come to settle his account. Jefford instantly recognized the delicacy of the issue.

"Is there something that I was supposed to, or not supposed to know, *brother?*" Jefford's tone bore a hint of sarcasm. "Are you using me to facilitate some clandestine plot to destroy the woman who by her kindness has made me very happy and has restored my self- worth?"

"It's a very long and complicated story, Jeff," Pigeon explained. "However, there is nothing underhanded about any of it – at least nothing that would incriminate you or cause you any inconvenience or shame – whatsoever – or cause you to appear ungrateful to this woman who has restored your self-esteem, whatever that means. I know that there might be photographs of her in that roll, but…all that I can say to you is that you have to trust me. Why are you asking me such a question, however?"

Jefford studied his friend briefly before responding. "There are no photographs of her. Who took the photographs…you?"

"Yes," Pigeon lied. "Why?"

Jefford paused.

"I know...," Pigeon continued with an embarrassing smile. "The nude photograph of me on the floor...I could explain how..."

"That was you lying there!?" Jefford intercepted with mild amusement and shock.

Pigeon was now more perplexed than ever. He contemplated his friend with an uncertain smile and a knitted brow.

"I would never have known. As a matter of fact, nobody *could* know. The face was not photographed – only from the chest down to the knees," Jefford continued. "The reason I asked was that you have several photographs of that fellah who was murdered in Westminster Lane...ah...Gaskin, I think...yes, Wilberforce Gaskin, that was his name...a few photographs of him...lying half naked, bare chested and asleep on the couch, wearing what looks like a funny pair of leopard skin boxers. You knew him?"

Pigeon was petrified. However, he quickly regained composure. "Yes," he struggled to answer. "Casually. But someone might have used my camera to take those photos...I...I don't recall taking photographs of him. Why the hell would I want to do that anyway?"

"Anyway," Jefford responded, "here they are. I developed them myself, so no one else has seen them." He handed Pigeon a large, brown envelope, which bore the *Superflash* emblem.

"Thank you," Pigeon nervously received the envelope with a feigned smile. "I'm afraid that I must be going now, my brother. I have a nine thirty appointment with a prospective client."

"Do you know that it was broadcast one week ago that Gaskin's sister, who flew in to the island from England for the funeral, was offering a three thousand dollar reward for any information leading to the arrest of her brother's killer? I'd like to get my hands on that!"

"Really?" Pigeon replied. "Anyway, I have to go. Thanks, again."

The two friends embraced onec more and Pigeon departed, with his mind in turmoil as the cool drizzle descended upon him like heavenly sprinklers to cool his searing anger.

Jefford returned to his office and telephoned Maggie to inform her that the photographs were ready. However, he advised her not to come to the studio for fear of any possible altercation with Pigeon, who he said, had called earlier to say that he was going to stop by some time during the day to collect the photographs. He therefore arranged to meet her at her home that evening.

* * *

Shortly before his appointed meeting, Pigeon arrived at his office. The receptionist calmly informed him that the gentleman whom he had scheduled to meet had arrived and was waiting in the conference room. Pigeon nevertheless retired momentarily to his office and closed the door so as to fully compose himself after his harrowing meeting with Jefford. Before inviting his client to his office, he viewed the photographs and then consumed a potent shot of brandy to calm his nerves.

"Ms. Neptune," the agitated Pigeon called from his opened door, "Please send the gentleman inside."

"Yes, sir," she replied and proceeded to the conference room. She soon returned and tapped on the door. "Sir, they're here," she spoke gently as she peered in the room.

"They...?" Pigeon whispered.

Ms. Neptune shook her head in the affirmative and ushered the two men into the office. The two men entered, and Pigeon recognized the other one as the man who had offered his wife a seat at the service. He expressed great delight at seeing both men again.

"Mr. Huntley!" Pigeon exclaimed as they shook hands. "It's so good to see you again!"

"Please. Call me Burtland. No need to be so formal," he replied.

The shorter of the two extended his arm, "Scott...Scott Fielding."

"A pleasure!" Pigeon replied. "Do have a seat. Coffee...tea...or brandy, perhaps?"

The men opted for the brandy, after which they spoke of superficial topics regarding the unstable weather and Pigeon's plans for the church as senior warden. However, Pigeon sensed some uneasiness during the conversation and therefore hastened to get to the purpose of what he believed to be an official visit.

"Well, how may I help you gentlemen today, in spite of the many challenges that I'm already facing in my role as senior warden?" Pigeon artfully swung the conversation.

The two men briefly observed each other. The taller of the two then straightened up and spoke. "Well...you probably have been seeing us together...ah...at church...and perhaps at other places..."

"You know, it's a shame that the first time I actually noticed you at the church was the day you offered your seats to my wife and me," Pigeon confessed. "I guess that this is one of the drawbacks of a large congregation; we don't know each another as we should."

"But we know *you*, Mr. Goodfellow, and we know *of* you. Your reputation as a brilliant lawyer precedes you. Furthermore, you were recommended to us by a good friend of ours whom you successfully represented a few years ago," Scott replied.

"He's right," Burtland agreed, then, without any further hesitation, he plunged right into the issue at hand. "We are, well, *married* to each other, for lack of a better word, and we want to raise two children, ah...adopt and raise them...as our own. I will adopt one as mine, who will bear my last name, and Scotty will adopt the other and give him his surname. I'll adopt the girl and Scotty will adopt the boy. In this way, our...well... *marriage*, will not become...ah...too public. We would like you to be our legal counselor in our attempt to get these children and raise them as our own."

A gut wrenching silence followed the stunning revelation. Pigeon had never before heard of such a relationship – at least not to the extent of being described as a marriage, let alone desiring to raise a family. However, at this point he realized that he would need every iota of support from the members of the church as he sought to defeat the enemy within and destroy the BOARD. Pigeon was therefore judicious enough not to reveal any sign of awkwardness or appear judgemental towards the two persons sitting before him. Furthermore, he remembered their acts of kindness towards his wife and him.

"Well," Pigeon finally responded, "I must confess that your request threw a googly at me. However, if I can help you, I certainly will do so. But tell me, as a matter of interest, if your...marriage...was...well...celebrated as a ceremony, like you know, a...ah... "

"A normal one, like that of a man and a woman?" Scotty interjected with a gentle smile.

"Yes," Pigeon awkwardly replied.

"In one sense, no, and in another sense, yes," Scott replied. "We had a simple ceremony where we exchanged our own vows and then the priest gave us his blessing. After the service, we held a small reception in our home. That was it. It was nothing more than a declaration of our love in front of a few close friends, and the church's approval, that's all. We don't need to flaunt our relationship. We realize that such a thing as this has never been heard of in Ischalton, and therefore not many people will approve of our relationship. So we have to be respectful of their opinion. Nevertheless, we must do what we feel is good and right for us to do. Of course, if you would rather not provide the legal service for us, we would understand perfectly."

"My service is not an issue. I shall be happy to perform the legal counseling. I just need a basic platform of information to stand on, Pigeon assured the men. "So, tell me; did you ...people...ah...well..."

"...Men," Scotty interjected jocularly. "I know that this is most awkward for you, but we are still men. Neither of us has had a sex change."

"You're absolutely right. So, did you gentlemen *marry* in England before you came to Ischalton?" Pigeon further inquired.

"No," Burtland replied. "We made our vows here, at St Patrick's. Fr. Perths performed the ceremony…after months of counseling. We will always be grateful to him. I don't know if any other priest would have granted us such a favor."

"Well, I offer belated congratulations and wish you all the best of British luck in your endeavor to adopt the children. I am sure that you will make excellent parents," Pigeon responded.

After several minutes of further pertinent conversation, the men shook hands again and Pigeon promised to immediately begin the adoption process. Furthermore, the men requested that Pigeon swear to secrecy before any further arrangements be made. Pigeon thus raised a prayer book which he always kept on his desk for his private devotion and swore to the required secrecy. Subsequent consultations were arranged and the men departed in good spirits, expressing abundant joy that their request would be honored by one whom they felt they could trust.

Pigeon closed the door and sat in his chair, overwhelmed as a result of the conversation with the two men. Ambivalence rocked his mind to and fro as he pondered on all of the possibilities that lay bare before him. Once more he opened the brown the envelope and studied the photographs which Jefford had given him. He found it difficult to believe that Maggie, a mere woman of the demi-monde, had bamboozled him. He knew that the adoption process was going to prove quite a challenge for him, but the photographs of a man whose death had made the headlines only a few weeks ago was going to pose an even greater challenge if he were to be found with them. Immediately he picked up the receiver and telephoned Maggie.

"Hello," the euphonious voice answered on the other side.

"You bitch…you evil, nasty, bloodsucking bitch!" Pigeon exploded with rage.

"And good morning to you too, Mr. Goodfellow. How lovely to hear your voice," Maggie replied with sarcasm.

"Listen to me, you succubus; if I lay my hands on you, I'll strangle you!" Pigeon yelled. "You made an ass of me,, and I don't like to be made to look stupid, you hear me! What's the point of bringing this roll of film to me when there is no proof that it is I who is lying naked on the floor? You just wanted me to go back on my word to help you destroy that weasel Pilchard. And incidentally, you ask me to develop films as my own with pictures of Mr. Gaskin in his underwear?!"

A sinister laughter resounded on the other side and Pigeon flew into a blazing rage. "You think it funny, eh, you think it funny, you crabdog!"

"No. It's not funny at all, if you know what I mean," Maggie nonchalantly replied.

"What the hell do you mean? Explain what you mean, swine!" Pigeon demanded.

"Let me tell you what I mean – in the spirit of true friendship. Leave Mr. Pilchard alone, you hear me. Good morning, Mr. Goodfellow." Maggie's tone was icy and threatening as she calmly hung up the receiver.

"Hello...hello..." Pigeon paused and took several deep breaths before quietly replacing the receiver. He interpreted Maggie's threat as a vain attempt to humiliate him, and her surrender of the roll of films as an appeasement into forgetting their plot to avenge the judge. He thus dismissed her threat as foam on the ebbing tide.

Pigeon suddenly felt the world closing in on him, and even though he had developed a liking for the two gentlemen who had just left his office, he realized that it would have been futile to surrender his trust to them. Suddenly, after a brief but profound consideration, the thought registered that the married men would be the weapon with which he could inflict the final and fatal blow to the vicar, who in his opinion had joined with the enemy and turned on him like a vicious, rabid, wild dog. Pigeon was now so filled with hatred that his wrath and desire for vengeance no longer recognized any boundaries. Slowly, incessantly, insidiously, the mental disease began to consume him like a deadly pestilence, and thus life assumed a new purpose – to utterly destroy anyone whom he perceived as a threat to him and his position as senior warden. Without therefore ceasing to reconsider the ramifications or consequences of his plan, the irrational lawyer donned his rain coat and hat and departed with haste to Bishop's Court.

High winds and heavy rain launched a hostile onslaught on the island as the silver jaguar made its way through the flexuous streets of mid-town Georgetown, on its way to Bishop's Court. Pigeon showed scant regard for the stop signs as he battled the weather with his competent vehicle to reach the place where he would begin his ruthless crusade against the church.

On arriving at Bishop's Court, Pigeon had no Gilbert to greet him. The rain was pouring as heavily as when he left his office, but now it was accompanied by flashes of lightning and peals of thunder that seemed to rock the foundations of the Georgian structure. He dashed towards the main door and pressed the bell. Within a few seconds, dainty footsteps hurried down the stairs and opened the door. Mrs. Watts stood there – the image of culinary royalty – in her starched, bleached, frilled apron over a grey, pin-stripped dress. She was sensibly shod in a pair of flat, black shoes which boasted ostentatious, gold colored buckles at the top. Her slender legs were oiled and her thick, greying hair was neatly tucked under a burgundy and white wrap. She smiled demurely at him as their eyes met.

"Good morning, good sir," she greeted Pigeon in her quasi-British accent as he wrestled desperately with his umbrella to keep the wind from destroying it and the rain from soaking him.

"Good morning, Mrs. Watts. Is Bishop Addington here?" Pigeon's voice trembled as he made a mild attempt to enter the building. However, Mrs. Watts had positioned herself firmly in the center of the doorway, which inhibited any further movement by him as he shivered from the damp coolness of the inclement weather.

"Yes. What is your name, may I aks, so that I can announce that you has arriven?" the stately cook inquired.

"Let de man in, Watty. The man getting' wet!" a familiarly gruff voice shouted from the guard hut.

"Kindly shut up and mind your business, Gilbert," Mrs. Watts replied in her practiced accent. Nettie is doin' something for madam, and so I has to give the gentleman the same formularities like any other gues'ses; so bug off!"

"Aww, go boil yo' 'ead, yo' cantankerous, ole cow!" the voice boomed from the hut.

"I'm going to report you to the Bishop," Mrs. Watts threatened Gilbert as she stepped aside to allow Pigeon in the foyer. "Do come in from the rain, sir. I will infirm his Lordship that you has arriven. Please to give me your name, please?"

"Peter Goodfellow. You *have* met me before, Mrs. Watts. I came to your home before to speak with Philbert. I'm the senior warden of St. Patrick's in Abertswaithe," Pigeon calmly responded.

"The senior warden of St Patrick's…in Abersths?"

"Yes. Effective this year," Pigeon added.

"Is someone there, Ms Watts?" a polished voice floated downstairs.

"Yes, madam, the senior warden of St. Patrick's," the rehearsed British accent soared up the stairs.

"Please, do come up, Mr. Goodfellow. Bishop will see you in a minute. Get him a towel, Ms. Watts," the considerate voice gave a gentle command from above as Pigeon mounted the stairs. "We can't have our guest contract a cold on account of this inclemency, can we?"

"Good morning, Mrs. Addington," Pigeon greeted the gracious hostess.

"O dear me," the slighty rotund but dainty woman remarked. "You have been drenched! Haven't you got a brolly?"

"I do, but Mrs. Watts took some time to recognize me," Pigeon explained. "Consequently, a few drops caught me."

"Do have a seat in the drawing room. My husband will see you momentarily. May I offer you a cup of tea, perhaps?" Mrs. Addington inquired.

"Thank you. Very gracious of you," Pigeon replied.

"And your family; are they well?" Mrs. Addington asked as she sat erect at the edge of the antique chair opposite him, with her hands clasped and resting on her right thigh and her legs drawn together sideways and tucked slightly under the chair.

"Yes. Their only problem seems to be the fact that I am now the senior warden of St. Patrick's....you know, the politics involved…"

"Oh yes. I have been hearing quite a lot about St. Patrick's lately," she revealed.

"Have you?"

"Yes. As a matter of fact, my husband…"

At that very moment, Bishop Addington entered the room. Mrs. Addington stopped speaking abruptly, and after an incoherent remark about the weather, excused herself and exited.

"Ahh…the Good fellow!" Bishop Addington warmly greeted Pigeon. "How do you do, my learned friend?"

"My Lord!" Pigeon returned the cordiality.

"It must be a matter of some urgency that has brought you out in this awful weather," the Bishop remarked in a jovial tone.

The remark seemed oddly accurate and Pigeon interpreted it as a subtle caveat about the aftermath of the meeting at *Brad's Palace*, or perhaps some subversive act against him in his office as senior warden – which Bishop Addington might have overheard. This supposition was further justified by Mrs. Addington's incomplete remark that clearly was indicative of some aggressive and pending action which her husband might be in the process of taking.

"It is, my lord; urgent, and twice as serious," Pigeon replied with a sober expression as he looked squarely into the face of the senior ecclesiastic. "Blasphemy, my lord… blasphemy!"

"What are you talking about, my good man?" The Bishop's tone and expression gradually began to assume an aura of seriousness. His eyes addressed Pigeon's.

Gentle footsteps approached the room and Pigeon paused as Antoinette entered with a tray comprising accoutrements for tea and two chicken volauvents. Her tender simplicity brought an air of effervescence to the room as she carefully laid the tray on the coffee table and poured the tea.

"You remember Mr. Goodfellow, Nettie?" Bishop Addington asked as she served the puffed, chicken pastry. "He is the new senior warden of St. Patrick's church in Abersthwaithe, effective January."

Antoinette smiled respectfully, and after briefly inquiring about the comfort of the two men, left the room. She hurried to the kichen, deeply troubled, and reported to Mrs. Watts that Mr. Goodfellow had had an infection since January. Her concern was whether it was contagious and whether she had contracted any germs as a result of her mild contact with him as she served him the refreshments.

"This…blasphemy, Mr. Goodfellow, what is it referring to?" Bishop Addington continued in his wonted dignity.

"My Lord, I have been informed that Fr. Perths performed some kind of…of…well, it was compared to…marriage…some ceremony between two men whereby they speak of it as…well, as a marriage."

Neither of the two men said a solitary word for the following few seconds. Eventually, it was the bishop who uttered something that seemed almost unintelligible.

"There is no such arrange…ment...ceremony…I don't know…what do you mean…ahh…I have never…what exactly are you trying to tell me, Mr. Goodfellow?" Bishop Addington's expression remained calm as his eyes penetrated Pigeon's.

"Fr. Perths performed a ceremony – a reconstructed rite of marriage between two men, right in the church, St. Patrick's, that is…" Pigeon testified.

Bishop Addington remained silent as Pigeon contemplated him in anticipation of some subtle, but deadly outburst. However, the Bishop continued to display a disciplined and almost supernatural calmness.

"How were you made aware of such a thing, even if it were indeed so?" Bishop Addington asked as he continued to stare at Pigeon in a pensive expression.

"The two men came to me this morning to solicit my legal counsel for an adoption," Pigeon replied. "They are planning to raise a family – two children – by the process of adoption."

"Hardly by procreation," Bishop Addington muttered.

"They will adopt separately, as two separate individuals, and each child will be given the surname of his or her respective parent," Pigeon further explained.

"I know that you will not come to sit before me to tell me a lie, but I find all that you have just said to be rather incredulous," the bishop remarked.

"I'm afraid it's true, my lord," Pigeon swore.

"I must immediately summon Fr. Perths to a meeting. I must learn from his own lips whether what you have just said is true," the bishop calmly remarked. "Do you have any tangible proof of what you have said…you know, any paperwork that supports your claim?" Bishop Addington inquired.

"I have some paperwork, but not enough evidence to hold up in court; that is, if you – or they – choose to take any legal action. My advice is that you wait until I have gathered enough evidence of their ...*marriage*...before you summon Fr. Perths or do anything drastic. I shall be meeting the two men again next week. I will expedite matters so as to furnish you with all evidence needed. However my lord, I will ask but one favor of you," Pigeon requested.

"I'll be happy to oblige," Bishop Addington responded with a gentle smile.

"I would like this information to be highly confidential," he besought the bishop. "You must pretend that your knowledge of this...*marriage*... was acquired from some other source. I am, afterall, being hired to facilitate an adoption. The marriage is only incidental. Technically, there is nothing to support such a union. The children are being adopted by two individuals, not by a married couple."

"I understand," Bishop Addington replied. "And I will so oblige," he promised.

"Thank you," Pigon beamed as he took one last bite of his pastry.

After several minutes of light bantering, Bishop Addington rose and graciously excused himself so as to attend to other pending matters. Pigeon thanked the bishop for affording him the time to listen to his grave concern and hastened through the showers to his car. Once inside the luxurious vehicle, he whispered a thanksgiving prayer for the opportunity to topple the BOARD and the vestry by aiming at what he had deemed the source – Reverend Perths. He was, he thought, the senior warden of the most powerful church in Ischalton, and he desired a vestry that was going to be faithful to him only, one that would pay obeisance to him and no other. It therefore became necessary to attack the one person whose demise would be crucial to his ultimate victory.

The torrential rain mercilessly assaulted the sleek, silver vehicle as it maneuvered confidently through the now flooding streets of the city. Pigeon bore a wry grin as he cruised through the streets, confident that he was now set to crush the enemy and finally receive what was divinely his – the seat of ultimate power and control at St. Patrick's Anglican Church. This devilish feeling of accomplishment thus motivated him to passionately embark on the relentless pursuit of the destruction of all persons whom he had perceived to be the enemy. Bishop Addington's readiness to believe his story and to act upon it was the trumpet that heralded the divine approval of an imminent and just war against the enemy. Now, therefore, there was nothing more to consider, nothing else to fear. Pigeon was convinced that he had received divine authority to declare war against the foe, and he was going to be unyielding in mercy, tenacious in his quest for vengeance, athirst for the blood of those who had wronged him. He thus returned to his office to begin working on the adoption papers, rejoicing that he had won the day.

* * *

Darkness fell swiftly that evening as grey, tempestuous clouds glided slowly across the unpredictable sky. Most of the flooding in the low lying areas like Brewster's village had subsided considerably and the villagers were hurrying to their humble abodes before the second spate of torrential rains descended upon the island. Under the threat of an awful inclemency, the streets in Brewster's village were desolate, except for the few who dared to meet secretly at *Brad's Palace* for a meeting concerning the building of the church in the village. Adolph Pilchard, who was chairing the meeting, had requested that *Brad's Palace* remain closed for the duration of the meeting. Some of the others who were in attendance were Mrs. Ramgolam, Fenton Skeete, Nathaniel Francios, Fritz Batty, Bill Jones, Laurent Faulkner, Tessie Shoehorn, Rudy 'Shark' Killpatrick who was going to employed to construct the building, Jason Coleman, a few other men from the village who were going to be under Shark's supervision – and Philbert Watts. This venue was chosen for the meeting because of Shark and the other men from Brewster's village and Slough who were going to construct the building. Tessie had advised Mr. Faulkner that it would be wise to keep that caliber of persons from his home, despite the formality of the gathering.

The group discussed the architectural drawing and the proposed site for the church. They also set the tentative dates of completion and dedication as well as addressed other pertinent issues, including names of persons eligible to sit on the Bishop's committee. Laurent Faulkner made a motion to have Bishop Addington install Mrs. Ramgolam as the senior warden during the service of consecration. Additional names were suggested for the junior warden and the rest of the Bishop's committee. However, only Mrs. Ramgolam's position was voted upon and passed by the small gathering. The BOARD, in conjunction with the vestry, was subsequently going to make the recommendations for the committee to the Bishop.

Pending the bishop's approval, construction was set to begin on the twenty fifth of January, with completion on or about the end of April. Mr. Pilchard had already procured the building permit which was issued after Bishop Addington signed his approval for the structure to be erected. After the discussions had concluded, Mr. Faulkner ordered drinks – the best that were available at a place like *Brad's Palace* – and the group toasted their success.

* * *

While the celebration was in progress at *Brad's*, tension was building in Maggie's home. Jefford had arrived mildly drunk and earlier than expected with the photographs, and was demanding from Maggie what she had promised him upon receipt of the developed films. Maggie vehemently denied that she had made such a promise. Furthermore, she derided Jefford's performance when she visited his office, and ridiculed his lack of finesse and control. In addition, she poked fun at what she described as his excessive mass of blotchy cytoplasm which trembled like vibrating jello when his limp, exhausted body sank to the floor amidst the gasps and panting of estacy. Jefford became intensely furious, not so much at Maggie's blunt refusal to reward him with her favors, but at her flagrant contempt at what he had considered to be one of his most impressive skills. Consequently, he immediately transferred his plan of betrayal from Pigeon to Maggie, but sought to disguise his embarrassment and wrath by making one last attempt to win her sweet surrender. Jefford thus began to slow dance to the music which was being softly played on Maggie's stereo. Maggie watched in quiet amusement and mild disgust as Jefford began to unbutton his shirt until the garment parted to reveal the pale, blotchy protrusion of fat which sagged slightly over his trouser waist. The pallid mass shook vigorously as he hopped and turned rhythmiclessly to the samba. Maggie continued to observe the rotund little man divest himself of his undergarments as he slowly gyrated his pelvis, and when he was left only in a pair of grimy jock-straps, and had positioned himself directly in front of her, she rose seductively and began to dance around him as she slowly slipped the spaghetti straps from her shoulders. She maintained an alluring gaze at him as she twirled and likewise gyrated her pelvis while running her fingers through her hair. Jefford returned the gaze and turned round and round as she danced before him. Soon the music stopped, and Maggie began to hum another tune while she drew close to Jefford, and taking his hand in hers, led him to the sofa. She placed him in a reclining position and propped his head on one of the large, velvet covered cusions as she ran her impeccably manicured fingers along his heaving chest and the surface of his lips which were parted to reveal tobacco stained dentures as he gasped ecstatically. The rubicund complexion of his face became flushed with excitement as he firmly gripped the edges of the cushion and tossed his short, fat legs aimlessly and uncontrollably in the grip of rapture. When Maggie realized that she had taken him to the pinnacle of febrile emotion, she took a few steps back and stooped gracefully to the floor where she took up his clothes and rolled them under her arm.

"Just stay there, sweetie," she whispered, "whilst I go yonder to the bathroom, and slip into something that will paralyse you with desire."

Jefford remained on the sofa in the throes of ecstacy and searing anticipation of what was to come. He closed his eyes so as to make his lover's sudden appearance more dramatic, and whispered a prayer that his performance would make Maggie retract her cruel comments about his sexual ineptitude.

Suddenly, Jefford heard growling sound obehind him, coming from the direction of the kitchen. He whispered a brief prayer of gratitude and rose and turned to face the object of his desire. His heart pounded intemperately as he turned, but upon opening his eyes, he became stupefied with horror. There at the entrance to the kitchen stood Maggie, fully dressed, with Basil the ferocious mastiff by her side, barring his terrifying fangs and tugging desperately to launch a deadly attack.

"Get out, now!" Maggie ordered the semi-nude playboy.

Jefford was too petrified to move, and in the wake of such terrifying fear, urinated himself as Maggie beheld him with disdain.

"Go!" she demanded as she pretended to loose the chain which kept the fierce animal constrained.

The frightened man turned in a desperate effort to retrieve his clothing and to take up the envelope containing the photographs.

"Your clothes are outside. I threw them over the gate. And you *will* leave those photographs just where they are," Maggie warned. "Now I tell you for the last time; go!"

Without one more second of hesitancy, Jefford turned and darted towards the stairs in a frenzied attempt to escape the jaws of the savage animal, which Maggie had now released to ignominiously escort him to the road. The short, fat man raced towards the gate, oblivious to the stare and raucous laughter from the neighbor who had inadvertently stepped out on his verandah in the adjacent house that cool, wet evening and witnessed the hasty retreat. Once outside the gate, Jefford turned and hurled a dose of emetic profanities towards Maggie as the vicious animal threw itself at the iron bars in a final attempt to maul the lascivious intruder. Eventually, Jefford grabbed his clothes and darted off down the street, and donned his attire behind one of the large flambouyant trees that lined the street. Maggie and her neighbor shared no conversation when she appeared at the door to restrain the animal, for the man retreated inside – perhaps too embarrassed to face his lubricious neighbor.

Jefford slammed his car door and sped off towards Baker Street, to the home of one of his close acquaintances, Mike Burberry, a detective who often served as his partner on the squash court of the Flamingo Sports Club.

* * *

Shortly before midnight, Mr. Pilchard received a telephone call from Philbert Watts. Philbert had decided that it would be unwise to accept the position of junior warden in the wake of Bill Jones' resignation.

"What's brought on this sudden decision, Watts?" the appalled judge inquired.

"I just don't want to be involved in the politics," Philbert confessed.

"But surely, it must be more than that," the judge insisted. "There must be some other reason which you are not telling me. I mean…you ran for the position of warden of St. Patrick's, perhaps the most powerful position a lay person can hold in the ecclesiastical arena, now you tell me that you don't want to be involved in the politics? Look, Watts, we're both grown men. I'd appreciate your candidness."

"Gloysis Ramgolam, that's what," Philbert charged. "You invite me to a meeting about the church which is being built in Brewster's village, and right in front of me you all decide to make a recommendation to the bishop to commission a titmouse like Mrs. Ramgolam as senior warden. I felt like a fool, your honor, grossly insulted!"

"Is that it, Watts? You bear a grudge towards Mrs. Ramgolam over an insignificant position like senior warden of a village church? I would think that the position which has been offered to you at St. Patrick's would be cause for celebration," the judge cried.

"Face it, your honor," Philbert remonstrated, "the position at St. Patrick's would make me nothing more than the protagonist in a puppet show, with the BOARD members pulling the strings."

The judge sighed. "Tell me, Watts, what would please you – junior warden at St. Patrick's or warden at a small village church?"

"Neither, your honor, all due respects," Philbert replied. "Furthermore, if I am to assume any such position, it must be as a result of the people's vote, not the decision of an illegal, covert group of despots attempting to subvert the vestry."

A period of piercing silence followed Philbert's scathing remark.

"Tell me, Philbert, have you been speaking with Pigeon Goodfellow? That remark sounds awfully characteristic of Goodfellow."

Philbert remained silent.

"You have been speaking with him, haven't you?" the judge reiterated.

"That's totally beside the point," Philbert responded. "Furthermore, am I not entitled to speak with whomever I wish without suspicion or admonition from you or any other member of the BOARD?"

"Your defensive response and evasion of the question prove your guilt, Watts," the judge proclaimed. "You have to decide where your allegiance lies if you want to assume social status…if you want to mingle with the fat cats,

Watts. You have to learn to play the game and not be so naïve. We are placing you in a position that would make you somebody in society, Watts. Don't be a dunderhead!"

"I would rather remain with the alley cats, your honor, and let the high culture fat cats scratch each other silly and gouge each other's eyes out in their struggle for power. Furthermore, your honor, with all due respects, I *am* somebody in society, by dint of my name and talents," Philbert assured the judge.

"Very well, my good man," the judge responded dismissively. "I will unilaterally rescind the offer to elevate you to junior warden of St.Patrick's. I shall speak with Fr. Perths in the morning about your decision and he and I shall appoint someone more deserving to fill the position."

"Thank you. Very much," Philbert replied in a dignified tone and hung up before the judge could utter another word.

"Son of a bitch!" the judge swore as he slammed the receiver. Immediately he telephoned Laurent Faulkner, and after the two men had called Philbert and Pigeon names that were redolent of every kind of refuse, he made an appointment to see the vicar early the following day.

*   *   *

Precisely at one thirty in the morning, Maggie was awakened by the sound of her door bell and Basil's frantic barking as he dashed up and down the stairs. Alarmed and a trifle afraid, Maggie wrapped herself in her purple floor length duster and slipped her dainty feet into a pair of high heeled slippers. She hurriedly passed the comb through her hair and applied a little lip stick before cautiously descending the stairs.

"Who is it?" she inquired as she switched on the foyer light and the impressive lanterns which adorned both sides of the massive, polished mahogany door.

"The police," a polished, baritone voice echoed from the outside. Maggie froze, but subsequently took a deep breath before answering.

"Just a minute. I have to lock the dog in the bedroom before I open. I'd hate to have you suffer an unfriendly, canine welcome," Maggie shouted in feigned pleasantry from behind the door.

As she proceeded to lock the animal in the room, her thoughts raced like galloping horses through her head. She was convinced that the sudden and unexpected visit had something to do with Wilberforce's death. Maggie had always been haunted by thoughts of the police interrogating her about her relationship with Wilberforce – a thought which terrified her because of her fear of losing the judge's love if she were ever forced to reveal the intimate details of her friendship with Wilberforce. She had been tormented many a night by thoughts of her scandalous affair with the judge being brought to the surface through Wilberforce's inquest. However, she would eventually slip into peaceful slumber by seeing the embarrassing situation as the gate through which she would eventually claim the judge as her own. Before returning to the door, Maggie therefore braced herself for the worst and made up her mind that this perhaps was the last chance she might have to finally lay full claim to her lover.

"Do come in," Maggie greeted the detective and the two officers.

The detective was the first to enter, and respectfully removed his hat. "Good morning. I'm detective Burberry. I'm sorry to have appeared like a phantom in the dead of night to speak with you Ms...."

"Billings. Margaret Billings." Maggie led the men to the drawing room and offered them tea and assorted biscuits. "Whatever seems to be the matter…that you should appear like this? Is there something wrong?" Maggie sat comfortably in her Queen Anne chair, erect and dignified, with her hands clasped and her legs crossed. She maintained a calm disposition and spoke in a subdued tone.

Mr. Burberry was succinct and precise in the purpose of his visit. "Ms. Billings, we are in the possession of some photographs which we understand were taken ahh…in this house…photographs of the late Wilberforce Gaskin…in pajamas and …well, one of them was taken with him in his underpants. We are not accusing you of anything, of course, but we think that you might be able to help us in our investigation." The detective revealed the photographs to Maggie.

"These…these photographs were taken by Mr. Pilchard…Adolph Pilchard, the judge, one night when they were over here for dinner…joking around, just having fun. Why would these photographs warrant an urgent, nocturnal visit?" Maggie inquired in a calm voice.

"They were discreetly taken to the studio by Mr. Peter Goodfellow, to be used as some form of evidence, I suppose, or for some other reason which… you know…," the detective explained.

"Peter Goodfellow indeed. I had asked him to develop them for me. His photograph is also in this set…" Maggie replied as she fumbled through the photographs.

"Was his photograph taken the same time as Mr. Gaskin's?" one of the officers interjected.

"Look," Maggie suddenly rose from her chair and handed the photographs back to Mr. Burberry, "I am not sure what you are trying to do, Mr. Burberry, but I will not entertain this interrogation about Mr. Gaskin's death, of which I know nothing, without the presence of my attorney. You have no right to impose on me like this in the dead of night. I'm afraid I'll have to ask you to leave."

"Hardly an imposition, Ms. Billings, when we have snippets of evidence of your romantic affair with the descesased," Mr. Burberry charged as he fixed a firm stare in Maggie's eyes.

"I will politely ask you once more to remove yourselves from my premises, or I will have no recourse but to have judge Pilchard speak very sternly to you about this," Maggie warned the seemingly adamant detective.

"Save yourself the time and energy, mam. I shall speak to judge Pilchard myself. This visit hardly warrants such hostility, unless of course, there is some delicate trace of guilt. Good morning," the detective remarked as he rose from his chair and tipped his fedora.

The men left without exchanging another word with the now distraught woman. As soon as they exited the gate, Maggie rushed to the telephone and, after a few moments of hesitancy, dialed Mr. Pilchard's number.

"Pilchard's," the dignified, but sleepy voice greeted the terrified woman.

"Adolph…Adolph…the detective and two officers were just here…and they were interrogating me…forcing me to admit to having an affair with Mr. Gaskin…and they…!"

"…Maggie, calm down, calm down," Mr. Pilchard interjected. "Tell me, slowly and clearly, what has happened."

"The detective was here, I tell you. He brought some photographs of Mr. Gaskin, which I had taken to *Superflash Studios* to have developed. They were photographs which I had taken a long time ago, but took them to have them developed so that I can have something to remind me of my friend, that's all. Now they come over here, at this ungodly hour, to interrogate me." Maggie's voice shook with fear as she related the details of the unexpected visit.

"How did they get those films?" the judge asked.

"They didn't say, but I believe that it must have been one of the girls working at the studio who recognized Mr. Gaskin and, because of the monetary reward which Mr. Gaskin's sister is offering, might have called the police," Maggie reasoned.

"Is there anything unusual about the pictures?" the judge further inquired.

"No. Not at all; just regular pictures of him in different clothing. But I told the detective that you and I had taken them one night while we were having dinner over here, and that we were just clowning around…having a good time. So, you must say exactly the same thing, you hear me!" Maggie warned her lover.

"What?!" the judge exclaimed in utter shock and anger.

"Just do as I say if they ever ask you anything, that's all," Maggie pleaded.

"What in the blazes is wrong with you, woman? Why the bloody hell would you say such a thing?" the judge replied in a loud whisper.

"Look, Adolph, they wouldn't come after you. They would never come to you. You know that once your name is mentioned, no one would dare take another step," Maggie tried to calm the infuriated judge.

"Look, Maggie, who was the detective? What is his name? I'll go talk to him in the morning," the judge promised.

"Burberry, I think. A tall, dark skinned fellah with wavy hair," Maggie responded.

"My goodness…my God, have mercy…" the judge's voice cried in despair.

"Adolph…?"

"You told Mike Burberry that I was involved in taking those photographs?" the judge cried.

"What's wrong, Adolph?"

"I had told him during an incidental conversation on the golf course, shortly after Gaskin's death that I had never heard of the man," the judge declared.

A deadly period of silence followed. It was Maggie who finally broke the silence.

"What do we do now?" she cried.

"What do we do now? I think what you mean is what do *I* do now. I am going to stick to my story. I have never seen or met the man. That's my story, Maggie. So whatever you conjured up about my taking Gaskin's photographs, you will have to admit to lying. I'm not going to go to the gallows for a blatant lie, Maggie. Why the hell did you say something like that, woman? My bloody reputation is at stake here!" Pilchard yelled in a subdued tone as he stood in the dark behind the door to his study.

"You wouldn't bale out on me like this, Adolph, after all I have done for you, after all we have gone through. You will never bale out on me like this!" Maggie begged.

"Like bloody hell I would, Maggie! You have nothing to lose. I have my reputation, my status, my marriage, my dignity Maggie!" the judge continued to rant and rave as he paced around the dark room.

"…And me," the frightened woman added. "You don't speak of losing me, or that doesn't count?"

"I love you, Maggie, you know that I do, with all my heart," the judge confessed. "But I have a wife. I have an image to upkeep. What kind of happiness could we enjoy if something disastrous was to come out of all this…this lie that you hatched? You act as if it is just a matter of packing up and leaving home and moving in with you. Maggie, things are beautiful as they are. Don't let us spoil it with unrealistic ideas. My advice is that you summon Mr. Burberry to a private meeting and tell him that you were afraid and confused, that you hatched this lie about me and you taking any photographs of Gaskin. As far as you are concerned, Maggie, I have never met the man, you hear me; never!"

Maggie mentioned nothing more, but the judge could hear his distraught mistress sobbing on the other side.

"Maggie, sweetheart, stop...stop crying. I will speak to Burberry in the morning. I promise. Nothing is going to happen to you. Nor is anything going to destroy our relationship, you hear me. You and I will get through this, o.k. Nothing withstands the test of time than love. And we've got that, o.k., darling. It's going to be fine. And tomorrow, I'll find a way to come over. We'll have dinner and spend a wonderful evening together. I'll love all of your fears away...alright..." the judge swore.

"I look forward. I'll be fine as long as I have your love, I know that I'll be fine," Maggie whispered as she tried to compose herself.

"And that you do, darling. *That* you do have...all of my love. So stop crying. There is no more need to cry like this. You know that if I could have come over now, I would have been there to wrap my arms around you and comfort you," Mr. Pilchard continued to comfort his mistress. "Be patient. I'm going to make this wait worthwhile, o.k. Go. Go and get some sleep, Maggie. I'll see you tonight. I have to get back to bed... goodnight, sweetheart."

The judge carefully and quietly switched off the phone and turned to exit the room. As he swung out to the corridor, he gasped and froze in absolute terror and shock; the receiver dropped to the floor and his mouth fell open. Mrs. Pilchard was standing there, with her hands clasped and her eyes fixed firmly on her unfaithful husband.

"You need not wait until tonight to go comfort your *kept* woman, Adolph. You may go right now. Afterall, it would be quite difficult, or should I say, impossible, for you to wrap your arms around her all the way from here, don't you think?" Mrs. Pilchard said in her polished, velvet voice.

The judge lost his ability to speak for a moment and stared stupidly at his wife who remained as dignified and calm as ever.

"I have always suspected something beyond the superficial façade you have tried to portray, Adolph. I have been told many times about your relationship with Maggie Billings, but I have always given you the benefit of the doubt. I always told myself that if I am to find out anything like this, it must be you who must reveal it to me, then I will know that it is the truth. Now I know – straight from the horse's mouth. So you may go, Adolph, and do hurry. Tonight might be too late." Mrs. Pilchard turned and proceeded to the bedroom.

The judge remained exactly where he was for another minute before making even a single step. When he finally returned to the room, Mrs. Pilchard was in bed with the blanket pulled up to her shoulders. The lamp on his side of the bed was turned on, and on his pillow was the prayer book, opened to the page which contained the marriage vows. The object struck a sudden and powerful blow to the judge's heart. He threw himself across the bed and burst into tears. Mrs. Pilchard remained steadfast under the blanket and shortly slipped into a deep slumber.

*   *   *

Dark, heavily saturated clouds shrouded the island as the bells of St. Patrick's Cathedral welcomed the dawn of another day. However, for Mr. Pilchard, the chimes seemed to toll the arrival of judgment day. The tolling woke him from a very disturbing dream. He was on trial for adultery, and the court was packed with members of the society who had held him in very high esteem. When the judge entered the courtroom, everyone stood. However, he could not stand, for he was already strapped and bound to the chair to which he had condemned many a criminal in his role as judge. Everyone seemed drastically taller than he, and as he looked up at the sinister grins of the distorted faces of the jury which surrounded him, he felt as though he was in a deep, dark hole, awaiting execution by sinking into an abyss of non-existence. The people then sat and he turned to behold the judge who was going to pronounce his fate. The judge's face was concealed behind a black cloth which covered the entire head, but Adolph could see that the face was beholding him, even from behind the opaque veil. Then one of the jurors proceeded to the bench and lifted the veil so that judgment could be pronounced. There was no hearing – no opportunity for exoneration – just punishment for his grave sin. As Adolph sat there, frozen in fear of his impending doom, the jurist lifted the veil. There before him, glaring at him with an expression worse than his fate was the judge – Wilberforce Gaskin. However, before the judgment could be pronounced, the jurist took up a large bell which he always tolled before a death sentence is passed. It was the bell which awakened the terrified judge. He rose from the terrifying dream in beads of sweat and rushed to the toilet, where he regurgitated all that he had consumed the previous evening.

Mrs. Pilchard prepared her husband's breakfast as usual that morning, as well as his attire for work as she was wont to do. She never allowed the maid to attend to these duties. They were hers, and she executed them joyfully and sincerely – almost ritually. Mrs. Pilchard's continued faithfulness and dignified reticence caused the judge much discomfort. It drove him almost to the point of insanity when she made him a full English breakfast that morning. However, Mrs. Pilchard did not sit at the table to carry out the morning ritual of chatting with her husband. Instead, she retired to the drawing room with her bible and prayer book. The judge could not consume that which was placed so lovingly before him, and after a few minutes of sitting at the table, immersed in a tempestuous sea of embarrassment, guilt and fear, he rose and got dressed, and departed without the courage or heart to say anything to his wife.

* * *

Mr. Pilchard was unusually quiet when he and Laurent Faulkner arrived at the vicarage. Fr. Perths was pleased to see them, for it was a powerful reminder that he was restored to favor among the members of the *Gold Circle*. He immediately put on the kettle.

"Goodfellow's struck again," Mr. Faulkner informed the malleable clergyman. "This time it's Watts, the bloody imbecile!"

"What's he done with Watts?" Fr. Perths inquired.

"Talked him out of accepting the position of junior warden," Faulkner explained.

"I call it a blessing…in disguise," the vicar rejoined.

"Hardly a blessing," the judge added.

"Why?" Fr. Perths asked as he placed the teacups and saucers on the coffee table.

"It was through Watts that we would have controlled the brutes, contained them like bridled mules," Mr. Pilchard remonstrated, "now Goodfellow's upturned the whole bloody jackass cart."

"If Mrs. Ramgolam had even the slightest semblance of basic human common sense, I would be the first to recommend her," Mr. Faulkner added, "but the poor woman lacks even the simplest of human mental characteristics. Attach a tail to her rear end and she could easily be mistaken for one of Uncle Ed's mules."

The men burst into throes of laughter. However, the judge quickly regained his composure and interjected a proposal that caught the other two men by surprise.

"I will assume the position until the next election," he suggested, "for I am in fact the only person who has the ability to subdue Goodfellow."

"You can't!" Mr. Faulkner exclaimed.

"And why not?" Fr. Perths inquired.

"The man's just lost his bid for the position of senior warden," Faulkner protested. "He got the lowest score, even lower than Watts. What do you think would happen? The congregation would see clearly through this. Don't insult their intelligence."

"Are we talking about the whole congregation, you know, the members from Brewsters' and Slough…?" Fr. Perths asked.

"No. Just the full humans – the real members," Faulkner replied with a smirk.

"You have a point," the pitiful clergyman agreed.

"Nevertheless, I believe that I am the best person for the position – you will just have to trust that I can do the job. If you believe that I can't, then it's obvious that I have no business sitting on the BOARD."

"You're taking this personally, Pilchard." Mr. Faulkner stated. "You know for yourself that you and Goodfellow can't work together on anything. What do you hope to achieve by this, eh? Pardon my saying this, Pilchard, but it all sounds to me like a bid to satisfy the ego."

"I am *the* most powerful man on this island, Faulkner," the angry judge bellowed. "I resent your insinuation. I don't need a mediocre position like this to boost my ego. I am the honorable Adolph Pilchard – a man respected and revered by the people of this island. I am here trying to do what I think is best for St. Patrick's. Is there something wrong with that? Or do you want the position? Why the bloody hell don't you just admit it, Faulkner? I would gladly step back and let you have it – all of it – for you are the one who needs this position to boost your bloody ego!"

The judge's angry outburst shocked the two men, and Mr. Faulkner responded in like manner. "Since when did you become the most respected and revered man in Ischalton, Pilchard? And with regards to your power, there are many who don't give a damn about you or your position on the bench. Who the hell do you think you are, Pilchard? We are in a crisis and all you can think about is yourself and your bloody ego…!"

"Now you listen to me…" the judge shouted as he rose angrily from his chair.

"No. You listen to me, Pilchard!" Mr. Faulkner rose and stood directly before the judge, "this is not a bid for office. I am not in competition with you over this position. So there is no need to for this puerile outburst. I am merely being practical!"

"Well, Faulkner, you and your practicality can kiss my ass! I realize that I am in the minority here, so I wouldn't prolong the discussion. You can have it, Faulkner, or offer it to another of your *specie*!" The judge donned his raincoat and hat and headed towards the door. "Gentlemen," he said in a calm voice as he tipped his hat. He closed the door gently and departed.

Mr. Faulkner, still shocked at the judge's unwarranted outburst, collected his hat and umbrella and stormed out behind his comrade. He bade the vicar no farewell, and slammed the door behind him.

"How do you like your tea, gentlemen?" the vicar shouted with sarcasm after them.

Mr. Faulkner hurried towards the judge's vehicle and tapped on the window as the car slowly rolled passed him. The judge stopped the car and rolled down the window.

"You mind telling me what that was all about, Pilchard?" Faulkner's hurt was obvious in his tone and his eyes.

"I'm sorry, but I'm a bit tense…" the judge apologized.

"Something's wrong?" Faulkner inquired.

The judge perceived that his friend's concern was sincere, and thus invited him to join him at *Phauphen's Tavern* for a quiet drink. Mr. Faulkner returned to his vehicle and soon the two cars pulled up in front of the pub. The room was relatively quiet, with only two other men having a conversation at one of the tables. Mr. Hauklyn was not available to personally greet his distinguished guests, but Winston, the manager, extended a cordial greeting to the men as they entered, and escorted them to a table on the far side of the room. The judge ordered two draught beers and a platter of fishcakes.

"My life's falling apart, Faulkner," the judge began as he took the first sip of the ice cold beverage.

"Professional…?"

"Would that it were!" the judge sighed. "Domestic…marital, to be precise."

"Maggie Billings," Faulkner stated flatly.

The judge recoiled in astonishment.

"It was bound to happen," Faulkner continued. "It always somehow rises to the surface…always comes to a bitter climax…always."

"You mean…you…"

"We all knew, Pilchard," Faulkner revealed as he sampled one of the delectable fishcakes. "That affair has often been the topic of discussion among discreet circles."

"And you never cautioned me about it?" the judge responded in a delicately reprimanding tone.

"You never confided in me about the affair," Faulkner stated. "As far as I was concerned, it never existed. In any case, what would I have done in such a case, tell you to be more careful? Would you have severed the relationship even if I had advised you to do so? I hardly think so."

"Well, Sylvia's found out about Maggie. She heard me on the phone last night…damn!" the judge swore.

"What are you going to do?"

"Don't know. Sylvia's reticence is more deadly than a viper's bite," the judge proclaimed as he stared into the air with unfocused eyes.

"Do you love Maggie?"

"I suppose I do…though in a different way, of course. My biggest fear is not Sylvia's reaction. It's my reputation – or loss of…" Pilchard admitted.

"Well old buddy, it's already out there – the whole shebang. So what worse could happen? The ball is now in your court. However, even though you profess love for Maggie, Sylvia's still you wife, and that makes all the difference. Go home and tell her that you're sorry. Don't try to deny anything; you'll only make it worse. Go home. Look Sylvia straight in the face, admit your guilt and beg her forgiveness." Faulkner advised.

"You sound convinced that everything will fall into place. If only it were that easy and straightforward," the judge sighed and shook his head in despair.

"It wouldn't fall into place immediately, but the process will begin. And that's all you want. It worked for me," Faulkber revealed.

"What?" Mr. Pilchard reeled in shock.

"Hey, I'm a man – and a damn good catch at that. I've got looks, so I'm told, and I've got the bucks to go with it," Faulkner jocularly boasted.

"I never thought that…well…you…"

"Well, you're wrong. I played the field. I got caught once. I repented. And that's that," Faulkner confessed. "I never denied anything, even the things that were untrue. I just let Cynthia seize the day. I sat there like a grammar school boy in the principal's office and let her badger me with words and threats. But soon it was all over."

"Never again, eh."

"Never got *caught* again. I just play by different rules now," Faulkner explained. "I just keep everything on a casual level. I promise nothing. They expect nothing. It's come. Dine. Leave."

"Well it's not that simple here, Faulkner. I am in love with the woman… Maggie, I mean," Pilchard admitted. "She lights my fire in ways that, well, Sylvia can't – or chooses not to do."

"Yes. I've heard about her great skill in lighting fires," Faulkner nonchalantly remarked and took another sip of the refreshing beer.

"Sorry?" the astonished judge whispered in disbelief.

"Pyromanic…no insult intended. Maggie has a reputation of lighting fires everywhere. Many men, I understand, have been severely burnt – some to cinders – their ego, that is," Faulkner revealed and gulped the remaining beer until the glass was empty. "Sorry to, well, put it this way, but I thought you should know before you make the wrong decision, friend."

"Are you saying that…" the judge echoed slowly in disbelief.

"Right. She plays the field. Got it first hand from Jason Coleman," Faulkner testified.

"Maggie…unfaithful…to me? Jason tells you such a blatant lie and you believe him?"

"Pilchard. Wake up," Faulkner advised his friend. "Maggie is as unfaithful to you as you are to your old lady."

"What the hell does Coleman mean by spreading such a lie about…"

"Plichard, this is not about Coleman," Faulkner sternly interjected. "This is about Maggie, and you are making a serious mistake in loving her the way you do. It's about you destroying your marriage because of her, about you walking out on your old lady for someone who is unfaithful now and will be unfaithful later. Your reputation is the least of your worries. Everybody already knows of your affair with Maggie. Tell me, Pilchard, did you honestly think that your affair with Maggie was discreet? You're a tall man, an imposing figure in society; a famous and respected man among men. Do you honestly think that the cloak of the dark night shrouded you from the eyes of the people on Westminster Lane?"

"Do the members of the BOARD know of it?"

"The stories came from there. Perhaps that's why you lost in the elections. The members probably lost confidence in you; yet none of them would have brought this up. I'm just…well… hypothesizing."

Faulkner then raised his hand and ordered another round of beer.

The judge sank into a profoundly pensive mood as Mr. Faulkner continued to enlighten him about the wherewithal of his illicit and not so discreet affair.

"Word has it that that fellah, Gaskin, who was murdered that night on Westminster Lane, was Maggie's lover. It is said that he was on his way from her house when he got into the accident," Faulkner stated.

Pilchard began to feel dizzy as Faulkner revealed the sordid details of Maggie's unfaithfulness. He propped his elbow on the table and rested his head in his palm.

"Did you ever see any of these blokes at Maggie's house? I mean, you must have at least suspected something at sometime. Everybody knows of Maggie's promiscuity. I even heard of Bill Jones' one night stand – from Jason," Faulkner reported.

"That's enough, Faulkner. That's enough. It all may be nothing more than rumors…mere speculation. But tell me, does Goodfellow know anything about any of this… I mean, Maggie's purported relationships… with Jason…or Gaskin?" the judge's expression was stamped with fear and desperation as he fixed his eyes on Faulkner.

Faulkner paused and stared at his friend on the opposite side of the table. He was suddenly overwhelmed with pity for the distraught judge, who refused to fully comprehend the ramifications of his exposed relationship with one of St. Patrick's most talked about members. He straightened up and looked Pilchard squarely in the face, "Goodfellow told his wife that he suspects that you know something about the details of Gaskin's death."

"Poppycock!" the infuriated but frightened judge snapped. "Anyway, how do you know this…that he told his wife such a thing, I mean?"

"The idle wives of the rich have much time to spend chit-chatting on the phone, Pilchard," Faulkner replied. "It's through the same means that Cynthia found out about me and …that woman. To answer your question, Goodfellow's wife told my wife. She asked me if I had heard anything about it. For all you know, Goodfellow might be carrying out some private investigation. Pilchard, when I disagreed with your proposal to assume the position of junior warden, I was acting out of concern for you. I know what would come out of it if you and Goodfellow were to butt heads. Trust me. We have won the fight to build the church in Brewster's village. Leave it at that. Avoid that son of a bitch like the plague."

"Thank you. Thank you, Faulkner," Pilchard responded in a solemn tone.

After completing their drinks, the two men departed – one to *Faulkner & Babbit* – the other to his home, to admit to the sin of adultery and seek forgiveness and restitution for the sake of his reputation. He vowed that he would subsequently exercise more caution in his insatiable desire for carnal pleasure.

On his way back home, the judge purchased a bouquet comprising red roses, as well as six African violets which Mrs.Pilchard had loved so much. He turned into his driveway, but Archie the caretaker was not there to meet him. Mr. Pilchard thus opened the door himself and mounted the stairs with the two bouquets. Dharmattie the maid met him at the top of the stairs and relieved him of the flowers, which he surrendered reluctantly after insisting that he wished to present the violets himself to Mrs. Pilchard. Daharmattie therefore took the bouquet of roses to the kitchen and placed it in a glass vase before finally placing it on the table. The judge proceeded to the bedroom and then to the study, but soon returned to the drawing room, still holding the violets.

"Where is Mrs. Pilchard?" he calmly inquired of Dharmattie.

The highly emotional domestic turned from ostensibly admiring the flowers and faced him, with tears in her eyes. "Madam gone, sir. She pack up she t'ings an' lef'. She say to give yo dhis envelope." Upon delivering the envelope to the judge, the emotionally delicate housekeeper burst into a torrent of tears, and threw herself on the floor in front of the judge, rolling around, wailing and pounding the floor like a widow in the throes of uncontrollable grief.

"Get up, Dharmattie, and stop making yourself a fool," the judge quietly ordered the dramatic servant.

Immediately, Dharmattie composed herself and returned to the kitchen to continue watching her favorite television sitcom, as if nothing had ever happened. The judge took the letter to the bedroom, closed the door and sat on the bed where he proceeded to unfold the letter. It was a relatively brief but caustic note, and the contents were crippling enough to evoke a gush of tears from the most powerful man in Ischalton. Upon composing himself, he read the contents again.

Dear Adolph

Life has hurled me a crushing blow. Thanks to you. I should have expected this, however. Your excessive late nights at the 'office' and the rumors foreshadowed this awful day. I wish I were less naïve. However, I'm glad that I have not taken action based on rumours, but on solid truth. I myself have heard you profess your love for Maggie Billings. You may comfort her tonight as you plan to do, and you may stay with her to comfort her for the rest of her miserable life. I will never lower my dignity to compete for the affection of an unfaithful husband – at least not with a slut like Maggie. Don't bother searching for me. I will not listen to the empty confessions of a mendacious tongue. I trust that Maggie Billings will always be there to satisfy your unnatural, unreasonable demands. You have greatly disappointed me, Adolph. And more so, you have disappointed the many people who have always held you in such high esteem. However, don't worry. I will do nothing to shame you. You will do a much better job of it by yourself.

Sylvia.

The judge sighed and shook his head in bitter remorse. However, the evil apparition of ambivalence performed its death dance before him, and he sat on the cold, lonely marriage bed for almost an hour, trying to decide on a course of action. He wanted his marriage restored – for the sake of his image; he wanted Maggie's love, for the satisfaction of his concupiscence. After a protracted period of profound thought, he picked up the telephone and dialed the number to his travel agent and booked a flight to Aruba, ostensibly to spend a week with his ailing sister and her husband, where he could think clearly about his actions and decide on a plan to restore his marriage. He made a few more telephone calls to reschedule all pending court cases for that week before giving Dharmattie a ride back to Slough in the pouring rain. He gave her and Archie the week off during the time he would be in Aruba, and warned the loquacious domestic to maintain her reticence. The stage was therefore set for the deadly plan which he had conjured up while he was sitting on the bed. The cunning judge thus returned home to refine the plot which he was going to execute – a plot which he firmly believed would arrest the decay of his reputation and restore the glory of his social status – a plot which he had deemed necessary to save his own life.

*   *   *

Just before the stroke of three o' clock, Mike Burberry and two police officers arrived at Pigeon's office. Pigeon was on the phone when the receptionist tapped on the door and announced the arrival of the men. After the formal greetings and reception, and some trivial comments about the incessant rain and floods affecting the low lying areas, the men sat down to address the issue which warranted the unexpected visit.

"I understand that you took a roll of films to *Superflash Studios* to be developed a couple o'days ago…containing photographs of Wilberforce Gaskin, you know, the gentleman who …" Mr. Burberry began.

"…I know of the incident," Pigeon calmly interjected.

"I suppose that you knew him," Mr. Burberry assumed.

"Not really. It was Maggie Billings who brought the film here. She came to see me about a legal matter and forgot it, so I offered to take them to the studio for her. It was raining heavily that day, and I didn't want her to have to come back through that weather just to do that. Why do you ask?"

"Well, the intimate nature of the photographs suggest a little more than just, well, a casual friendship, you know, pictures of him in pajamas and underpants, and another photograph of someone's genitals exposed…his, maybe?"

"What are you talking about? We can't be talking about the same roll of films, of course," Pigeon replied.

"I think that we are, actually," the astute detective rejoined as he pulled out an envelope from his blazer pocket. "Here, see if you recognize these photographs."

Pigeon examined the photographs carefully as if he were indeed seeing them for the first time. The detective quietly observed him.

"They're exactly the same as the ones you took to be developed," Mr. Burberry stated. "I understand that it was you who took the photographs. And I further understand that the nude person in the photo is actually you."

Pigeon became instantly enraged. "What the hell are you insinuating, Mr. Burberry?"

"I'm not insinuating anything, Mr. Goodfellow. I know better enough than to insinuate anything to a practing member of the legal profession, especially one as prominent and brilliant as you...," Mr. Burberry declared with a wry smile.

"I trust that you do," Pigeon rejoined.

"I'm *stating* a fact, sir. I have evidence, highly reliable evidence, that it was you who took those photographs and that it is your exposed genitals in this photograph. It might interest you to know that Ms. Billings also has a copy of these very films...films of which you also have a set."

Pigeon remained silent. He instantly realized that Jefford had betrayed him. "Jefford's betrayed me, eh, for thirty pieces of silver?" he whined. "...Developed another set for Maggie Billings, eh?"

"Worse than that. We have reason to believe that you can assist us in the investigation surrounding Mr. Gaskin's death," Mr. Burberry stated. "I'm afraid that I'll have to ask you to accompany us to headquarters."

"What?" Pigeon exclaimed in utter disbelief as the two officers rose and unlocked a pair of handcuffs. He offered no resistance, but swore to file a massive lawsuit against *Superflash Studios* and Maggie Billings.

A small crowd witnessed the prominent lawyer being escorted to the waiting police vehicle as Ms. Neptune stood at the entrance to the posh building, wailing and admonishing the policemen for humiliating and disgracing a man of such respectability in public view.

Within minutes, word had circulated among the elite that Pigeon Goodfellow had been taken into custody for questioning. Mrs. Goodfellow immediately telephoned Mr. Pilchard to solicit his assistance, but on receiving no response, dialed the number to the vicarage. Fr. Perths seemed strangely unperturbed, but nevertheless agreed to meet her at the police headquarters.

Copious telephone calls continued to pour in at the Goodfellow residence as Mrs. Goodfellow, in a most lachrymose state, scrambled to make herself presentable enough to appear at the police station. Their son had already reached the home when the first news of his father's indictment was broadcast and flashed across the television screen. As Pigeon's supporters received word of his arrest, they made their way to Weston Avenue and stood in front of the headquarters in the drizzling rain. When Mrs. Goodfellow arrived, she was greeted with cheers and words of moral support from the embittered crowd.

In Brewster's village, violence broke out on the street in front of the building site between some of Pigeon's supporters and the group of men who had already begun to construct the church. Pigeon's supporters had arrived at the site and had begun to torpedo the frame and the carpenters with a hail of bottles and stones. The workers responded in like manner, but the expletives which were hurled across the enemy line were more damaging than the objects. Another small group of Pigeon's supporters attacked *Brad's Palace* with sticks and stones as Mr. Bradshaw, on hearing of the melee at the building site, attempted to close the pub. Further away, pandemonium broke out in the market as a small, riotous band of men pounced on Pissy Ragnaugth and began to destroy Ram's merchandise and throw them in the air. As the confusion continued, Ram and his wife arrived on an old bicycle, bearing cutlasses and swearing indiscriminately at the panicing crowd. One of the men, Thelma Mullins' husband, who was affiliated neither with Pigeon nor his supporters, but who sought to take advantage of the situation to avenge his enemies, threw a coconut at Ram. The hard-shelled seed connected to Ram's forehead and knocked him off the bicycle. Mrs. Ramgolam went sprawling on the ground at the impact, and rising almost instantaneously, charged forward towards Mullins with the cutlass raised for assault. Mullins turned and darted off down the wet, dirt road with Ram's wife in close pursuit. A small crowd followed, pleading with the 'Public Relations Afficah' to 'pull herself together', and not make an ass of herself, lest she be relieved of her prominent position and lose the golden opportunity to become the senior warden of the new church. Mullins managed to outrun the angry woman, and having scaled the fence surrounding one of the more modest homes in the village, dropped his trousers and exposed himself to the fuming woman. In her blinding, uncontrollable rage, Mrs. Ramgolam flung the cutlass with all her might at the coarse, half naked jester. The deadly weapon missed the vulgar exhibitionist by what seemed to be a fraction of an inch and connected to the bark of a tree where it stuck. Mullins pulled up his trousers and grabbed the weapon, and with lightning speed, charged forward towards Mrs. Ramgolam, who, in similar rapidity dashed up the street, screaming for her husband. Two men grabbed Mullins and threw him to the ground, and having subdued him, confiscated the weapon. They subsequently gave him a sound beating for having exposed himself in front of Mrs. Ramgolam, who in spite of the opprobrium she brought to herself by chasing after Mullins, was nevertheless their Public Relations officer and deserved the honor of protection and respect. Furthermore, Mullins' scurrilousity was considered a gross insult to all women, and therefore evoked a volcano of anger among the men of the village. The two men thus further humiliated and disgraced Mullins by stripping him and commanding him to run back to his home by way of the main street. In order to ensure obedience to their command, they chased after him as he bolted through the muddy street, hurling stones and resonating expletives. A large crowd followed, jeering at the retreating coward.

Almost immediately, the sound of approaching sirens sent the crowds fleeing desperately to their respective homes for fear of the merciless policemen and their indiscriminate truncheons.

Bishop Addington received word of Pigeon's arrest about an hour after he was apprehended and hastened to the police headquarters. The angry crowd that had braved the weather and gathered in front of the building burst into applause as the bishop's vehicle approached the headquarters and stopped. Bishop Addington gave a curt but dignified wave to the small crowd as he disembarked and entered the building. The mob remained subdued for the first few minutes that the bishop was inside until someone in the crowd, an old woman who was boasting that she was an Anglican all her life, raised her voice to the tune of '*What a friend we have in Jesus.*' Those familiar with the hymn joined in full chorous, with the said old woman shouting the words ahead of each line. The policemen who stood watch over the crowd in order to keep them under control did not prohibit them from singing, for the hymn of praise was more pleasing to the ear than the litany of resentment against the police or the sporadic obscenities which sailed through the air from unidentifiable individuals.

After what seemed like hours had elapsed, a tsunamious applause assaulted the air as Pigeon emerged from the building with Bishop Addington and Mrs. Goodfellow at this side. Pigeon was exonerated after a protracted period of interrogation and passionate pleading from Bishop Addington. Pigeon vehemently denied that the nude torso was his, and insisted that it was Maggie Billings who had given him the films to be developed. The prominent lawyer also suffered the haunting humiliation of being taken to a room where he was asked to remove his clothing so as to compare his genitals with the one in the photograph. However, his story proved credulous because the angle from which the photograph was taken falsified the proportions of his manhood. Furthermore, Mrs. Goodfellow's testimony convinced the examining officer that the photograph was not an authentic representation of her husband's organ.

Pigeon did not disclose any of his findings or suspicions regarding Judge Pilchard to the officers. He only wisely responded to the questions posed, and with Bishop Addington's appearance and input, was released after a plethora of apologies from the detective and officers.

As the Goodfellows were escorting the bishop to his vehicle, the people surged forward to congratulate Mr. Goodfellow on his release and to pledge their support. The crowd hailed the senior ecclesiastic as he made his way to his vehicle, and swore to honor him as long as God granted them life. Suddenly, the people became very quiet, and turned their attention to a figure in a black raincoat approaching the Goodfellows. The bishop had already departed before the figure reached the Goodfellows, but as he drew close, Pigeon recognized him instantly.

"Good afternoon, Fr. Perths," Pigeon greeted the reverend gentleman.

"My brother in Christ! How good to see you here! Tell me, have you been freed?" the vicar asked in his practiced sanctimonious voice.

"Yes," Pigeon responded curtly. "Their suspicions were groundless."

"Of course. Oh, hello, Mrs. Goodfellow. Such demonstrated faithfulness!" he beamed.

"Good afternoon, Fr. Perths," Mrs. Goodfellow responded with wonted dignity and immediately clutched her son's arm and proceeded to the car. She neither smiled nor showed any joy at having seen the perfidious cleric. The crowd likewise respectfully acknowledged his presence but offered no distinct expressions of joy at seeing him. In fact, they discreetly and privately chided him for failing to be present at his senior warden's side in such a time of distress.

* * *

Fog and a notoriously irritating drizzle prevailed throughout the evening as people hurried to their respective homes before the onslaught of the torrential rains that were forecast for the night. However, the wet, melancholy night provided the golden opportunity for the judge to crouch undetected through the darkness and desolation of Westminster Lane to his mistress' house. Hastily, he stole his way past the spot where Wilberforce died to Maggie's door and turned the key. Maggie was expecting him, for he had telephoned her earlier in the day to inform her that he was going to Aruba to visit his ailing sister. He further explained that Mrs. Pilchard was going to spend the time of his absence with his sister. Upon ascending the stairs, the judge met his mistress at the top of the stairs and they embraced and kissed passionately.

"You are a powerful man, Adolph. You speak and it's like the whole world obeys your command," Maggie hailed her lover as they held hands and approached the dining table where she had placed the settings for a romantic dinner.

"And aren't you glad that this powerful man is yours?" the judge replied and kissed his mistress once more.

"So, you are going off to Aruba…leaving me in this mess? What will happen if the police come after me…to interrogate me about those photographs?" Maggie whined.

"The judge has spoken, sweetheart. I've spoken with Burberry. You're out of the woods, trust me. No one can harm you," the judge swore.

"But Goodfellow's been freed. What good has your talk with Burberry done? You'll be gone and Goodfellow is freed. I'm afraid, Adolph. I'm terrified of that man. He's dangerous…very dangerous," Maggie complained as her tear filled eyes searched the Judge's.

On sensing the desperation in his mistress' eyes, the judge drew her towards him and held her firmly in his arms, "Then come with me, to Aruba. You will follow me on the next day's flight and book into the Hilton for two nights. Then on the third day, you will fly to Curacao for the rest of the week. I shall hop over for the few days and return to Aruba before coming home. You will return to Ischalton first and I will come back two days later. How's that?"

"O Adolph!" Maggie cried and wrapped her arms around the judge. "That would be wonderful...me and you, alone on the sun drenched beaches of Curacao. And who knows, we might decide to remain there for the rest of our lives, in pure bliss! O Adolph, Adolph, if only it were true that I was the only one in your life!"

"Don't get carried away, Maggie. Let's eat," the judge replied as he gently released the enraptured woman and directed her to the kitchen. "I'm famished!"

During the dinner, as the judge sat savoring the delectable meal of pineapple chunks served over braised lamb chops and vegetable pasta, the telephone rang and the elated hostess hurried to the bedroom and picked up the receiver.

"Good evening. The Billings' residence," Maggie answered in her usual sultry tone.

"I hope that you're satisfied, Maggie, now that you have broken up the Pilchard's home," the voice hissed from the other side.

"Who is this, may I ask?" Maggie replied in a somber tone.

"Never mind, you slut! You aren't satisfied that you caused the death of a good, decent man. You now have destroyed a good marriage," the enraged voice continued. "Where is he now, you tramp? Is he crying with his head in your lap, or is he chained to your bed post?"

"Listen to me, whoever you are," Maggie warned, "I don't know what or whom you're talking about, but if you call this house once more, I shall have the police on your tail, you idle, meddlesome bitch!"

Maggie slammed the receiver and sat on the edge of the bed, staring in horror at the talking object which moments earlier had plunged a dagger of fear through her heart and tossed her mind into an abyss of despair. She was too terrified to move, and after a short while, the tears began to flow incessantly down her cheeks as she muffled the sounds of grave distress.

Several minutes had passed before the judge realized that Maggie's absence was strangely prolonged. He called but received no answer. He thus rose from the table and cautiously proceeded towards the bedroom. The judge froze in shock on beholding his lover seated on the bed in the height of mental anguish.

"My goodness, Maggie!" he exclaimed. "What's wrong?"

The distraught woman made no reply but hung her head and burst into tears. Adolph approached the bed and sat beside her. He gently placed his arms around her as she continued crying pitifully.

"Maggie," he gently pleaded, "what's wrong? Has something happened to one of your relatives?"

"Someone…someone just accused me of destroying your marriage, and …and…"

"And what? Maggie, speak to me; and what…?" the judge implored.

"And causing Wilberforce's death. She said that *I* caused Wilberforce's death!"

"She who? Whose voice was it? Did you recognize the voice? For heaven's sake, speak to me, Maggie," the judge besought the distressed woman.

"I don't know the voice!" she snapped.

Maggie rose and proceeded to the vanity where she took a white hankerchief and began to dry her eyes and pat the mascaraed tears from her cheeks. She turned and beheld the judge, as if awaiting some explanation.

"There is something that I should have shared with you, Maggie. Come, sit," he requested.

"What is it, Adolph?" she asked with suspicion aglow in her eyes, without approaching the now troubled judge.

"Sylvia. She's left. She overheard our conversation last night. I'm sorry. I should have told you," the judge confessed.

"You should have? You should have?" Maggie screamed and turned her back on her agitated lover.

The judge rose and approached the terrified woman and placed his hands on her shoulders. "Maggie, I'm sorry. I was wrong for not disclosing this to you, but…"

"But what? I'll tell you but what!" she yelled as she spun to face the cunning judge. "You thought that I was going to ask you your intentions, or make some kind of demand on you, didn't you…well, didn't you!?"

"I thought no such thing, Maggie!" the judge firmly replied. "I thought it best not to say anything so as not to alarm you. Look at you now. This is the exact reason that I chose not to say anything. She might come back home tomorrow, for all we know, Maggie. So what good would it have been to tell you…and raise your hopes?"

"You are nothing more than a dog, Adolph…a double-dealing, unethical dog!" Maggie hissed. "You want to eat your cake and have it too,eh?"

"Maggie, please!" the judge pleaded. "You're bordering on paralogism. Listen to yourself. I love you, sweetheart. I adore you, you know that!"

"Maybe you do and maybe you don't. Tell me, Adolph, what happens if your dear wife does not return home? What happens if she asks for a divorce? What will you do?" Maggie asked in a sardonic tone.

"I take that to be a rhetorical question," the judge responded in a somber expression as his eyes pierced Maggie.

"No. Adolph," she replied. "I want an answer. What will you do if she doesn't return? I imagine that this is the first time that she has done such a thing. You don't know what will ultimately happen. So I need to know now what you will do should she decide not to return home or ask for a divorce."

"I prefer not to answer, Maggie. I will not be forced into any sort of commitment," the judge replied after a brief period of silence.

"Just as I thought; exactly as I thought," Maggie snarled. "You never believed that this day would come. It was convenient for you to have your wife in your castle and your mistress stached away in some dark, forbidden hole to satisfy your desires. Now you have to choose, you're in a quandary. This tells me one thing, Adolph. You will never choose me over your wife. And from your response a few seconds ago, it doesn't seem as if you'd choose me over anybody. I've been a fool, Adolph. A fool to be pitied, scorned, mocked, used, abused...."

"Maggie! Stop talking like a fool!" the judge snapped. "You are asking me to make a decision that shows scant regard for the sacredness of my marriage vows."

"Shows what, Adolph?" Maggie responded in a rancorous tone. "You have the nerve to tell me about the sacredness of marriage? You leave your darling wife's bed at night to come over here to nestle in mine, and then leave my bed to go back to your marriage bed and tuck yourself in as if nothing has happened. Now you tell me about my disregard for the sacredness of your marriage vows? If you have no regard for your own blasted vows, why the hell should I have any? You know, Adolph, all of this is my fault. I should have known that you would never leave your wife for me. I spurned the love of a man who worshipped the ground I walked on because of you and what I thought I had with you. I could have been married to a man whose word was his honor and whose love was pure and undefiled...and shared with no one else but me. Now I have not only lost him forever, but I am being accused of causing his death. I am going to say this to you now Adolph, and listen carefully. I gave my life to you. I lost true love because of you. I cannot now go to Mr. Gaskin's grave and present myself as a bride to her bridegroom, but I can make you do what you led me to believe you would do, and that's to make me yours and yours alone. I will not lose the second time. And honestly, if Wilberforce were still alive and this had happened, I would have told you to go to hell!"

"You talk like a fool, Maggie," the judge began his defense. "I have never given you any reason to believe that I would leave my wife for you. If she were to die, then yes, I would contemplate marriage to you, or if she asks for a divorce and would not withdraw the request, then perhaps I would think of marriage. But neither of the two has happened. So stop window wishing. Enjoy things as they are. We love each other. Isn't this enough to keep us together?"

"It's convenient for you, Adolph. As you say, *if* she dies, then you would *contemplate* marriage," Maggie rejoined. "I might have thought that you would say that you would certainly marry. Mr. Gaskin has died. I have no one now, no certainties, not even you. If your lady wife dies, you would merely contemplate marriage. I need guarantees, Adolph, and since you will not offer me any, I will establish my own. I will watch what happens. And I will give you one month to make a decision if she does not return. If she doesn't, and you do not offer me marriage, I will sever this relationship. If she returns, and you take her back, I will walk away from everything."

"You are making an unreasonable demand of me, Maggie. You must understand that…"

"Understand what?" Maggie interjected. "…That I must be content to be your kept woman, your dog at the side of your table – for you to throw your scraps of food when you find it unsuitable for consumption?"

"Maggie, please…" the judge pleaded as he attempted to embrace her once more.

"Get away from me, Adolph," she sternly advised him. "Perhaps you should go."

"You don't mean that, sweetheart; so don't say things that you will regret later. Let's talk about this…" the judge begged.

"There is nothing more to discuss, Adolph. I am convinced that you never would have told me that your wife has left you because you have no intention of honoring what you have led me to believe, so go. I will pick up the pieces and get on with my life while I still stand a chance." Maggie straightened herself to her full height and turned abruptly to lead her lover to the door.

"Like hell I'll leave!" the judge shouted as he grabbed his mistress and spun her around.

"Take your hands off me, Adolph!" Maggie snarled and struggled with the ferocity of a wild cat.

"Sit your ass down!" the angry judge commanded the svelte woman as he tossed her towards the bed. The force sent her tumbling across the bed. She grabbed one of the posts so as to prevent herself from landing on the floor on the other side.

"Get out, Adolph! Get out of my house this instant!" she warned as she pushed back the now ruffled, blond colored hair from her face.

"You think that I haven't heard about you and your promiscuity, eh, you tart! Marriage? Is that what you ask of me? I know about you and the company you've been entertaining!" the irate judge shouted as he pointed his index accusingly at his distraught mistress. "Now you make demands of me?"

"Get out of this house now, Adolph, before I call the police!" Maggie again warned her lover.

"Police? To tell them what, Maggie, that you and Jason defiled holy ground the many times that you went on your rendezvous at St. Michael's monastry…eh…on your so-called retreats…or about your affair with Bill Jones? And heaven knows what you did with Gaskin!" Pilchard continued to yell as he threw his bony arms listlessly in the air. "Do you know how embarrassing…how hurtful it has been hearing all of these awful things you were doing behind my back? I love you, Maggie. And I have been as faithful to you as I could – in spite of my wife. You knew of Sylvia, and we both agreed to develop our relationship in spite of my marriage. But you knew that I had a wife. I did not swear loyalty to you alone and covertly carry on with someone else. So in that respect I have been faithful to you. Couldn't you have been the same to me, eh…bitch?"

"And I love you too, Adolph," Maggie confessed. "But I will not continue to be the other woman. You led me to believe that you would leave your wife if you had the opportunity. Now you do, and you come over here and look me in the face and say nothing…nothing! If I did not receive that telephone call, I would have packed up my things and hurried off to Aruba and Curacao to be your wench, for you to build up my hopes even higher and then when we return you thrust me back into the hole – like a dog buries a bone…until you feel like *gnawing* at something? Well its over, Adolph!"

"You know you enjoy me gnawing at you, Maggie," the judge responded. "So please don't make it sound like…"

"Yes. I agree. Your gnawing *is* rather enjoyable," Maggie agreed. "Comparatively speaking…in spite of its brevity."

Maggie's sarcastic remark threw the aging judge into a fit of fury, and instantaneously he grabbed the lamp from the night stand closer to him and hurled it towards his mistress. The object missed its intended target and crashed against the wall with such force that it broke into what seemed like hundreds of tiny pieces. Adolph stormed out of the house, slamming the door behind him. Having heard the door slam shut, she rushed to the verandah and shouted after the enraged judge who was just approaching the gate, "On your way back to your lonely bed, you might consider stopping by

Jason, or Bill, and letting them tell you what it takes to qualify as a real man, you know what I mean?"

Maggie's sarcasm hit the judge like a cannon ball to the chest. He turned and studied her momentarily without uttering a solitary word, and calmly closed the gate behind him.

The pain in the judge's eyes pierced Maggie like a poison dagger to the heart. She stumbled back into the house, slid the glass doors shut and drew the drapes.

On reaching his vehicle, the judge hastily closed the door and sat in the dark automobile, blowing heavily in an attempt to mitigate his anger and allow judiciousness to take custody of his brain. The preponderance of his rage, however, was on Jason, whose rejuvenated charm, dark, chiseled handsomeness and popularity among the young and upcoming female members of St. Patrick's had often provoked a hint of discreet jealousy within him. Now that Maggie had so callously verified what he had often imagined, and having heard Faulkner testify against the brazen woman, the enraged judge ignited the engine and slowly reversed from the back of the dark blue station wagon which was parked unreasonably close to the front of his vehicle. As Pilchard skillfully maneuvered the automobile between the two vehicles which had sandwiched his, a figure appeared outside his window. The terrified judge gasped and raised his hands to indicate an instant surrender. The figure smiled and tapped on the glass, and the judge breathed a sigh of relief on recognizing the face with several missing teeth. The vagrant who haunted the alley at night had come to renew his acquaintance.

"What do you want?" the judge snapped.

"I see you visitin' yo' bird again, eh?" the man commented as he flashed a semi-toothless grin.

"What's that to do with you?" the irritable judge replied as he held his breath against the fleeting odor of urine and spoilt cabbage.

"A lot o'mens huntin' dhat bird, yeah. I sees dhem wit' me own two eyes dhem, yeah. She' a' nice bird, though. I'd like to get me 'hands on 'er, he he he …..I'd roast 'er over a slow fire, yeah, he he he …. Gimme a dollar, if you has…"

'Go to hell…go to bloody hell!" the judge yelled as he swerved the massive vehicle. The car almost crushed the vagrant's poorly shod feet. He jumped aside, but the vehicle still was not able to clear the limited space between the two automobiles that were parked in front and behind it respectively. The vagrant thus had another opportunity to plead for charity by pounding desperately on the glass. However, the now furious judge lowered the window and hurled a round of uncensored expressions which aroused the derelict's anger. In response to the judge's harsh refusal, the vagrant kicked the vehicle with his heavy, weathered boot and pointed accusingly at the man behind the wheel.

"You ole' black dog!" he yelled. "You killed dhat man wid' yer car…I see you…you kill 'im wid' your car!"

By this time, the judge had successfully maneuvered his car from between the two vehicles, and without saying another word pressed the accelerator and sped away. His heart pounded with fear as he sped along the dark, desolate street. His head began to spin as he considered the awful verity of his secret – a secret which was no longer his to bear. There was a witness – regardless of his reliability – to the utterly odious crime he had committed that night. Judge Pilchard had always relished his fame and the high esteem lavished upon him by the members of all walks of society. He had always celebrated and indiscriminately flaunted his power and authority. He was afraid of no one, and had considered himself socially invincible. However, on passing a lonely stretch on Cane View Drive, he stopped momentarily at the side of the road to compose himself and to confront the ramifications of the vagrant's terrifying accusation. As the frightened judge considered the awful possibilities of his crime, he closed his eyes in prayer, beseeching the Almighty God to vindicate him from any blame or possible suspicion, for he knew that even mere suspicion had the power to cripple the reputation of one of such high social standing – even if the suspicions were ultimately to be proved false. However, the judge felt alone, the shuddering victim of an unanswered prayer. He felt the sensation of falling with rapid force towards the earth, into a mire of reverberating shame and resonating disgrace. Furthermore, he considered the irony of the man who could bring about his downfall – a malodorous vagabond, thought of as being cursed by the very God whose mercy he had earlier petitioned – the fool whom God would use to shame the wise. A gush of irrational fear thus seized the trembling judge. He thus opened the car boot and removed a large wrench from his tool kit, after which he ignited the engine once more and drove off, slowly, menacingly, towards Westminster Lane, one last time, to erase every trace of his heinous crime perpetrated against one whom he had considered to be the archrival in his forbidden affair.

The car turned on to Westminster Lane and the judge switched off the lights as the vehicle rolled ominously through the dark, tree lined street towards the enrance to the alleyway. On reaching the alley, the judge stopped the car and rolled down the window to attract the attention of the vagrant who was about to settle in under a makeshift, cardboard tent for the night. Judge Pilchard waved a five dollar bill to the unsuspecting man and beckoned to him. As the man approached the vehicle, the judge leaned across and opened the door. The vagrant entered. Judge Pilchard politely ordered him to close the door and the car sped off down the quiet street once more.

"Nice car you got, yeah," the vagrant remarked with a smile as he observed the details of the comparatively superior vehicle. The judge rolled down the windows slightly, despite the consistent drizzle, so as to make the atmosphere in the vehicle more salubrious.

"Here," Judge Pilchard said as he handed the vagrant the five dollar bill. "Let this last you for the week. I will give you another five dollar bill next week, and after that I will give you the same amount every week when I come to visit my bird."

The man was filled with immense happiness at the promise of a consistent monetary support. "T'anks, t'anks. You's a good man, your honor. God bless you!"

A brief period of quiet followed during which the vagrant studied the five dollar note. The car continued along the dark streets, many of which were unfamiliar to the guest in the judge's car.

"I want you to do something for me," Judge Pilchard requested.

"Anyt'ing, your honor. Whatever you wants, I do fo' you," the elated man replied.

"I am going to take you to a house on the next street. When we get there, I will stop further down the street, away from the house. I am going to give you this wrench. Take it and go to the house I will show you. Knock on the door. When the man comes and opens, I want you to hit him in his head, several times, right here in the temple," the judge explained in a low monotone. "Don't stop hitting him until he's stopped moving. Alright? When you come back, I'll give you fifty dollars."

The vagrant's face became aglow with excitement and enthusiasm. "Fifty dollars? Fifty dollars, your honor? Anything for you, your honor; anything. Show me the 'ouse."

Judge Pilchard was thrilled at the vagrant's willingness to so easily execute the deadly task. The vehicle turned on to Amsterdam Drive, and Judge Pilchard extinguished the lights as he did on Westminster Lane. The car rolled stealthily past Jason's home. Light was shining on the ground floor where Jason did his accounting and the upper floor was dimly lit. Jason's car was parked in the driveway. The judge therefore thought it reasonable to assume that Jason had no company and that the path was clear to carry out his deadly plan. He drove around the block once more so as to make sure that there was no sign of movement in the houses closest to Jason's. The car rolled past Jason's home the second time and stopped a few houses away. The vagrant disembarked and approached the gate. He quietly and cautiously opened it and entered the yard, bearing the weapon unobtrusively at this side, and pressed the bell. Muffled footsteps in bedroom slippers approached the door.

"Goodnight," Jason greeted the visitor as he addressed him suspiciously. "Hey, I recognize your face, but…but where… Anyway, can I help you?"

As Jason stood at the half opened door, holding his breath in order to avoid the assault of the stench emanating from the strange visitor, the vagrant, with lightning speed, swung the wrench ungainfully towards his unsuspecting victim. Instinctively, Jason raised his arm to ward off the deadly blow and the weapon connected to his arm and bounced off to the floor. Upon realizing that the weapon was out of his reach, the vagrant launched forward and threw Jason against the hard, wooden floor. The brass lamp and the coffee table crashed to the floor with the sudden impact of the two falling figures struggling fervently in a passionate attempt to subdue each other. The vagrant fought with the ferocity of a mad dog, snarling and punching unmethodically, while trying desperately to retrieve the wrench with one hand and pin his victim to the floor with the other. Jason struggled relentlessly to save his life, but the stench that reeked from the vagrant's unwashed body and dirty clothing proved its own powerful weapon as the men wrestled fiercely on the floor. During the scuffle, Jason made several attempts to shout for assistance from his neighbor, but each time he opened his mouth the vagrant pressed his dirty hand against his mouth and muffled the sound. The two men rolled across the floor towards the desk where the wrench had fallen. By dint of his larger size and pungent odor, the vagrant was able to pin Jason to the floor, and reaching out his hand, grabbed the wrench and raised it to inflict the fatal blow. Jason grabbed his assailant's arm with one hand and sank his fingers into his lower jaw with the other hand and pushed his head as far back as he could. The vagrant struggled passionately to free his neck and lower jaw from Jason's deadly grip. In his endeavour to break free he swung the wrench awkwardly and it missed Jason's head and connected to the floor. Instantaneously, Jason grabbed the weapon and began to inflict a fleet of painful blows across the vagrant's body with all his might. The intruder struggled to break free from the blows, and when the opportunity arose, he spat in Jason's face, and with flashing speed jumped up and darted through the door. Jason chased after him, while shouting for assistance. The neighbor's dogs began barking viciously and throwing themselves against the fence as the two men raced along the short driveway. Jason raised the wrench and hurled it towards his retreating assailant as he struggled desperately to open the gate. The object hurtled through the air like a torpedo and struck a fatal blow to the vagrant's right temple. He made a few short steps and fell to the ground, took one last, heaving breath and closed his eyes. Jason stopped abruptly upon realizing that the object had struck such a deadly blow. He was too petrified to move, and although the commotion had attracted the attention of Jason's two closest neighbors, he could not hear them calling out to him. Seconds passed into minutes and the vagrant did not move an inch. One of the neighbors reached the gate and cautiously stooped to examine the body which lay on the wet grass beside the concrete wall. He pressed his finger against the pulse of the vagrant's neck but felt no beat.

"I think he's dead, Coleman," the neighbor said calmly as he raised his eyes towards Jason, who remained in the same spot, trembling and breathing heavily. The tears flowed profusely down his cheeks and he struggled to keep his jaws from chattering.

"You've killed the man, Coleman. He's dead," the neighbor reiterated with equal nonchalance.

At the second declaration of the vagrant's demise, Jason came to the full realization of what had happened so quickly, and having lost all self control, threw himself upon the bonnet of his white BMW and began crying hysterically. The neighbor, a man in his mid sixties, approached Jason and rested his hand comfortingly on his shoulder.

"It's alright, Coleman. It's going to be alright. Just take a deep breath and compose yourself. We'll have to call the police, but it's going to be alright," the neighbor assured the highly agitated Jason as he continued to cover his face with his arms and cry pitifully.

"Who is this man, Coleman, and what was he doing here?" the neighbor asked as he stood beside Jason, patting him gently on the shoulder.

"Don't…don't …know, Mr. Lickorish," Jason responded without raising his head.

By this time, a few more people had assembled at the entrance to Jason's yard and had flocked around the body. One of the men went home and returned with a sheet with which he covered the body.

"That's Patrick Mullins…," a voice soared across to Jason's ear. "They call him 'Bunzo', man. He always hangs around in front of *El Dorado Bakery*, you know…with a bag full o' coconut buns. You know that woman from Brewster's village…she used to be in charge of the Fellowship Committee before Nellie Sweetwine got the post?"

"You mean Thelma Mullins?" another voice interjected.

"Yeah…she and her husband had that big fight in the church yard with some men during the Annual General Meeting…," the voice responded.

Harold Persaud, who owned a variety store on Grant Street in Georgetown, and who had given Bunzo due respect by covering his body, exclaimed in shock, " O rass, is Thelma Mullins' son?"

"He had parents?" another voice added.

Harold turned in shock and momentarily contemplated the individual. "Yes. He had to have parents, like all of us standing here. He was somebody's child; somebody's son. He didn't just drop outta a tree, you know; don't mind how crazy or wretched he was."

No one uttered another word after Harold chided the seemingly callous individual. They all stood gazing at the body and shaking their heads in disbelief.

"I can't believe that he had parents," the voice repeated.

Suddenly, the sound of police sirens filled the air and two cars swung the corner. The sirens and the flashing lights attracted the attention of dozens of people in the quiet, middle class neighborhood and some more of them flocked to the scene. Others peered from behind their drapes or stood on their verandahs. Five policemen emerged from the vehicles and approached the body.

"I know this fellah," one of the policemen stated as he stared at Bunzo's body lying sideways, facing the wall. The murder weapon was a few feet away and another policeman carefully placed it in a plastic bag. The two officers entered the yard and approached Jason and Mr. Lockorish.

Jason was still in the throe of anguish and seemed confused when the officer began to ask him questions.

"What happened here...?" the officer inquired.

"The man out there attacked him...that's all I know," Mr. Lickorish testified. "I didn't see what actually happened, I only heard Mr. Coleman shouting for help. Next thing I know was that the man fell to the ground as he was running away."

"He was running away when he died?" the officer further inquired.

"Dunno. Maybe," Mr. Lockorish replied. "You godda ask him."

"I need a lawyer," Jason cried. "I am not saying anything until I speak with my lawyer."

One of the constables, the one who was acquainted with Bunzo, approached the four men. "The ambulance is comin', sir. Looks like a blow to the head. The head is swollen and he is bleeding through his nose. What the hell was he doing in this neighborhood...how did he reach all the way here?"

"That's a mystery," the officer replied. "We're goin' to have to take him in."

"I need to call my lawyer before I leave," Jason requested.

One of the policemen waited at the door while Jason proceeded to the desk and dialled.

"Good evening. Goodfellows...," the familiar voice answered on the other side.

"Hello...hello, Pigeon. This is Jason...your ole' mate."

Complete silence followed Jason's identification of himself.

"Hello...," Jason repeated.

"I'm hearing you, Jason," the cold, flat voice responded.

"Look...I...I'm sorry to bother you," Jason stuttered as he held back the tears, "but...but I...I need you to come over to ...to ...the police ...police ..."

"What's wrong, Jason?" Pigeon's voice maintained its insouciance.

"The ...the...police...they are take...taking...me to the station.... I need...I need you to come....please...please...," Jason besought his one time friend and burst into tears.

"Jason," Pigeon advised his former friend after a short period had elapsed, "wait there...let them wait. I'm coming over right away."

During the telephone conversation, the ambulance had arrived and the paramedics were attending to Bunzo. Jason remained in the house, for he could not face the covered body of his assailant being put into the vehicle. The crowd had grown much larger because many of them had thought that it was Jason who might have the victim of some awful crime. Upon realizing that it was merely a homeless man, some of them returned to their homes and went back to bed as if nothing had happened.

"I thought that somebody had died," one of them remarked.

"Somebody *has* died," a woman from the house adjacent to Jason's answered.

"Well, I mean, *somebody*, you know...one of us...," the individual explained and turned away.

"One of us *has* died, Mr. Sealy...," the woman replied in a tone that reeked with disgust.

Another car turned the corner and stopped about twenty five feet behind the ambulance. The distinguished figure of Pigeon Goodfellow emerged and approached the small crowd. Greetings were exchanged with those who knew him personally, and he entered Jason's house and introduced himself to the officer. Jason was intensely grateful to Pigeon for his faithfulness as a true friend, but equally humiliated by his own lack of sincerity. His conscience tormented him; he had betrayed Pigeon, but now sought his assistance. Pigeon's kindness was like coals of fire upon his head, and it profoundly disturbed him. Suddenly, as if propelled by some powerful, unseen force, he rose from the chair and threw his arms around Pigeon in a passionate embrace of resuscitated brotherhood. However, Pigeon remained unresponsive, and stood with his arms hanging listlessly at his side as Jason hugged him. Tears streamed down Jason's face once more as he expressed effusive gratitude to Pigeon for responding to his urgent plea for help. The policemen stood by, seemingly unimpressed and unmoved by the fulsome display of spurious affection and exaggerated display of appreciation.

"Perhaps we should leave now, sir?" the officer suggested as Jason was about to return to his seat.

One of the constables put the handcuffs on Jason and the men left the house. Mr. Lickorish locked the door behind them and promised Jason that he would keep an eye on the house. Pigeon advised Jason to answer no questions while in the private custody of the officers in the vehicle. Pigeon remained for a while after the police vehicles had departed so as to gather any pertinent information from the by-standers. No one seemed to have noticed anything unusual that evening, nor did anybody observe any strange persons or vehicles in the street. However, they all seemed to entertain the same question about the vagrant's presence in that neighborhood on such a damp, cool evening.

"How on earth did he get here, so far from his domain?" one individual asked.

"The bigger question is *why* was he in this neighborhood, and moreso, why was he at Coleman's house? What's going on, Goodfellow?" another asked.

No one could make sense of the incident, so Pigeon politely excused himself from the dispersing crowd and departed for the police headquarters.

*   *   *

Mr. Pilchard had just entered his house when the telephone rang. He dashed up the stairs and took up the receiver. "Pilchard's…"

"Faulkner here. I just got a call from Galloway. Seems like Jason is in some kind of trouble…with the police…"

"What? What's happened?" the cunning judge asked in feigned ignorance.

"Someone…some homeless man, I understand, apparently attacked him in his home and he killed him," Faulkner replied.

"My goodness! When did this happen?"

"Apparently a few minutes ago. Galloway just returned from the scene. He said that the man lay dead at Jason's gate. They found a wrench by his side…the murder weapon, I assume. Anyway, they've taken Jason into custody or something like that. I hear that Goodfellow is representing him." Faulkner added.

"Who?"

"Your good friend, Pigeon," Faulkner reiterated. "He was out there at the scene. Apparently Jason's solicited his counsel."

"Is Jason mad?" the judge yelled. "Why the hell didn't he call me? I would have directed him to someone. Of all people, he solicits that crook,

Goodfellow? Look, I'm going to try to go down to the headquarters right now because I wouldn't see him for a couple o' days. I'm leaving in the morning for Aruba. But tell me, didn't anyone see anything strange in the street, you know, I mean, like any strange persons or so. How did this homeless man know where to go…why Jason's home, or was it a random attack?"

"No one seemed to know or have seen anything unusual," Faulkner replied.

Judge Pilchard breathed a sigh of relief at Mr. Faulkner's response. "Well, thank you for the information. I'll try to see Jason as soon as I have finished packing."

As soon as the judge hung up the telephone, he threw himself forward across the bed and thanked God for answering his fervent prayer to spare him the agony of blame or suspicion. He also thanked God for helping him to execute his plan much better than he could ever have imagined or asked. Mr. Pilchard sat up at the side of the bed and smiled to himself as he mused over the plan which he had made, but which took a different turn – a different path which fell in his favor. He thought of the possible outcome of the original plan, which was to take the vagrant over to Amsterdam Avenue to kill Jason. Following that, he would take the vagrant to a secluded place and kill him by throwing a handful of coins in front of the car. When the unsuspecting man stoops to gladly pick up the coins, he would knock him down and crush him beneath the wheels of the vehicle. In that way, he would have settled matters with the man whose virility and boyish charm he had discreetly envied so intensely – the impertinent gigolo who had dared to seduce his mistress and whose amorousness she had so highly praised. He also would have silenced the wandering simpleton whose testimony could have brought his downfall. He had succeeded in the latter, but he was nevertheless content with the fate of the former, for Jason's apprehension was enough to bring about his ultimate downfall.

Judge Pilchard was further comforted by the possibility of certain exoneration, due to the fact that he was always regarded by the public as being above reproof and being a man of the highest integrity. He smiled again as he remembered Faulkner's report of the absence of witnesses. Furthermore, he thought, he had committed murder before and had escaped suspicion, and now he had silenced the only witness to the heinous crime. The reprobate judge smiled for the third time, for he firmly believed that his social status had set him on the pinnacle of vindication; the indurate vice chairman of the BOARD smiled because he was not in the least troubled by a guilty conscience or remorse; but moreso, Judge Pilchard smiled because he had proved to himself that he was indeed a powerful man. He then rose and proceeded to the closet from which he removed a black suitcase.

By nine o'clock the following morning, Judge Pilchard was airborne and the news of the murder and Jason's arrest had already been broadcast several times. However, the full report of Pigeon's apprehension earlier the previous day, supported by photographs of the same, had been printed across the front page of the *Argosy*, and concerned members of the *Gold Circle* subsequently became engaged in conversation over the telephone with Fr. Perths. Many of them had supported Pigeon in the election but were now having ambivalent feelings towards their new senior warden. Jason's arrest caused grave concern for the parishioners also, especially the members of the BOARD. However, he was not their warden, thus expulsion from the unlawful group, unless he be proved innocent, was not a difficult decision for them to make since it did not warrant any ecclestiastical proceedings.

* * *

Pigeon arrived at his office shortly after ten o' clock, exhausted and fatigued after the long, harrowing night at the police headquarters. He had managed to get Jason released on a five thousand dollar bail and was going to represent him at the trial which was set for late August. As he ambled towards his office, Ms. Culley warmly greeted him and offered to make him a cup of tea. Shortly after he entered his office, she followed, bearing a teacup and saucer in one hand and a white envelope in the other.

"Here you are, sir. Oh, by the way, one of the two men who came to see you last week…the short, plumpish one…"

"Oh…Mr. Fielding…ahh, yes…I was expecting this…," Pigeon interjected as he took the envelope. "Thank you."

He placed the teacup and saucer on his desk and proceeded to open the envelope while humming the tune, "Morning has broken." Suddenly, the humming stopped and his jaw fell open as he read the contents of the note. It was a rescission of the adoption proceedings by Burtland Huntley and Scott Fielding, on the ground that his suspicious involvement with Mr. Gaskin's death had caused a conflict of interest and as such may flagrantly hinder or prevent the adoption.

"Thundering Pansies!" Pigeon clamoured and tossed the letter on the floor. He stormed outside to Ms. Culley. "When did Mr. Fielding deliver this envelope?"

"This morning," she replied. "As I entered the building, he approached me and asked me to deliver it to you. He was waiting when I arrived. He said that the note was urgent."

"And it bloody is. Sons o' bitches," Pigeon swore.

"Something wrong, Mr. Goodfellow?" Ms. Culley asked in a concerned tone.

"No. Nothing unusual, except those two bloody friends of Dorothy," he snapped. "Apart from that, everything's alright."

"Dorothy who?"

"They want to adopt two children as raise them as their own, you know, like a normal family with a mother and a father...a husband and a wife...," Pigeon explained. "That's what is meant by the term 'friends of Dorothy'. Figure it out."

"You mean, like when two men..."

"Yes, Miss Culley..." Pigeon interjected.

"O dear," the frail woman exclaimed in shock. "So what will you do?"

"Nothing," Pigeon explained. "They no longer wish to retain my services for fear that the article in the newspapers would hinder the adoption process...a conflict of interest, they claim...the bloody poofs!"

"Well, count your blessings, Mr. Goodfellow. Your services to them for such a thing might instead have caused you *your* reputation," Miss Culley replied in an attempt to console the nevertheless disappointed and hurt barrister.

"You know, Miss Culley," Pigeon remarked, "it seems like no one is worth the effort any more. One gives oneself wholly in friendship, in trust, in sincerity – only to be tenderized and then devoured like a piece of wild meat from a camp fire; or be used and then tossed aside like a pair of tattered, dingy drawers; or be embraced, only to later be castigated like a waif who plunders the garbage in the backyard of the rich to fill his protrudent gut; or hailed for a moment and then forgotten like a fallen hero. This has been my life story, Miss Culley...one disappointment after another, one insult following the other...huh..."

"Like Jesus," Miss Culley added as she shook her head, "a mental crucifixion which mere mortals must endure if they must eventually be glorified. So don't worry. Furthermore, there are some whose colors remain the same."

"Miss Cully!?" Pigeon exclaimed in shock. "Since when did you become so philosophical?"

"Don't be fooled by my reticence or my aura of simplicity, Mr. Goodfellow. I am profoundly religious," Miss Culley humbly confessed with a gentle smile.

"I'm impressed," Pigeon admitted. "You've been working here for over fifteen years and I have never considered you more than anything else than a wonderful receptionist...a good and faithful secretary, a young woman from the crude village of Slough. Yet here you are, a true and affectionate being, wise beyond your years and profound in your faith. It is a true saying indeed, that there is none so blind as those who will not see, and as in my case, *cannot* see. Thank you, Miss Culley, for your comforting words. Now, if you will excuse me, there is something that I must do."

"You're most welcome, sir. And thank you too for your kind remarks," Miss Culley replied. "Oh, Mr. Goodfellow…what are you going to do about this awful article in the *Argosy*?

"As the proverb states, Miss Culley, fire is a good servant but a bad master. I will not allow that fire to consume me. *I* will control it; *I* will dictate what, or whom it consumes. Then I will let it extinguish itself. I will not feed it. I will do nothing or say nothing. Even the biggest and wildest blaze is eventually extinguished," he assured the deeply concerned receptionist and returned to his office. He gathered the Fielding/ Huntley Adoption File and headed out of the office.

*   *   *

Sunday morning brought a relentless struggle for predominance between the brilliant hues of the morning sun and the sombrous monotone of the saturated clouds which issued sporadic threats of scattered downpours. A strange uneasiness hung like a pall over St. Patrick's as the congregation assembled for the principal mass. The Goodfellows arrived about five minutes before the start of the service. From the moment of their arrival Pigeon sensed an uncanny uneasiness. Familiar faces gently nodded; acquaintances merely smiled and waved politely and hurried away before any words could be exchanged; friends became conveniently preoccupied with trivial things or issues as he and Mrs.Goodfellow approached. Those who dared to exchange any words were condescending in their remarks, much to the chagrin of the ostracized couple. Nevertheless, the Goodfellows proceeded to their regular pew and knelt in prayer. The members adjacent to them remained unusually meditative, with their hands clasped tightly and their heads bowed in humble adoration or raised in contemplation of the huge crucifix which hung over the altar.

At the beginning of the service, Pigeon cast discreet glances around him in search of Jason, but he was nowhere to be seen. The procession filed by in solemn dignity, and as Pigeon focused his attention on the words to the opening hymn, a large, comforting hand rested gently on his shoulder. Upon turning, his eyes rested upon Philbert Watts, who winked assuringly at him.

"Be strong, brother. You're not alone," he whispered without stopping.

The words sent a wave of joy through Pigeon. Philbert's encouragement was the only expression of support for the man for whom many of those who were now snobbing him had voted and pledged their support. During the entire sermon, Pigeon noticed that Fr. Perths was averting his attention from them even though they had sat in the third row on the pulpit side. Subsequently, during the reading of the notices, Fr. Perths announced that there was an emergency vestry meeting to be held in the common room immediately after the service. Pigeon also noticed that the vicar never looked at him or his wife during the administration of the holy sacraments.

After the service, those who shared fellowship with the Goodfellows avoided the topic of Mr. Gaskin's death altogether. However, Mrs. Ramgolam, whose fugacious association with the BOARD had given her some false sense of security and power, superimposed by delusions of grandeur, audaciously approached Pigeon in the presence of the few members who were genuinely concerned about his welfare.

"I was t'inkin' all through the service dhat you should go talk to the parson 'bout whu you knows 'bout Mr. Gaskin' death. Is' always good to talk to the pries' 'bout t'ings dhat deh pun yo' conscience. You does feel good aftah…" Mrs. Ramgolam advised.

The group turned and contemplated her in a variety of expressions.

"Gloysis, why you doesn't hush up you beak and mind yo' business," Ram reprimanded his wife. "Nobody ain't aks you nothin'. Come leh we go 'ome 'fore you gets yo'self in trouble like you did pun new year's mornin'."

"I is the Public Relations Afficah and I got the right to talk to the peoples dhem," she responded. "So shut yo' damn mouth and go outside and wait."

"He' right, Gloysis," Dotty Cambridge warned the impudent Public Relations officer. "Go 'long and mine you business before I tek me 'andbag and wrap it 'roung you throat."

"You talkin' to me, Dotty?" Mrs. Ramgolam asked the modestly attired woman who had dared to oppose her and publicly challenge her authority.

Dotty placed her hands on both hips and scrutinized the Public Relations Officer. "Everybody put all yo' hands pun you hip and wine if all yo' t'ink I talkin' to somebody else."

"Gloysis, come alang 'fore you gets yo'self in trouble. You deh in the chu'ch and you mekin' story wid people," Ram besought his obstinate wife. "You jes' now tek communion and you ready fuh pick a story wid people… right in de chu'ch. God goin' strike you down, Gloysis! Come leh we go 'ome. Ah warnin' yo'. You ain't got no right to aks de man he business."

"But she the Dotty ain't got no right to threaten me 'bout she goin' wrap she 'andbag 'round me throat!" Mrs. Ramgolam protested. "I wasn't talkin' to she. She should learn to mind she business and tek she mout' outta people' business; the big bubby cow!"

"Me bubby don't keep me back, sweetheart; so whu you say don't bother me," Dotty replied.

"I knows dhat, love," Mrs. Ramgolam responded. "Dhem does only get in the way."

In a sudden burst of anger at Mrs. Ramgolam's response, Dottie forced her way through the small group in an attempt to physically assault the Public Relations Officer. "Hold me' prayer book, Effie, leh me show she what dhis…"

"Stop it, Dottie. You deh in church, man; don't bother widh she. Wait 'till we reach back in the village," Effie intercepted and besought the angry woman.

"Don't stop she, Effie," Mrs. Ramgolam advised. "Leh she through…leh she come…"

"Gloysis!" Ram yelled and made an abrupt turn and strode angrily towards the door. He turned once more towards his wife, "When the Lord strike you fuh' rowin' wid people while you deh in the chu'ch, eh, pun holy ground, is you alone 'e goin' to strike. I gone!"

"Whenever you ready fuh wrap you 'andbag 'round me throat, Dotty, you can come. I ready fuh you any time. When you goin' home from church and you passin' me house, I goin' to be waitin' fuh you to wrap you 'andbag round me throat!" Mrs. Ramgolam promised and excused herself.

The small group contemplated her in total shock as she exited the building behind her husband. While they were watching the boisterous woman leave the building, Rex approached Pigeon and advised him that the vicar and vestry were already assembled in the common room and were waiting for him.

"When was this meeting decided, Rex?" Pigeon inquired of the petulant, old sexton.

"Dunno," he curtly replied and turned away.

"Don't say anything, dear. Just go." Mrs. Goodfellow advised her husband. "You might be gald that you did."

Some of the others who were standing with the Goodfellows concurred and likewise encouraged him. Pigeon thus excused himself and reluctantly proceeded to the common room. The vestry members, as well as a few members from the BOARD, were gathered together behind closed doors. The tension loomed over the room like a haunting mist as Pigeon turned the knob and entered.

"Mr. Goodfellow," Fr. Perths greeted the solemn, suspicious warden, "it's rather good of you to come. I'm sorry to have inconvenienced you with my sudden announcement of this urgent meeting."

"When did you decide to call this meeting, Fr.?" Pigeon asked as he fixed the vicar a piercing stare.

"Well…I decided a few days ago," the tense vicar replied, "but I only got in touch with some of the people yeaterday. I'm sorry that I missed a few people. It became too late to continue the calls, so I thought it best just to make a general announcement this morning. No disrespect intended, my good man. Do sit."

"Don't you think that you should have at least notified Mr. Goodfellow before anyone else, vicar? Afterall, he *is* our senior warden, regardless of his circumstances," Bart Knuckles commented.

"Please, Mr. Knuckles, don't let us turn this meeting into a verbal civil war. We are here to discuss an important matter. Please. Let's concentrate on that and not get personal issues in the way," Ruthel Pollard responded from the front row.

"Did you say that this was a vestry meeting, vicar?" Pigeon asked.

"Yes. Primarily," Fr. Perths replied. "However, I have invited a few others …well…mainly to share their opinion and their counsel. Afterall, the vestry has a couple of relatively new, inexperienced persons. I'm sure that they will appreciate the good counsel of our experienced friends. It was awfully kind of them to sacrifice their time to join us for this very…"

"…Don't insult the intelligence of the people here, Fr.," Pigeon interjected. "You have invited these people to support your agenda. All of these other people here are BOARD members. Am I to believe that you called them to notify them of this meeting before you consulted me, as your senior warden? I insist that they leave before any discussion takes place."

"I respectfully beg to disagree, Mr. Goodfellow, but these persons are here at my behest. Haven't I the prerogative as your vicar to invite anyone I choose to a vestry meeting, which is always open to the congregation?"

"I will not spend the morning exchanging words with you, Fr. Perths," Pigeon declared with a serious expression, "so let's continue with the meeting so that I can be on my way."

"Again, my brothers and sisters, I thank you for responding to my request at such short notice," Fr. Perths began. "I promise that I will address the issue as expeditiously as possible. Mr. Goodfellow, this actually has to do with your position as senior warden."

Absolute silence engulfed the room. Pigeon stared at the vicar with a stern expression.

"Please believe me when I say this, Peter. We are speaking out of a genuine concern for your welfare and out of our love for you as a member of this parish," Fr. Perths continued. "I have, after conversation with Bishop Addington and the advice of some of the concerned members gathered here, that you should relinquish your position as senior warden …because… ahhh…in light of what has been taking place, with respect to…ahh…your …ahh…arrest and …ahhh…the article in the newspapers. Trust me, we are very concerned about your…your …ahh…sanity. These things can be very stressful, and we would prefer that you don't take on the extra burden of wardenship of such a large parish, you know what I mean…with all that is going on here…the building of the church in Brewster's village…you follow?

"Have you quite finished, Reverend Perths?" Pigeon inquired as he stared unflinchingly at the visibly agitated vicar.

"In a nutshell…that's what we have called this meeting to discuss," he replied. "Yes. I have finished, more or less… Yes, as a matter of fact I have."

Joe Persaud rose from his seat without seeking permission to speak. "Fr. Perths, is this how we deal with members here in this church…on this vestry? I mean, if Mr. Goodfellow had had a problem functioning as senior warden, I'm sure that he would have come to you himself and told you. Why would you, or anyone else sitting here as a matter of fact, simply assume that this man cannot deal with the pressures of this office and his own private issues. Furthermore, he has not been charged with anything. He is as free as anyone else sitting here. Why are we doing this?"

"You are relatively new on this vestry, Joe, and you have no concept of the pressure that the position of warden places upon the head. My advice is that you sit down and allow those who are more experienced to deal with this matter," Ruthel Pollard responded.

"The man is a first class, top rated, respected lawyer. If he can deal with maintaining such a high profile, what is a meager position like senior warden to him?" Joe rejoined.

Ruthel Pollard rose impetuously from her chair and turned towards Joe. "Why are we turning this into a litany of defences? The man needs our support. Overlook your sentiments and let us be practical!" she yelled in her strident cackle.

"Please, sit down and take it easy, Ruthel," Bart Knuckles chimed in. "There's no need to get your drawers in a twist. If we're going to come here making assumptions about…"

"I do *not* wear drawers!" Ruthel snarled as she turned and glared at Bart.

"Well," Bart retorted, "don't get your bloomers in a twist."

"I do not *weeaaar* bloomers!" Ruthel hissed.

"What *do* you wear?" Joe joined in to taunt the tetchy old woman.

The gaunt, irritable senior straightened to her full height and opened her excessively painted eyes wide at the disputatious new member, "None of your damn business!" she snapped and fixed Joe a harsh, cold stare. She scrutinized him threateningly before turning and taking her seat. A wave of supressed laughter gushed across the room from the rear. The agitated old woman turned and cast a disapproving look at the small group that dared to mock her.

"Brothers and sisters, let us get a grip of ourselves, "Laurent Faulkner intervened. "We are dealing with a serious matter. Our church has become the focus of negative attention because of a public scandal. We have a duty to protect our parish home, and all we are suggesting is that Mr. Goodfellow, in his capacity as *your* senior warden, relinquish his position for his own good and for the good of our church. Is this an unreasonable request? This is not a personal attack on Mr. Goodfellow. It's a decision we are forced to make for the good of all. Let's not waste time turning this into a public execution. We are not a firing squad standing here with verbal machine guns to riddle this man with bullets. We just think it wise that he remove himself from the public's eye until all of this blows over. Of course, he is free to run again for this office next year when most people would have long forgotten the scandal."

"I still don't see what one thing has to do with the other," Joe insisted. "As such I don't support your recommendation. Sorry."

"Faulkner," Bart Knuckles added as he rose from his chair, "Mr. Goodfellow might have his peculiarities and we might have our differences with him, but this is not the way to go about this. All due respects, Fr. Perths, but as the vicar you should have called Mr. Goodfellow to a private meeting and discussed this with him. The decision to relinquish the position should ultimately be his, not ours. We shouldn't be here wasting our time with this on a Sunday morning. If I had known that this was the matter to be discussed, I never would have come to the meeting. This is underhand work, Faulkner. And I know that this was not Fr. Perth's idea."

"Agreed!" Joe echoed.

"May I say something?" Tessie Shoehorn asked and stood up to face Bart. "You can stand here and talk a lot o' nonsense about underhandedness and all that, but if you had any degree of intelligence, you would be sitting there quietly, considering the ramifications of this whole thing rather than standing here and talking a lot o' foolishness. We have a responsibility to …"

"Go to hell, fat girl!" Bart yelled contemptuously. "For your information, I have already considered the ramifications of this whole thing. My advice to you is that *you* forget the ramifications of this whole thing and focus on the ramifications of your gross overweight…"

Tessie drew a deep breath and heaved her chest as she considered Bart with rabid scorn. She then took her seat again without saying another word. A brief period of unnerving silence followed.

"This is going too far," Bart continued. "I am convinced that this is just the seizing of an opportunity to get this man out of office. This has nothing to do with his welfare. It has to do with your agenda. The man won the election fairly, by an overwhelming majority. Have you sought the opinion of the people who voted for him? Or is this just the whim and fancy of a select few? You all come here, minutes after receiving communion, and stand in front a group of intelligent people to inveigle them into joining you in this wickedness? This is iniquity, Faulkner...Fr. Perths, and you know it!"

"The height of impertinence!" Laurent Faulkner roared. "How dare you accuse us of such base misconduct!"

"He's out of order!" Ruthel echoed.

"Aww, go boil your head, Ruthel. You miserable old bat! I'm out of order, and you are out of your mind – all of you!" Bart retorted.

"He is the one whom we should be asking to relinquish his position!" Tessie barked.

"Go to hell, all of you!" Bart responded and headed towards the closed door. "Go to bloody hell!" He opened the door and turned towards Tessie, "And you Tessie, as long as I am in this church, say nothing more to me, you hear me, nothing, until you lose at least a hundred and fifty pounds!" The irate man slammed the door so hard that the sound reverberated throughout the undercroft.

No one said another word for about fifteen seconds. Joe then rose from his seat and approached the door. "I'm with Bart. Count me out of this. This man is a lawyer, a top rated lawyer. Figure out what I mean. Good morning." Joe closed the door quietly behind him.

Midgelyn Underwood, another vestry member, and the owner of *"Midgeland Car Dealers"* in Georgetown, rose and asked to be excused. She made no comment. She quietly left the room. Seven other persons left the room without uttering a solitary word. Eventually, there were only eight persons remaining in the room, of which only three were members of the vestry.

"Thank you all for you gracious support," Laurent Faulkner shouted sarcastically from the door as the seven persons left en masse.

"It's my turn to speak now, ladies and gentlemen, and Reverend Perths," Pigeon calmly said as Faulkner reentered the room. "I am going to be brief and succinct. I will do as you are asking me to do. I shall relinquish my position. It's clear that the sinister force at work in this church knows no boundary and I have no intention of spending my time and exhausting my energy in arguing and fighting in the Lord's house. However, the consequences of your actions today, and my decision to submit, will cause ecclesiastical tremors across this church that will be felt by many and remembered by all for years to come. Good morning."

"Is that a threat, Goodfellow?" Laurent Faulkner asked as he stared Pigeon squarely in the face.

"No," he quietly replied. "It's a guaranteed promise."

Pigeon took gracious leave of what he subsequently called 'the brood of sanctimonious vipers' and proceeded to his vehicle where Mrs. Goodfellow sat waiting paitently for him.

Chapter Eight

Judgment Day

Judge Pilchard's precipitate departure aroused no public suspicion since he often made such impetuous trips abroad to attend to personal or professional business. However, Mrs. Pilchard's grave distress at the discovery of her husband's infidelity was creating mounting tension in the Hudson home in Versailles. Dorset Hudson could no longer bear to see her sister in the pangs of such intense, emotional distress and reluctantly confessed to having had knowledge of her brother-in-law's adulterous affair with Maggie Billings. The apparent breach of sisterhood created in Mrs. Pilchard a mild antagonism towards her sister.

"You must understand, Sylvia," Dorset sought to explain, "that knowledge of such relationships is best left unsaid if the result produces more harm than good. What good would have come out of it if I had revealed it to you sooner?"

"Your loyalty to me as your sister, that's what," Mrs. Pilchard replied as she dried her eyes and patted her nose with a cotton, lace trimmed hankerchief. "Your loyalty to me as your sister is more important than loyalty to my husband. You hid this from me all these years. This is what hurts more than anything else. Adolph is a man, and by virtue of his manhood, he is potential lecher like every man is. But you are my sister, and your loyalty is due to me by dint of sisterhood."

Dorset approached the sofa on which her sister was sitting and sat beside her, and rested her hand comfortably on her sister's hand. She made no further attempt to justify her delay in making her sister aware of the relationship between her husband and Maggie, but sat there quietly – her reticence placing more credulity to her remorse than any word could have expressed.

"I want a divorce," Mrs. Pilchard suddenly blurted and rose from the chair. She found her way across the room to the window and sood there, looking towards the hazy sky and breathing heavily.

"Surely, you don't mean that, Sylvie," Dorset whispered in utter shock.

"Yes, Dorset," Mrs. Pilchard tersely replied as she turned to face her sister who sat erect at the edge of the chair in total shock. "I feel dirty, cheated, used…the epitome of a woman scorned."

Dorset could see that her sister's eyes were filled with pain and rabid hate for the man whom she had loved and trusted so deeply.

"You are angry now, Sylvie, but do not let your anger dictate your actions. Deep inside, you must have known that Adolph was prone to such a thing. He is one of the most admired citizens on this island, a man feared and respected by many and held in high esteem by virtually all of the people."

"Yes, Dorset. As an admired citizen, as a man feared and respected, I suppose that he would be prone to such a thing and perhaps to succumb to it – as a man. But as a Christian, no," Mrs. Pilchard remonstrated.

"Nevertheless", Dorset continued, "Don't you think that he would have flaunted his image? Didn't you think that some brazen woman would have sought his affection some day? Didn't you think that he might have succumbed to such a temptation one day? Of course I am equally shocked and disappointed that he would yield to such a thing; but face it, Sylvie, every married woman must carry this reality in the deep recesses of her mind. Certainly it never becomes a reality in many instances, but sometimes it just happens. Do you think that I do not entertain such thoughts about my husband? Sure I do. But if it should ever happen – or has happened and it comes to my attention, I will find a way to address it without rushing into divorce. What good will a divorce serve anyway? You will still be married to him – in the eyes of the church."

"I cannot ever let that man touch me again, Dorset, after he has been with that tramp, Maggie Billings…the fetid, gungy, iniquitous wretch!" Mrs. Pilchard hissed. "I'll choke her and pull out every strand of her hair when I see her!"

"You will need three more pairs of hands to do that, Dorset. In any case, you will do no such thing. You will maintain your dignity through it all. I will not allow you to stoop to such vile misconduct to claim your right to your husband's affections," Dorset assured her distraught sister. "You will lose the sympathy of the public by disgracing yourself like that. Remember, it is the sympathy of the people that will give you victory over Maggie – and Adolph. Use it, girl, to your fullest advantage! Furthermore, remember that Maggie could only have done what Adolph allowed her to do. A man in your husband's position would never have allowed himself to be caught up in such a potentially scandalous thing unless he himself had encouraged it and nurtured it. So redirect your anger against Maggie. In different degrees, Adolph has been as unfaithful to her as he has been to you."

"What you say isn't quite accurate, but I get your point, Dorset," Mrs. Pilchard replied after a moment of deep thought. "If it's not a howling inconvenience, I shall remain here, in this house, until I can figure out what exactly I should do."

"Of course, Sylvie. But let me deal with Maggie. I don't have as much to lose as you. George and I don't carry the degree of public prominence as you and Adolph. Let me deal with her, for I know that you will always carry this resentment for Maggie in your heart. Let me at least talk to her so that you can be relieved of the unnecessary burden of anger and desire for revenge. They will wear you out if they are not lifted. Let me be to you what Simon of Cyrene was to Jesus."

"A poor analogy, but you can do whatever you like," Mrs. Pilchard agreed. "I will not stain my hand with the muck from around her scrawny neck."

The two sisters threw their arms around each other's neck and laughed hysterically.

* * *

Shortly after nine o'clock that Tuesday morning, Fr. Perths received a call from Bishop Addington, requesting and urgent meeting with him that very day at four o'clock. The request filled the priest with a wave of anxiety. Pigeon's threat immediately came to mind, but he dismissed all fear because he had the support of some of the church's most powerful members – Adolph Pilchard, Laurent Faulkner, Ruthel Pollard and the other members of the BOARD. If the meeting with the bishop involved the erection of the church in Brewster's Village, then he feared no adverse consequences, for the judge himself was overseeing the project which members of the BOARD were financing. Reverend Perths thus shrugged off all thoughts of any possible reprimand. Nevertheless, the cowardly parson thought it wise to notify Laurent Faulkner of the Bishop's urgent request and seek his counsel.

"Good morning. *Faulkner & Babbit*," the strident voice answered. "May I help you?"

"Mr. Faulkner, please."

"Certainly. One minute, please," the voice responded.

"Mr. Faulkner's office, Madge speaking. Can I help you?" the sultry voice responded.

"Mr. Faulkner, please." The tone of Fr. Perth's voice was tinged with impatience with the unnecessary formalities.

"Who is calling, please," the voice inquired.

"Reverend Perths...from St. Patrick's."

"Ahh, St.Patrick's. Please hold, Reverend," the voiced advised cheerfully and respectfully.

The protracted period of waiting allowed the impatient man of the cloth to realize how intimidated he was of the usually gentle bishop. He had never before been so urgently summoned by the bishop. In addition, Pigeon's threat drove some degree of fear into him – a fear which he refused to acknowledge for fear of ridicule from the members of the BOARD.

"Fr. Perths, how do you do?" Mr. Faulkner's distinguished voice and mildly British accent rang through the receiver.

"Reasonably well, my dear friend...rather...fine," the timid voice replied.

"Is something wrong, Fr.? The tone in your voice sounds slightly troubled," the sensitive chairman of the BOARD inquired.

"Bishop Addington...he...he's called me to an...urgent meeting..."

"When?"

"Today. This afternoon at four," the trembling vicar replied.

A brief period of silence followed.

"What about?" Mr. Faulkner asked.

"Not sure. Pigeon's threat comes to mind," the frightened vicar admitted.

"Poppycock! Don't take his threat seriously. What the hell could he do to you or any one of us on the BOARD? His threat is nothing more than a weak ploy to intimidate you. Lift you head high, vicar. Go sit confidently before the bishop and stare him squarely in the face and talk to him," Mr. Faulkner advised.

"Perhaps, I should take you with me, under the pretence that you have given me a ride," Fr. Perths suggested.

"No. He's requested your presence. You should go alone. Look, vicar, it might be nothing at all to warrant this fear. Just relax. Bishop Addington is a gracious man. One can always get over a gracious man. If he accuses you of anything, regardless of what it is, plead guilty; that will totally disarm him. If he is offering you another position, agree to it. That will please him and perhaps make him change his mind. If he is seeking your counsel on an important ecclesiastical decision, give prudent advice, it might earn you a promotion in the diocese. Hey, Archdeacon Perths doesn't sound too bad at all, eh…"

The two men laughed and then hung up. Fr. Perths felt a surge of confidence and empowerment sweeping through him. He smiled at the thought of the purple trimmings on his cassock and prayed that the purpose of the urgent meeting with his Lordship might be to notify him of such a promotion.

* * *

Later that day, shortly before three o'clock, Bunzo was buried in the cemetery in Brewster's village. Fr. Perths had read of the death, but on the advice of Laurent Faulkner, dissociated himself from any involvement with the Mullins family or the obsequies. Uncle Ed had called the vicar earlier the previous day to request that he make himself available to the grieving family, but was told of the advice to stay away because of Mr. Mullins' hostility towards the members of St. Patrick's. Uncle Ed chided the callous vicar for his insensitivity towards a 'poor, insignificant family in crisis', and further pointed out that such an unchristian response would never have been made had it been a family of some prominence. Consequently, Uncle Ed discreetly undertook the financial responsibilities for the funeral and Bart Knuckles, through conversation with Uncle Ed, provided the free, well made coffin. Many villagers prepared food for the wake, which was held on Monday night, and *Brad's Palace* supplied the drinks. However, they did not offer any alcohol or include prune juice.

Not many people in the village had known that Bunzo was the Mullins' son, but on receipt of such knowledge, immediately offered the family their support. Even the villagers with whom the Mullins had had altercations demonstrated their sympathy by attending the wake and the funeral. Some, however, were gravely disappointed or peeved by the absence of liquor, but nevertheless remained at the wake so as to execute the ritual of singing, guzzling the traditional funerary dishes and slamming dominoes on the makeshift tables. In the absence of liquor, the squabbles and fights were considerably less.

There was whispered talk among some of the mourners regarding the Mullins' neglect of their late son. Even as they ate and drank, sang and prayed, they spoke disparagingly of Thelma Mullins whose breach of her maternal instinct, they cried, was an abysmal shame. It was the guilt of this maternal infringement, they later remarked, that caused Mrs. Mullins to wail so pitifully and scream her son's name so hysterically, and hold on so tenaciously to his coffin as it was being lowered into the grave. Mr. Mullins wandered off in solitude towards the bark of a tree, the branches of which had been severely damaged by the mischievious, pubescent boys who frequented the burial ground on their way home from school most afternoons. He began to viciously punch the partly rotted bark before some of his friends were able to constrain him and comfort him. Mrs. Mullins fainted from grief and exhaustion before her daughter and two of her older sons managed to finally release her firm grip from the polished, pinewood box. The pastor and self appointed bishop from the *Jordan River Pentecostal Church* was thus able to complete the committal and thereupon immediately approach Uncle Ed to receive his compensation.

* * *

Reverend Perths' mild imbibition served to settle his nerves and relax his mind as he turned into Bishop's Court shortly before the appointed time of his meeting. Gilbert was standing outside the guard hut when the mentally agitated shepherd of St.Patrick's flock arrived, and greeted him respectfully.

"Good aft'noon, Father Perks. How is you today?" Gilbert inquired with a broad smile as he opened the door of the vehicle.

"Perths, not Perks," the vicar corrected the courteous watchman as he locked the door. He neither smiled nor responded to the question regarding his welfare.

"Bishop is inside…in his office," Gilbert informed him. "Let me escort you to the door."

"That would not be necessary. I know the way," the supercilious vicar curtly replied.

"Very well, sir," Gilbert said quietly and politely, and returned to the guard hut.

Lidya, the Bishop's secretary, invited the tense vicar into the office and offered him a seat while she notified the bishop of his arrival. Fr. Perths politely refused the tea which Lidya offered him when she returned from the bishop's office.

Time seemed to stand still as the vicar nervously awaited the bishop's entrance. He tapped his feet impatiently and closed his eyes in deep thought as he envisioned himself being offered some new clerical position. He had always boasted to Laurent Faulkner that by virtue of his English extraction and his white skin he automatically had been stamped with the seal of superiority over the native clergy of the mere colony. In addition, he remembered the rumor that Archdeacon Blinkinsopp was contemplating retirement and planning to return to England. However, that rumor had been in circulation for several months and he had no claim to its authenticity. Nevertheless, he prayed passionately that it might be so, and that his being summoned so urgently by the bishop would mark the beginning of his natural escalation to the top of the ecclesiastical ladder which was his, he swore, by culturally divine right.

The pompous vicar was suddenly awakened from his ambitious daydream by the roar of the engine of another vehicle entering the compound and Gilbert's voice soaring across the beat of the engine. Fr. Perths assumed that the individual entering the compound was merely making an incidental visit. However, after a momentary period of more profound thought, he began to imagine himself sitting before a select panel interviewing him for some senior position. He thus smiled for the first time since his arrival at Bishop's Court.

A tap on the door attracted his attention. He turned to acknowledge the individual whose wise counsel the bishop might have been soliciting in his consideration of the individual to fill the prospective, imaginary post. However, he froze as the individual entered the office.

"Reverend Perths! How good it is to see you!" the individual cordially greeted him as he extended his arm for a handshake.

"Li...like...wise, Mr. Go...Good...fellow," the confused vicar managed to utter as he awkwardly rose and feebly extended his arm.

"Please, sit down, Father," Pigeon dismissively instructed the bewildered reverend gentleman and turned towards the desk. "How are you, Lidya?" he inquired as he approached the desk and gently kissed the conservatively attired secretary on the cheek.

"I'm well, Mr. Goodfellow," Lidya replied. "I'll let Bishop know that you have arrived."

Bishop Addington entered the front office immediately behind Lidya and warmly greeted both gentlemen, after which he invited them into his office and shut the door. He further instructed Lydia not to disturb him during the course of the meeting. Upon assuming his place behind his desk, Bishop Addington expressed gratitude to the man of the cloth and the senior warden for their obedient response to his urgent summons. The two men sat in adjacent chairs which faced the desk, and the bishop began the meeting with a short prayer. At the conclusion of the prayer, Bishop Addington opened a file and placed it on the desk in front of him. He subsequently leaned back in his black leather chair and fixed Fr. Perths a firm but nevertheless gentle stare.

"Are you familiar with the names Burtland Huntley and Scott Fielding, Fr. Perths?"

"Yes," the tense vicar answered after a moment of absolute silence, during which he felt the blood rush to his head and his body become warm and faint. As he returned the bishop's stare his face became flushed with anxiety.

He knew that if he were standing when the bishop had hurled the question at him he would have fallen.

"Could you tell me a little about them?" Bishop Addington asked without averting his gaze.

"Well, they…they are relatively new members of the church…St. Patrick's, that is. By relatively new I mean…about three years of …sporadic visits, but they later became more frequent in their attendance," the vicar explained.

"I'm sure that you know more about them than that," the bishop stated with a wry smile.

"Well, my Lord, Mr. Huntley is from Manchester in the U.K. and Mr. Fielding is a local Ischaltonese, but of English extraction," Fr. Perths further explained.

"When they came to the church, did they come together, or did they meet each other there?" Bishop Addington continued to interrogate the terrified vicar.

'I…I…believe that they came at the same time…"

"Where do they live?" the bishop asked.

"In Dartmoth…"

"Together, or separately?"

"Don't know, my Lord."

"Tell me, Fr. Perths; when they came to the church, were they already Anglicans or were they received from some other denomination?"

The frightened priest immediately suspected that the bishop might have been made aware of the ceremony he had performed between the two men and was merely cross examining him. Consequently, he appealed to mendacity to deliver him from the prospect of some manner of severe discipline. "Mr. Fielding was Roman Catholic. Mr. Huntley was relatively unchurched. So I performed a special, private service to welcome them to St. Patrick's. They were going to formally be received into the Anglican Communion when you come for confirmation next year. That was the plan. I have been meeting with them for private confirmation classes. "

"Why on earth would you do that?" the bishop inquired. "Such a welcoming should be public…on a Sunday in front of the congregation. And why would you decide to conduct private comfirmation classes?"

"They…they wanted it like that, my Lord," the lying priest responded. "I guess that they felt that it would be, well, a trifle embarrassing to be welcomed in front of the whole congregation, or sit with children in a confirmation class. I merely acquiesced to their request for privacy."

"Well, I can understand the embarrassment of sitting in a class comprising twelve year olds. But don't you think it odd that they would be a trifle embarrassed to be welcomed in front of the congregation, but bold enough to approach Mr. Goodfellow in his capacity as lawyer, to seek his counsel regarding the adoption of children…as a couple?" Bishop Addington's tone was gentle, but penetrating.

"Sorry?" the mortified priest straightened up and knitted his brow as he thrust ejaculatory, unintelligible utterances at the warden and the Bishop. "They..sakii..asking…couples..for chi…they….wa…"

"They approached Mr. Goodfellow as a couple for legal counsel. They are in the process of adopting children – as a couple," the bishop reiterated as he maintained his piercing stare at the visibly shaken vicar.

"I…I don't know about that, my Lord," Fr. Perths cried as he forced an awkward and stupid smile across his face.

"Don't know about what; the adoption or the unity?" Bishop Addington inquired.

"Either, my lord," Fr. Perths swore. "I know of no such thing!"

"That so called service which you conducted, was it indeed a private welcoming service, or the blessing of a forbidden and blasphemous thing?" Bishop Addington continued to cross examine him.

"Who could have given you the impression of such a thing, my Lord?" Fr. Perths questioned the gentle diocesan.

"That's beside the point, Fr. Perths," the bishop quietly but seriously responded. "My question to you is – did you or did you not perform a ceremony uniting those two men as a supposed couple?"

"Any report regarding such a ceremony could be no more than a blatant lie and therefore hearsay," Reverend Perths protested. "Mr. Goodfellow is merely assuming that the men are a couple because they are living together in the same home and adopting children to share their home. He cannot simply assume that such a ceremony was performed because they are posing as a couple and because they are members of St. Patrick's…or even because a private welcoming ceremony was performed. I vehemently uphold my innocence, my lord. No such ceremony was ever performed, my Lord."

"Then how do you account for Mr. Goodfellow's testimony?"

"About what?" the vicar asked in a hostile tone.

"Fr. Perths," the bishop stated flatly, "I have asked Mr. Goodfellow here to speak plainly and truthfully about what he knows. I do not wish to address this serious issue as if it were a mere rumor being weighed and analysed for authenticity. I want this matter addressed and resolved as truthfully, as discreetly and as fairly as possible. Mr. Goodfellow, would you please reveal to Fr. Perths what you were told?"

The rejected senior warden turned and addressed the vicar of St. Patrick's squarely in the face, "Mr. Huntley and Mr. Fielding confided in me that you performed a ceremony uniting them in what they referred to as *a marriage* and subsequently pronounced the church's blessing on the same. What I say to you is the gospel truth, and I am prepared to face any ecclesiastical or legal court in my defence of my testimony."

The cornered reverend became livid with rage. He rose impetuously from his chair and pounded his cuffed hand on the desk. "You are a liar, Peter Goodfellow…a confounded liar! My Lord, this man is fabricating a nasty lie against me and blaspheming against the church by sitting here and saying such a terrible thing!"

"I hardly think so, Father…" the bishop nonchalantly responded.

"It's his word against mine, that's all it is!" the irate clergyman yelled as he pointed accusingly at Pigeon. "He can never prove that in court, my lord. What evidence does he bring to support such a filthy lie?!"

"Enough to indict you, my friend," Pigeon calmly retorted with a derisive grin.

"My Lord, this man has a personal vendetta against me and against St. Patrick's because he was asked to relinquish his position as senior warden… because of his suspected involvement in the death of Mr. Gaskin. Such a thing brings negative attention to the church, my Lord. His accusation is nothing more than a cowardly act of vengeance!" Fr. Perths continued in his defense.

"You might wish to take your seat, Father, and lower your voice," Bishop Addington quietly warned the tempestuous vicar. "I doubt that Mr. Goodfellow, who happens to be one of the most famous lawyers on this island, would deign to gamble with his reputation by making such a baseless accusation on a clergyman of your status. Don't you think that he would first seriously consider the ramifications of such a twisted testimony? Would such a man come before his bishop and craft such a lie?"

"I would neither swear for his intelligence nor vouch for his sense of decency, my Lord. All I ask is that you pray for the soul of this man who sits here crafting such a terrible lie against me – and worse – the church. God's church, my Lord; God's holy church!"

"Sit down, Father," Bishop Addington abruptly commanded the irrational cleric.

The barefaced cleric immediately arrested his outburst and sat quietly. His heavy breathing suggested an attempt to suppress his temper, but neither the bishop nor Pigeon seemed moved by his emotional outburst or his desperate appeal for exoneration, for they showed no signs of sympathy.

"Now, Fr. Perths, I shall ask you once more. Did you perform a ceremony to unite Mr. Fielding and Mr. Huntley in a supposed marriage and pronounce the church's blessing on that so called union?"

"I did indeed perform a ceremony to welcome them," Fr. Perths admitted. "But no, my Lord, I did not perform any such supposed marriage ceremony. There is no evidence of such a thing recorded in the parish register."

"Of course not. You would not dare record such a blasphemy!" Bishop Addington remarked.

"My Lord, you speak as though this man's accusations were true!" Fr. Perths remonstrated.

"My Lord," Pigeon added, "the gentlemen also told me that they had received counseling. I am sure that this is what the good Reverend was referring to when he spoke earlier of private confirmation classes?"

"My Lord," Fr. Perths requested, "I beg to be excused until this man leaves this room. I shall not be accused, humiliated or disgraced in front of you for something of which I know nothing!"

"You will be excused at the conclusion of this meeting," the bishop responded. "Until then, I expect you to answer me truthfully with regards to a very serious accusation. I will treat this whole thing as nothing more than a report. However, I will conduct further investigation, and I pray, all due respects to you Mr. Goodfellow, that you are wrong."

"I stand firmly on my word, bishop, and my word is my honor. I am ready to swear in any court that my testimony is true," Pigeon swore.

"And I do the same," the lying vicar maintained. "I vehemently deny all that you have so wickedly accused me of doing. My word, too, is my honor."

"Of course you must know, vicar, that denial is not synonomous with innocence," Pigeon remarked with a sarcastic smile.

"Well, gentlemen," Bishop Addington interjected as he rose from his chair and extended his arm for a parting handshake, "I appreciate your coming at such short notice. I guess that there is nothing more than can be said at this point. However, I shall be making some discreet inquiry, and based upon my findings, I shall be contacting either of you. Furthermore, I trust that both of you will respect my wish for utmost confidentiality in this matter."

After both men had sworn to confidentiality, they departed without saying a solitary word to each other. Pigeon made a brief stop at his office on his way home, and on his desk he found a note from Miss Culley informing him that Jason had called and had expressed the need to speak with him urgently. He returned the call and promised his former friend that he would visit him before the week was over.

Meanwhile, the cunning vicar diverted from his route to Abersthwaithe, and in the shaded cloak of the dusk turned on to Midland Highway and headed towards the ritzy, south coast of the island – to Dartmoth.

* * *

Maggie Billings sat in her living room early that cloudy evening, sipping her third glass of wine. The pain of emptiness and the agony of a lonely heart, compounded by the fear generated by the telephone call which she had received the last night that the judge was with her, awakened in her the desire for immediate comfort from any of the many men who had secretly made sporadic visits to her home and shared her bed when the judge was occupied with his wife. She had previously thought of inviting Howard 'Howie' Callender, the Treasurer of the diocese who worshipped at the cathedral in Georgetown where she had begun worshipping, and with whom she had had a brief but torrid affair the week after she had begun attending the church. However, the remembrance of Mrs. Callender's cold, forbidding stare drove her from that thought, and she decided instead to seek the company of one less likely to provoke spousal wrath; thus she picked up the telephone and dialed Archie Carchide's number. Archie was the head usher at the cathedral and he was in the process of a bitter divorce because of his infidelity. Immediately, Archie responded to the invitation and soon arrived at Maggie's home, clothed in a pair of faded blue jeans and a red and white plaid shirt, over which he threw a dark blue balzer.

Dinner was prepared and was being kept warm on the stove when Archie arrived. After a passionate embrace and a short period of fervent kissing, Maggie fixed herself and her gentleman caller a drink and they retired to the sofa for conversation. During their confabulation, Maggie revealed the nature of her emotional pain and her need to find someone with whom she can settle while she was still in control of her mental faculty and while she still had some physical appeal. Archie thus seized the day and promised faithfully to fill the emptiness of her lonely heart. This immensely pleased Maggie and she leaned her head on his shoulder and likewise promised to love him until death do them part. Minutes later, they were gasping and panting like a pair of exhausted foxhounds after the futile pursuit of a fortunate hare. Subsequently, they drew to the dining table, clothed only in their underwear. However, Maggie draped herself in a flowing silk duster and donned a pair of high heeled slippers after they had finished the barley soup and before she served the main course. The pompadour which had graced her head on Archie's arrival had fallen in wild disarray after the physical expression of the covenant they had made, and she gathered it and tied it in a bun at the nape of her long, slender neck.

Maggie replenished their drinks, and in the course of the dinner, she continued to reveal the sordid details of her painful relationship with the judge, and was in the process of sharing his account of Mr. Gaskin's death with her when she heard the front door softly close and footsteps gently ascend the stairs. However, before she could rise to investigate what was happening, the judge appeared, bearing two long stemmed roses and a bottle of wine covered in a black and gold felt bag. He froze as his eyes rested on the semi-nude male figure sitting at the table, with his back towards him.

"A...Ado...Adolph...I ...wasn't expect...ing you...back...so soon...tonight..." the mortified woman uttered as she clasped the front of her untied duster to cover her partly naked body.

"I'm sure," the judge quipped. "Who the bloody hell is that at the table?"

"A friend. We...we were...just having...dinner," she sheepishly replied.

"Looks to me like he's already had dessert," the irate judge responded as he calmly approached the table to address the half naked guest who never averted his eyes from his dinner. "Dinner eh, my friend? You're having dinner in your underpants, with my woman?"

"Adolph, please!" Maggie implored.

"How could you do this, Maggie? Is this what you've been doing behind my back all these years?" The judge's voice was shaking with anger and pain. "You have proved yourself the perfect, two-timing slut, as I heard you were!"

Immediately, Archie rose from the table and confronted the judge. "Who the blazes you' calling a slut? Look, Maggie invited me here for dinner. Furthermore, we are in love; so bug off, grandaddy. Your *woman* needs a real man in her life, not a skinny, toothless, decrepit old fool."

"Listen, you asshole, I don't know who you are, but it's obvious that..."

"But I know who you are, Judge Pilchard," Archie interjected quietly with a smirk as he stood erect with his arms folded across his muscular chest. Does your wife know about your woman? Is the public aware of your extra-marital affair?"

In a sudden gush of irrational fear and uncontrollable anger and jealousy, the judge swung the felt covered wine bottle across Archie's forehead with all his might. The object connected to his rival's cranium with crippling force, but Archie merely staggered momentarily like a drunkard in the wind before launching forward, and in the wake, dashing the lean, lanky judge against the dining table before they went tumbling to the floor. The sound of glass, chinaware and stainless steel cutlery reverberated across the room as they came crashing down upon the polished, greenheart floor in a tight grip. Basil, who was already locked in Maggie's bedroom for the night began to bark viciously at the sound of the impact. Maggie neither screamed nor summoned her neighbor for assistance because of the embarrassing nature of the scuffle. Instead, she pleaded desperately with the two rivals to immediately stop the fight. Archie was struggling defensively, but the judge continued wrestling aggressively in what Maggie knew was an obvious effort to severely injure the man who she knew could publicly expose his infidelity, had insulted his masculinity – like she did during his last visit, and could in a solitary day, completely demolish his fame and respect. Furthermore, she trembled at the thought of the repercussions of an altercation between Archie and one of the island's most prominent and feared socialites, and as such pleaded with Archie not to retaliate in like manner. As Maggie continued to beseech the men to end the scuffle, she grabbed Archie by the arm in an attempt to release him from the judge's tight grip around his neck. However, as Archie broke free and was in the process of rising from the floor, the judge swung a powerful right hook which connected to his jaw. The unexpected blow threw Archie into a paroxysm of rage and he lost all self control. He pounced on the judge, knocking him back to the floor with a crippling left hook. As the judge fell back to the floor, Archie subdued him by sitting on his chest and arresting his arms by constraining them under his knees. He further confined the judge's head by gripping him tightly around the neck. Then, with his free left hand, Archie began to fetch the now exhausted judge a few stinging slaps across the face as he sharply admonished and humiliated him in front of the woman upon whom they both were lavishing their affections.

"You blistering, old fool!" Archie cursed his rival as he fetched him another slap. "If you were a real man, I'd punch you in your ugly face. You have the nerve to fight with me, eh?" He swung another slap. "You are a married man. The whole @@%&# island thinks that you are an honorable man, a man of integrity; and look where you are, in a brawl in a woman's house, you adulterous dog!" Another slap was hurled. "If you had any real strength like a man, I would have punched out your false teeth right in this house, and let you go home to your wife and muffle an explanation of what happened to them. But I respect your poor wife, Mr. Pilchard, that's why I've spared you. She is the one I respect, not you, you fool…" Archie berated the judge as he fetched him another slap. "Let me tell you something, I am the man of this house, you hear me? I, Archie Carchide, big, black, muscular Archie…I am the one who makes Maggie glad that she is a woman, so bug off while you are able, eh; piss off!" Archie tossed a final slap across the judge's chin and lower lip and rose quickly from the floor.

Judge Pilchard lay on the floor momentarily as he regained his strength. His breathing was labored and his eyes were ablaze with the rage of a consuming fire. Maggie knew that he had never before experienced such humiliation, and therefore understood why his anger had exploded like the fury of a volcanic eruption. She grabbed Archie around the waist after he rose from the floor and pulled him towards the sofa where she had placed his clothing. While she was helping him to quickly get dressed, the judge rose from the hard floor, panting and leaning slightly forward, and headed slowly for the chair which was close to the sofa. Maggie was not worried by his approach, nor did she think that Archie was under any threat, for she realized that the judge was exhausted and obviously too weak to continue the fight. However, as Archie bent over to slip his feet into his trousers, the judge, with the speed and precision of a deadly cobra, sprang forward and plunged one of the steak knives into the left side of Archie's back. The weapon penetrated with so much force that it punctured Archie's lung and he sank slowly to the floor. As he fell, he turned and looked helplessly and pitifully at Maggie. His expression bore the desperate plea for assistance. However, as his powerful body landed on the floor, he took one last breath and closed his eyes.

Maggie turned and contemplated the judge in horror. Tears began welling up in her eyes and flowing down her cheeks as she backed away from him. She tried to speak, but no sound was emanating from her cherry red lips. Her lover stood over the body of the man who had threatened to hurl him in disgrace from the top of the social ladder and who had trampled his masculinity before the woman who previously had often professed her undying love for him. Suddenly, the judge raised his eyes and studied the woman who had betrayed him. His icy stare penetrated her and she could feel her blood run cold. He then stepped over Archie's bleeding body and began to slowly approach the terrified woman.

"Maggie, come here. We have to talk. Look what you have caused, because of your unfaithfulness to me…because of your harlotry. Look!" he growled as he drew closer.

"Get away from me, Adolph!" she warned as she retreated in terror. "We have nothing more to talk about. You've made it clear to me that I'll be nothing more than your mistress. Look what you've done…for the second time!"

"What the hell do you mean by the second time? You saw for yourself that he tried to harm me. You bloodywell saw!" the judge yelled as he stopped in order to reason with the exasperated woman.

"You are a dog, Adolph!" Maggie screamed, "a nasty, murderous, jealous dog, you! When you though that Wilberforce was honorable enough to offer me something permanent, you got rid of him. I know that you caused his death!"

"What?!"

"*You* killed him!" Maggie reiterated. "I never believed your cock and bull story about some car turning the corner behind you when you drove off. It was your car that killed Wilberforce, I'm sure. That man who used to come to the alley at night saw your car; he saw you! He told me when had I stopped to give him some money on Christmas night, but I kept my quiet because I loved you, Adolph. I loved you enough to bear the burden of denying the truth about the death of a man who earnestly was in love with me. I used to give that man in the alley money every time I saw him so that he would not tell anyone that he saw you…your car. He knew you, Adolph, he knew you. And now you've come again, and killed another man. And you know what else; my intuition tells me that you had something to do with the incident at Jason's house. Somehow or the other, you were involved in that attack on Jason..." Maggie began to cry as she pointed accusingly her lover.

"I don't know what's come over you, Maggie. You have been drinking. It's obvious that you have been drinking and you don't know what you are saying," the judge replied as he calmly tried to dismiss Maggie's suspicions. "Come here, please. We need to talk."

Maggie somehow began to doubt her lover's sincerity as he approached her. She began to step further back in fear and desperation towards her bedroom door. "Adolph, stay away from me...or I'll call the police...stay away!"

Basil began to bark more fiercely, as if he too had sensed that Maggie was in danger.

"Come here, Maggie," the judge continued to beg. "Don't go and lock yourself in the bedroom. We have to talk!"

Maggie stepped back once more, but the judge made a sudden dash forward and snatched the delicate woman by the arm. However, before he could tug her away from the door, she grabbed the knob and pushed the door open. He seized her and tossed her to the floor. The reading lamp on the side table came crashing down to the floor as she tried to break the fall.

"Oh...so he is the man who makes you glad you are a woman, eh? So he is the man of the house, eh? Well, this man has come back to state his claim, bitch. I'm going to show you who the real man is around here!" the judge bellowed as he began to undo his shirt buttons.

"Adolph, please...!" Maggie begged.

Suddenly, a terrifying growl was heard and Basil, sensing the danger and the death in the house, rushed out of the room and sprang on the judge. The cowardly assailant and the vicious animal fell to the floor. The judge, in his fierce desperation to defend himself from the savage animal, inadvertently provoked it to a state of uncontrollable ferocity. Maggie quickly rose and instinctively tried to pull the animal from on top of the struggling judge, but she suddenly stepped back in a malevolent joy as the animal began to overpower him by snarling and sinking its deadly fangs into his flesh.

"Maggie...pull the bastard off...Maggie...ahhhh......the son of a bitch...I'll kill this @@#% animal.....get him...off...please....Maggie....!" the judge screamed in agony.

The animal continued to growl and bite savagely as the judge screamed for mercy. Maggie remained motionless as she braced the china cabinet, too terrified and exhausted to run, and too crapulent to give way to rationality.

After a few more terrifying minutes, the judge's cries gradually became weaker until they eventually ceased and his limbs became limp. He succumbed to the attack of the vicious animal. The dog then turned and scuttled across the floor to his mistress. Maggie remained standing with her head hung sideways and her arms hanging listlessly to her side. Her hair was now in complete disarray and the heavy make-up was smudged indelicately across her face. She stood there for more than ten minutes, gazing at the two dead, bloodied bodies sprawled across her polished floor. Some of the blood that oozed from the judge's body had meandered across to the Persian rug and had saturated a part of it. Basil remained faithfully by her side, panting and growling intermittently as he kept his eyes fixed on the body of the judge.

The ringing of the telephone seemed to snap Maggie from her trance. The canine began to bark fiercely. However, Maggie made no attempt to answer the phone, but turned and descended the stairs, with zombie-like precision. She unlocked the front door and proceeded towards the gate, with Basil by her side. Having unlocked the gate, she turned left on Westminster Lane and headed along the desolate, tree lined street in the drizzling rain – with her companion by her side. Soon they reached Midland Avenue and turned left again. However, they now began to attract the attention of the passersby who were driving along the main street or hurrying along under umbrellas. Some of the people began to follow them, although they kept their distance because of the dog, whose mouth and teeth were stained with the blood of his victim. As they proceeded further, the number of people following increased. Some of them knew Maggie well and some were mildly acquainted with her. They followed in awe as Maggie, barefooted and clothed only in a pair of lace underwear and an untied, silk duster which revealed her enviable and delicate proportions, with her dog trailing slightly behind her, ambled along in an aimless gait through the street. She stared blankly into the night as she continued down the road, oblivious to the traffic or the people. Her demise brought tears to the eyes of the women who knew her and who followed her as they tried to make sense of what was happening. Someone eventually called the police, and as Maggie and her companion approached Finchley Square, three police cars with screaming sirens and flashing lights surrounded her. Having been cautioned about the fierce animal by her side, the police came with the necessary appurtenance to subdue it before throwing a sheet over Maggie's shoulders and putting her into the car. She offered no resistance as they surrounded her and placed her in the vehicle. Sadness and mystery engulfed the atmosphere as the wailing sirens filled the air and the flashing lights disappeared around the corner.

Thus the woman who once socialized with the elite now walked alone. She, whose impeccable sense of fashion was often the conversation piece among the women of high social standing, was whisked away, draped in a plain, dingy white sheet. She who sat in the company of some of the island's most sophisticated and desirable men now sat among a squad of unrefined, sweaty policemen. Maggie Billings, once the target of both admiration and hatred among married women of consequence, was now the object of pity and derision. The house on Westminister lane which formerly gave pleasure to several eligible bachelors and married men of ignoble character, now served as a temporary morgue – to house the bodies of two adulterous husbands whose wives may hardly mourn their passing.

*   *   *

Reverend Perths spent that evening making telephone calls to all of the guests who had attended the blessing of the unholy union between Burtland Huntley and Scott Fielding. He judiciously began to make contact immediately upon leaving Bishop Addington's office, and so he was able to speak with Maggie Billings before her unfortunate circumstance. He had instructed them to vehemently deny any such ceremony should the Bishop make contact with them. He further advised them to say that the service was held to privately welcome the two men to St. Patrick's, and that they were being privately prepared for reception into the Anglican Communion during the upcoming sacrament of confirmation. However, there was one other witness to the celebration whom the dastardly vicar did not warn – an uninvited guest who merely wandered into the church and furtively observed the sacrilegious rite from behind the intricately designed iron gate which led to the basement – the unscrupulous sexton, Rexworth Davis. It was only after the bishop had exhausted all of the persons whom he assumed might know or might have witnessed the celebration that he considered Rex, in his capacity as the sexton. However, Bishop Addington was not able to contact Maggie that night.

Shortly after half past eight that evening, Bishop Addington obtained Rex's telephone number from Bill Jones. Upon establishing contact with Rex, the bishop invited him to Bishop's Court early the following day and issued strict instructions that their meeting was to be highly confidential.

*   *   *

The storm clouds which brought the incessant drizzle soon dissipated, and under the glistening foliage caused by the haunting light of the half moon and the subdued light from the street lanterns on the wet leaves, a black Pontiac cruised along the tree lined street and turned into the Pilchards' driveway. Mrs. Pilchard, along with her sister and her husband, stepped out and entered the dark, desolate house. The absence of the Mercedes and the lingering scent of Old Spice in the master bedroom served to comfirm Mrs.

Pilchard's suspicion that her husband had just left the house and had perhaps gone to perform his nocturnal rite in Westminster Lane. Mrs. Pilchard removed most of her clothing, as well as much of her personal belongings. The telephone rang several times during the time that they were in the house, but Mrs. Pilchard chose not to answer. Before exiting the house, she scribbled a note to her husband to inform him that she had removed her belongings. She also stressed the hurt and embarrassment he had caused her, as well as the gravity of her disappointment, but further stated that she had forgiven him. Nevertheless, she stated, she was going to remain at Dorset's home until he earnestly repents of his sin and becomes totally transformed from a life of adultery. Finally, she advised him not to call or visit her sister's home until such time that he shall have embraced a life of moral rectitude and spiritual wholesomeness.

Mrs. Pilchard and the Hudsons departed quietly. None of them spoke a word until the vehicle turned on to King Edward Drive, when Dorset suggested that they pass Maggie's home to see if Adolph's car was parked on Westminster Lane. Mr. Hudson was not in favor of the idea, but nevertheless turned on to Midland Avenue towards Maggie's home. Upon turning on to Westminster Lane, they spotted the car discreetly parked between a grey Vauxhall van and blue Datsun, about two hundred and fifty feet from Maggie's house. However, further down the lane, a crowd had gathered in front of one of the houses and there were police cars and flashing lights. Two ambulances were also parked in front of the house and the police had cordoned off that section of the street. Mr. Hudson thus reversed and they proceeded north along Midland Avenue to Versailles. Tears flowed down Mrs. Pilchard's face as the car sped away, and she confessed for being foolish enough to have left left the note on her husband's desk.

Restlessness resulting from thoughts of the unfaithful judge physically expressing his love for Maggie caused Mrs. Pilchard to turn on the television shortly after one o'clock in the morning. She began switching channels indiscriminately to find a program on which she could focus in order to rid her thoughts of her husband's shameless infidelity. For the first time, since overhearing the conversation between Maggie and her husband, Mrs. Pilchard began to feel the pangs of resentment building up in her. In a sudden fit of infernal anger, she wished him dead so that her life could be restored to normalcy – without the burden of worry about the whereabouts of an unfaithful husband.

Suddenly, Mrs. Pilchard froze and became like a dead woman as the news the double homicide flashed across the screen. When she regained some degree of composure, she tried to scream but no sound would issue forth from her lips. Subsequently, she rose, and with her last ounce of strength managed to grope through the dark corridor to Dorset's room by leaning against the wall for support. Upon reaching the bedroom, she knocked on the door with the ghastly persistence of a zombie. Dorset opened, and immediately, Mrs. Pilchard collapsed on the floor. Dorset's terrifying scream awoke Mr. Hudson, and he picked up his sister-in-law and lifted her bodily back to her bed. It was while they were in the room desperately trying to find out what had happened that the newsflash of the double murder flashed across the screen again. Dorset emitted a blood curdling scream and fainted at the side of the bed. Mr. Hudson immediately summoned his neighbors who rushed over to nurse the women while he got dressed and hurried over to Westminster Lane.

* * *

By sunrise the following morning, the entire island was thrown into a state of grief and confusion as the news of the horrible homicide was broadcast and the television flashed pictures of the bodies being taken into the ambulance. Rumors that Maggie had hinted at a taedium vitae began to circulate like a whirlwind. Consequently, she was placed in the psychiatric ward in the Queen Mary Public Hospital and put on suicide watch. The bells of St. Patrick's began to toll as the news reached Abersthwaithe and the flag in front of the Supreme Court was flown at half mast. Several reporters flocked Bishop's Court for comments from Bishop Addington. However, he sagaciously dismissed them without giving any comments other than to ask the public to pray for the Pilchard and Carchide family members, and to cast no judgment on the deceased or the individual or persons responsible for their deaths.

Immediately upon receiving word of the judge's demise, Mrs. Ramgolam donned a black dress and covered her face with a piece of black mosquito netting which she kept in a trunk under her bed for attending the funerals of socialites. She urgently proceeded to St. Patrick's so as to receive information regarding the judge's funeral service in order to inform the people of Brewster's village and Slough in a timely manner. As she was passing one of the shanty liquor bars in the village, a group of men who had gathered there for their morning ritual jeered her as she rode past on her bicycle.

"Y'all rass don't got nothing to do when the marnin' come but to 'ang 'round a blasted rum shop drinkin' rum and interferin' wid' people," she yelled abusively as she stopped a few yards from the shack.

The men began to mercilessly mock her, calling her 'Monkey pun iron', 'Blondie, the village idiot' and 'St. Patrick's circus clown.' Mrs. Ramgolam hurled a few piercing expletives before mounting her bicycle again and riding off towards Abersthwaithe. A beer bottle and an empty milk can followed her through the air and landed on the ground beside the bicycle, followed by a round of uproarious laughter.

*   *   *

In spite of the confusion and sadness caused by the shocking news of the murders, Rex nevertheless rose early that morning, put on his best suit and caught the bus to Bishop's Court. Gilbert met him at the gate. Immediately, the two men braced themselves for some kind of mutual hostility.

Rex approached the gate which was shut to prevent the unnecessary flow of reporters flocking to the court for the Bishop's comments regarding the murder of one of the most prominent members of the church. He neither waited for Gilbert to open the gate to let him in nor acknowledged his presence. He merely glanced at the aging watchman and made his way towards the building.

"You ain't supposed to come in here widhout getting' pa'mission from me," Gilbert snapped.

"Go to hell!" Rex retorted.

"Who you talkin' to, yo' ugly, stupid, ol' jackass?" Gilbert replied as he turned to follow the retreating sexton.

"You. Ah talkin' to you, yo' thunderin' ol' fool!" Rex replied and turned to face the advancing watchman.

"I'd cuff you in you damn mouth," Gilbert threatened the unflinching Rex as he approached him.

Sensing assault, Rex bent over and picked up a huge stone from the driveway, "Come…come nah…," he besought Gilbert who immediately refrained from taking another step forward, "I'd smash in you' face widh dhis rock. It would be three people who geh' kill' today… "

"Why you doesn't put down dhat brick and fight han' to han' like a man, ya' flippin' antie-man…" Gilbert challenged his heavily armed opponent.

Just then, Antoinette appeared at the door, "Gilbert, Bishop say to send the man to the office." However, she realized after relaying the message that the two men were apparently involved in an altercation.

"Gilbert…whu happening there?" she shouted.

"Nothin'. Is 'e… 'e come here vex widh me…jus' like dhat…vex widh me fuh nothin'…" Gilbert replied.

Antoinette closed the door and hurried up the stairs to Mrs. Addington, who was watching the news on the television. "Mam…!" she cried with a desperate look on her face.

"Oh dear me. What is it, Nettie?" the alarmed Mrs. Addington inquired.

"God's wrath is upon dhis house, mam…fire and brimstone!" she continued with alarm.

"Nettie! Calm down and tell me what has happened!" Mrs. Addington besought the almost hysterical house keeper.

"Sodom and Gomorrah, mam, Sodom and Gomorrah…right in dhis yard…!"

"What on earth do you mean by that, Nettie?"

"Dhat man who come to see Bishop, mam, he want to have sex widh Gilbert. He jes' now tell me so!" she reported in a state of agitation. "He want to have sex widh Gilbert – right our dhere in the yard, mam, fuh nothing!"

Mrs. Addington, aware of Antoinette's hearing impairment, rose calmly and went to the door. "Where is the gentleman, Gilbert?"

"He gone to the office, mam. He gone inside." Gilbert replied.

"What was he saying to you?" she inquired.

"Nothing, mam. He vex widh me for no reason, mam. I ain't never do him nothing. He jes' vex widh me…jes like dhat, 'cause I didn't open the gate for 'im," Gilbert explained.

"Well, thank you for explaining, Gilbert. I'm glad to know that that was all that it was," Mrs. Addington said with relief and closed back the door.

Bishop Addington explained to Rex that in light of all that was happening, he did not expect to see him, but nevertheless was glad that he had respectfully considered his request to have audience and traveled so far to keep the appointment. In order to show his appreciation for Rex's response, notwithstanding, Bishop Addington instructed his chauffeur to take Rex back to Brewster's village in his Morris Oxford.

"I'm sure that you are as shocked about the news of the deaths of Judge Pilchard and Mr. Carchide," Bishop Addington began after Mrs. Watts served Rex a pot of tea and two cucumber sandwiches.

"Yes, me' Lord," Rex replied. "It's a shame, me Lord, a shame…"

"What do you mean?"

"Judge Pilchard, me Lord, and Maggie Billings," Rex explained. "Them two was in love."

"You shouldn't make such statements, Rex, unless you can prove what you say. You can find yourself in a lot of trouble, you know," the Bishop advised the sexton.

"I has proof, me Lord. I has proof," Rex assured the Bishop.

"Someone told you?"

"No, me Lord. I see them…wid me own two eyes. Them was kissin' in the undercroft and I see them," Rex reported, "and…and Judge Pilchard… he…he say that if I I tell anybody, he goin' to make me redundant…"

"What were you doing down there to be able to see that?" Bishop Addington asked with a gentle, but doubtful smile. "Surely they would have been particularly careful…discreet, you know …"

"The place was dark, me Lord, and the vestry had a meetin' and I was waitin in the choir room with me radio, and I fall off to sleep. I did turn off the lights so they didn't see me 'till they switch on the lights, and the keys drop outta Ms. Billings' han', me Lord. They did come for hymn books to sing before they went home. I see them, me Lord. They kiss up one another for a long time before they see me lyin' down …sittin' down pun the chair," Rex testified.

"Well, that's rather unfortunate that you should be a witness to such a terrible thing," Bishop Addington added and changed the conversation. "Rex, I know that the homicide will consume much of my time today, so I will hasten to the purpose of the meeting. I need to ask you something of grave importance," the bishop began as he fixed a disarming stare at the simple minded sexton. "It was never my intention to involve you in this, but I have exhausted the names on the list and I still have no definite answer to this very troubling report. You are my last hope to knowing the truth, and I know that you will tell me just that if you have any knowledge of it, for you are a man of great moral rectitude."

Bishop Addington's cajolement might have been above Rex's comprehension, but he nevertheless was mollified by it.

"Anything you wants to know 'bout St. Patrick's, I can tell you, me Lord…anything," Rex boasted as he threw his arms in the air convincingly.

"Tell me, Rex, as the sexton of St. Patrick's, your responsibility will involve opening the church for any service and closing up after it, wouldn't it?"

"Yes, me Lord," Rex proudly answered. "Nothin' don't happen there unless I knows of it. I is in charge of all the services, me Lord."

"Tell me, then," Bishop Addington inquired. "Were you aware of a private service some time ago, where Fr. Perths welcomed two men to St. Patrick's…"

"I doesn't know what you means by dhat, Bishop," Rex responded after a period of deep thought.

"I mean, did you see any service going on, where two men were given a special welcome to St Patrick's…It might have taken place some time…"

"Oh…two men….wait, me Lord, it's on the tip o' me tongue…yes, two white men, "Rex interjected.

"Ahh, you remember!" Bishop Addington exclaimed with relief.

"Yes…I think…it…was…ohh, that's what it was! I now remember," Rex recalled. "They was dressed up in white and one o' then had a bunch o' flowers and …and…"

"Yes…?"

"He…he kissed the other one, and …and…that woman, Ms. Billings, she take out they photographs…and they was comin' towards me, and I dash back downstairs in the undercroft and run outside behind a vault, by some bush, and Fr.Perths come outside, but he didn't see me."

"But…why did you run? Weren't you the one who opened the church?"

"I didn't know that they was havin' a service, me Lord. I was passin' and I see some fancy cars in front the church. Only a lil' bit o' light was on in the church and the door was locked, but I had me' keys, and so I went in through the undercroft. And then I hear voices upstairs and I see some lights on, and I creep up the steps, and I see them…I remember now, Bishop…it was two white men and they was dressed up nice. And After Fr. Perths come outside lookin' to see who it was, everybody dash out and run to the cars and drive away, and Fr.Perths went back in the church, and I run home."

"What do you suppose they were doing, Rex? I mean, what kind of service was taking place before your eyes?"

"If one o' dhem was a woman, I would 'ave thought that it was a weddin', me Lord. They was dressed up in white and one o' dhem had flowers and they was kissin', jes like a weddin'. But it wasn't dhat, me Lord. I doesn't know what kind o' service it was. I ain't' never see a service like dhat." Rex testified.

"I guess you're right, Rex. It couldn't have been a wedding. Afterall…" Bishop Addington concluded. "Well, my good man, I thank you for coming to see me today. I have thoroughly enjoyed your company. I shall get my driver to take you home," he said as he rose and headed towards the door.

*   *   *

Rex was soon on his way to Brewster's village. He rode in the rear seat with one arm stretched across the backrest. His arrival home attracted a large crowd of people who thought that it was Bishop Addington who perhaps had come to inspect the new church which was still under construction. Rex had instructed the driver to close the windows and turn on the air condition system as he rode, so that he could fully enjoy the amenities of the luxury vehicle.

The chauffeur, in his crisp, tailored uniform and black hat, stepped out of the impressive automobile and opened the rear door. Rex emerged from the vehicle and strutted across the old wooden bridge which led to his home. He strode erect and neither acknowledged the crowd nor thanked the driver. The refined chauffer nevertheless gave a slight bow of the head as Rex exited the vehicle. He said nothing or acknowledged no one, but entered the vehicle and drove off. Immediately, Rex's status soared to new heights and word began to circulate in the village that Rex had become a 'big shot.'

*　　　*　　　*

A pall of gloom and a haunting calm hoovered over Aberstwaithe during next few days following the murders. The double homicide dominated the newspaper headlines for almost three days following the incident. Several articles pertaining to the judge's impressive life and career continued to flood the front page of the main newspapers. Incidental articles about Archie Carchide's estranged relationship with his wife and his meager stint at the cathedral appeared in some unobtrusive parts of two of the newspapers several days after the murder. The speculation which prevailed was that Maggie had murdered the two men – by stabbing one and having her dog fatally attack the other. However, her confinement in the observation ward and the heavy medication which was being administered halted any further investigation into the brutal slaying of one of the island's most illustrious citizens.

On the eve of judge Pilchard's funeral, Pigeon reluctantly went to visit Jason at his home. The gruesome murders had overwhelmed him, and his brotherly affection for Jason had dissipated. Earlier that morning, feigning close friendship with Maggie, he had visited the mentally troubled woman in the hospital in an attempt to gather information regarding the murder and to offer his legal counsel for a modest fee. However, visitors outside the few, immediate family were strictly prohibited. Furthermore, Maggie was under police viligance. The futility of Pigeon's trip to the hospital had thrown him into a disgruntled mood, for he had believed that his status would have made him exempt from the restrictions placed on the visitations.

Jason placed a decanter containing whiskey, a bottle of Ginger Ale and two glasses containing ice on the coffee table. After taking a toast, he plunged into the reason for his request to have Pigeon visit him so urgently.

"I want to apologize for my behavior these last couple 'o weeks," he confessed. "I feel like a right idiot. I cannot believe that I acted that way towards you, a man whom I've trusted and loved like a brother. I'm ashamed of myself and I just want to let you know that."

"Jason," Pigeon replied, "I don't know how to interpret your apology, but I have forgiven you, mate. I simply reminded myself of the complexities of the human mind, and the fact that these mental complications sometimes cause a person to vacillate like a pendulum – switch allegiances like an unscrupulous trader on the stock exchange. Your apology may be more necessary than genuine, Jason. You are in a quandary now. You need my support. So it would be to your best interest to apologize. Hey, there's no need to do this. I'm dealing with you from a professional perspective. What you have done will not affect my good counsel. I'm here, aren't I? I promised you that I will represent your case to the best of my ability, haven't I? I do my job, you pay me, we respect each other and that's all I ask."

"Pigeon", Jason continued, "I need to feel forgiven, so that I can move on. What you have just said does not convince me that we are like we were before. I need that assurance."

"We can never be like before, Jason. After our long years of close friendship, you saw fit to betray our friendship for the sake of a group of people who you knew hated me. You joined with them to crush me, friend. Remember? And after all of that, I have come to help you. I responded to your desperate cry for assistance when you called that night. I brought up nothing of what you did. Doesn't all of this say that I do not hold any animosity against you? I will always be here for you, Jason, but I could never be as trusting towards you as I was before. This is the only difference. Perhaps in time I will learn to trust you again, but right now, I am extending my friendship to you – a friendship that is based on a sense of duty rather than trust. Let's leave it at that, Jason. Let time determine the course of our friendship."

Jason remained silent and stared at Pigeon with an expression that begged for mercy. However, Pigeon's heart was hardened against Jason, and he realized at that moment that in spite of what he had explained to Jason, he was doing himself a favor because of the significant income which he was going to derive from responding to him – not because of his sense of duty.

"Would you understand how serious and sincere I am if I reveal a secret about judge Pilchard?" the desperate Jason begged.

"What secret could you possibly hold for a dead man, Jason?"

"He was planning to kill you…have you killed. Maggie Billings told me. He had believed that you knew that he was having an affair with her and that you were going to expose him," Jason revealed. "Furthermore, they didn't want you to be the senior warden, so they inveigled Fr. Perths into asking you to relinquish your position. He and Faulkner were planning to give you a very difficult time if you hadn't relinquished your position. They also wanted to…"

"…Jason," Pigeon interjected by raising his hand, "I have not relinquished my position as senior warden. I never submitted a resignation. Furthermore, you are revealing things to me that you otherwise would have kept secret if judge Pilchard had not died. You sat and plotted against me with them; now you are revealing secrets to me. This is what I mean about your vacillating mind. What will happen if I were to die now? Would you divulge all that I say against the BOARD if I were to say something negative about them now? My advice to you, Jason, is to reserve your speech. You might say something that will turn me completely against you. Let us just deal with each other like lawyer and client – like members of the church, you know – drawn together for the sake of a common purpose. Such a relationship will negate the need for friendship and thus remove any possibility of betrayal."

Jason made no response but stared at Jason with the expression of a puppy after a harsh reprimand. Pigeon then rose and took one last gulp of whiskey before thanking his former friend for his hospitality and apology.

Pigeon tuned into the death announcements which were being broadcast as he drove back home. It was then that he received the details of the judge's funeral arrangements, since no one from the church had given him any information – even in his capacity as the senior warden. He thus spent the rest of his journey debating whether he should attend the service, and in what capacity he should attend – as the senior warden or as a mere parishioner. Diplomacy, he thought, would dictate that he attend, but he felt that his attendance would hurl him headlong into the same abyss of hypocrisy as the very BOARD members whom he had so intensely despised. In addition, he would have to face Fr. Perths whose ministry he was in the process of taking to task. Upon arriving home, the irresolute Pigeon discussed the issue with his wife, and she advised him to attend as she had planned to do, for the sake of Mrs. Pilchard.

Archie Carchide's funeral service was held the day before judge Pilchard's. However, his death seemed publicly insignificant in juxtaposition to the honorable Judge's, and no report or photographs of the funeral were placed in the newspapers as was done for the judge. The Carchide family was grateful for the lack of sensationalism and they laid Archie to rest peacefully after a glorious but lachrymose service at the Cathedral, which was filled to capacity. Bishop Addington presided over the proceedings.

The honorable Judge Pilchard's body was taken to St. Patrick's where it lay in state on a catafalque draped with purple and black satin. The highly polished mahogany casket was opened fully to reveal the entire body lying in repose beneath the inner glass cover. The judge maintained his dignified appearance even in death. He looked suave in his conservative ash grey, pin stripped wool suit and white, cotton shirt. His badly bruised neck was covered by the mauve and white silk ascot which was tucked elegantly in his shirt. A silk handkerchief comprising three matching pastel colors was folded stylishly in his pocket. His mustache was perfectly groomed and his partly grey hair was brushed backwards and carried a small part at the side. An assortment of scented roses covered his feet and his lower limbs. His total appearance was one of a gentle soul in peaceful slumber.

The crowd which had gathered outside the church when the body arrived was massive. Most of them had come from Brewster's village and Slough. They knew instinctively that they would not have been allowed inside the church during the service, and as such they walked with their chairs and umbrellas. Rex seized the opportunity to parade in his cassock and to direct the long line of people who came to pay their respects to their fallen hero. The sky was overcast, but it was not saturated enough for even the slightest drizzle. It was as if nature herself were paying her respects that dismal afternoon, for when sunset approached, the clouds gave way to the crimson brilliance and monochromatic tones of the blue and grey evening sky.

Mrs. Pilchard conducted herself with utmost dignity even in the visible display of intense grief, and the people shed their tears with her – and for her, however, as they tried to make sense of the horrible crime which, as far as they had been made to believe, Maggie had executed upon the two men. However, even as the people mourned the judge's passing with Mrs. Pilchard, they indulged in malicious talk all during the service. They prayed and they whispered; they sang and they speculated; they cried and they cast aspersions. Nevertheless, they were there in full force – the old and the young, the rich and the poor alike, every race and nationality that lived on the island.

About fifteen minutes before the start of service, the Ramgolams arrived in a weathered taxi, accompanied by the bodyguard. Mrs. Ramgolam had received special permission from the BOARD the day after the judge died to sit in the rear of the nave during the service. Her attire caused quite a stir as she strutted into the church and up the main aisle to view the body. Word circulated that she had instructed her husband to walk slightly behind her as a sign of respect for her ecclesiastical superiority, and he fearfully complied. The crowd stared in awe as she plodded with the ungainliness of a cow in high heels down the aisle. She acknowledged no one, but kept her attention focused on the huge cross which hung against the backdrop of the altar. The rustling of her imitation black silk dress demanded the mourners' attention. Her face was covered with the black net which was held in place by a huge white rose pinned to a black straw hat. She gripped a large gold bag with a hand that was covered with white gloves, over which she placed a profuse assortment of authentic gold bangles. As she approached the casket, she opened her handbag and removed an old, red hand towel. Suddenly, as if rehearsed a thousand times, she emitted a loud wail and threw herself forward to the floor. Ram and Bertie the bodyguard raised her to her knees in an attempt to help her to stand. However, she bluntly refused to stand, and approached the catafalque on her knees, bawling and weeping hysterically.

The crowd outside the church surged forward to witness the dramatic outpouring of grief by the Public Relations officer.

"Is whu happenin' in deh?" one of the the women asked as she fought her way to peer inside the church.

"Is Gloysis Ramgolam," a man answered, "mekin' sheself a damn fool as usual…walkin' pun she knees…mekin' sheself a blasted monkey."

Inside the church, the congregation was appalled and disgusted by such a course display of grief and Mr. Faulkner brought four men from outside to remove Mrs. Ramgolam from the casket. As soon as she saw the men approaching, she immediately composed herself and quietly paid her respects to the judge. None of the men dared touch her after she fixed them a threatening stare. She afterwards turned, kissed Mrs. Pilchard and assumed her seat in the rear. Ram was directed outside the building to take his place with the other members from the two villages.

During the service, which was conducted by the Dean of the cathedral and presided over by Bishop Addington, Fr. Perths announced that the church had lost one of Ischalton's most eminent men. He further stated in his remarks that Judge Pilchard was the man whom he had appointed to assume the office of senior warden after the elected warden had been advised to relinquish his position, because of his purported involvement surrounding Mr. Gaskin's death. Some of the congregation turned and gave Pigeon a puzzled stare, which Pigeon interpreted as a sign of their ignorance of such a decision on the vicar's part. Later in the service, Laurent Faulkner paid tribute to his fallen comrade by speaking of his contribution to society and the church, and his exemplary character. He was, according to Faulkner, a man who held the highest regard for family values and his church, and who was the 'quintessential Christian husband.' After a dynamic sermon by the Dean, the service continued with an anthem by the choir. Philbert Watts sang the communion anthem, '*Safe in the Arms of Jesus*', with such passionate tenderness that many members of the congregation were moved to tears.

As the casket was bourne from the church, the choir burst into the Hallelujah Chorus as the bell tolled solemnly and the people outside stood quietly to pay their final respects to one of the island's most revered men. Men removed their hats and women gave a slight bow of the knees as the casket passed on its way to the judge's final resting place in the church yard.

Judge Pilchard's tomb was sealed just before sunset amidst the chorus of many traditional burial hymns which the villagers had raised. They took turns at calling the words for the sake of those who were not as familiar with the words as they. Even in the throes of grief, Mrs. Pilchard expressed sincere gratitude to those villagers who were still gathered around the grave, singing and lending their support to her – a woman whom they had always held in high esteem.

Reverend Perths escorted the Dean and Bishop Addington to their respective vehicles, and as the Bishop shook the vicar's hand, he requested that he report to Bishop's Court on Monday morning. This request, however, did not cause the vicar any stress or anxiety, because he had the word of all who had attended the blessing of the unholy union that they would vehemently deny that any such service took place. They all had promised that if called by the bishop, they would state that it was merely a private welcoming service. Those who were called did as promised. Fr. Perths thus resigned himself to the fact that the meeting was being called to receive an apology from his Lordship. On returning to the vicarage, he therefore celebrated his victory over Pigeon by imbibing almost a full bottle of imported wine with his dinner.

* * *

Sunday morning came two days after Judge Pilchard's funeral, and the services proceeded in their usual manner in spite of the mountain of semi-whithered flowers which was piled on the fresh, concrete tomb in the church yard – a grim reminder of the horror which had taken place in Westminster Lane a few nights earlier. Fr. Perths reiterated his profound sorrow at the passing of judge Pilchard, and quoted several passages from the book of Proverbs to warn all men of the danger involved in being enticed by one who plays the harlot; many persons in the congregation later voiced offence at his insensitive remark which they claimed was directed at Maggie Billings. He further announced that Bill Jones had resumed office as junior warden, especially since he had never accepted Bill's resignation, and that he had appointed Laurent Faulkner to fill the role of senior warden until the end of the term, after which the newly elected warden shall assume office. Mild applause among a few members of the BOARD followed the announcement. Others simply stared at the vicar with blank faces or expressions of simmering disapproval. In the absence of Mrs. Goodfellow, Pigeon raised his voice in angry protest from his pew in the middle of the nave. He subsequently closed his prayer book and stormed out of the church, yelling threats against the man of the cloth, whom he described as 'an odious and repulsive wretch.' Several members immediately rose and quietly followed the justly elected senior warden.

At the end of the service, Jason approached Laurent Faulkner and handed him a box containing the accounting files which Faulkner had brought to his home.

"Here, Mr. Faulkner," he said as he stared the illegally appointed senior warden squarely in the face, "I don't wish to do this any more. I think that it might be within your best interest – and mine – if someone else were to do your accounting." Jason's tone was flat and his expression was cold.

"What do you mean by this, Coleman?" Faulkner asked with a puzzled expression.

"I just said it. I don't wish to do this any more. I'm done with it," he reiterated.

"Who put you up to this, Coleman? Goodfellow?"

"Mr.Goodfellow has nothing to do with this. It's my decision…entirely my decision," Jason explained.

"You have not completed the job, Coleman. So if you choose to do this, you can consider yourself not paid," warned the now irate Faulkner.

"That's fine, Mr. Faulkner. You can keep your money. I'm not here to fight with you for money. The job is almost done, but you can keep your money. I'd rather have peace of mind than to stain my hand – and my soul – by accepting your money. Money might mean a lot to you, but I have grown past that, I'd like to think. Good morning." Jason turned and strode out of the Parish Hall.

"You can go to hell, Coleman!" Faulkner shouted as he followed Jason outside. "What is Goodfellow giving you for doing this, eh; ten dollars?"

Jason stopped abruptly and turned towards Faulkner and glared at him. "No. He's paying me the same amount that you paid Fr. Perths to bribe him into making you senior warden." He turned again and marched briskly to his car and ignited the engine.

"Asshole! Bloody no-good, fickle-minded asshole!" Faulkner yelled as Jason's car pulled off.

*   *   *

Very few people remained for fellowship that day, and by noon, the place was deserted. The cunning reverend thus made his way over to the Faulkners to discuss the possible protest by some of the parishioners who had walked out of the church in the wake of his announcement regarding Mr. Faulkner's appointment.

"We've got to stand united, Laurent, as white men," he advised after he had imbibed his third glass of whiskey and ginger ale. "We can't let these savages override our authority."

"Why are you worried about something like that," Faulkner asked.

"Some of them actually have functioning brainboxes, you know. We can't take anything for granted," the vicar warned the still sober Faulkner.

"Fr. Perths, I agree with you that as white men we should stand united. However, I don't quite think it respectful to refer to your parishioners as savages," the mildly irritated Faulkner remonstrated.

"I'm not talking about all of them, you know that. I would have thought that you would understand who I mean," Fr.Perths explained.

"I'm afraid I don't Fr. Whom are you talking about?"

"Isn't it obvious?"

"No."

"The natives. That's who I mean. They are many, and could outnumber us. We are Englishmen, Laurent; you are of English extraction. But more important, we are white men – the best of both worlds, we say."

"The natives, Fr.? Is this what you thought of judge Pilchard whose death you claim to mourn so deeply? Is this what you think of Bill Jones... Fritz Batty...Ruthel. Those are some of your biggest financial supporters, you know...more than a lot of the white people who come here," Faulkner contended.

"I'm not talking about Judge Pilchard and others like him. I mean the others... Judge Pilchard was different."

"In what way? He was a native Ischaltonese," Faulkner replied as he studied the vicar.

"Well...the Judge, Fritz...Bill...well, they're like us, you know...they are the exceptions," the vicar sought to clarify his point.

"I see," Faulkner replied. "I see."

Faulkner artfully digressed from the conversation, and about ten minutes later excused himself under the pretense that he had to make an urgent trip to Georgetown.

"So I take it that we're an indomitable force, eh...two British subjects... hic...a...against the ...hic...army of ...hic...natives...ha ha ha ... strike up the band, my friend...hic...raise the Union Jack!" Fr. Perths saluted and took a final gulp of his whiskey before slamming his glass against the wooden table.

Faulkner stared at the bordering drunkard in disgust. "Fr. Perths," he stated, "I am beginning to have serious reservations about accepting the position as warden. I am not too sure about this whole thing, especially in the wake of Pilchard's sudden death and after what took place this morning in church. I believe that I'll be more effective behind the scene."

The vicar stared at Faulkner with unfocused, glassy eyes. His face beamed flushed with fatigue from the excessive alcohol. "You...hic...are not afraid of ...hic...being the warden. You...hic...are...af...afraid...of that your... your...covert prejudice would one day rise...hic...to the surface under the ...hic...pressure. You...you...are afraid of ...hic...ex...exposing your own subtle bigotry. That's what...hic..."

The enraged Faulkner made no comment, but placed his hand on Fr. Perth's shoulder and directed him to his vehicle.

*   *   *

The orange and green hues of the dawn and the chiming of St. Patrick's bells seemed to lift the pall of gloom that had hoovered over the village of Abersthwaithe and the surrounding villages during the last week. A passing cloud sprinkled asperges over St. Patrick's and the surrounding villages just before the morning bustle when the people were still engaged in their private morning devotions.

Monday morning came like the glory of death on horseback. It was the day of reckoning; it was the day of freedom. It was the day of joy; it was the day of doom. It was the day of war; it was the day of peace. It was the end of the old era; it was the beginning of the new age. The judge lay buried in his grave in the very churchyard where the political and social Armageddon was going to take place. The brilliant sun which illuminated the morning sky did not portend judgment on this day when the people set about their wonted daily chores.

Reverend Perths donned his clerical attire and set out for Bishop's Court. Instead of following his ritual of listening to the talk show which was aired at nine o'clock on IBC, he drove quietly as he pondered all of the possibilities of his meeting with the bishop. It was his day, he thought, to assert himself as *the* archetypical English vicar in a colony where the people still considered themselves as remnants of British sovereignty, and who still paid obeisance to citizens of the mother country or to those who were of English extraction. He also considered the purported advantage of being a clergyman – a white man of the cloth who had custody of the people's spiritual lives – and as such, many aspects of their secular lives. However, his greatest affirmation was his vicarial office at St Patrick's, long recognized and respected as the island's most prestigious house of worship. He thus smiled and began to humm the hymn, "Now thank we all our God." Fr. Perths soon turned into Bishop's Court, as confident as the sun that rules the day – but completely oblivious to the certainty of night fall which puts the light of day to flight.

"Do come right in, Fr.," Lidya greeted the unsuspecting vicar. "His Lordship will see you momentarily. He's engaged on the phone at present. Shall I pour you a cup of tea?"

"I shall be much obliged. Thank you," Fr. Perths replied and sat on the chair closest to the door.

Immediately upon the vicar's completion of the hot beverage, Bishop Addington emerged from his office and welcomed him with a firm handshake and a broad, but dignified smile.

"Please, step right into the office, Fr.," the Bishop indicated with a brief sweep of his hand.

Bishop Addington's cordiality convinced the vicar that all was well, and he smiled at the thought of having won the day. "I thank you for this great privilege, my Lord," Fr. Perths remarked as he sat.

"Fr. Perths," the bishop began without making any response to the vicar's expression of gratitude, "I've asked you here this morning to address a very serious issue that potentially holds grave ramifications for the church..."

"I am indeed grateful that you would deign to seek the counsel of a mere vicar, my Lord. I do hope that I can offer even a soupcon of prudent advice," Fr. Perths interjected with a submissive smile as he sought to appease the patient diocesan.

"Fr. Perths, please listen to what I have to say to you without interrupting me," the bishop gently insisted.

The pangs of uneasiness suddenly began to gnaw at the vicar's mind and spirit. He could see, for the first time since his arrival, the signs of seriousness and resignation on the bishop's face. His face instantly became flushed and he began to feel dizzy.

"I am giving you the opportunity, one last time, to tell me the truth regarding Mr. Huxley and Mr. Fielding. Did you or didn't you perform the ...*rite*, for the lack of a better term, of a civil union between the two gentlemen.?" The bishop's stare was piercing as he fixed his attention on the trembling vicar.

"I...I do so...so... swear, my Lord, that no such rite was ever performed," the lying vicar again testified. "You may call Ruthel Pollard, John Bratsfuningsworth, Ella..."

"I have already done so, Father," the bishop interjected, "but it's not their testimony that has caused me to summon you here today, for I am sure that they were bound to secrecy. It's the testimony of the one uninvited guest whom none of you saw that day. It is that person's evidence that I hold to be true."

"And who might that be, my Lord?"

"That's immaterial," Bishop Addington replied. "I have heard all of the sordid, blasphemous details of the service, from the bouquet of flowers to the unholy kiss in front of the altar; from the attire of the couple to the description of the guests."

Immediately, the enraged, terrified vicar began to viciously asperse Pigeon Goodfellow for concocting such a ghastly lie. He then began to berate Jason

Coleman whom he now mildly suspected as a result of his sudden change of allegiance towards Laurent Faulkner. The judicious bishop remained quiet as Fr.Perths continued to hurl a litany of curses on the persons whom he suspected as having informed him of the nature of the service. Fr. Perths accused them of distorting the truth with warts of disgusting lies in order to avenge their anger over his decision to appoint Laurent Faulkner as the interim senior warden.

"These names whom you've just called," the bishop inquired, "were any of them among the congregation that day?"

"No, my Lord," the vicar answered curtly.

"Then why would you even assume that one of them is responsible for giving me the information? When this so called welcoming service was taking place, was the church locked?" Bishop Addington continued to interrogate the vicar.

"Yes…I think so, my Lord."

"Why would you decide to perform such a service so discreetly?" the bishop inquired.

"To protect their privacy, my Lord. They requested a private service."

"I'm sure," his lordship responded sarcastically. "Tell me, Fr, who else in the church would have keys?"

"Rex…the wardens…ahh…oh,…Mr. Mertins…yes indeed, Mr.Mertins…Nollie Mertins. The man is a fabulist!"

"Who told you that it was Mr. Mertins who supplied the information?"

"It has to be. Probably his anger at not being invited, I'm sure. Who among the others with a key would do such a thing? Furthermore, he is perhaps the most likely to be acquainted with any of the persons who witnessed the welcoming service," Fr. Perths reasoned.

"You can't accuse a man so unjustly, Fr. Perths. Mr. Mertins made no such report."

"Wait a minute, my Lord. When the BOARD was formed, I think…yes, Mr. Faulkner and judge Pilchard were given keys. That's right. They had keys and access to the building," the vicar calculated.

"Seems like everyone in the church had keys," Bishop Addington remarked with a slight smile. "This makes it extremely difficult to determine who it was that discreetly witnessed the whole affair, doesn't it?"

"Are you telling me, my Lord, that it was judge Pilchard who told you such a thing?"

"Why would you automatically assume that it was he to revealed the secret to me?" the bishop asked.

"Because Mr. Faulkner would never do that. I know that he would never do such a thing," Fr. Perths swore.

"Well now that you have hauled every one whom you've suspected through the gauntlet, let us return to the matter at hand. Remember, Fr., that this meeting is not to discuss any person whom you believe to be a nark. It is to address your inappropriate conduct, first in performing such a blasphemy and second in lying so boldly and unashamedly; in the vernacular of the streets, you sat here twice and told me a barefaced lie…served me a right whopper! You did perform such a ceremony, didn't you? Who on earth carries a bouquet of flowers to a welcoming service; which man does that, at least? Who dresses in white suits to be welcomed into a parish? Where does kissing fit in such a ceremony? Answer me, Fr. You *did* perform such a blasphemy, didn't you!?" Bishop Addington's tone was serious and harsh.

The persistent vicar no longer deemed it wise to prolong the charade. He burst into tears and confessed to having performed the ceremony of an unholy union in the name of the church.

"I…I was…mere…merely…blessing their friendship…, my…my Lord," the vicar managed to articulate as he sniveled, with his hands covering the lower part of his face. "This is being blown completely out of proportion."

"You mocked the sanctity of marriage Father. You blasphemed the sacrament of Holy Matrimony. And to aggravate an already serious situation, you lied to me; and worse than that, you inveigled others to lie! Some of the people whom I called, who *were* at the ceremony, including the two men in question, vehemently denied that such a ceremony took place – because you obviously made them swear to secrecy!"

Bishop Addington's pallid complexion became almost purple with rage as he reprimanded the quasi-penitent vicar.

"I have summoned you here today, Fr. Perths, to inform you that I am removing you from office as vicar of St. Patrick's, and revoking your licence – with immediate effect."

The vicar gasped as the bishop declared his intention. He raised his head and fixed the bishop a blank stare. His jaw dropped and he remained as motionless as a statue for a few seconds.

"However, in order to protect your honor – and the sanctity of the church," Bishop Addington continued, "I suggest that *you* initiate the process by sending me a letter of your intention to relinquish your position for reasons which you prefer not to mention. My further advice is that you return to England for a reasonable period of time until any possible negative reaction to your resignation shall have blown over. If the persons who witnessed the ceremony are really your faithful friends, they will never divulge what you had them swear to. You and I will have to trust that they will not ever divulge this blasphemy, for both of our sakes. I have not discussed my decision with anyone else, so you have the opportunity to leave with your dignity."

Neither Reverend Perth's reticence nor his wounded expression evoked any sympathy or remorse from his Lordship. Bishop Addington did not prolong the conversation, for he was adamant about his decision.

"My Lord," Fr. Perths began to plead, "If I have offended…"

"Go." Bishop Addington firmly interjected. "I will give you no opportunity to beg for forgiveness or to suggest any form of reparation. What you have done is most repulsive in the sight of God. It is to him you must plead for mercy and forgiveness!"

The greatly perturbed vicar glared at the bishop as the tears rolled down his now flushed cheeks. Suddenly, he made an abrupt turn and stormed out of the office, and slammed the door behind him. Bishop Addington completely ignored Fr. Perth's arrant display of insolence and went back into his office. Fr. Perths returned to his vehicle, embarrassed and intensely angry but nevertheless happy and convinced that Bishop Addington had arrested a potentially destructive and embarrassing situation before it became a public scandal. Having closed the door, however, he began to cry like a humiliated toddler.

Gilbert was sitting in the guard hut when Fr. Perths angrily strode past to his car. Upon realizing that the dismissed vicar was in emotional turmoil, he quietly approached the vehicle and tapped on the window.

"Is you alright, vicar?" the inquisitive watchman inquired.

Reverend Perths slowly raised his head to reveal his flushed, tear stained face. "I'll be fine. Bastards, all of them! The people I trusted…there was a Judas among them. How much I feel like the Lord. I served them well, yet one of them turned against me…came and told the bishop a lie. I have my suspicions about who it was that came to see the bishop."

Gilbert stared at the forlorn cleric without uttering a solitary word.

"I've decided to give the Bishop my resignation, Gilbert. That's what I came to tell him today. He was begging me to stay, but I can't. I cannot in good conscience break bread with those people…ever again! If I ever lay my hands on that person, Gilbert…"

The malicious watchman looked furtively around and then leaned forward, pushing his entire head through the window, "Listen, don't say nothin', ya 'ear. But if somebody do that to you, I think that it was Davis who done it…Rexworth Davis." Gilbert pulled his head outside the car and checked the surroundings again before leaning into the vehicle once more. "I see 'im wid me own two eyes las' week. And then the Bishop send 'im back 'ome in 'is car. The chauffeur take 'im back to Brewster's village. Bishop ain't never take me nowhere in 'is car…nowhere, but 'e send dhat crabdog Davis 'ome in 'is car…to stink it out!"

The gullible vicar reeled back in shock. "Rex…Rexworth…you mean Mr. Davis…?"

"Yessss! I see 'im widh me own two eyes. I jes knows dhat it was 'im who tell dhat lie pun you. 'e got the face of a liar!" Gilbert reported.

Reverend Perths thanked Gilbert for the information and ignited the engine.

"ow 'bout a raise for a real frien', vicar?" Gilbert asked as he flashed a satisfied smile.

The grateful vicar opened his wallet and offered Gilbert twenty dollars. The watchman's face glowed with the brightness of the noonday sun and he kissed the money and expressed gratitude to God for making the vicar such a good priest.

"Vicar," he charged the clergyman as he reversed out the driveway, "don't say nothin' that I tell you, eh?"

"And you don't tell anyone what we discussed, Gilbert; alright?" Fr. Perths replied and headed out of the driveway.

The sullen English clergyman turned right upon leaving Bishop's Court and headed for *Faulkner & Babbit*.

*   *   *

By three o'clock that afternoon, the news of Fr. Perth's resignation had reached most of Abersthwaithe and the two surrounding villages. The ostensible reason given for the sudden, drastic action was 'to attend to urgent family matters in England.' However, the members of the upper circles were not convinced that his reason was authentic, for they could not recall even a solitary mention of any particularly close family members in the former mother country.

Ironically, it was the proletariat from Brewster's village in particular who were able to analyse the situation and taper their suspicions to Rex, for they too believed that the vicar's reason was a fabrication. They had suspected that something was reported to the bishop, but they had limited the subject to the building of the church in the village. It was Rex's pompous return to Brewster's village in the bishop's vehicle earlier the previous week which had stimulated their suspicions. Soon, therefore, news of Rex's supposed betrayal began to spread across the village and ultimately reach Abersthwaithe. Copious telephone calls to the vicarage to express shock and sorrow at Fr. Perth's sudden resignation and disappointment in the ungrateful sexton kept the vicar busy that evening. Reverend Perths thus became intensely angry with Gilbert for breaking his promise. However, as he thought of the conversation with the bishop and with Gilbert, he suddenly remembered that someone had entered the building during the service in question and had tumbled down the stairs in an attempt to escape when the couple were about to leave the church. His suspicion now became fixed on the loquacious sexton. Therefore, the crafty vicar sought to slightly distort the truth in order to protect his honor and that of Burtland Huntley and Scott Fielding, especially since the people did not find his reason for resignation to be credulous.

"Rex told the bishop that I had performed what he thought was a private marriage ceremony between two divorcees without diocesan permission," the wily vicar told Darlene Burrows during their telephone conversation. He advised her that their conversation was confidential because he knew that such an advice would become the impetus for an immediate divulgence to others in similar confidentiality, not resulting from maliciousness, however, but from the desire to to create some imaginary intimacy between herself and himself. Consequently, Rex became an instant target of the people's wrath. That night, they stoned his house with a hail of rocks and bottles. The police were summoned and the small crowd of militants dispersed. Rumor circulated that it was the Public Relations Officer who had instigated the attack on Rex's home.

While the situation at St. Patrick's was becoming more heated that evening, a grave crisis was taking place at the Queen Mary Hospital in Georgetown. Maggie Billings had attempted to commit suicide by swallowing an overdose of painkillers and sleeping pills which she had requested over the course of the time she was in the hospital but pretended to have drunk when they were delivered. She apparently had hidden them in the drawer containing her toiletry, to be consumed when she had acquired enough to inflict a fatal dose. News of the foiled attempt was broadcast on the radio and television later that night. The following morning, Reverend Perth's resignation appeared in the headlines of the island's three main newspapers and the news of the same was broadcast on the air and television. The *Argosy* bore the caption, "St. Patrick's steeple is falling down, my *fear* vicar." One of the relatively popular tabloids contained an article entitled, "The Fall of the Anglican Empire", while another newspaper bore the headline, "*Judge*ment Day" followed by the article which implied that judge Pilchard's ghost had returned to declare the verdict of doom upon the souls that had sentenced him to the haunting darkness of the lonely tomb. The Pilchard family took profound offence at this article and subsequently demanded an apology from the printery.

News of the vicar's departure to England early the following week caused a riot on the grounds of the church that Sunday morning. The BOARD members, with the cooperation of some of the members from Brewster's village and Slough, determined to host a farewell celebration that Sunday and made plans to reject the priest whom Bishop Addington had sent to temporarily replace Fr. Perths. They set up tables and chairs outside on the front lawn and in the garden on the opposite side of the burial ground. Members of the upper circles were going to be seated at the tables on the lawn and in the garden. They were going to be served their meal on chinaware, with stainless steel cutlery and glasses containing a variety of beverages. The privileged members of the lower circles who were selected to serve were going to partake of their meal downstairs in the undercroft after the favored guests had been served. The other guests from the lower circles were going to be seated in the undercroft and partake of a simpler meal in sanitary containers, with plastic spoons and disposable paper cups. The Ramgolams, however, were going to be seated outside among the *Gold* and *Silver Circles*.

Threatening looks addressed Rex as he executed his tasks. However, the cocky sexton was not the least intimidated by them, for he had the assumed protection of the police who had dispersed the mob that had stoned his house. Furthermore, he had the earned a new social status by dint of his new relationship with the bishop, whose chauffeur driven vehicle had brought him back to Brewster's village.

Shortly before six o'clock that Sunday morning, the militants, about eight in number, arrived at the church to execute their plan of rejection. At the stroke of six o'clock, a blue Vauxhall slowly approached the church and stopped in front of the main entrance. A tall, dark man attired in a black suit and black clerical shirt, and an impressive garment bag and bible in his hand, stepped out of the vehicle and approached the group. His face bore a gentle, pleasant countenance, and his short, matted hair bore hints of grey at the temples.

"Good morning," he greeted the group in his refined, East African accent. His polite smile revealed two rows of perfect, white teeth. As he approached the hostile group, they could not help but freeze in amazement at his uncompromising dignity and striking resemblance to the late judge. None of them could muster the courage or audacity to intercept him as he strode with the elegance of a kabaka towards the entrance.

A few members of the group managed to sheepishly acknowledge his greeting as the imposing figure drew closer. Still, no one made any attempt to move.

"What a delightful morning!" he exclaimed in his polished baritone.

"Yes, indeed," Nathaniel Francois replied with a forced smile.

"How do you do? I am Fr. Weronde," he said as he extended his arm to Nathaniel. "I'll be the supply priest for the next few weeks until Bishop Addington makes alternative arrangements for you."

"Pleased to meet you, Fr." Nathaniel responded.

"I suppose that you are Mr. Goodfellow...the senior warden?" the clergyman asked.

"No, Reverend. We don't expect Mr. Goodfellow this morning."

"What are you people doing out here so early? Are you preparing for a celebration of some kind?" the priest inquired as he looked around at the furniture set out on the lawn.

The group cast furtive glances at each other for they could not muster up the courage to tell the reverend gentleman the true purpose of their mission. As they stood awkwardly contemplating the minister, with stupid, blank smiles pasted across their faces, another vehicle arrived and parked behind the clergyman's Vauxhall. Two figures emerged; one was Bill Jones – the other was Laurent Faulkner.

"What time is your first service?" Fr. Weronde inquired with a puzzled expression. "I didn't expect to see so many of you this early."

"Seven o'clock," Leroy Alleyne, one of the members of the *Iron Circle* selected to assist in rejecting the minister replied. "But you..."

Nathaniel gave Leroy a slight jab on his arm with his elbow to direct him to remain silent. Mr. Faulkner approached the group.

"Good morning, Reverend. May I help you?" Faulkner's tone was cold and he bore an unfriendly expression.

"Ahhh...Good morning! I suppose that you are the senior warden?" Fr. Weronde warmly acknowledged Mr. Faulkner's greeting and extended his arm.

"Yes," Faulkner replied abruptly without extending his arm.

"I am Fr. Weronde. It's indeed a pleasure to meet you in person, Mr. Goodfellow!"

"I am not Mr. Goodfellow," Faulkner snapped. "I am Laurent Faulkner, *Mr.* Laurent Faulkner – *the* senior warden; and this is Jones, the junior warden."

"But...but... I thought..."

"I'm sure you have. But I *am* the senior warden," Faulkner rudely interjected with a wry smile. "I think that there is some mistake here. Fr. Perths is celebrating both masses today."

"Are you sure?" the perplexed cleric replied. "I spoke at length with Bishop Addington – and Mr. Goodfellow – last night, and my impression was that I will be doing both services here for a few weeks..."

"Perhaps, but not today, sir. *Our* vicar is celebrating today," Faulkner reiterated. "Now I'm sure that I have explained the situation simply enough for you to understand, Reverend?"

Reverend Weronde straightened to his full height and fixed Mr. Faulkner a hard stare. "Am I to assume that you are in defiance of his Lordship's orders?"

"All due respects, Reverend Sir, but we are the ones who are responsible for the financial soundness of this parish. It's our money that pays our minister. Furthermore, it's the money from this parish that maintains other churches which can't pay their diocesan asking; so I think that it is reasonable for us to defy his Lordship's orders if we do not agree to them," Faulkner arrogantly stated.

"I see," Fr. Weronde responded.

As they spoke, three more cars arrived. The passengers quickly exited and hurried towards the entrance. Leading the group was Pigeon Goodfellow. Among the group were Jason and Ralph Baxter whose help Pigeon had solicited to assist in transporting the members from Slough and Brewster's village. There were thirteen of them in all.

"Fr. Weronde...!" Pigeon warmly greeted the tense clergyman.

"Good morning..." the priest responded with some uncertainty.

"Mr. Goodfellow...the senior warden. We spoke last night. How are you?" Pigeon smiled brightly as he extended his arm.

"There seems to be some confusion with regards to my duties here today," Fr. Weronde complained.

"No, Reverend. There is no confusion. *You* are celebrating mass here today," Pigeon affirmed.

"This gentleman has just told me that..."

"Disregard what he's just told you, Reverend," Pigeon interjected. "Do come in, Fr."

"Fr. Perths will be conducting the mass here today, Mr. Goodfellow," Faulkner decreed.

"Mr. Faulkner is the senior warden here, Fr. You have to follow *his* instructions," Bill warned the confused priest.

"What you people are doing here is wrong, Faulkner!" Pigeon suddenly bellowed as he pointed an accusing finger at the opposing group of 'Faulknerites.' "I had heard that you were planning to do this, and I came here this morning hoping that it would have been nothing but a rumor. But I see that what I heard was right. You *are* a troublemaker, Faulkner...a bloody insurrectionist!"

"I have the people's support in this and I will dictate things around here from now on, Goodfellow! This church needs judicious direction from one who is competent enough to give it; not from a mudhead!" Faulkner stated defiantly

By this time, several members had already arrived for the 7.00 a.m. service and were merely standing around, observing the heated exchange. Rex had long arrived and had opened the building, but remained inside.

Suddenly, one of the members who had arrived in Pigeon's vehicle, a young man in his early twenties, boldly stepped forward directly in front of Faulkner.

"This man you've just called a mudhead is my godfather, one of the island's most prominent lawyers, who makes his money by protecting and defending the innocent people in this society from vultures like you, Mr. Faulkner; crooks like you who push inferior merchandise on people for outrageous prices!"

"It must be obvious to you, *boy*, that my store was not meant to attract customers of your base, social status," Faulkner replied contemptuously.

"Go to hell, Mr. Faulkner!" the young man replied.

Immediately, with an innate impulsiveness, Mr. Faulkner fetched the impertinent young man a powerful slap which sent him reeling backwards into Pigeon. The shocking assault left everyone momentarily petrified.

"How dare you strike that young man you arrogant, impertinent jackass!" Fr. Weronde exclaimed in shock and horror.

Pigeon gripped his godson firmly so as to prevent him from retaliating. "Don't do a thing, Eric. I'll take care of this in court. Furthermore, we're on holy ground. Don't worry; I'll attend to this in court! Come let me take you to the car."

None of the witnesses said a word for fear of opposing one whom they might have hated but nevertheless respected because of his English extraction and his wealth. Faulkner thus seized the day.

"Come on, folks, get into the church. Fr. Perths will soon be here to conduct the mass. And you, sir," Faulkner said as he turned towards Fr. Weronde, "you need not stay."

"I was sent here by the Bishop and I shall remain and do what he has sent me here to do!" Fr. Weronde sternly replied.

"You don't go nowhere, parson!" shouted Oscar 'Cabbage' Alleyne who lived in Slough and who had a small farm on which he cultivated cabbage. He had just arrived in time to hear about the assault on Pigeon's godson and witness Mr. Faulkner dismissing the minister who was sent by the bishop.

"You have something to say, Mr. Alleyne?" Faulkner addressed the short, portly man who was attired in his Sunday best and sported a fedora with a feather on the side. His gold teeth and thick gold chain which hung obtrusively round his neck dazzled in the morning sunlight and he held a slightly tattered bible in his hand.

"Yes, I does!" he replied as he approached Mr. Faulkner. "Who the rass you thinks you is, eh, tellin' the parson 'bout he got to go; and slappin' dhat young boy out dhere? Whu right you got to do dhat?"

"Isn't it obvious, Mr. Alleyne?" Faulkner knew that his remark would be beyond the comprehension of most of the people who were already gathered there. In addition, he knew that the others who would understand would not entertain any though of responding to his implied superiority. Furthermore, since his assault on the young man had provoked no hostile, physical response, he felt at ease in daring to repeat the same action on Cabbage Alleyne if necessary.

"You is a nasty, wicked man!" Cabbage shouted accusingly. "...a redneck bully!"

This time, however, Faulkner did not slap the impertinent man. He stepped forward instead, and pushed Cabbage backward with such force that he slipped and fell against the hedge that separated the entrance where they were standing from the garden where the furniture was set. "Get the blazes out of here, you bloody vagabond!" Faulkner yelled.

Cabbage rose impetuously and handed Jason the bible, then with lightning speed charged forward and knocked Mr. Faulkner to the ground. He pounced on him and began to rapidly connect his fists to his face which such speed and viciousness that before anyone could remove him, Mr. Faulkner sported two puffed eyes and a swollen, bleeding bottom lip.

It was the assault on Mr. Faulkner, however, that triggered the churchyard melee. Winston Broomes, who had arrived earlier that morning with Nathaniel's group, descended upon Cabbage with a fleet of blows that sent him tumbling to the ground. Cabbage managed to grab his assailant in a chokehold and the two men began a violent fight that ended up in the garden. The furniture began to tumble as the men slammed each other into them. Another man from Nathaniel's group joined in the fight and began to kick Cabbage as he and Winston wrestled on the ground. This unfair, double assault on Cabbage aroused the anger of some of the men from Pigeon's group, and they pounced on the two men who were attacking Cabbage. Their intervention provoked rage in the men from Nathaniel's group and soon a shameless brawl broke out in the churchyard. Some of the women began running wildly up the street and in the church, screaming for help as the men and some of the women whose spouses were involved in the scuffle turned on each other and began to throw chairs and tables at one other. Rex, in grave panic for fear that they would soon turn on him, locked the church doors and began to manually ring the church bells with such desperation that some of the neighbors in the de luxe homes opposite the church opened their bedroom windows and began to hurl a chain of expletives at the members. Upon realizing that there was a riot in progress, one of them summoned the police. The noise from the cursing and fighting, superimposed by the loud, cacophonus clangling of the bells, was so loud that none of them heard the police sirens approaching. There were about fifteen persons involved in the fight. Reverend Wreonde was hurriedly escorted back to his car and instructed to return safely to his home. A large, intimidating woman from Slough, who was known by many only by the name 'Grizzly', had earlier grabbed Mr. Faulkner and dragged him into the church before Rex could have closed the door. Within the hallowed walls of the worship space, she battered him with her home-made, macramé handbag in which she carried her smelling-salts, prayer book and hymnal, and ripped his shirt before returning to the outside and releasing her frustrations on Monty Sookram, a short, half Indian man who was participating in the skirmish – and who had abandoned her several years earlier in favor of a charwoman named Matty Austin.

Reverend Perths was on his way to the church to conduct the mass, as instructed by Mr.Faulkner, but was warned to return to the vicarage until the skirmish was over. During the fight, someone ran over to the burial ground and gathered some of the decaying wreaths from Judge Pilchard's tomb and began to throw them towards those involved in the fight. Those who had realized where the flowers came from got up and ran hastily down the street, for they believed that if decaying flowers from a grave touched them, they would be visited in the night by the deceased or suffer bad luck. Consequently, many of them had already gone by the time the police arrived.

A huge crowd had already gathered in front of the church before the police arrived, but had scattered after the withered flowers began to sail through the air.

"Is whu happenin here?" an appalled spectator inquired of one of the church members from Slough.

"Whu else?" she replied. "The white man ain't even gone yet and everybody doin' they own t'ing. The white man ain't even gone yet, and already is a whole lot o'confusion. I ain't comin' back to dhis chu'ch unless the bishop send annadah white pries'."

The spectator became more dismayed by her answer than by the melee itself, and studied her momentarily before articulating his utter disgust at her simplicity and gross stupidity.

Many of the people involved in the fight were subsequently arrested. However, some of the members who were in the church during the fight hid Mr. Faulkner in the bell tower. As a result, he was not taken to the police station that morning. Meanwhile, the police cancelled the farewell function and two of them remained at the rear of the church during the celebration of the one mass which was conducted by Fr.Perths. At the end of the service, the members were instructed to leave immediately – with their pots and their food – for their respective homes. Rex then secured the building and departed, under the protection of the police.

By noon, the news of the riot at St. Patrick's had spread across the island. Bishop Addington immediately sent the police to remove Fr. Perths from the vicarage and escort him to one of the hotels in Georgetown for his own safety. The diocese paid the bill.

That week, the irreverent clergyman departed unceremoniously for England. It would be the last time that the parishioners would see him or hear from him.

EPILOGUE

Superfical order was finally restored at St. Patrick's, for Bishop Addington conducted mass there for the next few weeks following the disturbance. He never discussed the issue pertaining to Fr. Perth's *resignation* with the vestry or congregation, or entertained any questions regarding the same. Furthermore, he temporarily suspended the vestry until he would officially meet with them about one month later. During the mass which was held the following week, Pigeon Goodfellow was officially reinstated to his rightful place as senior warden. However, Bill Jones' was respectfully asked to relinquish his position because of his involvement in the brawl and by dint of his earlier resignation, and his office was given to Philbert Watts who would function in that position until the next election. Some of the vestry members who were loyal to the BOARD resigned after Philbert's appointment.

One week after the reinstitution of the vestry, Bishop Addington requested that the members of the BOARD attend the second mass as a group and sit together in the first few pews. This appeal immensely pleased the members and they responded in full force. The church was filled that day, for after the melee, the numbers had dwindled significantly, partly in protest over Fr. Perth's resignation and partly because of the embarrassment of the riot on the church grounds. A smaller proportion of those who had refrained from attending had been due to the homicide on Westminister Lane.

At the end of the announcements, which were read by Pigeon, Bishop Addington approached the lectern and invited the BOARD to take their place at the chancel step. The vestry members and those who had resigned because of Philbert's appointment smiled as the BOARD members stood and approached the center of the chancel. They were subsequently invited to turn and face the congregation. Their faces beamed with pride and radiated with the joy of final defeat. Based on remarks which some of the members had made after the bishop's request, they felt justified, invincible and ready to relentlessly pursue their devilish, ambitious agenda of social cleansing and ecclesiastical tyranny. The congregation burst into applause, and even though some of them did not agree to the formation of the BOARD, or had absolutely no knowledge of the existence of such a group, they nevertheless displayed spurious appreciation or blind affection for the group which they respectively had hated so passionately or of whom they were so pathetically ignorant. Bishop Addington raised his right hand with the dignity of a monarch as he gestured to the congregation to cease their applause. A pious quiet instantly engulfed the worship space.

"My brothers and sisters," Bishop Addington began, "some time in the early part of last year, a group of like-minded members of St. Patrick's embarked on a mission to establish some sort of leadership…an advisory board that would serve to give counsel to the vestry and direct the order of affairs in this famous house of worship. Sadly, however, it has become incumbent upon me to say that in the wake of their existence and control, they unilaterally have brought this parish of St. Patrick's, as well as the Anglican Communion as a whole, simultaneously to the pinnacle of embarrassment and the valley of disgrace."

The group froze in shock. Ruthel Pollard, who was placed in the center of the front line as a mark of respect for her age and social status, and whose poise mirrored that of a graceful ballerina, gasped and had to be physically supported by Bill Jones, who was standing to her immediate right. Some of the others hung their heads in virulent shame and began to twiddle their fingers or tap their feet. A deathlike silence crept across the nave as the large congregation turned their attention on the brood that stood before them in the agony of reverberating ignominy. Tessie Shoehorn suddenly became dizzy and had to be taken into the sacristy.

"Not a damn t'ing ain't wrong wid she, eh," whispered Daisy Mae Hercules, a middle aged woman who sold cassava bread and black-pudding at one of the street corners in Brewster's village. "Is shame she shame mek she pretend dhat she ain't feelin' good."

"Nuttin ain't wrong wid dhat woman, me Lord," yelled Leila Agard, an Indian woman who was famous for her roti and other Indian delicacies which she sold from her crudely constructed stand in Slough. "Is shame she shame mek she fly out like dhat. Mek she come back outside and listen!"

"Fly? Who, Tessie? Ha!" someone remarked from the pew behind Leila. "That would be the day when that three hundred pound thickhead could fly anywhere."

Bishop Addington immediately arrested the potential uproar and bubbling animosity. "Please, my friends, there is no need to be hostile towards her. Pray for her, instead."

The rising noise from the congregation was soon abated and silence prevailed once more.

"I must perspicuously state my utter disappointment in this group of intelligent people who might have used their mental prowess to build up, rather than tear down. The things that have taken place here over the past months have caused many persons to question the role of the church. I therefore stand here as your bishop, to appeal to your sense of order and decency, in the name of the church and in the holy name of God, to put an immediate end to your despotism, and be transformed to a spirit of humility, gentleness and love. This BOARD which you have formed is not recognized as a legal entity by me as your bishop or by the diocese, and is therefore dissolved with immediate effect."

Many in the congregation, especially in the rear, burst into applause. Some stood as they expressed their appreciation. Again, the bishop raised his hand to command quiet.

"My beloved," the Bishop continued, "my asking you to stand here is not to publicly disgrace you, but to help you to realize the ugliness of your illegal, unchristian undertaking..."

"I'm sure that if Ruthel was not standing there, the bishop would 'a chosen another word to describe the 'illegal, unchristian undertaking'," Uncle Ed whispered to Petulia Nobles who was seated next to him. Petulia buried her face in her palms to contain her amusement.

"...and," his Lordship continued, "to ask the other members of this congregation, even in the midst of our own shortcomings, to join me in praying for you and for this parish as we prepare for another era in our ministry."

Thus Bishop Addington offered a prayer for the restoration of order, respect and forgiveness. Additionally, he prayed for the completion of the construction of the church in Brewster's village and guidance in the election of its officers. At the end of the prayer, the congregation responded with a resonating 'Amen.'

The silence which followed the 'Amen' was harrowing – piercing to the core of the heart. There they stood – the brood of arrogant, insensitive despots, the now defunct BOARD – in front of the congregation like a condemned platoon of self-serving crusaders before the firing squad; there they remained, under a pall of suffocating disgrace as they awaited His Lordship's direction to return to their seats – the aristocrats, the bon viveurs, the socialites, the upper echelon of the ecclesiastical circles – as the congregation contemplated them in an infernal silence; there they were, like refugees at the gate of Hades, seeking asylum from the judgment passed on them by those whom they had condemned as societal dross.

After an agonizing period of prolonged and tormenting silence, they were exonerated by the blessing from His Lordship and instructed to return to their seats. That day, beginning in the hallowed walls of St. Patrick's, Bishop Addington won the intense hatred of the once highly favored few who felt that their status had given them immunity to reprimand.

The mass continued wonderfully. However, only a few members of the defunct BOARD remained for fellowship in the Parish Hall. The others made a hasty exit after the prayer of dismissal.

As Laurent Faulkner and Bill hurried from the building, Faulkner paused and gazed momentarily at judge Pilchard's tomb. "For a moment," he confessed, "as I stood in front of the congregation, I wished that it was I who was resting in my grave, and that it was Pilchard who had to bear the agonizing disgrace and humiliation of standing before the congregation as the death sentence was passed against the BOARD."

*   *   *

Construction of the church in Brewster's village had come to a halt the week following judge Pilchard's burial. Funding for the project was being donated by members of the BOARD, and the late judge and Laurent Faulkner were the largest contributors. The two men were so passionately determined to permanently segregate the worshippers that they had offered substantial amounts to expeditiously bring the plan to fruition. According to the contract, payments were to be made in thirds. Mr. Faulkner had committed to making the entire first payment and judge Pilchard had pledged to make the second payment. The other members had collectively pledged to make the final payment. Work on the building stopped when the payment for the second stage was not honored. Mr. Faulkner was not willing to provide the additional funds. An emergency meeting was thus called at Mr. Faulkner's home two nights after the embarrassing Sunday incident.

The meeting was planned to begin at eight o'clock, and Effie the Faulkner's cook, prepared Bambury cakes and a variety of volauvents which were served with tea and imported red wine. However, nine o'clock was approaching and only half of the BOARD members were present. After some telephone calls had been made, the members present were informed by Mr. Faulkner that the absentees had severed their association with them because of Sunday's humiliating reprimand by His Lordship. The news caused panic among those present, for they were earlier advised that the purpose of the meeting was to request a pledge increase in order to complete the project in the wake of judge Pilchard's demise.

Laurent Faulkner nevertheless called the meeting to order after most of the delectable pastries were consumed and the members had had their fill of wine and tea. Anxiety swept across the room and the expression on the faces of those present were like the countenance of a woman standing on the shore, awaiting the arrival of a husband engaged in warfare in some distant land – knowing deep inside that he may never return. They knew that they did not have the means to pledge more generously as they had led each other to believe, and that the time had come for the truth to be unearthed. The withdrawal of half of the membership now posed embarrassing threats to what was left of their image, and they knew that they could not now refuse the financial burden – or impossibility – which would now be placed upon them by dint of their intemperance. As Mr. Faulkner presented the progress report and calculated the additional amount required from each of those present, some of them immediately began to suffer from acute indigestion.

Sam Galloway, whose stomach was on fire, raised his hand in a desperate attempt to avoid finding the additional sum. "Mr. Faulkner, I think that it would be a gross insult to Mrs. Pilchard to deny her the privilege of contributing to this worthwhile project. I firmly believe that she should be invited to contribute in the name of her husband. Afterall, this project was his dream. Perhaps, she will be honored to donate the full amount pledged by judge Pilchard."

"Here here!" Ruthel Pollard concurred. "I'm sure that he's left her a handsome legacy."

"Is she back home?" Darleyne Burrows whispered.

"I think she is now," Ruthel replied.

"Brilliant idea!" Faulkner agreed. "I had thought of it, but subsequently dismissed the idea for fear of being construed as insensitive. However, since you deem it wise to include her, I'll call her right away."

Faulkner retired to the quiet of his study to make the call. The members immediately rose from their seats and pounced on the remaining pastries and wine. Their shameless voracity knew no boundary, and upon Faulkner's return, a request was made for more pastry and another bottle of wine, 'in anticipation of Mrs. Pilchard's frabjous agreement.'

"Pigs!" Ruthel hissed disdainfully as she stared disapprovingly at the crowd gathered around the table. "Guzzlers in a pig sty!"

"Yes, you're right," Urselle Joseph concurred. "Imagine forcing their way ahead of a senior member." Urselle cast a furtive glance at Ruthel.

"A rather common lot, my mother used to say!" Ruthel further remarked.

"Would you like another volauvent, Ruthel?" Urselle Joseph asked in a mellifluous tone of piercing sarcasm.

Ruthel assumed an erect posture and fixed Urselle a perforating stare. "Certainly not!" she snapped.

Faulkner returned with another bottle of wine. However, he apologized for not having had any more pastries, and explained that Effie had already retired to her quarters for the night. As he spoke and opened the wine, his face was flushed and his movement was languid.

Ruthel supposed that the fatigue of overseeing the construction without the presence and assistance of the late judge was now becoming problematic, and shared her feelings with Urselle. "Laurent seems overwhelmed by the demands of the project. He now misses Pilchard, I'm sure. He doesn't seem himself."

"Perhaps," Urselle replied. "I think that it might be that his conversation with Mrs. Pilchard has brought him to the reality of judge Plichard's death. You know how men grieve…differently. Maybe the denial has just worn off and the anger or grief has just stepped in. Mrs. Pilchard's grief might have stimulated his."

After everyone's glass was replenished, Laurent Faulkner stood up in the center of the large room and requested silence. "I have just spoken with Mrs. Pilchard and she has sent her warmest regards."

"Is she giving us the money?" the pragmatic Fritz Batty inquired.

"No." Faulkner answered abruptly.

"O shit," Sam groaned quietly and rested his head in the palm of his hand.

"Why?" Nathaniel barked.

"She was never in agreement with the project," Faulkner replied with a sigh.

"Why?" Sam yelled. "We're giving the mules their own stable to worship in!"

"She is not in disagreement with the construction proper. It's our motives that she finds 'morally contemptible.' She *claims* that if our motives were different, she would have willingly contributed whatever we asked."

"Aww, let her go to hell. We don't need any dead man's money anyway!" Sam growled.

"Wait…I have an idea," Maurice Chan interjected. "Let us begin a memorial fund at the church in memory of judge Pilchard. We can use the funds for precisely that – to finish the church. Bishop Addington is not coming back here in a hurry. The supply priest is not going to be concerned about this. He's only going to be here for a couple o' weeks the most. What do you say?"

"Good idea, Chan," Faulkner agreed, "but the bishop is not the problem."

"Who is?" another member asked.

"*Your* senior warden," Faulkner replied. "You'll have to get his approval."

"Why didn't Maggie's dog maul *him* instead of judge Pilchard?" Sam again hurled a sardonic remark.

"*He* wasn't having an affair with her, that's why," Darleyne Burrows remarked.

Everyone turned and contemplated her for a few moments. She instantly hung her head and took another sip of wine.

"Furthermore, we cannot solicit any funds in the judge's name unless Mrs. Pilchard gives her stamp of approval," Faulkner added.

"Well, if she refuses to give the money which her *husband* promised, then the least she can do is to agree to the memorial fund," Ruthel declared.

"Who will bell the cat?" Faulkner asked.

"Let Ruthel do it. Mrs. Pilchard will respect her," someone suggested from the far corner.

Everyone agreed with the suggestion and Ruthel was subsequently led to the study to once again seek Mrs. Pilchard's assistance. Ruthel expressed mild reservations but nevertheless proceeded because of the flattering remark about the widow's possible respect for her.

It was almost ten thirty when Ruthel made the call. The voice on the other end of the line was somnolent and slightly petulant. "Goodnight, Mrs. Pilchards' residence. May I help you?"

"Sylvie love...?"

"No. This is her sister, Dorset – Mrs. Hudson. Mrs. Pilchard is asleep."

"This is Ruthel, Ruthel Pollard, the Prime Minister's aunt."

"How may I help you, Ms. Pollard?"

Dorset's flat tone mildly angered Ruthel who thought it highly impertinent of Mrs. Hudson to be unimpressed by her social status. She rolled her eyes and sighed and immediately assumed a harsh, businesslike tone.

"I have a rather urgent matter to discuss with Mrs. Pilchard," Ruthel stated in her usual abrupt manner, "which demands her immediate response. I would be obliged if you would kindly wake her so that I can speak to her."

"I will do no such thing, Ms. Pollard," Mrs. Hudson firmly but gently replied. "My sister has been under great emotional stress since her husband's tragic death, so I will not wake her to undertake any additional pressure or fatigue. What is it you wish to speak to her so urgently about? Perhaps I can help you."

"The members of the board of directors at St. Patrick's would like to start a memorial fund in honor of Mr. Pilchard, and we are seeking her permission to do so."

"A memorial fund for what? What is the money being collected for, Ms. Pollard?" Mrs. Hudson inquired in a voice of hushed dignity.

"For the construction of the church in Brewster's village. We feel that..."

"Ms. Pollard," Mrs. Hudson interjected, "someone called a few minutes ago in an attempt to solicit funds from my sister towards this very project, and my sister clearly explained, for reasons which I'm sure you already know, that she will have no part in such a despicable act of blatant prejudice. I will answer for her and state firmly that she will never agree to such a base solicitation of funds in her husband's name. You all should be ashamed of yourselves...and worse, you are attempting to drag my late brother-in-law's name into this sordid mess!"

"I hardly think that we can put him in a bigger mess than he had put himself in, Mrs. Hudson," Ruthel rejoined in her high pitched, agitated tone, "so your remark is hardly necessary; furthermore, it does not inflict any scathing wounds on the integrity of this BOARD!"

Dorset drew a deep breath at Ruthel's audacity. "Is a festering sore affected by purulence? Do maggots exacerbate a decomposing corpse, Ms. Pollard? Let me tell you something, you callous, unsympathetic, scatophagous old bat," Dorset replied in a sharp and moderately loud tone, "my sister will no longer be worshipping at St. Patricks'. She has severed her membership from that religious club. As such, please do not ever call this number to solicit any more money from her, do you hear me? Furthermore, I don't care if you are the Prime Minister or the Prime Minister's mother or the Prime Minister's wife; don't ever call this number again!" Mrs. Hudson slammed the receiver.

Ruthel paused as the pangs of Dorset's insults penetrated to the core of her being. "O.k., my dear; do have a good night's rest," she finally managed to say as she gently hung up the telephone.

"What nonsense has she been telling you?" Faulkner inquired as she turned to exit the room.

Ruthel gasped, for she did not realize that he was close enough to overhear some of Dorset's hostile reaction. "She refused to put Sylvia on the phone and...well...she...she said..."

"Mrs. Pilchard does not approve..." he interjected.

"Yes. What do I say to the group? They were depending on me...to... to at least..."

"Tell them the truth, Ruthel," Faulkner advised. "Don't beat about the bush. They'll have to come up with the difference, that's all."

Faulkner entered the room with the aged ambassador by his side. He put her to sit on the closest chair.

"Is a toast in order?" Sam greeted them with opened arms and a broad smile as they entered.

"Put down your glass, Sam. She's refused," Faulkner informed the group.

Silence instantly engulfed the room.

"What? What did she say?" Fritz asked with a withering expression stamped across his delicately sagging face.

"Well," Faulkner reported, "she didn't even come to the phone. It was her sister who told Ruthel..."

"Told Ruthel what?" Fritz impatiently reiterated.

"Well, she just about told her to get stuffed," Faulkner explained and poured himself a glass of wine.

Another period of silence followed, during which time some of the members sipped their wine in an attempt to conceal the awkwardness.

"I'm nevertheless taking a private toast," Barry Murphy whispered to Nathaniel. "I've often wanted to tell that crabby old crone the same thing. So I'm happy that someone's actually done so."

The two men nudged each other and suppressed their laughter.

"What do we do now, Faulkner?" Dr. Coaksley asked in a surly voice.

"We all have to increase our pledge, that's all," Faulkner snapped.

"By how much?" someone asked.

"Well, divide the amount we need by the number present here. I would say approximately nine hundred to a thousand dollars each," Faulkner calmly replied. "That should cover the unexpected expenses which came up and which are likely to arise."

For the third time, silence spread across the room. However, no one gave any hint of his or her inability to meet the new financial obligation.

"Let us sign for a thousand each. In this case we can't go wrong," Faulkner commanded as he distributed the pledge sheets. "Of course, I shall not be required to increase mine since I covered the entire first part of the project – which already has been completed."

They all signed and returned the sheets to Faulkner who expressed effusive gratitude to them for their understanding and their determination to complete the project in spite of all attempts to hinder its progress. Sam protested the exclusion of those who had severed their membership after Bishop Addington's visit. His opinion was that they all were a part of the project and that they should be made to honor their commitment, even if they were no longer members.

"I'm sure that Sam is making so much damn noise because he can't meet the financial demand made of him," Faulkner whispered to Ruthel.

By the close of the meeting, Faulkner had received nine thousand dollars in pledges, and the meeting concluded with a song of praise. However, he received no checks or cash.

*   *   *

Sam Westwater drove off in a mildly inebriated state, but yet rational enough to decide that this was his last day as a member of the BOARD. Fritz Batty prayed all the way home that there might urgently be a few more deaths around the villages so as to prevent him from borrowing money to honor his commitment. Dr. Coaksley made a unilateral decision to secretly approach a select number of *Gold* and *Silver Circle* members and solicit funds which ultimately would reduce the amount that he had just pledged to give – funds which he would surreptitiously present as his own. Ruthel shuddered at the thought of having to approach her parsimonious nephew, the Prime Minister, for assistance in meeting her obligation – her pledge of support for a project to which he was sharply opposed by dint of his blatant disdain for the arrogant, ostentatious members of St. Patrick's – and in particular, the late judge.

Laurent Faulkner retired to bed that night, mentally exhausted, but proud that he would singlehandedly bring the project to fruition, thus proving his superiority over the members of the BOARD. He stretched himself partly under the printed cotton sheet, rested his head on his palms and smiled as he contemplated what he believed in time would be his greatest joy – the eradication of the plebs.

*   *   *

The deadline for the submission of the additional funds came and went twice, and the pangs of frustration began to gnaw at Mr. Faulkner. His failure began to jeer at him. The situation was further aggravated by the persistent calls from the contractor who threatened to seek counsel from Pigeon Goodfellow with regards to a 'breach of contract.' Faulkner thus penned a letter to the members of the now defunct BOARD – all who had become members from its inception – stating that he was ready to 'wash his hands of the whole venture, and let the *mules* take over St. Patrick's.' He further stated that 'should such a repulsive thing happen, he would immediately sever his membership from St. Patrick's' and assume the same at Holy Trinity in South Hamdensville. The letter provoked intense anger among some of the members who knew Holy Trinity to be a very exclusive parish on the south coast. Most of the members of the small, wealthy parish were Caucasians of American and English extraction who were socially aloof from the middle and lower class Ischaltonese. Dr. Coaksley, in particular, was offended by the letter, and after making a few telephone calls to a select group of BOARD members, decided to relinquish his membership. Those whom he called, among them Sam Westwater, also immediately severed their membership. However, their response was not so much a reaction to Mr.

Faulkner's threatening letter as it was an opportunity to evade the heavy financial obligation which was placed upon them. Thus they sent their respective responses to Faulkner by way of writing, expressing their anger and their disappointment in him as their president, along with their resignation from the long defunct BOARD. Their feigned anger lent credence and legitimacy to their resignation, and consequently spared them the burden of a mortifying embarrassment. Three days later, Faulkner sent another letter to the members tendering his resignation as president of the BOARD and informing them of his decision to acquire membership at Holy Trinity. He concluded his letter by 'wishing them all the best in their fellowship with the rustics.'

*   *   *

Maggie Billings' mental condition continued to deteriorate, and she was later transferred to a mental institution in Rosehall for extended psychiatric treatment. Bishop Addington had paid her several pastoral visits, during which time he made subtle attempts to elicit information regarding the homicide, but was unsuccessful. Her maundering offered him no conclusiveness. Rumor was being circulated that judge Pilchard and Archie Carchide were involved in a scuffle over Maggie and that it was Maggie who inflicted the fatal wound on the more powerful of the two men in order to defend the man she loved. Judge Pilchard's death was believed to be a mere accident caused by the canine who probably felt that his owner was in danger by her presence or participation in the deadly duel.

"Unless Maggie regain a state of rationality, this rumor would assume credulity and consequently become the reliable evidence of an unknown informer," Pigeon complained to the bishop during a telephone conversation. Pigeon, under the guise of a dear friend, was able to visit the institution in a covert attempt to extract any detail that could help to quell the rumor and establish the truth concerning the character of the late judge. However, all he managed to get was the rambling of a bordering lunatic.

Jason and Pigeon maintained a casual acquaintance – though more on a professional level as the latter prepared to represent his once closest friend in court. Perhaps in time, pity and gratitude will bring the two men together again, *dei gratia*, to a lifelong bond of brotherhood.

Meanwhile, some semblance of order was restored at St.Patrick's as supply clergy continued to conduct services on Sundays. The few remaining members of the defunct BOARD began to lose control and the walls which discreetly had separated the *Circles* were broken down – much to the charign of the members who had enjoyed the privileges that were formerly bestowed upon them. Peasants and aristocrats – they shared a common pew; mules and horses – they partook of fellowship at the same stable; the sinful and the sanctimonious – they groped frantically in the darkness of ignorance for the light of truth; mud and gold dust – they co-mingled to form an indistinguishable identity. However, in spite of all of this, the people continued to pray perseveringly – each according to his or her own purpose – that God in his infinite goodness would restore to them, or bestow upon them, what they vehemently believed was inherently theirs.

*   *   *

Late one melancholy Sunday afternoon, several weeks after the dissolution of the BOARD, Pigeon drove into Brewster's Village. The persistent drizzle and the swampy dirt roads seemed to have sentenced the villagers to the confines of their modest homes. Consequently, the sleek, silver jaguar was able to plough unobtrusively through the mud in the early evening mist as Pigeon dextrously negotiated the pot holes on Wiggins Road. On reaching the site of the controversial house of worship, he stopped momentarily to observe its progress. The wooden, skeletal structure seemed far from completion, and there were piles of lumber and zinc sheets on the side. As Pigeon stood on the crude wooden bridge which was built to facilitate the process, a man approached him and told him that he had been hired by the white man 'to keep a' eye pun the place 'cause the villagers dhem was thiefin' the material at night', but was subsequently fired when Mrs. Ramgolam accused him of stealing the material himself and selling it to his friends. He vehemently denied the accusation and then called the Public Relations Officer a 'hignorant, bow leg' proboscis monkey.'

Pigeon shared a light banter with the villager before turning towards his vehicle. Before igniting the engine, he turned once more to observe the unfinished structure. There it stood before him, dying a slow death even before it had attained life; condemned by the very people who contended to bring it into existence; abandoned by those who proved unfaithful to the cause. Like the BOARD itself, its past must sink into oblivion and its future must remain a dismal prospect.

The senior warden turned the key and drove off west towards the setting sun. The dark, saturated clouds scudded insidiously across the evening sky as a solitary ray of golden sunlight penetrated the whispering mist in relentless defiance of whatever lay ahead. Pigeon knew that he would have to stand guard like a sentinel, lest that which appears moribund rise like a phoenix – to begin a new life of contradiction.